"ASK MOM
or
THE RICHEST COMMOI
By R.S. Sι

.

PREFACE TO THE ORIGINAL EDITION.

IT may be a recommendation to the lover of light literature to be told, that the following story does not involve the complication of a plot. It is a mere continuous narrative of an almost everyday exaggeration, interspersed with sporting scenes and excellent illustrations by Leech.

March 31, 1858.

CHAPTER I. OUR HERO AND CO.—A SLEEPING PARTNER.

CONSIDERING that Billy Pringle, or Fine Billy, as his good-natured friends called him, was only an underbred chap, he was as good an imitation of a Swell as ever we saw. He had all the airy dreaminess of an hereditary high flyer, while his big talk and off-hand manner strengthened the delusion.

It was only when you came to close quarters with him, and found that though he talked in pounds he acted in pence, and marked his fine dictionary words and laboured expletives, that you came to the conclusion that he was "painfully gentlemanly." So few people, however, agree upon what a gentleman is, that Billy was well calculated to pass muster with the million. Fine shirts, fine ties, fine talk, fine trinkets, go a long way towards furnishing the character with many. Billy was liberal, not to say prodigal, in all these. The only infallible rule we know is, that the man who is always talking about being a gentleman never is one. Just as the man who is always talking about honour, morality, fine feeling, and so or never knows anything of these qualities but the name.

Nature had favoured Billy's pretensions in the lady-killing way. In person he was above the middle height, five feet eleven or so, slim and well-proportioned, with a finely-shaped head and face, fair complexion, light brown hair, laughing blue eyes, with long lashes, good eyebrows, regular pearly teeth and delicately pencilled moustache. Whiskers he did not aspire to. Nor did Billy abuse the gifts of Nature by disguising himself in any of the vulgar groomy gamekeepery style of dress, that so effectually reduce all mankind to the level of the labourer, nor adopt any of the "loud" patterns that have lately figured so conspicuously in our streets. On the contrary, he studied the quiet unobtrusive order of costume, and the harmony of colours, with a view of producing a perfectly elegant general effect. Neatly-fitting frock or dress coats, instead of baggy sacks, with trouser legs for sleeves, quiet-patterned vests and equally quiet-patterned trousers. If he could only have been easy in them he would have done extremely well, but there was always a nervous twitching, and jerking, and feeling, as if he was wondering what people were thinking or saying of him.

In the dress department he was ably assisted by his mother, a lady of very considerable taste, who not only fashioned his clothes but his mind, indeed we might add his person, Billy having taken after her, as they say; for his father, though an excellent man and warm, was rather of the suet-dumpling order of architecture, short, thick, and round, with a neck that was rather difficult to find. His name, too, was William, and some, the good-natured ones again of course, used to say that he might have been called "Fine Billy the first," for under the auspices of his elegant wife he had assumed a certain indifference to trade; and when in the grand strut at Ramsgate or Broadstairs, or any of his watering-places, if appealed to about any of the things made or dealt in by any of the concerns in which he was a "Co.," he used to raise his brows and shrug his shoulders, and say with a very deprecatory sort of air, "'Pon my life, I should say you're right," or "'Deed I should say it was so," just as if he was one of the other Pringles,—the Pringles who have nothing to do with trade,—and in noways connected with Pringle & Co.; Pringle & Potts; Smith, Sharp & Pringle; or any of the firms that the Pringles carried on under the titles of the original founders. He was neither a tradesman nor a gentleman. The Pringles—like the happy united family we meet upon wheels; the dove nestling with the gorged cat, and so on—all pulled well together when there was a common victim to plunder; and kept taking their hands in by what they called taking fair advantages of each other, that is to say, cheating each other, when there was not.

Nobody knew the ins and outs of the Pringles. If they let their own right hands know what their left hands did, they took care not to let anybody else's right hand know. In multiplicity of concerns they rivalled that great man "Co.," who the country-lad coming to London said seemed to be in partnership with almost everybody. The author of "Who's Who?" would be puzzled to post people who are Brown in one place, Jones in a second, and Robinson in a third. Still the Pringles were "a most respectable family," mercantile morality being too often mere matter of moonshine. The only member of the family who was not exactly "legally honest,"—legal honesty being much more elastic than common honesty,—was cunning Jerry, who thought to cover by his piety the omissions of his practice. He was a fawning, sanctified, smooth-spoken, plausible, plump little man, who seemed to be swelling with the milk of human kindness, anxious only to pour it out upon some deserving object. His manner was so frank and bland, and his front face smile so sweet, that it was cruel of his side one to contradict the impression and show the cunning duplicity of his nature. Still he smirked and smiled, and "bless-you, dear" and "hope-your-happy," deared the women, that, being a bachelor, they all thought it best to put up with his "mistakes," as he called his peculations, and sought his favour by frequent visits with appropriate presents to his elegant villa at Peckham Rye. Here he passed for quite a model man; twice to church every Sunday, and to the lecture in the evening, and would not profane the sanctity of the day by having a hot potato to eat with his cold meat.

He was a ripe rogue, and had been jointly or severally, as the lawyers say, in a good many little transactions that would not exactly bear inspection; and these "mistakes" not tallying with the sanctified character he assumed, he had been obliged to wriggle out of them as best he could, with the loss of as few feathers as possible. At first, of course, he always tried the humbugging system, at which he was a great adept; that failing, he had recourse to bullying, at which he was not bad, declaring that the party complaining was an ill-natured, ill-conditioned, quarrelsome fellow, who merely wanted a peg to hang a grievance upon, and that Jerry, so far from defrauding him, had been the best friend he ever had in his life, and that he would put him through every court in the kingdom before he would be imposed upon, by him. If neither of these answered, and Jerry found himself pinned in a corner, he feigned madness, when his solicitor, Mr. Supple, appeared, and by dint of legal threats, and declaring that if the unmerited persecution was persisted in, it would infallibly consign his too sensitive client to a lunatic asylum, he generally contrived to get Jerry out of the scrape by some means or other best known to themselves. Then Jerry, of course, being clear, would inuendo his own version of the story as dexterously as he could, always taking care to avoid a collision with the party, but more than insinuating that he (Jerry) had been infamously used, and his well-known love of peace and quietness taken advantage of; and though men of the world generally suspect the party who is most anxious to propagate his story to be in the wrong, yet their number is but small compared to those who believe anything they are told, and who cannot put "that and that" together for themselves.

So Jerry went on robbing and praying and passing for a very proper man. Some called him "cunning Jerry," to distinguish him from an uncle who was Jerry also; but as this name would not do for the family to adopt, he was generally designated by them as "Want-nothin'-but-what's-right Jerry," that being the form of words with which he generally prefaced his extortions. In the same way they distinguished between a fat Joe and a thin one, calling the thin one merely "Joe," and the fat one "Joe who can't get within half a yard of the table;" and between two clerks, each bearing the not uncommon name of Smith, one being called Smith, the other "Head-and-shoulders Smith,"—the latter, of course, taking his title from his figure.

With this outline of the Pringle family, we will proceed to draw out such of its members as figure more conspicuously in our story.

With Mrs. William Pringle's (*née* Willing) birth, parentage, and education, we would gladly furnish the readers of this work with some information, but, unfortunately, it does not lie in our power so to do, for the simple reason, that we do not know anything. We first find her located at that eminent Court milliner and dressmaker's, Madame Adelaide Banboxeney, in Furbelow Street, Berkeley Square, where her elegant manners, and obliging disposition, to say nothing of her taste in torturing ribbons and wreaths, and her talent for making plain girls into pretty ones, earned for her a very distinguished reputation. She soon became first-hand, or trier-on, and unfortunately, was afterwards tempted into setting-up for herself, when she soon found, that though fine ladies like to be cheated, it must be done in style, and by some one, if not with a carriage, at all events with a name; and that a bonnet, though beautiful in Bond Street, loses all power of attraction if it is known to come out of Bloomsbury. Miss Willing was, therefore, soon sold up; and Madame Banboxeney (whose real name was Brown, Jane Brown, wife of John Brown, who was a billiard-table marker, until his wife's fingers set him up in a gig), Madame Banboxeney, we say, thinking to profit by Miss Willing's misfortunes, offered her a very reduced salary to return to her situation; but Miss Willing having tasted the sweets of bed, a thing she very seldom did at Madame Banboxeney's, at least not during the season, stood out for more money; the consequence of which was, she lost that chance, and had the benefit of Madame's bad word at all the other establishments she afterwards applied to. In this dilemma, she resolved to turn her hand to lady's-maid-ism; and having mastered the science of hair-dressing, she made the rounds of the accustomed servant-shops, grocers, oilmen, brushmen, and so on, asking if they knew of any one wanting a perfect lady's-maid.

As usual in almost all the affairs of life, the first attempt was a failure. She got into what she thoroughly despised, an untitled family, where she had a great deal more to do than she liked, and was grossly "put upon" both by the master and missis. She gave the place up, because, as she said, "the master would come into the missis's room with nothing but his night-shirt and spectacles on," but, in reality, because the missis had some of her things made-up for the children instead of passing them on, as of right they ought to have been, to her. She deeply regretted ever having demeaned herself by taking such a situation. Being thus out of place, and finding the many applications she made for other situations, when she gave a reference to her former one, always resulted in the ladies declining her services, sometimes on the plea of being already suited, or of another "young person" having applied just before her, or of her being too young (they never said too pretty, though one elderly lady on seeing her shook her head, and said she "had sons"); and, being tired of living on old tea leaves, Miss Willing resolved to sink her former place, and advertise as if she had just left Madame Banboxeney's. Accordingly she drew out a very specious advertisement, headed "*to the nobility*," offering the services of a lady's-maid, who thoroughly understood millinery, dress-making, hair-dressing, and getting up fine linen, with an address to a cheese shop, and made an arrangement to give Madame Banboxeny a lift with a heavy wedding order she was busy upon, if she would recommend her as just fresh from her establishment.

This advertisement produced a goodly crop of letters, and Miss Willing presently closed with the Honourable Mrs. Cavesson, whose husband was a good deal connected with the turf, enjoying that certain road to ruin which so many have pursued; and it says much for Miss Willing's acuteness, that though she entered Mrs. Cavesson's service late in the day, when all the preliminaries for a smash had been perfected, her fine sensibilities and discrimination enabled her to anticipate the coming evil, and to deposit her mistress's jewellery in a place of safety three-quarters of an hour before the bailiffs entered. This act of fidelity greatly enhanced her reputation, and as it was well known that "poor dear Mrs. Cavesson" would not be able to keep her, there were several great candidates for this "treasure of a maid." Miss Willing had now nothing to do but pick and choose; and after some consideration, she selected what she called a high quality family, one where there was a regular assessed tax-paper establishment of servants, where the butler sold his lord's wine-custom to the highest bidder, and the heads of all the departments received their "reglars" upon the tradesmen's bills; the lady never demeaning herself by wearing the same gloves or ball-shoes twice, or propitiating the nurse by presents of raiment that was undoubtedly hers—we mean the maid's. She was a real lady, in the proper acceptation of the term.

This was the beautiful, and then newly married, Countess Delacey, whose exquisite garniture will still live in the recollection of many of the now bald-headed beaux of that period. For these delightful successes, the countess was mainly indebted to our hero's mother, Miss Willing, whose suggestive genius oft came to the aid of the perplexed and exhausted milliner. It was to the service of the Countess Delacey that Miss Willing was indebted for becoming the wife of Mr. Pringle, afterwards "Fine Billy the first,"—an event that deserves to be introduced in a separate chapter.

CHAPTER II. THE ROAD.

IT was on a cold, damp, raw December morning, before the emancipating civilisation of railways, that our hero's father, then returning from a trading tour, after stamping up and down the damp flags before the Lion and Unicorn hotel and posting-house at Slopperton, waiting for the old True Blue Independent coach "comin' hup," for whose cramped inside he had booked a preference seat, at length found himself bundled into the straw-bottomed vehicle, to a very different companion to what he was accustomed to meet in those deplorable conveyances. Instead of a fusty old farmer, or a crumby basket-encumbered market-woman, he found himself opposite a smiling, radiant young lady, whose elegant dress and ring-bedizened hand proclaimed, as indeed was then generally the case with ladies, that she was travelling in a coach "for the first time in her life."

This was our fair friend, Miss Willing.

The Earl and Countess Delacey had just received an invitation to spend the Christmas at Tiara Castle, where the countess on the previous year had received if not a defeat, at all events had not achieved a triumph, in the dressing way, over the Countess of Honiton, whose maid, Miss Criblace, though now bribed to secrecy with a full set of very little the worse for wear Chinchilla fur, had kept the fur and told the secret to Miss Willing, that their ladyships were to meet again. Miss Willing was now on her way to town, to arrange with the Countess's milliner for an annihilating series of morning and evening dresses wherewith to extinguish Lady Honiton, it being utterly impossible, as our fair friends will avouch, for any lady to appear twice in the same attire. How thankful men ought to be that the same rule does not prevail with them!

Miss Willing was extremely well got up; for being of nearly the same size as the countess, her ladyship's slightly-worn things passed on to her with scarcely a perceptible diminution of freshness, it being remarkable how, in even third and fourth-rate establishments, dresses that were not fit for the "missus" to be seen in come out quite new and smart on the maid.

On this occasion Miss Willing ran entirely to the dark colours, just such as a lady travelling in her own carriage might be expected to wear. A black terry velvet bonnet with a single ostrich feather, a dark brown Levantine silk dress, with rich sable cuffs, muff, and boa, and a pair of well-fitting primrose-coloured kid gloves, which if they ever had been on before had not suffered by the act.

Billy—old Billy that is to say—was quite struck in a heap at such an unwonted apparition, and after the then usual salutations, and inquiries how she would like to have the window, he popped the old question, "How far was she going?" with very different feelings to what it was generally asked, when the traveller wished to calculate how soon he might hope to get rid of his *vis-à-vis* and lay up his legs on the seat.

"To town," replied the lady, dimpling her pretty cheeks with a smile. "And you?" asked she, thinking to have as good as she gave.

"Ditto," replied the delighted Billy, divesting himself of a great coarse blue and white worsted comforter, and pulling up his somewhat dejected gills, abandoning the idea of economising his Lincoln and Bennett by the substitution of an old Gregory's mixture coloured fur cap, with its great ears tied over the top, in which he had snoozed and snored through many a long journey.

Miss Willing then drew from her richly-buckled belt a beautiful Geneva watch set round with pearls, (her ladyship's, which she was taking to town to have repaired), and Billy followed suit with his substantial gold-repeater, with which he struck the hour. Miss then ungloved the other hand, and passed it down her glossy brown hair, all smooth and regular, for she had just been scrutinising it in a pocket-mirror she had in her gold-embroidered reticule.

Billy's commercial soul was in ecstacies, and he was fairly over head and ears in love before they came to the first change of horses. He had never seen sich a sample of a hand before, no, nor sich a face; and he felt quite relieved when among the multiplicity of rings he failed to discover that thin plain gold one that intimates so much.

Whatever disadvantages old stage coaches possessed, and their name certainly was legion, it must be admitted that in a case of this sort their slowness was a recommendation. The old True Blue Independent did not profess to travel or trail above eight miles an hour, and this it only accomplished under favourable circumstances, such as light loads, good roads, and stout steeds, instead of the top-heavy cargo that now ploughed along the woolly turnpike after the weak, jaded horses, that seemed hardly able to keep their legs against the keen careering wind. If, under such circumstances, the wretched concern made the wild-beast-show looking place in London, called an inn, where it put up, an hour or an hour and a half or so after its time, it was said to be all very well, "considering,"—and this, perhaps, in a journey of sixty miles.

Posterity will know nothing of the misery their forefathers underwent in the travelling way; and whenever we hear—which we often do—unreasonable grumblings about the absence of trifling luxuries on railways, we are tempted to wish the parties consigned to a good long ride in an old stage coach. Why the worst third class that ever was put next the engine is infinitely better than the inside of the best of them used to be, to say nothing of the speed. As to the outsides of the old coaches, with their roastings, their soakings, their freezings, and their smotherings with dust, one cannot but feel that the establishment of railways was a downright prolongation of life. Then the coach refreshments, or want of refreshments rather; the turning out at all hours to breakfast, dine, or sup, just as the coach reached the house of a proprietor "wot oss'd it," and the cool incivility of every body about the place. Any thing was good enough for a coach passenger.

On this auspicious day, though Miss Willing had her reticule full of macaroons and sponge biscuits, and Fine Billy the first had a great bulging paper of sandwiches in his brown overcoat pocket, they neither of them felt the slightest approach to hunger, ere the lumbering vehicle, after a series of clumsy, would-be-dash-cutting lurches and evolutions over the rough inequalities of the country pavement, pulled up short at the arched doorway of the Salutation Inn—we beg pardon, hotel—in Bramfordrig, and a many-coated, brandy-faced, blear-eyed guard let in a whole hurricane of wind while proclaiming that they "dined there and stopped half an hour." Then Fine Billy the first had an opportunity of showing his gallantry and surveying the figure of his innamorata, as he helped her down the perilous mud-shot iron, steps of the old Independent, and certainly never countess descended from her carriage on a drawing-room day with greater elegance than Miss Willing displayed on the present occasion, showing a fettle circle of delicate white linen petticoat as she protected her clothes from the mud-begrimed wheel, and just as

4

much fine open-worked stocking above the fringed top of her Adelaide boots. On reaching the ground, which she did with a curtsey, she gave such a sweet smile as emboldened our Billy to offer his arm; and amid the nudging of outsiders, and staring of street-loungers, and "make way"-ing of inn hangers-on, our Billy strutted up the archway with all the dignity of a drum-major. His admiration increased as he now became sensible of the lady's height, for like all little men he was an admirer of tall women. As he caught a glimpse of himself in the unbecoming mirror between the drab and red fringed window curtains of the little back room into which they were ushered, he wished he had had on his new blue coat and bright buttons, with a buff vest, instead of the invisible green and black spot swansdown one in which he was then attired.

The outside passengers having descended from their eminences, proceeded to flagellate themselves into circulation, and throw off their husks, while Billy strutted consequentially in with the lady on his arm, and placed her in the seat of honour beside himself at the top of the table. The outsides then came swarming in, jostling the dish-bearers and seating themselves as they could. All seemed bent upon getting as much as they could for their money.

Pork was the repast. Pork in various shapes: roast at the top, boiled at the bottom, sausages on one side, fry on the other; and Miss Willing couldn't eat pork, and, curious coincidence! neither could Billy. The lady having intimated this to Billy in the most delicate way possible, for she had a particular reason for not wishing to aggravate the new landlord, Mr. Bouncible, Billy gladly sallied forth to give battle as it were on his own account, and by way of impressing the household with his consequence, he ordered a bottle of Teneriffe as he passed the bar, and then commenced a furious onslaught about the food when he got into the kitchen. This reading of the riot act brought Bouncible from his "Times," who having been in the profession himself took Billy for a nobleman's gentleman, or a house-steward at least—a class of men not so easily put upon as their masters. He therefore, after sundry regrets at the fare not being 'zactly to their mind, which he attributed to its being washing-day, offered to let them have a: "himional" of i'hi'im', the first turn at a very nice dish of hashed venison that was then simmering on the fire for Mrs. B. and himself, provided our travellers would have the goodness to call it hashed mutton, so that it might not be devoured by the outsiders, a class of people whom all landlords held in great contempt. To this proposition Billy readily assented, and returned triumphantly to the object of his adoration. He then slashed right and left at the roast pork, and had every plate but hers full by the time the hashed mutton made its appearance. He then culled out all the delicate tit-bits for his fair partner, and decked her hot plate with sweet sauce and mealy potatoes. Billy's turn came next, and amidst demands for malt liquor and the arrival of smoking tumblers of brown brandy and water, clatter, patter, clatter, patter, became the order of the day, with an occasional suspicious, not to say dissatisfied, glance of a pork-eating passenger at the savoury dish at the top of the table. Mr. Bonncible, however, brought in the Teneriffe just at the critical moment, when Billy having replenished both plates, the pork-eaters might have expected to be let in; and walked off with the dish in exchange for the decanter. Our friends then pledged each other in a bumper of Cape. The pork was followed by an extremely large strong-smelling Cheshire cheese, in a high wooden cradle, which in its turn was followed by an extremely large strong-smelling man in a mountainous many-caped greatcoat, who with a bob of his head and a kick out behind, intimated that paying time was come for him. Growls were then heard of its not being half an hour, or of not having had their full time, accompanied by dives into the pockets and reticules for the needful—each person wondering how little he could give without a snubbing.

Quite "optional" of course. Billy, who was bent on doing the magnificent, produced a large green-and-gold-tasseled purse, almost as big as a stocking, and drew therefrom a great five-shilling piece, which having tapped imposingly on his plate, he handed ostentatiously to the man, saying, "for this lady and me," just as if she belonged to him; whereupon down went the head even with the table, with an undertoned intimation that Billy "needn't 'urry, for he would make it all right with the guard." The waiter followed close on the heels of the coachman, drawing every body for half-a-crown for the dinner, besides what they had had to drink, and what they "pleased for himself," and Billy again anticipated the lady by paying for both. Instead, however, of disputing his right so to do, she seemed to take it as a matter of course, and bent a little forward and said in a sort of half-whisper, though loud enough to be heard by a twinkling-eyed, clayey-complexioned she-outsider, sitting opposite, dressed in a puce-coloured cloth pelisse and a pheasant-feather bonnet, "I fear you will think me very troublesome, but do you think you could manage to get me a finger-glass?" twiddling her pretty taper fingers as she spoke.

"Certainly!" replied Billy, all alacrity, "certainly."

"With a little tepid water," continued Miss Willing, looking imploringly at Billy as he rose to fulfil her behests.

"Such airs!" growled Pheasant-feathers to her next neighbour with an indignant toss of her colour-varying head.

5

Billy presently appeared, bearing one of the old deep blue-patterned finger-glasses, with a fine damask napkin, marked with a ducal coronet—one of the usual perquisites of servitude.

Miss then holding each pretty hand downwards, stripped her fingers of their rings, just as a gardener strips a stalk of currants of its fruit, dropping, however, a large diamond ring (belonging to her ladyship, which she was just airing) skilfully under the table, and for which fat Billy had to dive like a dog after an otter.

"Oh, dear!" she was quite ashamed at her awkwardness and the trouble she had given, she assured Billy, as he rose red and panting from the pursuit.

"Done on purpose to show her finery," muttered Pheasant-feather bonnet, with a sneer.

Miss having just passed the wet end of the napkin across her cherry lips and pearly teeth, and dipped her fingers becomingly in the warm water, was restoring her manifold rings, when the shrill *twang, twang, twang* of the horn, with the prancing of some of the newly-harnessed cripples on the pavement as they tried to find their legs, sounded up the arch-way into the little room, and warned our travellers that they should be reinvesting themselves in their wraps. So declining any more Teneriffe, Miss Willing set the example by drawing on her pretty kid gloves, and rising to give the time to the rest. Up they all got.

CHAPTER III. THE ROAD RESUMED.—MISS PHEASANT-FEATHERS.

THE room, as we said before, being crammed, and our fair friend Miss Willing taking some time to pass gracefully down the line of chair-backs, many of whose late occupants were now swinging their arms about in all the exertion of tying up their mouths, and fighting their ways into their over-coats, Mr. . Pringle, as he followed, had a good opportunity of examining her exquisite *tournure*, than which he thought he never saw anything more beautifully perfect. He was quite proud that a little more width of room at the end of the table enabled him to squeeze past a robing, Dutch-built British-lace-vending pack-woman, and reclaim his fair friend, just as a gentleman does his partner at the end of an old country dance. How exultingly he marched her through the line of inn hangers-on, hostlers, waiters, porters, post-boys, coachmen, and insatiable Matthews-at-home of an inn establishment, "Boots," a gentleman who will undertake all characters in succession for a consideration. How thankful we ought to be to be done with these harpies!

Bouncible, either mistaking the rank of his guests, or wanting to have a better look at the lady, emerged from his glass-fronted den of a bar, and salaam'd them up to the dirty coach, where the highly-fee'd coachman stood door in hand, waiting to perform the last act of attention for his money. In went Billy and the beauty, or rather the beauty and Billy, bang went the door, the outsiders scrambled up on to their perches and shelves as best they could. "*All right! Sit tight!*" was presently heard, and whip, jip, crack, cut, three blind 'uns and a bolter were again bumping the lumbering vehicle along the cobble-stoned street, bringing no end of cherry cheeks and corkscrew ringlets to the windows, to mark chat important epoch of the day, the coach passing by.

Billy, feeling all the better for his dinner, and inspirited by sundry gulps of wine, proceeded to make himself comfortable, in order to open fire as soon as ever the coach got off the stones. He took a rapid retrospect of all the various angels he had encountered, those who had favoured him, those who had frowned, and he was decidedly of opinion that he had never seen anything to compare to the fair lady before him. He was rich and thriving and would please himself without consulting Want-nothin'-but-what's-right Jerry, Half-a-yard-of-the-table Joe, or any of them. It wasn't like as if they were to be in Co. with him in the lady. She would never come into the balance sheets. No; she was to be all his, and they had no business with it. He believed Want-nothin'-but-what's-right would be glad if he never married. Just then the coach glid from the noisy pavement on to the comparatively speaking silent macadamised road, and Billy and the lady opened fire simultaneously, the lady about the discomforts of coach-travelling, which she had never tried before, and Billy about the smack of the Teneriffe, which he thought very earthy. He had some capital wine at home, he said, as everybody has. This led him to London, the street conveniences or inconveniences as they then were of the metropolis, which subject he plied for the purpose of finding out as well where the lady lived as whether her carriage would meet her or not; but this she skilfully parried, by asking Billy where he lived, and finding it was Doughty Street, Russell Square, she observed, as in truth it is, that it was a very airy part of the town, and proceeded to expatiate on the beauty of the flowers in Covent Garden, from whence she got to the theatres, then to the opera, intimating a very considerable acquaintance as well with the capital as with that enchanted circle, the West-end, comprising in its contracted limits what is called the world. Billy was puzzled. He wished she mightn't be a cut above him—such lords, such ladies, such knowledge of the court—could she be a maid-of-honour? Well, he didn't care. No ask no have, so he proceeded with the pumping process again. "Did she live in town?"

Fair Lady.—"Part of the year."

Billy.—"During the season I 'spose?"

Fair Lady.—"During the sitting of parliament."

"There again!" thought Billy, feeling the expectation-funds fall ten per cent, at least. "Well, faint heart never won fair lady," continued he to himself, considering how next he should sound her. She was very beautiful—what pretty pearly teeth she had, and such a pair of rosy lips—such a fair forehead too, and *such* nice hair—he'd give a fipun note for a kiss!—he'd give a tenpun note for a kiss!—dashed if he wouldn't give a fifty-pun for a kiss. Then he wondered what Head-and-shoulders Smith would think of her. As he didn't seem to be making much progress, however, in the information way, he now desisted from that consideration, and while contemplating her beauty considered how best he should carry on the siege. Should he declare who and what he was, making the best of himself of course, and ask her to be equally explicit, or should he beat about the bush a little longer and try to fish out what he could about her.

They had a good deal of day before them yet, dark though the latter part of it would be; which, however, on second thoughts, he felt might be rather favourable, inasmuch as she wouldn't see when he was taken aback by her answers. He would beat about the bush a little longer. It was very pleasant sport.

"Did you say you lived in Chelsea?" at length asked Billy, in a stupid self-convicting sort of way.

"No," replied the fair lady with a smile; "I never mentioned Chelsea."

"Oh, no; no more you did," replied Billy, taken aback, especially as the lady led up to no other place.

"Did she like the country?" at length asked he, thinking to try and fix her locality there, if he could not earth her in London.

"Yes, she liked the country, at least out of the season—there was no place like London in the season," she thought.

Billy thought so too; it was the best place in summer, and the only place in winter.

Well, the lady didn't know, but if she had to choose either place for a permanency, she would choose London.

This sent the Billy funds up a little. He forgot his intention of following her into the country, and began to expatiate upon the luxuries of London, the capital fish they got, the cod and hoyster sauce (for when excited, he knocked his h's about a little), the cod and hoyster sauce, the turbot, the mackerel, the mullet, that woodcock of the sea, as he exultingly called it, thinking what a tuck-out he would have in revenge for his country nice abstinence. He then got upon the splendour of his own house in Doughty Street—the most agreeable in London. Its spacious entrance, its elegant stone staircase; his beautiful drawingroom, with its maroon and rose-coloured brocaded satin damask curtains, and rich Toumay carpet, its beautiful chandelier of eighteen lights, and Piccolo pianoforte, and was describing a most magnificent mirror—we don't know what size, but most beautiful and becoming—when the pace of the vehicle was sensibly felt to relax; and before they had time to speculate on the cause, it had come to a stand-still.

"Stopped," observed Billy, lowering the window to look out for squalls.

No sooner was the window down, than a head at the door proclaimed mischief. The *tête-à-tête* was at an end. The guard was going to put Pheasant-feather bonnet inside. Open sesame — *W-h-i-s-h*. In came the cutting wind—oh dear what a day!

"Rum for a leddy?" asked the guard, raising a great half-frozen, grog-blossomy face out of the blue and white coil of a shawl-cravat in which it was enveloped,—"Git in" continued he, shouldering the leddy up the steps, without waiting for an answer, and in popped Pheasant-feathers; when, slamming-to the door, he cried "*right!*" to the coachman, and on went the vehicle, leaving the enterer to settle into a seat by its shaking, after the manner of the omnibus cads, who seem to think all they have to do is to see people past the door. As it was, the new-comer alighted upon Billy, who cannoned her off against the opposite door, and then made himself as big as he could, the better to incommode her. Pheasant-feathers, however, having effected an entrance, seemed to regard herself as good as her neighbours, and forthwith proceeded to adjust the window to her liking, despite the eyeing and staring of Miss Willing. Billy was indignant at the nasty peppermint-drop-smelling woman intruding between the wind and his beauty, and inwardly resolved he would dock the guard's fee for his presumption in putting her there. Miss Willing gathered herself together as if afraid of contamination; and, forgetting her *role*, declared, after a jolt received in one of her seat-shiftings, that it was just the "smallest coach she had ever been in." She then began to scrutinise her female companion's attire.

A cottage-bonnet, made of pheasant-feathers; was there ever such a frightful tiling seen,—all the colours of the rainbow combined,—must be a poacher's daughter, or a poulterer's. Paste egg-coloured ribbons; what a cloth pelisse,—puce colour in some parts,—bath-brick colour in others,—nearly drab in others,—thread-bare all over. Dare say she thought herself fine, with her braided waist, up to her ears. Her glazy gloves might be any colour—black, brown, green, gray. Then a qualm shot across Miss Willing's mind that she had seen the pelisse before. Yes, no, yes; she believed it was the very one she had sold to Mrs. Pickles' nursery governess for eighteen shillings. So it was. She had stripped the fur edging off herself, and there were the marks. Who could the wearer be? Where could she have got it? She could not recollect ever having seen her unwholesome face before. And yet the little ferrety, white-lashed eyes settled upon her as if they knew her. Who could she be? What, if she had lived fellow—(we'll not say what)—with the creature somewhere. There was no knowing people out of their working clothes, especially when they set up to ride inside of coaches. Altogether, it was very unpleasant.

Billy remarked his fair friend's altered mood, and rightly attributed it to the intrusion of the nasty woman, whose gaudy headgear the few flickering rays of a December sun were now lighting up, making the feathers, so beautiful on a bird, look, to Billy's mind, so ugly on a bonnet, at least on the bonnet that now thatched the frightful face beside him. Billy saw the fair lady was not accustomed to these sort of companions, and wished he had only had the sense to book the rest of the inside when the coach stopped to dine. However, it could not be helped now; so, having ascertained that Pheasant-feathers was going all the way to "Lunnnn," as she called it, when the sun sunk behind its massive leade'on'loud, preparatory to that long reign of darkness with which travellers were oppressed,—for there were no oil-lamps to the roofs of stage-coaches,—Billy being no longer able to contemplate the beauties of his charmer, now changed his seat, for a little confidential conversation by her side.

He then, after a few comforting remarks, not very flattering to Pheasant-feathers' beauty, resumed his expatiations about his splendid house in Doughty Street. Russell Square, omitting, of course, to mention that it had been fitted up to suit the taste of another lady, who had jilted him. He began about his dining-room, twenty-five feet by eighteen, with a polished steel fender, and "pictors" all about the walls; for, like many people, he fancied himself a judge of the fine arts, and, of course, was very frequently fleeced.

This subject, however, rather hung fire, a dining-room being about the last room in a house that a lady cares to hear about, so she presently cajoled him into the more genial region of the kitchen, which, unlike would-be fine ladies of the present day, she was not ashamed to recognise. From the kitchen they proceeded to the store-room, which Billy explained was entered by a door at the top of the back stairs, six feet nine by two feet eight, covered on both sides with crimson cloth, brass moulded in panels and mortise latch. He then got upon the endless, but "never-lady-tiring," subject of bed-rooms—his best bed-room, with a most elegant five-feet-three canopy-top, mahogany bedstead, with beautiful French chintz furniture, lined with pink, outer and inner valance, trimmed silk tassel fringe, &c., &c., &c. And so he went maundering on, paving the way most elaborately to an offer, as some men are apt to do, instead of getting briskly to the "ask-mamma" point, which the ladies are generally anxious to have them at.

To be sure, Billy had been bowled over by a fair, or rather unfair one, who had appeared quite as much interested about his furniture and all his belongings as Miss Willing did, and who, when she got the offer, and found he was not nearly so well off as Jack Sanderson, declared she was never so surprised in her life as when Billy proposed; for though, as she politely said, every one who knew him must respect him, yet he had never even entered her head in any other light than that of an agreeable companion. This was Miss Amelia Titterton, afterwards Mrs. Sanderson. Another lady, as we said before (Miss Bowerbank), had done worse; for she had regularly jilted him, after putting him to no end of expense in furnishing his house, so that, upon the whole, Billy had cause to be cautious. A coach, too, with its jolts and its jerks, and its brandy-and-water stoppages, is but ill calculated for the delicate performance of offering, to say nothing of having a pair of nasty white-lashed, inquisitive-looking, ferrety eyes sitting opposite, with a pair of listening ears, nestling under the thatch of a pheasant-feather bonnet. All things considered, therefore, Billy may, perhaps, stand excused for his slowness, especially as he did not know but what he was addressing a countess.

And so the close of a scarcely dawned December day, was followed by the shades of night, and still the jip, jip, jipping; whip, whip, whipping; creak, creak, creaking of the heavy lumbering coach, was accompanied by Billy's maunderings about his noble ebony this, and splendid mahogany that, varied with, here and there, a judicious interpolation of an "indeed," or a "how beautiful," from Miss Willing, to show how interested she was in the recital; for ladies are generally good listeners, and Miss Willing was essentially so.

The "demeanour of the witness" was lost, to be sure, in the chancery-like darkness that prevailed; and Billy felt it might be all blandishment, for nothing could be more marked or agreeable than the interest both the other ladies had taken in his family, furniture, and effects. Indeed, as he felt, they all took much the same course, for, for cool home-questioning, there is no man can compete with an experienced woman. They get to the "What-have-you-got, and What-will-you-do" point, before a man has settled upon the line of inquiry—very likely before he has got done with that interesting topic—the weather.

At length, a sudden turn of the road revealed to our friends, who were sitting with their faces to the horses, the first distant curve of glow-worm-like lamps in the distance, and presently the great white invitations to "try warren's," or "day and martin's blacking," began to loom through the darkness of the dead walls of the outskirts of London. They were fast approaching the metropolis. The gaunt elms and leafless poplars presently became fewer, while castellated and sentry-box-looking summer-houses stood dark in the little paled-off gardens. At last the villas, and semi-detached villas, collapsed into one continuous gas-lit shop-dotted street. The shops soon became better and more frequent,—more ribbons and flowers, and fewer periwinkle stalls. They now got upon the stones. Billy's heart jumped into his mouth at the jerk, for he knew not how soon his charmer and he might part, and as yet he had not even ascertained her locality. Now or never, thought be, rising to the occasion, and, with difficulty of utterance, he expressed a hope that he might have the pleasure of seeing her 'ome.

"Thank you, *no*," replied Miss Willing, emphatically, for it was just the very thing she most dreaded, letting him see her reception by the servants.

"Humph!" grunted Billy, feeling his funds fall five-and-twenty per cent.—".Miss Titterton or Miss Bowerbank over again," thought he.

"Not but that I most fully appreciate your kindness," whispered Miss Willing, in the sweetest tone possible, right into his ear, thinking by Billy's silence that her vehemence had offended him; "but," continued she, "I'm only going to the house of a friend, a long way from you, and I expect a servant to meet me at the Green Man in Oxford Street."

"Well, but let me see you to the"—(puff, gasp)—"Green Man," ejaculated Billy, the funds of hope rising more rapidly than his words.

"It's very kind," whispered Miss Willing, "and I feel it *very, very* much, but"—

"But if your servant shouldn't come," interrupted Billy, "you'd never find your way to Brompton in this nasty dense yellow fog," for they had now got into the thick of a fine fat one.

"Oh, but I'm not going to Brompton," exclaimed Miss Willing, amused at this second bad shot of Billy's at her abode.

"Well, wherever you are going, I shall only be too happy to escort you," replied Billy, "I know Lunnun well."

"So do I," thought Miss Willing, with a sigh. And the coach having now reached that elegant hostelry, the George and Blue Badger, in High Holborn, Miss showed her knowledge of it by intimating to Billy that that was the place for him to alight; so taking off her glove she tendered him her soft hand, which Billy grasped eagerly, still urging her to let him see her home, or at all events to the Green Man, in Oxford Street.

Miss, however, firmly but kindly declined his services, assuring him repeatedly that she appreciated his kindness, which she evinced by informing him that she was going to a friend's at No. —, Grosvenor Square, that she would only be in town for a couple of nights; but that if he *really* wished to see her again,—"*really* wished it," she repeated with an emphasis, for she didn't want to be trifled with,—she would be happy to see him to tea at eight o'clock on the following evening.

"*Eight o'clock!*" gasped Billy. "No. ——, Gruvenor Square," repeated he. "I knows it—I'll be with you to a certainty—I'll be with you to a"—(puff)—"certainty." So saying, he made a sandwich of her fair taper-fingered hand, and then responded to the inquiry of the guard, if there was any one to "git oot there," by alighting. And he was so excited that he walked off, leaving his new silk umbrella and all his luggage in the coach, exclaiming, as he worked his way through the fog to Doughty Street, "No.——, Gruvenor Square—eight o'clock—eight o'clock—No.——, Gruvenor Square—was there ever such a beauty!—be with her to a certainty, be with her to a certainty." Saying which, he gave an ecstatic bound, and next moment found himself sprawling a-top of a murder!—crying apple-woman in the gutter. Leaving him there to get up at his leisure, let us return to his late companion in the coach.

Scarcely was the door closed on his exit, ere a sharp shrill "*You don't know me!—you don't know me!*" sounded from under the pheasant-feather bonnet, and shot through Miss Willing like a thrill.

"Yes, no, yes; who is it?" ejaculated she, thankful they were alone.

9

"Sarey Grimes, to be sure," replied the voice, in a semi-tone of exultation.

"Sarah Grimes!" exclaimed Miss Willing, recollecting the veriest little imp of mischief that ever came about a place, the daughter of a most notorious poacher. "So it is! Why, Sarah, who would ever have thought of seeing you grown into a great big woman."

"I thought you didn't know me," replied Sarah; "I used often to run errands for you," added she.

"I remember," replied Miss Willing, feeling in her reticule for her purse. Sarah had carried certain delicate missives in the country that Miss Willing would now rather have forgotten, how thankful she was that the creature had not introduced herself when her fat friend was in the coach. "What are you doing now?" asked Miss Willing, jingling up the money at one end of the purse to distinguish between the gold and the silver.

Sarey explained that being now out of place (she had been recently dismissed from a cheesemonger's at Lutterworth for stealing a copper coal-scoop, a pound of whitening, and a pair of gold spectacles, for which a donkey-travelling general merchant had given her seven and sixpence), the guard of the coach, who was her great-uncle, had given her a lift up to town to try what she could do there again; and Miss Willing's quick apprehension seeing that there was some use to be made of such a sharp-witted thing, having selected a half-sovereign out of her purse, thus addressed her:

"Well, Sarah, I'm glad to see you again. You are very much improved, and will be very good-looking. There's half a sovereign for you," handing it to her, "and if you'll come to me at six o'clock to-morrow evening in Grosvenor Square, I dare say I shall be able to look out some things that may be useful to you."

"Thanke, mum; thanke!" exclaimed Sarey, delighted at the idea. "I'll be with you, you may depend."

"You know Big Ben," continued Miss Willing, "who was my lord's own man; he's hall-porter now, ring and tell him you come for me, and he'll let you in at the door."

"Certainly, mum, certainly," assented Pheasant-feathers, thinking how much more magnificent that would be than sneaking down the area.

And the coach having now reached the Green Man, Miss Willing alighted and took a coach to Grosvenor Square, leaving Miss Grimes to pursue its peregrinations to the end of its journey.

And Billy Pringle having, with the aid of the "pollis," appeased the basket-woman's wrath, was presently ensconced in his beautiful house in Doughty Street.

So, *tinkle, tinkle, tinkle*,—down goes the curtain on this somewhat long chapter.

CHAPTER IV. A GLASS COACH.—MISS WILLING (EN GRAND COSTUME)

NEXT day our friend Billy was buried in looking after his lost luggage and burnishing up the gilt bugle-horn buttons of the coat, waist-coat, and shorts of the Royal Epping Archers, in which he meant to figure in the evening. Having, through the medium of his "Boyle," ascertained the rank of the owner of the residence where he was going to be regaled, he ordered a glass-coach—not a coach made of glass, juvenile readers, in which we could see a gentleman disparting himself like a gold-fish in a glass bowl, but a better sort of hackney coach with a less filthy driver, which, by a "beautiful fiction" of the times, used to be considered the hirer's "private carriage."

It was not the "thing" in those days to drive up to a gentleman's door in a public conveyance, and doing the magnificent was very expensive: for the glass fiction involved a pair of gaunt raw-boned horses, which, with the napless-hatted drab-turned-up-with-grease-coated-coachman, left wry little change out of a sovereign. How thankful we ought to be to railways and Mr. Fitzroy for being able to cut about openly at the rate of sixpence a mile. The first great man who drove up St. James's Street at high tide in a Hansom, deserves to have his portrait painted at the public expense, for he opened the door of common sense and utility.

What a follow-my-leader-world it is! People all took to street cabs simultaneously, just as they did to walking in the Park on a Sunday when Count D'Orsay set up his "'andsomest ombrella in de vorld," being no longer able to keep a horse. But we are getting into recent times instead of attending Mr. Pringle to his party. He is supposed to have ordered his glass phenomenon.

Now Mr. Forage, the job-master, in Lamb's Conduit Street, with whom our friend did his magnificence, "performed funerals" also, as his yard-doors indicated, and being rather "full," or more properly speaking, empty, he acted upon the principle of all coaches being black in the dark, and sent a mourning one, so there was a striking contrast between the gaiety of the Royal Epping Archers' uniform—pea-green coat with a blue collar, salmon-coloured vest and shorts—

in which Mr. Pringle was attired, and the gravity of the vehicle that conveyed him. However, our lover was so intent upon taking care of his pumps, for the fog had made the flags both slippery and greasy, that he popped in without noticing the peculiarity, and his stuttering knock-knee'd hobble-de-hoy, yclept "Paul," having closed the door and mounted up behind, they were presently jingling away to the west, Billy putting up first one leg and then the other on to the opposite seat to admire his white-gauze-silk-encased calves by the gas and chemists' windows as they passed. So he went fingering and feeling at his legs, and pulling and hauling at his coat,—for the Epping Archer uniform had got rather tight, and, moreover, had been made on the George-the-Fourth principle, of not being easily got into—along Oxford Street, through Hanover Square, and up Brook Street, to the spacious region that contained the object of his adoration. The coach presently drew up at a stately Italian-column porticoed mansion: down goes Paul, but before he gets half through his meditated knock, the door opens suddenly in his face, and he is confronted by Big Ben in the full livery,—we beg pardon,—uniform of the Delacey family, beetroot-coloured coat, with cherry-coloured vest and shorts, the whole elaborately bedizened with gold-lace.

The unexpected apparition, rendered more formidable by the blazing fire in the background, throwing a lurid light over the giant, completely deprived little Paul of his breath, and he stood gaping and shaking as if he expected the monster to address him.

"Who may you please to want?" at length demanded Ben, in a deep sonorous tone of mingled defiance and contempt.

"P—p—p—please, wo—wo—wo—want," stuttered little Paul, now recollecting that he had never been told who to ask for.

"Yes, who do you wish to see?" demanded Ben, in a clear explanatory tone, for though he had agreed to dress up for the occasion on the reciprocity principle of course—Miss Willing winking at his having two nephews living in the house—he by no means undertook to furnish civility to any of the undergraduates of life, as he called such apologies as Paul.

"I—I—I'll ask," replied Paul, glad to escape back to the coach, out of which the Royal Archer's bull-head was now protruding, anxious to be emancipated.

"Who—ho—ho am I to a—a—ask for, pa—pa—per—please?" stuttered Paul, trembling all over with fear and excitement, for he had never seen such a sight except in a show.

"Ask for!" muttered Billy, now recollecting for the first time that the fair lady and he were mutually ignorant of each other's names. "Ask for! What if it should be a hoax?" thought he; "how foolish he would look!"

While these thoughts were revolving in Billy's mind, Big Ben, having thrust his hands deep into the pockets of his cherry-coloured shorts, was contemplating the dismal-looking coach in the disdainful cock-up-nose sort of way that a high-life Johnny looks at what he considers a low-life equipage; wondering, we dare say, who was to be deceived by such a thing.

Billy, seeing the case was desperate, resolved to put a bold face on the matter, especially as he remembered his person could not be seen in the glass coach; so, raising his crush hat to his face, he holloaed out, "*I say! is this the Earl of Delacey's?*"

"It is," replied Ben, with a slight inclination of his gigantic person.

"Then, let me out," demanded Billy of Paul. And this request being complied with, Billy skipped smartly across the flags, and was presently alongside of Ben, whispering up into his now slightly-inclined ear, "*I say, was there a lady arrived here last night from the country?*" (He was going to say "by the coach," but he checked himself when he got to the word country.)

"There was, sir," replied Ben, relaxing into something like condescension.

"Then I'm come to see her," whispered Billy, with a grin.

"Your name, if you please, sir?" replied Ben, still getting up the steam of politeness.

"Mr. Pringle—Mr. William Pringle!" replied Billy with firmness.

"All right, sir," replied the blood-red monster, pretending to know more than he did; and, motioning Billy onward into the black and white marble-flagged entrance hall, he was about to shut him in, when Billy, recollecting himself, holloaed, "'*Ome!*" to his coachman, so that he mightn't be let in for the two days' hire. The door then closed, and he was in for an adventure.

It will be evident to our fair friends that the Archer bold had the advantage over the lady, in having all his raiment in town, while she had all hers, at least all the pick of hers,—her first-class things,—in the country. Now every body knows that what looks very smart in the country looks very seedy in London, and though the country cousins of life do get their new things to take back with them there, yet regular town-comers have theirs ready, or ready at all events to try on against they arrive, and so have the advantage of looking like civilised people while they are up. London, however, is one excellent place for remedying any little deficiency of any sort, at least if a person has only either money or credit, and a lady or gentleman can soon be rigged out by driving about to the different shops.

11

Now it so happened that Miss Willing had nothing of her own in town, that she felt she would be doing herself justice to appear before Billy in, and had omitted bringing her ladyship's keys, whereby she might have remedied the deficiency out of that wardrobe; however, with such a commission as she held, there could be no difficulty in procuring the loan of whatever was wanted from her ladyship's milliner. We may mention that on accepting office under Lady Delacey, Miss Willing, with the greatest spirit of fairness, had put her ladyship's custom in competition among three distinguished modistes, viz. her old friend Madame Adelaide Banboxeney, Madame Celeste de Montmorency, of Dover Street, and Miss Julia Freemantle, of Cowslip Street, May Fair; and Miss Freemantle having offered the same percentage on the bill (15 L.) as the other two, and 20 L. a year certain money more than Madame Banboxeney, and 25 L. more than Madame Celeste de Montmorency, Miss Freemantle had been duly declared the purchaser, as the auctioneers say, and in due time (as soon as a plausible quarrel could be picked with the then milliner) was in the enjoyment of a very good thing, for though the Countess Delacey, in the Gilpin-ian spirit of the age, tried to tie Miss Freemantle down to price, yet she overlooked the extras, the little embroidery of a bill, if we may so call it, such as four pound seventeen and sixpence for a buckle, worth perhaps the odd silver, and the surreptitious lace, at no one knows what, so long as they were not all in one item, and were cleverly scattered about the bill in broken sums, just as the lady thought the ribbon dear at a shilling a yard, but took it when the counter-skipper replied, "S'pose, marm, then, we say thirteen pence"—Miss Willing having had a consultation with Miss Freemantle as to the most certain means of quashing the Countess of Honiton, broached her own little requirements, and Miss Freemantle, finding that she only wanted the dress for one night, agreed to lend her a very rich emerald-green Genoa velvet evening-dress, trimmed with broad Valenciennes lace, she was on the point of furnishing for Alderman Boozey's son's bran-new wife; Miss Freemantle feeling satisfied, as she said, that Miss Willing would do it no harm; indeed, would rather benefit it by the sit her fine figure would give it, in the same way as shooters find it to their advantage to let their keepers have a day or two's wear out of their new shoes in order to get them to go easy for themselves.

The reader will therefore have the goodness to consider Miss Willing arrayed in Alderman Boozey's son's bran-new wife's bran-new Genoa velvet dress, with a wreath of pure white camellias on her beautiful brown Madonna-dressed hair, and a massive true-lover's-knot brooch in brilliants at her bosom. On her right arm she wears a magnificent pearl armlet, which Miss Freemantle had on sale or return from that equitable diamond-merchant, Samuel Emanuel Moses, of the Minories, the price ranging, with Miss Freemantle, from eighty to two hundred and fifty guineas, according to the rank and paying properties of the inquirer, though as between Moses and "Mantle," the price was to be sixty guineas, or perhaps pounds, depending upon the humour Moses might happen to be in, when she came with the dear £. s. d. The reader will further imagine an elegant little boudoir with its amber-coloured silk fittings and furniture, lit up with the united influence of the best wax and Wallsend, and Miss Willing sitting at an inlaid centre-table, turning over the leaves of Heath's "Picturesque Annual" of the preceding year. Opposite the fire are large white and gold folding-doors, opening we know not where, outside of which lurks Pheasant-feathers, placed there by Miss Willing on a service of delicacy.

CHAPTER V. THE LADY'S BOUDOIR.—A DECLARATION.

THIS way, sir,—please, sir,—yes, sir," bowed the now obsequious Ben, guiding Billy by the light of a chamber candle through the intricacies of the halflit inner entrance. "Take care, sir, there's a step, sir," continued he, stopping and showing where the first stumbling-block resided. Billy then commenced the gradual accent of the broad, gently-rising staircase, each step increasing his conviction of the magnitude of the venture, and making him feel that his was not the biggest house in town. As he proceeded he wondered what Nothin'-but-what's-right Jerry, or Half-a-yard-of-the-table Joe, above all Mrs. Half-a-yard-of-the-table, would say if they could see him thus visiting at a nobleman's house, it seemed more like summut in a book or a play than downright, reality. Still there was no reason why a fine lady should not take a fancy to him— many deuced deal uglier fellows than he had married fine ladies, and he would take his chance along with the rest of them—so he laboured up after Ben, hoping he might not come down stairs quicker than he went up.

The top landing being gained, they passed through lofty folding-doors into the suite of magnificent but now put-away drawing-rooms, whose spectral half collapsed canvas bags, and covered statues and sofas, threw a Kensal-Green-Cemetery sort of gloom over Billy's spirits;

speedily, however, to be dispelled by the radiance of the boudoir into which he was now passed through an invisible door in the gilt-papered wall. "Mr. William Pringle, ma'm," whispered Ben, in a tone that one could hardly reconcile to the size of the monster: and Miss Willing having risen at the sound of the voice, bowing, Billy and she were presently locked hand in hand, smiling and teeth-showing most extravagantly. "I'll ring for tea presently," observed she to Ben, who seemed disposed to fuss and loiter about the room. "If you please, my lady," replied Ben, bowing himself backwards through the panel. Happy Billy was then left alone with his charmer, save that beetroot-coloured Ben was now listening at one door on his own account, and Pheasant-feathers at the other on Miss Willing's.

Billy was quite taken aback. If he had been captivated in the coach what chance had he now, with all the aid of dress, scenery, and decorations. He thought he had never seen such a beauty— he thought he had never seen such a bust—he thought he had never seen such an arm! Miss Titterton—pooh!—wasn't to be mentioned in the same century—hadn't half such a waist. "Won't you be seated?" at length asked Miss Willing, as Billy still stood staring and making a mental inventory of her charms. "Seat"—(puff)—"seat" (wheeze), gasped Billy, looking around at the shining amber-coloured magnificence by which he was surrounded, as if afraid to venture, even in his nice salmon-coloured shorts. At length he got squatted on a gilt chair by his charmer's side, when taking to look at his toes, she led off the ball of conversation. She had had enough of the billing and cooing or gammon and spinach of matrimony, and knew if she could not bring him to book at once, time would not assist her. She soon probed his family circle, and was glad to find there was no "mamma" to "ask," that dread parent having more than once been too many for her. She took in the whole range of connection with the precision of an auctioneer or an equity draftsman.

There was no occasion for much diplomacy on her part, for Billy came into the trap just like a fly to a "Ketch-'em-alive O!" The conversation soon waxed so warm that she quite forgot to ring for the tea; and Ben, who affected early hours in the winter, being slightly asthmatical, as a hall-porter ought to be, at length brought it in of his own accord. Most polite he was; "My lady" and "Your ladyship-ing" Miss Willing with accidental intention every now and then, which raised Billy's opinion of her consequence very considerably. And so he sat, and sipped and sipped, and thought what a beauty she would be to transfer to Doughty Street. Tea, in due time, was followed by the tray—Melton pie, oysters, sandwiches, anchovy toast, bottled stout, sherry and Seltzer water, for which latter there was no demand.

A profane medicine-chest-looking mahogany case then made its appearance, which, being opened, proved to contain four cut-glass spirit-bottles, labelled respectively, "Rum," "Brandy," "Whiskey," "Gin," though they were not true inscriptions, for there were two whiskey's and two brandy's. A good old-fashioned black-bottomed kettle having next mounted a stand placed on the top bar, Miss intimated to Ben that if they had a few more coals, he need not "trouble to sit up;" and these being obtained, our friends made a brew, and then drew their chairs together to enjoy the feast of reason and the flow of soul; Miss slightly raising Alderman Boozey's son's bran-new wife's bran-new emerald-green velvet dress to show her beautiful white-satin slippered foot, as it now rested on the polished steel fender.

The awkwardness of resuming the interrupted addresses being at length overcome by sundry gulphs of the inspiring fluid, our friend Mr. Pringle was soon in full fervour again. He anathematised the lawyers and settlements, and delay, and was all for being married off-hand at the moment.

Miss, on her part, was dignified and prudent. All she would say was that Mr. William Pringle was not indifferent to her,—"No," sighed she, "he wasn't"—but there were many, many considerations, and many, many points to be discussed, and many, many questions to be asked of each other, before they could even begin to *talk* of such a thing as immediate—"hem"—(she wouldn't say the word) turning away her pretty head.

"*Ask away, then!*" exclaimed Billy, helping himself to another beaker of brandy—for he saw he was approaching the "Ketch-'em-alive O." Miss then put the home-question whether his family knew what he was about, and finding they did not, she saw there was no time to lose; so knocking off the expletives, she talked of many considerations and points, the main one being to know how she was likely to be kept,—whether she was to have a full-sized footman, or an under-sized stripling, or a buttony boy of a page, or be waited upon by that greatest aversion to all female minds, one of her own sex. Not that she had the slightest idea of saying "No," but her experience of life teaching her that all early grandeur may be mastered by footmen, she could very soon calculate what sort of a set down she was likely to have by knowing the style of her attendant. "Show me your footman, and I will tell you what you are," was one of her maxims. Moreover, it is well for all young ladies to have a sort of rough estimate, at all events, of what they are likely to have,—which, we will venture to say, unlike estimates in general, will fall very far short of the reality. Our friend Billy, however, was quite in the promising mood, and if she had asked for half-a-dozen Big Bens he would have promised her them, canes, powder, and all.

"Oh! she should have anything, everything she wanted! A tall man with good legs, and all right about the mouth,—an Arab horse, an Erard harp, a royal pianoforte, a silver tea-urn, a gold coffee-pot, a service of gold—*eat gold*, if she liked," and as he declared she might eat gold if she liked, he dropped upon his salmon-coloured knees, and with his glass of brandy in one hand, and hers in the other, looked imploringly up at her, a beautiful specimen of heavy sentimentality; and Miss, thinking she had got him far enough, and seeing it was nearly twelve o'clock, now urged him to rise, and allow her maid to go and get him a coach. Saying which, she disengaged her hand, and slipping through the invisible door, was presently whispering her behests to the giggling Pheasant-feathers, on the other side of the folding ones. A good half-hour, however, elapsed before one of those drowsy vehicles could be found, during which time our suitor obtained the fair lady's consent to allow him to meet her at her friend Mrs. Freemantle's, as she called her, in Cowslip Street, May Fair, at three o'clock in the following afternoon; and the coach having at length arrived, Miss Willing graciously allowed Mr. Pringle to kiss her hand, and then accompanied him to the second landing of the staircase, which commanded the hall, in order to check any communication between Pheasant-feathers and him.

The reader will now perhaps accompany us to this famed milliner, dress and mantle-maker's, who will be happy to execute any orders our fair ones may choose to favour her with.

Despite the anathemas of a certain law lord, match-forwarding is quite the natural prerogative and instinct of women. They all like it, from the duchess downwards, and you might as well try to restrain a cat from mousing as a woman from match-making. Miss Freemantle (who acted Mrs. on this occasion) was as fond of the pursuit as any one. She looked Billy over with a searching, scrutinising glance, thinking what a flat he was, and wondered what he would think of himself that time twelvemonths. Billy, on his part, was rather dumb-foundered. Talking before two women was not so easy as talking to one; and he did not get on with the immediate matrimony story half so well as he had done over-night. The ladies saw his dilemma, and Miss Willing quickly essayed to relieve him. She put him through his pleadings with all the skill of the great Serjeant Silvertougue, making Billy commit himself most irretrievably.

"Mamma" (Miss Freemantle that is to say) then had her innings.

She was much afraid it couldn't be done off-hand—indeed she was. There was a place on the Border—Gretna Green—she dare say'd he'd heard of it; but then it was a tremendous distance, and would take half a lifetime to get to it. Besides, Miss p'raps mightn't like taking such a journey at that time of year.

Miss looked neither yes nor no. Mamma was more against it than her, Mamma feeling for the countess's coming contest and her future favours. Other difficulties were then discussed, particularly that of publicity, which Miss dreaded more than the journey to Gretna. It must be kept secret, whatever was done. Billy must be sworn to secrecy, or Miss would have nothing to say to him. Billy was sworn accordingly.

Mamma then thought the best plan was to have the banns put up in some quiet church, where no questions would be asked as to where they lived, and it would be assumed that they resided within the parish, and when they had been called out, they could just go quietly and get married, which would keep things square with the countess and everybody else. And this arrangement being perfected, and liberty given to Billy to write to his bride, whose name and address were now furnished him, he at length took his departure; and the ladies having talked him over, then resolved themselves into a committee of taste, to further the forthcoming tournament. And by dint of keeping all hands at work all night, Miss Willing was enabled to return to the countess with the first instalment of such a series of lady-killing garments as mollified her heart, and enabled her to sustain the blow that followed, which however was mitigated by the assurance that Mr. and Mrs. William Pringle were going to live in London, and that Madam's taste would always be at her ladyship's command.

We wish we could gratify our lady readers with a description of the brilliant attire that so completely took the shine out of the Countess of Honiton as has caused her to hide her diminished head ever since, but our pen is unequal to the occasion, and even if we had had a John Leech to supply our deficiencies, the dresses of those days would look as nothing compared to the rotatory haystacks of the present one.

What fair lady can bear the sight of her face painted in one of the old poke bonnets of funner days? To keep things right, the bonnet ought to be painted to the face every year or two.

But to the lovers.

In due time "Mamma" (Miss Freemantle) presented her blooming daughter to the happy Billy, who was attended to the hymeneal alter by his confidential clerk, Head-and-shoulders Smith. Big Ben, who was dressed in a blue frock coat with a velvet collar, white kerseymere trousers, and varnished boots, looking very like one of the old royal dukes, was the only other person present at the interesting ceremony, save Pheasant-feathers, who lurked in one of the pews.

The secret had been well kept, for the evening papers of that day and the morning ones of the next first proclaimed to the "great world," that sphere of one's own acquaintance, that William Pringle, Esquire, of Doughty Street, Bussell Square, was married to Miss Emma Willing, of—the papers did not say where.

CHAPTER VI. THE HAPPY UNITED FAMILY.—CURTAIN CRESCENT.

THE PRINGLES of course were furious when they read the announcement of Billy's marriage. Such a degradation to such a respectable family, and communicated in such a way. We need scarcely say that at first they all made the worst of it, running Mrs. William down much below her real level, and declaring that Billy though hard enough in money matters, was soft enough in love affairs. Then Mrs. Half-a-yard-of-the-table Joe, who up to that time had been the *belle* of the family, essayed to pick her to pieces, intimating that she was much indebted to her dress—that fine feathers made fine birds—hoped that Billy would like paying for the clothes, and of spoiling it. Joe looked as if he was to perpetuate the family name. By-and-by, when it became known that the Countess Delacey's yellow carriage, with the high-stepping greys and the cocked-up-nose beet-root-and-cherry-coloured Johnnies, was to be seen astonishing the natives in Doughty Street, they began to think better of it; and though they did not stint themselves for rudeness (disguised as civility of course), they treated her less like a show, more especially when Billy was present. Still, though they could not make up their minds to be really civil to her, they could not keep away from her, just as the moth will be at the candle despite its unpleasant consequences. Indeed, it is one of the marked characteristics of Snobbism, that they won't be cut. At least, if you do get a Snob cut, ten to one but he will take every opportunity of rubbing up against you, or sitting down beside you in public, or overtaking you on the road, or stopping a mutual acquaintance with you in the street, either to show his indifference or his independence, or in the hope of its passing for intimacy. There are people who can't understand any coolness short of a kick. The Pringles were tiresome people. They would neither be in with Mrs. William, nor out with her. So there was that continual knag, knag, knagging going on in the happy united family, that makes life so pleasant and enjoyable. Mrs. William well knew, when any of them came to call upon her, that her sayings and doings would furnish recreation for the rest of the cage. It is an agreeable thing to have people in one's house acting the part of spies. One day Mrs. Joe, who lived in Guildford Street, seeing the Countess's carriage-horses cold-catching in Doughty Street, while her ladyship discussed some important millinery question with Mrs. William, could not resist the temptation of calling, and not being introduced to the Countess, said to Mis. William, with her best vinegar sneer, the next time they met. She "'oped she had told her fine friend that the vulgar woman she saw at her 'ouse was no connection of her's." But enough of such nonsense. Let us on to something more pleasant.

Well, then, of course the next step in our story is the appearance of our hero, the boy Billy——Fine Billy, aforesaid. Such a boy as never was seen! All other mammas went away dissatisfied with theirs, after they had got a peep of our Billy. If baby-shows had been in existence in those days, Mrs. Billy might have scoured the country and carried away all the prizes. Everybody was struck in a heap at the sight of him, and his sayings and doings were worthy of a place in Punch. So thought his parents, at least. What perfected their happiness, of course, operated differently with the family, and eased the minds of the ladies, as to the expediency of further outward civility to Mrs. William, who they now snubbed at all points, and prophesied all sorts of uncharitableness of. Mrs., on her side, surpassed them all in dress and good looks, and bucked Billy up into a very produceable-looking article. Though he mightn't exactly do for White's bay-window on a summer afternoon, he looked uncommonly well on "'Change," and capitally in the country. Of course, he came in for one of the three cardinal sources of abuse the world is always so handy with, viz., that a man either behaves ill to his wife, is a screw, or is out-running the constable, the latter, of course, being Billy's crime, which admitted of a large amount of blame being laid on the lady, though, we are happy to say, Billy had no trial of speed with the constable, for his wife, by whose permission men thrive, was a capital manager, and Billy slapped his fat thigh over his beloved balance-sheets every Christmas, exclaiming, as he hopped joyously round on one leg, snapping his finger and thumb, "*Our Billy shall be a gent! Our Billy shall be a gent!*" And he half came in to the oft-expressed wish of his wife, that he might live to see him united to a quality lady: Mr. and Lady

Arabella Pringle, Mr. and Lady Sophia Pringle, or Mr. and Lady Charlotte Elizabeth Pringle, as the case might be.

Vainglorious ambition! After an inordinate kidney supper, poor Billy was found dead in his chair. Great was the consternation among the Pringle family at the lamentable affliction. All except Jerry, who, speculating on his habits, had recently effected a policy on his life, were deeply shocked at the event. They buried him with all becoming pomp, and then, Jerry, who had always professed great interest in the boy Billy—so great, indeed, as to induce his brother (though with no great opinion of Jerry, but hoping that his services would never be wanted, and that it might ingratiate the nephew with the bachelor uncle,) to appoint him an executor and guardian—waited upon the widow, and with worlds of tears and pious lamentations, explained to her in the most unexplanatory manner possible, all how things were left, but begging that she would not give herself any trouble about her son's affairs, for, if she would attend to his spiritual wants, and instil high principles of honour, morality, and fine feeling into his youthful mind, he would look after the mere worldly dross, which was as nothing compared to the importance of the other. "Teach him to want nothin' but what's right," continued Jerry, as he thought most impressively. "Teach him to want nothin' but what's right, and when he grows up to manhood marry him to some nice, pious respectable young woman in his own rank of life, with a somethin' of her own; gentility is all very well to talk about, but it gets you nothin' at the market," added he, forgetting that he was against the mere worldly dross.

But Mrs. Pringle, who knew the value of the article, intimated at an early day, that she would like to be admitted into the money partnership as well, whereupon Jerry waxing wroth, said with an irate glance of his keen grey eyes, "My dear madam, these family matters, in my opinion, require to be treated not only in a business-like way, but with a very considerable degree of delicacy, an undisputed dogma, acquiring force only by the manner in which it was delivered." So the pretty widow saw she had better hold her tongue, and hope for the best from the little fawning bully.

The melancholy catastrophe with which we closed our last chapter found our hero at a preparatory school, studying for Eton, whither papa proposed sending him on the old principle of getting him into good society; though we believe it is an experiment that seldom succeeds. The widow, indeed, took this view of the matter, for her knowledge of high life caused her to know that though a "proud aristocracy" can condescend, and even worship wealth, yet that they are naturally clannish and exclusive, and tenacious of pedigree. In addition to this, Mrs. Pringle's experience of men led her to think that the solemn pedantic "Greek and Latin ones," as she called them, who know all about Julius Cæsar coming, "*summa diligentia*," on the top of the diligence, were not half so agreeable as those who could dance and sing, and knew all that was going on in the present-day world; which, in addition to her just appreciation of the delicate position of her son, made her resolve not to risk him among the rising aristocracy at Eton, who, instead of advancing, might only damage his future prospects in life, but to send him to Paris, where, besides the three R's,—"reading, riting, and rithmetic,"—he would acquire all the elegant accomplishments and dawn fresh upon the world an unexpected meteor.

This matter being arranged, she then left Dirty Street, as she called Doughty Street, with all the disagreeable Pringle family espionage, and reminiscences, and migrated westward, taking up her abode in the more congenial atmosphere of Curtain Crescent, Pimlico, or Belgravia, as, we believe the owners of the houses wish to have it called. Here she established herself in a very handsome, commodious house, with porticoed doorway and balconied drawing-rooms—every requisite for a genteel family in short; and such a mansion being clearly more than a single lady required, she sometimes accommodated the less fortunate, through the medium of a house-agent, though both he and she always begged it to be distinctly understood that she did not let lodgings, but "apartments;" and she always requested that the consideration might be sent to her in a sealed envelope by the occupants, in the same manner as she transmitted them the bill. So she managed to make a considerable appearance at a moderate expense, it being only in the full season that her heart yearned towards the houseless, when of course a high premium was expected. There is nothing uncommon in people letting their whole houses; so why should there be anything strange in Mrs. Pringle occasionally letting a part of one? Clearly nothing. Though Mrs. Joe did say she had turned a lodging-house keeper, she could not refrain from having seven-and-sixpence worth of Brougham occasionally to see how the land lay.

It is but justice to our fair friend to say that she commenced with great prudence. So handsome unprotected a female being open to the criticisms of the censorious, she changed her good-looking footman for a sedate elderly man, whose name, Properjohn, John Properjohn, coupled with the severe austerity of his manners, was enough to scare away intruders, and to keep the young girls in order, whom our friend had consigned to her from the country, in the hopes that her drilling and recommendation would procure them admission into quality families.

16

Properjohn had been spoiled for high service by an attack of the jaundice, but his figure was stately and good, and she sought to modify his injured complexion by a snuff-coloured, Quaker-cut coat and vest, with claret-coloured shorts, and buckled shoes. Thus attired, with his oval-brimmed hat looped up with gold cord, and a large double-jointed brass-headed cane in his hand, he marched after his mistress, a damper to the most audacious. Properjohn, having lived in good families until he got spoiled by the jaundice, had a very extensive acquaintance among the aristocracy, with whom Mrs. Pringle soon established a peculiar intercourse. She became a sort of ultimate Court of Appeal, a *Cour de Cassation*, in all matters of taste in apparel,—whether a bonnet should be lilac or lavender colour, a dress deeply flounced or lightly, a lady go to a ball in feathers or diamonds, or both—in all those varying and perplexing points that so excite and bewilder the female mind: Mrs. Pringle would settle all these, whatever Mrs. Pringle said the fair applicants would abide by, and milliners and dress-makers submitted to her judgment. This, of course, let her into the privacies of domestic life. She knew what husbands stormed at the milliners' and dress-makers' bills, bounced at the price of the Opera-box, and were eternally complaining of their valuable horses catching cold. She knew who the cousin was who was always to be admitted in Lavender Square, and where the needle-case-shaped note went to after it had visited the toy-shop in Arcadia Street. If her own information was defective, Properjohn could supply the deficiency. The two, between them, knew almost everything.

Nor was Mrs. Pringle's influence confined to the heads of houses, for it soon extended to many of the junior members also. It is a well known fact that, when the gorgeous Lady Rainbow came to consult her about her daughter's goings on with Captain Conquest, the Captain and Matilda saw Mamma alight from the flaunting hammer-clothed tub, as they stood behind the figured yellow tabaret curtains of Mrs. Pringle's drawing-room window, whither they had been attracted by the thundering of one of the old noisy order of footmen. Blessings on the man, say we, who substituted bells for knockers—so that lovers may not be disturbed, or visitors unaccustomed to public knocking have to expose their incompetence.

We should, however, state, that whenever Mrs. Pringle was consulted by any of the juveniles upon their love affairs, she invariably suggested that they had better "Ask Mamma," though perhaps it was only done as a matter of form, and to enable her to remind them at a future day, if things went wrong, that she had done so. Many people make offers that they never mean to have accepted, but still, if they are not accepted, *they made them you know.* If they are accepted, why then they wriggle out of them the best way they can. But we are dealing in generalities, instead of confining ourselves to Mrs. Pringle's practice. If the young lady or gentleman—for Mrs. Pringle was equally accessible to the sexes—preferred "asking" her to "Asking Mamma," Mrs. Pringle was always ready to do what she could for them; and the fine Sèvres and Dresden china, the opal vases, the Bohemian scent-bottles, the beautiful bronzes, the or-molu jewel caskets, and Parisian clocks, that mounted guard in the drawing-room when it was not "in commission" (occupied as apartments), spoke volumes for the gratitude of those she befriended. Mrs. Pringle was soon the repository of many secrets, but we need not say that the lady who so adroitly concealed Pheasant Feathers on her own account was not likely to be entrapped into committing others; and though she was often waited upon by pleasant conversationalists on far-fetched errands, who endeavoured to draw carelessly down wind to their point, as well as by seedy and half-seedy gentlemen, who proceeded in a more business-like style, both the pleasant conversationalists and the seedy and the half-seedy gentlemen went away as wise as they came. She never knew anything; it was the first she had heard of anything of the sort.

Altogether, Mrs. Pringle was a wonderful woman, and not the least remarkable trait in her character was that, although servants, who, like the rest of the world, are so ready to pull people down to their own level, knew her early professional career, yet she managed them so well that they all felt an interest in elevating her, from the Duke's Duke, down to old quivering-calved Jeames de la Pluche, who sipped her hop champagne, and told all he heard while waiting at table—that festive period when people talk as if their attendants were cattle or inanimate beings.

The reader will now have the goodness to consider our friend, Fine Billy, established with his handsome mother in Curtain Crescent—not Pimlico, but Belgravia—with all the airs and action described in our opening chapter. We have been a long time in working up to him, but the reader will not find the space wasted, inasmuch as it has given him a good introduction to "Madam," under whose auspices Billy will shortly have to grapple with the "Ask Mamma" world. Moreover, we feel that if there has been a piece of elegance overlooked by novelists generally, it is the delicate, sensitive, highly-refined lady's-maid. With these observations, we now pass on to the son He had exceeded, if possible, his good mother's Parisian anticipations, for if he had not brought away any great amount of learning, if he did not know a planet from a fixed star, the difference of oratory between Cicero and Demosthenes, or the history of Cupid and the minor heathen deities, he was nevertheless an uncommonly good hand at a polka, could be matched to waltz with any

17

one, and had a tremendous determination of words to the mouth. His dancing propensities, indeed, were likely to mislead him at starting; for, not getting into the sort of society Mrs. Pringle wished to see him attain, he took up with Cremorne and Casinos, and questionable characters generally.

Mrs. Pringle's own establishment, we are sorry to say, soon furnished her with the severest cause of disquietude; for having always acted upon the principle of having pretty maids—the difference, as she said, between pretty and plain ones being, that the men ran after the pretty ones, while the plain ones ran after the men—having always, we say, acted upon the principle of having pretty ones, she forgot to change her system on the return of her hopeful son; and before she knew where she was, he had established a desperate *liaison* with a fair maid whose aptitude for breakage had procured for her the *sobriquet* of Butter Fingers. Now, Butter Fingers, whose real name was Disher—Jane Disher—was a niece of our old friend, Big Ben, now a flourishing London hotel landlord, and Butter Fingers partook of the goodly properties and proportions for which the Ben family are distinguished. She was a little, plump, fair, round-about thing, with every quality of a healthy country beauty.

Fine Billy was first struck with her one Sunday afternoon, tripping along in Knightsbridge, as she was making her way home from Kensington Gardens, when the cheap finery—the parasol, the profusely-flowered white gauze bonnet, the veil, the machinery laced cloak, the fringed kerchief, worked sleeves, &c., which she kept at Chickory the greengrocer's in Sun Street., and changed there for the quiet apparel in which she left Mrs. Pringle's house in Curtain Crescent—completely deceived him; as much as did the half-starting smile of recognition she involuntarily gave him on meeting. Great was his surprise to find that such a smart, neat-stepping, well-set-up, *bien chaussée* beauty and he came from the same quarters. We need not say what followed: how Properjohn couldn't see what everybody else saw; and how at length poor Mrs. Pringle, having changed her mind about going to hear Mr. Spurgeon, caught the two sitting together, on her richly carved sofa of chaste design, in the then non-commissioned put-away drawing room. There was Butter Fingers in a flounced book-muslin gown with a broad French sash, and her hair clubbed at the back *à la* crow's-nest. It was hard to say which of the three got the greatest start, though the blow was undoubtedly the severest on the poor mother, who had looked forward to seeing her son entering the rank of life legitimately in which she had occupied a too questionable position. The worst of it was, she did not know what to do—whether to turn her out of the house at the moment, and so infuriate the uncle and her son also, or give her a good scolding, and get rid of her on the first plausible opportunity. She had no one to consult. She knew what "Want-nothin'-but-what's-right Jerry" would say, and that nothing would please Mrs. Half-a-yard-of-the-table Joe more than to read the marriage of Billy and Butter Fingers.

Mrs. Pringle was afraid too of offending Big Ben by the abrupt dismissal of his niece, and dreaded if Butter Fingers had gained any ascendancy over William, that he too might find a convenient marrying place as somebody else had done.

Altogether our fair friend was terribly perplexed. Thrown on the natural resources of her own strong mind, she thought, perhaps, the usual way of getting young ladies off bad matches, by showing them something better, might be tried with her son. Billy's *début* in the metropolis had not been so flattering as she could have wished, but then she could make allowances for town exclusiveness, and the pick and choice of dancing activity which old family connections and associations supplied. The country was very different; there, young men were always in request, and were taken with much lighter credentials.

If, thought she, sweet William could but manage to establish a good country connection, there was no saying but he might retain it in town; at all events, the experiment would separate him from the artful Butter Fingers, and pave the way for her dismissal.

To accomplish this desirable object, Mrs. Pringle therefore devoted her undivided attention.

CHAPTER VII. THE EARL OF LADYTHORNE.—MISS DE GLANCEY.

AMONG Mrs. Pringle's many visitors was that gallant old philanthropist, the well-known Earl of Ladythorne, of Tantivy Castle, Feather-bedfordshire and Belvedere House, London.

His lordship had known her at Lady Delacey's, and Mrs. Pringle still wore and prized a ruby ring he slipped upon her finger as he met her (accidentally of course) in the passage early one morning as he was going to hunt. His saddle-horses might often be seen of a summer afternoon, tossing their heads up and down Curtain Crescent, to the amusement of the inhabitants of that locality. His lordship indeed was a well-known general patron of all that was fair and fine and handsome in creation, fine women, fine houses, fine horses, fine hounds, fine pictures, fine statues, fine every thing. No pretty woman either in town or country ever wanted a friend if he was aware of it.

He had long hunted Featherbedfordshire in a style of great magnificence, and though latterly his energies had perhaps been as much devoted to the pursuit of the fair as the fox, yet, as he found the two worked well together, he kept up the hunting establishment with all the splendour of his youth. Not that he was old: as he would say, "*far from it!*" Indeed, to walk behind him down St..James's Street (he does not go quite so well up), his easy jaunty air, tall graceful figure, and elasticity of step, might make him pass for a man in that most uncertain period of existence the "prime of life," and if uncivil, unfriendly, inexorable time has whitened his pow, his lordship carries it off with the aid of gay costume and colour. He had a great reputation among the ladies, and though they all laughed and shook their heads when his name was mentioned, from the pretty simpering Mrs. Ringdove, of Lime-Tree Grove, who said he was a "naughty man," down to the buxom chambermaid of the Rose and Crown, who giggled and called him a "gay old gentleman," they all felt pleased and flattered by his attentions.

Hunting a country undoubtedly gives gay old gentlemen great opportunities, for, under pretence of finding a fox, they may rummage any where from the garret to the cellar.

In this interesting pursuit, his lordship was ably assisted by his huntsman, Dicky Boggledike. Better huntsman there might be than Dicky, but none so eminently qualified for the double pursuit of the fox and the fine. He had a great deal of tact and manner, and looked and was essentially a nobleman's servant. He didn't come blurting open-mouthed with "I've seen a davilish," for such was his dialect, "I've seen a davilish fine oss, my lord," or "They say Mrs. Candle's cow has gained another prize," but he would take an opportunity of introducing the subject neatly and delicately, through the medium of some allusion to the country in which they were to be found, some cover wanting cutting, some poacher wanting trouncing, or some puppy out, at walk, so that if his lordship didn't seem to come into the humour of the thing, Dicky could whip off to the other scent as if he had nothing else in his mind. It was seldom, however, that his lordship was not inclined to profit by Dicky's experience, for he had great sources of information, and was very careful in his statements, His lordship and Dicky had now hunted Featherbedfordshire together for nearly forty years, and though they might not be so Ex. gra., as we say in the classics. "A Fox Run into a Lady's Dressing-Room.—The Heythrop hounds met at Ranger's Lodge, within about a mile of Charlbury, found in Hazell Wood, and went away through Great Cran well, crossing the park of Cornbury, on by the old kennel to Live Oak, taking the side hill, leaving Leafield (so celebrated for clay-pipes) to his left, crossed the bottom by Five Ashes; then turned to the right, through King's Wood. Smallstones, Knighton Copse, over the plain to Ranger's Lodge, with the hounds close at his brush, where they left him in a mysterious manner. After the lapse of a little time he was discovered by a maid-servant in the ladies' dressing-room, from which he immediately bolted on the appearance of the petticoats, without doing the slightest damage to person or property."—*Bell's Life*. What a gentlemanly fox! punctual in the mornings, or so late in leaving off in the evenings, as they were; and though his lordship might come to the meet in his carriage and four with the reigning favourite by his side, instead of on his neat cover hack, and though Dicky did dance longer at his fences than he used, still there was no diminution in the scale of the establishment, or in Dicky's influence throughout the country. Indeed, it would rather seem as if the now well-matured hunt ran to show instead of sport, for each succeeding year brought out either another second horseman (though neither his lordship nor Dicky ever tired one), or another man in a scarlet and cap, or established another Rose and Crown, whereat his lordship kept dry things to change in case he got wet. He was uncommonly kind to himself, and hated his heir with an intensity of hatred which was at once the best chance for longevity and for sustaining the oft-disappointed ambitious hopes of the fair.

Now Mrs. Pringle had always had a very laudable admiration of fox-hunters. She thought the best introduction for a young man of fortune was at the cover side, and though Jerry Pringle (who looked upon them as synonymous) had always denounced "gamblin' and huntin'" as the two greatest vices of the day, she could never come in to that opinion, as far as hunting was concerned.

She now thought if she could get Billy launched under the auspices of that distinguished sportsman, the Earl of Ladythorne, it might be the means of reclaiming him from Butter Fingers, and getting him on in society, for she well knew how being seen at one good place led to another, just as the umbrella-keepers at the Royal Academy try to lead people into giving them something in contravention of the rule above their heads, by jingling a few half-pence before their faces. Moreover, Billy had shown an inclination for equitation—by nearly galloping several of Mr. Spavin, the neighbouring livery-stable-keeper's horses' tails off; and Mrs. Pringle's knowledge of hunting not being equal to her appreciation of the sport, she thought that a muster of hounds

19

found all the gentlemen who joined his hunt in horses, just as a shooter finds them in dogs or guns, so that the thing would be managed immediately.

Indeed, like many ladies, she had rather a confused idea of the whole thing, not knowing but that one horse would hunt every day in the week; or that there was any distinction of horses, further than the purposes to which they were applied. Hunters and racehorses she had no doubt were the same animals, working their ways honestly from year's end to year's end, or at most with only the sort of difference between them that there is between a milliner and a dressmaker. Be that as it may, however, all things considered, Mrs. Pringle determined to test the sincerity of her friend the Earl of Ladythorne: and to that end wrote him a gossiping sort of letter, asking, in the postscript, when his dogs would be going out, as her son was at home and would "*so like*" to see them.

Although we introduced Lord Ladythorne as a philanthropist, his philanthropy, we should add, was rather lop-sided, being chiefly confined to the fair. Indeed, he could better stand a dozen women than one man. He had no taste or sympathy, for the hirsute tribe, hence his fields were very select, being chiefly composed of his dependents and people whom he could d—— and do what he liked with. Though the Crumpletin Railway cut right through his country, making it "varry contagious," as Harry Swan, his first whip, said, for sundry large towns, the sporting inhabitants thereof preferred the money-griping propensities of a certain Baronet—Sir Moses Mainchance—whose acquaintance the reader will presently make, to the scot-free sport with the frigid civilities of the noble Earl. Under ordinary circumstances, therefore, Mrs. Pringle had made rather an unfortunate selection for her son's*début*, but it so happened that her letter found the Earl in anything but his usual frame of mind.

He was suffering most acutely for the hundred and twentieth time or so from one of Cupid's shafts, and that too levelled by a hand against whose attacks he had always hitherto been thought impervious. This wound had been inflicted by the well-known—perhaps to some of our readers too well-known—equestrian coquette, Miss de Glancey of Half-the-watering-places-in-England-and-some-on-the-Continent, whose many conquests had caused her to be regarded as almost irresistible, and induced, it was said—with what degree of truth we know not—a party of England's enterprising sons to fit her out for an expedition against the gallant Earl of Ladythorne under the Limited Liability Act.

Now, none but a most accomplished, self-sufficient coquette, such as Miss de Glancey undoubtedly was, would have undertaken such an enterprise, for it was in direct contravention of two of the noble Earl's leading principles, namely, that of liking large ladies (fine, coarse women, as the slim ones call them.) and of disliking foxhunting ones, the sofa and not the saddle being, as he always said, the proper place for the ladies; but Miss de Glancey prided herself upon her power of subjugating the tyrant man, and gladly undertook to couch the lance of blandishment against the hitherto impracticable nobleman. In order, however, to understand the exact position of parties, perhaps the reader will allow us to show how his lordship came to be seized with his present attack, and also how he treated it.

Well, the ash was yellow, the beech was brown, and the oak ginger coloured, and the indomitable youth was again in cub-hunting costume—a white beaver hat, a green cut-away, a buff vest, with white cords and caps, attended by Boggledike and his whips in hats, and their last season's pinks or purples, disturbing the numerous litters of cubs with which the country abounded, when, after a musical twenty minutes with a kill in Allonby Wood, his lordship joined horses with Dicky, to discuss the merits of the performance, as they rode home together.

"Yas, my lord, yas," replied Dicky, sawing away at his hat, in reply to his lordship's observation that they ran uncommonly well; "yas, my lord, they did. I don't know that I can ever remember bein' better pleased with an entry than I am with this year's. I really think in a few more seasons we shall get 'em as near parfection as possible. Did your lordship notish that Barbara betch, how she took to runnin' to-day? The first time she has left my oss's eels. Her mother, old Blossom, was jest the same. Never left my oss's eels the first season, and everybody said she was fit for nothin' but the halter; but my!" continued he, shaking his head, "what a rare betch she did become."

"She did that," replied his lordship, smiling at Dicky's pronunciation.

"And that reminds me," continued Dicky, emboldened by what he thought the encouragement, "I was down at Freestone Banks yesterday, where Barbara was walked, a seein' a pup I have there now, and I think I seed the very neatest lady's pad I ever set eyes on!"—Dicky's light-blue eyes settling on his lordship's eagle ones as he spoke. "Aye! who's was that?" asked the gay old gentleman, catching at the word "lady."

"Why, they say she belongs to a young lady from the south—a Miss Dedancey, I think they call her," with the aptitude people have for mistaking proper names.

"Dedancey," repeated his lordship, "Dedancey; never heard of the name before—what's set her here?"

"She's styin' at Mrs. Roseworth's, at Lanecroft House, but her osses stand at the Spread Heagle, at Bush Dill—Old Sam 'Utchison's, you know."

Indomitable Youth. Horses! what, has she more than one? *Dicky.* Two, a bay and a gray,—it's the bay that takes my fancy most:—the neatest stepper, with the lightest month, and fairest, freeest, truest action I ever seed.

Indomitable Youth. What's she going to do with them?

Dicky. Ride them, ride them! They say she's the finest oss-woman that ever was seen.

"In-deed," mused his lordship, thinking over the *pros* and *cons* of female equestrianism,—the disagreeableness of being beat by them,—the disagreeableness of having to leave them in the lurch,—the disagreeableness of seeing them floored,—the disagreeableness of seeing them all running down with perspiration;—the result being that his lordship adhered to his established opinion that women have no business out hunting.

Dicky knew his lordship's sentiments, and did not press the matter, but drew his horse a little to the rear, thinking it fortunate that all men are not of the same way of thinking. Thus they rode on for some distance in silence, broken only by the occasional flopping and chiding of Harry Swan or his brother whip of some loitering or refractory hound. His lordship had a great opinion of Dicky's judgment, and though they might not always agree in their views, he never damped Dicky's ardour by openly differing with him. He thought by Dicky's way of mentioning the lady that he had a good opinion of her, and, barring the riding, his lordship saw no reason why he should not have a good opinion of her too. Taking advantage of the Linton side-bar now bringing them upon the Somerton-Longville road, he reined in his horse a little so as to let Dicky come alongside of him again.

"What is this young lady like?" asked the indomitable youth, as soon as they got their horses to step pleasantly together again.

"Well now," replied Dicky, screwing up his mouth, with an apologetic touch of his hat, knowing that that was his weak point, "well now, I don't mean to say that she's zactly—no, not zactly, your lordship's model,—not a large full-bodied woman like Mrs. Blissland or Miss Poach, but an elegant, *very* elegant, well-set-up young lady, with a high-bred hair about her that one seldom sees in the country, for though we breeds our women very beautiful—uncommon 'andsome, I may say—we don't polish them hup to that fine degree of parfection that they do in the towns, and even if we did they would most likely spoil the 'ole thing by some untoward unsightly dress, jest as a country servant spoils a London livery by a coloured tie, or goin' about with a great shock head of 'air, or some such disfigurement; but this young lady, to my mind, is a perfect pictor, self, oss, and seat,—all as neat and perfect as can be, and nothing that one could either halter or amend. She is what, savin' your lordship's presence, I might call the 'pink of fashion and the mould of form!'—Dicky sawing away at his hat as he spoke.

"Tall, slim, and genteel, I suppose," observed his lordship drily.

"Jest so," assented Dicky, with a chuck of the chin, making a clean breast of it, "jest so adding, at least as far as one can judge of her in her 'abit, you know."

"Thought so," muttered his lordship.

And having now gained one of the doors in the wall, they cut across the deer-studded park, and were presently back at the Castle. And his lordship ate his dinner, and quaffed his sweet and dry and twenty-five Lafitte without ever thinking about either the horse, or the lady, or the habit, or anything connected with the foregoing conversation, while the reigning favourite, Mrs. Moffatt, appeared just as handsome as could be in his eyes.

CHATTER VIII. CUB-HUNTING.

THOUGH his lordship, as we said before, would stoutly deny being old, he had nevertheless got sufficiently through the morning of life as not to let cub-hunting get him out of bed a moment sooner than usual, and it was twelve o'clock on the next day but one to that on which the foregoing conversation took place, that Mr. Boggledike was again to be seen standing erect in his stirrups, yoiking and coaxing his hounds into Crashington Gorse. There was Dicky, cap-in-hand, in the Micentre ride, exhorting the young hounds to dive into the strong sea of gorse. "*Y-o-o-icks! wind him! y-o-o-icks! pash him up!*" cheered the veteran, now turning his horse across to enforce the request. There was his lordship at the high corner as usual, ensconced among the clump of weather-beaten blackthorns—thorns that had neither advanced nor receded a single inch since he first knew them,—his eagle eye fixed on the narrow fern and coarse grass-covered dell down which Reynard generally stole. There was Harry Swan at one corner to head the fox back from the beans, and Tom Speed at the other to welcome him away over the corn-garnered open. And now the whimper of old sure-finding Harbinger, backed by the sharp "yap" of the terrier, proclaims that our friend is at home, and presently a perfect hurricane of melody bursts from the agitated gorse,—every hound is in the paroxysm of excitement, and there are five-and-twenty couple of them, fifty musicians in the whole!

"*Tally-ho!* there he goes across the ride!"

"*Cub!*" cries his lordship.

"*Cub!*" responded Dicky.

"*Crack!*" sounds the whip.

Now the whole infuriated phalanx dashed across the ride and dived into the close prickly gorse on the other side as if it were the softest, pleasantest quarters in the world. There is no occasion to coax, and exhort, and ride cap-in-hand to them now. It's all fury and commotion. Each hound seems to consider himself personally aggrieved,—though we will be bound to say the fox and he never met in their lives,—and to be bent upon having immediate satisfaction. And immediate, any tyro would think it must necessarily be, seeing such preponderating influence brought to bear upon so small an animal. Not so, however: pug holds his own; and, by dint of creeping, and crawling, and stopping, and listening, and lying down, and running his foil, he brings the lately rushing, clamorous pack to a more plodding, pains-taking, unravelling sort of performance.

Meanwhile three foxes in succession slip away, one at Speed's corner, two at Swan's; and though Speed screeched, and screamed, and yelled, as if he were getting killed, not a hound came to see what had happened. They all stuck to the original scent.

"Here he comes again!" now cries his lordship from his thorn-formed bower, as the cool-mannered fox again steals across the ride, and Dicky again uncovers, and goes through the capping ceremony. Over come the pack, bristling and lashing for blood—each hound looking as if he would eat the fox single-handed. Now he's up to the high corner as though he were going to charge his lordship himself, and passing over fresh ground the hounds get the benefit of a scent, and work with redoubled energy, making the opener gorse bushes crack and bend with their pressure. Pug has now gained the rabbit-burrowed bank of the north fence, and has about made up his mind to follow the example of his comrades, and try his luck in the open, when a cannonading crack of Swan's whip strikes terror into his heart, and causes him to turn tail, and run the moss-grown mound of the hedge. Here he unexpectedly meets young Prodigal face to face, who, thinking that rabbit may be as good eating as fox, has got up a little hunt of his own, and who is considerably put out of countenance by the *rencontre*; but pug, not anticipating any such delicacy on the part of a pursuer, turns tail, and is very soon in the rear of the hounds, hunting them instead of their hunting him. The thing then becomes more difficult, businesslike, and sedate—the sages of the pack taking upon them to guide the energy of the young. So what with the slow music of the hounds, the yap, yap, yapping of the terriers, and the shaking of the gorse, an invisible underground sort of hunt is maintained—his lordship sitting among his blackthorn bushes like a gentleman in his opera-stall, thinking now of the hunt, now of his dinner, now of what a good thing it was to be a lord, with a good digestion and plenty of cash, and nobody to comb his head.

At length pug finds it too hot to hold him. The rays of an autumnal sun have long been striking into the gorse, while a warm westerly wind does little to ventilate it from the steam of the rummaging inquisitive pack. Though but a cub, he is the son of an old stager, who took Dicky and his lordship a deal of killing, and with the talent of his sire, he thus ruminates on his uncomfortable condition.

"If," says he, "I stay here, I shall either be smothered or fall a prey to these noisy unrelenting monsters, who seem to have the knack of finding me wherever I go. I'd better cut my stick as I did the time before, and have fresh air and exercise at all events, in the open." so saying he made a dash at the hedge near where Swan was stationed, and regardless of his screams and the cracks of his whip, cut through the beans and went away, with a sort of defiant whisk of his brush.

What a commotion followed his departure! How the screeches of the men mingled with the screams of the hounds and the twangs of the horn! In an instant his lordship vacates his opera-stall and is flying over the ragged boundary fence that separates him from the beans; while Mr. Boggledike capers and prances at a much smaller place, looking as if he would fain turn away were it not for the observation of the men. Now Dicky is over! Swan and Speed take it in their stride, just as the last hound leaves the gorse and strains to regain his distant companions. A large grass field, followed by a rough bare fallow, takes the remaining strength out of poor pug; and, turning short to the left, he seeks the friendless shelter of a patch of wretched oats. The hounds overrun the scent, but, spreading like a rocket, they quickly recover it; and in an instant, fox, hounds, horses, men, are among the standing corn,—one ring in final destruction of the beggarly crop, and poor pug is in the hands of his pursuers. Then came the grand *finale*, the *who hoop!* the baying, the blowing, the beheading, &c. Now Harry Swan, whose province it is to magnify sport and make imaginary runs to ground, exercises his calling, by declaring it was five-and-thirty minutes (twenty perhaps), and the finest young fox he ever had hold of. Now his lordship and Dicky take out their *tootlers* and blow a shrill reverberating blast; while Swan stands straddling and yelling, with the mangled remains high above his head, ready to throw it into the sea of mouths that are baying around to receive it. After a sufficiency of noise, up goes the carcase; the wave of hounds breaks against it as it falls, while a half-ravenous, half-indignant, growling worry succeeds the late clamourous outcry.

"Tear 'im and eat 'im!" cries Dicky.

"Tear 'im and eat 'im!" shouts his lordship.

"Tear 'im and eat 'im!" shrieks Speed.

"*Hie worry! worry! worry!*" shouts Swan, trying to tantalize the young hounds with a haunch, which, however, they do not seem much to care about.

The old hounds, too, seem as if they had lost their hunger with their anger; and Marmion lets Warrior run off with his leg with only a snap and an indignant rise of his bristles.

Altogether the froth and effervescence of the thing has evaporated; so his lordship and Dicky turning their horses' heads, the watchful hounds give a bay of obedient delight as they frolic under their noses; and Swan having reclaimed his horse from Speed, the onward procession is formed to give Brambleton Wood a rattle by way of closing the performance of the day.

His lordship and Dicky ride side by side, extolling the merits of the pack and the excellence of Crashington Gorse. Never was so good a cover. Never was a better pack. Mainchance's! *pooh!* Not to be mentioned in the same century. So they proceed, magnifying and complimenting themselves in the handsomest terms possible, down Daisyfield lane, across Hill House pastures, and on by Duston Mills to Broomley, which is close to Brambleton Wood.

Most of our Featherbedfordshire friends will remember that after leaving Duston Mills the roads wind along the impetuous Lime, whose thorn and broom-grown banks offer dry, if not very secure, accommodation for master Reynard; and the draw being pretty, and the echo fine, his lordship thought they might as well run the hounds along the banks, not being aware that Peter Hitter, Squire Porker's keeper, had just emerged at the east end as they came up at the west. However, that was neither here nor there, Dicky got his *Y-o-o-icks*, his lordship got his view, Swan and Speed their cracks and canters, and it was all in the day's work. No fox, of course, was the result. "*Tweet, tweet, tweet,*" went the horns, his lordship taking a blow as well as Dicky, which sounded up the valley and lost itself among the distant hills. The hounds came straggling leisurely out of cover, as much as to say, "You know there never *is* a fox there, so why bother us?"

All hands being again united, the cavalcade rose the hill, and were presently on the Longford and Aldenbury turnpike. Here the Featherbedfordshire reader's local knowledge will again remind him that the Chaddleworth lane crosses the turnpike at right angles, and just as old Ringwood, who, as usual, was trotting consequentially in advance of the pack, with the fox's head in his mouth, got to the finger-post, a fair equestrian on a tall blood bay rode leisurely past with downcast eyes in full view of the advancing party. Though her horse whinnied and shied, and seemed inclined to be sociable, she took no more notice of the cause than if it had been a cart, merely coaxing and patting him with her delicate primrose-coloured kid gloves. So she got him past without even a sidelong look from herself.

But though she did not look my lord did, and was much struck with the air and elegance of everything—her mild classic features—her black-felt, Queen's-patterned, wide-awake, trimmed with lightish-green velvet, and green cock-feathered plume, tipped with straw-colour to match the ribbon that now gently fluttered at her fair neck,—her hair, her whip, her gloves, her *tout ensemble*. Her lightish-green habit was the quintessence of a fit, and altogether there was a high-bred finish about her that looked more like Hyde Park than what one usually sees in the country.

"Who the deuce is that, Dicky?" asked his lordship, as she now got out of hearing.

"That be *her*, my lord," whispered Dicky, sawing away at his hat. "That be *her*," repeated he with a knowing leer.

"*Her!* who d'ye mean?" asked his lordship, who had forgotten all Dicky's preamble.

"Well,—Miss—Miss—What's her name—Dedancev, Dedancey,—the lady I told you about."

And the Earl's heart smote him, for he felt that he had done injustice to Dicky, and moreover, had persevered too long in his admiration of large ladies, and in his repudiation of horsemanship.

He thought he had never seen such a graceful seat, or such a piece of symmetrical elegance before, and inwardly resolved to make Dicky a most surprising present at Christmas, for he went on the principle of giving low wages, and of rewarding zeal and discretion, such as Dicky's, profusely. And though he went and drew Brambleton Wood, he was thinking far more of the fair maid, her pensive, downcast look, her long eyelashes, her light silken hair, her graceful figure, and exquisite seat, than of finding a fox; and he was not at all sorry when he heard Dicky's horn at the bridle-gate at the Ashburne end blowing the hounds out of cover. They then went home, and his lordship was very grumpy all that evening with his fat fair-and-forty friend, Mrs. Moffatt, who could not get his tea to his liking at all.

We dare say most of our readers will agree with us, that when a couple want to be acquainted there is seldom much difficulty about the matter, even though there be no friendly go-between to mutter the cabalistic words that constitute an introduction; and though Miss de Glancey did ride so unconcernedly past, it was a sheer piece of acting, as she had long been waiting at Carlton Clumps, which commands a view over the surrounding country, timing herself for the exact spot where she met the too susceptible Earl and his hounds.

No one knew better how to angle for admiration than this renowned young lady,—when to do the bold—when the bashful—when the timid—when the scornful and retiring, and she rightly calculated that the way to attract and win the young old Earl was to look as if she didn't want to have anything to say to him. Her downcast look, and utter indifference to that fertile source of introduction, a pack of hounds, had sunk deeper into his tender heart than if she had pulled up to up to admire them collectively, and made in matters of this sort—how the fair creatures can express their feelings by their fondness. And if one dog can be so convenient, by how much more so can a whole pack of hounds be made!

CHAPTER IX. A PUP AT WALK.—IMPERIAL JOHN.

WE all know how useful a dog can be of dressers, was to be seen in regular St. James's Street attire, viz. a bright blue coat with gilt buttons, a light blue scarf, a buff vest with fawn-coloured leathers, and brass heel spurs, capering on a long-tailed silver dun, attended by a diminutive rosy-cheeked boy—known in the stables as Cupid-without-Wings—on a bay.

He was going to see a pup he had at walk at Freestone Banks, of which the reader will remember Dicky had spoken approvingly off a previous day; and the morning being fine and sunny, his lordship took the bridle-road over Ashley Downs, and along the range of undulating Heathmoor Hills, as well for the purpose of enjoying the breeze as of seeing what was passing in the vale below. So he tit-up'd and tit-up'd away, over the sound green sward, on his flowing-tailed steed, his keen far-seeing eye raking all the roads as he went. There seemed to be nothing stirring but heavy crushing waggons, with doctor's gigs and country carts, and here and there a slow-moving steed of the grand order of agriculture.

When, however, he got to the broken stony ground where all the independent hill tracks join in common union to effect the descent into the vale, his hack pricked his ears, and looking a-head to the turn of the lane into which the tracks ultimately resolved themselves, his-lordship first saw a fluttering, light-tipped feather, and then the whole figure of a horsewoman, emerge from the concealing hedge as it were on to the open space beyond. Miss, too, had been on the hills, as the Earl might have seen by her horse's imprints, if he had not been too busy looking abroad; and she had just had time to effect the descent as he approached. She was now sauntering along as unconcernedly as if there was nought but herself and her horse in the world. His lordship started when he saw her, and a crimson flush suffused his healthy cheeks as he drew his reins, and felt his hack gently with his spur to induce him to use a little more expedition down the hill. Cupid-without-Wings put on also, to open the rickety gate at the bottom, and his lordship telling him, as he passed through, to "shut it gently," pressed on at a well-in-hand trot, which he could ease down to a walk as he came near the object of his pursuit. Miss's horse heard footsteps coming and looked round, but she pursued the even tenour of her way apparently indifferent to everything—even to a garotting. His lordship, however, was not to be daunted by any such coolness; so stealing quietly alongside of her, he raised his hat respectfully, and asked, in his mildest, blandest tone, if she had "seen a man with a hound in a string?"

"*Hound! me! see!*" exclaimed Miss de Glancey, with a well feigned start of astonishment. "*No, sir, I have not,*" continued she haughtily, as if recovering herself, and offended by the inquiry.

"I'm afraid my hounds startled your horse the other day," observed his lordship, half inclined to think she didn't know him.

"Oh, no, they didn't," replied she with an upward curl of her pretty lip; "my horse is not so easily startled as that; are you, Cock Robin?" asked she, leaning forward to pat him.

Cock Robin replied by laying back his ears, and taking a snatch at his lordship's hack's silver mane, which afforded him an opportunity of observing that Cock Robin was not very sociable.

"*Not with strangers,*" pouted Miss de Glancey, with a flash of her bright hazel eyes. So saying, she touched her horse lightly with her gold-mounted whip, and in an instant she was careering away, leaving his lordship to the care of the now grinning Cupid-without-Wings.

And thus the minx held the sprightly youth in tow, till she nearly drove him mad, not missing any opportunity of meeting him, but never giving him too much of her company, and always pouting at the suggestion of *her* marrying a "*mere fox-hunter.*" The whole thing, of course, furnished conversation for the gossips, and Mr. Boggledike, as in duty bound, reported what he heard. She puzzled his lordship more than any lady he had ever had to do with, and though he often resolved to strike and be free, he had only to meet her again to go home more subjugated than ever. And so what between Miss de Glancey out of doors and Mrs. Moffatt in, he began to have a very unpleasant time of it. His hat had so long covered his family, that he hardly knew how to set about obtaining his own consent to marry; and yet he felt that he ought to marry if it was only to spite his odious heir—*old* General Binks; for his lordship called him old though the General was ten years younger than himself; but still he would like to look about him a little longer. What he would now wish to do would be to keep Miss de Glancey in the country, for he felt interested in her, and thought she would be ornamental to the pack. Moreover, he liked all that was handsome, *piquant*, and gay, and to be joked about the Featherbedfordshire witches when he went to town. So he resolved himself into a committee of ways and means, to consider how the object was to be effected, without surrendering himself. That must be the last resource at all events, thought he.

Now upon his lordship's vast estates was a most unmitigated block-head called Imperial John, from his growing one of those chin appendages. His real name was Hybrid—John Hybrid, of Barley Hill Farm; but his handsome sister, "Imperial Jane," as the wags called her, having attracted his lordship's attention, to the danger as it was thought of old Binks, on leaving her furnishing seminary at Turnham Green, John had been taken by the hand, which caused him to lose his head, and make him set up for what he called "a gent." He built a lodge and a portico to Barley Hill Farm, rough cast, and put a pine roof on to the house, and then advertised in the "Featherbedfordshire Gazette," that letters and papers were for the future to be addressed to John Hybrid, Esquire, Barley Hill Hall, and not Farm as they had hitherto been. And having done so much for the place, John next revised his own person, which, though not unsightly, was coarse, and a long way off looking anything like that of a gentleman. He first started the imperial aforesaid, and not being laughed at as much as he expected for that, he was emboldened to order a red coat for the then approaching season. Mounting the pink is a critical thing, for if a man does not land in the front rank they will not admit him again into the rear, and he remains a sort of red hat for the rest of his life,—neither a gentleman nor a farmer.

John, however, feeling that he had his lordship's countenance, went boldly at it, and the first day of the season before that with which we are dealing, found him with his stomach buttoned consequentially up in a spic and span scarlet with fancy buttons, looking as bumptious as a man with a large balance at his banker's. He sat bolt upright, holding his whip like a field-marshal's bâton, on his ill-groomed horse, with a tight-bearing rein chucking the Imperial chin well in the air, and a sort of half-defiant "you'd better not laugh at me" look. And John was always proud to break a fence, or turn a hound, or hold a horse, or do anything his lordship bid him, and became a sort of hunting aide-de-camp to the great man. He was a boasting, bragging fool, always talking about m-o-y hall, and m-o-y lodge, and m-o-y plate in m-o-y drawing-room, for he had not discovered that plate was the appendage of a dining-room, and altogether he was very magnificent.

Imperial Jane kept old Binks on the fret for some time, until another of his lordship's tenants, young Fred Poppyfield, becoming enamoured of her charms, and perhaps wishing to ride in scarlet too, sought her fair hand, whereupon his lordship, acting with his usual munificence, set them up on a farm at so low a rent that it acquired the name of Gift Hall Farm. This arrangement set Barley Hall free so far as the petticoats were concerned, and his lordship little knowing how well she was "up" in the country, thought this great gouk of a farmer, with his plate in his drawingroom, might come over the accomplished Miss de Glancey,—the lady who sneered at himself as "a mere fox-hunter." And the wicked monkey favoured the delusion, which she saw through the moment his lordship brought the pompous egotist up at Newington Gorse, and begged to be allowed to introduce his friend, Mr Hybrid, and she inwardly resolved to give Mr. Hybrid a benefit. Forsaking his lordship therefore entirely, she put forth her most seductive allurements at Imperial John, talked most amazingly to him, rode over whatever he recommended, and seemed quite smitten with him.

And John, who used to boast that somehow the "gals couldn't withstand him," was so satisfied with his success, that he presently blundered out an offer, when Miss de Glancey, having led him out to the extreme length of his tether, gave such a start and shudder of astonishment as Fanny Kemble, or Mrs. Siddons herself, might have envied.

"O, Mr. Hybrid! O, Mr. Hybrid!" gasped she, opening wide her intelligent eyes, as if she had but just discovered his meaning. "O, Mr. Hybrid!" exclaimed she for the third time, "*you—you— you*," and turning aside as if to conceal her emotion, she buried her face in her laced-fringed, richly-cyphered kerchief.

John, who was rather put out by some women who were watching him from the adjoining turnip-field, construing all this into the usual misfortune of the ladies not being able to withstand him, returned to the charge as soon as he got out of their hearing, when he was suddenly brought up by such a withering "*Si-r-r-r! do you mean to insult me?*" coupled with a look that nearly started the basket-buttons of his green cut-away, and convinced him that Miss de Glancey, at all events, could withstand him. So his Majesty slunk off, consoling himself with the reflection, that riding-habits covered a multitude of sins, and that if he was not much mistaken, she would want a deal of oil-cake, or cod liver oil, or summut o' that sort, afore she was fit to show.

And the next time Miss met my lord (which, of course, she did by accident), she pouted and frowned at the "mere fox-hunter," and intimated her intention of leaving the country—going home to her mamma, in fact.

It was just at this juncture that Mrs. Pringle's letter arrived, and his lordship's mind being distracted between love on his own account, dread of matrimony, and dislike of old Binks, he caught at what he would in general have stormed at, and wrote to say that he should begin hunting the first Monday in November, and if Mrs. Pringle's son would come down a day or two before, he would "put him up" (which meant mount him), and "do for him" (which meant board and lodge him), all, in fact, that Mrs. Pringle could desire. And his lordship inwardly hoped that Mr. Pringle might be more to Miss de Glancey's liking than his Imperial Highness had proved. At all events, he felt it was but a simple act of justice to himself to try. Let us now return to Curtain Crescent.

CHAPTER X. JEAN ROUGIER, OR JACK ROGERS.

WE need not say that Mrs. Pringle was overjoyed at the receipt of the Earl's letter. It was so kind and good, and so like him. He always said he would do her a good turn if he could: but there are so many fine-weather friends in this world that there is no being certain of any one. Happy are they who never have occasion to test the sincerity of their friends, say we.

Mrs. Pringle was now all bustle and excitement, preparing Billy for the great event.

His wardrobe, always grand, underwent revision in the undergarment line. She got him some magnificently embroidered dress shirts, so fine that the fronts almost looked as if you might blow them out, and regardful of the *rôle* he was now about to play, she added several dozen with horses, dogs, birds, and foxes upon them, "suitable for fishing, shooting, boating, &c.," as the advertisements said. His cambric kerchiefs were of the finest quality, while his stockings and other things were in great abundance, the whole surmounted by a splendid dressing-case, the like of which had ne'er been seen since the days of Pea-Green Haine. Altogether he was capitally provided, and quite in accordance with a lady's-maid's ideas of gentility.

Billy, on his part, was active and energetic too, for though he had his doubts about being able to sit at the jumps, he had no objection to wear a red coat; and mysterious-looking boys, with blue bags, were constantly to be found seated on the mahogany bench, in the Curtain Crescent passage, waiting to try on his top boots; while the cheval glass up-stairs was constantly reflecting his figure in scarlet, *à la* Old Briggs. The concomitants of the chase, leathers, cords, whips, spurs, came pouring in apace. The next thing was to get somebody to take care of them.

It is observable that the heads of the various branches of an establishment are all in favour of "master" spending all his money on their particular department. Thus, the coachman would have him run entirely to carriages, the groom to horses, the cook to the *cuisine*, the butler to wines, the gardener to grapes, &c., and so on.

Mrs. Pringle, we need hardly say, favoured lady's-maids and valets. It has been well said, that if a man wants to get acquainted with a gentleman's private affairs, he should either go to the lawyer or else to the valet that's courting the lady's-maid; and Mrs. Pringle was quite of that opinion. Moreover, she held that no man with an efficient, properly trained valet, need ever be catspawed or jilted, because the lady's-maid would feel it a point of honour to let the valet know how the land lay, a compliment he would return under similar circumstances. To provide Billy with this, as she considered, most essential appendage to a gentleman, was her next consideration—a valet that should know enough and not too much—enough to enable him to blow his master's trumpet properly, and not too much, lest he should turn restive and play the wrong tune.

At length she fixed upon the Anglo-Frenchman, whose name stands at the head of this chapter—Jean Rougier, or Jack Rogers. Jack was the son of old Jack Rogers, so well known as the enactor of the Drunken Huzzar, and similar characters of Nutkins's Circus; and Jack was entered to his father's profession, but disagreeing with the clown, Tom Oliver, who used to give him sundry most unqualified cuts and cuffs in the Circus, Jack, who was a tremendously strong fellow, gave Oliver such a desperate beating one night as caused his life to be despaired off. This took place at Nottingham, from whence Jack fled for fear of the consequences; and after sundry vicissitudes he was next discovered as a post-boy, at Sittingbourne, an office that he was well adapted for, being short and stout and extremely powerful. No brute was ever too bad for Jack's riding: he would tame them before the day was over. Somehow he got bumped down to Dover, when taking a fancy to go "foreign," he sold his master's horses for what they would fetch; and this being just about the time that the late Mr. Probert expiated a similar mistake at the Old Bailey, Jack hearing of it, thought it was better to stay where he was than give Mr. Calcraft any trouble. He therefore accepted the situation of boots to the Albion Hotel, Boulogne-sur-mer; but finding that he did not get on half so well as he would if he were a Frenchman, he took to acquiring the language, which, with getting his ears bored, letting his hair and whiskers grow, and adopting the French costume in all its integrity, coupled with a liberal attack of the small-pox, soon told a tale in favour of his fees. After a long absence, he at length returned at the Bill Smith Revolution; and vacillating for some time between a courier and a valet, finally settled down to what we now find him.

We know not how it is, if valets are so essentially necessary, that there should always be so many out of place, but certain it is that an advertisement in a morning paper will always bring a full crop to a door.

Perhaps, being the laziest of all lazy lives, any one can turn his hand to valeting, who to dig is unable, and yet to want is unwilling.

Mrs. Pringle knew better than hold a levee in Curtain Crescent, letting all the applicants pump Properjohn or such of the maids as they could get hold of; and having advertised for written applications, stating full particulars of previous service, and credentials, to be addressed to F. P. at Chisel the baker's, in Yeast Street, she selected some half-dozen of the most promising ones, and appointed the parties to meet her, at different hours of course, at the first-class waiting-room of the great Western Station, intimating that they would know her by a bunch of red geraniums she would hold in her hand. And the second applicant, Jean Rougier, looked so like her money, having a sufficient knowledge of the English language to be able to understand all that was said, and yet at the same time sufficiently ignorant of it to invite confidential communications to be made before him; that after glancing over the testimonials bound up in his little parchment-backed passport book, she got the name and address of his then master, and sought an interview to obtain Monsieur's character. This gentleman, Sir Harry Bolter, happening to owe Jack three-quarters of a year's wages, which he was not likely to pay, spoke of him in the highest possible terms, glossing over his little partiality for drink by saying that, like all Frenchmen, he was of a convivial turn; and in consequence of Sir Harry's and Jack's own recommendations, Mrs. Pringle took him.

The reader will therefore now have the kindness to consider our hero and his valet under way, with a perfect pyramid of luggage, and Monsieur arrayed in the foraging cap, the little coatee, the petticoat trowsers, and odds and ends money-bag of his long adopted country, slung across his ample chest.

Their arrival and reception at Tantivy Castle will perhaps be best described in the following letter from Billy to his mother:—

Tantivy Castle.

My dearest Mamma,

I write a line to say that I arrived here quite safe by the 5-30 train, and found the Earl as polite as possible. I should tell you that I made a mistake at starting, for it being dark when I arrived, and getting confused with a whole regiment of footmen, I mistook a fine gentleman who came forward to meet me for the Earl, and made him a most respectful bow, which the ass returned, and began to talk about the weather; and when the real Earl came in I took him for a guest, and was going to weather him. However he soon put all matters right, and introduced me to

Mrs. Moffatt, a very fine lady, who seems to ride the roast here in grand style. They say she never wears the same dress twice.

There are always at least half-a-dozen powdered footmen, in cerulean blue lined with rose-coloured silk, and pink silk stockings, the whole profusely illustrated with gold lace, gold aigulets, and I don't know what, lounging about in the halls and passages, wailing for company which Rougier says never comes. This worthy seems to have mastered the ins and outs of the place already, and says, "my lor has an Englishman to cook his beef-steak for breakfast, a Frenchman to cook his dinner, and an Italian confectioner; every thing that a 'my lord' ought to have" It is a splendid place,—as you will see by the above picture, * more like Windsor than anything I ever saw, and there seems to be no expense spared that could by any possibility be incurred. I've got a beautiful bedroom with warm and cold baths and a conservatory attached.

* Our friend was writing on Castle-paper, of course.

To-morrow is the first day of the season, and all the world and his wife will be there to a grand déjeuner à la Fourchette. The hounds meet before the Castle. His lordship says he will put me on a safe, steady hunter, and I hope he will, for I am not quite sure that I can sit at the jumps. However I'll let you know how I come on. Meanwhile as the gong is sounding for dressing, believe me, my dearest mamma,

Ever your truly affectionate son,

Mrs. Pringle, Wm. PRINGLE.

Curtain Crescent, Belgrade Square, London.

CHAPTER XI. THE OPENING DAY.—THE HUNT BREAKFAST.

REVERSING the usual order of things, each first Monday in November saw the sporting inmates of Tantivy Castle emerge from the chrysalis into the butterfly state of existence. His lordship's green-duck hunter and drab caps disappeared, and were succeeded by a spic-and-span span new scarlet and white top; Mr. Roggledike's last year's pink was replaced by a new one, his hat was succeeded by a cap; and the same luck attended the garments of both Swan and Speed. The stud-groom, the pad-groom, the sending-on groom, all the grooms down to our little friend, Cupid-without-Wings, underwent renovation in their outward men. The whole place smelt of leather and new cloth. The Castle itself on this occasion seemed to participate in the general festivity, for a bright sun emblazoned the quarterings of the gaily flaunting flag, lit up the glittering vanes of the lower towers, and burnished the modest ivy of the basements. Every thing was bright and sunny, and though Dicky Boggledike did not "zactly like" the red sunrise, he "oped the rine might keep off until they were done, 'specially as it was a show day." Very showy indeed it was, for all the gentlemen out of livery,—those strange puzzlers—were in full ball costume; while the standard footmen strutted like peacocks in their rich blue liveries with rose-coloured linings, and enormous bouquets under their noses, feeling that for once they were going to have something to do.

The noble Earl, having got himself up most elaborately in his new hunting garments, and effected a satisfactory tie of a heart's-ease embroidered blue satin cravat, took his usual stand before the now blazing wood and coal fire in the enormous grate in the centre of his magnificent baronial hall, ready to receive his visitors and pass them on to Mrs. Moffat in the banqueting room. This fair lady was just as fine as hands could make her, and the fit of her rich pale satin dress, trimmed with swan's-down, reflected equal credit on her milliner and her maid. Looking at her as she now sat at the head of the sumptuously-furnished breakfast table, her plainly dressed hair surmounted by a diminutive point-lace cap, and her gazelle-like eye lighting up an intelligent countenance, it were hardly possible to imagine that she had ever been handsomer, or that beneath that quiet aspect there lurked what is politely called a "high spirit," that is to say, a little bit of temper.

That however is more the Earl's look-out than ours, so we will return to his lordship at the entrance hall fire.

Of course this sort of gathering was of rather an anomalous character,—some coming because they wanted something, some because they "dirsn't" stay away, some because they did not know Mrs. Moffat would be there, some because they did not care whether she was or not. It was a show day, and they came to see the beautiful Castle, not Mrs. Anybody.

The first to arrive were the gentlemen of the second class, the agents and dependents of the estate,—Mr. Cypher, the auditor, he who never audited; Mr. Easylease, the land agent; his son, Mr. John Easylease, the sucking land agent; Mr. Staple, the mining agent; Mr. James Staple, the sucking mining agent; Mr. Section, the architect; Mr. Pillerton, the doctor; Mr. Brick, the builder; &c., who were all very polite ard obsequious, "your lordship" and my "my lording" the Earl at every opportunity. These, ranging themselves on either side of the fire, now formed the nucleus of the court, with the Earl in the centre.

Presently the rumbling of wheels and the grinding of gravel was succeeded by the muffled-drum sort of sound of the wood pavement of the grand covered portico, and the powdered footmen threw back the folding-doors as if they expected Daniel Lambert or the Durham Ox to enter. It was our old friend Imperial John, who having handed his pipeclayed reins to his ploughman-groom, descended from his buggy with a clumsy half buck, half hawbuck sort of air, and entered the spacious portals of the Castle hall. Having divested himself of his paletot in which he had been doing "the pride that apes humility," he shook out his red feathers, pulled up his sea-green-silk-tied gills, finger-combed his stiff black air, and stood forth a sort of rough impersonation of the last year's Earl. His coat was the same cut, his hat was the same shape, his boots and breeches were the same colour, and altogether there was the same sort of resemblance between John and the Earl that there is between a cart-horse and a race-horse.

Having deposited his whip and paletot on the table on the door-side of a tall, wide-spreading carved oak screen, which at once concealed the enterers from the court, and kept the wind from that august assembly, John was now ready for the very obsequious gentleman who had been standing watching his performances without considering it necessary to give him any assistance. This bland gentleman, in his own blue coat with a white vest, having made a retrograde movement which cleared himself of the screen, John was presently crossing the hall, bowing and stepping and bowing and stepping as if he was measuring off a drain.

His lordship, who felt grateful for John's recent services, and perhaps thought he might require them again, advanced to meet him and gave him a very cordial shake of the hand, as much as to say, "Never mind Miss de Glancey, old fellow, we'll make it right another time." They then fell to conversing about turnips, John's Green Globes having turned out a splendid crop, while his Swedes were not so good as usual, though they still might improve.

A more potent wheel-roll than John's now attracted his lordship's attention, and through the far windows he saw a large canary-coloured ark of a coach, driven by a cockaded coachman, which he at once recognised as belonging to his natural enemy Major Yammerton, "five-and-thirty years master of haryers," as the Major would say, "without a subscription." Mr. Boggledike had lately been regaling his lordship with some of the Major's boastings about his "haryars" and the wonderful sport they showed, which he had had the impudence to compare with his lordship's fox hounds. Besides which, he was always disturbing his lordship's covers on the Roughborough side of the country, causing his lordship to snub him at all opportunities. The Major, however, who was a keen, hard-bitten, little man, not easily choked off when he wanted anything, and his present want being to be made a magistrate, he had attired himself in an antediluvian swallow-tailed scarlet, with a gothic-arched collar, and brought his wife and two pretty daughters to aid in the design. Of course the ladies were only coming to see the Castle.

The cockaded coachman having tied his reins to the rail of the driving-box, descended from his eminence to release his passengers, while a couple of cerulean-blue gentlemen looked complacently on, each with half a door in his hand ready to throw open as they approached, the party were presently at the hall table, where one of those indispensable articles, a looking-glass, enabled the ladies to rectify any little derangement incidental to the joltings of the journey, while the little Major run a pocket-comb through a fringe of carroty curls that encircled his bald head, and disposed of a cream-coloured scarf cravat to what he considered the best advantage. Having drawn a doeskin glove on to the left hand, he offered his arm to his wife, and advanced from behind the screen with his hat in his ungloved right hand ready to transfer it to the left should occasion require.

"Ah Major Yammerton!" exclaimed the Earl, breaking off in the middle of the turnip dialogue with Imperial John. "Ah, Major Yammerton, I'm delighted to see you" (getting a glimpse of the girls). "Mrs. Yammerton, this is indeed extremely kind," continued he, taking both her hands in his; "and bringing your lovely daughters," continued he, advancing to greet them.

Mrs. Yammerton here gave the Major a nudge to remind him of his propriety speech. "The gi—gi—girls and Mrs. Ya—Ya—Yammerton," for he always stuttered when he told lies, which was pretty often; "the gi—gi—girls and Mrs. Ya—Ya—Yammerton have done me the honour—"

Another nudge from Mrs. Yammerton.

"I mean to say the gi—gi—girls and Mrs. Ya—Ya—Yammerton," observed he, with a stamp of the foot and a shake of the head, for he saw that his dread enemy, Imperial John, was laughing at him, "have done themselves the honour of co—co—coming, in hopes to be allowed the p—p—p—pleasure of seeing your mama—magnificent collection of pi—pi—pictors." the Major at length getting out what he had been charged to say.

"By all means!" exclaimed the delighted Earl, "by all means; but first let me have the pleasure of conducting you to the refreshment-room;" saying which his lordship offered Mrs. Yammerton his arm. So passing up the long gallery, and entering by the private door, he popped her down beside Mrs. Moffatt before Mrs. Yammerton knew where she was.

Just then our friend Billy Pringle, who, with the aid of Rougier, had effected a most successful *logement* in his hunting things, made his appearance, to whom the Earl having assigned the care of the young ladies, now beat a retreat to the hall, leaving Mrs. Yammerton lost in astonishment as to what her Mrs. Grundy would say, and speculations as to which of her daughters would do for Mr. Pringle.

Imperial John, who had usurped the Earl's place before the fire, now shied off to one side as his lordship approached, and made his most flexible obeisance to the two Mr. Fothergills and Mr. Stot, who had arrived during his absence. These, then, gladly passed on to the banqueting-room just as the Condor-like wings of the entrance hall door flew open and admitted Imperial Jane, now the buxom Mrs. Poppyfield. She came smiling past the screen, magnificently attired in purple velvet and ermine, pretending she had only come to warm herself at the "'All fire while Pop looked for the groom, who had brought his 'orse, and who was to drive her 'ome;" but hearing from the Earl that the Yammertons were all in the banqueting-room, she saw no reason why she shouldn't go too; so when the next shoal of company broke against the screen, she took Imperial John's arm, and preceded by a cloud of lackeys, cerulean-blue and others, passed from the hall to the grand apartment, up which she sailed majestically, tossing her plumed head at that usurper Mrs. Moffatt; and then increased the kettle of fish poor Mrs. Yammerton was in by seating herself beside her.

"Impudent woman," thought Mrs. Yammerton, "if I'd had any Idea of this I wouldn't have come;" and she thought how lucky it was she had put the Major up to asking to see the "pictors." it was almost a pity he was so anxious to be a magistrate. Thought he might be satisfied with being Major of such a fine regiment as the Featherbedfordshire Militia. Nor were her anxieties diminished by the way the girls took the words out of each other's mouths, as it were, in their intercourse with Billy Pringle, thus preventing either from making any permanent impression.

The great flood of company now poured into the hall, red coats, green coats, black coats, brown coats, mingled with variously-coloured petticoats. The ladies of the court, Mrs. Cypher, Mrs. Pillerton, Mrs. and the Misses Easylease, Mrs. Section, and others, hurried through with a shivering sort of step as if they were going to bathe. Mr. D'Orsay Davis, the "we" of the Featherbedfordshire Gazette, made his bow and passed on with stately air, as a ruler of the roast ought to do. The Earl of Stare, as Mr. Buckwheat was called, from the fixed protuberance of his eyes—a sort of second edition of Imperial John, but wanting his looks, and Gameboy Green, the hard rider of the hunt, came in together; and the Earl of Stare, sporting scarlet, advanced to his brother peer, the Earl, who, not thinking him an available card, turned him over to Imperial John who had now returned from his voyage with Imperial Jane, while his lordship commenced a building conversation with Mr. Brick.

A lull then ensuing as if the door had done its duty, his lordship gave a wave of his hand, whereupon the trained courtiers shot out into horns on either side, with his lordship in the centre, and passed majestically along to the banqueting-room.

The noble apartment a hundred feet long, and correspondingly proportioned, was in the full swing of hospitality when the Earl entered. The great influx of guests for which the Castle was always prepared, had at length really arrived, and from Mrs. Moffatt's end of the table to the door, were continuous lines of party-coloured eaters, all engaged in the noble act of deglutition. Up the centre was a magnificent avenue of choice exotics in gold, silver, and china vases, alternating with sugar-spun Towers, Temples, Pagodas, and Rialtos, with here and there the more substantial form of massive plate, *épergnes*, testimonials, and prizes of different kinds. It was a regular field day for plate, linen, and china.

The whole force of domestics was now brought to bear upon the charge, and the cerulean-blue gentlemen vied with the gentlemen out of livery in the assiduity of their attentions. Soup, game, tea, coffee, chocolate, ham, eggs, honey, marmalade, grapes, pines, melons, ices, buns, cakes, skimmed and soared, and floated about the room, in obedience to the behests of the callers. The only apparently disengaged person in the room, was Monsieur Jean Rougier, who, in a blue coat with a velvet collar and bright buttons, a rolling-collared white vest, and an amplified lace-tipped black Joinville, stood like a pouter pigeon behind Mr. Pringle's chair, the *beau idéal* of an indifferent spectator. And yet he was anything but an indifferent spectator; for beneath his stubbly hair were a pair of little roving, watchful eyes, and his ringed ears were cocked for whatever they could catch. The clatter, patter, clatter, patter of eating, which was slightly interrupted by the entrance of his lordship was soon in full vigour again, and all eyes resumed the contemplation of the plates.

30

Presently, the "fiz, pop, bang" of a champagne cork was heard on the extreme right, which was immediately taken up on the left, and ran down either side of the table like gigantic crackers. Eighty guests were now imbibing the sparkling fluid, as fast as the footmen could supply it. And it was wonderful what a volubility that single glass a-piece (to be sure they were good large ones) infused into the meeting; how tongue-tied ones became talkative, and awed ones began to feel themselves sufficiently at home to tackle with the pines and sugar ornaments of the centre. Grottoes and Pyramids and Pagodas and Rialtos began to topple to their fall, and even a sugar Crystal Palace, which occupied the post of honour between two flower-decked Sèvres vases, was threatened with destruction. The band and the gardeners were swept away immediately, and an assault on the fountains was only prevented by the interference of Mr. Beverage, the butler. And now a renewed pop-ponading commenced, more formidable, if possible, than the first, and all glasses were eagerly drained, and prepared to receive the salute.

All being ready, Lord Ladythorne rose amid the applause so justly due to a man entertaining his friends, and after a few prefatory remarks, expressive of the pleasure it gave him to see them all again at the opening of another season, and hoping that they might have many more such meetings, he concluded by giving as a toast, "Success to fox-hunting!"—which, of course, was drunk upstanding with all the honours.

All parties having gradually subsided into their seats after this uncomfortable performance, a partial lull ensued, which was at length interrupted by his lordship giving Imperial John, who sat on his left, a nod, who after a loud throat-clearing *hem!* rose bolt upright with his imperial chin well up, and began, "Gentlemen and Ladies!" just as little weazeley Major Yammerton commenced "Ladies and gentlemen!" from Mrs. Moffatt's end of the table. This brought things to a stand still—some called for Hybrid, some for Yammerton, and each disliking the other, neither was disposed to give way. The calls, however, becoming more frequent for Yammerton, who had never addressed them before, while Hybrid had, saying the same thing both times, the Earl gave his Highness a hint to sit down, and the Major was then left in that awful predicament, from which so many men would be glad to escape, after they have achieved it, namely,—the possession of the meeting.

However, Yammerton had got his speech well off, and had the heads of it under his plate; so on silence being restored, he thus went away with it:—

"Ladies and gentlemen,—(cough)—ladies and gentlemen,—(hem) I rise, I assure you—(cough)—with feelings of considerable trepidation—(hem)—to perform an act—(hem)—of greater difficulty than may at first sight appear—(hem, hem, haw)—for let me ask what it is I am about to do? ("You know best," growled Imperial John, thinking how ill he was doing it.) I am going to propose the health of a nobleman—(applause)—of whom, in whose presence, if I say too much, I may offend, and if I say too little, I shall most justly receive your displeasure (renewed applause). But, ladies and gentlemen, there are times when the 'umblest abilities become equal to the occasion, and assuredly this is one—(applause). To estimate the character of the illustrious nobleman aright, whose health I shall conclude by proposing, we must regard him in his several capacities—(applause)—as Lord-Lieutenant of the great county of Featherbedford, as a great and liberal landlord, as a kind and generous neighbour, and though last, not least, as a brilliant sportsman—(great applause, during which Yammerton looked under his plate at his notes.)—As Lord-Lieutenant," continued he, "perhaps the greatest praise I can offer him, the 'ighest compliment I can pay him, is to say that his appointments are so truly impartial as not to disclose his own politics—(applause)—as a landlord, he is so truly a pattern that it would be a mere waste of words for me to try to recommend him to your notice,—(applause)—as a neighbour, he is truly exemplary in all the relations of life,—(applause)—and as a sportsman, having myself kept haryers five-and-thirty years without a subscription, I may be permitted to say that he is quite first-rate,—(laughter from the Earl's end of the table, and applause from Mrs. Moffatt's.)—In all the relations of life, therefore, ladies and gentlemen,"—continued the Major, looking irately down at the laughers—"I beg to propose the bumper toast of health, and long life to our 'ost, the noble Earl of Ladythorne!"

Whereupon the little Major popped down on his chair, wondering whether he had omitted any thing he ought to have said, and seeing him well down, Imperial John, who was not to be done out of his show-off, rose, glass in hand, and exclaimed in a stentorian voice,

"Gentlemen and Ladies! Oi beg to propose that we drink this toast up standin' with all the honours!—Featherbedfordshire fire!" upon which there was a great outburst of applause, mingled with demands for wine, and requests from the ladies, that the gentlemen would be good enough to take their chairs off their dresses, or move a little to one side, so that they might have room to stand up; Crinoline, we should observe, being very abundant with many of them.

31

A tremendous discharge of popularity then ensued, the cheers being led by Imperial John, much to the little Major's chagrin, who wondered how he could ever have sat down without calling for them.

Now, the Earl, we should observe, had not risen in the best of moods that morning, having had a disagreeable dream, in which he saw old Binks riding his favourite horse Valiant, Mazeppa fashion, making a drag of his statue of the Greek slave, enveloped in an anise-seeded bathing-gown; a vexation that had been further increased when he arose, by the receipt of a letter from his "good-natured friend" in London, telling him how old Binks had been boasting at Boodle's that he was within an ace of an Earldom, and now to be clumsily palavered by Yammerton was more than he could bear.

He didn't want to be praised for anything but his sporting propensities, and Imperial John knew how to do it. Having, however, a good dash of satire in his composition, when the applause and the Crinoline had subsided, he arose as if highly delighted, and assured them that if anything could enhance the pleasure of that meeting, it was to have his health proposed by such a sportsman as Major Yammerton, a gentleman who he believed had kept harriers five-and-thirty years, a feat he believed altogether unequalled in the annals of sporting—(laughter and applause)—during which the little Major felt sure he was going to conclude by proposing his health with all the honours, instead of which, however, his lordship branched off to his own department of sport, urging them to preserve foxes most scrupulously, never to mind a little poultry damage, for Mr. Boggledike would put all that right, never to let the odious word Strychnine be heard in the country, and concluded by proposing a bumper to their next merry meeting, which was the usual termination of the proceedings. The party then rose, chairs fell out of line, and flying crumpled napkins completed the confusion of the scene.

CHAPTER XII. THE MORNING FOX.—THE AFTERNOON FOX.

THE day was quite at its best, when the party-coloured bees emerged from the sweets of Tantivy Castle, to taint the pure atmosphere with their nasty cigars, and air themselves on the terrace, letting the unadmitted world below see on what excellent terms they were with an Earl. Then Imperial John upbraided Major. Yammerton for taking the words out of his mouth, as it were, and the cockey Major turned up his nose at the "farmer fellow" for presuming to lector him. Then the emboldened ladies strolled through the picture-galleries and reception-rooms, regardless of Mrs. Moffatt or any one else, wondering where this door led to and where that. The hounds had been basking and loitering on the lawn for some time, undergoing the inspection and criticisms of the non-hunting portion of the establishment, the gardeners, the gamekeepers, the coachmen, the helpers, the housemaids, and so on. They all pronounced them as perfect as could be, and Mr. Hoggledike received their compliments with becoming satisfaction, saying, with a chuck of his chin, "Yas, Yas, I think they're about as good as can be! Parfaction. I may say!"

Having abused the cigars, we hope our fair friends will now excuse us for saying that we know of few less agreeable scenes than a show meet with fox-hounds. The whole thing is opposed to the wild nature of hunting. Some people can eat at any time, but to a well-regulated appetite, having to undergo even the semblance of an additional meal is inconvenient; while to have to take a *bonâ fide* dinner in the morning, soup, toast, speeches and all, is perfectly suicidal of pleasure. On this occasion, the wine-flushed guests seemed fitted for Cremorne or Foxhall, as they used to pronounce Vauxhall, than for fox-hunting. Indeed, the cigar gentry swaggered about with a very rakish, Regent Street air. His lordship alone seemed impressed with the importance of the occasion; but his anxiety arose from indecision, caused by the Binks' dream and letter, and fear lest the Yammerton girls might spoil Billy for Miss de Glancey, should his lordship adhere to his intention of introducing them to each other. Then he began to fidget lest he might be late at the appointed place, and Miss de Glancey go home, and so frustrate either design.

"*To horse! to horse!*" therefore exclaimed he, now hurrying through the crowd, lowering his Imperial Jane-made hat-string, and drawing on his Moffatt-knit mits. "*To horse! to horse!*" repeated he, flourishing his cane hunting-whip, causing a commotion among the outer circle of grooms. His magnificent black horse, Valiant (the one he had seen old Binks bucketing), faultless in shape, faultless in condition, faultless every way, stepped proudly aside, and Cupid-without-Wings dropping himself off by the neck, Mr. Beanley, the stud groom, swept the coronetted rug over the horse's bang tail, as the superb and sensible animal stepped forward to receive his rider, as the Earl came up. With a jaunty air, the gay old gentleman vaulted lightly into the saddle, saying as he drew the thin rein, and felt the horse gently with his left leg, "Now get Mr. Pringle his horse." His lordship then passed on a few paces to receive the sky-scraping salutes of the servants, and at a jerk of his head the cavalcade was in motion.

Our friend Billy then became the object of attention. The dismounted Cupid dived into the thick of the led horses to seek his, while Mr. Beanley went respectfully up to him, and with a touch of his flat-brimmed hat, intimated that "his oss was at 'and."

"What sort of an animal is it?" asked the somewhat misgiving Billy, now bowing his adieus to the pretty Misses Yammerton.

"A very nice oss, sir," replied Mr. Beanley, with another touch of hat; "yes, sir, a very nice oss—a perfect 'unter—nothin' to do but sit still, and give 'im 'is 'ead, he'll take far better care o' you than you can of 'im." So saying, Mr. Beanley led the way to a very sedate-looking, thorough-bred bay, with a flat flapped saddle, and a splint boot on his near foreleg, but in other respects quite unobjectionable. He was one of Swan's stud, but Mr. Beanley, understanding from the under butler, who had it from Jack Rogers,—we beg his pardon,—Monsieur Rougier himself, that Mr. Pringle was likely to be a good tip, he had drawn it for him. The stirrups, for a wonder, being the right length, Billy was presently astride, and in pursuit of his now progressing lordship, the gaping crowd making way for the young lord as they supposed him to be—for people are all lords when they visit at lords.

Pop, pop, bob, bob, went the black caps of the men in advance, indicating the whereabouts of the hounds, while his lordship ambled over the green turf on the right, surrounded by the usual high-pressure toadies. Thus the cavalcade passed through the large wood-studded, deer-scattered park, rousing the nearer herds from their lairs, frightening the silver-tails into their holes, and causing the conceited hares to scuttle away for the fern-browned, undulating hills, as if they had the vanity to suppose that this goodly array would condescend to have anything to do with them. Silly things! Peppercorn, the keeper, had a much readier way of settling their business. The field then crossed the long stretch of smooth, ornamental water, by the old gothic-arched bridge, and passed through the beautiful iron gates of the south lodge, now wheeled back by grey-headed porters, in cerulean-blue plush coats, and broad, gold-laced hats. Meanwhile, the whereabouts of the accustomed hunt was indicated by a lengthening line of pedestrians and small cavalry, toiling across the park by Duntler the watcher's cottage and the deer sheds, to the door in the wall at the bottom of Crow-tree hill, from whence a bird's-eye view of the surrounding country is obtained. The piece had been enacted so often, the same company, the same day, the same hour, the same find, the same finish, that one might almost imagine it was the same fox On this particular occasion, however, as if out of pure contradiction, Master Reynard, by a series of successful manoeuvres, lying down, running a wall, popping backwards and forwards between Ashley quarries and Warmley Gorse, varied by an occasional trip to Crow-tree hill, completely baffled Mr. Boggledike, so that it was afternoon before he brought his morning fox to hand, to the great discomfort of the Earl, who had twice or thrice signaled Swan to "who hoop" him to ground, when the tiresome animal popped up in the midst of the pack. At length Boggledike mastered him; and after proclaiming him a "cowardly, short-running dastardly traitor, no better nor a 'are," he chucked him scornfully to the hounds, decorating Master Pillerton's pony with the brush, while Swan distributed the pads among others of the rising generation.

The last act of the "show meet" being thus concluded, Mr. Boggledike and his men quickly collected their hounds, and set off in search of fresh fields and pastures new.

The Earl, having disposed of his show-meet fox—a bagman, of course—now set up his business-back, and getting alongside of Mr. Boggledike, led the pack at as good a trot as the hounds and the state of the line would allow. The newly laid whinstone of the Brittleworth road rather impeded their progress at first; but this inconvenience was soon overcome by the road becoming less parsimonious in width, extending at length to a grass siding, along which his lordship ambled at a toe in the stirrup trot, his eagle-eye raking every bend and curve, his mind distracted with visions of Binks, and anxiety for the future.

He couldn't get over the dream, and the letter had anything but cheered him.

"Very odd," said he to himself, "very odd," as nothing but drab-coated farmers and dark-coated grooms lounging leisurely "on," with here and there a loitering pedestrian, broke the monotony of the scene. "Hope she's not tired, and gone home," thought he, looking now at his watch, and now back into the crowd, to see where he had Billy Pringle. There was Billy riding alongside of Major Yammerton's old flea-bitten grey, whose rider was impressing Billy with a sense of his consequence, and the excellence of his "haryers," paving the way for an invitation to Yammerton Grange. "D-a-ash that Yammerton," growled his lordship, thinking how he was spoiling sport at both ends; at the Castle by his uninvited eloquence, and now by his fastening on to the only man in the field he didn't want him to get acquainted with. And his lordship inwardly resolved that he would make Easylease a magistrate before he would make the Major one. So settling matters in his own mind, he gave the gallant Valiant a gentle tap on the shoulder with his whip, and shot a few paces ahead of Dicky, telling the whips to keep the crowd off the hounds—meaning off himself. Thus he ambled on through the quiet little village of Strotherdale, whose inhabitants all rushed out to see the hounds pass, and after tantalising poor Jonathan Gape, the turnpike-gate man, at the far end, who thought he was going to get a grand haul, he turned short to the left down the tortuous green lane leading to Quarrington Gorse.

"There's a footmark," said his lordship to himself, looking down at the now closely eaten sward. "Ah! and there's a hat and feather," added he as a sudden turn of the lane afforded a passing glimpse. Thus inspirited, he mended his pace a little, and was presently in sight of the wearer. There was the bay, and there was the wide-awake, and there was the green trimming, and there was the feather; but somehow, as he got nearer, they all seemed to have lost *caste*. The slender waist and graceful upright seat had degenerated into a fuller form and lazy slouch; the habit didn't look like her habit, nor the bay horse like her bay horse, and as he got within speaking distance, the healthy, full-blown face of Miss Winkworth smiled upon him instead of the mild, placid features of the elegant de Glancey.

"Ah, my dear Miss Winkworth!" exclaimed his half-disgusted, half-delighted lordship, raising his hat, and then extending the right-hand of fellowship; "Ah, my dear Miss Winkworth, I'm charmed to see you" (inwardly wondering what business women had out hunting). "I hope you are all well at home," continued he (most devoutly wishing she was there); and without waiting for an answer, he commenced a furious assault upon Benedict, who had taken a fancy to follow him, a performance that enabled General Boggledike to come up with that army of relief, the pack, and engulf the lady in the sea of horsemen in the rear.

"If that had been *her*," said his lordship to himself, "old Binks would have had a better chance;" and he thought what an odious thing a bad copy was.

Another bend of the land and another glimpse, presently put all matters right. The real feather now fluttered before him. There was the graceful, upright seat, the elegant air, the well-groomed horse, the *tout ensemble* being heightened, if possible, by the recent contrast with the coarse, country attired Miss Winkworth.

The Earl again trotted gently on, raising his hat most deferentially as he came along side of her, as usual, unaverted head.

"Good morning, my Lord!" exclaimed she gaily, as if agreeably surprised, tendering for the first time her pretty, little, primrose-coloured kid-gloved hand, looking as though she would condescend to notice a "mere fox-hunter."

The gay old gentleman pressed it with becoming fervour, thinking he never saw her looking so well before.

They then struck up a light rapid conversation.

Miss perhaps never did look brighter or more radiant, and as his lordship rode by her side, he really thought if he could make up his mind to surrender his freedom to any woman, it would be to her. There was a something about her that he could not describe, but still a something that was essentially different to all his other flames.

He never could bear a riding-woman before, but now he felt quite proud to have such an elegant, piquant attendant on his pack.—Should like, at all events, to keep her in the country, and enjoy her society.—Would like to add her to the collection of Featherbedfordshire witches of which his friends joked him in town.—"Might have done worse than marry Imperial John," thought his lordship. John mightn't he quite her match in point of manner, but she would soon have polished him up, and John must be doing uncommonly well as times go—cattle and corn both selling prodigiously high, and John with his farm at a very low rent. And the thought of John and his beef brought our friend Billy to the Earl's mind, and after a sort of random compliment between Miss de Glancey and her horse, he exclaimed, "By the way! I've got a young friend out I wish to introduce to you," so rising in his saddle and looking back into the crowd he hallooed out, "Pringle!" a name that was instantly caught up by the quick-eared Dicky, a "Mister" tacked to it and passed backward to Speed, who gave it to a groom; and Billy was presently seen boring his way through the opening crowd, just as a shepherd's dog bores its way through a flock of sheep.

"Pringle," said his lordship, as the approach of Billy's horse caused Valiant to lay back his ears, "Pringle! I want to introduce you to Miss de Glancey, Miss de Glancey give me leave to introduce my friend Mr. Pringle," continued he, adding *soto voce*, as if for Miss de Glancey's ear alone, "young man of very good family and fortune—*richest Commoner, in England, they say*." But before his lordship got to the richest Commoner part of his speech, a dark frown of displeasure had overcast the sweet smile of those usually tranquil features, which luckily, however, was not seen by Billy; and before he got his cap restored to his head after a sky scraping salute, Miss de Glancey had resumed her wonted complacency,—inwardly resolving to extinguish the "richest Commoner," just as she had done his lordship's other "friend Mr. Hybrid." Discarding the Earl, therefore, she now opened a most voluble battering on our good-looking Billy who, to do him justice, maintained his part so well, that a lady with less ambitious views might have been very well satisfied to be Mrs. Pringle. Indeed, when his lordship looked at the two chattering and ogling and simpering together, and thought of that abominable old Binks and the drag, and the letter from the Boodleite, his heart rather smote him for what he had done; for young and fresh as he then felt himself, he knew that age would infallibly creep upon him at last, just as he saw it creeping upon each particular friend when he went to town, and he questioned that he should ever find any lady so eminently qualified to do the double duty of gracing his coronet and disappointing the General. Not but that the same thought had obtruded itself with regard to other ladies; but he now saw that he had been mistaken with respect to all of them, and that this was the real, genuine, no mistake, "right one." Moreover, Miss de Glancey was the only lady who according to his idea had not made up to him—rather snubbed him in fact. Mistaken nobleman! There are, many ways of making up to a man. But as with many, so with his lordship, the last run was always the finest, and the last lady always the fairest—the most engaging. With distracting considerations such as these, and the advantage of seeing Miss de Glancey play the artillery of her arts upon our young friend, they reached the large old pasture on the high side of Quarrington Gorse, a cover of some four acres in extent, lying along a gently sloping bank, with cross rides cut down to the brook. Mr. Boggledike pulled up near the rubbing-post in the centre of the field, to give his hounds a roll, while the second-horse gentlemen got their nags, and the new comers exchanged their hacks for their hunters. Judging by the shaking of hands, the exclamations of "halloo! old boy is that you?"

"I say! where are you from?" and similar inquiries, there were a good many of the latter—some who never went to the Castle, some who thought it too far, some who thought it poor fun. Altogether, when the field got scattered over the pasture, as a shop-keeper scatters his change on the counter, or as an old stage coachman used to scatter his passengers on the road with an upset, there might be fifty or sixty horsemen, assmen, and gigmen.

Most conspicuous was his lordship's old eye-sore, Hicks, the flying hatter of Hinton (Sir Moses Mainchance's "best man"), who seemed to think it incumbent upon him to kill his lordship a hound every year by his reckless riding, and who now came out in mufti, a hunting-cap, a Napoleon-grey tweed jacket, loose white cords, with tight drab leggings, and spurs on his shoes, as if his lordship's hounds were not worth the green cut-a-way and brown boots he sported with Sir Moses. He now gave his cap-peak a sort of rude rap with his fore-finger, as his lordship came up, as much as to say, "I don't know whether I'll speak to you or not," and then ran his great raking chestnut into the crowd to get at his old opponent Gameboy Green, who generally rode for the credit of the Tantivy hunt. As these sort of cattle always hunt in couples, Hicks is followed by his shadow, Tom Snowdon, the draper—or the Damper, as he is generally called, from his unhappy propensity of taking a gloomy view of everything.

To the right are a knot of half-horse, half-pony mounted Squireen-looking gentlemen, with clay pipes in their mouths, whose myrtle-green coats, baggy cords, and ill-cleaned tops, denote as belonging to the Major's "haryers." And mark how the little, pompons man wheels before them, in order that Pringle may see the reverence they pay to his red coat. He raises his punt hat with all the dignity of the immortal Simpson of Vauxhall memory, and passes on in search of further compliments.

His lordship has now settled himself into the "Wilkinson and Kidd" of Rob Roy, a bay horse of equal beauty with Valiant, but better adapted to the country into which they are now going, Imperial John has drawn his girths with his teeth, D'Orsay Davis has let down his hat-string, Mr. John Easylease has tightened his curb, Mr. Section drawn on his gloves, the Damper finished his cigar, and all things are approximating a start.

"*Elope, lads! Elope!*" cries Dicky Boggledike to his hounds, whistling and waving them together, and in an instant the rollers and wide-spreaders are frolicking and chiding under his horse's nose. "*G-e-e-ntly, lads! g-e-ently!*" adds he, looking the more boisterous ones reprovingly in the face—"gently lads, gently," repeats he, "or you'll be rousin' the gem'lman i' the gos." This movement of Dicky and the hounds has the effect of concentrating the field, all except our fair friend and Billy, who are still in the full cry of conversation, Miss putting forth her best allurements the sooner to bring Billy to book.

At a chuck of his lordship's chin, Dicky turns his horse towards the gorse, just as Billy, in reply to Miss de Glancey's question, if he is fond of hunting, declares, as many a youth has done who hates it, that he "doats upon it!"

A whistle, a waive, and a cheer, and the hounds are away. They charge the hedge with a crash, and drive into the gorse as if each hound had a bet that he would find the fox himself.

Mr. Boggledike being now free of his pack, avails himself of this moment of ease, to exhibit his neat, newly clad person of which he is not a little proud, by riding along the pedestrian-lined hedge, and requesting that "you fut people," as he calls them, "will have the goodness not to 'alloa, but to 'old up your 'ats if you view the fox;" and having delivered his charge in three several places, he turns into the cover by the little white bridle-gate in the middle, which Cupid-without-Wings is now holding open, and who touches his hat as Dicky passes.

The scene is most exciting. The natural inclination of the land affords every one a full view of almost every part of the sloping, southerly-lying gorse, while a bright sun, with a clear, rarified atmosphere, lights up the landscape, making the distant fences look like nothing. Weak must be the nerves that would hesitate to ride over them as they now appear.

Delusive view! Between the gorse and yonder fir-clad hills are two bottomless brooks, and ere the dashing rider reaches Fairbank Farm, whose tall chimney stands in bold relief against the clear, blue sky, lies a tract of country whose flat surface requires gulph-like drains to carry off the surplus water that rushes down from the higher grounds. To the right, though the country looks rougher, it is in reality easier, but foxes seem to know it, and seldom take that line; while to the left is a strongly-fenced country, fairish for hounds, but very difficult for horses, inasmuch as the vales are both narrow and deep. But let us find our fox and see what we can do among them. And as we are in for a burst, let us do the grand and have a fresh horse.

CHAPTER XIII. GONE AWAY!

SEE! a sudden thrill shoots through the field, though not a hound has spoken; no, not even a whimper been heard. It is Speed's new cap rising from the dip of the ground at the low end of the cover, and now having seen the fox "right well away," as he says, he gives such a ringing view halloa as startles friend Echo, and brings the eager pack pouring and screeching to the cry—

"*Tweet! tweet! tweet!*" now goes cantering Dicky's superfluous horn, only he doesn't like to be done out of his blow, and thinks the "fut people" may attribut' the crash to his coming.

All eyes are now eagerly strained to get a view of old Reynard, some for the pleasure of seeing him, others to speculate upon whether they will have to take the stiff stake and rise in front, or the briar-tangled boundary fence below, in order to fulfil the honourable obligation of going into every field with the hounds. Others, again, who do not acknowledge the necessity, and mean to take neither, hold their horses steadily in hand, to be ready to slip down Cherry-tree Lane, or through West Hill fold-yard, into the Billinghurst turnpike, according as the line of chase seems to lie.

"*Talli-ho!*" cries the Flying Hatter, as he views the fox whisking his brush as he rises the stubble-field over Fawley May Farm, and in an instant he is soaring over the boundary-fence to the clamorous pack just as his lordship takes it a little higher up, and lands handsomely in the next field. Miss de Glancey then goes at it in a canter, and clears it neatly, while Billy Pringle's horse, unused to linger, after waiting in vain for an intimation from his rider, just gathers himself together, and takes it on his own account, shooting Billy on to his shoulder.

"He's off! no, he's on; he hangs by the mane!" was the cry of the foot people, as Billy scrambled back into his saddle, which he regained with anything but a conviction that he could sit at the jumps. Worst of all, he thought he saw Miss de Glancey's shoulders laughing at his failure.

The privileged ones having now taken their unenviable precedence, the scramble became general, some going one way, some another, and the recent frowning fences are soon laid level with the fields.

A lucky lane running parallel with the line, along which the almost mute pack were now racing with a breast-high scent, relieved our friend Billy from any immediate repetition of the leaping inconvenience, though he could not hear the clattering of horses' hoofs behind him without shuddering at the idea of falling and being ridden over. It seemed very different he thought to the first run, or to Hyde Park; people were all so excited, instead of riding quietly, or for admiration, as they do in the park. Just as Billy was flattering himself that the leaping danger was at an end, a sudden jerk of his horse nearly chucked him into Imperial John's pocket, who happened to be next in advance. The fox had been headed by the foot postman between Hinton and Sambrook; and Dicky Boggledike, after objurgating the astonished man, demanding, "What the daval business he had there?" had drawn his horse short across the lane, thus causing a sudden halt to those in the rear.

The Flying Hatter and the Damper pressing close upon the pack as usual, despite the remonstrance of Gameboy Green and others, made them shoot up to the far-end of the enclosure, where they would most likely have topped the fence but for Swan and Speed getting round them, and adding the persuasion of their whips to the entreaties of Dicky's horn. The hounds sweep round to the twang, lashing and bristling with excitement.

"*Yo doit!*" cries Dicky, as Sparkler and Pilgrim feather up the lane, trying first this side, then that. Sparkler speaks! "He's across the lane."

"*Hoop! hoop! tallio! tallio!*" cries Dicky cheerily, taking off his cap, and sweeping it in the direction the fox has gone, while his lordship, who has been bottling up the vial of his wrath, now uncorks it as he gets the delinquents within hearing.

"Thank you, Mr. Hicks, for pressing on my hounds! Much obleged to you, Mr. Hicks, for pressing on my hounds! Hang you, Mr. Hicks, for pressing on my hounds!" So saying, his lordship gathered Rob Roy together, and followed Mr. Boggledike through a very stiff bullfinch that Dicky would rather have shirked, had not the eyes of England been upon him.

S-w-ic-h! Dicky goes through, and the vigorous thorns close again like a rat-trap.

"Allow me, my lord!" exclaims Imperial John from behind, anxious to be conspicuous.

"Thank 'e, no," replied his lordship, carelessly thinking it would not do to let Miss de Glancey too much into the secrets of the hunting field. "Thank 'e, no," repeated he, and ramming his horse well at it, he gets through with little more disturbance of the thorns than Dicky had made. Miss de Glancey comes next, and riding quietly up the bank, she gives her horse a chuck with the curb and a touch with the whip that causes him to rise well on his haunches and buck over without injury to herself, her hat, or her habit. Imperial John was nearly offering his services to break the fence for her, but the "*S-i-r-r!* do you mean to insult me?" still tingling in his ears, caused him to desist. However he gives Billy a lift by squashing through before him, whose horse then just rushed through it as before, leaving Billy to take care of himself. A switched face was the result, the pain, however, being far greater than the disfigurement.

While this was going on above, D'Orsay Davis, who can ride a spurt, has led a charge through a weaker place lower down; and when our friend had ascertained that his eyes were still in his head, he found two distinct lines of sportsmen spinning away in the distance as if they were riding a race. Added to this, the pent-up party behind him having got vent, made a great show of horsemanship as they passed.

"Come along!" screamed one.

"Look alive!" shouted another.

"Never say die!" cried a third, though they were all as ready to shut up as our friend.

Billy's horse, however, not being used to stopping, gets the bit between his teeth, and scuttles away at a very overtaking pace, bringing him sufficiently near to let him see Gameboy Green and the Flying Hatter leading the honourable obligation van, out of whose extending line now a red coat, now a green coat, now a dark coat drops in the usual "had enough" style.

In the ride-cunning, or know-the-country detachment, Miss de Glancey's flaunting habit, giving dignity to the figure and flowing elegance to the scene, might be seen going at perfect ease beside the noble Earl, who from the higher ground surveys Gameboy Green and the Hatter racing to get first at each fence, while the close-packing hounds are sufficiently far in advance to be well out of harm's way.

"C—a—a—tch 'em, if you can!" shrieks his lordship, eyeing their zealous endeavours.

"C—a—a—tch 'em, if you can!" repeats he, laughing, as the pace gets better and better, scarce a hound having time to give tongue.

"Yooi, over he goes!" now cries his lordship, as a spasmodic jerk of the leading hounds, on Alsike water meadow, turns Trumpeter's and Wrangler's heads toward the newly widened and deepened drain-cut, and the whole pack wheel to the left. What a scramble there is to get over! Some clear it, some fall back, while some souse in and out.

Now Gameboy, seeing by the newly thrown out gravel the magnitude of the venture, thrusts down his hat firmly on his brow, while Hicks gets his chesnut well by the head, and hardening their hearts they clear it in stride, and the Damper takes Foundings for the benefit of those who come after. What a splash he makes!

And now the five-and-thirty years master of "haryers" without a subscription coming up, seeks to save the credit of his quivering-tailed grey by stopping to help the discontented Damper out of his difficulty, whose horse coming out on the wrong side affords them both a very fair excuse for shutting up shop.

The rest of the detachment, unwilling to bathe, after craning at the cut, scuttle away by its side down to the wooden cattle-bridge below, which being crossed, the honourable obligationers and the take-care-of-their-neckers are again joined in common union. It is, however, no time to boast of individual feats, or to inquire for absent friends, for the hounds still press on, though the pace is not quite so severe as it was. They are on worse soil, and the scent does not serve them so well. It soon begins to fail, and at length is carried on upon the silent system, and looks very like failing altogether.

Mr. Boggledike, who has been riding as cunning as any one, now shows to the front, watching the stooping pack with anxious eye, lest he should have to make a cast over fences that do not quite suit his convenience.

"G—e—ntly, urryin'! gently!" cries he, seeing that a little precipitancy may carry them off the line. "Yon cur dog has chased the fox, and the hounds are puzzled at the point where he has left him."

"Ah, sarr, what the daval business have you out with a dog on such an occasion as this?" demands Dicky of an astonished drover who thought the road was as open to him as to Dicky.

"O, sar! sar! you desarve to be put i' the lock-up," continues Dicky, as the pack now divide on the scent.

"O, sar! sar! you should be chaasetised!" added he, shaking his whip at the drover, as he trotted on to the assistance of the pack.

The melody of the majority however recalls the cur-ites, and saves Dicky from the meditated assault.

While the brief check was going on, his lordship was eyeing Miss de Glancey, thinking of all the quiet captivating women he had ever seen, she was the most so. Her riding was perfection, and he couldn't conceive how it was that he had ever entertained any objection to sports-women. It must have been from seeing some clumsy ones rolling about who couldn't ride; and old Binks's chance at that moment was not worth one farthing.

"Where's Pringle?" now asked his lordship, as the thought of Binks brought our hero to his recollection.

"Down," replied Miss de Glancey carelessly, pointing to the ground with her pretty amethyst-topped whip.

"Down, is he!" smiled the Earl, adding half to himself and half to her, "thought he was a mull'."

Our friend indeed has come to grief. After pulling and hauling at his horse until he got him quite savage, the irritated animal, shaking his head as a terrier shakes a rat, ran blindfold into a bullfinch, shooting Billy into a newly-made manure-heap beyond. The last of the "harrver" men caught his horse, and not knowing who he belonged to, just threw the bridle-rein over the next gatepost, while D'Orsay Davis, who had had enough, and was glad of an excuse for stopping, pulls up to assist Billy out of his dirty dilemma.

Augh, what a figure he was!

But see! Mr. Boggledike is hitting off the scent, and the astonished drover is spurring on his pony to escape the chasetisement Dicky has promised him.

At this critical moment, Miss de Glancey's better genius whispered her to go home. She had availed herself of the short respite to take a sly peep at herself in a little pocket-mirror she carried in her saddle, and found she was quite as much heated as was becoming or as could be ventured upon without detriment to her dress. Moreover, she was not quite sure but that one of her frizettes was coming out.

So now when the hounds break out in fresh melody, and the Flying Hatter and Gameboy Green are again elbowing to the front, she sits reining in her steed, evidently showing she is done.

"Oh, come along!" exclaimed the Earl, looking back for her. "Oh, come along," repeated he, waving her onward, as he held in his horse.

There was no resisting the appeal, for it was clear he would come back for her if she did, so touching her horse with the whip, she is again cantering by his side.

"I'd give the world to see you beat that impudent ugly hatter," said he, now pointing Hicks out in the act of riding at a stiff newly-plashed fence before his hounds were half over.

And his lordship spurred his horse as he spoke with a vigour that spoke the intensity of his feelings.

The line of chase then lay along the swiftly flowing Arrow banks and across Oxley large pastures, parallel with the Downton bridle-road, along which Dicky and his followers now pounded; Dicky hugging himself with the idea that the fox was making for the main earths on Bringwood moor, to which he knew every yard of the country.

And so the fox was going as straight and as hard as ever he could, but as ill luck would have it, young Mr. Nailor, the son of the owner of Oxley pastures, shot at a snipe at the west corner of the large pasture just as pug entered at the east, causing him to shift his line and thread Larchfield plantations instead of crossing the pasture, and popping down Tillington Dean as he intended.

38

Dicky had heard the gun, and the short turn of the hounds now showing him what had happened, he availed himself of the superiority of a well-mounted nobleman's huntsman in scarlet over a tweed-clad muffin-capped shooter, for exclaiming at the top of his voice as he cantered past, horn in hand,

"O ye poachin' davil, what business 'ave ye there!"

"O ye nasty sneakin' snarin' ticket-o'-leaver, go back to the place from whence you came!" leaving the poor shooter staring with astonishment.

A twang of the horn now brings the hounds—who have been running with a flinging catching side-wind scent on to the line, and a full burst of melody greets the diminished field, as they strike it on the bright grass of the plantation.

"For—rard! for—rard!" is the cry, though there isn't a hound but what is getting on as best as he can.

The merry music reanimates the party, and causes them to press on their horses with rather more freedom than past exertions warrant.

Imperial John's is the first to begin wheezing, but his Highness feeling him going covers a retreat of his hundred-and-fifty-guineas-worth, as he hopes he will be, under shelter of the plantation.

****

"I think the 'atter's oss has about 'ad enough," now observes Dicky to his lordship, as he holds open the bridle-gate at the end of the plantation into the Benington Lane for his lordship and Miss de Glancey to pass.

"Glad of it," replied the Earl, thinking the Hatter would not be able to go home and boast how he had cut down the Tantivy men and hung them up to dry.

"Old 'ard, one moment!" now cries Dicky, raising his right hand as the Hatter comes blundering through the quickset fence into the hard lane, his horse nearly alighting on his nose.

"Old 'ard, please!" adds he, as the Hatter spurs among the road-stooping pack.

"Hooick to Challenger! Hooick to Challenger!" now hollas Dicky, as Challenger, after sniffing up the grassy mound of the opposite hedge, proclaims that the fox is over; and Dicky getting his horse short by the head, slips behind the Hatter's horse's tail for his old familiar friend the gap in the corner, while the Hatter gathers his horse together to fulfil the honourable obligation of going with, the hounds.

"C—u—r—m up!" cries he, with an *obligato* accompaniment of the spur rowels, which the honest beast acknowledges by a clambering flounder up the bank, making the descent on his head on the field side that he nearly executed before. The Hatter's legs perform a sort of wands of a mill evolution.

"Not hurt, I hope!" hollas the Earl, who with Miss de Glancey now lands a little above, and seeing the Hatter rise and shake himself he canters on, giving Miss de Glancey a touch on the elbow, and saying with a knowing look, "*That's capital!* get rid of him, leggings and all!"

His lordship having now seen the last of his tormentors, has time to look about him a little.

"Been a monstrous fine run," observes he to the lady, as they canter together behind the pace-slackening pack.

"Monstrous," replies the lady, who sees no fun in it at all.

"How long has it been?" asks his lordship of Swan, who now shows to the front as a whip-aspiring huntsman is wont to do.

"An hour all but five minutes, my lord," replies the magnifier, looking at his watch. "No—no—an hour 'zactly, my lord," adds he, trotting on—restoring his watch to his fob as he goes.

"An hour best pace with but one slight check—can't have come less than twelve miles," observes his lordship, thinking it over.

"Indeed," replied Miss de Glancey, wishing it was done.

"Grand sport fox-hunting, isn't it?" asked his lordship, edging close up to her.

"Charming!" replied Miss de Glancey, feeling her failing frizette.

The effervescence of the thing is now about over, and the hounds are reduced to a very plodding pains-taking pace. The day has changed for the worse, and heavy clouds are gathering overhead. Still there is a good holding scent, and as the old saying is, a fox so pressed must stop at last, the few remaining sportsmen begin speculating on his probable destination, one backing him for Cauldwell rocks, another for Fulford woods, a third for the Hawkhurst Hills.

"'Awk'urst 'ills for a sovereign!" now cries Dicky, hustling his horse, as, having steered the nearly mute pack along Sandy-well banks, Challenger and Sparkler strike a scent on the track leading up to Sorryfold Moor, and go away at an improving pace.

"'Awk'urst 'ills for a fi'-pun note!" adds he, as the rest of the pack score to cry.

"Going to have rine!" now observes he, as a heavy drop beats upon his up-turned nose. At the same instant a duplicate drop falls upon Miss de Glancey's fair cheek, causing her to wish herself anywhere but where she was.

Another, and another, and another, follow in quick succession, while the dark, dreary moor offers nothing but the inhospitable freedom of space. The cold wind cuts through her, making her shudder for the result. "He's for the hills!" exclaims Gameboy Green, still struggling on with a somewhat worse-for-wear looking steed.

"He's for the hills!" repeats he, pointing to a frowning line in the misty distance.

At the same instant his horse puts his foot in a stone-hole, and Gameboy and he measure their lengths on the moor.

"That comes of star-gazing," observed his lordship, turning his coat-collar up about his ears. "That comes of star-gazing," repeats he, eyeing the loose horse scampering the wrong way.

"We'll see no more of him," observed Miss de Glancey, wishing she was as well out of it as Green.

"Not likely, I think," replied his lordship, seeing the evasive rush the horse gave, as Speed, who was coming up with some tail hounds, tried to catch him.

The heath-brushing fox leaves a scent that fills the painfully still atmosphere with the melody of the hounds, mingled with the co-beck——-co-beck co-lurk of the startled grouse. There is a solemn calm that portends a coming storm. To Miss de Clancey, for whom the music of the hounds has no charms, and the fast-gathering clouds have great danger, the situation is peculiarly distressing. She would stop if she durst, but on the middle of a dreary moor how dare she.

An ominous gusty wind, followed by a vivid flash of lightning and a piercing scream from Miss de Glancey, now startled the Earl's meditations.

"Lightning!" exclaimed his lordship, turning short round to her assistance. "Lightning in the month of November—never heard of such a thing!"

But ere his lordship gets to Miss de Glancey's horse, a most terrific clap of thunder burst right over head, shaking the earth to the very centre, silencing the startled hounds, and satisfying his lordship it *was* lightning.

Another flash, more vivid if possible than the first, followed by another pealing crash of thunder, more terrific than before, calls all hands to a hurried council of war on the subject of shelter.

"We must make for the Punch-bowl at Rockbeer," exclaims General Boggledike, flourishing his horn in an ambiguous sort of way, for he wasn't quite sure he could find it.

"*You* know the Punch-bowl at Rockbeer!" shouts he to Harry Swan, anxious to have some one on whom to lay the blame if he went wrong.

"I know it when I'm there," replied Swan, who didn't consider it part of his duty to make imaginary runs to ground for his lordship.

"Know it when you're there, man," retorted Dicky in disgust; "why any————" the remainder of his sentence being lost in a tremendously illuminating flash of lightning, followed by a long cannonading, reverberating roll of thunder.

Poor Miss de Glancey was ready to sink into the earth.

"*Elope, hounds! elope!*" cried Dicky, getting his horse short by the head, and spurring him into a brisk trot. "*Elope, hounds! elope!*" repeated he, setting off on a speculative cast, for he saw it was no time for dallying.

And now,

"From cloud to cloud the rending lightnings rage; Till in the furious elemental war Dissolved, the whole precipitated mass, Unbroken floods and solid torrents pour."

Luckily for Dicky, an unusually vivid flash of lightning so lit up the landscape as to show the clump of large elms at the entrance to Rockbeer; and taking his bearings, he went swish swash, squirt spurt, swish swash, squirt spurt, through the spongy, half land, half water moor, at as good a trot as he could raise. The lately ardent, pressing hounds follow on in long-drawn file, looking anything but large or formidable. The frightened horses tucked in their tails, and looked fifty per cent, worse for the suppression. The hard, driving rain beats downways, and sideways, and frontways, and backways—all ways at once. The horses know not which way to duck, to evade the storm. In less than a minute Miss de Glancey is as drenched as if she had taken a shower-bath. The smart hat and feathers are annihilated; the dubious frizette falls out, down comes the hair; the bella-donna-inspired radiance of her eyes is quenched; the Crinoline and wadding dissolve like ice before the fire; and ere the love-cured Earl lifts her off her horse at the Punch-bowl at Rockbeer, she has no more shape or figure than an icicle. Indeed she very much resembles one, for the cold sleet, freezing as it fell, has encrusted her in a rich coat of ice lace, causing her saturated garments to cling to her with the utmost pertinacity. A more complete wreck of a belle was, perhaps, never seen.

40

"*What an object!*" inwardly ejaculated she, as Mrs. Hetherington, the landlady, brought a snivelling mould candle into the cheerless, fireless little inn-parlour, and she caught a glimpse of herself in the—at best—most unbecoming mirror. What would she have given to have turned back!

And as his lordship hurried up stairs in his water-logged boots, he said to himself, with a nervous swing of his arm, "I was right!—women *have* no business out hunting." And the Binks chance improved amazingly.

The further *denouement* of this perishing day will be gleaned from the following letters.

CHAPTER XIV. THE PRINGLE CORRESPONDENCE.
MR WILLIAM TO HIS MAMMA.

"Tantivy Castle, November.

"My dearest Mamma,

"*Though I wrote to you only the other day, I take up my pen, stiff and sore as I am and scarcely able to sit, to tell you of my first day's hunt, which, I assure you, was anything but enjoyable. In fact, at this moment I feel just as if I had been thumped by half the pugilists in London and severely kicked at the end. To my fancy, hunting is about the most curious, unreasonable amusement that ever was invented. The first fox was well enough, running backwards and forwards in an agreeable manner, though they all abused him and called him a cowardly beggar, though to my mind it was far pluckier to do what he did, with fifty great dogs after him, than to fly like a thief as the next one did. Indeed I saw all the first run without the slightest inconvenience or exertion, for a very agreeable gentleman, called Major Hammerton, himself an old keeper of hounds, led me about and showed me the country.*

"*I don't mean yo say that he led my horse, but he showed me the way to go, so as to avoid the jumps, and pointed out the places where I could get a peep of the fox. I saw him frequently. The Major, who was quite polite, asked me to go and stay with him after I leave here, and I wouldn't mind going if it wasn't for the hounds, which, however, he says are quite as fine as his lordship's, without being so furiously and inconveniently fast. For my part, however, I don't see the use of hunting an animal that you can shoot, as they do in France. It seems a monstrous waste of exertion. If they were all as sore as I am this morning, I'm sure they wouldn't try it again in a hurry. I really think racing, where you pay people for doing the dangerous for you, is much better fun, and prettier too, for you can choose any lively colour you like for your jacket, instead of having to stick to scarlet or dark clothes.*

"*But I will tell you about fox No. 2. I was riding with a very pretty young lady, Miss de Glancey, whom the Earl had just introduced me to, when all of a sudden everybody seemed to be seized with an uncontrollable galloping mania, and set off as hard as ever their horses could lay legs to the ground. My horse, who they said was a perfect hunter, but who, I should say, was a perfect brute, partook of the prevailing epidemic, and, though he had gone quite quietly enough before, now seized the bit between his teeth, and plunged and reared as though he would either knock my teeth down my throat, or come back over upon me. 'Drop your hand!' cried one. 'Ease his head!' cried another, and what was the consequence? He ran away with me and, dashing through a flock of turkeys, nearly capsized an old sow.*

"*Then the people, who had been so civil before, all seemed to be seized with the rudes. It was nothing but 'g-u-u-r along, sir! g-u-u-r along! Hang it! don't you see the hounds are running!' just as if I had made them run, or as if I could stop them. My good friend, the Major, seemed to be as excited as any body: indeed, the only cool person was Miss de Glancey, who cantered away in a most unconcerned manner. I am sorry to say she came in for a desperate ducking. It seems that after I had had as much as I wanted, and pulled up to come home, they encountered a most terrific thunder-storm in crossing some outlandish moor, and as his lordship, who didn't get home till long after dark, said she all at once became a dissolving view, and went away to nothing. Mrs. Moffatt, who is stout and would not easily dissolve, seemed amazingly tickled with the joke, and said she supposed she would look like a Mermaid—which his lordship said was exactly the case. When the first roll of thunder was heard here, the Earl's carriage and four was ordered out, with dry things, to go in quest of him; but they tried two of his houses of call before they fell in with him. It then had to return to take the Mermaid to her home, who had to borrow the publican's wife's Sunday clothes to travel in.*

"*After dinner, the stud-groom came in to announce the horses for to-day; and hearing one named for me, I begged to decline the honour, on the plea of having a great many letters to write, so Mrs. Moffatt accompanied his lordship to the meet, some ten miles north of this, in his carriage and four, from whence she has just returned, and says they went away with a brilliant scent from Foxlydiate Gorse, meaning, I presume, with another such clatter as we had yesterday. I am glad I didn't go, for I don't think I could have got on to a horse, let alone sit one, especially at the jumps, which all the Clods in the country seem to have clubbed their ideas to concoct. Rougier says people are always stiff after the first day's hunting; but if I had thought I should be as sore and stiff as I am, I don't think I would ever have taken a day, because Major Hammerlon says it is not necessary to go out hunting in the morning to entitle one to wear the dress uniform in the evening—which is really all I care for.*

41

"*The servants here seem to live like fighting-cocks, from Rougier's account; breakfasts, luncheons, dinners, teas, and suppers. They sit down, ten or a dozen at the second table, and about thirty or so in the hall, besides which there are no end of people out of doors. Rougier says they have wine at the second table, and eau de vie punch at night at discretion, of which, I think, he takes more than is discreet, for he came swaggering into my room at day-break this morning, in his evening dress, with his hat on, and a great pewter inkstand in his hand, which he set down on the dressing-table, and said, 'dere, sir, dere is your shavin' rater!' Strange to say, the fellow speaks better English when he's drunk than he does when he's sober. However, I suppose I must have a valet, otherwise I should think it would be a real kindness to give the great lazy fellows here something to do, other than hanging about the passages waylaying the girls, I'll write you again when I know what I'm going to do, but I don't think I shall stay here much longer, if I'm obliged to risk my neck after these ridiculous dogs. Ever, my dearest Mamma your most affectionate, but excruciatingly sore, son.*

"Wm. PRINGLE."

The following is Mrs. Pringle's answer; who, it will be seen, received Billy's last letter while she was answering his first one:—

"25, Curtain Crescent, "Belgrave Square, London.

"My own dearest William,

"*I was overjoyed, my own darling, to receive your kind letter, and hear that you had arrived safe, and found his lordship so kind and agreeable. I thought you had known him by sight, or I would have prevented your making the mistake by describing him to you. However, there is no harm done. In a general way, the great man of the place is oftentimes the least.—The most accessible, that is to say. The Earl is an excellent, kind-hearted man, and it will do you great good among your companions to be known to be intimate with him, for I can assure you it is not every one he takes up with. Of course, there are people who abuse him, and say he is this and that, and so on; but you must take people—especially great ones—as you find them in this world; and he is quite as good as his whites of their eyes turning-up neighbours. Don't, however, 'presume on his kindness by attempting to stay beyond what he presses you to do, for two short visits tell better than one long one, looking as though you had been approved of. You can easily find out from the butler or the groom of the chambers, or some of the upper servants, how long you are expected to stay, or perhaps some of the guests can tell you how long they are invited for.*

"*I had written thus far when your second welcome letter arrived, and I can't tell you how delighted I am to hear you are safe and well, though I'm sorry to hear you don't like hunting, for I assure you it is the best of all possible sports, and there is none that admits of such elegant variety of costume.*

"*Look at a shooter,—what a ragamuffin dress his is, hardly distinguishable from a keeper; and yachters and cricketers might be taken for ticket-of-leave men. I should be very sorry indeed if you were not to persevere in your hunting; for a red coat and leathers are quite your become, and there is none, in my opinion, in which a gentleman looks so well, or a snob so ill. Learning to hunt can't be more disagreeable than learning to sail or to smoke, and see how many hundreds—thousands I may say—overcome the difficulty every year, and blow their clouds, as they call them, on the quarterdeck, as though they had been born sailors with pipes in their mouths. Remember, if you can't manage to sit your horse, you'll be fit for nothing but a seat in Parliament along with Captain Catlap and the other incurables. I can't think there can be much difficulty in the matter, judging from the lumpy wash-balley sort of men one hears talking about it. I should think if you had a horse of your own, you would be able to make better out. Whatever you do, however, have nothing to do with racing. It's only for rogues and people who have more money than they know what to do with, and to whom it doesn't matter whether they win or they lose. We musn't have you setting up a confidential crossing-sweeper with a gold eyeglass. No gentleman need expect to make money on the turf, for if you were to win they wouldn't pay you, whereas, if you lose it's quite a different thing. One of the beauties of hunting is that people have no inducement to poison each other; whereas in racing, from poisoning horses they have got to poisoning men, besides which one party must lose if the other is to win. Mutual advantage is impossible. Another thing, if you were to win ever so, the trainer would always keep his little bill in advance of your gains, or he would be a very bad trainer.*

"*I hope Major Hammerton is a gentleman of station, whose acquaintance will do you good, though the name is not very aristocratic—Hamilton would have been better. Are there any Miss H's? Remember there are always forward people in the world, who think to advance themselves by taking strangers by the hand, and that a bad introduction is far worse than none. Above all, never ask to be introduced to a great man. Great people have their eyes and ears about them just as well as little ones, and if they choose to know you, they will make the advance. Asking to be introduced only prejudices them against you, and generally insures a cut at the first opportunity.*

"*Beware of Miss de Glancey. She is a most determined coquette, and if she had fifty suitors, wouldn't be happy if she saw another woman with one, without trying to get him from her. She hasn't a halfpenny. If you see her again, ask her if she knows Mr. Hotspur Smith, or Mr. Enoch Benson, or Mr. Woodhorn, and tell me how she looks. What is she doing down there? Surely she hasn't the vanity to think she can captivate the Earl. You needn't mention me to Mrs. Moffatt, but I should like to know what she has on, and also if there are any new dishes for dinner. Indeed, the less you talk about your belongings the better; for the world has but two ways, that of running people down much below their real level, or of extolling them much beyond their deserts. Remember, well-bred people always take breeding for granted, 'one of us,' as they say in others when they find them at good houses,*

42

and as you have a good name, you have nothing to do but hold your tongue, and the chances are they will estimate you at far more than your real worth.

"A valet is absolutely indispensable for a young gentleman. Bless you! you would be thought nothing of among the servants if you hadn't one. They are their masters' trumpeters. A valet, especially a French one, putting on two clean shirts a day, and calling for Burgundy after your cheese, are about the most imposing things in the lower regions. In small places, giving as much trouble as possible, and asking for things you think they haven't got, is very well; but this will not do where you now are. In a general way, it is a bad plan taking servants to great houses, for, as they all measure their own places by the best they have ever seen, and never think how many much worse ones there are, they come back discontented, and are seldom good for much until they have undergone a quarter's starving or so, out of place. It is a good thing when the great man of a country sets an example of prudence and economy, for then all others can quote him, instead of having the bad practices of other places raked up as authority for introducing them into theirs. The Earl, however, would never be able to get through half his income if he was not to wink at a little prodigality, and the consumption of wine in great houses would be a mere nothing if it was not for the assistance of the servants. Indeed, the higher you get into society, the less wine you get, until you might expect to see it run out to nothing at a Duke's. I dare say Rougier will be fond of drink, and the English servants will perhaps be fond of plying him with it; but, so long as he does not get incompetent, a little jollity on his part will make them more communicative before him, and it is wonderful what servants can tell. They know everything in the kitchen—nothing in the parlour. His lordship, I believe, doesn't allow strange servants to wait except upon very full occasions, otherwise it might be well to put Rougier under the surveillance of Beverage, the butler, lest he should come into the room drunk and incompetent, which would be very disagreeable.

"I enclose you a gold fox-head pin to give Mr. Boggledike, who doesn't take money, at least nothing under 5 L., and this only costs 18s. He is a favourite with his lordship, and it will be well to be in with him. You had better give the men who whip the hounds a trifle, say 10s. or half-a-sovereign each—gold looks better than silver. If you go to Major Hammertons you must let me know; but perhaps you will inquire further before you fix. And now, hoping that you will stick to your hunting, and be more successful on another horse after a quieter fox, believe me ever, my own dearest William, your most truly and sincerely affectionate mother,

"Emma Pringle.

"P.S.—Don't forget the two clean shirts.

"P.S.—When you give Dicky Boggledike the pin, you can compliment him on his talents as a huntsman (as Mr. Redpath the the actor); and as they say he is a very bad one, he will be all the more grateful for it.

"P.S.—I have just had another most pressing letter from your uncle Jerry, urging me to go and look through all the accounts and papers, as he says it is not fair throwing such a heavy responsibility upon him. Poor man! He need not be so pressing. He little knows how anxious I am to do it. I hope now we shall get something satisfactory, for as yet I know no more than I did before your poor father died.

"P.S.—Don't forget to tell me if there are any Miss H.'s, and whatever you do, take care of Dowb, that is, yourself."

But somehow Billy forgot to tell his Mamma whether there were any Miss H.'s or not, though he might have said "No," seeing they were Miss "Y.'s."

And now, while our hero is recovering from his bruises, let us introduce the reader further to his next host, Major Y.

CHAPTER XV. MAJOR YAMMERTON'S COACH STOPS THE WAY.

MAJOR Yammerton was rather a peculiar man, inasmuch as he was an Ass, without being a Fool. He was an Ass for always puffing and inflating himself, while as regarded worldly knowledge, particularly that comprised in the magic letters £. s. d., few, if any, were his equals. In the former department, he was always either on the strut or the fret, always either proclaiming the marked attention he had met with, or worrying himself with the idea that he had not had enough. At home, instead of offering people freely and hospitably what he had, he was continually boring them with apologies for what he had not. Just as if all men were expected to have things alike, or as if the Major was an injured innocent who had been defrauded of his rights. If he was not boring and apologising, then he was puffing or praising everything indiscriminately—depending, of course, upon who he had there—a great gun or a little one.

He returned from his Tantivy Castle hunt, very much pleased with our Billy, who seemed to be just the man for his money, and by the aid of his Baronetage he made him out to be very highly connected. Mrs. Yammerton and the young ladies were equally delighted with him, and it was unanimously resolved that he should be invited to the Grange, for which purpose the

43

standing order of the house "never to invite any one direct from a great house to theirs," was suspended. A very salutary rule it is for all who study appearances, seeing that what looks very well one way may look very shady the other; but this being perhaps a case of "now or never," the exception would seem to have been judiciously made. The heads of the house had different objects in view; Mamma's, of course, being matrimonial, the Major's, the laudable desire to sell Mr. Pringle a horse. And the mention of Mamma's object leads us to the young ladies.

These, Clara, Flora, and Harriet, were very pretty, and very highly educated—that is to say, they could do everything that is useless—play, draw, sing, dance, make wax-flowers, bead-stands, do decorative gilding, and crochet-work; but as to knowing how many ounces there are in a pound of tea, or how many pounds of meat a person should eat in a day, they were utterly, entirely, and most elegantly ignorant. Towards the close of the last century, and at the beginning of the present one, ladies ran entirely to domesticity, pickling, preserving, and pressing people to eat. Corded petticoats and patent mangles long formed the staple of a mid life woman's conversation. Presently a new era sprang up, which banished everything in the shape of utilitarianism, and taught the then rising generation that the less they knew of domestic matters the finer ladies they would be, until we really believe the daughters of the nobility are better calculated for wives, simply because they are generally economically brought up, and are not afraid of losing *caste*, by knowing what every woman ought to do. No man thinks the worse of a woman for being able to manage her house, while few men can afford to marry mere music-stools and embroidery frames. Mrs. Yammerton, however, took a different view of the matter. She had been brought up in the patent mangle and corded petticoat school, and inwardly resolved that her daughters should know nothing of the sort—should be "real ladies," in the true kitchen acceptation of the term. Hence they were mistresses of all the little accomplishments before enumerated, which, with making calls and drinking tea, formed the principal occupation of their lives. Not one of them could write a letter without a copy, and were all very uncertain in their spelling—though they knew to a day when every King and Queen began to reign, and could spout all the chief towns in the kingdom. Now this might have been all very well, at least bearable, if the cockey Major had had plenty of money to give them, but at the time they were acquiring them, the "contrary was the case," as the lawyers say. The Major's grandfather (his father died when he was young) had gone upon the old annexation principle of buying land and buying land simply because "it joined," and not always having the cash to pay for it with, our Major came into an estate (large or small, according as the reader has more or less of his own saddled with a good, stout, firmly setting mortgage.) Land, however, being the only beast of burthen that does not show what it carries, our orphan—orphan in top-boots to be sure—passed for his best, and was speedily snapped up by the then beautiful. Italian like Miss Winnington, who consoled herself for the collapse of his fortune, by the reflection that she had nothing of her own. Perhaps, too, she had made allowance for the exaggeration of estimates, which generally rate a man at three or four times his worth. The Winningtons, however, having made a great "crow" at the "catch," the newly-married couple started at score as if the estate had nothing to carry but themselves.

In due time the three graces appeared,—Clara, very fair, with large languishing blue eyes and light hair; Flora, with auburn hair and hazel eyes; and Harriet, tall, clear, and dark, like Mamma. As they grew up, and had had their heads made into Almanacs at home, they were sent to the celebrated Miss Featherey's finishing and polishing seminary at Westbourne Grove, who for 200 L, a-year, or as near 200 L. as she could get, taught them all the airs and graces, particularly how to get in and out of a carriage properly, how to speak to a doctor, how to a counter-skipper, how to a servant, and so on. The Major, we may state, had his three daughters taken as two. Well, just as Miss Harriet was supplying the place of Miss Clara (polished), that great agricultural revolution, the repeal of the corn laws, took place, and our Major, who had regarded his estate more with an eye to its hunting and shooting capabilities than to high farming, very soon found it slipping away from him, just as Miss de Glancey slipped away from her dress in the thunder-storm. Up to that time, his easy-minded agent, Mr. Bullrush, a twenty stone man of sixty years of age, had thought the perfection of management was not to let an estate go back, but now the Major's seemed likely to slip through its girths altogether. To be sure, it had not had any great assistance in the advancing line, and was just the same sour, rush-grown, poachy, snipe-shooting looking place that it was when the Major got it; but this was not his grandfather's fault, who had buried as many stones in great gulf-like drains, as would have carried off a river and walled the estate all round into the bargain; but there was no making head against wet land with stone drains, the bit you cured only showing the wetness of the rest. The blotchy March fallows looked as if they had got the small pox, the pastures were hardly green before Midsummer, and the greyhound-like cattle that wandered over them were evidently of Pharaoh's lean sort, and looked as if they would *never* be ready for the butcher. Foreign cattle, too, were coming in free, and the old cry of "down corn, down horn," frightened the fabulously famed "stout British farmer" out of his wits.

Then those valuable documents called leases—so binding on the landlord, were found to be wholly inoperative on the tenants, who threw up their farms as if there were no such things in existence.

If the Major wouldn't take their givings up, why then he might just do his "warst;" meanwhile, of course, they would "do their warst," by the land. With those who had nothing (farming and beer-shop keeping being about the only trades a man can start with upon nothing), of course, it was of no use persisting, but the awkward part of the thing was, that this probing of pockets showed that in too many eases the reputed honesty of the British farmer was also mere fiction; for some who were thought to be well off, now declared that their capital was their aunt's, or their uncle's, or their grandmother's, or some one else's, so that the two classes, the have-somethings, and the have-nothings, were reduced to a level. This sort of thing went on throughout the country, and landlords who could not face the difficulty by taking their estates in hand, had to submit to very serious reductions of rent, and rent once got down, is very difficult to get up again, especially in countries where they value by the rate-book, or where a traditionary legend attaches to land of the lowest rent it has ever been let for.

Our Major was sorely dispirited, and each market-day, as he returned from Mr. Bullrush's with worse and worse news than before, he pondered o'er his misfortunes, fearing that he would have to give up his hounds and his horses, withdraw his daughters from Miss Featherey's, and go to Boulogne, and as he contemplated the airy outline of their newly-erected rural palace of a workhouse, he said it was lucky they had built it, for he thought they would all very soon be in it. Certainly, things got to their worst in the farming way, before they began to mend, and such land as the Major's—good, but "salivated with wet," as the cabman said of his coat—was scarcely to be let at any price.

In these go-a-head days of farming, when the enterprising sons of trade are fast obliterating the traces of the heavy-heel'd order of easy-minded Hodges who,

———*"held their farms and lived content While one year paid another's rent,"*

without ever making any attempt at improvement, it may be amusing to record the business-like offer of some of those indolent worthies who would bid for a pig in a poke. Thus it runs:—It should have been dated April 1, instead of 21:—

TO MAJOR YAMMERTON.

"Onard Sir,

"Hobnail Hill, April 21.

"Wheas We have, considered n'e shall give you for Bonnyrig's farme the som £100 25 puns upon condishinds per year if you should think it to little we may perhaps advance a little as we have not looked her carefully over her and for character Mr. Soicerby will give you every information as we are the third giniration that's been under the Sowerbys.

"Yours sincerely,

"Henerey Brown,

"Homfray Brown—Co.

"If you want anye otes I could sell you fifteen bowels of verye fine ones."

Now the "som £100 25 puns" being less than half what the Major's grandfather used to get for the farm:—viz. "£200 63 puns,"—our Major was considerably perplexed; and as "Henerey and Homfray"'s offer was but a sample of the whole, it became a question between Boulogne and Bastile, as those once unpopular edifices, the workhouses, were then called. And here we may observe, that there is nothing perhaps, either so manageable or so unmanageable as land—nothing easier to keep right than land in good order, and nothing more difficult to get by the head, and stop, than land that has run wild; and it may be laid down as an infallible rule, that the man who has no taste for land or horses should have nothing to do with either. He should put his money in the funds, and rail or steam when he has occasion to travel. He will be far richer, far fatter, and fill the bay window of his club far better, than by undergoing the grinding of farmers and the tyranny of grooms. Land, like horses, when once in condition is easily kept so, but once let either go down, and the owner becomes a prey to the scratchers and the copers.

If, however, a man likes a little occupation better than the eternal gossip, and *"who's that?"* of the clubs, and prefers a smiling improving landscape to a barren retrograding scene, he will find no pleasanter, healthier, or more interesting occupation than improving his property. And a happy thing it was for this kingdom, that Prince Albert who has done so much to refine and elevate mankind, should have included farming in the list of his amusements,—bringing the before despised pursuit into favour and fashion, so that now instead of land remaining a prey to the "Henerey Browns & Co." of life, we find gentlemen advertising for farms in all directions, generally stipulating that they are to be on the line of one or other of the once derided railways.

45

But we are getting in advance of the times with our Major, whom we left in the slough of despond, consequent on the coming down of his rents. Just when things were at their worst, the first sensible sunbeam of simplicity that ever shone upon land, appeared in the shape of the practical, easy-working Drainage Act, an act that has advanced agriculture more than all previous inventions and legislation put together. But our gallant friend had his difficulties to contend with even here.

Mr. Bullrush was opposed to it. He was fat and didn't like trouble, so he doubted the capacity of such a pocket companion as a pipe to carry off the superfluous water, then he doubted the ability of the water to get into the pipe at such a depth, above all he doubted the ability of the tenants to pay drainage interests. "How could they if they couldn't pay their rents?" Of course, the tenants adopted this view of the matter, and were all opposed to making what they called "experiences," at their own expense; so upon the whole, Mr. Bullrush advised the Major to have nothing to do with it. It being, however, a case of necessity with the Major, he disregarded Mr. Bullrush's advice which led to a separation, and being now a free agent, he went boldly at the government loan, and soon scared all the snipes and half the tenants off his estate. The water poured off in torrents; the plump juicy rushes got the jaundice, and Mossington bog, over which the Major used to have to scuttle on foot after his "haryers," became sound enough to carry a horse. Then as Mr. Bullrush rode by and saw each dreary swamp become sound ground, he hugged himself with the sloven's consolation that it "wouldn't p-a-a-y." Pay, however, it did, for our Major next went and got some stout horses, and the right sort of implements of agriculture, and soon proved the truth of the old adage, that it is better to follow a sloven than a scientific farmer. He worked his land well, cleaned it well, and manured it well; in which three simple operations consists the whole science of husbandry, and instead of growing turnips for pickling, as his predecessors seemed to do, he got great healthy Swedes that loomed as large as his now fashionable daughter's dresses. He grew as many "bowels" of oats upon one acre of land as any previous tenant had done upon three. So altogether, our Major throve, and instead of going to Boulogne, he presently set up the Cockaded Coach in which we saw him arrive at Tantivy Castle. Not that he went to a coachmaker's and said, "Build me a roomy family coach regardless of expense," but, finding that he couldn't get an inside seat along with the thirty-six yard dresses in the old chariot, he dropped in at the sale of the late Squire Trefoil's effects, who had given some such order, and, under pretence of buying a shower-bath, succeeded in getting a capital large coach on its first wheels for ten pounds,—scarcely the value of the pole.

As a contrast to Henerey Brown and Co.'s business-like offer for the farm, and in illustration of the difference between buying and selling, we append the verbose estimate of this ponderous affair. Thus it runs—

HENRY TREFOIL, ESQ.

To CHALKER AND CHARGER COACHMAKERS, BY APPOINTMENT, TO THE EMPEROR OF CHINA, Emperor of Morocco, the King of Oude, the King of the Cannibal Islands, &c., &c., &c., &c.

Long Acre, London.

(Followed by all the crowns, arms, orders, flourish, and flannel, peculiar to aristocratic tradesmen.)

Three hundred and ninety pounds! And to think that the whole should come to be sold for ten sovereigns. Oh, what a falling off was there, my coachmakers! Surely the King of the Cannibal Islands could never afford to pay such prices as those! Verily, Sir Robert Peel was right when he said that there was no class of tradespeople whose bills wanted reforming so much as coachmakers. What ridiculous price they make wood and iron assume, and what absurd offers they make when you go to them to sell!

CHAPTER XVI. THE MAJOR'S MENAGE.

AND first about the "haryers!"

"Five-and-thirty years master of haryers without a subscription!"

This, we think, is rather an exaggeration, both as regards time and money, unless the Major reckons an undivide d moiety he had in an old lady-hound called "Lavender" along with the village blacksmith of Billinghurst when he was at school. If he so calculates, then he would be right as to time, but wrong as to money, for the blacksmith paid his share of the tax, and found the greater part of the food. For thirty years, we need hardly tell the reader of sporting literature, that the Major had been a master of harriers—for well has he blown the horn of their celebrity during the whole of that long period—never were such harriers for finding jack hares, and pushing them through parishes innumerable, making them take rivers, and run as straight as railways, putting the costly performances of the foxhounds altogether to the blush. Ten miles from point to point, and generally without a turn, is the usual style of thing, the last run with this distinguished pack being always unsurpassed by any previous performance. Season after season has the sporting world been startled with these surprising announcements, until red-coated men, tired of blanks and ringing foxes, have almost said, "Dash my buttons, if I won't shut up shop here and go and hunt with these tremendous harriers," while other currant-jelly gentlemen, whose hares dance the fandango before their plodding pack, have sighed for some of these wonderful "Jacks" that never make a curve, or some of the astonishing hounds that have such a knack at making them fly.

Well, but the reader will, perhaps, say it's the blood that does it—the Major has an unrivalled, unequalled strain of harrier blood that nobody else can procure. Nothing of the sort! Nothing of the sort! The Major's blood is just anything he can get. He never misses a chance of selling either a single hound or a pack, and has emptied his kennel over and over again. But then he always knows where to lay hands on more; and as soon as ever the new hounds cross his threshold they become the very "best in the world"—better than any he ever had before. They then figure upon paper, just as if it was a continuous pack; and the field being under pretty good command, and, moreover, implicated in the honour of their performances, the thing goes on smoothly and well, and few are any the wiser. There is nothing so popular as a little fuss and excitement, in which every man may take his share, and this it is that makes scratch packs so celebrated. Their followers see nothing but their perfections. They are

"To their faults a little blind, And to their virtues ever kind."

At the period of which we are writing, the Major's pack was rather better than usual, being composed of the pick of three packs,—"cries of dogs" rather—viz., the Corkycove harriers, kept by the shoemakers of Waxley; the Bog-trotter harriers (four couple), kept by some moor-edge miners; the Dribbleford dogs, upon whom nobody would pay the tax; and of some two or three couple of incurables, that had been consigned from different kennels on condition of the Major returning the hampers in which they came.

The Major was open to general consignments in the canine line—Hounds, Pointers, Setters, Terriers, &c.—not being of George the Third's way of thinking, who used to denounce all "presents that eat." He would take anything; anything, at least, except a Greyhound, an animal that he held in mortal abhorrence. What he liked best was to get a Lurcher, for which he soon found a place under a pear-tree.

The Major's huntsman, old Solomon, was coachman, shepherd, groom, and gamekeeper, as well as huntsman, and was the cockaded gentleman who drove the ark on the occasion of our introduction. In addition to all this, he waited at table on grand occasions, and did a little fishing, hay-making, and gardening in the summer. He was one of the old-fashioned breed of servants, now nearly extinct, who passed their lives in one family and turned their hands to whatever was wanted. The Major, whose maxim was not to keep any cats that didn't catch mice, knowing full well that all gentlemen's servants can do double the work of their places, provided they only get paid for it, resolved, that it was cheaper to pay one man the wages of one-and-a-half to do the work of two men, than to keep two men to do the same quantity; consequently, there was very little hissing at bits and curb-chains in the Major's establishment, the hard work of other places being the light work, or no work at all, of his. Solomon was the *beau idéal* of a harrier huntsman, being, as the French say, *d'un certain age*, quiet, patient, and a pusillanimous rider.

Now about the subscription.

It is true that the Major did not take a subscription in the common acceptation of the term, but he took assistance in various ways, such as a few days ploughing from one man, a few "bowels" of seed-wheat from another, a few "bowels" of seed-oats from a third, a lamb from a fourth, a pig from a fifth, and to which, he had all the hounds walked during the summer, so that his actual expenses were very little more than the tax. This he jockeyed by only returning about two-thirds the number of hounds he kept; and as twelve couple were his hunting maximum, his taxing minimum would be about eight—eight couple—or sixteen hounds, at twelve shillings a-piece, is nine pound twelve, for which sum he made more noise in the papers than the Quorn, the Belvoir, and the Cottesmore all put together. Indeed the old adage of "great cry and little wool," applies to packs as well as flocks, for we never see hounds making a great "to-do" in the papers without suspecting that they are either good for nothing, or that the fortunate owner wants to sell them.

With regard to horses, the Major, like many people, had but one sort—the best in England— though they were divided into two classes, viz., hunters and draught horses. Hacks or carriage horses he utterly eschewed. Horses must either hunt or plough with him; nor was he above putting his hunters into the harrows occasionally. Hence he always had a pair of efficient horses for his carriage when he wanted them, instead of animals that were fit to jump out of their skins at starting, and ready to slip through them on coming home.

Clothing he utterly repudiated for carriage horses, alleging, that people never get any work out of them after they are once clothed.

The hunters were mostly sedate, elderly animals, horses that had got through the "morning of life" with the foxhounds, and came to the harriers in preference to harness. The Major was always a buyer or an exchanger, or a mixer of both, and would generally "advance a little" on the neighbouring job-master's prices. Then having got them, he recruited the veterans by care and crushed corn, which, with cutting their tails, so altered them, that sometimes their late groom scarcely knew them again.

Certainly, if the animals could have spoken, they would have expressed their surprise at the different language the Major held as a buyer and as a seller; as a buyer, when like Gil Blas' mule, he made them out to be all faults, as a seller when they suddenly seemed to become paragons of perfection. He was always ready for a deal, and would accommodate matters to people's convenience—take part cash, part corn, part hay, part anything, for he was a most miscellaneous barterer, and his stable loft was like a Marine Store-dealer's shop. Though always boasting that his little white hands were not "soiled with trade," he would traffic in anything (on the sly) by which he thought he could turn a penny. His last effort in the buying way had nearly got him into the County Court, as the following correspondence will show, as also how differently two people can view the same thing.

Being in town, with wheat at 80s. and barley and oats in proportion, and consequently more plethoric in the pocket than usual, he happened to stray into a certain great furniture mart where two chairs struck him as being cheap. They were standing together, and one of them was thus ticketed:

No. 8205. 2 Elizabethan chairs. India Japanned. 43 s.

The Major took a good stare at them, never having seen any before. Well, he thought they could not be dear at that; little more than a guinea each. Get them home for fifty shillings, say There was a deal of gold, and lacker, and varnish about them. Coloured bunches of flowers, inlaid with mother of pearl, Chinese temples, with "insolent pig-tailed barbarians," in pink silk jackets, with baggy blue trowsers, and gig whips in their hands, looking after the purple ducks on the pea-green lake—all very elegant.

He'd have them, dashed if he wouldn't! Would try and swap them for Mrs. Rocket Larkspur's Croydon basket-carriage that the girls wanted. Just the things to tickle her fancy. So he went into the office and gave his card most consequentially, with a reference to Pannell, the sadler in Spur Street, Leicestor-square, desiring that the chairs might be most carefully packed and forwarded to him by the goods train with an invoice by post.

When the invoice came, behold! the 43s. had changed into 86s.

"Hilloa!" exclaimed the astonished Major. This won't do! 86s. is twice 43s.; and he wrote off to say they had made a mistake. This brought the secretary of the concern, Mr. Badbill, on to the scene. He replied beneath a copious shower of arms, orders, flourish, and flannel, that the mistake was the Major's—that they, "never marked their goods in pairs," to which the Major rejoined, that they had in this instance, as the ticket which he forwarded to Pannell for Badbill's inspection showed, and that he must decline the chairs at double the price they were ticketed for.

Badbill, having duly inspected the ticket, retorted that he was surprised at the Major's stupidity, that two meant one, in fact, all the world over.

The Major rejoined, that he didn't know what the Reform Bill might have done, but that two didn't mean one when he was at school; and added, that as he declined the chairs at 86s. they were at Badhill's service for sending for.

Badbill wrote in reply—

"*We really cannot understand how it is possible, for any one to make out that a ticket on an article includes the other that may stand next it. Certainly the ticket you allude to referred only to the chair on which it was placed.*"

And in a subsequent letter he claimed to have the chairs repacked at the Major's expense, as it was very unfair saddling them with the loss arising entirely from the Major's mistake.

To which our gallant friend rejoined, "that as he would neither admit that the mistake was his, nor submit to the imputation of unfairness, he would stick to the chairs at the price they were ticketed at."

Badbill then wrote that this declaration surprised them much—that they did not for a moment think he "intentionally misunderstood the ticket as referring to a pair of chairs, whereas it only gave the price of one chair," and again begged to have them back; to which the Major inwardly responded, he "wished they might get them," and sent them an order for the 43s.

48

This was returned with expressions of surprise, that after the explanation given, the Major should persevere in the same "course of error," and hoped that he would, without further delay, favour the Co. with the right amount, for which Badbill said they "anxiously waited," and for which the Major inwardly said, they "might wait."

In due time came a lithographed circular, more imposingly flourished and flanneled than ever, stating the terms of the firm were "cash on delivery;" and that unless the Major remitted without further delay, he would be handed over to their solicitor, &c.; with an intimation at the bottom, that that was the "third application"—of which our gallant friend took no notice.

Next came a written,

"Sir,

"*I am desired by this firm to inform you, that unless we hear from you by return of post respecting the payment of our account, we shall place the matter in the hands of our solicitors without further notice, and regret you should have occasioned us so much trouble through your own misunderstanding.*"

Then came the climax. The Major's solicitor went, ticket in hand, and tendered the 43s., when the late bullying Badbill was obliged to write as follows:—

"*It appears you are quite correct rejecting the ticket, and we are in error. Our ticketing clerk had placed the figure in the wrong part of the card, the figure 'two' referring to the number of chairs in stock, and not as understood to signifying chairs for 43s.;*" and Badbill humorously concluded by expressing a hope that the Major would return the chairs and continue his custom—two very unlikely events, as we dare say the reader will think, to happen.

Such, then, was the knowing gentleman who now sought the company of Fine Billy; and considering that he is to be besieged on both sides, we hope to be excused for having gone a little into his host and hostess' pedigree and performances.

The Major wrote Billy a well-considered note, saying, that when he could spare a few days from his lordship and the foxhounds, it would afford Mrs. Yammerton and himself great pleasure if he would come and pay them a visit at Yammerton Grange, and the Major would be happy to mount him, and keep his best country for him, and show him all the sport in his power, adding, that they had been having some most marvellous runs lately—better than any he ever remembered.

Now, independently of our friend Billy having pondered a good deal on the beauty of the young lady's eyes, he could well spare a few days from the foxhounds, for his lordship, being quite de Glancey-cured, and wishing to get rid of him, had had him out again, and put him on to a more fractious horse than before, who after giving him a most indefinite shaking, had finally shot him over his head.

The Earl was delighted, therefore, when he heard of the Major's invitation, and after expressing great regret at the idea of losing our Billy, begged he would "come back whenever it suited him:" well knowing that if he once got him out of the house, he would be very sly if he got in again. And so Billy, who never answered Mamma's repeated inquiries if there were any "Miss H's" engaged himself to Yammerton Grange, whither the reader will now perhaps have the kindness to accompany him.

CHAPTER XVII. ARRIVAL AT YAMMERTON GRANGE.—A FAMILY PARTY.

AILWAYS have taken the starch out of country magnificence, as well as out of town.

Time was when a visitor could hardly drive up to a great man's door in the country in a po'chay—now it would be considered very magnificent—a bliss, or a one-oss fly being more likely the conveyance. The Richest Commoner in England took his departure from Tantivy Castle in a one-horse fly, into which he was assisted by an immense retinue of servants. It was about time for him to be gone for Mons. Jean Rougier had been what he called "boxing" with the Earl's big watcher, Stephen Stout, to whom having given a most elaborate licking, the rest of the establishment were up in arms, and would most likely have found a match for Monsieur among them. Jack—that is to say, Mons. Jean—now kissed his hand, and grinned, and bowed, and *bon-jour'd* them from the box of the fly, with all the affability of a gentleman who has had the best of it.

Off then they ground at as good a trot as the shaky old quadruped could raise.

It is undoubtedly a good sound principle that Major and Mrs. Yammerton went upon, never to invite people direct from great houses to theirs; it dwarfs little ones so. A few days ventilation at a country inn with its stupid dirty waiters, copper-showing plate, and wretched cookery, would be a good preparation, only no one ever goes into an inn in England that can help it. Still, coming down from a first-class nobleman's castle to a third-class gentleman's house, was rather a trial upon the latter. Not that we mean to say anything disrespectful of Yammerton Grange, which, though built at different times, was good, roomy, and rough-cast, with a man-boy in brown and yellow livery, who called himself the "Butler," but whom the women-servants called the "Bumbler." The above outline will give the reader a general idea of the "style of thing," as the insolvent dandy said, when he asked his creditors for a "wax candle and eau-de-Cologne" sort of allowance. Everything at the Grange of course was now put into holiday garb, both externally and internally—gravel raked, garden spruced, stables strawed, &c. All the Major's old sheep-caps, old hare-snares, old hang-locks, old hedging-gloves, pruning-knives, and implements of husbandry were thrust into the back of the drawer of the passage table, while a mixed sporting and military trophy, composed of whips, swords and pistols, radiated round his Sunday hat against the wall above it.

The drawing-room, we need not say, underwent metamorphose, the chairs and sofas suddenly changing from rather dirty print to pea-green damask, the druggeted carpet bursting into cornucopias of fruit and gay bouquets, while a rich cover of many colours adorned the centre table, which, in turn, was covered with the proceeds of the young ladies' industry. The room became a sort of exhibition of their united accomplishments. The silver inkstand surmounted a beautiful unblemished blotting-book, fresh pens and paper stood invitingly behind, while the little dictionary was consigned, with other "sundries," to the well of the ottoman.

As the finishing preparations were progressing, the Major and Mrs. Yammerton carried on a broken discussion as to the programme of proceedings, and as, in the Major's opinion,

"There's nothing can compare, To hunting of the hare,"

he wanted to lead off with a *gallope*, to which Mrs. Yammerton demurred. She thought it would be a much better plan to have a quiet day about the place—let the girls walk Mr. Pringle up to Prospect Hill to see the view from Eagleton Rocks, and call on Mrs. Wasperton, and show him to her ugly girls, in return for their visit with Mr. Giles Smith. The Major, on the contrary, thought if there was to be a quiet day about the place, he would like to employ it in showing Billy a horse he had to sell; but while they were in the midst of the argument the click of front gate sneck, followed by the vehement bow-wow-wow-wow-wow bark of the Skye terrier, Fury, announced an arrival, and from behind a ground-feathering spruce, emerged the shaky old horse, dragging at its tail the heavily laden cab. Then there was such a scattering of crinoline below, and such a gathering of cotton above, to see the gentleman alight, and such speculations as to his Christian name, and which of the young ladies he would do for.

"I say his name's Harry!" whispered Sally Scuttle, the housemaid, into Benson's—we beg pardon—Miss Benson's, the ladies'-maid's ear, who was standing before her, peeping past the faded curtains of the chintz-room.

"I say it's John!" replied Miss Benson, now that Mr. Pringle's head appeared at the window.

"I say it's Joseph!" interposed Betty Bone, the cook, who stood behind Sally Scuttle, at which speculation they all laughed.

"Hoot, no! he's not a bit like Joseph," replied Sally, eyeing Billy as he now alighted.

"Lank! he's quite a young gent," observed Bone.

"*Young!* to be sure!" replied Miss Henson; "you don't s'pose we want any old'uns here."

"He'll do nicely for Miss;" observed Sally.

"And why not for Miss F.?" asked Henson, from whom she had just received an old gown.

"Well, either," rejoined Sally; "only Miss had the last chance."

"Oh, curates go for nothin'!" retorted Benson; "if it had been a captin it would have been something like."

"Well, but there's Miss Harriet; you never mention Miss Harriet, why shouldn't Miss Harriet have a chance?" interposed the cook.

"Oh, Miss Harriet must wait her turn. Let her sisters be served first. They can't all have him, you know, so it's no use trying."

Billy having entered the house, the ladies' attention was now directed to Monsieur.

"What a thick, plummy man he is!" observed Benson, looking down on Rougier's broad shoulders.

"He looks as if he got his vittles well," rejoined Bone, wondering how he would like their lean beef and bacon fare.

"Where will he have to sleep?" asked Sally Scuttle.

"O, with the Bumbler to be sure," replied Bone.

"Not *he!*" interposed Miss Benson, with disdain. "You don't s'pose a reg'lar valley-de-chambre 'ill condescend to sleep with a footman! You don't know them—if you think that."

"He's got mouse catchers," observed Sally Scuttle, who had been eyeing Monsieur intently.

"Ay, and a beard like a blacking brush," whispered Bone.

"He's surely a foreigner," whispered Benson, as Monsieur's, "*I say!* take *vell* care of her!—*leeaft* her down j-e-a-ntly" (alluding to his own carpet bag, in which he had a bottle of rum enveloped in swaddling clothes of dirty linen) to the cabman, sounded upstairs.

"So he is," replied Benson, adding, after a pause, "Well, anybody may have him for me;"—saying which she tripped out of the room, quickly followed by the others.

Our Major having, on the first alarm, rushed off to his dirty Sanctum, and crowned himself with a drab felt wide-a-wake, next snatched a little knotty dog-whip out of the trophy as he passed, and was at the sash door of the front entrance welcoming our hero with the full spring tide of hospitality as he alighted from his fly.

The Major was overjoyed to see him. It was indeed kind of him, leaving the castle to "come and visit them in their 'umble abode." The Major, of course, now being on the humility tack.

"Let me take your cloak!" said he; "let me take your cap!" and, with the aid of the Bumbler, who came shuffling himself into his brown and yellow livery coat, Billy was eased of his wrapper, and stood before the now thrown-open drawing-room door, just as Mrs. Yammerton having swept the last brown holland cover off the reclining chair, had stuffed it under the sofa cushion. She, too, was delighted to see Billy, and thankful she had got the room ready, so as to be able presently to subside upon the sofa, "Morning Post" in hand, just as if she had been interrupted in her reading. The young ladies then dropped in one by one; Miss at the passage door, Miss Flora at the one connecting the drawingroom with the Sanctum, and Miss Harriet again at the passage door, all divested of their aprons, and fresh from their respective looking-glasses. The two former, of course, met Billy as an old acquaintance, and as they did not mean to allow Misa Harriet to participate in the prize, they just let her shuffle herself into an introduction as best she could. Billy wasn't quite sure whether he had seen her before or he hadn't. At first he thought he had; then he thought he hadn't; but whether he had or he hadn't, he knew there would be no harm in bowing, so he just promiscuated one to her, which she acknowledged with a best Featherey curtsey. A great cry of conversation, or rather of random observation, then ensued; in the midst of which the Major slipped out, and from his Sanctum Monsieur getting up much the same sort of entertainment in the kitchen. There was such laughing and giggling and "*he-hawing*" among the maids, that the Major feared the dinner would be neglected.

The Major's dining-room, though small, would accommodate a dozen people, or incommode eighteen, which latter number is considered the most serviceable-sized party in the country where people feed off their acquaintance, more upon the debtor and creditor system, than with a view to making pleasant parties, or considering who would like to meet. Even when they are what they call "alone," they can't be "alone," but must have in as many servants as they can raise, to show how far the assertion is from the truth.

Though the Yammertons sat down but six on the present occasion, and there were the two accustomed dumb-waiters in the room, three live ones were introduced, viz., Monsieur, the Bumbler, and Solomon, whose duty seemed to consist in cooling the victuals, by carrying them about, and in preventing people from helping themselves to what was before them, by taking the dishes off the steady table, and presenting them again on very unsteady hands.

No one is ever allowed to shoot a dish sitting if a servant can see it. How pleasant it would be if we were watched in all the affairs of life as we are in eating!

Monsieur, we may observe, had completely superseded the Bumbler, just as a colonel supersedes a captain on coming up.

"Oi am Colonel Crushington of the Royal Plungers," proclaims the Colonel, stretching himself to his utmost altitude.

"And I am Captain Succumber, of the Sugar-Candy Hussars," bows the Captain with the utmost humility; whereupon the Captain is snuffed out, and the Colonel reigns in his stead.

"I am Monsieur Jean Rougier, valet-de-chambre to me lor Pringle, and I sail take in de potage,—de soup," observed Rougier, coming down stairs in his first-class clothes, and pushing the now yellow-legged Bumbler aside.

And these hobble-de-hoys never being favourites with the fair, the maids saw him reduced without remorse.

So the dinner got set upon the table without a fight and though Monsieur allowed the Bumbler to announce it in the drawing-room, it was only that he might take a suck of the sherry while he was away. But he was standing as bolt upright as a serjeant-major on parade when "me lor" entered the dining-room with Mrs. Yammerton on his arm, followed by the Graces, the Major having stayed behind to blow out the composites.

They were soon settled in their places, grace said, and the assault commenced.

The Major was rather behind Imperial John in magnificence, for John had got his plate in his drawing-room, while the Major still adhered to the good old-fashioned blue and red, and gold and green crockery ware of his youth.

Not but that both Mamma and the young ladies had often represented to him the absolute necessity of having plate, but the Major could never fall in with it at his price—that of German silver, or Britannia metal perhaps.

We dare say Fine Billy would never have noticed the deficiency, if the Major had not drawn attention to it by apologising for its absence, and fearing he would not be able to eat his dinner without; though we dare say, if the truth were known our readers—our male readers at least—will agree with us, that a good, hot well-washed china dish is a great deal better than a dull, lukewarm, hand-rubbed silver one. It's the "wittles" people look to, not the ware.

Then the Major was afraid his wine wouldn't pass muster after the Earl's, and certainly his champagne was nothing to boast of, being that ambiguous stuff that halts between the price of gooseberry and real; in addition to which, the Major had omitted to pay it the compliment of icing it, so that it stood forth in all its native imperfection. However, it hissed, and fizzed, and popped, and banged, which is always something exciting at all events; and as the Major sported needle-case-shaped glasses which he had got at a sale (very cheap we hope), there was no fear of people getting enough to do them any harm.

Giving champagne is one of those things that has passed into custom almost imperceptibly. Twenty, or five-and-twenty years ago, a mid-rank-of-life person giving champagne was talked of in a very shake-the-head, solemn, "I wish-it-may-last," style; now everybody gives it of some sort or other. We read in the papers the other day of ninety dozen, for which the holder had paid 400 L., being sold for 13s. 6d. a doz.! What a chance that would have been for our Major. We wonder what that had been made of.

It was a happy discovery that giving champagne at dinner saved other wine after, for certainly nothing promotes the conviviality of a meeting so much as champagne, and there is nothing so melancholy and funereal as a dinner party without it. Indeed, giving champagne may be regarded as a downright promoter of temperance, for a person who drinks freely of champagne cannot drink freely of any other sort of wine after it: so that champagne may be said to have contributed to the abolition of the old port-wine toping wherewith our fathers were wont to beguile their long evenings. Indeed, light wines and London clubs have about banished inebriety from anything like good society. Enlarged newspapers, too, have contributed their quota, whereby a man can read what is passing in all parts of the world, instead of being told whose cat has kittened in his own immediate neighbourhood.—With which philosophical reflections, let us return to our party.

Although youth is undoubtedly the age of matured judgment and connoisseurship in everything, and Billy was quite as knowing as his neighbours, he accepted the Major's encomiums on his wine with all the confidence of ignorance, and, what is more to the purpose, he drank it. Indeed, there was nothing faulty on the table that the Major didn't praise, on the old horse-dealing principle of lauding the bad points, and leaving the good ones to speak for themselves. So the dinner progressed through a multiplicity of dishes; for, to do the ladies justice, they always give good fare:—it is the men who treat their friends to mutton-chops and rice puddings.

Betty Bone, too, was a noble-hearted woman, and would undertake to cook for a party of fifty,—roasts, boils, stews, soups, sweets, savouries, sauces, and all! And so what with a pretty girl along side of him, and two sitting opposite, Billy did uncommonly well, and felt far more at home than he did at Tantivy Castle with the Earl and Mrs. Moffatt, and the stiff dependents his lordship brought in to dine.

The Major stopped Billy from calling for Burgundy after his cheese by volunteering a glass of home-brewed ale, "bo-bo-bottled," he said, "when he came of age," though, in fact, it had only arrived from Aloes, the chemist's, at Hinton, about an hour before dinner. This being only sipped, and smacked, and applauded, grace was said, the cloth removed, the Major was presently assuring Billy, in a bumper of moderate juvenile port, how delighted he was to see him, how flattered he felt by his condescension in coming to visit him at his 'umble abode, and how he 'oped to make the visit agreeable to him. This piece of flummery being delivered, the bottles and dessert circulated, and in due time the ladies retired, the Misses to the drawing-room, Madam to the pantry, to see that the Bumbler had not pocketed any of the cheese-cakes or tarts, for which, boy-like, he had a propensity.

* * * *

The Major, we are ashamed to say, had no mirror in his drawing-room, wherein the ladies could now see how they had been looking; so, of course, they drew to that next attraction—the fire, which having duly stirred, Miss Yammerton and Flora laid their heads together, with each a fair arm resting on the old-fashioned grey-veined marble mantel-piece, and commenced a very laughing, whispering conversation. This, of course, attracted Miss Harrier, who tried first to edge in between them, and then to participate at the sides; but she was repulsed at all points, and at

52

length was told by Miss Yammerton to "*get away!*" as she had "nothing to do with what they were talking about."

"Yes I have," pouted Miss Harriet, who guessed what the conversation was about.

"No, you haven't," retorted Miss Flora.

"It's between Flora and me," observed Miss Yammerton dryly, with an air of authority.

"Well, but that's not fair!" exclaimed Miss Harriet.

"Yes it is!" replied Miss Yammerton, throwing up her head.

"Yes it *is!*" asserted Miss Flora, supporting her elder sister's assertion.

"No, it's *not!*" retorted Miss Harriet.

"You weren't there at the beginning," observed Miss Yammerton, alluding to the expedition to Tantivy Castle.

"That was not my fault," replied Miss Harriet, firmly; "Pa would go in the coach."

"Never mind, you were *not* there," replied Miss Yammerton tartly.

"Well, but I'll *ask mamma* if that's fair?" rejoined Miss Harriet, hurrying out of the room.

CHAPTER XVIII. A LEETLE, CONTRETEMPS.

THE Major having inducted his guest into one of those expensive articles of dining-room furniture, an easy chair—expensive, inasmuch as they cause a great consumption of candles, by sending their occupants to sleep,—now set a little round table between them, to which having transferred the biscuits and wine, he drew a duplicate chair to the fire for himself, and, sousing down in it, prepared for a *tête-à-tête* chat with our friend. He wanted to know what Lord Ladythorne said of him, to sound Billy, in fact, whether there was any chance of his making him a magistrate. He also wanted to find out how long Billy was going to stay in the country, and see whether there was any chance of selling him a horse; so he led up to the points, by calling upon Billy to fill a bumper to the "Merry haryers," observing casually, as he passed the bottle, that he had now kept them "live-and-thirty years without a subscription, and was as much attached to the sport as ever." This toast was followed by the foxhounds and Lord Ladythorne's health, which opened out a fine field for general dissertation and sounding, commencing with Mr. Boggledike, who, the Major not liking, of course, he condemned; and Mrs. Pringle having expressed an adverse opinion of him too, Billy adopted their ideas, and agreed that he was slow, and ought to be drafted.

With his magisterial inquiry the Major was not so fortunate, his lordship being too old a soldier to commit himself before a boy like Billy; and the Major, after trying every meuse, and every twist, and every turn, with the proverbial patience and pertinacity of a hare-hunter, was at length obliged to whip off and get upon his horses. When a man gets upon his horses, especially after dinner, and that man such an optimist as the Major, there is no help for it but either buying them in a lump or going to sleep; and as we shall have to endeavour to induce the reader to accompany us through the Major's stable by-and-bye, we will leave Billy to do which he pleases, while we proceed to relate what took place in another part of the house. For this purpose, it will be necessary to "*ease* her—*back* her," as the Thames steamboat boys say, our story a little to the close of the dinner.

Monsieur Jean Rougier having taken the general bearings of the family as he stood behind "me lor Pringle's" chair, retired from active service on the coming in of the cheese, and proceeded to Billy's apartment, there to arrange the toilette table, and see that everything was *comme il faut*. Billy's dirty boots, of course, he took downstairs to the Bumbler to clean, who, in turn, put them off upon Solomon.

Very smart everything in the room was. The contents of the gorgeous dressing-case were duly displayed on the fine white damask cloth that covered the rose-colour-lined muslin of the gracefully-fringed and festooned toilette cover, whose flowing drapery presented at once an effectual barrier to the legs, and formed an excellent repository for old crusts, envelopes, curlpapers, and general sweepings. Solid ivory hair-brushes, with tortoiseshell combs, cosmetics, curling fluids, oils and essences without end, mingled with the bijouterie and knick-nacks of the distinguished visitor. Having examined himself attentively in the glass, and spruced up his bristles with Billy's brushes, Jack then stirred the fire, extinguished the toilette-table candle, which he had lit on coming in, and produced a great blue blouse from the bottom drawer of the wardrobe, in which, having enveloped himself in order to prevent his fine clothes catching dust, he next crawled backwards under the bed. He had not lain there very long ere the opening and shutting of downstairs doors, with the ringing of a bell, was followed by the rustling of silks, and the light tread of airy steps hurrying along the passage, and stopping at the partially-opened door. Presently increased light in the apartment was succeeded by less rustle and tip-toe treads passing the bed, and making up to the looking-glass. The self-inspection being over, candles were then flashed about the room in various directions; and Jack having now thrown all his energies into his ears, overheard the following hurried *sotto voce* exclamations:—

First Voice. "Lauk! what a little dandy it is!"

Second Voice. "Look, I say! look at his boots—one, two, three, four, five, six, seven, eight, nine, ten: ten pair, as I live, besides jacks and tops."

First Voice. "And shoes in proportion," the speaker running her candle along the line of various patterned shoes.

Second Voice. (Advancing to the toilette-table). "Let's look at his studs. Wot an assortment! Wonder if those are diamonds or paste he has on."

First Voice. "Oh, *diamonds* to be sure" (with an emphasis on diamonds). "You don't s'pose such a little swell as that would wear paste. See! there's a pearl and diamond ring. Just fits me, I do declare," added she, trying it on.

Second Voice. "What beautiful carbuncle pins!"

First Voice. "Oh. what studs!"

Second Voice. "Oh. what chains!"

First Voice. "Oh, what pins!"

Second Voice. "Oh, what a love of a ring!" And so the ladies continued, turning the articles hastily over. "Oh, how happy he *must* be," sighed a languishing voice, as the inspection proceeded.

"See! here's his little silver shaving box," observed the first speaker, opening it.

"Wonder what *he* wants with a shaving box,—got no more beard than I have," replied the other, taking up Billy's badger-hair shaving-brush, and applying it to her own pretty chin.

"Oh! smell what delicious perfume!" now exclaimed the discoverer of the shaving-box. "Essence of Rondeletia, I do believe! No, extrait de millefleurs," added she, scenting her 'kerchief with some.

Then there was a hurried, frightened "*hush!*" followed by a "Take care that ugly man of his doesn't come."

"Did you ever *see* such a monster!" ejaculated the other earnestly.

"Kept his horrid eyes fixed upon me the whole dinner," observed the first speaker.

"Frights they are," rejoined the other.

"He must keep him for a foil," suggested the first.

"Let's go, or we'll be caught!" replied the alarmist; and forthwith the rustling of silks was resumed, the candles hurried past, and the ladies tripped softly out of the room, leaving the door ajar, with Jack under the bed to digest their compliments at his leisure.

* * * *

But Monsieur was too many for them. Miss had dropped her glove at the foot of the bed, which Jack found on emerging from his hiding place, and waiting until he had the whole party reassembled at tea, he walked majestically into the middle of the drawing-room with it extended on a plated tray, his "horrid eyes" combining all the venom of a Frenchman with the *hauteur* of an Englishman, and inquired, in a loud and audible voice, "Please, has any lady or shentleman lost its glo-o-ve?"

"Yes, I have!" replied Miss, hastily, who had been wondering where she had dropped it.

"Indeed, marm," replied Monsieur, bowing and presenting it to her on the tray, adding, in a still louder voice, "I found it in Monsieur Pringle's bed-room." And Jack's flashing eye saw by the brightly colouring girls which were the offenders.

Very much shocked was Mamma at the announcement; and the young ladies were so put about, that they could scarcely compose themselves at the piano, while Miss Harriet's voice soared exultingly as she accompanied herself on her harp.

CHAPTER XIX. THE MAJOR'S STUD.

MRS. Yammerton carried the day, and the young ladies carried paper-booted Billy, or rather walked him up to Mrs. Wasperton's at Prospect Hill, and showed him the ugly girls, and also the beautiful view from Eagleton Rocks, over the wide-spreading vale of Vernerley beyond, which, of course, Billy enjoyed amazingly, as all young gentlemen do enjoy views under such pleasant circumstances. Perhaps he might have enjoyed it more, if two out of three of the dear charmers

54

had been absent, but then things had not got to that pass, and Mamma would not have thought it proper—at least, not unless she saw her way to a very decided preference—which, of course, was then out of the question. Billy was a great swell, and the "chaws" who met him stared with astonishment at such an elegant parasol'd exquisite, picking his way daintily along the dirty, sloppy, rutty lanes. Like all gentlemen in similar circumstances, he declared his boots "wouldn't take in wet."

Of course, Mamma charged the girls not to be out late, an injunction that applied as well to precaution against the night air, as to the importance of getting Billy back by afternoon stable time, when the Major purposed treating him to a sight of his stud, and trying to lay the foundation of a sale.

Perhaps our sporting readers would like to take a look into the Major's stable before he comes with his victim, Fine Billy. If so, let them accompany us; meanwhile our lady friends can skip the chapter if they do not like to read about horses—or here; if they will step this way, and here comes the Dairymaid, they can look at the cows: real Durham short-horns, with great milking powers and most undeniable pedigrees. Ah, we thought they would tickle your fancy. The cow is to the lady, what the horse is to the gentleman, or, on the score of usefulness, what hare-hunting is to fox-hunting—or shooting to hunting. Master may have many horses pulled backwards out of his stable without exciting half the commiseration among the fair, that the loss of one nice quiet milk-giving cushy cow affords. Cows are friendly creatures. They remember people longer than almost any other animal, dogs not excepted. Well, here are four of them, Old Lily, Strawberry Cream, Red Rose, and Toy; the house is clean and sweet, and smells of milk, and well-made hay, instead of the nasty brown-coloured snuff-smelling stuff that some people think good enough for the poor cow.

The Major is proud of his cows, and against the whitewashed wall he has pasted the description of a perfect one, in order that people may compare the originals with the portrait. Thus it runs:—

She's long in the face, she's fine in the horn, She'll quickly get fat without cake or corn; She's clean in her jaws, anti full in her chine, She's heavy in flank, and wide in her loin; She's broad in her ribs, and long in her rump, A straight and flat back without ever a hump; She's wide in her hips, and calm in her eyes, She's fine in her shoulders, and thin in her thighs; She's light in her neck, and small in her tail, She's wide at the breast, and good at the pail. She's tine in her bone and silky of skin. She's a grazier's without, and a butcher's within.

Now for the stable; this way, through the saddle-room, and mind the whitening on the walls. Stoop yonr head, for the Major being low himself, has made the door on the principle of all other people being low too. There, there you are, you see, in a stable as neat and clean as a London dealer's; a Newmarket straw plait, a sanded floor with a roomy bench against the wall on which the Major kicks his legs and stutters forth the merits of his steeds. They are six in number, and before he comes we will just run the reader through the lot, with the aid of truth for an accompaniment.

This grey, or rather white one next the wall, White Surrey, as he calls him, is the old quivering tailed horse he rode on the de Glancey day, and pulled up to save, from the price-depressing inconvenience of being beat. He is eighteen years old, the Major having got him when he was sixteen, in a sort of part purchase, part swap, part barter deal. He gave young Mr. Meggison of Spoonbill Park thirteen pounds ten shillings, an old mahogany Piano-Forte, by Broadwood, six and a half octaves, a Squirrel Cage, two Sun-blinds, and a very feeble old horse called Nonpareil, that Tom Rivett the blacksmith declared it would be like robbing Meggison to put new shoes on to, for him. He is a game good shaped old horse, but having frequently in the course of a chequered career, been in that hardest of all hard places, the hands of young single horse owners, White Surrey has done the work of three or four horses. He has been fired and blistered, and blistered and fired, till his legs are as round and as callous as those of a mahogany dining-table; still it is wonderful how they support him, and as he has never given the Major a fall, he rides him as if he thought he never would. His price is sometimes fifty, sometimes forty, sometimes thirty, and there are times when he might be bought for a little less—two sovereigns, perhaps, returned out of the thirty. The next one to him—the white legged brown,—is of the antediluvian order too. He is now called Woodpecker, but he may be traced by half-a-dozen aliases through other stables—Buckhunter, Captain Tart, Fleacatcher, Sportsman, Marc Anthony, &c. He is nearly, if not quite thorough bred, and the ignoble purposes to which he has been subjected, false start making, steeple chasing, flat and hurdle racing, accounts for the number of his names. The Major got him from Captain Caret, of the Apple-pie huzzars, when that gallant regiment was ordered out to India,—taking him all away together, saddle, bridle, clothing, &c., for twenty-three pounds, a strong iron-bound chest, fit for sea purposes, as the Major described it, and a spying glass. This horse, like all the rest of them, indeed, is variously priced, depending upon the party asking, sometimes fifty, sometimes five-and-twenty would buy him.

The third is a mare, a black mare, called Star, late the property of Mr. Hazey, the horse-dealing master of the Squeezington hounds. Hazey sold her in his usual course of horse-dealing cheating to young Mr. Sprigginson, of Mary gold Lodge, for a hundred and twenty guineas (the shillings back), Hazey's discrimination enabling him to see that she was turning weaver, and Sprigginson not liking her, returned her on the warranty; when, of course, Hazey refusing to receive her, she was sent to the Eclipse Livery and Bait Stables at Hinton, where, after weaving her head off, she was sold at the hammer to the Major for twenty-nine pounds. Sprig then brought an action against Hazey for the balance, bringing half-a-dozen witnesses to prove that she wove when she came; Hazey, of course, bringing a dozen to swear that she never did nothin' 'o the sort with him, and must have learnt it on the road; and the jury being perplexed, and one of them having a cow to calve, another wanting to see his sweetheart, and the rest wanting their dinners, they just tossed up for it, "Heads!" for Sprig; "Tails!" for Hazey, and Sprig won. There she goes, you see, weaving backwards and forwards like a caged panther in a den. Still she is far from being the worst that the Major has; indeed, we are not sure that she is not about the best, only, as Solomon says, with reference to her weaving, she gets the "langer the warser."

Number four is a handsome whole coloured bright bay horse, "Napoleon the Great," as the Major calls him, in hopes that his illustrious name will sell him, for of all bad tickets he ever had, the Major thinks Nap is the worst. At starting, he is all fire, frisk, and emulation, but before he has gone five miles, he begins to droop, and in hunting knocks up entirely before he has crossed half-a-dozen fields. He is a weak, watery, washy creature, wanting no end of coddling, boiled corn, and linseed tea. One hears of two days a-week horses, but Napoleon the Great is a day in two weeks one. The reader will wonder how the Major came to get such an animal, still more how he came to keep him; above all, how he ever came to have him twice. The mystery, however, is explained on the old bartering, huckstering, half-and-half system. The Major got him first from Tom Brandysneak, a low public-house-keeping leather-plater, one of those sporting men, not sportsmen, who talk about supporting the turf, as if they did it like the noblemen of old, upon principle, instead of for what they can put into their own pockets; and the Major gave Sneak an old green dog-cart, a melon frame, sixteen volumes of the "Racing Calendar," bound in calf, a ton of seed-hay, fifty yards of Croggon's asphalt roofing felt, and three "golden sovereigns" for him. Nap was then doing duty under the title of Johnny Raw, his calling being to appear at different posts whenever the cruel conditions of a race required a certain number of horses to start in order to secure the added money; but Johnny enacted that office so often for the benefit of the "Honourable Society of Confederated Legs," that the stewards of races framed their conditions for excluding him; and Johnny's occupation being gone, he came to the Major in manner aforesaid. Being, however, a horse of prepossessing appearance, a good bay, with four clean black legs, a neat well set-on head, with an equally neat set-on tail, a flowing mane, and other &c's, he soon passed into the possession of young Mr. Tabberton, of Green Linnet Hill, whose grandmamma had just given him a hundred guineas wherewith to buy a good horse—a *real* good one he was to be—a hundred-guinea-one in fact. Tabberton soon took all the gay insolence out of Johnny's tail, and brought him back to the Major, sadly dilapidated—a sad satire upon his former self.

Meanwhile the Major had filled up his stall with a handsome rich-coloured brown mare, with a decidedly doubtful fore-leg; and the Major, all candour and affability, readily agreed to exchange, on condition of getting five-and-twenty pounds to boot. The mare presently went down to exercise, confirming the Major's opinion of the instability of her leg, and increasing his confidence in his own judgment. Napoleon the Great, late Johnny Raw, now reigns in her stead, and very well he looks in the straw. Indeed, that is his proper place; and as many people only keep their horses to look at, there is no reason why Napoleon the Great should remain in the Major's stables. He certainly won't if the Major can help it.

Number five is a vulgar looking little dun-duck-et-y mud-coloured horse, with long white stockings, and a large white face, called Bull-dog, that Solomon generally rides. Nobody knows how old he is, or how many masters he has had, or where he came from, or who his father was, or whether he had a grandfather, or anything whatever about him. The Major got him for a mere nothing—nine pounds—at Joe Seton's, the runaway Vet's sale, about five years ago, and being so desperately ugly and common looking, no one has ever attempted to deprive the Major of him either in the way of barter or sale. Still Bully is a capital slave, always ready either to hunt, or hack, or go in harness, and will pass anything except a public-house, being familiarly and favourably known at the doors of every one in the county. Like most horses, he has his little peculiarity; and his consists of a sort of rheumatic affection of the hind leg, which causes him to catch it up, and sends him limping along on three legs, like a lame dog, but still he never comes down, and the attack soon goes off. Solomon and he look very like their work together.

56

The next horse to Bull-dog, and the last in the stable, is Golden-drop, a soft, mealy chestnut—of all colours the most objectionable. He is a hot, pulling, hauling, rushing, rough-actioned animal, that gives a rider two days' exercise in one.

The worst of him is, he has the impudence to decline harness; for though he doesn't "mill," as they call it, he yet runs backwards as fast as forwards, and would crash through a plate-glass window, a gate, a conservatory, or anything else that happened to be behind. As a hack he is below mediocrity, for in his walk he digs his toes into the ground about every tenth step, and either comes down on his nose, or sets off at score for fear of a licking, added to which, he shies at every heap of stones and other available object on the road, whereby he makes a ten miles' journey into one of twelve. The Major got him of Mr. Brisket, the butcher, at Hinton, being taken with the way in which his hatless lad spun him about the ill-paved streets, with the meat-basket on his arm—the full trot, it may be observed, being the animal's pace—but having got him home, the more the Major saw of him the less he liked him. He had a severe deal for him too, and made two or three journeys over to Hinton on market-days, and bought a pennyworth of whipcord of one saddler, a set of spur-leathers of another, a pot of harness-paste of a third, in order to pump them about the horse ere he ventured to touch. He also got Mr. Paul Straddler, the disengaged gentleman of the place, whose greatest pleasure is to be employed upon a deal, to ferret out all he could about him, who reported that the horse was perfectly sound, and a capital feeder, which indeed he is, for he will attack anything, from a hayband down to a hedge-stake. You see he's busy on his bedding now.

Brisket knowing his man, and that the Major killed his own mutton, and occasionally beef, in the winter, so that there was no good to be got of him in the meat way, determined to ask a stiff price, viz., 25 L. (Brisket having given 14 L.), which the Major having beat down to 23 L. commenced on the mercantile line, which Brisket's then approaching marriage favoured, and the Major ultimately gave a four-post mahogany bedstead, with blue damask furniture, palliasse and mattress to match; a mahogany toilet-mirror, 23 inches by 28: a hot-water pudding-dish, a silver-edged cake-basket, a bad barometer, a child's birch-wood crib, a chess-board, and 2 L. 10 s. in cash for him, the 2 L. 1 s.. being, as the Major now declares (to himself, of course,) far more than his real worth. However, there the horse stands; and though he has been down twice with the Major, and once with the Humbler, these little fore paws (*faux pas*) as the Major calls them, have been on the soft, and the knees bear no evidence of the fact. Such is our friend's present stud, and such is its general character.

But stay! We are omitting the horse in this large family-pew-looking box at the end, whose drawn curtains have caused us to overlook him. He is another of the Major's bad tickets, and one of which he has just become possessed in the following way:—

Having—in furtherance of his character of a "thorrer sportsman," and to preserve the spirit of impartiality so becoming an old master of "haryers"—gone to Sir Moses Mainchance's opening day, as well as to my Lord's, Sir Moses, as if in appreciation of the compliment, had offered to give the horse on which his second whip was blundering among the blind ditches.

The Major jumped at the offer, for the horse looked well with the whip on him; and, as he accepted, Sir Moses increased the stream of his generosity by engaging the Major to dine and take him away. Sir Moses had a distinguished party to meet him, and was hospitality itself. He plied our Major with champagne, and hock, and Barsac, and Sauterne, and port, and claret, and compliments, but never alluded to the horse until about an hour after dinner, when Mr. Smoothley, the jackal of the hunt, brought him on the *tapis*.

"Ah!" exclaimed Sir Moses, as if in sudden recollection, "that's true! Major, you're quite welcome to 'Little-bo-peep,' (for so he had christened him, in order to account for his inquisitive manner of peering). Your *quite* welcome to 'Little-bo-peep,' and I hope he'll be useful to you."

"Thank'e, Sir Moses, thank'e!" bobbed the grateful Major, thinking what a good chap the baronet was.

"*Not a bit!*" replied Sir Moses, chucking up his chin, just as if he was in the habit of giving a horse away every other day in the week. "*Not a bit!* Keep him as long as you like—all the season if you please—and send him back when you are done."

Then, as if in deprecation of any more thanks, he plied the wine again, and gave the Major and his "harriers" in a speech of great gammonosity. The Major was divided between mortification at the reduction of the gift into a loan, and gratification at the compliment now paid him, but was speedily comforted by the flattering reception his health, and the stereotyped speech in which he returned thanks, met at the hands of the company. He thought he must be very popular. Then, when they were all well wined, and had gathered round the sparkling fire with their coffee or their Curaçoa in their hands, Sir Moses button-holed the Major with a loud familiar, "I'll tell ye what, Yammerton! you're a devilish good feller, and there shall be no

57

obligation between us—you shall just give me forty puns for 'Little-bo-peep,' and that's making you a present of him for it's a hundred less than I gave."

"'Ah! that's the way to do it!" exclaimed Mr. Smoothley, as if delighted at Sir Moses having dropped upon the right course. "Ah! *that's* the way to do it!" repented he swinging himself gaily round on his toe, with a loud snap of his finger and thumb in the air.

And Sir Moses said it in such a kind, considerate, matter-of-course sort of way, before company too, and Smoothley clenched it so neatly, that our wine-flushed Major, acute as he is, hadn't presence of mind to say "No." So he was saddled with "Little-bo-peep," who has already lost one eye from cataract, which is fast going with the other.

But see! Here comes Solomon followed by the Bumbler in fustian, and the boy from the farm, and we shall soon have the Major and Billy, so let us step into Bo-peep's box, an I hear the Major's description of his stud.

＊ ＊ ＊ ＊

Scarcely have the grooms dispersed the fast-gathering gloom of a November afternoon, by lighting the mould candles in the cord-suspended lanterns slung along the ceiling, and began to hiss at the straw, when the Major entered, with our friend Billy at his heels. The Bumbler and Chaw then put on extra activity, and the stable being presently righted, heads were loosened, water supplied, and the horses excited by Solomon's well-known peregrination to the crushed corn-bin. All ears were then pricked, eyes cast back, and hind-quarters tucked under to respond gaily to the "come over" of the feeder.

The late watchful whinnying restlessness is succeeded by gulping, diving, energetic eating. Our friend having passed his regiment of horses in silent review, while the hissing was going on, now exchanges a few confidential words with the stud groom, as if he left everything to him, and then passes upwards to where he started from. Solomon having plenty to do elsewhere, presently retires, followed by his helpers, and the Major and Billy seat themselves on the bench. After a few puffs and blows of the cheeks and premonitory jerks of the legs, the Major nods an approving "nice 'oss, that," to Napoleon the Great, standing opposite, who is the first to look up from his food, being with it as with his work, always in a desperate hurry to begin, and in an equally great one to leave off.

"Nice 'oss, that," repeats the Major, nodding again.

"Yarse, he looks like a nice 'orse;" replied Billy, which is really as much as any man can say under the circumstances.

"That 'oss should have won the D-d-d-derby in Nobbler's year," observed the Major; "only they d-d-drugged him the night before starting, and he didn't get half round the c-c-co-course," which was true enough, only it wasn't owing to any drugging, for he wasn't worth the expense.

"That 'oss should be in Le-le-le-leieestershire," observed the Major. "He has all the commandin' s-s-s-statur requisite to make large fences look s-s-s-small, and the s-s-s-smoothest, oiliest action i-ma-ma-maginable."

"Yarse;" replied Billy, wondering what pleasure there was in looking at a lot of blankets and hoods upon horses—which was about all he could see.

"He should be at Me-me-melton," observed the Major; still harping on Napoleon—"wasted upon haryers," added he.

"Yarse," replied Billy, not caring where he was.

The Major then took a nod at the Weaver, who, as if in aid of her master's design, now stood bolt upright, listening, as it were, instead of reeling from side to side.

"That's a sw-sw-swe-e-t mare," observed the Major, wishing he was rid of her. "I don't know whether I would rather have her or the horse (Nap);" which was true enough, though he knew which he would like to sell Billy.

"You'll remember the g-g-gray, the whi-white," continued he; looking on at the old stager against the wall. "That's the 'oss I rode with the Peer, on the Castle day, and an undeniable g-g-good one he is;" but knowing that he was not a young man's horse—moreover, not wanting to sell him, he returned to Napoleon, whose praises he again sounded considerably. Billy, however, having heard enough about him, and wanting to get into the house to the ladies, drew his attention to Bull-dog, now almost enveloped in blankets and straw; but the Major, not feeling inclined to waste any words on him either, replied, "That he was only a servant's 'oss." He, however, spoke handsomely of Golden-drop, declaring he was the fastest trotter in England, perhaps in Europe, perhaps in the world, and would be invaluable to a D-d-doctor, or any man who wanted to get over the ground. And then, thinking he had said about enough for a beginning, it all at once occurred to him that Billy's feet must be wet, and though our friend asserted most confidently that they were not, as all townsmen do assert who walk about the country in thin soles, the Major persisted in urging him to go in and change, which Billy at length reluctantly assented to do.

CHAPTER XX. CARDS FOR A SPREAD.

THE Major's ménage not admitting of two such great events as a hunt and a dinner party taking place on the same day, and market interfering as well, the hunt again had to be postponed to the interests of the table. Such an event as a distinguished stranger—the friend of an Earl, too—coming into the country could not but excite convivial expectations, and it would ill become a master of hounds and a mother of daughters not to parade the acquisition. Still, raising a party under such circumstances, required a good deal of tact and consideration, care, of course, being taken not to introduce any matrimonial competitor, at the same time to make the gathering sufficiently grand, and to include a good bellman or two to proclaim its splendour over the country. The Major, like a county member with his constituents, was somewhat hampered with his hounds, not being able to ask exactly who he liked, for fear of being hauled over the coals, viz. warned off the land of those who might think they ought to have been included, and altogether, the party required a good deal of management. Inclination in these matters is not of so much moment, it being no uncommon thing in the country for people to abuse each other right well one day, and dine together the next. The "gap" which the Major prized so much with his hounds, he strongly objected to with his parties.

Stopping gaps, indeed, sending out invitations at all in the country, so as not to look like stopping gaps, requires circumspection, where people seem to have nothing whatever to do but to note their neighbours' movements. Let any one watch the progress of an important trial, one for murder say, and mark the wonderful way in which country people come forward, long after the event, to depose to facts, that one would imagine would never have been noticed—the passing of a man with a cow, for instance, just as they dropped their noses upon their bacon plates, the suspension of payment by their clock, on that morning, or the post messenger being a few minutes late with the letters on that day, and so on. What then is there to prevent people from laying that and that together, where John met James, or Michael saw Mary, so as to be able to calculate, whether they were included in the first, second, or third batch of invitations? Towns-people escape this difficulty, as also the equally disagreeable one of having it known whether their "previous engagements" are real or imaginary; but then, on the other hand, they have the inconvenience of feeling certain, that as sure as ever they issue cards for a certain day, every one else will be seized with a mania for giving dinners on the same one. No one can have an idea of the extent of London hospitality—who has not attempted to give a dinner there. Still, it is a difficult world to please, even in the matter of mastication, for some people who abuse you if you don't ask them to dine, abuse you quite as much if you do. Take the Reverend Mr. Tightlace, the rector, and his excellent lady, for instance. Tightlace was always complaining, at least observing, that the Yammertons never asked them to dine—wondered "*why* the Yammertons never asked them to dine, was very odd they never asked them to dine," and yet, when Miss Yammerton's best copper-plate handwriting appeared on the highly-musked best cream-laid satin note-paper, "requesting, &c." Tightlace pretended to be quite put out at the idea of having to go to meet that wild sporting youth, who, "he'd be bound to say, could talk of nothing but hunting." Indeed, having most reluctantly accepted the invitation, he found it necessary to cram for the occasion, and having borrowed a copy of that veteran volume, the "British Sportsman," he read up all the long chapter on racing and hunting, how to prepare a horse for a hunting match or plate; directions for riding a hunting match or plate; of hunting the hare, and hunting the fox, with directions for the choice of a hunter, and the management of a hunter; part of which latter consisted in putting him to grass between May and Bartholomew-tide, and comforting his stomach before going out to hunt with toasted bread and wine, or toasted bread and ale, and other valuable information of that sort—all of which Tightlace stored in his mind for future use—thinking to reduce his great intellect to the level of Billy's capacity.

Mr. and Mrs. Rocket Larkspur, of Ninian Green, were also successfully angled for and caught; indeed, Mrs. Larkspur would have been much disappointed if they had not been invited, for she had heard of Billy's elegant appearance from her maid, and being an aspiring lady, had a great desire to cultivate an acquaintance with high life, in which Billy evidently moved. Rocket was a good slow sort of gentleman-farmer, quite a contrast to his fast wife, who was all fire, bustle, and animation, wanting to manage everybody's house and affairs for them. He had married her, it was supposed, out of sheer submission, because she had made a dead set at him, and would not apparently be said "nay" to. It is a difficult thing to manouvre a determined woman in the country, where your habits are known, and they can assail you at all points—

59

church, streets, fields, roads, lanes, all are open to them; or they can even get into your house under plea of a charity subscription, if needs be. Mrs. and Miss Dotherington, of Goney Garth, were invited to do the Morning Post department, and because there was no fear of Miss Dotherington, who was "very amiable," interfering with our Billy. Mrs. Dotherington's other *forte*, besides propagating parties, consisted in angling for legacies, and she was continually on the trot looking after or killing people from whom she had, or fancied she had, expectations. "I've just been to see poor Mrs. Snuff," she would say, drawing a long face; "she's looking *wretchedly* ill, poor thing; fear she's not long for this world;" or, with a grin, "I suppose you've heard old Mr. Wheezington has had another attack in the night, which nearly carried him off." Nothing pleased her so much as being told that any one from whom she had expectations was on the wane. She could ill conceal her satisfaction.

So far so good; the party now numbered twelve, six of themselves and six strangers, and nobody to interfere with Fine Billy. The question then arose, whether to ask the Blurkinses, or the Faireys, or the Crickletons, and this caused an anxious deliberation. Blurkins was a landowner, over whose property the Major frequently hunted; but then on the other hand, he was a most disagreeable person, who would be sure to tread upon every body's corns before the evening was over. Indeed, the Blurkins' family, like noxious vermin, would seem to have been sent into the world for some inscrutable purpose, their mission apparently being to take the conceit out of people by telling them home truths. "Lor' bless us! how old you have got! why you've lost a front tooth! declare I shouldn't have known you!" or "Your nose and your chin have got into fearful proximity," was the sort of salute Blurkins would give an acquaintance after an absence. Or if the "Featherbedfordshire Gazette," or the "Hit-im and Hold-im shire Herald" had an unflattering paragraph respecting a party's interference at the recent elections, or on any other subject, Blurkins was the man who would bring it under his notice. "There, sir, there; see what they say about you!" he would say, coming up in the news-room, with the paper neatly folded to the paragraph, and presenting it to him.

The Faireys of Yarrow Court were the most producible people, but then Miss was a beauty, who had even presumed to vie with the Yammertons, and they could not ask the old people without her. Besides which, it had transpired that a large deal box, carefully covered with glazed canvas, had recently arrived at the Rosedale station, which it was strongly suspected contained a new dinner dress from Madame Glace's in Hanover Street; and it would never do to let her sport it at Yammerton Grange against their girl's rather soiled—but still by candle-light extremely passable—watered silk ones. So, after due deliberation, the Faireys were rejected.

The Crickletons' claims were then taken into consideration.

Crick was the son of Crickleton, the late eminent chiropodist of Bolton Row, whom many of our readers will remember parading about London on his piebald pony, with a groom in a yellow coat, red plush breeches, and boots; and the present Crickleton was now what he called "seeking repose" in the country, which, in his opinion, consisted in setting all his neighbours by the ears. He rented Lavender Lodge and farm, and being a thorough Cockney, with a great inclination for exposing his ignorance both in the sporting and farming way, our knowing Major was making rather a good thing of him. At first there was a little rivalry between them, as to which was the greater man: Crickleton affirming that his father might have been knighted; the Major replying, that as long as he wasn't knighted it made no matter. The Major, however, finding it his interest to humour his consequence, compromised matters, by always taking in Mrs. Crickleton, a compliment that Crick returned by taking in Mrs. Yammerton. Though the Major used, when in the running-down tack, to laugh at the idea of a knight's son claiming precedence, yet, when on the running-up one, he used to intimate that his friend's father might have been knighted, and even sometimes assigned the honour to his friend himself. So he talked of him to our Billy.

The usual preponderating influence setting in in favour of acceptances, our host and hostess were obliged to play their remaining card with caution. There were two sets of people with equal claims—the Impelows of Buckup Hill, and the Baskyfields of Lingworth Lawn; the Impelows, if anything, having the prior claim, inasmuch as the Yammertons had dined with them last; but then, on the other hand, there was a very forward young Impelow whom they couldn't accommodate, that is to say, didn't want to have; while, as regarded the Baskyfields, old Basky and Crickleton were at daggers drawn about a sow Basky had sold him, and they would very likely get to loggerheads about it during the evening. A plan of the table was drawn up, to see if it was possible to separate them sufficiently, supposing people would only have the sense to go to their right places, but it was found to be impracticable to do justice to their consequence, and preserve the peace as well; so the idea of having the Baskyfields was obliged to be relinquished. This delay was fatal to the Impelows, for John Giles, their man-of-all-work, having seen Solomon scouring the country on horseback with a basket, in search of superfluous poultry, had reported the forthcoming grand spread at the Grange to his "Missis"; and after waiting patiently for an invitation, it at length came so late as to be an evident convenience, which they wouldn't submit to; so after taking a liberal allowance of time to answer, in order to prevent the Yammertons from playing the same base trick upon any one else, they declined in a stiff, non-reason-assigning note. This was the first check to the hitherto prosperous current of events, and showed our sagacious friends that the time was past for stopping gaps with family people, and threw them on the other resources of the district.

The usual bachelor stop-gaps of the neighbourhood were Tom Hetherington, of Bearbinder Park, and Jimmy Jarperson, of Fothergill Burn, both of whom had their disqualifications; Jarperson's being an acute nerve-shaking sort of laugh, that set every one's teeth on edge who heard it, and earned for him the title of the Laughing Hyæna; the other's misfortune being, that he was only what may be called an intermediate gentleman, that is to say, he could act the gentleman up to a pint of wine or so, after which quantity nature gradually asserted her supremacy, and he became himself again.

Our friend Paul Straddler, of Hinton, at one time had had the call of them both, but the Major, considering that Straddler had not used due diligence in the matter of Golden-drop, was not inclined to have him. Besides which, Straddler required a bed, which the Major was not disposed to yield, a bed involving a breakfast, and perhaps a stall for his horse, to say nothing of an out-of-place groom Straddler occasionally adopted, and who could eat as much as any two men. So the Laughing Hyæna and Hetherington were selected.

And now, gentle reader, if you will have the kindness to tell them off on your fingers as we call them over, we will see if we have got country, and as many as ever the Major can cram into his diningroom. Please count:—

Major, Mrs., three Misses Yammerton and Fine Billy...6 The Rev. Mr. and Mrs. Tightlace.....................2 Mr. and Mrs. Rocket Larkspur.........................2 Mrs. and Miss Dotherington............................2 Mr. and Mrs. Blurkins................................2 Mr. and Mrs. Crickleton..............................2 The Hyæna, and Hetherington...........................2 18

All right! eighteen; fourteen for dining-room chairs, and four for bedroom ones. There are but twelve Champagne needle-cases, but the deficiency is supplied by half-a-dozen ale glasses at the low end of the table, which the Major says will "never be seen."

So now, if you please, we will go and dress—dinner being sharp six, recollect.

CHAPTER XXI. THE GATHERING.—THE GRAND SPREAD ITSELF.

IF a dinner-party in town, with all the aids and appliances of sham-butlers, job-cooks, area-sneak-entrés, and extraneous confectionary, causes confusion in an establishment, how much more so must a party in the country, where, in addition to the guests, their servants, their horses, and their carriages, are to be accommodated. What a turning-out, and putting-up, and make-shifting, is there! What a grumbling and growling at not getting into the best stable, or at not having the state-vehicle put into the coach-house. If Solomon had not combined the wisdom of his namesake, with the patience of Job, he would have succumbed to the pressure from without. As it was, he kept persevering on until having got the last shandry-dan deposited under the hay house, he had just time to slip up-stairs to "clean himself," and be ready to wait at dinner.

But what a commotion the party makes in the kitchen! Everybody is in a state of stew, from the gallant Betty Bone down to the hind's little girl from Bonnyriggs Farm, whom they have "got in" for the occasion.

Nor do their anxieties end with the dishing-up of the dinner; for no sooner is it despatched, than that scarcely less onerous entertainment, the supper for the servants, has to be provided.

Then comes the coffee, then the tea, then the tray, and then the carriages wanted, then good night, good night, good night; most agreeable evening; no idea it was so late; and getting away. But the heat, and steam, and vapour of the kitchen overpowers us, and we gladly seek refuge in the newly "done-up" drawingroom.

In it behold the Major!—the Major in all the glory of the Yammerton harrier uniform, a myrtle-green coat, with a gold embroidered hare on the myrtle-green velvet collar, and puss with her ears well back, striding away over a dead gold surface, with a raised burnished rim of a button, a nicely-washed, stiffly-starched, white vest, with a yellow silk one underneath, black shorts, black silk stockings, and patent leather pumps. He has told off his very rare and singularly fine port wine, his prime old Madeira, matured in the West Indies; his nutty sherry, and excellently flavoured claret, all recently bought at the auction mart, not forgetting the ginger-pop-like champagne,—allowing the liberal measure of a pint for each person of the latter, and he is

61

now trying to cool himself down into the easy-minded, unconcerned, every-day-dinner-giving host.

Mrs. Yammerton too, on whom devolves the care of the wax and the modérateurs, is here superintending her department—seeing that the hearth is properly swept, and distributing the Punches, and Posts, and "Ask Mamma's" judiciously over the fine variegated table-cover. She is dressed in a rich silvery grey—with a sort of thing like a silver cow tie, with full tassels, twisted and twined serpent-like into her full, slightly streaked, dark hair.

The illumination being complete, she seats herself fan in hand on the sofa, and a solemn pause then ensues, broken only by Billy's and Monsieur's meanderings over-head, and the keen whistle of the November wind careering among the hollies and evergreens which the Major keeps interpreting into wheels.

Then his wife and he seek to relieve the suspense of the moment by speculating on who will come first.

"Those nasty Tightlaces for a guinea," observed the Major, polishing his nails, while Mrs. Yammerton predicted the Larkspurs.

"No, the Tights," reiterated the Major, jingling his silver; "Tights always comes first—thinks to catch one unprepared—"

At length the furious bark of the inhospitable terrier, who really seemed as if he would eat horses, vehicle, visitors, and all, was followed by a quick grind up to the door, and such a pull at the bell as made the Major fear would cause it to suspend payment for good—*ring-ring-ring-ring-ring* it went, as if it was never going to stop.

"Pulled the bell out of the socket, for a guinea," exclaimed the Major, listening for the letting down of steps, iron or recessed—recessed had it.

"Mrs. D." said the Major—figuring her old Landaulet in his mind.

"*Ladies* evidently," assented Mrs. Yammerton, as the rustle of silks on their way to the put-to-rights Sanctum, sounded past the drawing-room door. The Major then began speculating as to whether they would get announced before another arrival took place, or not.

****

Presently a renewed rustle was succeeded by the now yellow-logged, brown-backed Bumbler, throwing open the door and exclaiming in a stentorian voice, as if he thought his master and mistress had turned suddenly deaf, "Mrs. and Miss Dothering-ton!" and in an instant the four were hugging, and grinning, and pump-handling each other's arms as if they were going into ecstacies, Mrs. Dotherington interlarding her gymnastics with Mrs. Yammerton, with sly squeezes of the hand, suited to *soto voce* observations not intended for the Major's ears, of "so *'appy* to ear it! so glad to congratulate you! *So nice!*" with an inquisitive whisper of—"*which is it? which is it?* Do tell me!"

****

Bow-wow-wow-wow-wow-wow went the clamorous Fury again; *Ring-ring-ring-ring-ring-ring-ring* went the aggravated bell, half drowning Mrs. Yammerton's impressive "O dear! nothin' of the sort—nothin' of the sort, only a fox-hunting acquaintance of the Major's—only a fox-hunting acquaintance of the Major's." And then the Major came to renew his affectionate embraces, with inquiries about the night, and the looks of the moon—was it hazy, or was it clear, or how was it?

"Mr. and Mrs. Rocket Larkspur!" exclaimed the Bumbler, following up the key-note in which he had pitched his first announcement and forthwith the hugging and grinning was resumed with the new comers, Mrs. Larkspur presently leading Mrs. Yammerton off sofawards, in order to poke her inquiries unheard by the Major, who was now opening a turnip dialogue with Mr. Rocket—yellow bullocks, purple tops, and so on. "Well, tell me—*which is it* '?" ejaculated Mrs. Rocket Larkspur, looking earnestly, in Mrs. Yammerton's expressive eyes—"*which is it* repeated she, in a determined sort of take-no-denial tone.

"Oh dear! nothin' of the sort—nothin' of the sort, I assure you!" whispered Mrs. Yammerton anxiously, well knowing the danger of holloaing before you are out of the wood.

"Oh, *tell me—tell me*," whispered Mrs. Rocket, coaxingly; "I'm not like Mrs.————um there, looking at Mrs. Dotherington, who would blab it all over the country."

"*Really* I have nothing to tell," replied Mrs. Yammerton serenely.

"Why, do you mean to say he's not after one of the————um's?" demanded Mrs. Rocket eagerly.

"I don't know what you mean," laughed Mrs. Yammerton.

Bow-wow-wow-wow-wow-wow went the terrier again, giving Mrs. Yammerton an excuse for sidling off to Mrs. "um," who with her daughter were lost in admiration at a floss silk cockatoo, perched on an orange tree, the production of Miss Flora. "Oh, it was so beautiful! Oh, what a love of a screen it would make; what would she give if her Margaret could do such work," inwardly thinking how much better Margaret was employed making her own—we will not say what.

Bow-wow-wow-wow-wow-wow went Fury again, the proceeds of this bark being Mr. and Mrs. Tightlace, who now entered, the former "'oping they weren't late," as he smirked, and smiled, and looked round for the youth on whom he had to vent his "British Sportsman" knowledge—the latter speedily drawing Mrs. Yammerton aside—to the ladies know what. But it was "no go" again. Mrs. Yammerton really didn't know what Mrs. Tightlace meant. No; she *really* didn't. Nor did Mrs. Tightlace's assurance that it was "the talk of the country," afford any clue to her meaning—but Mrs. Tightlace's large miniature brooch being luckily loose, Mrs. Yammerton essayed to fasten it, which afforded her an opportunity of bursting into transports of delight at its beauty, mingled with exclamations as to its "*wonderful* likeness to Mr. T.," though in reality she was looking at Mrs. Tightlace's berthe, to see whether it was machinery lace, or real.

Then the grand rush took place; and Fury's throat seemed wholly inadequate to the occasion, as first Blurkins's Brougham, then Jarperson's Gig, next the corn-cutter's *calèche*, and lastly, Hetherington's Dog-cart whisked up to the door, causing a meeting of the highly decorated watered silks of the house, and the hooded enveloped visitors hurrying through the passage to the cloak-room.

By the time the young ladies had made their obeisances and got congratulated on their looks, the now metamorphosed visitors came trooping in, flourishing their laced kerchiefs, and flattening their *chapeaux mèchaniques* as they entered. Then the full chorus of conversation was established; moon, hounds, turnips, horses.

Parliament, with the usual—"Oi see by the papers that Her is gone to Osborne," or, "Oi see by the papers that the Comet is coming;" while Mrs. Rocket Larkspur draws Miss Yammerton aside to try what she can fish out of her. But here comes Fine Billy, and if ever hero realised an author's description of him. assuredly it is our friend, for he sidles as unconcernedly into the room as he would into a Club or Casino, with all the dreamy listlessness of a thorough exquisite, apparently unconscious of any change having taken place in the part. But if Billy is unconscious of the presence of strangers, his host is not, and forthwith he inducts him into their acquaintance—Hetherington's, Hyæna's, and all.

It is, doubtless, very flattering of great people to vote all the little ones "one of us," and not introduce them to anybody, but we take leave to say, that society is considerably improved by a judicious presentation. We talk of our advanced civilisation, but manners are not nearly so good, or so "at-ease-setting," as they were with the last generation of apparently stiffer, but in reality easier, more affable gentlemen of the old school. But what a note of admiration our Billy is! How gloriously he is attired. His naturally curling hair, how gracefully it flows; his elliptic collar, how faultlessly it stands; his cravat, how correct; his shirt, how wonderfully fine; and, oh! how happy he must be with such splendid sparkling diamond studs—such beautiful amethyst buttons at his wrists—and such a love of a chain disporting itself over his richly embroidered blood-stone-buttoned vest. Altogether, such a first-class swell is rarely seen beyond the bills of mortality. He looks as if he ought to be kept under a glass shade. But here comes the Bumbler, and now for the agony of the entertainment.

The Major, who for the last few minutes has been fidgetting about pairing parties off according to a written programme he has in his waistcoat pocket, has just time to assign Billy to Mrs. Rocket Larkspur, to assuage her anguish at not being taken in before Mrs. Crickleton, when the Bumbler's half-fledged voice is heard proclaiming at its utmost altitude—"dinner is sarved!" Then there is such a bobbing and bowing, and backing of chairs, and such inward congratulations, that the "'orrid 'alf'our" is over, and hopes from some that they may not get next the fire—while others wish to be there. Though the Major could not, perhaps, manage to get twenty thousand men out of Hyde Park, he can, nevertheless, manouvre a party out of his drawing-room into his dining-room, and forthwith he led the way, with Mrs. Crickleton under his arm, trusting to the reel winding off right at the end. And right it would most likely have wound off had not the leg-protruding Bumbler's tongue-buckle caught the balloon-like amplitude of Mrs. Rocket Larkspur's dress and caused a slight stoppage—in the passage,—during which time two couples slipped past and so deranged the entire order of the table. However, there was no great harm done, as far as Mrs. Larkspur's consequence was concerned, for she got next Mr. Tightlace, with Mr. Pringle between her and Miss Yammerton, whom Mrs. Larkspur had just got to admit, that she wouldn't mind being Mrs. P————, and Miss having been thus confidential, Mrs. was inclined, partly out of gratitude,—partly, perhaps, because she couldn't help it—to befriend her. She was a great mouser, and would promote the most forlorn hope, sooner than not be doing.

We are now in the dining-room, and very smart everything is. In the centre of the table, of course, stands the Yammer ton testimonial,—a "Savory" chased silver plated candelabrum, with six branches, all lighted up, and an ornamental centre flower-basket, decorated with evergreens and winter roses, presented to our friend on his completing his "five and twentieth year as master of harriers," and in gratitude for the unparalleled sport he had uniformly shown the subscribers.

Testimonialising has become quite a mania since the Major got his, and no one can say whose turn it may be next. It is not everybody who, like Mr. Daniel Whittle Harvey with the police force one, can nip them in the bud; but Inspector Field, we think, might usefully combine testimonial-detecting with his other secret services. He would have plenty to do—especially in the provinces. Indeed London does not seem to be exempt from the mania, if we may judge by Davis the Queen's huntsman's recent attempt to avert the intended honour; neatly informing the projectors that "their continuing to meet him in the hunting field would be the best proof of their approbation of his conduct." However, the Major got his testimonial; and there it stands, flanked by two pretty imitation Dresden vases decorated with flowers and evergreens also. And now the company being at length seated and grace said, the reeking covers are removed from the hare and mock turtle tureens, and the confusion of tongues gradually subsides into sip-sip-sipping of soup. And now Jarperson, having told his newly caught footman groom to get him hare soup instead of mock turtle, the lad takes the plate of the latter up to the tureen of the former, and his master gets a mixture of both—which he thinks very good.

And now the nutty sherry comes round, which the Major introduces with a stuttering exordium that would induce anyone who didn't know him to suppose it cost at least 80s. a-dozen, instead of 36s. (bottles included); and this being sipped and smacked and pronounced excellent, "two fishes" replace the two soups, and the banquet proceeds, Mr. Tightlace trying to poke his sporting knowledge at Billy between heats, but without success, the commoner not rising at the bait, indeed rather shirking it.

A long-necked green bottle of what the Bumbler called "bluecellas," then goes its rounds; and the first qualms of hunger being appeased, the gentlemen are more inclined to talk and listen to the luncheon-dining ladies. Mrs. Rocket Larkspur has been waiting most anxiously for Billy's last mouthful, in order to interrogate him, as well as to London fashion, as to his opinions of the Miss "ums." Of course with Miss "um" sitting just below Billy, the latter must be done through the medium of the former,—so she leads off upon London.

"She supposed he'd been very gay in London?"

"Yarse," drawled Billy in the true dandified style, drawing his napkin across his lips as he spoke.

Mrs. Rocket wasn't so young as she had been, and Billy was too young to take up with what he profanely called "old ladies."

"He'd live at the west-end, she s'posed?"

"Yarse," replied Billy, feeling his amplified tie.

"Did he know Billiter Square?"

"Yarse," replied he, running his ringed fingers down his studs. "Was it fashionable?" asked Mrs. Rocket. (She had a cousin lived there who had asked her to go and see her.)

"Y-a-a-rse, I should say it is," drawled Billy, now playing with a bunch of trinkets, a gold miniature pistol, a pearl and diamond studded locket, a gold pencil-case, and a white cornelian heart, suspended to his watch-chain. "Y-a-a-rse, I should say it is," repeated he; adding "not so fashionable as Belgrave."

"Sceuse me, sare," interrupted Monsieur Jean Rougier from behind his master's chair, "Sceuse me, it is not fashionable, sare,—it is not near de Palace or de Park of Hyde, sare, bot down away among those dem base mechanics in de east—beyond de Mansion 'Ouse, in fact."

"Oh, ah, y-a-a-rse, true," replied Billy, not knowing where it was, but presuming from Mrs. Larkspur's inquiry that it was some newly sprung-up square on one of the western horns of the metropolis.

Taking advantage of the interruption, Mr. Tightlace again essayed to edge in his "British Sportsman" knowledge beginning with an inquiry if "the Earl of Ladythorne had a good set of dogs this season?" but the Bumbler soon cut short the thread of his discourse by presenting a bottle of brisk gooseberry at his ear. The fizzing stuff then went quickly round, taxing the ingenuity of the drinkers to manoeuvre the frothy fluid out of their needlecase-shaped glasses. Then as conversation was beginning to be restored, the door suddenly flew open to a general rush of returning servants. There was Soloman carrying a sirloin of beef, followed by Mr. Crickleton's gaudy red-and-yellow young man with a boiled turkey, who in turn was succeeded by Mr. Rocket Larkspur's hobbledehoy with a ham, and Mr. Tightlace's with a stew. Pâtés and côtelettes, and minces, and messes follow in quick succession; and these having taken their seats, immediately vacate them for the Chiltern-hundreds of the hand. A shoal of vegetables and sundries alight on the side table, and the feast seems fairly under weigh.

But see! somehow it prospers not!

People stop short at the second or third mouthful, and lay down their knives and forks as if they had had quite enough. Patties, and cutlets, and sausages, and side-dishes, all share the same fate!

"Take round the champagne," says the Major, with an air, thinking to retrieve the character of his kitchen with the solids. The juicy roast beef, and delicate white turkey with inviting green stuffing, and rich red ham, and turnip-and-carrot-adorned stewed beef then made their progresses, but the same fate attends them also. People stop at the second or third mouthful;—some send their plates away slily, and ask for a little of a different dish to what they have been eating, or rather tasting. That, however, shares the same fate.

"Take round the champagne," again says the Major, trying what another cheerer would do. Then he invites the turkey-eaters—or leavers, rather—to eat beef; and the beef eaters—or leavers—to eat turkey: but they all decline with a thoroughly satisfied 'no-more-for-me' sort of shake of the head.

"Take away!" at length says the Major, with an air of disgust, following the order with an invitation to Mrs. Rocket Larkspur to take wine. The guests follow the host's example, and a momentary rally of liveliness ensues. Mrs. Rocket Larkspur and Mr. Tight-lace contend for Fine Billy's ear; but Miss Yammerton interposing with a sly whisper supersedes them both. Mrs. Rocket construes that accordingly. A general chirp of conversation is presently established, interspersed with heavy demands upon the breadbasket by the gentlemen. Presently the door is thrown open, and a grand procession of sweets enters—jellies, blancmanges, open tarts, shut tarts, meringues, plum pudding, maccaroni, black puddings,—we know not what besides: and the funds of conviviality again look up. The rally is, however, but of momentary duration. The same evil genius that awaited on the second course seems to attend on the third. People stop at the second or third mouthful and send away the undiminished plates slily, as before. Home venture on other dishes—but the result is the same—the plate vanishes with its contents. There is, however, a great run upon the cheese—Cheshire and Gloucester; and the dessert suffers severely. All the make-weight dishes, even, disappear; and when the gentlemen rejoin the ladies in the drawing-room they attack the tea as if they had not had any dinner.

At length a "most agreeable evening" is got through; and as each group whisks away, there is a general exclamation of "What a most extraordinary taste everything had of————" What do you think, gentle reader?

"Can't guess! can't you?"

"What do you think, Mrs. Brown?"

"What do you think, Mrs. Jones?

"What do you, Mrs. Robinson?"

"What! none of you able to guess! And yet everybody at table hit off directly!"

"All give it up?" Brown, Jones, and Robinson?

"Yes—yes—yes."

"Well then, we'll tell you":—

"Everything tasted of Castor oil!"

"*Castor oil!*" exclaims Mrs. Brown.

"Castor oil!" shrieks Mrs. Jones.

"Castor oil!" shudders Mrs. Robinson.

"O-o-o-o! how nasty!"

"But how came it there?" asks Mrs. Brown.

"We'll tell you that, too—"

The Major's famous cow Strawberry-cream's calf was ill, and they had tapped a pint of fine "cold-drawn" for it, which Monsieur Jean Rougier happening to upset, just mopped it up with his napkin, and chucking it away, it was speedily adopted by the hind's little girl in charge of the plates and dishes, who imparted a most liberal castor oil flavour to everything she touched.

And that entertainment is now known by the name of the "Castor Oil Dinner."

CHAPTER XXII. A HUNTING MORNING.—UNKENNELING.

WHAT a commotion there was in the house the next morning! As great a disturbance as if the Major had been going to hunt an African Lion, a royal Bengal Tiger, or a Bison itself. *Ring-ring-ring-ring* went one bell, *tinkle-tinkle-tinkle* went another, *ring-ring-ring* went the first again, followed by exclamations of "There's master's bell again!" with such a running down stairs, and such a getting up again. Master wanted this, master wanted that, master had carried away the buttons at his knees, master wanted his other pair of White what-do-they-call-ems—not cords, but moleskins—that treacherous material being much in vogue among masters of harriers. Then master's boots wouldn't do, he wanted his last pair, not the newly-footed ones, and they were on the trees, and the Bumbler was busy in the stable, and Betty Bone could not skin the trees, and altogether there was a terrible hubbub in the house. His overnight exertions, though coupled with the castor oil catastrophe, seemed to have abated none of his ardour in pursuit of the hare.

Meanwhile our little dandy, Billy, lay tumbling and tossing in bed, listening to the dread preparations, wishing he could devise an excuse for declining to join him. The recollection of his bumps, and his jumps, and his falls, arose vividly before him, and he would fain have said "no" to any more. He felt certain that the Major was going to give him a startler, more dreadful perhaps than those he had had with his lordship. Would that he was well out of it! What pleasure could there be in galloping after an animal they could shoot? In the midst of these reflections Mons. Rougier entered the apartment and threw further light on the matter by opening the shutters.

"You sall get up, sare, and pursue the vild beast of de voods—de Major is a-goin' to hont."

"Y-a-r-se," replied Billy, turning over.

"I sal get out your habit verd, your green coat, dat is to say."

"*No! no!*" roared Billy; "*the red! the red!*"

"*De red!*" exclaimed Monsieur in astonishment, "de red Not for de soup dogs! you only hont bold reynard in de red."

"Oh, yes, you do," retorted Billy, "didn't the Major come to the carstle in red?"

"Because he came to hont de fox," replied Monsieur; "if he had com' for to hont poor puss he would 'ave 'ad on his green or his grey, or his some other colour."

Billy now saw the difference, and his mortification increased. "Well, I'll breakfast in red at all events," said he, determined to have that pleasure.

"Vell, sare, you can pleasure yourself in dat matter; but it sall be moch ridicule if you pursue de puss in it."

"But why not?" asked Billy, "hunting's hunting, all the world over."

"I cannot tell you vy, sir; but it is not *etiquette*, and I as a professor of garniture, toggery vot you call, sid lose *caste* with my comrades if I lived with a me lor vot honted poor puss in de pink."

"*Humph!*" grunted Billy, bouncing out of bed, thinking what a bore it was paying a man for being his master. He then commenced the operations of the occasion, and with the aid of Monsieur was presently attired in the dread costume. He then clonk, clonk, clonked down stairs with his Jersey-patterned spurs, toes well out to clear the steps, most heartily wishing he was clonking up again on his return from the hunt.

Monsieur was right. The Major is in his myrtle-green coat—a coat, not built after the fashion of the scanty swallow-tailed red in which he appears at page 65 of this agreeable work, but with the more liberal allowance of cloth peculiar to the period in which we live. A loosely hanging garment, and not a strait-waistcoat, in fact, a fashion very much in favour of bunglers, seeing that anybody can make a sack, while it takes a tailor to make a coat. The Major's cost him about two pounds five, the cloth having been purchased at a clothier's and made up at home, by a three shilling a day man and his meat. We laugh at the ladies for liking to be cheated by their milliners; but young gentlemen are quite as accommodating to their tailors. Let any man of forty look at his tailor's bill when he was twenty, and see what a liberality of innocence it displays. And that not only in matters of taste and fashion, which are the legitimate loopholes of extortion, but in the sober articles of ordinary requirement. We saw a once-celebrated west-end tailor's bill the other day, in which a plain black coat was made to figure in the following magniloquent item:—

"A superfine black cloth coat, lappels sewed on" (we wonder if they are usually pinned or glued) "lappels sewed on, cloth collar, cotton sleeve linings, velvet handfacings," (most likely cotton too,) "embossed edges and fine wove buttons"—how much does the reader think? four guineas? four pound ten? five guineas? No, five pound eighteen and sixpence! An article that our own excellent tailor supplies for three pounds fifteen! In a tailor's case that was recently tried, a party swore that fourteen guineas was a fair price for a Taglioni, when every body knows that they are to be had for less than four. But boys will be boys to the end of the chapter, so let us return to our sporting Major. He is not so happy in his nether garments as he is in his upper ones; indeed he has on the same boots and moleskins that Leech drew him in at Tantivy Castle, for these lower habiliments are not so easy of accomplishment in the country as coats, and though most people have tried them there, few wear them out, they are always so ugly and unbecoming. As, however, our Major doesn't often compare his with town-made ones, he struts about in the comfortable belief that they are all right—very smart.

He is now in a terrible stew, and has been backwards and forwards between the house and the stable, and in and out of the kennel, and has called Solomon repeatedly from his work to give him further instructions and further instructions still, until the Major has about confused himself and every body about him. As soon as ever he heard by his tramp overhead that Billy had got into his boots, he went to the bottom of the stairs and holloaed along the passage towards the kitchen. "Betty! Betty! Betty! send in breakfast as soon as ever Mr. Pringle comes down!'" "Ah, dere is de Majur." observed Monsieur, pausing from Billy's hair-arranging to listen—"him kick up de deval's own dost on a huntin' mornin'."

"What's happened him?" asked Billy.

"Don't know—but von vould think he was going to storm a city—take Sebastopol himself," replied Monsieur, shrugging his broad shoulders. He then resumed his valeting operations, and crowned the whole by putting Billy into his green cut-away, without giving him even a peep of the pink.

Meanwhile, Mrs. Yammerton has been holding a court of inquiry in the kitchen and larder, as to the extent of the overnight mischief, smelling at this dish and that, criticising the spoons, and subjecting each castor-oily offender to severe ablution in boiling water. Of course no one could tell in whose hands the bottle of "cold drawn" had come "in two," and Monsieur was too good a judge to know anything about it; so as the mischief couldn't be repaired, it was no use bewailing it farther than to make a knot in her mind to be more careful of such dangerous commodities in future.

Betty Bone had everything—tea, coffee, bread, cakes, eggs, ham (fried so as to hide the spurious flavour), honey, jam, &c., ready for Miss Benson, who had been impressed into the carrying service, *vice* the Bumbler turned whip, to take in as soon as Mr. Pringle descended, a fact that was announced to the household by the Major's uproarious greeting of him in the passage. He was overjoyed to see him! He hoped he was none the worse for his over-night festivities; and without waiting for an answer to that, he was delighted to say that it was a fine hunting morning, and as far as human judgment could form an opinion, a good scenting one; but after five-and-thirty years' experience as a master of "haryers," he could conscientiously say that there was nothing so doubtful or ticklish as scent, and he made no doubt Mr. Pringle's experience would confirm his own, that many days when they might expect it to be first-rate, it was bad, and many days when they might expect it to be bad, it was first-rate; to all which accumulated infliction Billy replied with his usual imperturbable "Yarse," and passed on to the more agreeable occupation of greeting the young ladies in the dining-room. Very glad they all were to see him as he shook hands with all three.

The Major, however, was not to be put off that way; and as he could not get Billy to talk about hunting, he drew his attention to breakfast, observing that they had a goodish trot before them, and that punctuality was the politeness of princes. Saying which, he sat down, laying his great gold watch open on a plate beside him, so that its noisy ticking might remind Billy of what they had to do. The Major couldn't make it out how it was that the souls of the young men of the present day are so difficult to inflame about hunting. Here was he, turned of————, and as eager in the pursuit as ever. "Must be that they smoke all their energies out," thought he; and then applied himself vigorously to his tea and toast, looking up every now and then with irate looks at his wife and daughters, whose volubility greatly retarded Billy's breakfast proceedings. He, nevertheless, made sundry efforts to edge in a hunting conversation himself, observing that Mr. Pringle mustn't expect such an establishment as the Peer's, or perhaps many that he was accustomed to—that they would have rather a shortish pack out, which would enable them to take the field again at an early day, and so on; all of which Billy received with the most provoking indifference, making the Major wish he mightn't be a regular crasher, who cared for nothing but riding. At length, tea, toast, eggs, ham, jam, all had been successively taxed, the Major closed and pocketed his noisy watch, and the doomed youth rose to perform the dread penance with the pack. "Good byes," "good mornings," "hope you'll have good sport," followed his bowing spur-clanking exit from the room.

A loud crack of the Major's hammer-headed whip now announced their arrival in the stable-yard, which was at once a signal for the hounds to raise a merry cry, and for the stable-men to loosen their horses' heads from the pillar-reins. It also brought a bevy of caps and curl-papers to the back windows of the house to see the young Earl, for so Rougier had assured them his master was—(heir to the Earldom of Ladythorne)—mount. At a second crack of the whip the stable-door flew open, and as a shirt-sleeved lad receded, the grey-headed, green-coated sage Solomon advanced, leading forth the sleek, well-tended, well-coddled, Napoleon the Great.

Amid the various offices filled by this Mathews-at-home of a servant, there was none perhaps in which he looked better or more natural than in that of a huntsman. Short, spare, neat, with a bright black eye, contrasting with the sobered hue of his thin grey hair, no one would suppose that the calfless little yellow and brown-liveried coachman of the previous night was the trim, neatly-booted, neatly-tied huntsman now raising his cap to the Richest Commoner in England,

and his great master Major Yammerton—Major of the Featherbedfordshire Militia, master of "haryers," and expectant magistrate.

"Well, Solomon," said the Major, acknowledging his salute, as though it was their first meeting of the morning, "well, Solomon, what do you think of the day?"

"Well, sir, I think the day's well enough," replied Solomon, who was no waster of words.

"I think so too," said the Major, drawing on his clean doeskin gloves. The pent-up hounds then raised another cry.

"That's pretty!" exclaimed the Major listening

"That's *beautiful!*" added he, like an enthusiastic admirer of music at the opera.

Imperturbable Billy spoke not.

"Pr'aps you'd like to see them unkenneled?" said the Major, thinking to begin with the first act of the drama.

"Yarse," replied Billy, feeling safe as long as he was on foot.

The Major then led the way through a hen-house-looking door into a little green court-yard, separated by peeled larch palings from a flagged one beyond, in which the expectant pack were now jumping and frisking and capering in every species of wild delight.

"Ah, you beauties!" exclaimed the Major, again cracking his whip. He then paused, thinking there would surely be a little praise. But no; Billy just looked at them as he would at a pen full of stock at a cattle show.

"Be-be-beauties, ar'n't they?" stuttered the Major.

"Yarse," replied Billy; thinking they were prettier than the great lounging, slouching foxhounds.

"Ca-ca-capital hounds," observed the Major.

No response from Billy.

"Undeniable b-b-blood," continued our friend.

No response again.

"F-f-foxhounds in mi-mi-miniature," observed the Major.

"Yarse," replied Billy, who understood that.

"Lovely! Lovely! Lovely! there's a beautiful bitch," continued the Major, pointing to a richly pied one that began frolicking to his call.

"Bracelet! Bracelet! Bracelet!" holloaed he to another; "pretty bitch that—pure Sir Dashwood King's blood, just the right size for a haryer—shouldn't be too large. I hold with So-so-somerville," continued the Major, waxing warm, either with his subject, or at Billy's indifference, "that one should

'*A di-di-different hound for every chase Select with judgment; nor the timorous hare, O'ermatch'd, destroy; but leave that vile offence To the mean, murderous, coursing crew, intent On blood and spoil.*'"

"Yarse," replied Billy, turning on his heel as though he had had enough of the show.

At this juncture, the Major drew the bolt, open flew the door, and out poured the pack; Ruffler and Bustler dashing at Billy, and streaking his nice cream-coloured leathers down with their dirty paws, while Thunder and Victim nearly carried him off his legs with the couples. Billy was in a great fright, never having been in such a predicament before.

The Major came to the rescue, and with the aid of his whip and his voice, and his "for shame, Ruffler! for shame, Bustler!" with cuts at the coupled ones, succeeded in restoring order.

"Let's mount," said he, thinking to get Billy out of further danger; so saying he wheeled about and led the way through the outer yard with the glad pack gamboling and frisking around him to the stables.

The hounds raise a fresh cry of joy as they see Solomon with his horse ready to receive them.

CHAPTER XXIII. SHOWING A HORSE.—THE MEET.

THE Bumbler, like our Mathews-at-home of a huntsman, is now metamorphosed, and in lieu of a little footman, we have a capped and booted whip. Not that he *is* a whip, for Solomon carries the couples as well as the horn, and also a spare stirrup-leather slung across his shoulder; but our Major has an eye as well to show as to business, and thinks he may as well do the magnificent, and have a horse ready to change with Billy as soon as Napoleon the Great seems to have had enough. To that end the Bumbler now advances with the Weaver which he tenders to Billy, with a deferential touch of his cap.

"Ah, that's *your* horse!" exclaimed the Major, making for White Surrey, to avoid the frolics and favours of his followers; adding, as he climbed on, "you'll find her a ca-ca-capital hack and a first-rate hunter. Here, *elope, hounds, elope!*" added he, turning his horse's head away to get the course clear for our friend to mount unmolested.

Billy then effects the ascent of the black mare, most devoutly wishing himself safe off again. The stirrups being adjusted to his length, he gives a home thrust with his feet in the irons, and gathering the thin reins, feels his horse gently with his left leg, just as Solomon mounts Napoleon the Great and advances to relieve the Major of his charge. The cavalcade then proceed; Solomon, with the now clustering hounds, leading; the Major and Billy riding side by side, and the Bumbler on Bulldog bringing up the rear. Caps and curl-papers then disappear to attend to the avocations of the house, the wearers all agreeing that Mr. Pringle is a very pretty young gentleman, and quite worthy of the pick of the young ladies.

Crossing Cowslip garth at an angle they get upon Greenbat pasture, where the first fruits of idleness are shown by Twister and Towler breaking away at the cows.

"*Yow, yow!*" they go in the full enjoyment of the chase. It's a grand chance for the Bumbler, who, adjusting his whip-thong, sticks spurs into Bulldog and sets off as hard as ever the old horse can lay legs to the ground.

"Get round them, man! get round them," shouts the Major, watching Bully's leg-tied endeavours, the old horse being a better hand at walking than galloping.

At length they are stopped and chided and for shamed, and two more fields land our party in Hollington lane, which soon brings them into the Lingytine and Ewehurst-road, whose liberal width and ample siding bespeaks the neighbourhood of a roomier region. Solomon at a look from the Major now takes the grass siding with his hounds, while the gallant master just draws his young friend alongside of them on the road, casting an unconcerned eye upon the scene, in the hope that his guest will say something handsome at last. But no, Billy doesn't. He is fully occupied with his boots and breeches, whose polish and virgin purity he still deplores. There's a desperate daub down one side. The Major tries to engage his attention by coaxing and talking to the hounds. "Cleaver, good dog! Cleaver! Chaunter, good dog! Chaunter!" throwing them bits of biscuit, but all his efforts are vain. Billy plods on at the old post-boy pace, apparently thinking of nothing but himself.

Meanwhile Solomon ambles cockily along on Napoleon, with a backward and forward move of his leg to the horse's action, who ducks and shakes his head and plays good-naturedly with the hounds, as if quite delighted at the idea of what they are going to do. He shows to great advantage. He has not been out for a week, and the coddling and linseeding have given a healthy bloom to his bay coat, and he has taken a cordial ball with a little catechu, and ten grains of opium, to aid his exertions. Solomon, too, shows him off well. Though he hasn't our friend Dicky Boggledike's airified manner, like him he is little and light, sits neatly in his saddle, while his long coat-lap partly conceals the want of ribbing home of the handsome but washy horse. His boots and breeches, drab cords and brown tops, are good, so are his spurs, also his saddle and bridle.

There is a difference of twenty per cent, between the looks of a horse in a good, well-made London saddle, and in one of those great, spongy, pulby, puddingy things we see in the country. Again, what a contrast there is between a horse looking through a nice plain-fronted, plain-buckled, thin-reined, town-made bridle, and in one of those gaudy-fronted things, all over buckles, with reins thick enough for traces to the Lord Mayor's coach.

All this adornment, however, is wasted upon fine Billy, who hasn't got beyond the mane and tail beauties of a horse. Action, strength, stamina, symmetry, are as yet sealed subjects to him. The Major was the man who could enlighten him, if Billy would only let him do it, on the two words for himself and one for Billy principle. Do it he would, too, for he saw it was of no use waiting for Billy to begin.

"Nice 'oss that," now observed the Major casually, nodding towards Nap.

"Yarse," replied Billy, looking him over.

"That's the o-o-oss I showed you in the stable."

"Is it?" observed Billy, who didn't recognize him.

"Ought to be at M-m-melton, that oss," observed the Major.

"Why isn't he?" asked Billy, in the innocence of his heart.

"Don't know," replied the Major carelessly, with a toss of his head; "don't know. The fact is, I'm idle—no one to send with him—too old to go myself—haryers keep me at home—year too short to do all one has to do—see what a length he is—ord bless us he'd go over Ashby p-p-pastures like a comet."

Billy had now got his eyes well fixed upon the horse, which the Major seeing held his peace, for he was a capital seller, and had the great gift of knowing when he had said enough. He was not the man to try and bore a person into buying, or spoil his market by telling a youngster that the horse would go in harness, or by not asking enough. So with Solomon still to and froing with his little legs, the horse still lively and gay, the hounds still frisking and playing, the party proceeded through the fertility-diminishing country, until the small fields with live fences gradually gave way to larger, drabber enclosures with stone walls, and Broadstruther hill with its heath-burnt summit and quarry broken side at length announces their approach to the moors. The moors! Who does not feel his heart expand and his spirit glow as he comes upon the vast ocean-like space of moorland country? Leaving the strife, the cares, the contentions of a narrow, elbow-jostling world for the grand enjoyment of pure unrestricted freedom! The green streak of fertile soil, how sweet it looks, lit up by the fitful gleam of a cloud-obscured sun, the distant sky-touching cairn, how tempting to reach through the many intricacies of mountain ground—so easy to look at, so difficult to travel. The ink rises gaily in our pen at the thought, and pressing on, we cross the rough, picturesque, stone bridge over the translucent stream, so unlike the polished, chiseled structures of town art, where nothing is thought good that is not expensive; and now, shaking off the last enclosure, we reach the sandy road below the watcher's hill-ensconced hut, and so wind round into the panorama of the hills within.

"Ah! there we are!" exclaimed the Major, now pointing out the myrtle-green gentlemen with their white cords, moving their steeds to and fro upon the bright sward below the grey rocks of Cushetlaw hill.

"There we are," repeated he, eyeing them, trying to make out who they were, so as to season his greetings accordingly.

There was farmer Rintoul on the white, and Godfrey Faulder, the cattle jobber, on the grey; and Caleb Bennison, the horse-breaker, in his twilled-fustian frock, ready to ride over a hound as usual; and old Duffield, the horse-leech, in his low-crowned hat, black tops, and one spur; and Dick Trail, the auctioneer, on his long-tailed nag; and Bonnet, the billiard-table keeper of Hinton, in his odious white hat, grey tweed, and collar-marked screw; but who the cluster of men are on the left the Major can't for the life of him make out. He had hoped that Crickleton might have graced the meet with his presence, but there is no symptom of the yellow-coated groom, and Paul Straddler would most likely be too offended at not being invited to dine and have gone to Sir Moses's hounds at the Cow and Calf on the Fixton and Primrose-bank road. Still there were a dozen or fourteen sportsmen, with two or three more coming over the hill, and distance hiding the deficiencies as well of steeds as of costume, the whole has a very lively and inspiriting effect.

At the joyous, well-known "here they come!" of the lookers out, a move is perceptible among the field, who forthwith set off to meet the hounds, and as the advancing parties near, the Major has time to identify and appropriate their faces and their persons. First comes Captain Nabley, the chief constable of Featherbeds, who greets our master with the friendliness of a brother soldier, "one of us" in arms, and is forthwith introduced to our Billy. Next is fat farmer Nettlefold, who considers himself entitled to a shake of the hand in return for the Major's frequent comings over his farm at Carol-hill green, which compliment being duly paid the great master then raises his hat in return for the salutes of Faulder, Rennison, and Trail, and again stops to shake hands with an aged well-whiskered dandy in mufty, one Mr. Wotherspoon, now farming or starving a little property he purchased with his butlerage savings under the great Duke of Thunderdownshire. Wotherspoon apes the manners of high life with the brandified face of low, talks parliament, and takes snuff from a gold box with a George-the-Fourthian air. He now offers the Major a pinch, who accepts it with graceful concession.

The seedy-looking gentleman in black, on the too palpable three and sixpence a sider, is Mr. Catoheside, the County Court bailiff, with his pocket full of summonses, who thinks to throw a round with the Major into the day's hire of his broken-knee'd chestnut, and the greasy-haired, shining-faced youth with him, on the longtailed white pony, is Ramshaw, the butcher's boy, on the same sort of speculation. Then we have Mr. Meggison's coachman availing himself of his master's absence to give the family horse a turn with the hounds instead of going to coals, as he ought; and Mr. Dotherington's young man halting on his way to the doctor's with a note. He will tell his mistress the doctor was out and he had to wait ever so long till he came home. The four truants seem to herd together on the birds-of-a-feather principle. And now the reinforced party reach the meet below the grey ivy-tangled rocks, and Solomon pulls up at the accustomed spot to give his hounds a roll, and let the Major receive the encomiums of the encircling field. Then there is a repetition of the kennel scene: "Lovely! Lovely! Lovely!—beautiful bitch that—Chaunter. Chaunter! Chaunter!—there's a handsome hound—Bustler, good dog!" Only each man has his particular favourite or hound that he has either bred or walked, or knows the name of, and so most of the pack come in for more or less praise. It is agreed on all hands that they never looked better, or the establishment more complete. "Couldn't be better if it had cost five thousand a-year!"

Most grateful were their commendations to the Major after the dry, monotonous "yarses" of Billy, who sits looking unconcernedly on, a regular sleeping partner in the old established firm of

"Laudation and Co." The Major inwardly attributes his indifference to conceited fox-hunting pride. "Looks down upon haryers."

The field, however, gradually got the steam of praise up to a very high pitch. Indeed, had not Mr. Wotherspoon, who was only an air-and-exercise gentleman, observed, after a pompous pinch of snuff, that he saw by the papers that the House of Lords, of which he considered himself a sort of supernumerary member, were going to do something or not to do something, caused a check in the cry, there is no saying but they might altogether have forgotten what they had come out about. As it was, the mention of Mr. Wotherspoon's favourite branch of the legislature, from which they had all suffered more or less severely, operated like the hose of a fire-engine upon a crowd, sending one man one way, another another, until Wotherspoon had only Solomon and the hounds to finish off before. "Indeed, sir," was all the encouragement he got from Solomon. But let us get away from the insufferable Brummagem brandy-faced old bore by supposing Solomon transferred from Napoleon the Great to Bulldog, Billy mounted on the washy horse instead of the weaving mare, the Major's girths drawn, clay pipes deposited in the breast pockets of the owners, and thongs unloosened to commence the all-important operation of thistle-whipping.

At a nod from the Major, Solomon gives a wave of his hand to the hounds, and putting his horse on, the tide of sportsmen sweep after, and Cushetlaw rocks are again left in their pristine composure.

Despite Billy's indifference, the Major is still anxious to show to advantage, not knowing who Billy may relate his day's sport to, and has therefore arranged with Solomon not to cast off until they get upon the more favourable ground of Sunnylaws moor. This gives Billy time to settle in his new saddle, and scrape acquaintance with Napoleon, whom he finds a very complacent, easy-going horse. He has a light, playful mouth, and Billy doesn't feel afraid of him. Indeed, if it wasn't for the idea of the jumps, he would rather enjoy it. His mind, however, might have been easy on that score, for they are going into the hills instead of away from them, and the Major has scuttled over the ground so often that he knows every bog, and every crossing, and every vantage-taking line; where to view the hare, and where to catch up his hounds, to a nicety.

At length they reached a pretty, amphitheatreish piece of country, encircled by grassy hills, folding gracefully into each other, with the bolder outline of the Arkenhill moors for the background. A silvery stream meanders carelessly about the lowland, occasionally lost to view by sand wreaths and gravel beds thrown up by impetuous torrents rushing down from the higher grounds.

The field is here reinforced by Tom Springer, the generally out-of-place watcher, and his friend Joe Pitfall, the beer-shop keeper of Wetten hill, with their tenpenny wide-awakes, well-worn, baggy-pocketed shooting-coats, and strong oak staffs, suitable either for leaping or poking poles.

The Major returns their salute with a lowering brow, for he strongly suspects they are there on their own account, and not for the sake of enjoying a day with his unrivalled hounds. However, as neither of them have leave over the ground, they can neither of them find fault, and must just put up with each other.

So the Major, addressing Springer, says "I'll give you a shillin' if you'll find me a hare," as he turns to the Bumbler and bids him uncouple Billy's old friends Ruffler and Bustler. This done, the hounds quickly spread to try and hit off the morning scent, while the myrtle-greeners and others distribute themselves, cracking, Hopping, and hissing, here, there, and everywhere. Springer and Pitfall go poke, poke, tap, tap, peep, peep, at every likely bush and tuft, but both the Major and they are too often over the ground to allow of hares being very plentiful. When they do find them they are generally well in wind from work Meanwhile, Mr. Wotherspoon, finding that Billy Pringle is a friend of Lord Ladythorne's, makes up to him, and speaks of his lordship in the kind, encouraging way, so becoming a great man speaking of a lesser one. "Oh, he knew his lordship well, excellent man he was, knew Mrs. Moffatt, too—'andsome woman she was. Not so 'andsome, p'raps, as Mrs. Spangles, the actress, but still a v-a-a-ry 'andsome woman. Ah, he knew Mrs. Spangles, poor thing, long before she came to Tantivy—when she was on the stage, in fact." And here the old buck, putting his massive, gold-mounted riding-whip under his arm, heaved a deep sigh, as though the mention of her name recalled painful recollections, and producing his gold snuff-box, after offering it to Billy, he consoled himself with a long-drawn respiration from its contents. He then flourished his scarlet, attar-of-rose-scented bandana, and seemed lost in contemplation of the stripes down his trowsers and his little lacquered-toe'd boots. Billy rode silently on with him, making no doubt he was a very great man—just the sort of man his Mamma would wish him to get acquainted with.

CHAPTER XXIV. THE WILD BEAST ITSELF.

JUST as the old buck was resuming the thread of his fashionable high-life narrative, preparatory to sounding Billy about the Major and his family, the same sort of electric thrill shot through the field that characterised the terrible "g-n-r along—don't you see the hounds are running?" de Glancey day with the Earl. Billy felt all over he-didn't-know-how-ish—very wish-he-was-at-home-ish. The horse, too, began to caper.

The thrill is caused by a shilling's-worth of wide-awake on a stick held high against the sky-line of the gently-swelling hill on the left, denoting that the wild beast is found, causing the Major to hold up his hat as a signal of reply, and all the rest of the field to desist from their flopping and thistle-whipping, and rein in their screws for the coming conflict.

"Now s-s-sir!" exclaims the stuttering Major, cantering up to our Billy all flurry and enthusiasm. "Now, s-s-sir! we ha-ha-have her, and if you'll fo-fo-follow me, I'll show you her," thinking he was offering Billy the greatest treat imaginable. So saying the Major drops his hands on White Surrey's neck, rises in his stirrups, and scuttles away, bounding over the gorse bushes and broom that intervened between him and the still stick-hoisted tenpenny.

****

"*Where is she?*" demands the Major. "*Where is she!*" repeats he, coming up.

"A Major, he mun gi' us halfe-croon ony ho' this time," exclaims our friend Tom Springer, whose head gear it is that has been hoisted.

"Deed mun ye!" asserts Pitfall, who has now joined his companion.

"*No, no!*" retorts the Major angrily, "I said a shillin'—a shilling's my price, and you know it."

"Well, but consider what a time we've been a lookin' for her, Major," replied Springer, mopping his brow.

"Well, but consider that you are about to partake of the enjoyments as well as myself, and that I find the whole of this expensive establishment," retorted the Major, looking back for his hounds. "Not a farthin' subscription."

"Say two shillin's, then," replied Springer coaxingly.

"No, no," replied the Major, "a shillin's plenty."

"Make it eighteen-pence then," said Pitfall, "and oop she goes for the money."

"Well, come," snapped the Major hurriedly, as Billy now came elbowing up. "Where is she? Where is she?" demanded he.

"A, she's not here—she's not here, but I see her in her form thonder," replied Springer, nodding towards the adjoining bush-dotted hill.

"Go to her, then," said the Major, jingling the eighteen-pence in his hand, to be ready to give him on view of the hare.

The man then led the way through rushes, brambles, and briars, keeping a steady eye on the spot where she sate. At length he stopped. "There she's, see!" said he, *sotto voce*, pointing to the green hill-side.

"I have her!" whispered the Major, his keen eyes sparkling with delight. "Come here," said he to Billy, "and I'll show her to you. There," said he, "there you see that patch of gorse with the burnt stick stumps, at the low end—well, carry your eye down the slope of the land, past the old willow-tree, and you have her as plain as a pike-staff."

Billy shook his head. He saw nothing but a tuft or two of rough grass.

"O yes, you see her large eyes watching us," continued the Major, "thinking she sees us without our seeing her.

"No," our friend didn't.

"Very odd," laughed the Major, "very odd," with the sort of vexation a man feels when another can't be made to see the object he does.

"Will you give them a view now?" asked Springer, "or put her away quietly?"

"Oh, put her away quietly," replied the Major, "put her away quietly; and let them get their noses well down to the scent;" adding—"I've got some strange hounds out, and I want to see how they work."

The man then advanced a few paces, and touching one of the apparently lifeless tufts with his pole, out sprang puss and went stotting and dotting away with one ear back and the other forward, in a state of indignant perturbation. "Buck!" exclaims Pitfall, watching her as she goes.

"Doubt it," replied the Major, scrutinising her attentively.

"Nay look at its head and shoulders; did you iver see sic red shoulders as those on a doe?" asked Springer.

"Well," said the Major, "there's your money," handing Springer the eighteen-pence, "and I hope she'll be worth it; but mind, for the futur' a shillin's my price."

After scudding up the hill, puss stopped to listen and ascertain the quality of her pursuers. She had suffered persecution from many hands, shooters, coursers, snarers, and once before from the Major and his harriers. That, however, was on a bad scenting day, and she had not had much difficulty in beating them.

Meanwhile Solomon has been creeping quietly on with his hounds, encouraging such to hunt as seemed inclined that way, though the majority were pretty well aware of the grand discovery and lean towards the horsemen in advance. Puss however had slipped away unseen by the hounds, and Twister darts at the empty form thinking to save all trouble by a chop. Bracelet then strikes a scent in advance. Ruffler and Chaunter confirm it, and after one or two hesitating rashes and flourishes, increasing in intensity each time, a scent is fairly established, and away they drive full cry amid exclamations of "Beautiful! beautiful! never saw anything puttier!" from the Major and the field—the music of the hounds being increased and prolonged by the echoes of the valleys and adjacent hills.

The field then fall into line, Silent Solomon first, the Major of course next. Fine Billy third, with Wotherspoon and Nettlefold rather contending for his company. Nabley, Duffield, Bonnet, Reunison. Fanlder, Catcheside, truants, all mixed up together in heterogeneous confusion, jostling for precedence as men do when there are no leaps. So they round Hawthorn hill, and pour up the pretty valley beyond, each man riding a good deal harder than his horse, the hounds going best pace, which however is not very great.

"Give me,—" inwardly prays the Major, cantering consequentially along with his thong-gathered whip held up like a sword, "give me five and twenty minutes, the first fifteen a burst, then a fault well hit off', and the remaining ten without a turn," thinking to astonish the supercilious foxhunter. Then he takes a sly look to see how Napoleon is faring, it being by no means his intention to let Fine Billy get to the bottom of him.

On, on, the hounds press, for now is the time to enjoy the scent with a hare, and they have ran long enough together to have confidence in their leaders.

Now Lovely has the scent, now Lilter, now Ruffler flings in advance, and again is superseded by Twister.

They brush through the heathery open with an increasing cry, and fling at the cross-road between Birwell Mill and Capstone with something like the energy of foxhounds; Twister catches it up beyond the sandy track, and hurrying over it, some twenty yards further on is superseded by Lovely, who hits it off to the left.

Away she goes with the lead.

"Beautiful! beautiful!" exclaims the Major, hoping the fox-hunter sees it.

"Beautiful! beautiful!" echoes Nettlefold, as the clustering pack drop their sterns to the scent and push forward with renewed velocity.

The Major again looks for our friend Billy, who is riding in a very careless slack-rein sort of style, not at all adapted for making the most of his horse. However it is no time for remonstrance, and the music of the hounds helps to make things pleasant. On, on they speed; up one hill, down another, round a third, and so on.

One great advantage of hunting in a strange country undoubtedly is, that all runs are straight, with harriers as well as foxhounds, with some men, who ride over the same ground again and again without knowing that it is the same, and Billy was one of this sort. Though they rounded Hawthorn hill again, it never occurred to him that it was the second time of asking; indeed he just cantered carelessly on like a man on a watering-place hack, thinking when his hour will be out, regardless of the beautiful hits made by Lovely and Lilter or any of them, and which almost threw the Major and their respective admirers into ecstacies. Great was the praise bestowed upon their performances, it being the interest of every man to magnify the run and astonish the stranger. Had they but known as much of the Richest Commoner as the reader does, they would not have given themselves the trouble.

Away they pour over hill and dale, over soft ground and sound, through reedy rushes and sedgy flats, and over the rolling stones of the fallen rocks.

Then they score away full cry on getting upon more propitious ground. What a cry they make 1 and echo seemingly takes pleasure to repeat the sound!

Napoleon the Great presently begins to play the castanets with his feet, an ominous sound to our Major, who looks back for the Bumbler, and inwardly wishes for a check to favour his design of dismounting our hero.

Half a mile or so further on, and the chance occurs. They get upon a piece of bare heather burnt ground, whose peaty smell baffles the scent, and brings the hounds first to a check, then to a stand-still.

Solomon's hand in the air beckons a halt, to which the field gladly respond, for many of the steeds are eating new oats, and do not get any great quantity of those, while some are on swedes, and others only have hay. Altogether their condition is not to be spoken of.

The Major now all hurry scurry, just like a case of "second horses! second horses! where's my fellow with my second horse?" at a check in Leicestershire, beckons the Bumbler up to Billy; and despite of our friend's remonstrance, who has got on such terms with Napoleon as to allow of his taking the liberty of spurring him, and would rather remain where he is, insists upon putting him upon the mare again, observing, that he couldn't think of taking the only spare 'orse from a gen'lman who had done him the distinguished honour of leaving the Earl's establishment for his 'umble pack; and so, in the excitement of the moment, Billy is hustled off one horse and hurried on to another, as if a moment's hesitation would be fatal to the fray. The Major then, addressing the Bumbler in an undertone, says, "Now walk that 'orse quietly home, and get him some linseed tea, and have him done up by the time we get in." He then spurs gallantly up to the front, as though he expected the hounds to be off again at score. There was no need of such energy, for puss has set them a puzzle that will take them some time to unravel; but it saved an argument with Billy, and perhaps the credit of the bay. He now goes drooping and slouching away, very unlike the cock-horse he came out.

Meanwhile, the hounds have shot out and contracted, and shot out and contracted—and tried and tested, and tried and tested—every tuft and every inch of burnt ground, while Solomon sits motionless between them and the head mopping chattering field.

"Must be on," observes Caleb Rennison, the horse-breaker, whose three-year-old began fidgetting and neighing.

"Back, I say," speculated Bonnet, whose domicile lay to the rear.

"Very odd," observed Captain Nabley, "they ran her well to here."

"Hares are queer things," said old Duffield, wishing he had her by the ears for the pot.

"Far more hunting with a hare nor a fox," observed Mr. Rintoul, who always praised his department of the chase.

"Must have squatted," observes old "Wotherspoon, taking a pinch of snuff, and placing his double gold eye-glasses on his nose to reconnoitre the scene.

"Lies very close, if she has," rejoins Godfrey Faulder, flopping at a furze-bush as he spoke.

"Lost her, I fear," ejaculated Mr. Trail, who meant to beg her for a christening dinner if they killed.

The fact is, puss having, as we said before, had a game at romps with her pursuers On a bad scenting day, when she regulated her speed by their pace, has been inconveniently pressed on the present occasion, and feeling her strength fail, has had recourse to some of the many arts for which hares are famous. After crossing the burnt ground she made for a greasy sheep-track, up which she ran some fifty yards, and then deliberately retracing her steps, threw herself with a mighty spring into a rushy furze patch at the bottom of the hill. She now lies heaving and panting, and watching the success of her stratagem from her ambush, with the terror-striking pack full before her.

And now having accommodated Mr. Pringle with a second horse, perhaps the reader will allow us to take a fresh pen and finish the run in another Chapter.

CHAPTER XXV. A CRUEL FINISH.

EVERY hound having at length sniffed and snuffed, and sniffed and snuffed, to satiety, Solomon now essays to assist them by casting round the flat of smoke-infected ground. He makes the 'head good first, which manouvre hitting off the scent, he is hailed and applauded as a conqueror. Never was such a huntsman as Solomon! First harrier huntsman in England! Worth any money is a huntsman! The again clamorous pack bustle up the sheep-path, at such a pace as sends the leaders hurrying far beyond the scent. Then the rear rush to the front, and a general spread of bewildered, benighted, confusion ensues.

"Where *has* she got to?" is the question.

"Doubled!" mutters the disappointed Major, reining in his steed.

"Squatted!" exclaims Mr. Rintoul, who always sported an opinion.

"Hold hard!" cries Mr. Trail, though they were all at a standstill; but then he wished to let them know he was there.

The leading hounds retrace their steps, and again essay to carry the scent forward. The second effort is attended with the same result as the first. They cannot get it beyond the double.

74

"Cunning animal!" mutters the Major, eyeing their endeavours.

"Far more hunt with a hare nor a fox," now observes Mr. Bonnet, raising his white hat to cool his bald head.

"Far!" replies Mr. Faulder, thinking he must be off.

"If it weren't for the red coats there wouldn't be so many fox-hunters," chuckles old Duffield, who dearly loves roast hare.

Solomon is puzzled; but as he doesn't profess to be wiser than the hounds, he just lets them try to make it out for themselves. If they can't wind her, he can't: so the old sage sits like a statue.

At length the majority give her up.

And now Springer and Pitfall, and two or three other pedestrians who have been attracted from their work by the music of the hounds, and have been enjoying the panorama of the chase with their pipes from the summit of an inside hill, descend to see if they can either prick her or pole her.

Down go their heads as if they were looking for a pin.—The hounds, however, have obliterated all traces of her, and they soon have recourse to their staves.

Bang, bang, bang, they beat the gorse and broom and juniper bushes with vigorous sincerity. Crack, flop, crack, go the field in aid of their endeavours. Solomon leans with his hounds to the left, which is lucky for puss, for though she withstood the downward blow of Springer's pole on her bush, a well-directed side thrust sends her flying out in a state of the greatest excitement. What an outburst of joy the sight of her occasioned! Hounds, horses, riders, all seemed to participate in the common enthusiasm! How they whooped, and halloo'd and shouted! enough to frighten the poor thing out of her wits. Billy and the field have a grand view of her, for she darts first to the right, then to the left, then off the right and again to the left, ere she tucks her long legs under her and strides up Kleeope hill at a pace that looks quite unapproachable. Faulder alone remains where he is, muttering "fresh har" as she goes.

The Major and all the rest of the field hug their horses and tear along in a state of joyous excitement, for they see her life is theirs. They keep the low ground and jump with the hounds at the bridlegate between Greenlaw sheep-walks and Hindhope cairn just as Lovely hits the scent off over the boundary wall, and the rest of the pack endorse her note. They are now on fresh ground, which greatly aids the efforts of the hounds, who push on with a head that the Major thinks ought to procure them a compliment from Billy. Our friend, however, keeps all his compliments for the ladies, not being aware that there is anything remarkable in the performance, which he now begins to wish at an end. He has ridden as long as he likes, quite as much as Mr. Spavin, or any of the London livery stable-keepers, would let him have for half-a-guinea. Indeed he wishes he mayn't have got more than is good for him.

The Major meanwhile, all energy and enthusiasm, rides gallantly forward, for though he is no great hand among the enclosures, he makes a good fight in the hills, especially when, as now, he knows every yard of the country. Many's the towl he's had over it, though to look at his excited face one would think this was his first hunt. He'll now "bet half-a-crown they kill her!" He'll "bet a guinea they kill her!" He'll "bet a fi-pun note they kill her!" He'll "bet half the national debt they kill her!" as Dainty, and Lovely, and Bustler, after dwelling and hesitating over some rushy ground, at length proclaim the scent beyond.

Away they all sweep like the careering wind. On follow the field in glorious excitement. A flock of black-faced sheep next foil the ground—sheep as wild, if not wilder, than the animal the hounds are pursuing. We often think, when we see these strong-scented animals scouring the country, that a good beast of chase has been overlooked for the stag. Why shouldn't an old wiry black-faced tup, with his wild sparkling eyes and spiral horns, afford as good a run as a home-fed deer? Start the tup in his own rough region, and we will be bound to say he will give the hounds and their followers a scramble. The Major now denounces the flying flock—"Oh, those nasty muttons!" exclaims he, "bags of bone rather, for they won't be meat these five years. Wonder how any sane people can cultivate such animals."

The hounds hunt well through the difficulty, or the Major would have been more savage still. On they go, yapping and towling, and howling as before, the Major's confidence in a kill increasing at every stride.

The terror-striking shouts that greeted poor puss's exit from the bush, have had the effect as well of driving her out of her country as of pressing her beyond her strength; and she has no sooner succeeded in placing what she hopes is a comfortable distance between herself and her pursuers, than she again has recourse to those tricks with which nature has so plentifully endowed her. Sinking the hill she makes for the little enclosed allotments below, and electing a bare fallow—bare, except in the matter of whicken grass—she steals quietly in, and commences her performances on the least verdant part of it.

75

First she described a small circle, then she sprung into the middle of it and squatted. Next she jumped up and bounded out in a different direction to the one by which she had entered. She then ran about twenty yards up a furrow, retracing her steps backwards, and giving a roll near where she started from. Then she took three bounding springs to the left, which landed her on the hard headland, and creeping along the side of the wall she finally popped through the water-hole, and squeezed into an incredibly small space between the kerbstone and the gate-post. There she lay with her head to the air, panting and heaving, and listening for her dread pursuers coming. O what agony was hers!

Presently the gallant band came howling and towling over the hill, in all the gay delirium of a hunt without leaps—the Major with difficulty restraining their ardour as he pointed out the brilliance of the performance to Billy—"Most splendid running! most capital hunting! most superb pack!" with a sly "*pish*" and "*sham*" at foxhounds in general, and Sir Mosey's in particular. The Major hadn't got over the Bo-peep business, and never would.

The pack now reached the scene of Puss's frolics, and the music very soon descended from a towering tenour to an insignificant whimper, which at length died out altogether. Soloman and Bulldog were again fixtures, Solomon as usual with his hand up beckoning silence. He knew how weak the scent must be, and how important it was to keep quiet at such a critical period; and let the hounds hit her off if they could.

Puss had certainly given them a Gordian knot to unravel, and not all the hallooing and encouragement in the world could drive them much beyond the magic circle she had described. Whenever the hunt seemed likely to be re-established, it invariably resulted in a return to the place from whence they started. They couldn't get forward with it at all, and poked about, and tested the same ground over and over again.

It was a regular period or full stop.

"Very rum," observed Caleb Rennison, looking first at his three-year-old, then at his watch, thinking that it was about pudding-time.

"She's surely a witch," said Mr. Wotherspoon, taking a prolonged pinch of snuff.

"We'll roast her for one at all events," laughed Mr. Trail, the auctioneer, still hoping to get her.

"First catch your hare, says Mrs. Somebody," responded Captain Nabley, eyeing the sorely puzzled pack.

"O ketch her! we're sure to ketch her," observed Mr. Nettlefold, chucking up his chin and dismounting.

"Not so clear about that," muttered Mr. Rintoul, as Lovely, and Bustler, and Lilter, again returned to repeat the search.

"If those hounds can't own her, there are no hounds in England can," asserted the Major, anxious to save the credit of his pack before the—he feared—too critical stranger.

At this depressing moment, again come the infantry, and commence the same system of peering and poking that marked their descent on the former occasion.

And now poor puss being again a little recruited, steals out of her hiding-place, and crosses quietly along the outside of the wall to where a flock of those best friends to a hunted hare, some newly-smeared, white-faced sheep, were quietly nibbling at the halfgrass, half-heather, of the little moor-edge farm of Mossheugh-law, whose stone-roofed buildings, washed by a clear mountain stream, and sheltered by a clump of venerable Scotch firs, stand on a bright green patch, a sort of oasis in the desert. The sheep hardly deign to notice the hare, far different to the consternation bold Reynard carries into their camp, when they go circling round like a squadron of dragoons, drawing boldly up to charge when the danger's past. So poor, weary, foot sore, fur-matted puss, goes hobbling and limping up to the farm-buildings as if to seek protection from man against his brother man.

Now it so happened that Mrs. Kidwell, the half-farmer, halfshepherd's pretty wife, was in the fold-yard, washing her churn, along with her little chubby-faced Jessey, who was equally busy with her Mamma munching away at a very long slice of plentifully-buttered and sugar'd bread; and Mamma chancing to look up from the churn to see how her darling progressed, saw puss halting at the threshold, as if waiting to be asked in.

"It's that mad old Major and his dogs!" exclaimed Mrs. Kidwell, catching up the child lest its red petticoat might scare away the visitor, and popping into the dairy, she saw the hare, after a little demur, hobble into the cow-house. Having seen her well in, Mrs. Kidwell emerged from her hiding-place, and locking the door, she put the key in her pocket, and resumed her occupation with her churn. Presently the familiar melody—the yow, yow, yap, yap, yow, yow of the hounds broke upon her ear, increasing in strength as she listened, making her feel glad she was at hand to befriend the poor hare.

The hunt was indeed revived. The hounds, one and all, having declared their inability to make any thing more of it.

Solomon had set off on one of his cruises, which resulted in the yeomen prickers and he meeting at the gate, where the hare had squatted, when Lovely gave tongue, just as Springer, with his eyes well down, exclaimed, "*here she's!*" Bustler, and Bracelet, and Twister, and Chaunter, confirmed Lovely's opinion, and away they went with the feeble scent peculiar to the sinking animal. Their difficulties are further increased by the sheep, it requiring Solomon's oft-raised hand to prevent the hounds being hurried over the line—as it is, the hunt was conducted on the silent system for some little distance. The pace rather improved after they got clear of the smear and foil of the muttons, and the Major pulled up his gills, felt his tie, and cocked his hat jauntily, as the hounds pointed for the pretty farm-house, the Major thinking to show off to advantage before Mrs. Kidwell. They presently carried the scent up to the still open gates of the fold-yard. Lovely now proclaims where puss has paused. Things look very critical.

"Good mornin', Mrs. Kidwell," exclaimed the gallant Major, addressing her; "pray how long have you been at the churn?"

"O, this twenty minutes or more, Major," replied Mrs. Kidwell, gaily.

"You haven't got the hare in it, have you?" asked he.

"Not that I know of; but you can look if you like," replied Mrs. Kidwell, colouring slightly.

"Why, no; we'll take your word for it," rejoined the Major gallantly. "Must be on, Solomon; must be on," said he—nodding his huntsman to proceed.

Solomon is doubtful, but "master being master," Solomon holds his hounds on past the stable, round the lambing-sheds and stackyard, to the front of the little three windows and a doored farm-house, without eliciting a whimper, no, not even from a babbler.

Just at this moment a passing cloud discharged a gentle shower over the scene, and when Solomon returned to pursue his inquiries in the fold-yard, the last vestige of scent had been effectually obliterated.

Mrs. Kidwell now stood watching the inquisitive proceedings if the party, searching now the hen-house, now the pigstye, now the ash-hole; and when Solomon tried the cow-house door, she observed carelessly: "Ah, that's locked;" and he passed on to examine the straw-shed adjoining. All places were overhauled and scrutinized. At length, even Captain Nabley's detective genius failed in suggesting where puss could be.

"Where did you see her last?" asked Mrs. Kidwell, with well-feigned ignorance.

"Why, we've not seen her for some time; but the hounds hunted her up to your very gate," replied the Major.

"Deary me, how strange! and you've made nothin' of her since?" observed she.

"Nothin'," assented the Major, reluctantly.

"Very odd," observed Mr. Catcheside, who was anxious for a kill.

"Never saw nothin' like it," asserted Mr. Rintoul, looking again into the pigstye.

"She must have doubled back," suggested Mr. Nettlefold.

"Should have met her if she had," observed old Duffield.

"She must be somewhere hereabouts," observes Mr. Trail, dismounting, and stamping about on foot among the half-trodden straw of the fold-yard.

No puss there.

"Hard upon the hounds," observes Mr. Wotherspoon, replenishing his nose with a good charge of snuff.

"*Cruel*, indeed," assented the Major, who never gave them more than entrails.

"Never saw a hare better hunted!" exclaimed Captain Nabley, lighting a cigar.

"Nor I," assented fat Mr. Nettleford, mopping his brow.

"How long was it?" asked Mr. Rintoul.

"An hour and five minutes," replied the Major, looking at his watch (five-and-forty minutes in reality).

"V-a-a-ry good running," elaborates old dandy Wortherspoon. "I see by the *Post*, that——"

"Well, I s'pose we must give her up," interrupted the Major, who didn't want to have the contents of his own second-hand copy forestalled.

"Pity to leave her," observes Mr. Trail, returning to his horse.

"What can you do?" asked the Major, adding, "it's no use sitting here."

"None," assents Captain Nabley, blowing a cloud.

At a nod from the Major, Solomon now collects his hounds, and passing through the scattered group, observes with a sort of Wellingtonian touch of his cap, in reply to their condolence, "Yes, sir, but it takes a *slee* chap, sir, to kill a moor-edge hare, sir!"

So the poor Major was foiled of his fur, and when the cows came lowing down from the fell to be milked, kind Mrs. Kidwell opened the door and out popped puss, as fresh and lively as ever; making for her old haunts, where she was again to be found at the end of a week.

CHAPTER XXVI. THE PRINGLE CORRESPONDENCE.

THE reader will perhaps wonder what our fair friend Mrs. Pringle is about, and how there happens to be no tidings from Curtain Crescent. Tidings there were, only the Tantivy Castle servants were so oppressed with work that they could never find time to redirect her effusions. At length Mr. Beverage, the butler, seeing the accumulation of letters in Mr. Packwood, the house-steward's room, suggested that they might perhaps be wanted, whereupon Mr. Packwood huddled them into a fresh envelope, and sent them to the post along with the general consignment from the Castle. Very pressing and urgent the letters were, increasing in anxiety with each one, as no answer had been received to its predecessor. Were it not that Mrs. Pringle knew the Earl would have written, she would have feared her Billy had sustained some hunting calamity. The first letter merely related how Mrs. Pringle had gone to uncle Jerry's according to appointment to have a field-day among the papers, and how Jerry had gone to attend an anti-Sunday-band meeting, leaving seed-cake, and sponge-cake, and wine, with a very affectionate three-cornered note, saying how deeply he deplored the necessity, but how he hoped to remedy the delay by another and an early appointment. This letter enclosed a very handsome large coat-of-arms seal, made entirely out of Mrs. Pringle's own head—containing what the heralds call assumptive arms—divided into as many compartments as a backgammon board, which she advised Billy to use judiciously, hinting that Major H. (meaning our friend Major Y.) would be a fitter person to try it upon than Lord L. The next letter, among many other things of minor importance, reminded Billy that he had not told his Mamma what Mrs. Moffatt had on, or whether they had any new dishes for dinner, and urging him to write her full particulars, but to be careful not to leave either his or her letters lying about, and hoping that he emptied his pockets every night instead of leaving that for Rougier to do, and giving him much other good and wholesome advice. The third letter was merely to remind him that she had not heard from him in answer to either of her other two, and begging him just to drop her a single line by return of post, saying he was well, and so on. The next was larger, enclosing him a double-crest seal, containing a lion on a cap of dignity, and an eagle, for sealing notes in aid of the great seal, and saying that she had had a letter from uncle Jerry, upbraiding her for not keeping her appointment with him, whereas she had never made any, he having promised to make one with her, and again urging Billy to write to her, if only a single line, and when he had time to send her a full account of what Mrs. Moffatt had on every day, and whether they had any new dishes for dinner, and all the news, sporting and otherwise, urging him as before to take care of Dowb (meaning himself), and hoping he was improving in his hunting, able to sit at the jumps, and enjoying himself generally..

The fifth, which caused the rest to come, was a mere repetition of her anxieties and requests for a line, and immediately produced the following letter:—

MR. WILLIAM TO HIS MAMMA.

"Yammerton Grange.

"My dearest Mamma,

"Your letters have all reached me at once, for though both Rougier and I especially charged the butler and another fine fellow, and gave them heads to put on, to send all that came immediately, they seem to have waited for an accumulation so as to make one sending do. It is very idle of them.

"The seals are beautiful, and I am very much obliged to you for them. I will seal this letter with the large one by way of a beginning. It seems to be uncommonly well quartered—quite noble.

"I will now tell you all my movements.

"I have been here at Major Yammerton"s,—not Hammerton's as you called him—for some days enjoying myself amazingly, for the Major has a nice pack of harriers that go along leisurely, instead of tearing away at the unconscionable pace the Earl's do. Still, a canter in the Park at high tide in my opinion is a much better thing with plenty of ladies looking on. Talking of cantering reminds me I've bought a horse of the Major's,—bought him all except paying for him, so you had better send me the money, one hundred guineas; for though the Major says I may pay for him when I like, and seems quite easy about it, they say horses are always ready money, so I suppose I must conform to the rule. It is a beautiful bay with four black legs, and a splendid mane and tail—very blood-like and racing; indeed the Major says if I was to put him into some of the spring handicaps I should be sure to win a hatful of money with him, or perhaps a gold cup or two. The Major is a great sportsman and has kept hounds for a great number of years, and altogether he is very agreeable, and I feel more at home here than I did at the Castle, where, though everything was very fine, still there was no fun and only Mrs. Moffatt to talk to, at least in the lady way, for though she always professed to be expecting lady callers, none ever came that I saw or heard of.

"I really forget all about the dinners there, except that they were very good and lasted a long time. We had a new dish here the other night, which if you want a novelty, you can introduce, namely, to flavour the plates with castor oil; you will find it a very serviceable one for saving your meat, as nobody can eat it. Mrs. Moffatt was splendidly dressed every day, sometimes in blue, sometimes in pink, sometimes in green, sometimes in silk, sometimes in satin, sometimes in velvet with a profusion of very lovely lace and magnificent jewelry. Rougier says, 'she makes de hay vile the son does shine.'

"I don't know how long I shall stay here, certainly over Friday, and most likely until Monday, after which I suppose I shall go back to the Castle. The Major says I must have another day with his hounds, and I don't care if I do, provided he keeps in the hills and away from the jumps, as I can manage the galloping well enough. It's the jerks that send me out of my saddle. A hare is quite a different animal to pursue to a fox, and seems to have some sort of consideration for its followers. She stops short every now and then and jumps up in view, instead of tearing away like an express train on a railway.

"The girls here are very pretty—Miss Yammerton extremely so,—fair, with beautiful blue eyes, and such a figure; but Rougier says they are desperately bad-tempered, except the youngest one, who is dark and like her Mamma; but I shouldn't say Monsieur is a particular sweet-tempered gentleman himself. He is always grumbling and grouting about what he calls his 'grob' and declares the Major keeps his house on sturdied mutton and stale beer. But he complained at the Castle that there was nothing but port and sherry, and composite candles to go to bed with, which he declared was an insult to his station, which entitles him to wax.

"You can't, think how funny and small this place looked after the Castle. It seemed just as if I had got into a series of closets instead of rooms. However, I soon got used to it, and like it amazingly. But here comes Monsieur with my dressing things, so I must out with the great seat and bid you good bye for the present, for the Major is a six o'clock man, and doesn't like to be kept waiting for his dinner, so now, my dearest Mamma, believe me. to remain ever your most truly affectionate son,

"Wm. Pringle,"

To which we need scarcely say the delighted Mrs. Pringle replied by return of post, writing in the following loving and judicious strain.

"25, Curtain Crescent,

"Belgrave Square.

"My own Beloved Darling,

"I was so overjoyed you can't imagine, to receive your most welcome letter, for I really began to be uneasy about you, not that I feared any accident out hunting, but I was afraid you might have caught cold or be otherwise unwell—mind, if ever you feel in the slightest degree indisposed send for the doctor immediately. There is nothing like taking things in time. It was very idle of the servants at Tantivy Castle to neglect your instructions so, but for the future you had better always write a line to the post-master of the place where you are staying, giving him your next address to forward your letters to; for it is the work for which they are paid, and there is no shuffling it off on to anybody elses shoulders. The greatest people are oftentimes the worst served, not because the servants have any particular objection to them personally—but because they are so desperately afraid of being what they call put upon by each other, that they spend double the time in fighting off doing a thing that it would take to do it. This is one of the drawbacks upon rank. Noblemen must keep a great staff of people, whom in a general way they cannot employ, and who do nothing but squabble and fight with each other who is to do the little there is, the greatest man among servants being he who does the least. However, as you have got the letters at last we will say no more about it.

"I hope your horse is handsome, and neighs and paws the ground prettily; you should be careful, however, in buying, for few people are magnanimous enough to resist cheating a young man in horses;—still, I am glad you have bought one if he suits you, as it is much better and pleasanter to ride your own horse than be indebted to other people for mounts. Nevertheless, I would strongly advise you to stick to either the fox or the stag, with either of which you can sport pink and look smart. Harriers are only for bottle-nosed old gentlemen with gouty shoes. I can't help thinking, that a day with a milder, more reasonable fox than the ones you had with Lord

Ladythorne, would convince you of the superiority of fox-hounds over harriers. I was asking Mr. Ralph Rasper, who called here the other day, how little Tom Stott of the Albany managed with the Queen's, and he said Tom always shoes his horses with country nails, and consequently throws a shoe before he has gone three fields, which enables him to pull up and lament his ill luck. He then gets it put on, and has a glorious ride home in red—landing at the Piccadilly end of the Albany about dusk. He then goes down to the Acacia or some other Club, and having ordered his dinner, retires to one of the dressing-rooms to change—having had, to his mind, a delightful day.

"Beware of the girls!—There's nothing so dangerous as a young man staying in a country house with pretty girls. He is sure to fall in love with one or other of them imperceptibly, or one or other of them is sure to fall in love with him; and then when at length he leaves, there is sure to be a little scene arranged, Miss with her red eye-lids and lace fringed kerchief, Mamma with her smirks and smiles, and hopes that he'll *soon return,* and so on. There are more matches made up in country houses than in all the west-end London ones put together,—indeed, London is always allowed to be only the cover for finding the game in, and the country the place for running it down. Just as you find your fox in a wood and run him down in the open. Be careful therefore what you are about.

"It is much easier to get entangled with a girl than to get free again, for though they will always offer to set a young man free, they know better than do it, unless, indeed, they have secured something better,—above all, never consult a male friend in these matters.

"The stupidest woman that ever was born, is belter than the cleverest man in love-affairs. In fact, no man is a match for a woman until he's married,—not all even then. The worst of young men is, they never know their worth until it is too late—they think the girls are difficult to catch, whereas there is nothing so easy, unless, as I said before, the girls are better engaged. Indeed, a young man should always have his Mamma at his elbow, to guard him against the machinations of the fair. As, however, that cannot be, let me urge you to be cautious what you are about, and as you seem to have plenty of choice, Don't be more attentive to one sister than to another, by which means you will escape the red eye-lids, and also escape having Mamma declaring you have trifled with Maria or Sophia's feelings, and all the old women of the neighbourhood denouncing your conduct and making up to you themselves for one of their own girls. Some ladies ask a man's intentions before he is well aware that he has any himself, but these are the spoil-sport order of women. Most of them are prudent enough to get a man well hooked before they hand him over to Papa, it is generally a case of 'Ask Mamma first. Beware of brothers!—I have known undoubted heiresses crumpled up into nothing by the appearance (after the catch) of two or three great heavy dragooners. Rougier will find all that out for you.

"Be cautious too about letter-writing. There is no real privacy about love-letters, any more than there is about the flags and banners of a regiment, though they occasionally furl and cover them up. The love letters are a woman's flags and banners, her trophies of success, and the more flowery they are, the more likely to be shown, and to aid in enlivening a Christmas tea-party. Then the girls' Mammas read them, their sisters read them, their maids read them, and ultimately, perhaps, a boisterous energetic barrister reads them to an exasperated jury, some of whose daughters may have suffered from simitar effusions themselves. Altogether, I assure you, you are on very ticklish ground, and I make no doubt if you could ascertain the opinion of the neighbourhood, you are booked for one or other of the girls, so again I say, my dearest boy, beware what you are about, for it is much easier to get fast than to get free again;—get a lady of rank, and not the daughter of a little scrubby squire; and whatever you do, don't leave this letter lying about, and mind, empty your pockets at nights, and don't leave it for Rougier to find.

"Now, about your movements. I think I wouldn't go back to Lord L.'s unless he asks you, or unless he named a specific day for your doing so when you came away. Mere general invitations mean nothing; they are only the small coin of good society. 'Sorry you're going. Hope we shall soon meet again. Hope we shall have the pleasure of seeing you to dinner some day,' is a very common mean-nothing form of politeness.

"Indeed, I question that your going to a master of harriers from Tantivy Castle would be any great recommendation to his Lordship; for masters of foxhounds and masters of harriers are generally at variance. Altogether, I think I would pause and consider before you decided on returning. I would not talk much about his Lordship where you now are, as it would look as if you were not accustomed to great people. You'll find plenty of friends ready to bring him in for you, just as Mr. Handycock brings in Lord Privilege in Peter Simple. We all like talking of titles. Remember, all noblemen under the rank of dukes are lords in common conversation. No earls or marquises then.

"It just occurs to me, that as you are in the neighbourhood, you might take advantage of the opportunity for paying a visit to Yawnington Hot Wells, where you will find a great deal of good society assembled at this time of year, and where you might pickup some useful and desirable acquaintances. Go to the best hotel whatever it is, and put Rougier on board wages, which will get rid of his grumbling. It is impertinent, no doubt, but still it carries weight in a certain quarter.

"As you have got a hunting horse, you will want a groom, and should try to get a nice-looking one. He should not be knocknee'd; on the contrary, bow-legged,—the sort of legs that a pig can pop through. Look an applicant over first, and if his appearance is against him. just put him off quietly by taking his name and address, and say that there are one or two before him, and that you will write to him if you are likely to require his services.

"You will soon have plenty to choose from, but it is hard to say whether the tricks of the town ones, or the gaucheries of the country ones are most objectionable. The latter never put on their boots and upper things properly. A slangy, slovenly-looking fellow should be especially avoided. Also men with great shock heads of hair. If they can't trim themselves, there will not be much chance of their trimming their horses. In short, I believe a groom—a man who really knows and cares anything about horses—is a very difficult person to get. There are plenty who can hiss and fuss, and be busy upon nothing, but very few who can both dress a horse, and dress themselves.

"I know Lord Ladythorne makes it a rule never to take one who has been brought up in the racing-stable, for he says they are all hurry and gallop, and for putting two hours' exercise into one. Whatever you do, don't take one without a character, for however people may gloss over their late servant's faults and imperfections, and however abject and penitent the applicants may appear, rely upon it, nature will out, and as soon as ever they yet up their condition, as they call it, or are installed into their new clothes, they begin to take liberties, and ultimately relapse into their old drunken dissolute habits. It is fortunate for the world that most of them carry their characters in their faces. Besides, it isn't fair to respectable servants to bring them in contact with these sort of profligates.

"Whatever you do, don't let him find his own clothes. There isn't one in twenty who can be trusted to do so, and nothing looks worse than the half-livery, half-plain, wholly shabby clothes some of them adopt.

"It is wonderful what things they will vote good if they have to find others themselves, things that they would declare were not fit to put on, and they couldn't be seen in if master supplied them. The best of everything then is only good enough for them.

"Some of them will grumble and growl whatever you give them; declare this man's cloth is bad, and another's boots inferior, and recommend you to go to Mr. Somebody else, who Mr. This, or Captain That, employs, Mr. This, or Captain That, having, in all probability, been recommended to this Mr. Somebody by some other servant. The same with the saddlers and tradespeople generally. If you employ a saddler who does not tip them, there will be nothing bad enough for his workmanship, or they will declare he does not do that sort of work, only farmer's work—cart-trappings, and such like things.

"The remedy for this is to pay your own bills, and give the servants to understand at starting that you mean to be master. They are to be had on your own terms, if you only begin as you mean to go on. If the worst comes to the worst, a month's notice, or a month's pay, settles all differences, and it is no use keeping and paying a servant that doesn't suit you. Perhaps you will think Rougier trouble enough, but he would be highly offended if you were to ask him to valet a horse. I will try if I can hear of anything likely to suit you, but the old saying, 'who shall counsel a man in the choice of a wife, or a horse,' applies with equal force to grooms.

"And now, my own dearest boy, having given you all the advice and assistance in my power, I will conclude by repeating what joy the arrival of your letter occasioned me, and also my advice to beware of the girls, and request that you will not leave this letter in your pockets, or lying about, by signing myself ever, my own dearest son, your most truly loving and affectionate Mamma,

"Emma Pringle.

"*P.S.—I will enclose the halves of two fifty-pound notes for the horse, the receipt of which please to acknowledge by return of post, when I will send the other halves.*

"P.S.—Mind the red eyelids! There's nothing so infectious

CHAPTER XXVII. SIR MOSES MAINCHANCE.

OUR friend Billy, as the foregoing letter shows, was now very comfortably installed in his quarters, and his presence brought sundry visitors, as well to pay their respects to him and the family, as to see how matters were progressing.

Mr. and Mrs. Rocket Larkspur, Mrs. Blurkins, and Mrs. Dotheringfcon, also Mrs. Crickleton came after their castor-oil entertainment, and Mrs. and Miss Wasperton, accompanied by their stiff friend Miss Freezer, who had the reputation of being very satirical. Then there were Mr. Tight and Miss Neate, chaperoned by fat Mrs. Plumberry, of Hollingdale Lodge, and several others. In fact Billy had created a sensation in the country, such godsends as a London dandy not being of every-day occurrence in the country, and everybody wanted to see the great "catch." How they magnified him! His own mother wouldn't have known him under the garbs he assumed; now a Lord's son, now a Baronet's, now the Richest Commoner in England; with, oh glorious recommendation! no Papa to consult in the matter of a wife. Some said not even a Mamma, but there the reader knows they were wrong. In proportion as they lauded Billy they decried Mrs. Yammerton; she was a nasty, cunning, designing woman, always looking after somebody.

Mrs. Wasperton, alluding to Billy's age, declared that it was just like kidnapping a child, and she inwardly congratulated herself that she had never been guilty of such meanness. Billy, on his part, was airified and gay, showing off to the greatest advantage, perfectly unconscious that he was the observed of all observers. Like Mrs. Moffatt he never had the same dress on twice, and was splendid in his jewelry.

Among the carriage company who came to greet him was the sporting Baronet, Sir Moses Mainchance, whose existence we have already indicated, being the same generous gentleman that presented Major Yammerton with a horse, and then made him pay for it.

Sir Moses had heard of Billy's opulence, and being a man of great versatility, he saw no reason why he should not endeavour to partake of it. He now came grinding up in his dog cart, with his tawdry cockaded groom (for he was a Deputy-Lieutenant of Hit-im and Holt-im shire), to lay the foundation of an invitation, and was received with the usual *wow, wow, wow, wow,* of Fury, the terrier, and the coat shuffling of the Bumbler.

If the late handsome Recorder of London had to present this ugly old file to the Judges as one of the Sheriffs of London and Middlesex, he would most likely introduce him in such terms as the following:—

"My Lords, I have the honour to present to your Lordships' (hem) notice Sir Moses Mainchance, (cough) Baronet, and (hem) foxhunter, who has been unanimously chosen by the (hem) livery of London to fill the high and important (cough) office of Sheriff of that ancient and opulent city. My Lords, Sir Moses, as his name indicates, is of Jewish origin. His great-grandfather, Mr. Moses Levy, I believe dealt in complicated penknives, dog-collars, and street sponges. His grandfather, more ambitious, enlarged his sphere of action, and embarked in the old-clothes line. He had a very extensive shop in the Minories, and dealt in rhubarb and gum arabic as well. He married a lady of the name of Smith, not an uncommon one in this country, who inheriting a large fortune from her uncle, Mr. Mainchance, Mr. Moses Levy embraced Christianity, and dropping the name of Levy became Mr. Mainchance, Mr. Moses Mainchance, the founder of the present most important and distinguished family. His son, the Sheriff elect's father, also carried on the business in the Minories, adding very largely to his already abundant wealth, and espousing a lady of the name of Brown.

"In addition to the hereditary trade he opened a curiosity shop in the west end of London, where, being of a highly benevolent disposition, he accommodated young gentlemen whose parents were penurious,—unjustly penurious of course,—with such sums of money as their stations in life seemed likely to enable them to repay.

"But, my Lords, the usury laws, as your Lordships will doubtless recollect, being then in full operation, to the great detriment of heirs-at-law, Mr. Mainchance, feeling for the difficulties of the young, introduced an ingenious mode of evading them, whereby *some* article of *vertu*— generally a picture or something of that sort—was taken as half, or perhaps three-quarters of the loan, and having passed into the hands of the borrower was again returned to Mr. Mainchance at its real worth, a Carlo Dolce, or a Coal Pit, as your Lordships doubtless know, being capable of representing any given sum of money. This gentleman, my Lords, the Sheriff elect's father, having at length paid the debt of nature—the only debt I believe that he was ever slow in discharging—the opulent gentleman who now stands at my side, and whom I have the honour of presenting to the Court, was enabled through one of those monetary transactions to claim the services of a distinguished politician now no more, and obtain that hereditary rank which he so greatly adorns. On becoming a baronet Sir Moses Mainchance withdrew from commercial pursuits, and set up for a gentleman, purchasing the magnificent estate of Pangburn Park, in Hit-im and Hold-im shire, of which county he is a Deputy-Lieutenant, getting together an unrivalled pack of foxhounds—second to none as I am instructed—and hunting the country with great circumspection; and he requests me to add, he will be most proud and happy to see your Lordships to take a day with his hounds whenever it suits you, and also to dine with him this evening in the splendid Guildhall of the ancient and renowned City of London.'"

The foregoing outline, coupled with Sir Moses' treatment of the Major, will give the reader some idea of the character of the gentleman who had sought the society of our hero. In truth, if nature had not made him the meanest, Sir Moses would have been the most liberal of mankind, for his life was a continual struggle between the magnificence of his offers and the penury of his performances. He was perpetually forcing favours upon people, and then backing out when he saw they were going to be accepted. It required no little face to encounter the victim of such a recent "do" as the Major's, but Sir Moses was not to be foiled when he had an object in view. Telling his groom to stay at the door, and asking in a stentorian voice if Mr. Pringle is at home, so that there may be no mistake as to whom he is calling upon, the Baronet is now ushered into the drawing-room, where the dandified Billy sits in all the dangerous proximity of three pretty girls without their Mamma. Mrs. Yammerton knew when to be out. "Good morning, young ladies!" exclaims Sir Moses gaily, greeting them all round—"Mr. Pringle," continued he, turning to Billy, "allow me to introduce myself—I believe I have the pleasure of addressing a nephew of my excellent old friend Sir Jonathan Pringle, and I shall be most happy if I can contribute in any way to your amusement while in this neighbourhood. Tell me now," continued he, without waiting for Billy's admission or rejection of kindred with Sir Jonathan, "tell me now, when you are not engaged in this delightful way," smiling round on the beauties, "would you like to come and have a day with my hounds?"

Billy shuddered at the very thought, but quickly recovering his equanimity, he replied, "Yarse, he should like it very much.

"Oh, Mr. Pringle's a mighty hunter!" exclaimed Miss Yammerton, who really thought he was.—"Very good!" exclaimed Sir Moses, "very good! Then I'll tell you what we'll do. We meet on Monday at the Crooked Billet on the Bushmead Road—Tuesday at Stubbington Hill—Thursday, Woolerton, by Heckfield—Saturday, the Kennels. S'pose now you come to me on Sunday, I would have said Saturday, only I'm engaged to dine with Lord Oilcake, but you wouldn't mind coming over on a Sunday, I dare say, would you?" and without waiting for an answer he went on to say, "Come on Sunday, I'll send my dogcart for you, the thing I have at the door, we'll then hunt Monday and Tuesday, dine at the Club at Hinton on Wednesday, where we always have a capital dinner, and a party of excellent fellows, good singing and all sorts of fun, and take Thursday at Woolerton, in your way home—draw Shawley Moss, the Withy beds at Langton, Tangleton Brake, and so on, but sure to find before we get to the Brake, for there were swarms of foxes on the moss the last time we were there, and capital good ones they are. Dom'd if they aren't. So know I think you couldn't be better Thursday, and I'll have a two-stalled stable ready for you on Sunday, so that's a bargain—ay, young ladies, isn't it?" appealing to our fair friends. And now fine Billy, who had been anxiously waiting to get a word in sideways while all this dread enjoyment was paraded, proceeded to make a vigorous effort to deliver himself from it. He was very much obliged to this unknown friend of his unknown uncle, Sir Jonathan, but he had only one horse, and was afraid he must decline. "Only one horse!" exclaimed Sir Moses, "only one horse!" who had heard he had ten, "ah, well, never mind," thinking he would sell him one. "I'll tell you what I'll do, I'll mount you on the Tuesday—I'll mount you on the Tuesday—dom'd if I won't—and that'll make it all right—and that'll make all right." So extending his hand he said, "Come on Sunday then, come on Sunday," and, bowing round to the ladies, he backed out of the room lest his friend the Major might appear and open his grievance about the horse. Billy then accompanied him to the door, where Sir Moses, pointing to the gaudy vehicle, said, "Ah, there's the dog-cart you see, there's the dog-cart, much at your service, much at your service," adding, as he placed his foot upon the step to ascend, "Our friend the Major here I make no doubt will lend you a horse to put in it, and between ourselves," concluded he in a lower tone, "you may as well try if you can't get him to lend you a second horse to bring with you." So saying, Sir Moses again shook hands most fervently with his young friend, the nephew of Sir Jonathan, and mounting the vehicle soused down in his seat and drove off with the air of a Jew bailiff in his Sunday best.

Of course, when Billy returned to the drawing-room the young ladies were busy discussing the Baronet, aided by Mamma, who had gone up stairs on the sound of wheels to reconnoitre her person, and was disappointed on coming down to find she had had her trouble for nothing.

If Sir Moses had been a married man instead of a widower, without incumbrance as the saying is, fine Billy would have been more likely to have heard the truth respecting him, than he was as matters stood. As it was, the ladies had always run Sir Moses up, and did not depart from that course on the present occasion. Mrs. Yammerton, indeed, always said that he looked a great deal older than he really was, and had no objection to his being talked of for one of her daughters, and as courtships generally go by contraries, the fair lady of the glove with her light sunny hair, and lambent blue eyes, rather admired Sir Moses' hook-nose and clear olive complexion than otherwise. His jewelry, too, had always delighted her, for he had a stock equal to that of any retired pawnbroker. So they impressed Billy very favourably with the Baronet's pretensions, far more favourably the reader may be-sure than the Recorder did the Barons of the Court of Exchequer.

CHAPTER XXVIII. THE HIT-IM AND HOLD-IM SHIRE HOUNDS.

DESCENDING Long Benningborough Hill on the approach from the west, the reader enters the rich vale of Hit-im and Hold-im shire, rich in agricultural productions, lavish of rural beauties, and renowned for the strength and speed of its foxes.

As a hunting country Hit-im and Hold-im shire ranks next to Featherbedfordshire, and has always been hunted by men of wealth and renown. The great Mr. Bruiser hunted it at one time, and was succeeded by the equally great Mr. Customer, who kept it for upwards of twenty years. He was succeeded by Mr. Charles Crasher, after whom came the eminent Lord Martingal, who most materially improved its even then almost perfect features by the judicious planting of gorse covers on the eastern or Droxmoor side, where woodlands are deficient.

It was during Lord Martingal's reign that Hit-im and Hold-im shire may be said to have attained the zenith of its fame, for he was liberal in the extreme, not receiving a farthing subscription, and maintaining the Club at the Fox and Hounds Hotel at Hinton with the greatest spirit and popularity. He reigned over Hit-im and Hold-im shire for the period of a quarter of a century, his retirement being at length caused by a fall from his horse, aggravated by distress at seeing his favourite gorses Rattle-ford and Chivington cut up by a branch-line of the Crumpletin railway.

On his lordship's resignation, the country underwent the degradation of passing into the hands of the well-known Captain Flasher, a gentleman who, instead of keeping hounds, as Lord Martingal had done, expected the hounds to keep him. To this end he organised a subscription— a difficult thing to realise even when men have got into the habit of paying, or perhaps promising one—but most difficult when, as in this case, they had long been accustomed to have their hunting for nothing. It is then that the beauties of a free pack are apparent. The Captain, however, nothing daunted by the difficulty, applied the screw most assiduously, causing many gentlemen to find out that they were just going to give up hunting, and others that they must go abroad to economise. This was just about the gloomy time that our friend the Major was vacillating between Boulogne and Bastille; and it so happened that Mr. Plantagenet Brown, of Pangburn Park, whose Norman-conquest family had long been pressing on the vitals of the estate, taking all out and putting nothing in, suddenly found themselves at the end of their tether. The estate had collapsed. Then came the brief summing-up of a long career of improvidence in the shape of an auctioneer's advertisement, offering the highly valuable freehold property, comprising about two thousand five hundred acres in a ring fence, with a modern mansion replete with every requisite for a nobleman or gentleman's seat, for sale, which, of course, brought the usual train of visitors, valuers, Paul-Pryers, and so on—some lamenting the setting, others speculating on the rising sun.

At the sale, a most repulsive, poverty-stricken looking little old Jew kept protracting the biddings when everybody else seemed done, in such a way as to cause the auctioneer to request an *imparlance*, in order that he might ascertain who his principal was; when the Jew, putting his dirty hands to his bearded mouth, whispered in the auctioneer's ear, "Shir Moshes Main-chance," whereupon the languid biddings were resumed, and the estate was ultimately knocked down to the Baronet.

Then came the ceremony of taking possession—the carriage-and-four, the flags, the band of music, the triumphal arch, the fervid address and heartfelt reply, amid the prolonged cheers of the wretched pauperised tenantry.

That mark of respect over, let us return to the hounds.

Captain Flasher did not give satisfaction, which indeed was not to be expected, considering that he wanted a subscription. No man would have given satisfaction under the circumstances, but the Captain least of all, because he brought nothing into the common stock, nothing, at least, except his impudence, of which the members of the hunt had already a sufficient supply of their own. The country was therefore declared vacant at the end of the Captain's second season, the Guarantee Committee thinking it best to buy him off the third one, for which he had contracted to hunt it. This was just about the time that Sir Moses purchased Pangburn Park, and, of course, the country was offered to him. A passion for hunting is variously distributed, and Sir Moses had his share of it. He was more than a mere follower of hounds, for he took a pleasure in their working and management, and not knowing much about the cost, he jumped at the offer, declaring he didn't want a farthing subscription, no, not a farthing: he wouldn't even have a cover fund—no, not even a cover fund! He'd pay keepers, stoppers, damage, everything himself,—dom'd if he wouldn't. Then when he got possession of the country, he declared that he found it absolutely indispensable for the promotion of sport, and the good of them all, that there should be a putting together of purses—every man ought to have a direct interest in the preservation of foxes, and, therefore, they should all pay five guineas,—just five guineas a-year to a cover fund. It wasn't fair that he should pay all the cost—dom'd if it was. He wouldn't stand it—dom'd if he would.

Then the next season he declared that five guineas was all moonshine—it would do nothing in the way of keeping such a country as Hit-im and Hold-im shire together—it must be ten guineas, and that would leave a great balance for him to pay. Well, ten guineas he got, and emboldened by his success, at the commencement of the next season he got a grand gathering together, at a hand-in-the-pocket hunt dinner at the Fox and Hounds Hotel at Hinton, to which he presented a case of champagne, when his health being drunk with suitable enthusiasm, he got up and made them a most elaborate speech on the pleasures and advantages of fox-hunting, which he declared was like meat, drink, washing and lodging to him, and to which he mainly attributed the very excellent health which they had just been good enough to wish him a continuance of in such complimentary terms, that he was almost overpowered by it. He was glad to see that he was not a monopoliser of the inestimable blessings of health, for, looking round the table, he thought he never saw such an assemblage of cheerful contented countenances—(applause)—and it was a great satisfaction to him to think that he in any way contributed to make them so—(renewed applause). He had been thinking since he came into the room whether it was possible to increase in any way the general stock of prosperity—(great applause)—and considering the success that had already marked his humble endeavours, he really thought that there was nothing like sticking to the same medicine, and, if possible, increasing the dose; for—(the conclusion of this sentence was lost in the general applause that followed). Having taken an inspiriting sip of wine, he thus resumed, "He now hunted the country three days a-week," he said, "and, thanks to their generous exertions, and the very judicious arrangement they had spontaneously made of having a hunt club, he really thought it would stand four days."—(Thunders of applause followed this announcement, causing the glasses and biscuits to dance jigs on the table. Sir Moses took a prolonged sip of wine, and silence being at length again restored, he thus resumed):—"It had always stood four in old Martingal's time, and why shouldn't it do so in theirs?—(applause). Look at its extent! Look at its splendid gorses! Look at its magnificent woodlands! He really thought it was second to none!" And so the company seemed to think too by the cheering that followed the announcement.

"Well then," said Sir Moses, drawing breath for the grand effort, "there was only one thing to be considered—one leetle difficulty to be overcome—but one, which after the experience he had had of their gameness and liberality, he was sure they would easily surmount."—(A murmur of "O-O-O's," with Hookey Walkers, and fingers to the nose, gradually following the speaker.)

"That *leetle* difficulty, he need hardly say, was their old familiar friend £ s. d.! who required occasionally to be looked in the face."—(Ironical laughter, with *sotto voce* exclamations from Jack to Tom and from Sam to Harry, of—) "I say! *three* days are *quite* enough—*quite* enough. Don't you think so?" With answers of "Plenty! plenty!" mingled with whispers of, "I say, this is what he calls hunting the country for nothing!"

"Well, gentlemen," continued Sir Moses, tapping the table with his presidential hammer, to assert his monopoly of noise, "Well, gentlemen, as I said before, I have no doubt we can overcome any difficulty in the matter of money—what's the use of money if it's not to enjoy ourselves, and what enjoyment is there equal to fox-hunting? (applause). None! none!" exclaimed Sir Moses with emphasis.

"Well then, gentlemen, what I was going to say was this: It occurred to me this morning as I was shaving myself——"

"That you would shave us," muttered Mr. Paul Straddler to Hicks, the flying hatter, neither of whom ever subscribed.

"—It occurred to me this morning, as I was shaving myself, that for a very little additional outlay—say four hundred a year—and what's four hundred a-year among so many of us? we might have four days a-week, which is a great deal better than three in many respects, inasmuch as you have two distinct lots of hounds, accustomed to hunt together, instead of a jumble for one day, and both men and horses are in steadier and more regular work; and as to foxes, I needn't say we have plenty of them, and that they will be all the better for a little more exercise.— (Applause from Sir Moses' men, Mr. Smoothley and others). Well, then, say four hundred a-year, or, as hay and corn are dear and likely to continue so, suppose we put it at the worst, and call it five—five hundred—what's five hundred a-year to a great prosperous agricultural and commercial country like this? Nothing! A positive bagatelle! I'd be ashamed to have it known at the 'Corner' that we had ever haggled about such a sum."

"You pay it, then," muttered Mr. Straddler.

"Catch him doing that," growled Hicks.

Sir Moses here took another sip of sherry, and thus resumed:—

"Well, now, gentlemen, as I said before, it only occurred to me this morning as I was shaving, or I would have been better prepared with some definite proposal for your consideration, but I've just dotted down here, on the back of one of Grove the fishmonger's cards (producing one from his waistcoat pocket as he spoke), the names of those who I think ought to be called upon to contribute;—and, waiter!" exclaimed he, addressing one of the lanky-haired order, who had just protruded his head in at the door to see what all the eloquence was about, "if you'll give me one of those mutton fats,—and your master ought to be kicked for putting such things on the table, and you may tell him I said so,—I'll just read the names over to you." Sir Moses adjusting his gold double eye glasses on his hooked nose as the waiter obeyed his commands.

"Well, now," said the Baronet, beginning at the top of the list, "I've put young Lord Polkaton down for fifty."

"But my Lord doesn't hunt, Sir Moses!" ejaculated Mr. Mossman, his Lordship's land-agent, alarmed at the demand upon a very delicate purse.

"Doesn't hunt!" retorted Sir Moses angrily. "No; but he might if he liked! If there were no hounds, how the deuce could he? It would do him far more good, let me tell him, than dancing at casinos and running after ballet girls, as he does. I've put him down for fifty, however," continued Sir Moses, with a jerk of his head, "and you may tell him I've done so."

"Wish you may get it," growled Mr. Mossman, with disgust.

"Well, then," said the Baronet, proceeding to the next name on the list, "comes old Lord Harpsichord. He's good for fifty, too, I should say. At all events, I've put him down for that sum;" adding, "I've no notion of those great landed cormorants cutting away to the continent and shirking the obligations of country life. I hold it to be the duty of every man to subscribe to a pack of fox-hounds. In fact, I would make a subscription a first charge upon land, before poor-rate, highway-rate, or any sort of rate. I'd make it payable before the assessed taxes themselves"— (laughter and applause, very few of the company being land-owners). "Two fifties is a hundred, then," observed Sir Moses, perking up; "and if we can screw another fifty out of old Lady Shortwhist, so much the better; at all events. I think she'll be good for a pony; and then we come to the Baronets. First and foremost is that confounded prosy old ass, Sir George Persiflage, with his empty compliments and his fine cravats. I've put him down for fifty, though I don't suppose the old sinner will pay it, though we may, perhaps, get half, which we shouldn't do if we were not to ask for more. Well, we'll call the supercilious old owls five-and-twenty for safety," added Sir Moses. "Then there's Sir Morgan Wildair; I should think we may say five-aud-twenty for him. What say you, Mr. Squeezely?" appealing to Sir Morgan's agent at the low end of the table.

"I've no instructions from Sir Morgan on the subject, Sir Moses," replied Mr. Squeezely, shaking his head.

"Oh, but he's a young man, and you must tell him that it's right—*necessary*, in fact," replied Sir Moses. "You just pay it, and pass it through his accounts—that's the shortest way. It's the duty of an agent to save his principal trouble. I wouldn't keep an agent who bothered me with all the twopenny-halfpenny transactions of the estate—dom'd if I would," said Sir Moses, resuming his eye-glass reading.

He then went on through the names of several other parties, who he thought might be coaxed or bullied out of subscriptions, he taking this man, another taking that, and working them, as he said, on the fair means first, and foul means principle afterwards.

"Well, then, now you see, gentlemen," said Sir Moses, pocketing his card and taking another sip of sherry prior to summing up; "it just amounts to this. Four days a-week, as I said before, is a dom'd deal better than three, and if we can get the fourth day out of these shabby screws, why so much the better; but if that can't be done entirely, it can to a certain extent, and then it will only remain for the members of the club and the strangers—by the way, we shouldn't forget them—it will only remain for the members of the club and the strangers to raise any slight deficiency by an increased subscription, and according to my plan of each man working his neighbour, whether the club subscription was to be increased to fifteen, or seventeen, or even to twenty pounds a-year will depend entirely upon ourselves; so you see, gentlemen, we have all a direct interest in the matter, and cannot go to work too earnestly or too strenuously; for believe me, gentlemen, there's nothing like hunting, it promotes health and longevity, wards off the gout and sciatica, and keeps one out of the hands of those dom'd doctors, with their confounded bills—no offence to our friend Plaister, there," alluding to a doctor of that name who was sitting about half-way down the table—"so now," continued Sir Moses, "I think I cannot do better than conclude by proposing as a bumper toast, with all the honours, Long life and prosperity to the Hit-im and Hold-im shire hounds!"

When the forced cheering had subsided, our friend—or rather Major Yammerton's friend—Mr. Smoothley, the gentleman who assisted at the sale of Bo-peep, arose to address the meeting amid coughs and knocks and the shuffling of feet. Mr. Smoothley coughed too, for he felt he had an uphill part to perform; but Sir Moses was a hard task-master, and held his "I. O. U.'s" for a hundred and fifty-seven pounds. On silence being restored, Mr. Smoothley briefly glanced at the topics urged, as he said, in such a masterly manner by their excellent and popular master, to whom they all owed a deep debt of gratitude for the spirited manner in which he hunted the country, rescuing it from the degradation to which it had fallen, and restoring it to its pristine fame and prosperity—(applause from Sir Moses and his *claqueurs*). "With respect to the specific proposal submitted by Sir Moses, Mr. Smoothley proceeded to say, he really thought there could not be a difference of opinion on the subject—(renewed applause, with murmurs of dissent here and there). It was clearly their interest to have the country hunted four days a week, and the mode in which Sir Moses proposed accomplishing the object was worthy the talents of the greatest financier of the day—(applause)—for it placed the load on the shoulders of those who were the best able to bear it—(applause). Taking all the circumstances of the case, therefore, into consideration, he thought the very least they could do would be to pass a unanimous vote of thanks to their excellent friend for the brilliant sport he had hitherto shown them, and pledge themselves to aid to the utmost of their power in carrying out his most liberal and judicious proposal.

"Jewish enough," whispered Mr. Straddler into the flying hatter's ear.

And the following week's Hit-im and Hold-im shire Herald, and also the Featherbedfordshire Gazette, contained a string of resolutions, embodying the foregoing, as unanimously passed at a full meeting of the members of the Hit-im and Hold-im shire hunt, held at the Fox and Hounds Hotel, in Ilinton, Sir Moses Main-chance, Bart., in the chair.

And each man set to work on the pocket of his neighbour with an earnestness inspired by the idea of saving his own. The result was that a very considerable sum was raised for the four days a-week, which, somehow or other, the country rarely or ever got, except in the shape of advertisements; for Sir Moses always had some excuse or other for shirking it,—either his huntsman had got drunk the day before, or his first whip had had a bad fall, or his second whip had been summoned to the small debts court, or his hounds had been fighting and several of them had got lamed, or the distemper had broken out in his stable, or something or other had happened to prevent him.

Towards Christmas, or on the eve of an evident frost, he came valiantly out, and if foiled by a sudden thaw, would indulge in all sorts of sham draws, and short days, to the great disgust of those who were not in the secret. Altogether Sir Moses Mainchance rode Hit-im and Hold-im shire as Hit-im and Hold-im shire had never been ridden before.

CHAPTER XXIX. THE PANGBURN PARK ESTATE.

THE first thing that struck Sir Moses Mainchance after he became a "laird" was that he got very little interest for his money. Here he was he who had always looked down with scorn upon any thing that would not pay ten per cent., scarcely netting three by his acres. He couldn't understand it—dom'd if he could. How could people live who had nothing but land? Certainly Mr. Plantagenet Smith had left the estate in as forlorn a condition as could well be imagined. Latterly his agent, Mr. Tom Teaser, had directed his attention solely to the extraction of rent, regardless of maintenance, to say nothing of improvements, consequently the farm buildings were dilapidated, and the land impoverished in every shape and way. Old pasture-field after old pasture-field had gradually succumbed to the plough, and the last ounce of freshness being extracted, the fields were left to lay themselves down to weeds or any thing they liked. As this sort of work never has but one ending, the time soon arrived when the rent was not raiseable.

Indeed it was the inability to make "both ends meet," as Paul By used to say, which caused Mr. Plantagenet Smith to retire from Burke's landed gentry, which he did to his own advantage, land being sometimes like family plate, valuable to sell, but unprofitable to keep.

Sir Moses, flushed with his reception and the consequence he had acquired, met his tenants gallantly the first rent-day, expecting to find everything as smooth and pleasant as a London house-rent audit. Great was his surprise and disgust at the pauperised wretches he encountered, creatures that really appeared to be but little raised above the brute creation, were it not for the uncommon keenness they showed at a "catch." First came our old friend Henerey Brown & Co., who, foiled in their attempt to establish themselves on Major Yammerton's farm at Bonnyrigs, and also upon several other farms in different parts of the county, had at length "wheas we have considered" Mr. Teaser to some better purpose for one on the Pangburn Park Estate.

This was Doblington farm, consisting of a hundred and sixty of undrained obdurate clay, as sticky as bird-lime in wet, and as hard as iron in dry weather, and therefore requiring extra strength to take advantage of a favourable season. Now Henerey Brown & Co. had farmed, or rather starved, a light sandy soil of some two-thirds the extent of Doblington, and their half-fed pony horses and wretched implements were quite unable to cope with the intractable stubborn stuff they had selected. Perhaps we can hardly say they selected it, for it was a case of Hobson's choice with them, and as they offered more rent than the outgoing tenant, who had farmed himself to the door, had paid, Mr. Teaser installed them in it. And now at the end of the year, (the farms being let on that beggarly pauper-encouraging system of a running half year) Henerey & Humphrey came dragging their legs to the Park with a quarter of a year's rent between them, Henerey who was the orator undertaking to appear, Humphrey paying his respects only to the cheer. Sir Moses and Mr. Teaser were sitting in state in the side entrance-hall, surrounded by the usual paraphernalia of pens, ink, and paper, when Henerey's short, square turnip-headed, vacant-countenanced figure loomed in the distance. Mr. Teaser trembled when he saw him, for he knew that the increased rent obtained for Henerey's farm had been much dwelt upon by the auctioneer, and insisted upon by the vendor as conducive evidence of the improving nature of the whole estate. Teaser, like the schoolboy in the poem, now traced the day's disaster in Henerey's morning face. However, Teaser put a good face on the matter, saying, as Henerey came diverging up to the table, "This is Mr. Brown, Sir Moses, the new tenant of Doblington—the farm on the Hill." he was going to add "with the bad out-buildings," but he thought he had better keep that to himself. *Humph* sniffed the eager baronet, looking the new tenant over.

"Your sarvent, Sir Moses," ducked the farmer, seating himself in the dread cash-extracting chair.

"Well, my man, and how dy'e do? I hope you're well—How's your wife? I hope she's well," continued the Baronet, watching Henerey's protracted dive into his corduroy breeches-pockets, and his fish up of the dirty canvas money-bag. Having deliberately untied the string, Henerey, without noticing the Baronet's polite enquiries, shook out a few local five pound notes, along with some sovereigns, shillings, and sixpence upon the table, and heaving a deep sigh, pushed them over towards Mr. Teaser. That worthy having wet his thumb at his mouth proceeded to count the dirty old notes, and finding them as he expected, even with the aid of the change, very short of the right amount, he asked Henerey if he had any bills against them?

"W-h-o-y no-a ar think not," replied Henerey, scratching his straggling-haired head, apparently conning the matter over in his mind. "W-h-o-y, yeas, there's the Income Tax, and there's the lime to 'loo off."

"Lime!" exclaimed the Baronet, "What have I to do with lime?"

"W-h-o-y, yeas, you know you promised to 'loo the lime," replied Hererey, appealing to Mr. Teaser, who frowned and bit his lip at the over-true assertion.

"Never heard of such a thing!" exclaimed Sir Moses, seeing through the deceit at a glance. "Never heard of such a thing," repeated he. "That's the way you keep up your rents is it?" asked he: "Deceive yourselves by pretending to get more money than you do, and pay rates and taxes upon your deceit as a punishment. That 'ill not do! dom'd if it will," continued the Baronet, waxing warm.

"Well, but the income tax won't bring your money up to anything like the right amount," observed Mr. Teaser to Henerey, anxious to get rid of the lime question.

"W-h-o-y n-o-a," replied Henerey, again scratching his pate, "but it's as much as I can bring ye to-day."

"To-day, man!" retorted Sir Moses, "Why, don't you know that this is the rent-day! the day on which the entire monetary transactions on the whole estate are expected to be settled."

Henerey—"O, w-h-o-y it 'ill make ne odds to ye, Sir Moses."

Sir Moses—"Ne odds to me! How do you know that?"

Henerey—(apologetically) "Oh, Sir Moses, you have plenty, Sir Moses."

Sir Moses—"Me plenty! me plenty! I'm the poorest crittur alive!" which was true enough, only not in the sense Sir Moses intended it.

Henerey—"Why, why, Sir Moses, ar'll bring ye some more after a bit; but ar tell ye," appealing to Teaser, "*Ye mun 'loo for the lime.*"

"The lime be hanged," exclaimed Sir Moses. "D'ye sp'ose I'm such a fool as to let you the land, and farm ye the land, and pay income tax on rent that I never receive? That won't do—dom'd if it will."

Henerey—(boiling up) "Well, but Sir Moses, wor farm's far o'er dear."

Sir Moses—(turning flesh-colour with fury) "O'er dear! Why, isn't it the rent you yourself offered for it?"

Henerey—"Why, why, but we hadn't looked her carefully over."

"Bigger fool you," ejaculated the Jew.

"The land's far worse nor we took it for—some of the plough's a shem to be seen—wor stable rains in desprate—there isn't a dry place for a coo—the back wall of the barn's all bulgin oot—the pigs get into wor garden for want of a gate—there isn't a fence 'ill turn a foal—the hars eat all wor tormots—we're perfectly ruined wi' rats," and altogether Henerey opened such a battery of grievances as completely drove Sir Moses, who hated anyone to talk but himself, from his seat, and made him leave the finish of his friend to Mr. Teaser.

As the Baronet went swinging out of the room he mentally exclaimed, "Never saw such a man as that in my life—dom'd if ever I did!"

Mr. Teaser then proceeded with the wretched audit, each succeeding tenant being a repetition of the first—excuses—drawbacks—allowances for lime—money no matter to Sir Moses—and this with a whole year's rent due, to say nothing of hopeless arrears.

"How the deuce," as Sir Moses asked, "do people live who have nothing but land?"

When Sir Moses returned, at the end of an hour or so, he found one of the old tenants of the estate, Jacky Hindmarch, in the chair. Jacky was one of the real scratching order of farmers, and ought to be preserved at Madame Tussaud's or the British Museum, for the information of future ages. To see him in the fields, with his crownless hat and tattered clothes, he was more like a scare-crow than a farmer; though, thanks to the influence of cheap finery, he turned out very shiney and satiney on a Sunday. Jacky had seventy acres of land,—fifty acres of arable and twenty acres of grass, which latter he complimented with an annual mowing without giving it any manure in return, thus robbing his pastures to feed his fallows,—if, indeed, he did not rob both by selling the manure off his farm altogether. Still Jacky was reckoned a cute fellow among his compatriots. He had graduated in the Insolvent Debtors' Court to evade his former landlord's claims, and emerged from gaol with a good stock of bad law engrafted on his innate knavery. In addition to this, Jacky, when a hind, had nearly had to hold up his hand at Quarter Sessions for stealing his master's corn, which he effected in a very ingenious way:—The granary being above Jacky's stable, he bored a hole through the floor, to which he affixed a stocking; and, having drawn as much corn as he required, he stopped the hole up with a plug until he wanted a fresh supply. The farmer—one Mr. Podmore—at length smelt a rat; but giving Jacky in charge rather prematurely, he failed in substantiating the accusation, when the latter, acting "under advice," brought an action against Podmore, which ended in a compromise, Podmore having to pay Jacky twenty pounds for robbing him! This money, coupled with the savings of a virtuous young woman he presently espoused, and who had made free with the produce of her master's dairy, enabled Jacky to take the farm off which he passed through the Insolvent Debtors' Court, on to the Pangburn Park estate, where he was generally known by the name of Lawyer Hindmarch.

Jacky and his excellent wife attempted to farm the whole seventy acres themselves; to plough, harrow, clean, sow, reap, mow, milk, churn,—do everything, in fact; consequently they were always well in arrear with their work, and had many a fine run after the seasons. If Jacky got his turnips in by the time other people were singling theirs, he was thought to do extremely well. To see him raising the seed-furrow in the autumn, a stranger would think he was ploughing in a green crop for manure, so luxuriant were the weeds. But Jacky Hindmarch would defend his system against Mr. Mechi himself; there being no creature so obstinate or intractable as a pig-headed farmer. A landlord had better let his land to a cheesemonger, a greengrocer, a draper, anybody with energy and capital, rather than to one of these selfsufficient, dawdling nincompoops. To be sure..Jacky farmed as if each year was to be his last, but he wouldn't have been a bit better if he had had a one-and-twenty years' lease before him. "Take all out and put nothing in," was his motto. This was the genius who was shuffling, and haggling, and prevaricating with Mr. Teaser when Sir Moses returned, and who now gladly skulked off: Henerey Brown not having reported very favourably of the great man's temper.

The next to come was a woman,—a great, mountainous woman—one Mrs. Peggy Turnbull, wife of little Billy Turnbull of Lowfield Farm, who, she politely said, was not fit to be trusted from home by hisself.—Mrs. Turnbull was, though, being quite a match for any man in the country, either with her tongue or her fists. She was a great masculine knock-me-down woman, round as a sugar-barrel, with a most extravagant stomach, wholly absorbing her neck, and reaching quite up to her chin. Above the barrel was a round, swarthy, sunburnt face, lit up with a pair of keen little twinkling beady black eyes. She paused in her roll as she neared the chair, at which she now cast a contemptuous look, as much as to say, "How can I ever get into such a thing as that?"

Mr. Teaser saw her dilemma and kindly gave her the roomier one on which he was sitting—while Sir Moses inwardly prepared a little dose of politeness for her.

"Well, my good woman," said he as soon as she got soused on to the seat. "Well, my good woman, how d'ye do? I hope you're well. How's your husband? I hope he's well;" and was proceeding in a similar strain when the monster interrupted his dialogue by thumping the table with her fist, and exclaiming at the top of her voice, as she fixed her little beady black eyes full upon him—

"*D'ye think we're ganninn to get a new B-a-r-r-u-n?*"

"Dom you and your b-a-r-r-n!" exclaimed the Baronet, boiling up. "Why don't you leave those things to your husband?"

"*He's see shy!*" roared the monster.

"You're not shy, however!" replied Sir Moses, again jumping up and running away.

And thus what with one and another of them, Sir Moses was so put out, that dearly as he loved a let off for his tongue, he couldn't bring himself to face his friends again at dinner. So the agreeable duty devolved upon Mr. Teaser, of taking the chair, and proposing in a bumper toast, with all the honours and one cheer more, the health of a landlord who, it was clear, meant to extract the uttermost farthing he could from his tenants.

And that day's proceedings furnished ample scope for a beginning, for there was not one tenant on the estate who paid up; and Sir Moses declared that of all the absurdities he had ever heard tell of in the whole course of his life, that of paying income-tax on money he didn't receive was the greatest. "Dom'd if it wasn't!" said he.

In fact the estate had come to a stand still, and wanted nursing instead of further exhaustion. If it had got into the hands of an improving owner—a Major Yammerton, for instance,—there was redemption enough in the land; these scratching fellows, only exhausting the surface; and draining and subsoiling would soon have put matters right, but Sir Moses declared he wouldn't throw good money after bad, that the rushes were meant to be there and there they should stay. If the tenants couldn't pay their rents how could they pay any drainage interest? he asked. Altogether Sir Moses declared it shouldn't be a case of over shoes, over boots, with him—that he wouldn't go deeper into the mud than he was, and he heartily wished he had the price of the estate back in his pocket again, as many a man has wished, and many a one will wish again—there being nothing so ticklish to deal with as land. There is no reason though why it should be so; but we will keep our generalities for another chapter.

Sir Moses's property went rapidly back, and soon became a sort of last refuge for the destitute, whither the ejected of all other estates congregated prior to scattering their stock, on failing to get farms in more favoured localities. As they never meant to pay, of course they all offered high rents, and then having got possession the Henerey Brown scene was enacted—the farm was "far o'er dear"—they could "make nouton't at that rent!" nor could they have made aught on them if they had had them for nothing, seeing that their capital consisted solely of their intense stupidity. Then if Sir Moses wouldn't reduce the rent, he might just do his "warst," meanwhile they pillaged the land both by day and by night. The cropping of course corresponded with the tenure, and may be described as just anything they could get off the land. White crop succeeded white crop, if the weeds didn't smother the seeds, or if any of the slovens did "try for a few turnips," as they called it, they were sown on dry spots selected here and there, with an implement resembling a dog's-meat man's wheelbarrow—drawn by one ass and steered by another.

Meanwhile Mr. Teaser's labours increased considerably, what with the constant lettings and leavings and watchings for "slopings." There was always some one or other of the worthies on the wing, and the more paper and words Mr. Teaser employed to bind them, the more inefficient and futile he found the attempt. It soon became a regular system to do the new landlord, in furtherance of which the tenants formed themselves into a sort of mutual aid association. Then when a seizure was effected, they combined not to buy, so that the sufferer got his wretched stock back at little or no loss.

Wretched indeed, was the spectacle of a sale; worn out horses, innocent of corn; cows, on whose hips one could hang one's hat; implements that had been "fettled oop" and "fettled oop," until not a particle of the parent stock remained; carts and trappings that seemed ready for a bonfire; pigs, that looked as if they wanted food themselves instead of being likely to feed any one else; and poultry that all seemed troubled with the pip.

The very bailiff's followers were shocked at the emptiness of the larders. A shank bone of salt meat dangling from the ceiling, a few eggs on a shelf, a loaf of bread in a bowl, a pound of butter in a pie-dish,—the whole thing looking as unlike the plentiful profusion of a farm-house as could well be imagined.

The arduous duties of the office, combined with the difficulty of pleasing Sir Moses, at length compelled Mr. Teaser to resign, when our "laird," considering the nature of the services required concluded that there could be no one so fit to fulfil them as one of the "peoplish." Accordingly he went to town, and after Consulting Levy this, and "Goodman" that, and Ephraim t'other, he at length fixed upon that promising swell, young Mr. Mordecai Nathan, of Cursitor-street, whose knowledge of the country consisted in having assisted in the provincial department of his father's catchpoll business in the glorious days of writs and sponging-houses.

In due time down came Mordecai, ringed and brooched and chained and jewelled, and as Sir Moses was now the great man, hunting the country, associating with Lord Oilcake, and so on, he gave Mordecai a liberal salary, four-hundred a year made up in the following clerical way:

Besides, which, Sir Moses promised him ten per cent, upon all recovered arrears, which set Mordecai to work with all the enthusiastic energy of his race.

CHAPTER XXX. COMMERCE AND AGRICULTURE.

ONE of the most distinguishing features between commerce and agriculture and agriculture undoubtedly is the marked indifference shown to the value of time by the small followers of the latter, compared to the respectful treatment it receives at the hands of the members of the commercial world. To look at their relative movements one would think that the farmer was the man who carried on his business under cover, instead of being the one who exposes all his capital to the weather. It is a rare thing to see a farmer—even in hay time—in a hurry. If the returns could be obtained we dare say it would be found that three-fourths of the people who are late for railway trains are farmers.

In these accelerated days, when even the very street waggon horses trot, they are the only beings whose pace has not been improved. The small farmer is just the same slowly moving dawdling creature that he was before the perfection of steam. Never punctual, never ready, never able to give a direct answer to a question; a pitchfork at their backs would fail to push some of these fellows into prosperity. They seem wholly lost to that emulative spirit which actuates the trader to endeavour to make each succeeding year leave him better than the last. A farmer will be forty years on a farm without having benefited himself, his family, his landlord, or any human being whatever. The last year's tenancy will find him as poor as the first, with, in all probability, his land a great deal poorer. In dealing, a small farmer is never happy without a haggle. Even if he gets his own price he reproaches hiself when he returns home with not having asked a little more, and so got a wrangle. Very often, however, they outwit themselves entirely by asking so much more than a thing is really worth, that a man who knows what he is about, and has no hopes of being able to get the sun to stand still, declines entering upon an apparently endless negotiation.

See lawyer Hindmarch coming up the High Street at Halterley fair, leading his great grey colt, with his landlord Sir Moses hailing him with his usual "Well my man, how d'ye do? I hope you're well, how much for the colt?"

The lawyer's keen intellect—seeing that it is his landlord, with whom he is well over the left—springs a few pounds upon an already exorbitant price, and Sir Moses, who can as he says, measure the horse out to ninepence, turns round on his heel with a chuck of his chin, as much as to say, "you may go on." Then the lawyer relenting says, "w—h—o—y, but there'll be summit to return upon that, you know, Sir Moses, Sir."

"I should think so," replies the Baronet, walking away, to "Well my man—how d'ye do? I hope you're well," somebody else.

A sale by auction of agricultural stock illustrates our position still further, and one remarkable feature is that the smaller the sale the more unpunctual people are. They seldom get begun under a couple of hours after the advertised time, and then the dwelling, the coaxing, the wrangling, the "puttings-up" again, the ponderous attempts at wit are painful and oppressive to any one accustomed to the easy gliding celerity of town auctioneers. A conference with a farmer is worse, especially if the party is indiscreet enough to let the farmer come to him instead of his going to the farmer.

The chances, then, are, that he is saddled with a sort of old man of the sea; as a certain ambassador once was with a gowk of an Englishman, who gained an audience under a mistaken notion, and kept sitting and sitting long after his business was discussed, in spite of his Excellency's repeated bows and intimations that he might retire.

Gowk seemed quite insensible to a hint. In vain his Excellency stood bowing and bowing—hoping to see him rise. No such luck. At length his Excellency asked him if there was anything else he could do for him?

"Why, noa." replied Gowk drily; adding after a pause, "but you haven't asked me to dine."

"Oh, I beg your pardon!" replied his Excellency, "I wasn't aware that it was in my instructions, but I'll refer to them and see," added he, backing out of the room.

Let us fancy old Heavyheels approaching his landlord, to ask if he thinks they are gannin to get a new barrun, or anything else he may happen to want, for these worthies have not discovered the use of the penny-post, and will trudge any distance to deliver their own messages. Having got rolled into the room, the first thing Heels does is to look out for a seat, upon which he squats like one of Major Yammerton's hares, and from which he is about as difficult to raise. Instead of coming out with his question as a trader would, "What's rum? what's sugar? what's indigo?" he fixes his unmeaning eyes on his landlord, and with a heavy aspiration, and propping his chin up with a baggy umbrella, ejaculates—"N-0-0," just as if his landlord had sent for him instead of his having come of his own accord.

"Well!" says the landlord briskly, in hopes of getting him on.

"It's a foine day," observes Heavyheels, as if he had nothing whatever on his mind, and so he goes maundering and sauntering on, wasting his own and his landlord's time, most likely ending with some such preposterous proposition as would stamp any man for a fool if it wasn't so decidedly in old Heavyheel's own favour.

To give them their due, they are never shy about asking, and have always a host of grievances to bait a landlord with who gives them an opportunity. Some of the women—we beg their pardon—ladies of the establishments, seem to think that a landlord rides out for the sake of being worried, and rush at him as he passes like a cur dog at a beggar.

Altogether they are a wonderful breed! It will hardly be credited hereafter, when the last of these grubbing old earthworms is extinct, that in this anxious, commercial, money-striving country, where every man is treading on his neighbour's heels for cash, that there should ever have been a race of men who required all the coaxing and urging and patting on the back to induce them to benefit themselves that these slugs of small tenant farmers have done. And the bulk of them not a bit better for it. They say "y-e-a-s," and go and do the reverse directly.

Fancy our friend Goodbeer, the brewer, assembling his tied Bonnifaces at a banquet consisting of all the delicacies of the season—beef, mutton, and cheese, as the sailor said—and after giving the usual loyal and patriotic toasts, introducing his calling in the urgent way some landlords do theirs—pointing out that the more swipes they sell the greater will be their profit, recommending them to water judiciously, keeping the capsicum out of sight, and, in lieu of some new implement of husbandry, telling them that a good, strong, salt Dutch cheese, is found to be a great promoter of thirst, and recommending each man to try a cheese on himself—perhaps ending by bowling one at each of them by way of a start.

But some will, perhaps, say that the interests of the landlord and tenant-farmer are identical, and that you cannot injure the latter without hurting the former.

Not more identical, we submit, than the interests of Goodbeer with the Bonnifaces; the land is let upon a calculation what each acre will produce, just as Goodbeer lets a public-house on a calculation founded on its then consumption of malt liquor; and whatever either party makes beyond that amount, either through the aid of guano, Dutch cheese, or what not, is the tenant's. The only difference we know between them is, that Goodbeer, being a trader, will have his money to the day; while in course of time the too easy landlord's rent has become postponed to every other person's claim. It is, "O, it will make ne matter to you, Sir Moses," with too many of them.

Then, if that convenient view is acquiesced in, the party submitting is called a "good landlord" (which in too many instances only means a great fool), until some other favour is refused, when the hundredth one denied obliterates the recollection of the ninety-nine conferred, and he sinks into a "rank bad un." The best landlord, we imagine, is he who lets his land on fair terms, and keeps his tenants well up to the mark both with their farming and their payments. At present the landlords are too often a sort of sleeping partners with their tenants, sharing with them the losses of the bad years without partaking with them in the advantages of the good ones.

"Ah, it's all dom'd well," we fancy we hear Sir Moses Main-chance exclaim, "saying, 'keep them up to the mark,' but how d'ye do it? how d'ye do it? can you bind a weasel? No man's tried harder than I have!"

We grant that it is difficult, but agriculture never had such opportunities as it has now. The thing is to get rid of the weasels, and with public companies framed for draining, building, doing everything that is required without that terrible investigation of title, no one is justified in keeping his property in an unproductive state. The fact is that no man of capital will live in a cottage, the thing therefore is to lay a certain number of these small holdings together, making one good farm of them all, with suitable buildings, and, as the saying is, let the weasels go to the wall. They will be far happier and more at home with spades or hoes in their hands, than in acting a part for which they have neither capital, courage, nor capacity. Fellows take a hundred acres who should only have five, and haven't the wit to find out that it is cheaper to buy manure than to rent land.

This is not a question of crinoline or taste that might be advantageously left to Mrs. Pringle; but is one that concerns the very food and well being of the people, and landlords ought not to require coaxing and patting on the back to induce them to partake of the cheese that, the commercial world offers them. Even if they are indifferent about benefiting themselves they should not be regardless of the interests for their country. But there are very few people who cannot spend a little more money than they have. Let them "up then and at" the drainage companies, and see what wonders they'll accomplish with their aid!

We really believe the productive powers of the country might be quadrupled.

CHAPTER XXXI. SIR MOSES'S MENAGE.—DEPARTURE OF FINE BILLY.

SIR MOSES, being now a magnate of the land, associating with Lord Oilcake, Lord Repartee, Sir Harry Fuzball and other great dons, of course had to live UP to the mark, an inconvenient arrangement for those who do not like paying for it, and the consequence was that he had to put up with an inferior article.—take first-class servants who had fallen into second-class circumstances. He had a ticket-of-leave butler. a *delirium tremens* footman, and our old friend pheasant-feathers, now calling herself Mrs. Margerum, for cook and house-keeper. And first, of the butler. He was indeed a magnificent man, standing six feet two and faultlessly proportioned, with a commanding presence of sufficient age to awe those under him, and to inspire confidence in an establishment with such a respectable looking man at the head. Though so majestic, he moved noiselessly, spoke in a whisper, and seemed to spirit the things off the table without sound or effort. Pity that the exigencies of gambling should have caused such an elegant man to melt his master's plate, still greater that he should have been found out and compelled to change the faultless white vest of upper service for the unbecoming costume of prison life. Yet so it was: and the man who was convicted as Henry Stopper, and sentenced to fourteen years' transportation, emerged at the end of four with a ticket-of-leave, under the assumed name of Demetrius Bankhead. Mr. Bankhead, knowing the sweets of office, again aspired to high places, but found great difficulty in suiting himself, indeed in getting into service at all.

People who keep fine gentlemen are very chary and scrupulous whom they select, and extremely inquisitive and searching in their inquiries.

In vain Mr. Bankhead asserted that he had been out of health and living-on the Continent, or that he had been a partner in a brewery which hadn't succeeded, or that his last master was abroad he didn't know where, and made a variety of similar excuses.

Though many fine ladies and gentlemen were amazingly taken with him at first, and thought he would grace their sideboards uncommonly, they were afraid to touch for fear "all was not right."

Then those of a lower grade, thought he wouldn't apply to them after having lived in such high places as he described, and this notwithstanding Bankhead's plausible assertion, that he wished for a situation in a quiet regular family in the country, where he could get to bed at a reasonable hour, instead of being kept up till he didn't know when. He would even come upon trial, if the parties liked, which would obviate all inquiries about character; just as if a man couldn't run off with the plate the first day as well as the last.

Our readers, we dare say, know the condescending sort of gentleman "who will accept of their situations," and who deprecate an appeal to their late masters by saying in an airified sort of way, with a toss of the head or a wave of the hand, that they told his Grace or Sir George they wouldn't trouble to ask them for characters. Just as if the Duke or Sir George were infinitely beneath their notice or consideration.

And again the sort of men who flourish a bunch of testimonials, skilfully selecting the imposing passages and evading the want of that connecting link upon which the whole character depends, and who talk in a patronising way of "poor lord this," or "poor Sir Thomas that," and what they would have done for them if they had been alive, poor men!

Mr. Demetrius Bankhead tried all the tricks of the trade—we beg pardon—profession— wherever he heard of a chance, until hope deferred almost made his noble heart sick. The "puts off" and excuses he got were curiously ingenious. However, he was pretty adroit himself, for when he saw the parties were not likely to bite, he anticipated a refusal by respectfully declining the situation, and then saying that he might have had so and so's place, only he wanted one where he should be in town half the year, or that he couldn't do with only one footman under him.

It was under stress of circumstances that Sir Moses Mainchance became possessed of Mr. Bankhead's services. He had kicked his last butler (one of the fine characterless sort) out of the house for coming in drunk to wait at dinner, and insisting upon putting on the cheese first with the soup, then with the meat, then with the sweets, and lastly with the dessert; and as Sir Moses was going to give one of his large hunt dinners shortly after, it behoved him to fill up the place— we beg pardon—office—as quickly as possible. To this end he applied to Mrs. Listener, the gossiping Register Office-keeper of Hinton, a woman well calculated to write the history of every family in the county, for behind her screen every particular was related, and Mrs. Listener, having paraded all the wretched glazey-clothed, misshapen creatures that always turn up on such occasions, Sir Moses was leaving after his last visit in disgust, when Mr. Bankhead walked in— "quite promiscuous," as the saying is, but by previous arrangement with Mrs. Listener. Sir Moses was struck with Bankhead's air and demeanour, so quiet, so respectful, raising his hat as he met Sir Moses at the door, that he jumped to the conclusion that he would do for him, and returning shortly after to Mrs. Listener, he asked all the usual questions, which Mrs. Listener cleverly evaded, merely saying that he professed to be a perfect butler, and had several most excellent testimonials, but that it would be much better for Sir Moses to judge for himself, for really Mrs. Listener had the comfort of Sir Moses so truly at heart that she could not think of recommending any one with whom she was not perfectly conversant, and altogether she palavered him so neatly, always taking care to extol Bankhead's personal appearance as evidence of his respectability, that the baronet was fairly talked into him, almost without his knowing it, while Mrs. Listener salved her own conscience with the reflection that it was Sir Moses's own doing, and that the bulk of his plate was "Brummagem" ware—and not silver. So the oft-disappointed ticket-of-leaver was again installed in a butlers pantry. And having now introduced him, we will pass over the delirium, tremens footman and arrive at that next important personage in an establishment, the housekeeper, in this case our old friend pheasant's-feathers. Mrs. Margerum, late Sarey Grimes, the early coach companion and confidante of our fair friend Mrs. Pringle—had undergone the world's "ungenerous scorn," as well for having set up an adopted son, as for having been turned away from many places for various domestic peculations. Mrs. Margerum, however, was too good a judge to play upon anything that anybody could identify, consequently though she was often caught, she always had an answer, and would not unfrequently turn the tables on her accusers—lawyer Hindmarch like—and make them pay for having been robbed. No one knew better than Mrs. Margerum how many feathers could be extracted from a bed without detection, what reduction a horse-hair mattress would stand, or how to make two hams disappear under the process of frying one. Indeed she was quite an adept in housekeeping, always however preferring to live with single gentlemen, for whom she would save a world of trouble by hiring all the servants, thus of course having them well under her thumb.

Sir Moses having suffered severely from waste, drunkenness and incapacity, had taken Mrs. Margerum on that worst of all recommendations, the recommendation of another servant—viz., Lord Oilcake's cook, for whom Mrs. Margerum had done the out-door carrying when in another situation. Mrs. Margerum's long career, coupled with her now having a son equal to the out-door department, established a claim that was not to be resisted when his lordship's cook had a chance, on the application of Sir Moses, of placing her.

Mrs. Margerum entered upon her duties at Pangburn Park, with the greatest plausibility, for not content with the usual finding fault with all the acts of her predecessors, she absolutely "reformed the butcher's bills," reducing them nearly a pound a-week below what they had previously been, and showed great assiduity in sending in all the little odds and ends of good things that went out. To be sure the hams disappeared rather quickly, but then they *do* cut so to waste in frying, and the cows went off in their milk, but cows are capricious things, and Mrs. Hindmarch and she had a running account in the butter and egg line, Mrs. Hindmarch accommodating her with a few pounds of butter and a few score of eggs when Sir Moses had company, Mrs. Margerum repaying her at her utmost convenience, receiving the difference in cash, the repayment being always greatly in excess of the advance. Still as Mrs. Margerum permitted no waste, and allowed no one to rob but herself, the house appeared to be economically kept, and if Sir Moses didn't think that she was a "charming woman," he at all events considered he was a most fortunate man, and felt greatly indebted to Lord Oilcake's cook for recommending her—"dom'd if he didn't."

But though Mrs. Margerum kept the servants well up to their tea and sugar allowances, she granted them every indulgence in the way of gadding about, and also in having their followers, provided the followers didn't eat, by which means she kept the house quiet, and made her reign happy and prosperous.

Being in full power when Mr. Bankhead came, she received him with the greatest cordiality, and her polite offer of having his clothes washed in Sir Moses's laundry being accepted, of course she had nothing to fear from Mr. Bankhead. And so they became as they ought to be, very good friends—greatly to Sir Moses's advantage.

Now for the out-door department of Sir Moses's ménage. The hunting establishment was of the rough and ready order, but still the hounds showed uncommon sport, and if the horses were not quite up to the mark, that perhaps was all in favour of the hounds. The horses indeed were of a very miscellaneous order—all sorts, all sizes, all better in their wind than on their legs—which were desperately scored and iron-marked. Still the cripples could go when they were warm, and being ridden by men whose necks were at a discount, they did as well as the best. There is nothing like a cheap horse for work.

Sir Moses's huntsman was the noted Tom Findlater, a man famous for everything in his line except sobriety, in which little item he was sadly deficient. Tom would have been quite at the top of the tree if it hadn't been for this unfortunate infirmity. "The crittur," as a Scotch huntsman told Sir Moses at Tattersall's, "could no keep itself sober." To show the necessities to which this degrading propensity reduces a man, we will quote Tom's description of himself when he applied to be discharged under the Insolvent Debtors' Act before coming to Sir Moses. Thus it ran— "John Thomas Findlater known also as Tom Find'ater, formerly huntsman to His Grace the Duke of Streamaway, of Stream-away Castle, in Streamaway-shire, then of No. 6, Back Row, Broomsfield, in the county of Tansey, helper in a livery stable, then huntsman to Sampson Cobbyford, Esq., of Bluntfield Park, master of the Hugger Mugger hounds in the county of Scramblington, then huntsman to Sir Giles Gatherthrong, Baronet, of Clipperley Park, in the county of Scurry, then huntsman to the Right Honourable Lord Lovedale, of Gayhurst Court, in the county of Tipperley, then of No. 11, Tan Yard Lane, Barrenbin, in the county of Thistleford, assistant to a ratcatcher, then huntsman to Captain Rattlinghope, of Killbriton Castle, in the County Steepleford, then whipper-in to the Towrowdeshire hounds in Derrydownshire, then helper at the Lion and the Lamb public-house at Screwford, in the County of Mucklethrift, then of 6 1/2 Union Street, in Screwford, aforesaid, moulder to a clay-pipe maker, then and now out of business and employ, and whose wife is a charwoman."

Such were the varied occupations of a man, who might have lived like a gentleman, if he had only had conduct. There is no finer place than that of a huntsman, for as Beckford truly says, his office is pleasing and at the same time flattering, he is paid for that which diverts him, nor is a general after a victory more proud, than is a huntsman who returns with his fox's head.

When Sir Moses fell in with Tom Findlater down Tattersall's entry, Tom was fresh from being whitewashed in the Insolvent Debtors' Court, and having only ninepence in the world, and what he stood up in, he was uncommonly good to deal with. Moreover, Sir Moses had the vanity to think that he could reclaim even the most vicious; and, provided they were cheap enough, he didn't care to try. So, having lectured Tom well on the importance of sobriety, pointing out to him the lamentable consequences of drunkenness—of which no one was more sensible than Tom—Sir Moses chucked him a shilling, and told him if he had a mind to find his way down to Pangburn Park, in Hit-im-and-Hold-im shire, he would employ him, and give him what he was worth; with which vague invitation Tom came in the summer of the season in which we now find him.

And now having sketched the ménage, let us introduce our friend Billy thereto. But first we must get him out of the dangerous premises in which he is at present located—a visit that has caused our handsome friend Mrs. Pringle no little uneasiness.

It was fortunate for Sir Moses Mainchance, and unfortunate for our friend Fine Billy, that the Baronet was a bachelor, or Sir Moses would have fared very differently at the hands of the ladies who seldom see much harm in a man so long as he is single, and, of course, refrains from showing a decided preference for any young lady. It is the married men who monopolise all the vice and improprieties of life. The Major, too, having sold Billy a horse, and got paid for him, was not very urgent about his further society at present, nor indisposed for a little quiet, especially as

Mrs. Yammerton represented that the napkins and table-linen generally were running rather short. Mamma, too, knowing that there would be nothing but men-parties at Pangburn Park, had no uneasiness on that score, indeed rather thought a little absence might be favourable, in enabling Billy to modify his general attentions in favour of a single daughter, for as yet he had been extremely dutiful in obeying his Mamma's injunctions not to be more agreeable to one sister than to another. Indeed, our estimable young friend did not want to be caught, and had been a good deal alarmed at the contents of his Mamma's last letter.

One thing, however, was settled, namely, that Billy was to go to the Park, and how to get there was the next consideration; for, though the Baronet had offered to convey him in the first instance, he had modified the offer into the loan of the gig at the last, and there would be more trouble in sending a horse to fetch it, than there would be in starting fair in a hired horse and vehicle from Yammerton Grange. The ready-witted Major, however, soon put matters right.

"I'll te te tell you wot," said he, "you can do. You can have old Tommy P-p-plumberg, the registrar of b-b-births, deaths, and marriages, t-t-trap for a trifle—s-s-say, s-s-seven and sixpence—only you must give him the money as a p-p-present, you know, not as it were for the hire, or the Excise would be down upon him for the du-du-duty, and p-p-p'raps fine him into the b-b-bargain."

Well, that seemed all right and feasible enough, and most likely would have been all right if Monsieur had proposed it; but, coming from master, of course Monsieur felt bound to object.

"It vouldn't hold alf a quarter their things," he said; "besides, how de deuce were they to manage with de horse?"

The Major essayed to settle that, too. There would be no occasion for Mr. Pringle to take all his things with him, as he hoped he would return to them from Sir Moses's and have another turn with the haryers—try if they couldn't circumvent the old hare that had beat them the other day, and the thing would be for Mr. Pringle to ride his horse quietly over, Monsieur going in advance with the gig, and having all things ready against Mr. Pringle arrived; for the Major well knew that the Baronet's promises were not to be depended upon, and would require some little manouvering to get carried out, especially in the stable department.

Still there was a difficulty—Monsieur couldn't drive. No, by his vord, he couldn't drive. He was *valet-de-chambre*, not coachman or grum, and could make nothing of horses. Might know his ear from his tail, but dat was all. Should be sure to opset, and p'raps damage his crown. (Jack wanted to go in a carriage and pair.) Well, the Major would accommodate that too. Tom Cowlick, the hind's lad at the farm, should act the part of charioteer, and drive Monsieur, bag, baggage and all. And so matters were ultimately settled, it never occurring to Billy to make the attempt on the Major's stud that the Baronet proposed, in the shape of borrowing a second horse, our friend doubtless thinking he carried persecution enough in his own nag. The knotty point of transit being settled, Billy relapsed into his usual easy languor among the girls, while Monsieur made a judicious draft of clothes to take with them, leaving him a very smart suit to appear in at church on Sunday, and afterwards ride through the county in. We will now suppose the dread hour of departure arrived.

It was just as Mrs. Pringle predicted! There were the red eye-lids and laced kerchiefs, and all the paraphernalia of leave-taking, mingled with the hopes of Major and Mrs. Yammerton, that Billy would soon return (after the washing, of course); for, in the language of the turf, Billy was anybody's game, and one sister had just as good a right to red eye-lids as another.

Having seen Billy through the ceremony of leave-taking, the Major then accompanied him to the stable, thinking to say a word for himself and his late horse 'ere they parted. After admiring Napoleon the Great's condition, as he stood turned round in the stall ready for mounting, the Major observed casually, "that he should not be surprised if Sir Moses found fault with that 'oss."

"Why?" asked Billy, who expected perfection for a hundred guineas.

"D-d-don't know," replied the Major, with a Jack Rogers' shrug of the shoulders. "D-d-don't know, 'cept that Sir Moses seldom says a good word for anybody's 'oss but his own."

The clothes being then swept over the horse's long tail into the manger, he stepped gaily out, followed by our friend and his host.

"I thought it b-b-better to send your servant on," observed the Major confidentially, as he stood eyeing the gay deceiver of a horse: "for, between ourselves, the Baronet's stables are none of the best, and it will give you the opportunity of getting the pick of them."

"Yarse," replied Billy, who did not enter into the delicacies of condition.

"That ho-ho-horse requires w-w-warmth," stuttered the Major, "and Sir Moses's stables are both d-d-damp and d-d-dirty;" saying which, he tendered his ungloved hand, and with repeated hopes that Billy would soon return, and wishes for good sport, not forgetting compliments to the Baronet, our hero and his host at length parted for the present.

96

And the Major breathed more freely as he saw the cock-horse capering round the turn into the Helmington road.

CHAPTER XXXII. THE BAD STABLE; OR, "IT'S ONLY FOR ONE NIGHT."

FROM Yammerton Grange to Pangburn Park is twelve miles as the crow flies, or sixteen by the road. The Major, who knows every nick and gap in the country, could ride it in ten or eleven; but this species of knowledge is not to be imparted to even the most intelligent head. Not but what the Major tried to put it into Billy's, and what with directions to keep the Helmington road till he came to the blacksmith's shop, then to turn up the crooked lane on the left, leaving Wanley windmill on the right, and Altringham spire on the left, avoiding the village of Rothley, then to turn short at Samerside Hill, keeping Missleton Plantations full before him, with repeated assurances that he couldn't miss his way, he so completely bewildered our friend, that he was lost before he had gone a couple of miles. Then came the provoking ignorance of country life,—the counter-questions instead of answers,—the stupid stare and tedious drawl, ending, perhaps, with "ars a stranger," or may be the utter negation of a place within, perhaps, a few miles of where the parties live. Billy blundered and blundered; took the wrong turning up the crooked lane, kept Wanley windmill on the left instead of the right, and finally rode right into the village of Rothley, and then began asking his way. It being Sunday, he soon attracted plenty of starers, such an uncommon swell being rare in the country; and one told him one way; another, another; and then the two began squabbling as to which was the right one, enlisting of course the sympathies of the bystanders, so that Billy's progress was considerably impeded. Indeed, he sometimes seemed to recede instead of advance, so contradictory were the statements as to distance, and the further be went the further he seemed to have to go.

If Sir Moses hadn't been pretty notorious as well from hunting the country as from his other performances, we doubt whether Billy would have reached Pangburn Park that night. As it was, Sir Moses's unpopularity helped Billy along in a growling uncivil sort of way, so different to the usual friendly forwarding that marks the approach to a gentleman's house in the country.

"Ay, ay, that's the way," said one with a sneer. "What, you're gannin to him—are ye?" asked another, in a tone that as good as said, I wouldn't visit such a chap. "Aye, that's the way—straight on, through Addingham town"—for every countryman likes to have his village called a town— "straight on through Addingham town, keep the lane on the left, and then when ye come to the beer-shop at three road ends, ax for the Kingswood road, and that'll lead ye to the lodges."

All roads are long when one has to ask the way—the distance seems nearly double in going to a place to what it does in returning, and Billy thought he never would get to Pangburn Park. The shades of night, too, drew on—Napoleon the Great had long lost his freedom and gaiety of action, and hung on the bit in a heavy listless sort of way. Billy wished for a policeman to protect and direct him. Lights began to be scattered about the country, and day quickly declined in favour of night. The darkening mist gathered perceptibly. Billy longed for those lodges of which he had heard so much, but which seemed ever to elude him. He even appeared inclined to compound for the magnificence of two by turning in at Mr. Pinkerton's single one. By the direction of the woman at this one, he at length reached the glad haven, and passing through the open portals was at length in Pangburn Park. The drab-coloured road directed him onward, and Billy being relieved from the anxieties of asking his way, pulled up into a walk, as well to cool his horse as to try and make out what sort of a place he had got to. With the exception, however, of the road, it was a confused mass of darkness, that might contain trees, hills, houses, hay-stacks, anything. Presently the melodious cry of hounds came wafted on the southerly breeze, causing our friend to shudder at the temerity of his undertaking. "Drat these hounds," muttered he, wishing he was well out of the infliction, and as he proceeded onward the road suddenly divided, and both ways inclining towards certain lights, Billy gave his horse his choice, and was presently clattering on the pavement of the court-yard of Pangburn Park.

Sir Moses's hospitality was rather of a spurious order; he would float his friends with claret and champagne, and yet grudge their horses a feed of corn. Not but that he was always extremely liberal and pressing in his offers, begging people would bring whatever they liked, and stay as long as they could, but as soon as his offers were closed with, he began to back out. Oh, he forgot! he feared he could only take in one horse; or if he could take in a horse he feared he couldn't take in the groom. Just as he offered to lend Billy his gig and horse and then reduced the offer into the loan of the gig only. So it was with the promised two-stalled stable. When Monsieur drove, or rather was driven, with folded arms into the court-yard, and asked for his "me lors stable," the half-muzzy groom observed with a lurch and a hitch of his shorts, that "they didn't take in (hiccup) osses there—leastways to stop all night."

"Veil, but you'll put up me lor Pringle's," observed Jack with an air of authority, for he considered that he and his master were the exceptions to all general rules.

"Fear we can't (hiccup) it," replied the blear-eyed caitiff; "got as many (hiccup) osses comin to-night as ever we have room for. Shall have to (hiccup) two in a (hiccup) as it is" (hiccup).

"Oh, you can stow him away somewhere," now observed Mr. Demetrius Bankhead, emerging from his pantry dressed in a pea-green wide-awake, a Meg Merrilies tartan shooting-jacket, a straw-coloured vest, and drab pantaloons.

"You'll be Mr. Pringle's gentleman, I presume," observed Bankhead, now turning and bowing to Jack, who still retained his seat in the gig.

"I be, sare," replied Jack, accepting the proffered hand of his friend.

"Oh, yes, you'll put him up somewhere, Fred," observed Bankhead, appealing again to the groom, "he'll take no harm anywhere," looking at the hairy, heated animal, "put 'im in the empty cow-house," adding "it's only for one night—only for one night."

"O dis is not the quadruped," observed Monsieur, nodding at the cart mare before him, "dis is a job beggar vot ve can kick out at our pleasure, but me lor is a cornin' on his own proper cheval, and he vill vant space and conciliation."

"Oh, we'll manage him somehow," observed Bankhead confidently, "only we've a large party to-night, and want all the spare stalls we can raise, but they'll put 'im up somewhere," added he, "they'll put 'im up somewhere," observing as before, "it's only for one night—only for one night. Now won't you alight and walk in," continued he, motioning Monsieur to descend, and Jack having intimated that his lor vould compliment their politeness if they took veil care of his 'orse, conceived he had done all that a faithful domestic could under the circumstances, and leaving the issue in the hands of fate, alighted from his vehicle, and entering by the back way, proceeded to exchange family "particulars" with Mr. Bankhead in the pantry.

Now the Pangburn Park stables were originally very good, forming a crescent at the back of the house, with coach-houses and servants' rooms intervening, but owing to the trifling circumstance of allowing the drains to get choked, they had fallen into disrepute. At the back of the crescent were some auxiliary stables, worse of course than the principal range, into which they put night-visitors' horses, and those whose owners were rash enough to insist upon Sir Muses fulfilling his offers of hospitality to them. At either end of these latter were loose boxes, capable of being made into two-stalled stables, only these partitions were always disappearing, and the roofs had long declined turning the weather; but still they were better than nothing, and often formed receptacles for sly cabby's, or postboys who preferred the chance of eleemosynary fare at Sir Moses's to the hand in the pocket hospitality of the Red Lion, at Fillerton Hill, or the Main-chance Arms, at Duckworth Bridge. Into the best of these bad boxes the gig mare was put, and as there was nothing to get in the house, Tom Cowlick took his departure as soon as she had eaten her surreptitious feed of oats. The pampered Napoleon the Great, the horse that required all the warmth and coddling in the world, was next introduced, fine Billy alighting from his back in the yard with all the unconcern that he would from one of Mr. Splint's or Mr. Spavins's week day or hour jobs. Indeed, one of the distinguishing features between the new generation of sportsmen and the old, is the marked indifference of the former to the comforts of their horses compared to that shown by the old school, who always looked to their horses before themselves, and not unfrequently selected their inns with reference to the stables. Now-a-days, if a youth gives himself any concern about the matter, it will often only be with reference to the bill, and he will frequently ride away without ever having been into the stable. If, however, fine Billy had seen his, he would most likely have been satisfied with the comfortable assurance that it was "only for one night," the old saying, "enough to kill a horse," leading the uninitiated to suppose that they are very difficult to kill.

"Ah, my dear Pringle!" exclaimed Sir Moses, rising from the depths of a rather inadequately stuffed chair (for Mrs. Margerum had been at it). "Ah, my dear Pringle, I'm delighted to see you!" continued the Baronet, getting Billy by both hands, as the noiseless Mr. Bankhead, having opened the library door, piloted him through the intricacies of the company. Our host really was glad of a new arrival, for a long winter's evening had exhausted the gossip of parties who in a general way saw quite enough, if not too much, of each other. And this is the worst of country visiting in winter; people are so long together that they get exhausted before they should begin.

They have let off the steam of their small talk, and have nothing left to fall back upon but repetition. One man has told what there is in the "Post," another in "Punch," a third in the "Mark Lane Express," and then they are about high-and-dry for the rest of the evening. From criticising Billy, they had taken to speculating upon whether he would come or not, the odds—without which an Englishmen can do nothing—being rather in favour of Mrs. Yammerton's detaining him. It was not known that Monsieur Rougier had arrived. The mighty problem was at length solved by the Richest Commoner in England appearing among them, and making the usual gyrations peculiar to an introduction. He was then at liberty for ever after to nod or speak or shake hands with or bow to Mr. George and Mr. Henry Waggett, of Kitteridge Green, both five-and-twenty pound subscribers to the Hit-im and Hold-im-shire hounds, to Mr. Stephen Booty, of Verbena Lodge, who gave ten pounds and a cover, to Mr. Silver-thorn, of Dryfield, who didn't give anything, but who had two very good covers which he had been hinting he should require to be paid for,—a hint that had procured him the present invitation, to Mr. Strongstubble, of Buckup Hill, and Mr. Tupman, of Cowslip Cottage, both very good friends to the sport but not "hand in the pocket-ites," to Mr. Tom Dribbler, Jun., of Hardacres, and his friend Captain Hurricane, of Her Majesty's ship Thunderer, and to Mr. Cuthbert Flintoff, commonly called Cuddy Flintoff, an "all about" sportsman, who professed to be of all hunts but blindly went to none. Cuddy's sporting was in the past tense, indeed he seemed to exist altogether upon the recollections of the chace, which must have made a lively impression upon him, for he was continually interlarding his conversation with view holloas, yoicks wind 'ims! yoick's push 'im ups! Indeed, in walking about he seemed to help himself along with the aid of for-rardson! for-rards on! so that a person out of sight, but within hearing, would think he was hunting a pack of hounds.

He dressed the sportsman, too, most assiduously, bird's-eye cravats, step-collared striped vests, green or Oxford-grey cutaways, with the neatest fitting trousers on the best bow-legs that ever were seen. To see him at Tattersall's sucking his cane, his cheesy hat well down on his nose, with his stout, well-cleaned doe-skin gloves, standing criticising each horse, a stranger would suppose that he lived entirely on the saddle, instead of scarcely ever being in one. On the present occasion, as soon as he got his "bob" made to our Billy, and our hero's back was restored to tranquillity, he at him about the weather,—how the moon looked, whether there were any symptoms of frost, and altogether seemed desperately anxious about the atmosphere. This inquiry giving the conversation a start in the out-of-doors line, was quickly followed by Sir Moses asking our Billy how he left the Major, how he found his way there, with hopes that everything was comfortable, and oh! agonising promise! that he would do his best to show him sport.

The assembled guests then took up the subject of their "magnificent country" generally, one man lauding its bottomless brooks, another its enormous bullfinches, a third its terrific stone walls, a fourth its stupendous on-and-offs, a fifth its flying foxes, and they unanimously resolved that the man who could ride over Hit-im and Hold-im-shire could ride over any country in the world. "*Any country in the world!*" vociferated Cuddy, slowly and deliberately, with a hearty crack of his fat thigh. And Billy, as he sat listening to their dreadful recitals, thought that he *had* got into the lion's den with a vengeance. Most sincerely he wished himself back at the peaceful pursuits of Yammerton Grange. Then, as they were in full cry with their boasting eulogiums, the joyful dressing-bell rang, and Cuddy Flintoff putting his finger in his ear, as if to avoid deafening himself, shrieked, "*hoick halloa! hoick.!*" in a. tone that almost drowned the sound of the clapper. Then when the "ticket of leaver" and the *delirium tremens* footman appeared at the door with the blaze of bedroom candles, Cuddy suddenly turned whipper-inv and working his right arm as if he were cracking a whip, kept holloaing, "*get away hoick! get away hoick.!*" until he drove Billy and Baronet and all before him.

****

"Rum fellow that," observed the Baronet, now showing Billy up to his room, as soon as he had got sufficient space put between them to prevent Cuddy hearing, "Rum fellow that," repeated he, not getting a reply from our friend, who didn't know exactly how to interpret the word "rum."

"That fellow's up to everything,—cleverest fellow under the sun," continued Sir Moses, now throwing open the door of an evident bachelor's bed-room. Not but that it was one of the best in the house, only it was wretchedly furnished, and wanted all the little neatnesses and knic-knaceries peculiar to a lady-kept house. The towels were few and flimsy, the soap hard and dry, there was a pincushion without pins, a portfolio without paper, a grate with a smoky fire, while the feather-bed and mattress had been ruthlessly despoiled of their contents. Even the imitation maple-wood sofa on which Billy's dress-clothes were now laid, had not been overlooked, and was as lank and as bare as a third-rate Margate lodging-house, one—all ribs and hollows.

"Ah, there you are!" exclaimed Sir Moses, pointing to the garments, "There you are!" adding, "You'll find the bell at the back of your bed," pointing to one of the old smothering order of four-posters with its dyed moreen curtains closely drawn, "You'll find the bell at the back of the bed, and when you come down we shall be in the same room as we were before." So saying, the Baronet retired, leaving our Billy to commence operations.

CHAPTER XXXIII. SIR MOSES'S SPREAD.

WE dare pay it has struck such of our readers as have followed the chace for more than the usual average allowance of three seasons, that hunts flourish most vigorously where there is a fair share of hospitality, and Sir Moses Mainchance was quite of that opinion. He found it answered a very good purpose as well to give occasional dinners at home as to attend the club meetings at Hinton. To the former he invited all the elite of his field, and such people as he was likely to get anything out of while the latter included the farmers and yeomen, the Flying Hatters, the Dampers, and so on, whereby, or by reason or means whereof, as the lawyers say, the spirit of the thing was well sustained. His home parties were always a great source of annoyance to our friend Mrs. Margerum, who did not like to be intruded upon by the job cook (Mrs. Pomfret, of Hinton), Mrs. Margerum being in fact more of a housekeeper than a cook, though quite cook enough for Sir Moses in a general way, and perhaps rather too much of a housekeeper for him—had he but known it. Mrs. Pomfret, however, being mistress of Mrs. Margerum's secret (viz., who got the dripping), the latter was obliged to "put up" with her, and taking her revenge by hiding her things, and locking up whatever she was likely to want. Still, despite of all difficulties, Mrs. Pomfret, when sober, could cook a very good dinner, and as Sir Moses allowed her a pint of rum for supper, she had no great temptation to exceed till then. She was thought on this occasion, if possible, to surpass herself, and certainly Sir Moses's dinner contrasted very favourably with what Billy Pringle had been partaking of at our friend Major Yammerton's, whose cook had more energy than execution. In addition to this, Mr. Bankhead plied the fluids most liberally, as the feast progressed, so that what with invitations to drink, and the regular course of the tide, the party were very happy and hilarious.

Then, after dinner, the hot chestnuts and filberts and anchovy toasts mingling with an otherwise excellent desert flavoured the wine and brought out no end of "yoicks wind 'ims" and aspirations for the morrow. They all felt as if they could ride—Billy and all!

"Not any more, thank you," being at length the order of the day, a move was made back to the library, a drawing-room being a superfluous luxury where there is no lady, and tea and coffee were rung for. A new subject of conversation was wanted, and Monsieur presently supplied the deficiency.

"That's a Frenchman, that servant of yours, isn't he, Pringle?" asked Sir Moses, when Monsieur retired with the tray.

"Yarse," replied Billy, feeling his trifling moustache after its dip in the cup.

"Thought so," rejoined Sir Moses, who prided himself upon his penetration. "I'll have a word with him when he comes in again," continued he.

Tea followed quickly on the heels of coffee, Monsieur coming in after Bankhead. Monsieur now consequentially drank, and dressed much in the manner that he is in the picture of the glove scene at Yammerton Grange.

"*Ah, Monsieur! comment vous portez-vous?*" exclaimed the Baronet, which was about as much French as he could raise.

"Pretty middlin', tenk you, sare," replied Jack, bowing and grinning at the compliment.

"What, you speak English, do you?" asked the Baronet, thinking he might as well change the language.

"I spake it, sare, some small matter, sare," replied Jack, with a shrug of his shoulders—"Not nothing like my modder's tongue, you knows."

"Ah! you speak it domd well," replied Sir Moses. "Let you and I have a talk together. Tell me, now, were you ever out hunting?"

Jean Rougier. "Oh, yes, sare, I have been at the chasse of de small dicky-bird—tom-tit—cock-robin—vot you call."

Sir Moses (laughing). "No, no, that is not the sort of chace I mean; I mean, have you ever been out fox-hunting?"

Jean Rougier (confidentially). "Nevare, sare—nevare."

Sir Moses. "Ah, my friend, then you've a great pleasure to come to—a great pleasure to come to, indeed. Well, you're a domd good feller, and I'll tell you what I'll do—I'll tell you what I'll do—I'll mount you to-morrow—domd if I won't—you shall ride my old horse, Cockatoo—carry you beautifully. What d'ye ride? Thirteen stun, I should say," looking Jack over, "quite up to that—quite up to that—stun above it, for that matter. You'll go streaming away like a bushel of beans."

"Oh, sare, I tenk you, sare," replied Jack, "but I have not got my hunting apparatus—my mosquet—my gun, my—no, not notin at all."

"Gun!" exclaimed Sir Moses, amidst the laughter of the company. "Why, you wouldn't shoot the fox, would ye?"

"*Certainement!*" replied Jack. "I should pop him over."

"Oh, the devil!" exclaimed Sir Moses, throwing up his hands in astonishment. "Why, man, we keep the hounds on purpose to hunt him."

"Silly fellers," replied Jack, "you should pepper his jacket."

"Ah, Monsieur, I see you have a deal to learn," rejoined Sir Moses, laughing. "However, it's never too late to begin—never too late to begin, and you shall take your first lesson to-morrow. I'll mount you on old Cockatoo, and you shall see how we manage these matters in England."

"Oh, sare, I tenk you moch," replied Jack, again excusing himself. "But I have not got no breeches, no boot-jacks—no notin, *comme il faut.*"

"I'll lend you everything you want,—a boot-jack and all," replied Sir Moses, now quite in the generous mood.

"Ah, sare, you are vure beautiful, and I moch appreciate your benevolence; bot I sud not like to risk my neck and crop outside an unqualified, contradictory quadruped."

"Nothing of the sort!" exclaimed Sir Moses, "nothing of the sort! He's the quietest, gentlest crittur alive—a child might ride him, mightn't it, Cuddy?"

"Safesthorse under the sun," replied Cuddy Flintoff, confidently. "Don't know such another. Have nothing to do but sit on his back, and give him his head, and he'll take far better care of you than you can of him. He's the nag to carry you close up to their stems. *Ho-o-i-ck, forrard, ho-o-i-ck!!* Dash my buttons, Monsieur, but I think I see you sailing away. Shouldn't be surprised if you were to bring home the brush, only you've got one under your nose as it is," alluding to his moustache.

Jack at this looked rather sour, for somehow people don't like to be laughed at; so he proceeded to push his tray about under the guests' noses, by way of getting rid of the subject. He had no objection to a hunt, and to try and do what Cuddy Flintoff predicted, only he didn't want to spoil his own clothes, or be made a butt of. So, having had his say, he retired as soon as he could, inquiring of Bankhead, when he got out, who that porky old fellow with the round, close-shaven face was.

When the second flight of tea-cups came in, Sir Moses was seated on a hardish chaise longue, beside our friend Mr. Pringle, to whom he was doing the agreeable attentive host, and a little of the inquisitive stranger; trying to find out as well about the Major and his family, as about Billy himself, his friends and belongings. The Baronet had rather cooled on the subject of mounting Monsieur, and thought to pave the way for a back-out.

"That's a stout-built feller of yours," observed he to Billy, kicking up his toe at Jack as he passed before them with the supplementary tray of cakes and cream, and so on.

"Yarse," drawled Billy, wondering what matter it made to Sir Moses.

"Stouter than I took him for," continued the Baronet, eyeing Jack's broad back and strong undersettings. "That man'll ride fourteen stun, I dessay."

Billy had no opinion on the point so began admiring his pretty foot; comparing it with Sir Moses's, which was rather thick and clumsy.

The Baronet conned the mount matter over in his mind; the man was heavy; the promised horse was old and weak; the country deep, and he didn't know that Monsieur could ride,—altogether he thought it wouldn't do. Let his master mount him if he liked, or let him stay at home and help Bankhead with the plate, or Peter with the shoes. So Sir Moses settled it in his own mind, as far as he was concerned, at least, and resumed his enquiries of our Billy. Which of the Miss Yammertons he thought the prettiest, which sang the best, who played the harp, if the Major indulged him with much hare-soup, and then glanced incidentally at his stud, and Bo-Peep.

He then asked him about Lord Ladythorne; if it was true that Mrs. Moffatt and he quarrelled; if his lordship wasn't getting rather slack; and whether Billy didn't think Dicky Boggledale an old woman, to which latter interrogatory he replied, "Yarse,"—he thought he was, and ought to be drafted.

While the *tête-à-tête* was going on, a desultory conversation ensued among the other guests in various parts of the room, Mr. Booty button-holeing Captain Hurricane, to tell him a capital thing out of "Punch," and receiving in return an exclamation of—"Why, man, I told you that myself before dinner." Tom Dribbler going about touching people up in the ribs with his thumb, inquiring with a knowing wink of his eye, or a jerk of his head, "Aye, old feller, how goes it;" which was about the extent of Tom's conversational powers. Henry Waggett talking "wool" to Mr. Tupman; while Cuddy Flintoff kept popping out every now and then to look at the moon, returning with a "hoick wind 'im; ho-ick!" or—

"*A southerly wind and a cloudy sky, Proclaimeth a hunting morning.*"

Very cheering the assurance was to our friend Billy Pringle, as the reader may suppose; but he had the sense to keep his feelings to himself.

At length the last act of the entertainment approached, by the door flying open through an invisible agency, and the *delirium tremens* footman appearing with a spacious tray, followed by Bankhead and Monsieur, with "Cardigans" and other the materials of "night-caps," which they placed on the mirth-promoting circle of a round table. All hands drew to it like blue-bottle-flies to a sugar-cask, as well to escape from themselves and each other, as to partake of the broiled bones, and other the good things with which the tray was stored.

"Hie, worry! worry! worry!" cried Cuddy Flintoff, darting at the black bottles, for he dearly loved a drink, and presently had a beaker of brandy, so strong, that as Silverthorn said, the spoon almost stood upright in it.

"Let's get chairs!" exclaimed he, turning short round on his heel: "let's get chairs, and be snug; it's as cheap sitting as standing," so saying, he wheeled a smoking chair up to the table, and was speedily followed by the rest of the party, with various shaped seats. Then such of the guests as wanted to shirk drinking took whiskey or gin, which they could dilute as much as they chose; while those who didn't care for showing their predilection for drink, followed Cuddy's example, and made it as strong as they liked. This is the time that the sot comes out undisguisedly. The form of wine-drinking after dinner is mere child's play in their proceedings: the spirit is what they go for.

At length sots and sober ones were equally helped to their liking; and, the approving sips being taken, the other great want of life—tobacco—then became apparent.

"Smoking allowed here," observed Cuddy Flintoff, diving into his side-pocket for a cigar, adding, as he looked at the wretched old red chintz-covered furniture, which, not even the friendly light of the *moderateur* lamps could convert into anything respectable: "No fear of doing any harm here, I think?"

So the rest of the company seemed to think, for there was presently a great kissing of cigar-ends and rising of clouds, and then the party seeming to be lost in deep reveries. Thus they sat for some minutes, some eyeing their cocked-up toes, some the dirty ceiling, others smoking and nursing their beakers of spirit on their knees.

At length Tom Dribbler gave tongue—"What time will the hounds leave the kennel in the morning, Sir Moses?" asked he.

"Hoick to Dribbler! Hoick!" immediately cheered Cuddy—as if capping the pack to a find.

"Oh, why, let me see," replied Sir Moses, filliping the ashes off the end of his cigar—"Let me see," repeated he—"Oh—ah—tomorrow's Monday; Monday, the Crooked Billet—Crooked Billet—nine miles—eight through Applecross Park; leave here at nine—ten to nine, say—nothing like giving them plenty of time on the road."

"Nothing," assented Cuddy Flintoff, taking a deep drain at his glass, adding, as soon as he could get his nose persuaded to come out of it again, "I *do* hate to see men hurrying hounds to cover in a morning."

"No fear of mine doing that," observed Sir Moses, "for I always go with them myself when I can."

"Capital dodge, too," assented Cuddy, "gets the fellers past the public houses—that drink's the ruin of half the huntsmen in England;" whereupon he took another good swig.

"Then, Monsieur, and you'll all go together, I suppose," interrupted Dribbler, who wanted to see the fun.

"Monsieur, Monsieur—oh, ah, that's my friend Pringle's valet," observed Sir Moses, drily; "what about him?"

"Why he's going, isn't he?" replied Dribbler.

"Oh, poor fellow, no," rejoined Sir Moses; "he doesn't want to go—it's no use persecuting a poor devil because a Frenchman."

"But I dare say he'd enjoy it very much," observed Dribbler.

"Well, then, will you mount him?" asked Sir Moses.

"Why I thought *you* were going to do it," replied Dribbler.

"*Me* mount him!" exclaimed Sir Moses, throwing out his ringed hands in well-feigned astonishment, as if he had never made such an offer—"*Me* mount him! why, my dear fellow, do you know how many people I have to mount as it is? Let me tell you," continued he, counting them off on his fingers, "there's Tom, and there's Harry, and there's Joe, and there's the pad-groom and myself, five horses out every day—generally six, when I've a hack—six horses a day, four days a week—if that isn't enough, I don't know what is—dom'd if I do," added he, with a snort and a determined jerk of his head.

"Well, but we can manage him a mount among us, somehow, I dare say," persevered Dribbler, looking round upon the now partially smoke-obscured company.

102

"Oh no, let him alone, poor fellow; let him alone," replied Sir Moses, coaxingly, adding, "he evidently doesn't wish to go—evidently doesn't wish to go."

"I don't know that," exclaimed Cuddy Flintoff, with a knowing jerk of his head; "I don't know that—I should say he's rather a y-o-o-i-cks wind 'im! y-o-i-cks push 'im up! sort of chap." So saying, Cuddy drained his glass to the dregs.

"1 should say you're rather a y-o-i-cks wind 'im—y-o-i-cks drink 'im up sort of chap," replied Sir Moses, at which they all laughed heartily.

Cuddy availed himself of the *divertissement* to make another equally strong brew—saying, "It was put there to drink, wasn't it?" at which they all laughed again.

Still there was a disposition to harp upon the hunt—Dribbler tied on the scent, and felt disposed to lend Jack a horse if nobody else would. So he threw out a general observation, that he thought they could manage a mount for Monsieur among them.

"Well, but perhaps his master mayn't, like it," suggested Sir Moses, in hopes that Billy would come to the rescue.

"O, I don't care about it," replied Billy, with an air of indifference, who would have been glad to hunt by deputy if he could, and so that chance fell to the ground.

"*Hoick to Governor! Hoick to Governor!*" cheered Cuddy at the declaration. "Now who'll lend him a horse?" asked he, taking up the question. "What say you, Stub?" appealing to Mr. Strongstubble, who generally had more than he could ride.

"He's such a beefey beggar," replied Strongstubble, between the whiffs of a cigar.

"Oh, ah, and a Frenchman too!" interposed Sir Moses, "he'll have no idea of saving a horse, or holding a horse together, or making the most of a horse."

"Put him on one that 'll take care of himself," suggested Cuddy; "there's your old Nutcracker horse, for instance," added he, addressing himself to Harry Waggett.

"Got six drachms of aloes," replied Waggett, drily.

"Or your Te-to-tum, Booty," continued Cuddy, nothing baffled by the failure.

"Lame all round," replied Booty, following suit.

"Hut you and your lames," rejoined Cuddy, who knew better—"I'll tell you what you must do then, Tommy," continued he, addressing himself familiarly to Dribbler, "you must lend him your old kicking chestnut—the very horse for a Frenchman," added Cutty, slapping his own tight-trousered leg—"you send the Shaver to the Billet in the morning along with your own horse, and old Johnny Crapaud will manage to get there somehow or other—walk if he can't ride: shoemaker's pony's very safe."

"Oh, I'll send him in my dog-cart if that's all," exclaimed Sir Moses, again waxing generous.

"That 'll do! That 'll do!" replied Cuddy, appealing triumphantly to the brandy. Then as the out-door guests began to depart, and the in-door ones to wind up their watches and ask about breakfast, Cuddy took advantage of one of Sir Moses' momentary absences in the entrance hall to walk off to bed with the remainder of the bottle of brandy, observing, as he hurried away, that he was "apt to have spasms in the night"; and Sir Moses, thinking he was well rid of him at the price, went through the ceremony of asking the "remanets" if they would take any more, and being unanimously answered in the negative, he lit the bedroom candles, turned off the *modérateurs*, and left the room to darkness and to Bankhead.

CHAPTER XXXIV. GOING TO COVER WITH THE HOUNDS.

HOW different a place generally proves to what we anticipate, and how difficult it is to recall our expectations after we have once seen it, unless we have made a memorandum beforehand. How different again a place looks in the morning to what we have conjectured over-night. What we have taken for towers perhaps have proved to be trees, and the large lake in front a mere floating mist.

Pangbum Park had that loose rakish air peculiar to rented places, which carry a sort of visible contest between landlord and tenant on the face of everything. A sort of "it's you to do it, not me" look. It showed a sad want of paint and maintenance generally. Sir Moses wasn't the man to do anything that wasn't absolutely necessary, "Dom'd if he was," so inside and outside were pretty much alike.

Our friend Billy Pringle was not a man of much observation in rural matters, though he understood the cut of a coat, the tie of a watch-ribbon cravat, or the fit of a collar thoroughly. We are sorry to say he had not slept very well, having taken too much brandy for conformity's sake, added to which his bed was hard and knotty, and the finely drawn bolsters and pillows all piled together, were hardly sufficient to raise his throbbing temples. As he lay tossing and turning about, thinking now of Clara Yammerton's beautiful blue eyes and exquisitely rounded figure, now of Flora's bright hair, or Harriet's graceful form, the dread Monsieur entered his shabbily furnished bed-room, with, "Sare, I have de pleasure to bring you your pink to-day," at once banishing the beauties and recalling the over-night's conversation, the frightful fences, the yawning ditches, the bottomless brooks, with the unanimous declaration that the man who could ride over Hit-im and Hold-im-shire could ride over any country in the world. And Billy really thought if he could get over the horrors of that day he would retire from the purgatorial pleasures of the chace altogether.

With this wise resolution he jumped out of bed with the vigorous determination of a man about to take a shower-bath, and proceeded to invest himself in the only mitigating features of the chace, the red coat and leathers. He was hardly well in them before a clamorous bell rang for breakfast, quickly followed by a knock at the door, announcing that it was on the table.

Sir Moses was always in a deuce of a hurry on a hunting morning. Our hero was then presently performing the coming downstairs feat he is represented doing at page 147, and on reaching the lower regions he jumped in with a dish of fried ham which led him straight to the breakfast room.

Here Sir Moses was doing all things at once, reading the "Post," blowing his beak, making the tea, stirring the fire, crumpling his envelopes, cussing the toast, and doming the footman, to which numerous avocations he now added the pleasing one of welcoming our Billy.

"Well done you! First down, I do declare!" exclaimed he, tendering him his left hand, his right one being occupied with his kerchief. "Sit down, and let's be at it," continued he, kicking a rush-bottomed chair under Billy as it were, adding "never wait for any man on a hunting morning." So saying, he proceeded to snatch an egg, in doing which he upset the cream-jug. "Dom the thing," growled he, "what the deuce do they set it there for. D'ye take tea?" now asked he, pointing to the tea-pot with his knife—"or coffee?" continued he, pointing to the coffee-pot with his fork, "or both praps," added he, without waiting for an answer to either question, but pushing both pots towards his guest, following up the advance with ham, eggs, honey, buns, butter, bread, toast, jelly, everything within reach, until he got Billy fairly blocked with good things, when he again set-to on his own account, munching and crunching, and ended by nearly dragging all the contents of the table on to the floor by catching the cloth with his spur as he got up to go away.

He then went doming and scuttling out of the room, charging Billy if he meant to go with the hounds to "look sharp."

During his absence Stephen Booty and Mr. Silverthorn came dawdling into the room, taking it as easy as men generally do who have their horses on and don't care much about hunting.

Indeed Silverthorn never disguised that he would rather have his covers under plough than under gorse, and was always talking about the rent he lost, which he estimated at two pounds an acre, and Sir Moses at ten shillings.

Finding the coast clear, they now rang for fresh ham, fresh eggs, fresh tea, fresh everything, and then took to pumping Billy as to his connection with the house, Sir Moses having made him out over night to be a son of Sir Jonathan Pringle's, with whom he sometimes claimed cousinship, and they wanted to get a peep at the baronetage if they could. In the midst of their subtle examination, Sir Moses came hurrying back, whip in one hand, hat in the other, throwing open the door, with, "Now, are you ready?" to Billy, and "morning, gentlemen," to Booty and Silverthorn.

Then Billy rose with the desperate energy of a man going to a dentist's, and seizing his cap and whip off the entrance table, followed Sir Moses through the intricacies of the back passages leading to the stables, nearly falling over a coal-scuttle as he went. They presently changed the tunnel-like darkness of the passage into the garish light of day, by the opening of the dirty back door.

Descending the little flight of stone steps, they then entered the stable-yard, now enlivened with red coats and the usual concomitants of hounds leaving home. There was then an increased commotion, stable-doors flying open, from which arch-necked horses emerged, pottering and feeling for their legs as they went. Off the cobble-stone pavement, and on to the grass grown soft of the centre, they stood more firm and unflinching. Then Sir Moses took one horse, Tom Findlater another, Harry the first whip a third, Joe the second whip a fourth, while the bine-coated pad groom came trotting round on foot from the back stables, between Sir Moses's second horse and Napoleon the Great.

Billy dived at his horse without look or observation, and the clang of departure being now at its height, the sash of a second-floor window flew up, and a white cotton night-capped head appeared bellowing out, "*Y-o-i-cks wind 'im! y-o-i-cks push 'im up!*" adding, "*Didn't I tell ye* it was going to be a hunting morning?"

"Ay, ay, Cuddy you did," replied Sir Moses laughing, muttering as he went: "That's about the extent of your doings."

"He'll be late, won't he?" asked Billy, spurring up alongside of the Baronet.

"Oh, he's only an afternoon sportsman that," replied Sir Moses; adding, "he's greatest after dinner."

"Indeed!" mused Billy, who had looked upon him with the respect due to a regular flyer, a man who could ride over Hit-im and Hold-im-shire itself.

The reverie was presently interrupted by the throwing open of the kennel door, and the clamorous rush of the glad pack to the advancing red coats, making the green sward look quite gay and joyful.

"Gently, there! gently!" cried Tom Findlater, and first and second whips falling into places, Tom gathered his horse together and trotted briskly along the side of the ill-kept carriage road, and on through the dilapidated lodges: a tattered hat protruding through the window of one, and two brown paper panes supplying the place of glass in the other. They then got upon the high road, and the firy edge being taken off both hounds and horses, Tom relaxed into the old post-boy pace, while Sir Moses proceeded to interrogate him as to the state of the kennel generally, how Rachael's feet were, whether Prosperous was any better, if Abelard had found his way home, and when Sultan would be fit to come out again.

They then got upon other topics connected with the chace, such as, who the man was that Harry saw shooting in Tinklerfield cover; if Mrs Swan had said anything more about her confounded poultry; and whether Ned Smith the rat-catcher would take half a sovereign for his terrier or not.

Having at length got all he could out of Tom, Sir Moses then let the hounds flow past him, while he held back for our Billy to come up. They were presently trotting along together a little in the rear of Joe, the second whip.

"I've surely seen that horse before," at length observed Sir Moses, after a prolonged stare at our friend's steed.

"Very likely," replied Billy, "I bought him of the Major."

"The deuce you did!" exclaimed Sir Moses, "then that's the horse young Tabberton had."

"What, you know him, do you?" asked Billy.

"Know him! I should think so," rejoined Moses; "everybody knows him."

"Indeed!" observed Billy, wondering whether for good or evil.

"I dare say, now, the Major would make you give thirty, or five-and-thirty pounds for that horse," observed Sir Moses, after another good stare.

"Far more!" replied Billy, gaily, who was rather proud of having given a hundred guineas.

"Far more!" exclaimed Sir Moses with energy; "far more! Ah!" added he, with a significant shake of the head, "he's an excellent man, the Major—an excellent man,—but a *leet*le too keen in the matter of horses."

Just at this critical moment Tommy Heslop of Hawthorndean, who had been holding back in Crow-Tree Lane to let the hounds pass, now emerged from his halting-place with a "Good morning, Sir Moses, here's a fine hunting morning?"

"Good morning, Tommy, good morning," replied Sir Moses, extending his right hand; for Tommy was a five-and-twenty pounder besides giving a cover, and of course was deserving of every encouragement.

The salute over, Sir Moses then introduced our friend Billy,—"Mr. Pringle, a Featherbedfordshire gentleman, Mr. Heslop," which immediately excited Tommy's curiosity—not to say jealousy—for the "Billet" was very "contagious," for several of the Peer's men, who always brought their best horses, and did as much mischief as they could, and after ever so good a run, declared it was nothing to talk of. Tommy thought Billy's horse would not take much cutting down, whatever the rider might do. Indeed, the good steed looked anything but formidable, showing that a bad stable, though "only for one night," may have a considerable effect upon a horse. His coat was dull and henfeathered; his eye was watery, and after several premonitory sneezes, he at length mastered a cough. Even Billy thought he felt rather less of a horse under him than he liked. Still he didn't think much of a cough. "Only a slight cold," as a young lady says when she wants to go to a ball.

Three horsemen in front, two black coats and a red, and two reds joining the turnpike from the Witch berry road, increased the cavalcade and exercised Sir Moses' ingenuity in appropriating backs and boots and horses. "That's Simon Smith," said he to himself, eyeing a pair of desperately black tops dangling below a very plumb-coloured, long-backed, short-lapped jacket. "Ah ! and Tristram Wood," added he, now recognising his companion. He then drew gradually upon them and returned their salutes with an extended wave of the hand that didn't look at all like money. Sir Moses then commenced speculating on the foremost group. There was Peter Linch and Charley Drew; but who was the fellow in black? He couldn't make out.

"Who's the man in black, Tommy?" at length asked he of Tommy Heslop.

"Don't know," replied Tommy, after scanning the stranger attentively.

"It can't be that nasty young Rowley Abingdon; and yet I believe it is," continued Sir Moses, eyeing him attentively, and seeing that he did not belong to the red couple, who evidently kept aloof from him. "It is that nasty young Abingdon," added he. "Wonder at his impittance in coming out with me. It's only the other day that ugly old Owl of a father of his killed me young Cherisher, the best hound in my pack," whereupon the Baronet began grinding his teeth, and brewing a little politeness wherewith to bespatter the young Owl as he passed. The foremost horses hanging back to let their friends the hounds overtake them, Sir Moses was presently alongside the black coat, and finding he was right in his conjecture as to who it contained, he returned the youth's awkward salute with, "Well, my man, how d'ye do? hope you're well. How's your father? hope he's well," adding, "dom 'im, he should be hung, and you may tell 'im I said so." Sir Closes then felt his horse gently with his heel, and trotted on to salute the red couple. And thus he passed from singles to doubles, and from doubles to triples, and from triples to quartets, and back to singles again, including the untold occupants of various vehicles, until the ninth milestone on the Bushmead road, announced their approach to the Crooked Billet. Tom Findlater then pulled up from the postboy jog into a wallk, at which pace he turned into the little green field on the left of the blue and gold swinging sign. Here he was received by the earthstopper, the antediluvian ostler, and other great officers of state. But for Sir Moses' presence the question would then have been "What will you have to drink?" That however being interdicted, they raised a discussion about the weather, one insisting that it was going to be a frost; another, that it was going to be nothing of the sort.

CHAPTER XXXV. THE MEET.

THE Crooked Billet Hotel and Posting house, on the Bushin ead road had been severed from society by the Crumpletin Railway. It had indeed been cut off in the prime of life: for Joe Cherriper, the velvet-collared doeskin-gloved Jehu of the fast Regulator Coach, had backed his opinion of the preference of the public for horse transit over steam, by laying out several hundred pounds of his accumulated fees upon the premises, just as the surveyors were setting out the line.

"A rally might be andy enough for goods and eavy marchandise," Joe said; "but as to gents ever travellin' by sich contraband means, that was utterly and entirely out of the question. Never would appen so long as there was a well-appointed coach like the Regulator to be ad." So Joe laid on the green paint and the white paint, and furbished up the sign until it glittered resplendent in the rays of the mid-day sun. But greater prophets than Joe have been mistaken.

One fine summer's afternoon a snorting steam-engine came puffing and panting through the country upon a private road of its own, drawing after it the accumulated rank, beauty, and fashion of a wide district to open the railway, which presently sucked up all the trade and traffic of the country. The Crooked Billet fell from a first-class way-side house at which eight coaches changed horses twice a-day, into a very seedy unfrequented place—a very different one to what it was when our hero's mother, then Miss Willing, changed horses on travelling up in the Old True Blue Independent, on the auspicious day that she captured Mr. Pringle. Still it was visited with occasional glimpses of its former greatness in the way of the meets of the hounds, when the stables were filled, and the long-deserted rooms rang with the revelry of visitors. This was its first gala-day of the season, and several of the Feather-bedfordshire gentlemen availed themselves of the fineness of the weather to see Sir Moses' hounds, and try whether they, too, could ride over Hit-im and Hold-im shire.

The hounds had scarcely had their roll on the greensward, and old black Challenger proclaimed their arrival with his usual deep-toned vehemence, ere all the converging roads and lanes began pouring in their tributaries, and the space before the bay-windowed red brick-built "Billet" was soon blocked with gentlemen on horseback, gentlemen in Malvern dog-carts, gentlemen in Newport Pagnells, gentlemen in Croydon clothesbaskets, some divesting themselves of their wraps, some stretching themselves after their drive, some calling for brandy, some for baccy, some for both brandy and baccy.

Then followed the usual inquiries, "Is Dobbinson coming?"

"Where's the Damper?"

"Has anybody seen anything of Gameboy Green?" Next, the heavily laden family vehicles began to arrive, containing old fat *paterfamilias* in the red coat of his youth, with his "missis" by his side, and a couple of buxom daughters behind, one of whom will be installed in the driving seat when papa resigns. Thus we have the Mellows of Mawdsley Hill, the Chalkers of Streetley, and the Richleys of Jollyduck Park, and the cry is still, "They come! they come!" It is going to be a bumper meet, for the foxes are famous, and the sight of a good "get away" is worth a dozen Legers put together.

See here comes a nice quiet-looking little old gentleman in a well-brushed, flat-brimmed hat, a bird's-eye cravat, a dark grey coat buttoned over a step-collared toilanette vest, nearly matching in line his delicate cream-coloured leathers, who everybody stares at and then salutes, as he lifts first one rose-tinted top and then the other, working his way through the crowd, on a thorough-bred suatlle-bridled bay. He now makes up to Sir Muses, who exclaims as the raised hat shows the familiar blue-eyed face, "Ah! Dicky my man! how d'ye do? glad to see you?" and taking off his glove the Baronet gives our old friend Boggledike a hearty shake of the hand. Dicky acknowledges the honour with becoming reverence, and then begins talking of sport and the splendid runs they have been having, while Sir Moses, instead of listening, cons over some to give him in return.

But who have we here sitting so square in the tandem-like dogcart, drawn by the high-stepping, white-legged bay with sky-blue rosettes, and long streamers, doing the pride that apes humility in a white Macintosh, that shows the pink collar to great advantage? Imperial John, we do believe?

Imperial John, it is! He has come all the way from Barley Hill Hall, leaving the people 011 the farm and the plate in the drawing-room to take care of themselves, starting before daylight, while his footman groom has lain ont over night to the serious detriment of a half sovereign. As John now pulls up, with a trace-rattling ring, he cocks his Imperial chin and looks round for applause—a "Well done, you!" or something of that sort, for coming such a distance. Instead of that, a line of winks, and nods, and nudges, follow his course, one man whispering another, "I say, here's old Imperial John," or "I say, look at Miss de Glancey's boy;" while the young ladies turn their eyes languidly upon him to see what sort of a hero the would-be Benedict is. His Highness, however, has quite got over his de Glancey failure, and having wormed his way after divers "with your leaves," and "by your leaves," through the intricacies of the crowd, he now pulls up at the inn door, and standing erect in his dog-cart, sticks his whip in the socket, and looks around with a "This is Mr. Hybrid the-friend-of-an-Earl" sort of air.

"Ah! Hybrid, how d'ye do?" now exclaims Sir Moses familiarly; "hope you're well?—how's the Peer? hope he's well. Come all the way from Barley Hill?"

"Barley Hill *Hall*," replies the great man with an emphasis on the Hall, adding in the same breath, "Oi say, ostler, send moy fellow!" whereupon there is a renewed nudging and whispering among the ladies beside him, of "That's Mr. Hybrid!"

"That's Imperial John, the gentleman who wanted to marry Miss de Glancey for though Miss de Glancey was far above having him, she was not above proclaiming the other."

His Highness then becomes an object of inquisitive scrutiny by the fair; one thinking he might do for Lavinia Edwards; another, for Sarah Bates; a third, for Rachel Bell; a fourth, perhaps, for herself. It must be a poor creature that isn't booked for somebody.

Still, John stands erect in his vehicle, flourishing his whip, hallooing and asking for his fellow.

"Ring the bell for moy fellow!—Do go for moy fellow!—Has anybody seen moy fellow? Have you seen moy fellow?" addressing an old smock-frocked countryman with a hoe in his hand.

"Nor, arm d—d if iver ar i did!" replied the veteran, looking him over, a declaration that elicited a burst of laughter from the bystanders, and an indignant chuck of the Imperial chin from our John.

"*Tweet, tweet, tweet!*" who have we here? All eyes turn up the Cherryburn road; the roused hounds prick their ears, and are with difficulty restrained from breaking away. It's Walker, the cross postman's gig, and he is treating himself to a twang of the horn. But who has he with him? Who is the red arm-folded man lolling with as much dignity as the contracted nature of the vehicle will allow? A man in red, with cap and beard, and all complete. Why it's Monsieur! Monsieur coming *in forma pauperis*, after Sir Moses' liberal offer to send him to cover,—Monsieur in a faded old sugar-loaf shaped cap, and a scanty coat that would have been black if it hadn't been red.

Still Walker trots him up like a man proud of his load amid the suppressed titters and "Who's this?" of the company. Sir Moses immediately vouchsafes him protection—by standing erect in his stirrups, and exclaiming with a waive of his right hand, "Ah, Monsieur! *comment vous portez-vous?*"

"Pretty bobbish, I tenk you, sare, opes you are veil yourself and all de leetle Mainchanees," replied Monsieur, rising in the gig, showing the scrimpness of his coat and the amplitude of his cinnamon-coloured peg-top trousers, thrust into green-topped opera-boots, much in the style of old Paul Pry. Having put something into Walker's hand, Monsieur alights with due caution and Walker whipping on, presently shows the gilt "V. R." on the back of his red gig as he works his way through the separating crowd. Walker claims to be one of Her Majesty's servants; if not to rank next to Lord Palmerston, at all events not to be far below him. And now Monsieur being left to himself, thrusts his Malacca cane whip stick under his arm, and drawing on a pair of half-dirty primrose-coloured kid gloves, pokes into the crowd in search of his horse, making up to every disengaged one he saw, with "Is dee's for me? Is dee's for me?"

Meanwhile Imperial John having emancipated himself from his Mackintosh, and had his horse placed becomingly at the step of the dog-cart, so as to transfer himself without alighting, and let everybody see the magnificence of the establishment, now souces himself into the saddle of a fairish young grey, and turns round to confront the united field; feeling by no means the smallest man in the scene. "Hybrid!" exclaims Sir Moses, seeing him approach the still dismounted Monsieur, "Hybrid! let me introduce my friend Rougier, Monsieur Rougier, Mr. Hybrid! of Barley Hill Hall, a great friend of Lord Ladythorne's," whereupon off went the faded sugar-loaf-shaped cap, and down came the Imperial hat, Sir Moses interlarding the ceremony with, "great friend of Louis Nap's, great friend of Louis Nap's," by way of balancing the Ladythorne recommendation of John. The two then struck up a most energetic conversation, each being uncommonly taken with the other. John almost fancied he saw his way to the Tuileries, and wondered what Miss "somebody" would say if he got there.

The conversation was at length interrupted by Dribbler's grinning groom touching Jack behind as he came up with a chestnut horse, and saying, "Please, Sir, here's your screw."

"Ah, my screw, is it!" replied Jack, turning round, "dat is a queer name for a horse—screw—hopes he's a good 'un."

"A good 'un, and nothin' but a good 'un," replied the groom, giving him a punch in the ribs, to make him form up to Jack, an operation that produced an ominous grunt.

"Vell" said Jack, proceeding to dive at the stirrup with his foot without taking hold of the reins; "if Screw is a good 'un I sail make you handsome present—tuppence a penny, p'raps—if he's a bad 'un, I sail give you good crack on the skoll," Jack flourishing his thick whipstick as he spoke.

"Will you!" replied the man, leaving go of the rein, whereupon down went the horse's head, up went his heels, and Jack was presently on his shoulder.

"Oh, de devil!" roared Jack, "he vill distribute me! he vill distribute me! I vill be killed! Nobody sall save me! here, garçon, grum!" roared he amid the mirth of the company. "Lay 'old of his 'ead! lay 'old of his 'ocks! lay 'old of 'eels! Oh, murder! murder!" continued he in well-feigned dismay, throwing out his supplicating arms. Off jumped Imperial John to the rescue of his friend, and seizing the dangling rein, chucked up the horse's head with a resolute jerk that restored Jack to his seat.

"Ah, my friend, I see you are not much used to the saddle," observed His Highness, proceeding to console the friend of an Emperor.

"Veil, sare, I am, and I am not," replied Jack, mopping his brow, and pretending to regain his composure, "I am used to de leetle 'orse at de round-about at de fair, I can carry off de ring ten time out of twice, but these great unruly, unmannerly, undutiful screws are more than a match for old Harry."

"Just so," assented His Highness, with a chuck of his Imperial chin, "just so;" adding in an under-tone, "then I'll tell you what we'll do—I'll tell you what we'll do—we'll pop into the bar at the back of the house, and have a glass of something to strengthen our nerves."

"By all means, sare," replied Jack, who was always ready for a glass. So they quietly turned the corner, leaving the field to settle their risible faculties, while they summoned the pretty corkscrew ringletted Miss Tubbs to their behests.

"What shall it be?" asked Imperial John, as the smiling young lady tripped down the steps to where they stood.

"Brandy," replied Jack, with a good English accent.

"Two brandies!" demanded Imperial John, with an air of authority.

"Cold, *with*?" asked the lady, eyeing Monsieur's grim visage.

"*Neat!*" exclaimed Jack in a tone of disdain.

"Yes, Sir," assented the lady, bustling away.

"*Shilling* glasses!" roared Jack, at the last flounce of her blue muslin.

Presently she returned bearing two glasses of very brown brandy, and each having appropriated one, Jack began grinning and bowing and complimenting the donor.

"Sare," said he, after smelling at the beloved liquor, "I have moch pleasure in making your quaintance. I am moch pleased, sare, with the expression of your mog. I tink, sare, you are de 'andsomest man I never had de pleasure of lookin' at. If, sare, dey had you in my country, sare, dey vod make you a King—Emperor, I mean. I drink, sare, your vare good health," so saying, Jack swigged off the contents oi his glass at a draught.

Imperial John felt constrained to do the same.

"Better now," observed Jack, rubbing his stomach as the liquid fire began to descend. "Better now," repeated he, with a jerk of his head, "Sare," continued he, "I sall return the compliment—I sall treat you to a glass."

Imperial John would rather not. He was a glass of sherry and a biscuit sort of man; but Monsieur was not to be balked in his liberality. "Oh, yes, sare, make me de pleasure to accept a glass," continued Jack, "Here! Jemima! Matilda! Adelaide! vot the doose do they call de young vomans—look sharp," added he, as she now reappeared. "Apportez, dat is to say, bring tout suite, directly; two more glasses; dis gentlemans vill be goode enough to drink my vare good 'ealth."

"Certainly," replied the smiling lady, tripping away for them.

"Ah, sare, it is de stoff to make de air corl," observed Jack, eyeing his new acquaintance. "Ye sall go like old chaff before the vind after it. Vill catch de fox myself."

The first glass had nearly upset our Imperial friend, and the second one appeared perfectly nauseous. He would give anything that Jack would drink them both himself. However, Monsieur motioned blue muslin to present the tray to John first, so he had no alternative but to accept. Jack then took his glass, and smacking his lips, said—"I looks, sare, towards you, sare, vith all de respect due to your immortal country. De English, sare, are de finest nation under de moon; and you, sare, and you are as fine a specimens of dat nation as never vas seen. Two such mans as you, sare, could have taken Sebastopol. You could vop all de ell ound savage Sepoys by yourself. So now, sare," continued Jack, brandishing his glass, "make ready, present, *fire!*" and at the word fire, he drained off his glass, and then held it upside down to show he had emptied it.

Poor Imperial John was obliged to follow suit.

The Imperial head now began to swim. Mr. Hybrid saw two girls in blue muslin, two Monsieurs, two old yellow Po-chaises, two water-carts with a Cochin-China cock a gollowing a-top of each.

Jack, on the contrary, was quite comfortable. He had got his nerves strung, and was now ready for anything. "S'pose, now," said he, addressing his staring, half-bewildered friend, "you ascend your gallant grey, and let us look after dese mighty chasseurs. But stop," added he, "I vill first pay for de tipple," pretending to dive into his peg-top trousers pocket for his purse. "*Ah! malheureusement,*" exclaimed he, after feeling them both. "I have left my blont, my tin, in my oder trousers pockets. Navare mind! navare mind," continued he, gaily, "'ve vill square it op some other day. Here," added he to the damsel, "dis gentlemens vill pay, and I vill settle vid him some oder day—some oder day." So saying, Jack gathered his horse boldly together, and spurred out of the inn-yard in a masterly way, singing *Partant pour la Syrie* as he went.

CHAPTER XXXVI. A BIRD'S EYE VIEW.

HE friends reappeared at the front of the Crooked Billet Hotel when the whole cavalcade had swept away, leaving only the return ladies, and such of the grooms as meant to have a drink, now that "master was safe." Sir Moses had not paid either Louis Napoleon's or Lord Ladythorne's friend, the compliment of waiting for them. On the contrary, having hailed the last heavy subscriber who was in the habit of using the Crooked Billet meet, he hallooed the huntsman to trot briskly away down Rickleton Lane, and across Beecham pastures, as well to shake off the foot-people, as to prevent any attempted attendance on the part of the carriage company. Sir Moses, though very gallant, was not always in the chattering mood; and, assuredly, if ever a master of hounds may be excused for a little abruptness, it is when he is tormented by the rival spirits of the adjoining hunt, people who always see things so differently to the men of the country, so differently to what they are meant to do.

It was evident however by the lingering looks and position of parties that the hunt had not been long gone—indeed, the last red coat might still be seen bobbing up and down past the weak and low parts of the Rickleton Lane fence. So Monsieur, having effected a satisfactory rounding, sot his horse's head that way, much in the old threepence a-mine and hopes for something over, style of his youth. Jack hadn't forgotten how to ride, though he might occasionally find it convenient to pretend to be a tailor. Indeed, his horse seemed to have ascertained the fact, and instead of playing any more monkey-tricks, he began to apply himself sedulously to the road. Imperial John was now a fitter subject for solicitude than Monsieur, His Highness's usual bumptious bolt-upright seat being exchanged for a very slouchy, vulgar roll. His saucy eyes too seemed dim and dazzled, like an owl's flying against the sun. Some of the toiling pedestrians, who in spite of Sir Moses's intention to leave them in the lurch, had started for the hunt, were the first overtaken, next two grinning boys riding a barebacked donkey, one with his face to the tail, doing the flagellation with an old hearth-brush, then a brandy-nosed horse-breaker, with a badly-grown black colt that didn't promise to be good for anything, next Dr. Linton on his dun pony, working his arms and legs most energetically, riding far faster than his nag; next Noggin, the exciseman, stealing quietly along on his mule as though he were bent on his business and had no idea of a hunt; and at length a more legitimate representative of the chace in the shape of young Mr. Hadaway, of Oakharrow Hill, in a pair of very baggy white cords, on but indifferent terms about the knees with his badly cleaned tops. They did not, however, overtake the hounds, and the great body of scarlet, till just as they turned off the Summersham road into an old pasture-field, some five acres of the low end of which had been cut off for a gorse to lay to the adjoining range of rocky hills whose rugged juniper and broom-dotted sides afforded very comfortable and popular lying for the foxes. It being, if a find, a quick "get away," all hands were too busy thinking of themselves and their horses, and looking for their usual opponents to take heed of anything else, and Jack and his friends entered without so much as an observation from any one.

Just at that moment up went Joe's cap on the top of the craig, and the scene changed to one of universal excitement. Then, indeed, had come the tug of war! Sir Moses, all hilarity, views the fox! Now Stephen Booty sees him, now Peter Lynch, and now a whole cluster of hats are off in his honour.

****

And now his honour's off himself—

"Shrill horns proclaim his flight." Oh dear! oh dear! where's Billy Pringle? Oh dear! oh dear! where's Imperial John? Oh dear! where's Jack Rogers?

Jack's all right! There he is grinning with enthusiasm, quite forgetting that he's a Frenchman, and hoisting his brown cap with the best of them. Another glass would have made him give a stunning view-halloa.

Imperial John stares like a man just awoke from a dream. Is he in bed, or is he out hunting, or how! he even thinks he hears Miss de Glancey's "*Si-r-r!* do you mean to insult me?" ringing in his ears.

Billy Pringle! poor Billy! he's not so unhappy as usual. His horse is very docile. His tail has lost all its elegant gaiety, and altogether he has a very drooping, weedy look: he coughs, too, occasionally. Billy, however, doesn't care about the coughs, and gives him a dig with his spur to stop it.

"Come along, Mr. Pringle, come along!" now shrieks Sir Moses, hurrying past, hands down, head too, hugging and spurring his horse as he goes. He is presently through the separating throng, leaving Billy far in the rear. "*Quick's*" the word, or the chance is lost. There are no reserved places at a hunt. A flying fox admits of no delay. It is either go or stay.

And now, Monsieur Jean Rougier having stuck his berry-brown conical cap tight on his bristly black head, crams his chestnut horse through the crowd, hallooing to his transfixed brandy friend, "Come along, old cock-a-doodle! come along, old Blink Bonny!"

Imperial John, who has been holding a mental conference with himself, poising himself in the saddle, and making a general estimate of his condition, thinking he is not so drunk as "all that," accepts the familiar challenge, and urges his horse on with the now flying crowd. He presently makes a bad shot at a gate on the swing, which catching him on the kneecap, contributes very materially to restore his sobriety, the pain making him first look back for his leg, which he thinks must be off, and then forward at the field. It is very large; two bustling Baronets, two Monsieurs, two huntsmen, two flying hatters—everybody in duplicate, in short.

Away they scud up Thorneycroft Valley at a pace that looks very like killing. The foremost rise the hill, hugging aud holding on by the manes.

"I'll go!" says his Highness to himself, giving up rubbing his kneecap, and settling himself in his saddle, he hustles his horse, and pushing past the undecided ones, is presently in the thick of the fray. There is Jack going, elbows and legs, elbows and legs, at a very galloping, dreary, done sort of pace, the roaring animal he bestrides contracting its short, leg-tied efforts every movement. Jack presently begins to objurgate the ass who lent it him; first wishes he was on himself, then declares the tanner ought to have him. he now sits sideways, and proceeds to give him a good rib-roasting in the old post-boy style.

110

And now there's a bobbing up and down of hats, caps, and horses' heads in front, with the usual deviation under the "hounds clauses consolidation act," where the dangerous fencing begins. A pair of white breeches are summersaulting in the air, and a bay horse is seen careering in a wild head in the air sort of way, back to the rear instead of following the hounds.

"That's lucky," said Jack Rogers to himself, as soon as he saw him coming towards him, and circumventing him adroitly at the corner of a turnip-field, he quits his own pumped-out animal and catches him. "That's good," said he, looking him over, seeing that he was a lively young animal in fairish condition, with a good saddle and bridle.

"Stirrups just my length, too, I do believe," continued he, preparing to mount. "All right, by Jove!" added he, settling himself into the saddle, feet well home, and gathering his horse together, he shot forward with the easy elasticity of breeding. It was a delightful change from the rolling cow-like action of the other.

"Let us see vot he as in his monkey," said Jack to himself, now drawing the flask from the saddle-case.

"Sherry, I fear," said he, uncorking it.

"Brandy, I declare," added he with delight, after smelling it. He then took a long pull at the contents.

"Good it is, too!" exclaimed he, smacking his lips; "better nor ve ad at de poblic;" so saying, he took another long suck of it.

"May as vell finish it," continued he, shaking it at his ear to ascertain what was left; and having secured the remainder, he returned the monkey to the saddle-case, and put on his horse with great glee, taking a most independent line of his own.

Jack's triumph, however, was destined to be but of short duration. The fox being hard pressed, abandoned his original point for Collington Woods, and swerving to the left over Stanbury Hundred, was headed by a cur, and compelled to seek safety in a drain in the middle of a fallow field. The hounds were presently feathering over the mouth in the usual wild, disappointed sort of way, that as good as says, "No fault of ours, you know; if he won't stay above ground, we can't catch him for you."

Such of the field as had not ridden straight for Collington Woods, were soon down at the spot; and while the usual enquiries, "Where's Pepper?" "Where's Viper?" "Where can we get a spade?" "Does anybody know anything about the direction of this drain?" were going on, a fat, fair, red-coated, flushed-faced pedestrian—to wit, young Mr. Threadcroft, the woolstapler's son of Harden Grange and Hinton, dived into the thick of the throng, and making up to Monsieur, exclaimed in an anger-choked voice, "This (puff) is my (gasp) horse! What the (gasp, puff) devil do you mean by riding away with him in this (puff-, gasp) way?" the youth mopping his brow with a yellow bandanna as he spoke.

"Your oss!" exclaimed Jack with the greatest effrontery, "on de loose can he be your os: I catched him fair! and I've a right to ride him to de end of de run;" a claim that elicited the uproarious mirth of the field, who all looked upon the young wool-pack, as they called him, as a muff.

"Nonsense!" retorted the youth, half frantic with rage. "How can that be?"

"Ow can dat be," repeated Jack, turning sideways in his saddle, and preparing to argue the case, "Ow can dat be? Dis hont, sare, I presume, sare, is condocted on de principle of de grand hont de Epping, vere every mans vot cotched anoder's oss, is entitled to ride him to the end of de ron," replied Jack gravely.

"Nonsense!" again retorted the youth, amidst the renewed laughter of the field. "We know nothing of Epping hunts here!"

"Nothin' of Epping onts here?" exclaimed Jack, throwing out his hands with well feigned astonishment. "Nothin' of Epping honts here! Vy, de grand hont de. Epping rules all the oder honts, jost as the grand Clob de Jockey at Newmarket rules all oder Jockey Clubs in de kingdom."

"Hoot, toot," sneered the fat youth, "let's have none of yonr jaw. Give me my horse, I say, how can he be yours?"

"Because, sare," replied Jack, "I tells you I cotched 'im fairly in de field. Bot for me he vod have been lost to society—to de vorld at large—eat up by de loup—by de volf—saddle, bridle, and all."

"Nothing of the sort!" retorted Mr. Treadcroft, indignantly, "you had no business to touch him."

Monsieur (with energy). I appeal to you, Sare Moses Baronet, de grand maître de chien, de master of all de dogs and all de dogs' vives, if I have not a right to ride 'im.

"Ah, I'm afraid, Monsieur, it's not the law of this country," replied Sir Moses, laughing. "It may be so in France, perhaps; but tell me, where's your own horse?"

Monsieur. Pomped out de beggar; had no go in 'im; left him in a ditch.

Sir Moses. That's a pity!—if you'd allowed me, I'd have sent you a good 'un.

Mr. Treadcroft, thus reinforced by Sir Moses's decision, returned to the charge with redoubled vigour. "If you don't give me up my horse, sir," says he, with firmness, "I'll give you in charge of the police for stealing him." Then

"Conscience, which makes cowards of us all,"

caused Jack to shrink at the recollection of his early indiscretion in the horse-stealing line, and instantly resolving not to give Jack Ketch a chance of taking any liberties with his neck, he thus addresses Mr. Treadcroft:—

"Sare, if Sare Moses Baronet, de grand maître de chien, do grandmodder of all de dogs and all de dogs' vives, says it is not a case of catch 'im and keep 'im 'cordin' to de rules of de grand hont de Epping, I must surrender de quadruped, but I most say it is dem un'andsome treatment, after I 'ave been at de trouble of catching 'im." So saying, Jack dropped off on the wrong side of the saddle, and giving the horse a slap on his side left his owner to take him.

"Tally-ho! there he goes!" now exclaimed a dozen voices, as out bounced the fox with a flourish of his well tagged brush that looked uncommonly defiant. What a commotion he caused! Every man lent a shout that seemed to be answered by a fresh effort from the flyer: but still, with twenty couple of overpowering animals after him, what chance did there seem for his life, especially when they could hunt him by his scent after they had lost sight. Every moment, however, improved his opportunity, and a friendly turn of the land shutting him out of view, the late darting, half-frantic pack were brought to their noses.

"Hold hard for *one*, minute!" is the order of the day.

"Now, catch 'em if you can!" is the cry.

Away they go in the settled determined way of a second start. The bolt taking place on the lower range of the gently swelling Culmington hills, that stretch across the north-east side of Hit-im and Hold-im shire, and the fox making for the vale below, Monsieur has a good bird's eye view of the scramble, without the danger and trouble of partaking of the struggle. Getting astride a newly stubbed ash-tree near the vacated drain mouth, he thus sits and soliloquises—"He's a pretty flyer, dat fox—if dey catch 'im afore he gets to de hills," eyeing a gray range uudulating in the distance, "they'll do well. That Moff of a man," alluding to Treadcroft, "'ill never get there. At all events," chuckled Jack, "his brandy vont. Dats 'im! I do believe," exclaimed Jack, "off again!" as a loose horse is now seen careering across a grass field. "No; dat is a black coat," continued Jack, as the owner now appeared crossing the field in pursuit of his horse. "Bot dat vill be 'im! dat vill be friend Moll'," as a red rider now measures his length on the greensward of a field in the rear of the other one; and Jack, taking off his faded cap, waives it triumphantly as he distinctly recognises the wild, staring running of his late steed. "Dash my buttons!" exclaims he, working his arms as if he was riding, "bot if it hadn't been for dat unwarrantable, unchristian-like cheek I'd ha' shown those red coats de vay on dat oss, for I do think he has de go in him and only vants shovin' along.—Ah Moff—my friend Moff!" laughed he, eyeing Treadcroft's vain endeavour to catch his horse, "you may as vell leave 'im where he is—you'll only fatigue yourself to no purpose. If you 'ad 'im you'd be off him again de next minute."

The telescope of the chace is now drawn out to the last joint, and Jack, as he sits, has a fine bird's eye view of the scene. If the hounds go rather more like a flock of wild geese than like the horses in the chariot of the sun, so do the field, until the diminutive dots, dribbling through the vale, look like the line of a projected railway.

"If I mistake not," continued Jack, "dat leetle shiny eel-like ting," eyeing a tortuous silvery thread meandering through the vale, "is vater, and dere vill be some fon by de time dey get there."

Jack is right in his conjecture. It is Long Brawlingford brook, with its rotten banks and deep eddying pools, describing all sorts of geographical singularities in its course through the country, too often inviting aspiring strangers to astonish the natives by riding at it, while the cautious countrymen rein in as they approach, and, eyeing the hounds, ride for a ford at the first splash.

Jack's friend, Blink Bonny, has ridden not amiss, considering his condition—at all events pretty forward, as may be inferred from his having twice crossed the Flying Hatter and come in for the spray of his censure. But for the fact of his Highness getting his hats of the flyer, he would most likely have received the abuse in the bulk. As it was, the hatter kept letting it go as he went.

And now as the hounds speed over the rich alluvial pastures by the brook, occasionally one throwing its tongue, occasionally another, for the scent is first-rate and the pace severe, there is a turning of heads, a checking of horses, and an evident inclination to diverge. Water is in no request.

"Who knows the ford?" cries Harry Waggett, who always declined extra risk.—"You know the ford, Smith?" continued he, addressing himself to black tops.

"Not when I'm in a hur-hur-hurry," ejaculates Smith, now fighting with his five-year-old bay.

"O'ill show ye the ford!" cries Imperial John, gathering his grey together and sending him at a stiff flight of outside slab-made rails which separate the field from the pack. This lands His Highness right among the tail hounds.

"Hold hard, Mr. Hybrid!" now bellows Sir Moses, indignant! at the idea of a Featherbedfordshire farmer thinking to cut down his gallant field.

"One minuit! and you may go as hard as iver you like!" cries Tom Findlater, who now sees the crows hovering over his fox as he scuttles away on the opposite side of the brook.

There is then a great yawing of mouths and hauling of heads and renewed inquiries for fords.—You know the ford, Brown? You know the ford, Green? *Who* knows the ford?

His Highness, thus snubbed and rebuked on all sides, is put on his mettle, and inwardly resolves not to be bullied by these low Hit-im and Hold-im shire chaps. "If they don't know what is due to the friend of an Earl, he will let them see that he does." So, regardless of their shouts, he shoves along with his Imperial chin well in the air, determined to ride at the brook—let those follow who will. He soon has a chance. The fox has taken it right in his line, without deviating a yard either way, and Wolds-man, and Bluecap, and Ringwood, and Hazard, and Sparkler are soon swimming on his track, followed by the body of the screeching, vociferating pack.

Old Blink Bonny now takes a confused, wish-I-was-well-over, sort of look at the brook, shuddering when he thought how far he was from dry clothes. It is however, too late to retreat. At it he goes in a half resolute sort of way, and in an instant the Imperial hat and the Imperial horse's head are all that appear above water.

"*Hoo-ray!*" cheer some of the unfeeling Hit-im and Hold-im shireites, dropping down into the ford a little below.

"*Hoo-ray!*" respond others on the bank, as the Red Otter, as Silverthorne calls His Highness, rises hatless to the top.

"Come here, and I'll help you out!" shouts Peter Linch, eyeing Mr. Hybrid's vain 'tarts first at the hat and then at the horse.

"Featherbed ford shire for ever!" cries Charley Drew, who doesn't at all like Imperial John.

And John, who finds the brook not only a great deal wider, but also a great deal deeper and colder than he expected, is in such a state of confusion that he lands on one side and his horse on the other, so that his chance of further distinction is out for the day. And as he stands shivering and shaking and emptying his hat, he meditates on the vicissitudes of life, the virtues of sobriety, and the rashness of coping with a friend of His Imperial brother, Louis Nap. His horse meanwhile regales upon grass, regardless of the fast receding field. Thus John is left alone in his glory, and we must be indebted to other sources for an account of the finish of this day's sport.

CHAPTER XXXVII. TWO ACCOUNTS OF A RUN; OR, LOOK ON THIS PICTURE.

MONSIEUR Jean Rougier having seen the field get small by degrees, if not beautifully less, and having viewed the quivering at the brook, thinking the entertainment over, now dismounted from his wooden steed, and, giving it a crack with his stick, saying it was about as good as his first one, proceeded to perform that sorry exploit of retracing his steps through the country on foot. Thanks to the influence of civilisation, there is never much difficulty now in finding a road; and, Monsieur was soon in one whose grassy hoof-marked sides showed it had been ridden down in chase. Walking in scarlet is never a very becoming proceeding; but, walking in such a scarlet as Jack had on, coupled with such a cap, procured him but little respect from the country people, who took him for one of those scarlet runners now so common with hounds. One man (a hedger) in answer to his question, "If he had seen his horse?" replied, after a good stare—"Nor— nor nobody else;" thinking that the steed was all imaginary, and Jack was wanting to show off: another said, "Coom, coom, that ill not de; you've ne horse." Altogether, Monsieur did not get much politeness from anyone; so he stumped moodily along, venting his spleen as he went.

The first thing that attracted his attention was his own pumped-out steed, standing with its snaffle-rein thrown over a gate-post; and Jack, having had about enough pedestrian exercise, especially considering that he was walking in his own boots, now gladly availed himself of the lately discarded mount.

"Wooay, ye great grunting brute!" exclaimed he, going up with an air of ownership, taking the rein off the post, and climbing on.

He had scarcely got well under way, ere a clattering of horses' hoofs behind him, attracted his attention; and, looking back, he saw the Collington Woods detachment careering along in the usual wild, staring, *which-way? which-way?* sort of style of men, who have been riding to points, and have lost the hounds. In the midst of the flight was his master, on the now woe-begone bay; who came coughing, and cutting, and hammer and pincering along, in a very ominous sort of way. Billy, on the other hand, flattered himself that they were having a very tremendous run, with very little risk, and he was disposed to take every advantage of his horse, by way of increasing its apparent severity, thinking it would be a fine thing to tell his Mamma how he had got through his horse. Monsieur having replied to their *which ways?* with the comfortable assurance "that they need not trouble themselves any further, the hounds being miles and miles away," there was visible satisfaction on the faces of some; while others, more knowing, attempted to conceal their delight by lip-curling exclamations of "What a bore!"

"Thought *you* knew the country, Brown." "Never follow you again, Smith," and so on. They then began asking for the publics. "Where's the Red Lion?"

"Does anybody know the way to the Barley Mow?"

"How far is it to the Dog and Duck at Westpool?"

"Dat oss of yours sall not be quite veil, I tink, sare," observed Jack to his master, after listening to one of its ominous coughs.

"Oh, yes he is, only a little lazy," replied Billy, giving him a refresher, as well with the whip on his shoulder, as with the spur on his side.

"He is feeble, I should say, sare," continued Jack, eyeing him pottering along.

"What should I give him, then?" asked Billy, thinking there might be something in what Jack said.

"I sud say a leetle gin vod be de best ting for im," replied Jack.

"Gin! but where can I get gin here?" asked Billy.

"Dese gentlemens is asking their vays to de Poblic ouses," replied Jack; "and if you follows dem, you vill laud at some tap before long."

Jack was right. Balmey Zephyr, as they call Billy West, the surgeon of Hackthorn, who had joined the hunt quite promiscuous, is leading the way to the Red Lion, and the cavalcade is presently before the well-frequented door; one man calling for Purl, another Ale, a third for Porter; while others hank their horses on to the crook at the door, while they go in to make themselves comfortable. Jack dismounting, and giving his horse in charge of his master, entered the little way-side hostelry; and, asking for a measure of gin, and a bottle of water, he drinks off the gin, and then proceeds to rinse Billy's horse's mouth out with the water, just as a training-groom rinses a horse's after a race.

"Dat vill do," at length said Jack, chucking the horse's head up in the air, as if he gets him to swallow the last drop of the precious beverage. "Dat vill do," repeated he, adding, "he vill now carry you ome like a larkspur." So saying, Jack handed the bottle back through the window, and, paying the charge, remounted his steed, kissing his hand, and *bon-jouring*the party, as he set off with his master in search of Pangburn Park.

Neither of them being great hands at finding their way about a country, they made sundry bad hits, and superfluous deviations, and just reached Pangburn Park as Sir Moses and Co. came triumphantly down Rossington hill, flourishing the brush that had given them a splendid fifty minutes (ten off for exaggeration) without a check, over the cream of their country, bringing Imperial John, Gameboy Green, and the flower of the Featherbedfordshire hunt, to the most abject and unmitigated grief.

"Oh, such a run!" exclaimed Sir Moses, throwing out his paws. "Oh, such a run! Finest run that ever was seen! Sort of run, that if old Thome (meaning Lord Ladythorne) had had, he'd have talked about it for a year." Sir Moses then descended to particulars, describing the heads up and sterns down work to the brook, the Imperial catastrophe which he dwelt upon with great *goût*, dom'd if he didn't; and how, leaving John in the lurch, they went away over Rillington Marsh, at a pace that was perfectly appalling, every field choking off some of those Featherbedfordshireites, who came out thinking to cut them all down; then up Tewey Hill, nearly to the crow trees, swinging down again into the vale by Billy Mill, skirting Laureston Plantations, and over those splendid pastures of Arlingford, where there was a momentary check, owing to some coursers, who ought to be hang, dom'd if they shouldn't. "This," continued Sir Moses, "let in some of the laggers, Dickey among the number; but we were speedily away again; and, passing a little to the west of Pickering Park, through the decoy, and away over Larkington Rise, shot down to the Farthing-pie House, where that great Owl, Gameboy Green, thinking to show off, rode at an impracticable fence, and got a cropper for his pains, nearly knocking the poor little Damper into the middle of the week after next by crossing him. Well, from there he made for the main earths in Purdoe Banks, where, of course, there was no shelter for him; and, breaking at the east end of

114

the dene, he set his head straight for Brace well Woods, good two miles off (one and a quarter, say); but his strength failing him over Winterttood Heath, we ran from scent to view, in the finest, openest manner imaginable,—dom'd if we didn't," concluded Sir Moses, having talked himself out of breath.

The same evening, just as Oliver Armstrong was shutting up day by trimming and lighting the oil-lamp at the Lockingford toll-bar, which stands within a few yards from where the apparently well-behaved little stream of Long Brawlingford brook divides the far-famed Hit-im and Hold-im shire from Featherbedfordshire, a pair of desperately mud-stained cords below a black coat and vest, reined up behind a well wrapped and buttoned-up gentleman in a buggy, who chanced to be passing, and drew forth the usual inquiry of "What sport?"

The questioner was no less a personage than Mr. Easylease, Lord Ladythorne's agent—we beg pardon, Commissioner—and Mr. Gameboy Green, the tenant in possession of the soiled cords, recognising the voice in spite of the wraps, thus replied—

"Oh, Mr. Easylease it's you, sir, is it? Hope you're well, sir," with a sort of move of his hat—not a take off, nor yet a keep on—"hope Mrs. Easylease is quite well, and the young ladies."

"Quite well, thank you; hope Mrs. G.'s the same. What sport have you had?" added the Commissioner, without waiting for an answer to the inquiry about the ladies.

"Sport!" repeated Gameboy, drawing his breath, as he conned the matter hastily over. "Sport!" recollecting he was as good as addressing the Earl himself—master of hounds—favours past—hopes for future, and so on. "Well," said he, seeing his line; "We've had a nice-ish run—a fair-ish day—five and twenty minutes, or so."

"Fast?" asked Mr. Easylease, twirling his gig-whip about, for he was going to Tantivy Castle in the morning, and thought he might as well have something to talk about beside the weather.

"Middlin'—nothin' partieklar," replied Green, with a chuck of the chin.

"Kill?" asked the Commissioner, continuing the laconics.

"Don't know," replied the naughty Green, who knew full well they had; for he had seen them run into their fox as he stood on Dinglebank Hill; and, moreover, had ridden part of the way home with Tommy Heslop, who had a pad.

"Why, you've been down!" exclaimed the Commissioner, starting round at the unwonted announcement of Gameboy Green, the best man of their hunt, not knowing if they had killed.

"Down, aye," repeated Gameboy, looking at his soiled side, which looked as if he had been at a sculptor's, having a mud cast taken of himself. "I'm indebted to the nasty little jealous Damper for that."

"The Damper!" exclaimed the Commissioner, knowing how the Earl hated him. "The Damper! that little rascally draper's always doing something wrong. How did he manage it?"

"Just charged me as I was taking a fence," replied Green, "and knocked me clean over."

"What a shame!" exclaimed the Commissioner, driving on. "What a shame," repeated he, whipping his horse into a trot.

And as he proceeded, he presently fell in with Dr. Pillerton, to whom he related how infamously the Hit-im and Hold-im shire chaps had used poor Green, breaking three of his ribs, and nearly knocking his eye out. And Dr. Pillerton, ever anxious, &c., told D'Orsay Davis, the great we of the Featherbedfordshire Gazette, who forthwith penned such an article on fox-hunting Jealousy, generally, and Hit-im and Hold-im shire Jealousy in particular, as caused Sir Moses to declare he'd horsewhip him the first time he caught him,—"dom'd if he wouldn't."

"Shall be w-h-a-w-t?" drawled our hero, dreading the reply.

"Down in de mouth—seek—onvell," replied Jack, depositing the top-boots by the sofa, and placing the shaving-water on the toilette table.

"Oh, is he!" said Billy, perking up, thinking he saw his way out of the dilemma. "What's the matter with him?"

"He coughs, sare—he does not feed, sare—and altogether he is not right."

"So-o-o," said Billy, conning the matter over—"then, p'raps I'd better not ride him?"

CHAPTER XXXVIII. THE SICK HORSE AND THE SICK MASTER.

YOUR oss sall be seek—down in de mouth dis mornin', sare," observed Monsieur to Billy, as the latter lay tossing about in his uncomfortable bed, thinking how he could shirk that day's hunting penance; Sir Moses, with his usual dexterity, having evaded the offer of lending him a horse, by saying that Billy's having nothing to do.

"Vot you think right, sare," replied Jack. "He is your quadruped, not mine; but I should not say he is vot dey call, op to snoff—fit to go."

"Ah," replied Billy. "I'll not ride 'im! hate a horse that's not up to the mark."

"Sare Moses Baronet vod perhaps lend you von, sare," suggested Jack.

"Oh, by no means!" replied Billy in a fright. "By no means! I'd just as soon not hunt to-day, in fact, for I've got a good many letters to write and things to do; so just take the water away for the present and bring it back when Sir Moses is gone." So saying, Billy turned over on his thin pillow, and again sought the solace of his couch. He presently fell into a delightful dreamy sort of sleep, in which he fancied that after dancing the Yammerton girls all round, he had at length settled into an interminable "Ask Mamma Polka," with Clara, from which he was disagreeably aroused by Jack Rogers' hirsute face again protruding between the partially-drawn curtains, announcing, "Sare Moses Baronet, sare, has cot his stick—is off."

"Sir Moses, *what!*" started Billy, dreading to hear about the hunt.

"Sare Moses Baronet, sare, is gone, and I've brought you your *l'eau chaude*, as you said."

"All right!" exclaimed Billy, rubbing his eyes and recollecting himself, "all right;" and, banishing the beauty, he jumped out of bed and resigned himself to Rogers, who forthwith commenced the elaborate duties of his office. As it progressed he informed Billy how the land lay. "Sare Moses was gone, bot Coddy was left, and Mrs. Margerum said there should be no *déjeuner* for Cod" (who was a bad tip), till Billy came down. And Jack didn't put himself at all out of his way to expedite matters to accommodate Cuddy.

At length Billy descended in a suit of those tigerish tweeds into which he had lapsed since he got away from Mamma, and was received with a round of tallihos and view-holloas by Cuddy, who had been studying *Bell's Life* with exemplary patience in the little bookless library, reading through all the meets of the hounds as if he was going to send a horse to each of them. Then Cuddy took his revenge on the servants by ringing for everything he could think of, demanding them all in the name of Mr. Pringle; just as an old parish constable used to run frantically about a fair demanding assistance from everybody in the name of the Queen. Mr. Pringle wanted devilled turkey, Mr. Pringle wanted partridge pie, Mr. Pringle wanted sausages, Mr. Pringle wanted chocolate, Mr. Pringle wanted honey, jelly and preserve. Why the deuce, didn't they send Mr. Pringle his breakfast in properly? And if the servants didn't think Billy a very great man, it wasn't for want of Cuddy trying to make them.

And so, what with Cuddy's exertions and the natural course of events, Billy obtained a very good breakfast. The last cup being at length drained, Cuddy clutched *Bell's Life*, and wheeling his semicircular chair round to the fire, dived into his side pocket, and producing a cigar-case, tendered Billy a weed. And Cuddy did it in such a matter-of-course way, that much as Billy disliked smoking, he felt constrained to accept one, thinking to get rid of it by a sidewind, just as he had got rid of old Wotherspoon's snuff, by throwing it away. So, taking his choice, he lit it, and prepared to beat a retreat, but was interrupted by Cuddy asking where "he was going?"

"Only into the open air," replied Billy, with the manner of a professed smoker.

"Open air, be hanged!" retorted Cuddy. "Open airs well enough in summer-time when the roses are out, and the strawberries ripe, but this is not the season for that kind of sport. No, no, come and sit here, man," continued he, drawing a chair alongside of him for Billy, "and let's have a chat about hunting."

"But Sir Moses won't like his room smoked in," observed Billy, making a last effort to be off.

"Oh, Sir Moses don't care!" rejoined Cuddy, with a jerk of his head; "Sir Moses don't care! can't hurt such rubbish as this," added he, tapping the arm of an old imitation rose-wood painted chair that stood on his left. "No old furniture broker in the Cut, would give ten puns for the whole lot, curtains, cushions, and all," looking at the faded red hangings around.

So Billy was obliged to sit down and proceed with his cigar. Meanwhile Cuddy having established a good light to his own, took up his left leg to nurse, and proceeded with his sporting speculations.

"Ah, hunting wasn't what it used to be (whiff), nor racing either (puff). Never was a truer letter (puff), than that of Lord Derby's (whiff), in which he said racing had got into the (puff) hands of (whiff) persons of an inferior (puff) position, who keep (puff) horses as mere instruments of (puff) gambling, instead of for (whiff) sport." Then, having pruned the end of his cigar, he lowered his left leg and gave his right one a turn, while he indulged in some hunting recollections. "Hunting wasn't what it used to be (puff) in the days of old (whiff) Warde and (puff) Villebois and (whiff) Masters. Ah no!" continued he, taking his cigar out of his mouth, and casting his eye up at the dirty fly-dotted ceiling. "Few such sportsmen as poor Sutton or Ralph Lambton, or that fine old fire-brick, Asseton Smith. People want to be all in the ring now, instead of sticking to one sport, and enjoying it thoroughly—yachts, manors, moors, race-horses, cricket, coaches, coursing, cooks—and the consequence is, they get blown before they are thirty, and have to live upon air the rest of their lives. Wasn't one man in fifty that hunted who really enjoyed it. See how glad they were to tail off as soon as they could. A good knock on the nose, or a crack on the crown settled half of them. Another thing was, there was no money to be made by it. Nothing an Englishman liked so much as making money, or trying to make it." So saying, Cuddy gave his cigar another fillip, and replacing it in his mouth, proceeded to blow a series of long revolving clouds, as he lapsed into a heaven of hunting contemplations.

From these he was suddenly aroused by the violent retching of Billy. Our friend, after experiencing the gradual growth of seasickness mingled with a stupifying headache, was at length fairly overcome, and Cuddy had just time to bring the slop-basin to the rescue. Oh, how green Billy looked!

****

"Too soon after breakfast—too soon after breakfast," muttered Cuddy, disgusted at the interruption. "Lie down for half an hour, lie down for half an hour," continued he ringing the bell violently for assistance.

"Send Mr. Pringle's valet here! send Mr. Pringle's valet here!" exclaimed he, as the half-davered footman came staring in, followed by the ticket-of-leave butler, "Here, Monsieur!" continued he, as Rougier's hairy face now peeped past the door, "your master wants you—eat something that's disagreed with him—that partridge-pie, I think, for I feel rather squeamish myself; and you, Bankhead," added he, addressing the butler, "just bring us each a drop of brandy, not that nasty brown stuff Mother Margermn puts into the puddings, but some of the white, you know—the best, you know," saying which, with a "now old boy!" he gave Billy a hoist from his seat by the arm, and sent him away with his servant. The brandy, however, never came, Bankhead declaring they had drunk all he had out, the other night. So Cuddy was obliged to console himself with his cigars and *Bell's Life*, which latter he read, marked, learned, and inwardly digested, pausing every now and then at the speculative passages, wondering whether Wilkinson and Kidd, or Messrs. Wilkinson and Co. were the parties who had the honour of having his name on their books, where Henry Just, the backer of horses, got the Latin for his advertisement from, and considering whether Nairn Sahib, the Indian fiend, should be roasted alive or carried round the world in a cage. He also went through the column and a quarter of the meets of hounds again, studied the doings at Copenhagen Grounds, Salford Borough Gardens, and Hornsea Wood, and finally finished off with the time of high-water at London Bridge, and the list of pedestrian matches to come. He then folded the paper carefully up and replaced it iu his pocket, feeling equal to a dialogue with anybody. Having examined the day through the window, he next strolled to his old friend the weather-glass at the bottom of the stairs, and then constituting himself huntsman to a pack of hounds, proceeded to draw the house for our Billy; "*Y-o-o-icks*, wind him! *y-o-o-icks*, push him up!" holloaed he, going leisurely up-stairs, "*E'leu in there! E'leu in!*" continued he, on arriving at a partially closed door on the first landing.

"*There's nobody here! There's nobody here!*" exclaimed Mrs. Margerum, hurrying out. "There's nobody here, sir!" repeated she, holding steadily on by the door, to prevent any one entering where she was busy packing her weekly basket of perquisites, or what the Americans more properly call "stealings."

"Nobody here! bitch-fox, at all events!" retorted Cuddy, eyeing her confusion—"where's Mr. Pringle's room?" asked he.

"I'll show you, sir; I'll show you," replied she, closing the room-door, and hurrying on to another one further along. "This is Mr. Pringle's room, sir," said she, stopping before it.

"All right!" exclaimed Cuddy, knocking at the door.

"Come in," replied a feeble voice from within; and in Cuddy went.

There was Billy in bed, with much such a disconsolate face as he had when Jack Rogers appeared with his hunting things. As, however, nobody ever admits being sick with smoking, Billy readily adopted Cuddy's suggestion, and laid the blame on the pie. Cuddy, indeed, was good enough to say he had been sick himself, and of course Billy had a right to be so, too. "Shouldn't have been so," said Cuddy, "if that beggar Bankhead had brought the brandy; but there's no getting anything out of that fellow." And Caddy and Billy being then placed upon terms of equality, the interesting invalids agreed to have a walk together. To this end Billy turned out of bed and re-established himself in his recently-discarded coat and vest; feeling much like a man after a bad passage from Dover to Calais. The two then toddled down-stairs together, Cuddy stopping at the bottom of the flight to consult his old friend the glass, and speculate upon the Weather.

"Dash it! but it's falling," said he, with a shake of the head after tapping it. "Didn't like the looks of the sky this morning—wish there mayn't be a storm brewing. Had one just about this time last year. Would be a horrid bore if hunting was stopped just in its prime," and talked like a man with half-a-dozen horses fit to jump out of their skins, instead of not owning one. And Billy thought it would be the very thing for him if hunting was stopped. "With a somewhat light heart, he followed Cuddy through the back slums to the stables.

"Sir Moses doesn't sacrifice much to appearances, does he?" asked Cuddy, pointing to the wretched rough-cast peeling off the back walls of the house, which were greened with the drippings of the broken spouts.

"No," replied Billy, staring about, thinking how different things looked there to what they did at the Carstle.

"Desperately afraid of paint," continued Cuddy, looking about. "Don't think there has been a lick of paint laid upon any place since he got it. Always tell him he's like a bad tenant at the end of a long lease," which observation brought them to the first stable-door. "Who's here?" cried Cuddy, kicking at the locked entrance.

"Who's there?" demanded a voice from within.

"Me! *Mr. Flintoff*!" replied Cuddy, in a tone of authority; "*open the door*" added he, imperiously.

The dirty-shirted helper had seen them coming; but the servants generally looking upon Cuddy as a spy, the man had locked the door upon him.

"Beg pardon, sir," now said the Catiff, pulling at his cowlick as he opened it; "beg pardon, sir, didn't know it was you."

"Didn't you," replied Cuddy, adding, "you might have known by my knock," saying which Cuddy stuck his cheesey hat down on his nose, and pocketing his hands, proceeded to scrutinise the stud.

"What's this 'orse got a bandage on for?" asked he about one. "Why don't ye let that 'orse's 'ead down?" demanded he of another. "Strip thisn'orse," ordered he of a third. Then Cuddy stood criticising his points, his legs, his loins, his hocks, his head, his steep shoulder, as he called it, and then ordered the clothes to be put on again. So he went from stable to stable, just as he does at Tattersall's on a Sunday, Cuddy being as true to the "corner" as the needle to the pole, though, like the children, he looks, but *never* touches, that is to say, "bids," at least not for himself. Our Billy, soon tiring of this amusement—if, indeed, amusement it can be called—availed himself of the interregnum caused by the outside passage from one set of stables to another, to slip away to look after his own horse, of whose health he suddenly remembered Rougier had spoken disparagingly in the morning. After some little trouble he found the Juniper-smelling head groom, snoring asleep among a heap of horse-cloths before the fire in the saddle-room.

It is said that a man who is never exactly sober is never quite drunk, and Jack Wetun was one of this order, he was always running to the "unsophisticated gin-bottle," keeping up the steam of excitement, but seldom overtopping it, and could shake himself into apparent sobriety in an instant. Like most of Sir Moses's people, he was one of the fallen angels of servitude, having lived in high places, from which his intemperate habits had ejected him; and he was now gradually descending to that last refuge of the destitute, the Ostlership of a farmer's inn. Starting out of his nest at the rousing shake of the helper, who holloaed in his ear that "Mr. Pringle wanted to see his 'orse," Wetun stretched his brawny arms, and, rubbing his eyes, at length comprehended Billy, when he exclaimed with a start, "Oss, sir? Oh, by all means, sir;" and, bundling on his greasy-collared, iron-grey coat, he reeled and rolled out of the room, followed by our friend. "That (hiccup) oss of (hiccup) yours is (hiccup) amiss, I think (hiccup), sir," said he, leading, or rather lurching the way. "A w-h-a-w-t?" drawled Billy, watching Weton's tack and half-tack gait.

"Amiss (hiccup)—unwell—don't like his (hiccup) looks," replied the groom, rolling past the stable-door where he was. "Oh, beg pardon," exclaimed he, bumping against Billy on turning short back, as he suddenly recollected himself; "Beg pardon, he's in here," added he, fumbling at the door. It was locked. Then, oh dear, he hadn't got the (hiccup) key, then (hiccup); yes, he had got the (hiccup) key, as he recollected he had his coat on, and dived into the pocket for it. Then he produced it; and, after making several unsuccessful pokes at the key-hole, at length accomplished an entry, and Billy again saw Napoleon the Great, now standing in the promised two-stalled stable along with Sir Moses's gig mare.

To a man with any knowledge of horses, Napoleon certainly did look very much amiss—more like a wooden horse at a harness-maker's, than an animal meant to go,—stiff, with his fore-logs abroad, and an anxious care-worn countenance continually cast back at its bearing flanks.

"Humph!" said Billy, looking him over, as he thought, very knowingly. "Not so much amiss, either, is he?"

"Well, sir, what you think," replied Wetun, glad to find that Billy didn't blame him for his bad night's lodgings.

"Oh, I dare say he'll be all right in a day or two," observed

Billy, half inclined to recommend his having his feet put into warm water.

"Ope so," replied Wetun, looking up the horse's red nostrils, adding, "but he's not (hiccup) now, somehow."

Just then a long reverberating crack sounded through the courtyard, followed by the clattering of *horses' hoofs, and Wetun exclaiming,* "Here be Sir Moses!" dropped the poor horse's head, and hurried ont to meet his master, accompanied by Billy.

"Ah, Pringle!" exclaimed Sir Moses, gaily throwing his leg over his horse's head as he alighted. "Ah, Pringle, my dear fellow, what, got you?"

"Well, what sport?" demanded Cuddy Flintoff, rushing up with eager anxiety depicted on his face.

"Very good," replied Sir Moses, stamping the mud off his boots, and then giving himself a general shake; "very good," repeated he; "found at Lobjolt Corse——ran up the banks and down the banks, and across to Beatie's Bog, then over to Deep-well Rocks, and back again to the banks."

"*Did you kill?*" demanded Cuddy, not wanting to hear any more about the banks—up the banks or down the banks either.

"Why, no," replied Sir Moses, moodily; "if that dom'd old Daddy Nevins hadn't stuck his ugly old mug right in the way, we should have forced him over Willowsike Pastures, and doubled him up in no time, for we were close upon him; whereas the old infidel brought us to a check, aud we never could get upon terms with him again; but, come," continued Sir Moses, wishing to cut short this part of the narrative, "let's go into the house and get ourselves warmed, for the air's cold, and I haven't had a bite since breakfast."

"Ay, come in!" cried Cuddy, leading the way; "come in, and get Mr. Pringle a drop of brandy, for he's eat something that's disagreed with him."

"Eat something that's disagreed with him. Sorry to hear that; what could it be?—what could it be?" asked Sir Moses, as the party now groped their way along the back passages.

"Why, I blame the partridge-pie," replied Cuddy, demurely.

"Not a bit of it!" rejoined Sir Moses—"not a bit of it! eat some myself—eat some myself—will finish it now—will finish it now."

"We've saved you that trouble," replied Cuddy, "for we finished it ourselves."

"The deuce you did!" exclaimed Sir Moses, adding, "and were *you* sick?"

"Squeamish," replied Cuddy—"Squeamish; not so bad as Mr. Pringle."

"But bad enough to want some brandy, I suppose," observed the Baronet, now entering the library.

"Quite so," said Cuddy—"quite."

"Why didn't you get some?—why didn't you get some?" asked the Baronet, moving towards the bell.

"Because Bankhead has none out," replied Mr. Cuddy, before Sir Moses rang.

"None out!" retorted Sir Moses—"none out!—what! have you finished that too!"

"Somebody has, it seems," replied Cuddy, quite innocently.

"Well, then, I'll tell you what you must do—I'll tell you what you must do," continued the Baronet, lighting a little red taper, and feeling in his pocket for the keys—"you must go into the cellar yourself and get some—go into the cellar yourself and get some;" so saying, Sir Moses handed Cuddy the candle and keys, saying, "shelf above the left hand bin behind the door," adding, "you know it—you know it."

"Better bring two when I'm there, hadn't I?" asked Cuddy.

"Well," said Sir Moses, dryly, "I s'pose there'll be no great harm if you do;" and away Cuddy went.

"D-e-e-a-vil of a fellow to drink—d-e-e-a-vil of a fellow to drink," drawled Sir Moses, listening to his receding footsteps along the passage. He then directed his blarney to Billy. "Oh dear, he was sorry to hear he'd been ill; what could it be? Lost a nice gallop, too—dom'd if he hadn't. Couldn't be the pie! Wondered he wasn't down in the morning." Then Billy explained that his horse was ill, and that prevented him.

"Horse ill!" exclaimed Sir Moses, throwing out his hands, and raising his brows with astonishment—"horse ill! O dear, but that shouldn't have stopped you, if I'd known—should have been most welcome to any of mine—dom'd if you shouldn't! There's Pegasus, or Atalanta, or Will-o'-the-Wisp, or any of them, fit to go. O dear, it was a sad mistake not sending word. Wonder what Wetun was about not to tell me—would row him for not doing so," and as Sir Moses went on protesting and professing and proposing, Cuddy Flintoff's footstep and "*for-rard on! for-rard on!*" were heard returning along the passage, and he presently entered with a bottle in each hand.

"There are a brace of beauties!" exclaimed he, placing them on the round table, with the dew of the cellar fresh on their sides—"there are a brace of blood-like beauties!" repeated he, eyeing their neat tapering necks, "the very race-horse of bottles—perfect pictures, I declare; so different to those great lumbering roundshouldered English things, that look like black beer or porter, or something of that sort." Then Cuddy ran off for glasses and tumblers and water; and Sir Moses, having taken a thimble-full of brandy, retired to change his clothes, declaring he felt chilly; and Cuddy, reigning in his stead, made Billy two such uncommonly strong brews, that we are sorry to say he had to be put to bed shortly after.

And when Mr. Bankhead heard that Cuddy Flintoff had been sent to the cellar instead of him, he declared it was the greatest insult that had ever been offered to a gentleman of his "order," and vowed that he would turn his master off the first thing in the morning.

CHAPTER XXXIX. MR. PRINGLE SUDDENLY BECOMES A MEMBER OF THE H. H. H.

NEXT day being a "dies non" in the hunting way, Sir Moses Mainchance lay at earth to receive his steward, Mr. Mordecai Nathan, and hear what sport he had had as well in hunting up arrears of rent as in the management of the Pangburn Park estate generally. Very sorry the accounts were, many of the apparent dullard farmers being far more than a match for the sharp London Jew. Mr. Mordecai Nathan indeed, declared that it would require a detective policeman to watch each farm, so tricky and subtile were the occupants. And as Sir Moses listened to the sad recitals, how Henery Brown & Co. had been leading off their straw by night, and Mrs. Turnbull selling her hay by day, and Jacky Hindmarch sowing his fallows without ever taking out a single weed, he vowed that they were a set of the biggest rogues under the sun, and deserved to be hung all in a row,—dom'd if they didn't! And he moved and seconded and carried a resolution in his own mind, that the man who meddled with land as a source of revenue was a very great goose. So, charging Mr. Mordecai Nathan to stick to them for the money, promising him one per cent, more (making him eleven) on what he recovered, he at length dissolved the meeting, most heartily wishing he had Pangburn Park in his pocket again. Meanwhile Messrs. Flintoff and Pringle had yawned away the morning in the usual dreamy loungy style of guests in country-houses, where the meals are the chief incidents of the day. Mr. Pringle not choosing to be tempted with any more "pie," had slipped away to the stable as soon as Cuddy produced the dread cigar-case after breakfast, and there had a conference with Mr. Wetun, the stud-groom, about his horse Napoleon the Great. The drunkard half laughed when Billy asked "if he thought the horse would be fit to come out in the morning, observing that he thought it would be a good many mornins fust, adding that Mr. Fleams the farrier had bled him, but he didn't seem any better, and that he was coming back at two o'clock, when p'raps Mr. Pringle had better see him himself." Whereupon our friend Billy, recollecting Sir Moses's earnest deprecation of his having stayed at home for want of a horse the day before, and the liberal way he had talked of Atalanta and Pegasus, and he didn't know what else, now charged Mr. Wetun not to mention his being without a horse, lest Sir Moses might think it necessary to mount him; which promise being duly accorded, Billy, still shirking Cuddy, sought the retirement of his chamber, where he indited an epistle to his anxious Mamma, telling her all, how he had left Major Yammerton's and the dangerous eyes, and had taken up his quarters with Sir Moses Mainchance, a great fox-hunting Hit-im and Hold-im shire Baronet at Pangburn Park, expecting she would be very much pleased and struck with the increased consequence. Instead of which, however, though Mrs. Pringle felt that he had perhaps hit upon the lesser evil, she wrote him a very loving letter by return of post, saying she was glad to hear he was enjoying himself, but cautioning him against "Moses Mainchance" (omitting the Sir), adding that every man's character was ticketed in London, and the letters "D. D." for "Dirty Dog" were appended to his. She also told him that uncle Jerry had been inquiring about him, and begging she would call upon him at an early day on matters of business, all of which will hereafter "more full and at large appear," as the lawyers say; meanwhile, we must back the train of ideas a little to our hero. Just as he was affixing the great seal of state to the letter, Cuddy Flintoff's "for-rard on! for-rard on!" was heard progressing along the passage, followed by a noisy knock, with an exclamation of "Pringle" at our friend's door.

"Come in!" cried he; and in obedience to the invitation, Flintoff stood in the doorway. "Don't forget," said he, "that we dine at Hinton to-day, and the Baronet's ordered the trap at four," adding, "I'm going to dress, and you'd better do the same." So saying, Cuddy closed the door, and hunted himself along to his own room at the end of the passage—"*E'leu in there! E'leu in!*" cried he as he got to the door.

Hinton, once the second town in Hit-im and Hold-im shire, stands at the confluence of the Long Brawlinerford and Riplinton brooks, whose united efforts here succeed in making a pretty respectable stream. It is an old-fashioned country place, whose component parts may be

120

described as consisting of an extensive market-place, with a massive church of the florid Gothic, or gingerbread order of architecture at one end, a quaint stone-roofed, stone-pillared market cross at the other, the Fox and Hounds hotel and posting-house on the north side, with alternating shops and public houses on the south.

Its population, according to a certain "sore subject" topographical dictionary, was 23,500, whilst its principal trade might have been described as "fleecing the foxhunters." That was in its golden days, when Lord Martingal hunted the country, holding his court at the Fox and Hounds hotel, where gentlemen stayed with their studs for months and months together, instead of whisking about with their horses by steam. Then every stable in the town was occupied at very remunerative rents, and the inhabitants seemed to think they could never build enough.

Like the natives of most isolated places, the Hintonites were very self-sufficient, firmly believing that there were no such conjurors as themselves; and, when the Grumpletin railway was projected, they resolved that it would ruin their town, and so they opposed it to a man, and succeeded in driving it several miles off, thus scattering their trade among other places along the line. Year by year the bonnet and mantle shops grew less gay, the ribbons less attractive, until shop after shop lapsed into a sort of store, hardware on one side, and millinery, perhaps, on the other. But the greatest fall of all was that of the Fox and Hounds hotel and posting-house. This spacious hostelry had apparently been built with a view of accommodating everybody; and, at the time of our story, it loomed in deserted grandeur in the great grass-grown market-place. In structure it was more like a continental inn than an English one; quadrangular, entered by a spacious archway, from whose lofty ceiling hung the crooks, from whence used to dangle the glorious legs and loins of four-year-old mutton, the home-fed hams, the geese, the ducks, the game, with not unfrequently a haunch or two of presentation venison. With the building, however, the similarity ended, the cobble-stoned courtyard displaying only a few water-casks and a basket-caged jay, in lieu of the statues, and vases, and fountains, and flower-stands that grace the flagged courts of the continent. But in former days it boasted that which in the eye of our innkeeper passes show, namely, a goodly line of two-horse carriages drawn across its ample width. In those days county families moved like county families, in great, caravan-like carriages, with plenty of servants, who, having drunk the "Park or Hall" allowance, uphold their characters and the honour of their houses, by topping up the measure of intemperance with their own money. Their masters and mistresses, too, considered the claims of the innkeepers, and ate and drank for the good of the house, instead of sneaking away to pastry-cooks for their lunches at a third of the price of the inn ones. Not that any landlord had ever made money at the Fox and Hounds hotel. Oh, no! it would never do to admit that. Indeed, Mr. Binny used to declare, if it wasn't "the great regard he had for Lord Martingal and the gents of his hunt, he'd just as soon be without their custom;" just as all Binnys decry, whatever they have—military messes, hunt messes, bar messes, any sort of messes. They never make anything by them—not they.

Now, however, that the hunt was irrevocably gone, words were inadequate to convey old Peter the waiter's lamentations at its loss. "Oh dear, sir!" he would say, as he showed a stranger the club-room, once the eighth wonder of the world, "Oh dear, sir! I never thought to see things come to this pass. This room, sir, used to be occupied night after night, and every Wednesday we had more company than it could possibly hold. Now we have nothing but a miserable three-and-sixpence a head once a month, with Sir Moses in the chair, and a shilling a bottle for corkage. Formerly we had six shillings a bottle for port and five for sherry, which, as our decanters didn't hold three parts, was pretty good pay." Then Peter would open the shutters and show the proportions of the room, with the unrivalled pictures on the walls: Lord Martingal on his horse, Lord Martingal off his horse; Mr. Customer on his horse, Mr. Customer off his horse, Mr. Customer getting drunk; Mr. Crasher on his horse, Mr. Crasher with a hound, &c., all in the old woodeny style that prevailed before the gallant Grant struck out a fresh light in his inimitable "Breakfast," and "Meet of the Stag-hounds." But the reader will perhaps accompany us to one of Sir Moses's "Wednesday evenings;" for which purpose they will have the goodness to suppose the Baronet and Mr. Flintoff arrayed in the dress uniform of the hunt—viz., scarlet coats with yellow collars and facings, and Mr. Pringle attired in the height of the fashion, bundling into one of those extraordinary-shaped vehicles that modern times have introduced. "*Right!*" cries the footman from the steps of the door, as Bankhead and Monsieur mount the box of the carriage, and away the well-muffled party drive to the scene of action.

The great drawback to the Hit-im and Hold-im shire hunt club-room at the Fox and Hounds hotel and posting-house at Hinton, undoubtedly was, that there was no ante or reception room. The guests on alighting from their vehicles, after ascending the broad straight flight of stairs, found themselves suddenly precipitated into the dazzling dining-room, with such dismantling accommodation only as a low screen before the door at the low-end of the room afforded. The effect therefore was much the or same as if an actor dressed for his part on the stage before the audience; a fox-hunter in his wraps, and a fox-hunter in his red, being very distinct and different beings. It was quite destructive of anything like imposing flourish or effect. Moreover the accumulation of steaming things on a wet night, which it generally was on a club dinner, added but little to the fragrance of the room. So much for generalities; we will now proceed to our particular dinner.

Sir Moses being the great gun of the evening, of course timed himself to arrive becomingly late—indeed the venerable post-boy who drove him, knew to a moment when to arrive; and as the party ascended the straight flight of stairs they met a general buzz of conversation coming down, high above which rose the discordant notes of the Laughing Hyæna. It was the first hunt-dinner of the season, and being the one at which Sir Moses generally broached his sporting requirements, parties thought it prudent to be present, as well as to hear the prospects of the season as to protect their own pockets. To this end some twenty or five-and-twenty variegated guests were assembled, the majority dressed in the red coat and yellow facings of the hunt, exhibiting every variety of cut, from the tight short-waisted swallow-tails of Mr. Crasher's (the contemporary of George the Fourth) reign, down to the sack-like garment of the present day. Many of them looked as if, having got into their coats, they were never to get out of them again, but as pride feels no pain, if asked about them, they would have declared they were quite comfortable. The dark-coated gentry were principally farmers, and tradespeople, or the representatives of great men in the neighbourhood. Mr. Buckwheat, Mr. Doubledrill, Mr. James Corduroys, Mr. Stephen Broadfurrow; Mr. Pica, of the "Hit-im and Hold-im shire Herald;" Hicks, the Flying Hatter, and his shadow Tom Snowdon the draper or Damper, Manford the corn-merchant, Smith the saddler. Then there was Mr. Mossman, Lord Polkaton's Scotch factor, Mr. Squeezeley, Sir Morgan Wildair's agent, Mr. Lute, on behalf of Lord Harpsichord, Mr. Stiff representing Sir George Persiflage, &c., &c. These latter were watching the proceedings for their employers, Sir Moses having declared that Mr. Mossman, on a former occasion (see page 188, ante), had volunteered to subscribe fifty pounds to the hounds, on behalf of Lord Polkaton, and Sir Moses had made his lordship pay it too—"dom'd if he hadn't." With this sketch of the company, let us now proceed to the entry.

Though the current of conversation had been anything but flattering to our master before his arrival, yet the reception they now gave him, as he emerged from behind the screen, might have made a less self-sufficient man than Sir Moses think he was extremely popular. Indeed, they rushed at him in a way that none but Briareus himself could have satisfied. They all wanted to hug him at once. Sir Moses having at length appeased their enthusiasm, and given his beak a good blow, proceeded to turn part of their politeness upon Billy, by introducing him to those around. Mr. Pringle, Mr. Jarperson—Mr. Pringle, Mr. Paul Straddler—Mr. Pringle, Mr. John Bullrush, and so on.

Meanwhile Cuddy Flintoff kept up a series of view halloas and hunting noises, as guest after guest claimed the loan of his hand for a shake. So they were all very hearty and joyful as members of a fox-hunting club ought to be.

The rules of the Hit-im and Hold-im-shire hunt, like those of many other hunts and institutions, were sometimes very stringent, and sometimes very lax—very stringent when an objectionable candidate presented himself—very lax when a good one was to be obtained. On the present occasion Sir Moses Mainchance had little difficulty in persuading the meeting to suspend the salutary rule (No. 5) requiring each new candidate to be proposed and seconded at one meeting, and his name placed above the mantelpiece in the club-room, until he was ballotted for at another meeting, in favour of the nephew of his old friend and brother Baronet, Sir Jonathan Pringle; whom he described as a most promising young sportsman, and likely to make a most valuable addition to their hunt. And the members all seeing matters in that light, Cuddy Flintoff was despatched for the ballot-box, so that there might be no interruption to the advancement of dinner by summoning Peter. Meanwhile Sir Moses resumed the introductory process, Mr. Heslop Mr. Pringle, Mr. Pringle Mr. Smoothley, Mr. Drew Mr. Pringle, helping Billy to the names of such faces as he could not identity for want of their hunting caps. Cleverer fellows than Billy are puzzled to do that sometimes.

Presently Mr. Flintoff returned with the rat-trap-like ballot-box under his arm, and a willow-pattern soup-plate with some beans in the bottom of it, in his hand.

"Make way!" cried he, "make way!" advancing up the room with all the dignity of a mace-bearer. "Where will you have it, Sir Moses?" asked he, "where will you have it, Sir Moses?"

"Here!" replied the Baronet, seizing a card-table from below the portrait of Mr. Customer getting drunk, and setting it out a little on the left of the fire. The ballot-box was then duly deposited on the centre of the green baize with a composite candle on each side of it.

Sir Moses, then thinking to make up in dignity what he had sacrificed to expediency, now called upon the meeting to appoint a Scrutineer on behalf of the club, and parties caring little who they named so long as they were not kept waiting for dinner, holloaed out "Mr. Flintoff!" whereupon Sir Moses put it to them if they were all content to have Mr. Flintoff appointed to the important and responsible office of Scrutineer, and receiving a shower of "yes-es!" in reply, he declared Mr. Flintoff was duly elected, and requested him to enter upon the duties of his office.

Cuddy, then turning up his red coat wrists, so that there might be no suspicion of concealed beans, proceeded to open and turn the drawers of the ballot-box upside down, in order to show that they were equally clear, and then restoring them below their "Yes" and "No" holes, he took his station behind the table with the soup-plate in his hand ready to drop a bean into each member's hand, as he advanced to receive it. Mr. Heslop presently led the way at a dead-march-in-Saul sort of pace, and other members falling in behind like railway passengers at a pay place, there was a continuous dropping of beans for some minutes, a solemn silence being preserved as if the parties expected to hear on which side they fell.

At length the constituency was exhausted, and Mr. Flintoff having assumed the sand-glass, and duly proclaimed that he should close the ballot, if no member appeared before the first glass was out, speedily declared it was run, when, laying it aside, he emptied the soup-plate of the remaining beans, and after turning it upside down to show the perfect fairness of the transaction, handed it to Sir Moses to hold for the result. Drawing out the "Yes" drawer first, he proceeded with great gravity to count the beans out into the soup-plate—one, two, three, four, five, six, seven, and so on, up to eighteen, when the inverted drawer proclaimed they were done.

"Eighteen Ayes," announced Sir Moses to the meeting, amid a murmur of applause.

Mr. Flintoff then produced the dread "No," or black-ball drawer, whereof one to ten white excluded, and turning it upside down, announced, in a tone of triumph, "*none!*"

"Hooray!" cried Sir Moses, seizing our hero by both hands, and hugging him heartily—"Hooray! give you joy, my boy! you're a member of the first club in the world! The Caledonian's nothing to it;—dom'd if it is." So saying, he again swung him severely by the arms, and then handed him over to the meeting.

And thus Mr. Pringle was elected a member of the Hit-im and Hold-im shire hunt, without an opportunity of asking his Mamma, for the best of all reasons, that Sir Moses had not even asked him himself.

CHAPTER XL. THE HUNT DINNER,

CARCELY were the congratulations of the company to our hero, on his becoming a member of the renowned Hit-im and Hold-im shire hunt, over, ere a great rush of dinner poured into the room, borne by Peter and the usual miscellaneous attendants at an inn banquet; servants in livery, servants out of livery, servants in a sort of half-livery, servants in place, servants out of place, post-boys converted into footmen, "boots" put into shoes. Then the carrot and turnip garnished roasts and boils, and stews were crowded down the table, in a profusion that would astonish any one who thinks it impossible to dine under a guinea a head. Rounds, sirloins middles, sucking-pigs, poultry, &c. (for they dispensed with the formalities of soup and fish), being duly distributed. Peter announced the fact deferentially to Sir Moses, as he stood monopolizing the best place before the fire, whereupon the Baronet, drawing his hands out of his trowser's pockets, let fall his yellow lined gloves and clapping his hands, exclaimed. "DINNER GENTLEMAN!" in a stentorian voice, adding, "PRINGLE you sit on my right! and CUDDY!" appealing to our friend Flintoff. "will you take the vice-chair?"

"With all my heart!" replied Cuddy, whereupon making an imaginary hunting-horn of his hand, he put it to his mouth, and went blowing and hooping down the room, to entice a certain portion of the guests after him. All parties being at length suited with seats, grace was said, and the assault commenced with the vigorous determination of over-due appetites.

If a hand-in-the-pocket-hunt-dinner possesses few attractions in the way of fare, it is nevertheless free from the restraints and anxieties that pervade private entertainments, where the host cranes at the facetious as he scowls at his butler, or madame mingles her pleasantries with prayers for the safe arrival of the creams, and those extremely capricious sensitive jellies. People eat as if they had come to dine and not to talk, some, on this occasion, eating with their knives, some with their forks, some with both occasionally. And so, what with one aid and another, they made a very great clatter.

The first qualms of hunger being at length appeased, Sir Moses proceeded to select subjects for politeness in the wine-taking way—men whom he could not exactly have at his own house, but who might be prevented from asking for cover-rent, or damages, by a little judicious flattery, or again, men who were only supposed to be lukewarmly disposed towards the great Hit-im and Hold-im shire hunt.

Sir Moses would rather put his hand into a chimney-sweep's pocket than into his own, but so long as anything could be got by the tongue he never begrudged it. So he "sherried" with Mossman and the army of observation generally, also with Pica, who always puffed his hunt, cutting at D'Orsay Davis's efforts on behalf of the Earl, and with Buckwheat (whose son he had recently dom'd à la Rowley Abingdon), and with Corduroys, and Straddler, and Hicks, and Doubledrill—with nearly all the dark coats, in short—Cuddy Flintoff, too, kept the game a-going at his end of the table, as well to promote conviviality as to get as much wine as he could; so altogether there was a pretty brisk consumption, and some of the tight-clad gentlemen began to look rather apoplectic. Cannon-ball-like plum-puddings, hip-bath-like apple-pies, and foaming creams, completed the measure of their uneasiness, and left little room for any cheese. Nature being at length most abundantly satisfied throughout the assembly, grace was again said, and the cloth cleared for action. The regulation port and sherry, with light—very light—Bordeaux, being duly placed upon the table, with piles of biscuits at intervals, down the centre, Sir Moses tapped the well-indented mahogany with his presidential hammer, and proceeded to prepare the guests for the great toast of the evening, by calling upon them to fill bumpers to the usual loyal and patriotic ones. These being duly disposed of, he at length rose for the all-important let off, amid the nudges and "now then's," of such of the party as feared a fresh attempt on their pockets—Mossman and Co., in particular, were all eyes, ears, and fears.

"Gentlemen!" cries Sir Moses, rising and diving his hands into his trouser's pockets—"Gentlemen!" repeated he, with an ominous cough, that sounded very like cash.

"*Hark to the Bar owl!—hark*" cheered Cuddy Flintoff from the other end of the room, thus cutting short a discussion about wool, a bargain for beans, and an inquiry for snuff in his own immediate neighbourhood, and causing a tapping of the table further up.

"Gentlemen!" repeated Sir Moses, for the third time, amid cries of "hear, hear," and "order, order,"—"I now have the pleasure of introducing to your notice the toast of the evening—a toast endeared by a thousand associations, and rendered classical by the recollection of the great and good men who have given in it times gone by from this very chair—(applause). I need hardly say, gentlemen, that that toast is the renowned Hit-im and Hold-im shire hunt—(renewed applause)—a hunt second to none in the kingdom; a hunt whose name is famous throughout the land, and whose members are the very flower and élite of society—(renewed applause). Never, he was happy to say, since it was established, were its prospects so bright and cheering as they were at the present time—(great applause, the announcement being considered indicative of a healthy exchequer)—its country was great, its covers perfect, and thanks to their truly invaluable allies—the farmers—their foxes most abundant—(renewed applause). Of those excellent men it was impossible to speak in terms of too great admiration and respect—(applause)—whether he looked at those he was blessed with upon his own estate—(laughter)—or at the great body generally, he was lost for words to express his opinion of their patriotism, and the obligations he felt under to them. So far from ever hinting at such a thing as damage, he really believed a farmer would be hooted from the market-table who broached such a subject—(applause, with murmurs of dissent)—or who even admitted it was possible that any could be done—(laughter and applause). As for a few cocks and hens, he was sure they felt a pleasure in presenting them to the foxes. At all events, he could safely say he had never paid for any—(renewed laughter). Looking, therefore, at the hunt in all its aspects—its sport past, present, and to come—he felt that he never addressed them under circumstances of greater promise, or with feelings of livelier satisfaction. It only remained for them to keep matters up to the present mark, to insure great and permanent prosperity. He begged, therefore, to propose, with all the honours, Success to the Hit-im and Hold-im shire hunt!"—(drunk with three times three and one cheer more). Sir Moses and Cuddy Flintoff mounting their chairs to mark time. Flintoff finishing off with a round of view halloas and other hunting noises.

When the applause and Sir Moses had both subsided, parties who had felt uneasy about their pockets, began to breathe more freely, and as the bottles again circulated, Mr. Mossman and others, for whom wine was too cold, slipped out to get their pipes, and something warm in the bar; Mossman calling for whiskey, Buckwheat for brandy, Broadfurrow for gin, and so on. Then as they sugared and flavoured their tumblers, they chewed the cud of Sir Moses's eloquence, and at length commenced discussing it, as each man got seated with his pipe in his mouth and his glass on his knee, in a little glass-fronted bar.

"What a man he is to talk, that Sir Moses," observed Buckwheat after a long respiration.

"He's a greet economist of the truth, I reckon," replied Mr. Mossman, withdrawing his pipe from his mouth, "for I've written to him till I'm tired, about last year's damage to Mrs. Anthill's sown grass."

124

"He's right, though, in saying he never paid for poultry," observed Mr. Broadfurrow, with a humorous shake of his big head, "but, my word, his hook-nosed agent has as many letters as would paper a room;" and so they sipped, and smoked, and talked the Baronet over, each man feeling considerably relieved at there being no fresh attempt on the pocket.

Meanwhile Sir Moses, with the aid of Cuddy Flintoff, trimmed the table, and kept the bottles circulating briskly, presently calling on Mr. Paul Straddler for a song, who gave them the old heroic one, descriptive of a gallant run with the Hit-im and Hold-im shire hounds, in the days of Mr. Customer, at which they all laughed and applauded as heartily as if they had never heard it before. They then drank Mr. Straddler's health, and thanks to him for his excellent song.

As it proceeded, Sir Moses intimated quietly to our friend Billy Pringle that he should propose his health next, which would enable Mr. Pringle to return the compliment by proposing Sir Moses, an announcement that threw our hero into a very considerable state of trepidation, but from which he saw no mode of escape. Sir Moses then having allowed a due time to elapse after the applause that followed the drinking of Mr. Straddler's health, again arose, and tapping the table with his hammer, called upon them to fill bumpers to the health of his young friend on his right (applause). "He could not express the pleasure it afforded him," he said, "to see a nephew of his old friend and brother Baronet, Sir Jonathan Pringle, become a member of their excellent hunt, and he hoped Billy would long live to enjoy the glorious diversion of fox-hunting," which Sir Moses said it was the bounden duty of every true-born Briton to support to the utmost of his ability, for that it was peculiarly the sport of gentlemen, and about the only one that defied the insidious arts of the blackleg, adding that Lord Derby was quite right in saying that racing had got into the hands of parties who kept horses not for sport, but as mere instruments of gambling, and if his (Sir Moses's) young friend, Mr. Pringle, would allow him to counsel him, he would say, Never have anything to do with the turf (applause). Stick to hunting, and if it didn't bring him in money, it would bring him in health, which was better than money, with which declaration Sir Moses most cordially proposed Mr. Pringle's health (drunk with three times three and one cheer more).

Now our friend had never made a speech in his life, but being, as we said at the outset, blessed with a great determination of words to the mouth, he rose at a hint from Sir Moses, and assured the company "how grateful he was for the honour they had done him as well in electing him a member of their delightful sociable hunt, as in responding to the toast of his health in the flattering manner they had, and he could assure them that nothing should be wanting on his part to promote the interests of the establishment, and to prove himself worthy of their continued good opinion," at which intimation Sir Moses winked knowingly at Mr. Smoothley, who hemmed a recognition of his meaning.

Meanwhile Mr. Pringle stood twirling his trifling moustache, wishing to sit down, but feeling there was something to keep him up: still he couldn't hit it off. Even a friendly round of applause failed to help him out; at length, Sir Moses, fearing he might stop altogether, whispered the words "*My health,*" just under his nose; at which Billy perking up, exclaimed, "Oh, aye, to be sure!" and seizing a decanter under him, he filled himself a bumper of port, calling upon the company to follow his example. This favour being duly accorded, our friend then proceeded, in a very limping, halting sort of way, to eulogise a man with whom he was very little acquainted amid the friendly word-supplying cheers and plaudits of the party. At length he stopped again, still feeling that he was not due on his seat, but quite unable to say why he should not resume it. The company thinking he might have something to say to the purpose, how he meant to hunt with them, or something of that sort, again supplied the cheers of encouragement. It was of no use, however, he couldn't hit it off.

****

"*All the honors!*" at length whispered Sir Moses as before.

"O, ah, to be sure! *all the honors!*" replied Billy aloud, amidst the mirth of the neighbours. "Gentlemen!" continued he, elevating his voice to its former pitch, "This toast I feel assured—that is to say, I feel quite certain. I mean," stammered he, stamping with his foot, "I, I, I."

"*Aye, two thou's i' Watlington goods!*" exclaimed the half-drunken Mr. Corduroys, an announcement that drew forth such a roar of laughter as enabled Billy to tack the words, "all the honors," to the end, and so with elevated glass to continue the noise with cheers. He then sate down perfectly satisfied with this his first performance, feeling that he had the germs of oratory within him.

A suitable time having elapsed, Sir Moses rose and returned thanks with great vigour, declaring that beyond all comparison that was the proudest moment of his life, and that he wouldn't exchange the mastership of the Hit-im and Hold-im shire hounds for the highest, the noblest office in the world—Dom'd if he would! with which asseveration he drank all their very good healths, and resumed his seat amidst loud and long continued applause, the timidest then feeling safe against further demands on their purses Another song quickly followed, and then according to the usual custom of society, that the more you abuse a man in private the more you praise him in public, Sir Moses next proposed the health of that excellent and popular nobleman the Earl of Ladythorne, whose splendid pack showed such unrivalled sport in the adjoining county of Featherbedford; Sir Moses, after a great deal of flattery, concluding by declaring that he would "go to the world's end to serve Lord Ladythorne—Dom'd if he wouldn't," a sort of compliment that the noble Earl never reciprocated; on the contrary, indeed, when he condescended to admit the existence of such a man as Sir Moses, it was generally in that well-known disparaging enquiry, "Who *is* that Sir Aaron Mainchance? or who is that Sir Somebody Mainchance, who hunts Hit-im and Hold-im shire?" He never could hit off the Baronet's Christian or rather Jewish name. Now, however, it was all the noble Earl, "my noble friend and brother master," the "noble and gallant sportsman," and so on. Sir Moses thus partly revenging himself on his lordship with the freedom.

When a master of hounds has to borrow a "draw" from an adjoining country, it is generally a pretty significant hint that his own is exhausted, and when the chairman of a hunt dinner begins toasting his natural enemy the adjoining master, it is pretty evident that the interest of the evening is over. So it was on the present occasion. Broad backs kept bending away at intervals, thinking nobody saw them, leaving large gaps unclosed up, while the guests that remained merely put a few drops in the bottoms of their glasses or passed the bottles altogether.

Sir Aaron, we beg his pardon—Sir Moses, perceiving this, and knowing the value of a good report, called on those who were left to "fill a bumper to the health of their excellent and truly invaluable friend Mr. Pica, contrasting his quiet habits with the swaggering bluster of a certain Brummagem Featherbedfordshire D'Orsay." (Drunk with great applause, D'Orsay Davis having more than once sneered at the equestrian prowess of the Hit-im aud Hold-im shire-ites.)

Mr. Pica, who was a fisherman and a very bad one to boot, then arose and began dribbling out the old stereotyped formula about air we breathe, have it not we die, &c., which was a signal for a general rise; not all Sir Moses and Cuddy Flintoff's united efforts being able to restrain the balance of guests from breaking away, and a squabble occurring behind the screen about a hat, the chance was soon irrevocably gone. Mr. Pica was, therefore, left alone in his glory. If any one, however, can afford to be indifferent about being heard, it is surely an editor who can report himself in his paper, and poor Pica did himself ample justice in the "Hit-im and Hold-im shire Herald" on the Saturday following.

CHAPTER XLI. THE HUNT TEA.—BUSHEY HEATH AND BARE ACRES.

THE 15th rule of the Hit-im and Hold-im shire hunt, provides that all members who dine at the club, may have tea and muffins ad libitum for 6 d. a head afterwards, and certainly nothing can be more refreshing after a brawling riotous dinner than a little quiet comfortable Bohea. Sir Moses always had his six-penn'orth, as had a good many of his friends and followers. Indeed the rule was a proposition of the Baronet's, such a thing as tea being unheard of in the reign of Mr. Customer, or any of Sir Moses's great predecessors. Those were the days of "lift him up and carry him to bed." Thank goodness they are gone! Men can hunt without thinking it necessary to go out with a headache. Beating a jug in point of capacity is no longer considered the accomplishment of a gentleman.

Mr. Pica's eloquence having rather prematurely dissolved the meeting, Sir Moses and his friends now congregated round the fire all very cheery and well pleased with themselves—each flattering the other in hopes of getting a compliment in return. "Gone off amazingly well!" exclaimed one, rubbing his hands in delight at its being over. "Capital party," observed another. "Excellent speech yours, Sir Moses," interposed a third. "Never heard a better," asserted a fourth. "Ought to ask to have it printed," observed a fifth. "O, never fear! Pica'll do that," rejoined a sixth, and so they went on warding off the awkward thought, so apt to arise of "what a bore these sort of parties are. Wonder if they do any good?"

The good they do was presently shown on this occasion by Mr. Smoothley, the Jackall of the hunt, whose pecuniary obligations to Sir Moses we have already hinted at, coming bowing and fawning obsequiously up to our Billy, revolving his hands as though he were washing them, and congratulating him upon becoming one of them. Mr. Smoothley was what might be called the head pacificator of the hunt, the gentleman who coaxed subscriptions, deprecated damage, and tried to make young gentlemen believe they had had very good runs, when in fact they had only had very middling ones.

126

The significant interchange of glances between Sir Moses and him during Billy's speech related to a certain cover called Waverley gorse, which the young Woolpack, Mr. Treadcroft, who had ascertained his inability to ride, had announced his intention of resigning. The custom of the hunt was, first to get as many covers as they could for nothing; secondly to quarter as few on the club funds as possible; and thirdly to get young gentlemen to stand godfathers to covers, in other words to get them to pay the rent in return for the compliment of the cover passing by their names, as Heslop's spiny, Linch's gorse, Benson's banks, and so on.

This was generally an after-dinner performance, and required a skilful practitioner to accomplish, more particularly as the trick was rather notorious. Mr. Smoothley was now about to try his hand on Mr. Pringle. The bowing and congratulations over, and the flexible back straightened, he commenced by observing that, he supposed a copy of the rules of the hunt addressed to Pangburn Park, would find our friend.

"Yarse," drawled Billy, wondering if there would be anything to pay. "Dash it, he wished there mightn't? Shouldn't be surprised if there was?"

Mr. Smoothley, however, gave him little time for reflection, for taking hold of one of his own red-coat buttons, he observed, "that as he supposed Mr. Pringle would be sporting the hunt uniform, he might take the liberty of mentioning that Garnett the silversmith in the market-place had by far the neatest and best pattern'd buttons."

"Oh, Garnett, oh, yarse," replied Billy, thinking he would get a set for his pink, instead of the plain ones he was wearing.

"His shop is next the Lion and the Lamb public house," continued Mr. Smoothley, "between it and Mrs. Russelton the milliner's, and by the way that reminds me," continued he, though we don't exactly see how it could, "and by the way that reminds me that there is an excellent opportunity for distinguishing yourself by adopting the cover young Mr. Treadcroft has just abandoned."

"The w-h-a-at?" drawled Billy, dreading a "do;" his mother having cautioned him always to be mindful after dinner.

"O, merely the gorse," continued Mr. Smoothley, in the most affable matter-of-course way imaginable, "merely the gorse—if you'll step this way, I'll show you," continued he, leading the way to where a large dirty board was suspended against the wall below the portrait of Lord Martingal on his horse.

"*Now he's running into him!*" muttered Sir Moses to himself, his keen eye supplying the words to the action.

"This, you see," explained Mr. Smoothley, hitching the board off its brass-headed nail, and holding it to the light—"this, you see, is a list of all the covers in the country—Screechley, Summer-field, Reddingfield, Bewley, Lanton Hill, Baxterley, and so forth. Then you see here," continned he, pointing to a ruled column opposite, "are the names of the owners or patrons— yes" (reading), "owners or patrons—Lord Oilcake, Lord Polkaton, Sir Harry Fuzball, Mr. Heslop, Lord Harpsichord, Mr. Drew, Mr. Smith. Now young Mr. Treadcroft, who has had as many falls as he likes, and perhaps more, has just announced his intention of retiring and giving up this cover," pointing to Waverley, with Mr. Treadcroft, Jun.'s name opposite to it, "and it struck me that it would be a capital opportunity for you who have just joined us, to take it before anybody knows, and then it will go by the name of Pringle's gorse, and you'll get the credit of all the fine runs that take place from it."

"Y-a-r-s-e," drawled Billy, thinking that that would be a sharp thing to do, and that it would be fine to rank with the lords.

"Then," continued Mr. Smoothley, taking the answer for an assent, "I'll just strike Treadey's name ont, and put yours in;" so saying, he darted at the sideboard, and seizing an old ink-clotted stump of a pen, with just enough go in it to make the required alteration, and substituted Mr. Pringle's name for that of Mr. Treadcroft. And so, what with his cover, his dinner, and his button, poor Billy was eased of above twenty pounds.

Just as Sir Moses was blowing his beak, stirring the fire, and chuckling at the success of the venture, a gingling of cups and tinkling of spoons was heard in the distance, and presently a great flight of tea-trays emerged from either side of the screen, conspicuous among the bearers of which were the tall ticket-of-leave butler and the hirsute Monsieur Jean Rougier. These worthies, with a few other "gentlemen's gentlemen," had been regaled to a supper in the "Blenheim," to which Peter had contributed a liberal allowance of hunt wine, the consumption of which was checked by the corks, one set, it was said, serving Peter the season. That that which is everybody's business is nobody's, is well exemplified in these sort of transactions, for though a member of the hunt went through the form of counting the cork-tops every evening, and seeing that they corresponded with the number set down in Peter's book, nobody ever compared the book with the cellar, so that in fact Peter was both check-keeper and auditor. Public bodies, however, are all considered fair game, and the Hit-im and Hold-im shire hunt was no exception to the rule. In addition to the wine, there had been a sufficient allowance of spirits in the "Blenheim" to set the drunkards to work on their own account, and Jack Rogers, who was quite the life of the party, was very forward in condition when the tea-summons was heard.

"Hush!" cried Peter, holding up his hand, aud listening to an ominous bell-peal, "I do believe that's for tea! So it is," sighed he, as a second summons broke upon the ear. "Tea at this hour!" ejaculated he, "who'd ha' thought it twenty years ago! Why, this is just the time they'd ha' been calling for Magnums, and beginnin' the evening—*Tea!* They'd as soon ha' thought of callin' for winegar!" added he, with a bitter sneer. So saying, Peter dashed a tear from his aged eye, and rising from his chair, craved the assistance of his guests to carry the degrading beverage up-stairs, to our degenerate party. "A set of weshenvomen!" muttered he, as the great slop-basin-like-cups stood ranged on trays along the kitchen-table ready for conveyance. "Sarves us right for allowing such a chap to take our country," added he, adopting his load, and leading the tea-van.

When the soothing, smoking beverage entered, our friend, Cuddy Flintoff, was "yoicking" himself about the club-room, stopping now at this picture, now that, holloaing at one, view-holloaing at another, thus airing his hunting noises generally, as each successive subject recalled some lively association in his too sensitive hunting imagination. Passing from the contemplation of that great work of art, Mr. Customer getting drunk, he suddenly confronted the tea-brigade entering, led by Peter, Monsieur, and the ticket-of-leave butler.

"Holloa! old Bushey Heath!" exclaimed Cuddy, dapping his hands, as Mousieur's frizzed face loomed congruously behind a muffin-towering tea-tray. "Holloa! old Bushey Heath!" repeated he, louder than before, "*What cheer there?*"

"Vot cheer there, Brother Bareacres?" replied Jack in the same familiar tone, to the great consternation of Cuddy, and the amusement of the party.

"Dash the fellow! but he's getting bumptious," muttered Cuddy, who had no notion of being taken up that way by a servant. "Dash the fellow! but he's getting bumptious," repeated he, adding aloud to Jack, "That's not the way you talked when you tumbled off your horse the other day!"

"Tombled off my 'oss, sare!" replied Jack, indignantly—"tombled off my 'oss, sare—nevare, sare!—nevare!"

"What!" retorted Cuddy, "do you mean to say you didn't tumble off your horse on the Crooked Billet day?" for Cuddy had heard of that exploit, but not of Jack's subsequent performance.

"No, sare, I jomp off," replied Jack, thinking Cuddy alluded to his change of horses with the Woolpack.

"*Jo-o-m-p* off! j-o-omp off!" reiterated Cuddy, "we all jomp off, when we can't keep on. Why didn't old Imperial John take you into the Crooked Billet, and scrape you, and cherish you, and comfort you, and treat you as he would his own son?" demanded Cuddy.

"Imperial John, sare, nevare did nothin' of the sort," replied Jack, confidently. "Imperial John and I retired to 'ave leetle drop drink together to our better 'quaintance. I met John there, *n'est-ce pas?* Monsieur Sare Moses, Baronet! Vasn't it as I say?" asked Jack, jingling his tea-tray before the Baronet.

"Oh yes," replied Sir Moses,—"Oh yes, undoubtedly; I introduced you there; but here! let me have some tea," continued he, taking a cup, wishing to stop the conversation, lest Lord Lady-thorne might hear he had introduced his right-hand man, Imperial John, to a servant.

Cuddy, however, wasn't to be stopped. He was sure Jack had tumbled off, and was bent upon working him in return for his Bareacres compliment.

"Well, but tell us," said he, addressing Jack again, "did you come over his head or his tail, when you jomp off?"

"Don't, Cuddy! don't!" now muttered Sir Moses, taking the entire top tier off a pile of muffins, and filling his mouth as full as it would hold; "don't," repeated he, adding, "it's no use (munch) bullying a poor (crunch) beggar because he's a (munch) Frenchman" (crunch). Sir Moses then took a great draught of tea.

Monsieur's monkey, however, was now up, and he felt inclined to tackle with Flintoff. "I tell you vot, sare Cuddy," said he, looking him full in the face, "you think yourself vare great man, vare great ossmaan, vare great foxer, and so on, bot I vill ride you a match for vot monies you please."

"Hoo-ray! well done you! go it, Monsieur! Who'd ha' thought it! Now for some fun!" resounded through the room, bringing all parties in closer proximity.

Flintoff was rather taken aback. He didn't expect anything of that sort, and though he fully believed Jack to be a tailor, he didn't want to test the fact himself; indeed he felt safer on foot than on horseback, being fonder of the theory than of the reality of hunting.

128

"Hut you and your matches," sneered he, thrusting his hands deep in his trousers' pockets, inclining to sheer of, adding, "go and get his Imperial Highness to ride you one."

"His Imperial Highness, sare, don't deal in oss matches. He is not a jockey, he is a gentlemans—great friend of de great lords vot rules de oder noisy dogs," replied Jack.

"*Humph*, grunted Sir Moses, not liking the language.

"In-deed!" exclaimed Cuddy with a frown, "In-deed! Hark to Monsieur! Hark!"

"Oh, make him a match, Cuddy! make him a match!" now interposed Paul Straddler, closing up to prevent Cuddy's retreat. Paul, as we said before, was a disengaged gentleman who kept a house of call for Bores at Hinton,—a man who was always ready to deal, or do anything, or go any where at any body else's expense. A great judge of a horse, a great judge of a groom, a great judge of a gig, a gentleman a good deal in Cuddy Flintoff's own line in short, and of course not a great admirer of his. He now thought he saw his way to a catch, for the Woolpack had told him how shamefully Jack had bucketed his horse, and altogether he thought Monsieur might be as good a man across country as Mr. Flintoff. At all events he would like to see.

"Oh, make him a match, Cuddy! make him a match!" now exclaimed he, adding in Flintoff's ear, "never let it be said you were afraid of a Frenchman."

"Afraid!" sneered Cuddy, "nobody who knows me will think that, I guess."

"Well then, *make* him a match!" urged Tommy Heslop, who was no great admirer of Cuddy's either; "*make* him a match, and I'll go your halves."

"And I'll go Monsieur's," said Mr. Straddler, still backing the thing up. Thus appealed to, poor Cuddy was obliged to submit, and before he knew where he was, the dread pen, ink and paper were produced, and things began to assume a tangible form. Mr. Paul Straddler, having seated himself on a chair at the opportune card-table, began sinking his pen and smoothing out his paper, trying to coax his ideas into order.

"Now, let us see," said he, "now let us see. Monsieur, what's his name—old Bushey-heath as you call him, agrees to ride Mr. Flintoff a match across country—now for distance, time, and stake! now for distance, time, and stake!" added he, hitting off the scent.

"Well, but how can you make a match? how can you make a match without any horses? how can you make a match without any horses?" asked Sir Moses, interposing his beak, adding "I'll not lend any—dom'd if I will." That being the first time Sir Moses was ever known not to volunteer one.

"O, we'll find horses," replied Tommy Heslop, "we'll find horses!" thinking Sir Moses's refusal was all in favor of the match. "Catch weights, catch horses, catch every thing."

"Now for distance, time, and stake," reiterated Mr. Straddler. "Now for distance, time, and stake, Monsieur!" continued he, appealing to Jack. "What distance would you like to have it?"

"Vot you please, sare," replied Monsieur, now depositing his tray on the sideboard; "vot you please, sare, much or little; ten miles, twenty miles, any miles he likes."

"O, the fellow's mad," muttered Cuddy, with a jerk of his head, making a last effort to be off.

"Don't be in a hurry, Cuddy, don't be in a hurry," interposed Heslop, adding, "he doesn't understand it—he doesn't understand it."

"O, I understands it, nicely, veil enough," replied Jack, with a shrug of his shoulders; "put us on to two orses, and see vich gets first to de money post."

"Aye, yes, exactly, to be sure, that's all right," asserted Paul Straddler, looking up approvingly at Jack, "and you say you'll beat Mr. Flintoff?"

"I say I beat Mr. Flintoff," rejoined Jack—"beat im dem veil too—beat his ead off—beat him *stupendous!*" added he.

"O, dash it all, we can't stand that, Caddy!" exclaimed Mr. Heslop, nudging Mr. Flintoff; "honor of the country, honor of the hunt, honor of England, honor of every thing's involved." Cuddy's bristles were now up too, and shaking his head and thrusting his hands deep into his trousers pockets, "he declared he couldn't stand that sort of language,—shot if he could."

"No; nor nobody else," continued Mr. Heslop, keeping him up to the indignity mark; "must be taught better manners," added he with a pout of the lip, as though fully espousing Caddy's cause.

"Come along, then! come along!" cried Paul Straddler, flourishing his dirty pen; "let's set up a school for grown sportsmen. Now for the guod boys. Master Bushey-heath says he'll ride Master Bareacres a match across country—two miles say—for, for, how much?" asked he, looking up.

This caused a pause, as it often does, even after dinner, and not the less so in the present instance, inasmuch as the promoters of the match had each a share in the risk. What would be hundreds in other people's cases becomes pounds in our own.

Flintoff and Straddler looked pacifically at each other, as much as to say, "There's no use in cutting each other's throats, you know."

"Suppose we say," (exhibiting four fingers and a thumb, slyly to indicate a five pound note), said Heslop demurely, after a conference with Cuddy.

129

"With all my heart," asserted Straddler, "glad it was no more."

"And call it fifty," whispered Heslop.

"Certainly!" assented Straddler, "very proper arrangement."

"Two miles for fifty pounds," announced Straddler, writing it down.

"P. P. I s'pose?" observed he, looking up.

"P. P." assented Heslop.

"Now, what next?" asked Paul, feeling that there was something more wanted.

"An umpire," suggested Mr. Smoothley.

"Ah, to be sure, an umpire," replied Mr. Straddler; "who shall it be?"

"Sir Moses!" suggested several voices.

"Sir Moses, by all means," replied Straddler.

"Content," nodded Mr. Heslop.

"It must be on a non-hunting day, then," observed the Baronet, speaking from the bottom of his tea-cup.

"Non-hunting day!" repeated Cuddy; "non-hunting day; fear that 'ill not do—want to be off to town on Friday to see Tommy White's horses sold. Have been above a week at the Park, as it is."

"You've been a fortnight to-morrow, sir," observed the ticket-of-leave butler (who had just come to announce the carriage) in a very different tone to his usual urbane whisper.

"Fortnight to-morrow, have I?" rejoined Cuddy sheepishly; "greater reason why I should be off."

"O, never think about that! O, never think about that! Heartily welcome, heartily welcome," rejoined Sir Moses, stuffing his mouth full of muffin, adding "Mr. Pringle will keep you company; Mr. Pringle will keep you company." (Hunch, munch, crunch.)

"Mr. Pringle *must* stop," observed Mr. Straddler, "unless he goes without his man."

"To besure he must," assented Sir Moses, "to be sure he must," adding, "stop as long as ever you like. I've no engagement till Saturday—no engagement till Saturday."

Now putting off our friend's departure till Saturday just gave a clear day for the steeple-chase, the next one, Thursday, being Woolerton by Heckfield, Saturday the usual make-believe day at the kennels; so of course Friday was fixed upon, and Sir Moses having named "noon" as the hour, and Timberlake toll-bar as the *rendezvous*, commenced a series of adieus as he beat a retreat to the screen, where having resumed his wraps, and gathered his tail, he shot down-stairs, and was presently re-ensconced in his carriage.

The remanets then of course proceeded to talk him and his friends over, some wishing the Baronet mightn't be too many for Billy, others again thinking Cuddy wasn't altogether the most desirable acquaintance a young man could have, though there wasn't one that didn't think that he himself was.

That topic being at length exhausted, they then discussed the projected steeple-chase, some thinking that Cuddy was a muff, others that Jack was, some again thinking they both were. And as successive relays of hot brandy and water enabled them to see matters more clearly, the Englishman's argument of betting was introduced, and closed towards morning at "evens," either jockey for choice.

Let us now take a look at the homeward bound party.

It was lucky for Billy that the night was dark and the road rough with newly laid whinstones, for both Sir Moses and Cuddy opened upon him most volubly and vehemently as soon as ever they got off the uneven pavement, with no end of inquiries about Jack and his antecedents. If he could ride? If he had ever seen him ride? If he had ever ridden a steeplechase? Where he got him? How long he had had him?

To most of which questions, Billy replied with his usual monosyllabic drawling, "yarses," amid jolts, and grinds, and gratings, and doms from Sir Moses, and cusses from Cuddy, easing his conscience with regard to Jack's service, by saying that he had had him "some time." Some time! What a line elastic period that is. We'd back a lawyer to make it cover a century or a season. Very little definite information, however, did they extract from Billy with regard to Jack for the best of all reasons, that Billy didn't know anything. Both Cuddy and Sir Moses interpreted his ignorance differently, and wished he mightn't know more than was good for them. And so in the midst of roughs and smooths, and jolts and jumps, and examinings, and cross-examinings, and re-examinings, they at length reached Pangburn Park Lodges, and were presently at home.

"Breakfast at eight!" said Sir Moses to Bankhead, as he alighted from the carriage.

"Breakfast at eight, Pringle!" repeated he, and seizing a flat candlestick from the half-drunken footman in the passage, he hurried up-stairs, blowing his beak with great vigour to drown any appeal to him about a horse.

He little knew how unlikely our young friend was to trouble him in that way.

CHAPTER XLII. MR. GEORDEY GALLON.

CUDDY Flintoff did not awake at all comfortable the next morning, and he distinctly traced the old copyhead of "Familiarity breeds contempt." in the hieroglyphic pattern of his old chintz bed-hangings. He couldn't think how he could ever be so foolish as to lay himself open to such a catastrophe; it was just the wine being in and the wit being out, coupled with the fact of the man being a Frenchman, that led him away—and he most devoutly wished he was well out of the scrape. Suppose Monsieur was a top sawyer! Suppose he was a regular steeple-chaser! Suppose he was a second Beecher in disguise! It didn't follow because he was a Frenchman that he couldn't ride. Altogether Mr. Flintoff repented. It wasn't nice amusement, steeple-chasing he thought, and the quicksilver of youth had departed from him; getting called Bareacres, too, was derogatory, and what no English servant would have done, if even he had called him Bushy Heath.

Billy Pringle, on the other hand, was very comfortable, and slept soundly, regardless of clubs, cover rents, over-night consequences, altogether. Each having desired to be called when the other got up, they stood a chance of lying in bed all day, had not Mrs. Margerum, fearing they would run their breakfast, and the servants'-hall dinner together, despatched Monsieur and the footman with their respective hot-water cans, to say the other had risen. It was eleven o'clock ere they got dawdled down-stairs, and Cuddy again began demanding this and that delicacy in the name of Mr. Pringle: Mr. Pringle wanted Yorkshire pie; Mr. Pringle wanted potted prawns; Mr. Pringle wanted bantams' eggs; Mr. Pringle wanted honey. Why the deuce didn't they attend to Mr. Pringle?

The breakfast was presently interrupted by the sound of wheels, and almost ere they had ceased to revolve, a brisk pull at the doorbell aroused the inmates of both the front and back regions, and brought the hurrying footman, settling himself into his yellow-edged blue-livery coat as he came.

It was Mr. Heslop. Heslop in a muffin cap, and so disguised in heather-coloured tweed, that Mr. Pringle failed to recognise him as he entered. Cuddy did, though; and greeting him with one of his best view holloas, he invited him to sit down and partake.

Heslop was an early bird, and had broke his fast hours before: but a little more breakfast being neither here nor there, he did as he was requested, though he would much rather have found Cuddy alone. He wanted to talk to him about the match, to hear if Sir Moses had said anything about the line of country, what sort of a horse he would like to ride, and so on.

Billy went munch, munch, munching on, in the tiresome, pertinacious sort of way people do when others are anxiously wishing them done,—now taking a sip of tea, now a bit of toast, now another egg, now looking as if he didn't know what he would take. Heslop inwardly wished him at Jericho. At length another sound of wheels was heard, followed by another peal of the bell; and our hero presently had a visitor, too, in the person of Mr. Paul Straddler. Paul had come on the same sort of errand as Heslop, namely, to arrange matters about Monsieur; and Heslop and he, seeing how the land lay, Heslop asked Cuddy if there was any one in Sir Moses's study; whereupon Cuddy arose and led the way to the sunless little sanctum, where Sir Moses kept his other hat, his other boots, his rows of shoes, his beloved but rather empty cash-box, and the plans and papers of the Pangburn Park estate.

Two anxious deliberations then ensued in the study and breakfast-room, in the course of which Monsieur was summoned into the presence of either party, and retired, leaving them about as wise as he found them. He declared he could ride, ride "dem veil too," and told Paul he could "beat Cuddy's head off;" but he accompanied the assertions with such wild, incoherent arguments, and talked just as he did to Imperial John before the Crooked Billet, that they thought it was all gasconade. If it hadn't been P. P., Pan! would have been off. Cuddy, on the other hand, gained courage; and as Heslop proposed putting him on his famous horse General Havelock, the reported best fencer in the country, Cuddy, who wasn't afraid of pace, hoped to be able to give a good account of himself. Indeed, he so far recovered his confidence, as to indulge in a few hunting noises—"*For-rard, on! For-rard on!*" cheered he, as if he was leading the way with the race well in hand.

Meanwhile Monsieur, who could keep his own counsel, communicated by a certain mysterious agency that prevails in most countries, and seems to rival the electric telegraph in point of speed, to enlist a confederate in his service. This was Mr. Geordey Gallon, a genius carrying on the trades of poacher, pugilist, and publican, under favour of that mistaken piece of legislation the Beer Act. Geordey, like Jack, had begun life as a post-boy, and like him had undergone various vicissitudes ere he finally settled down to the respectable calling we have named. He now occupied the Rose and Crown beershop at the Four Lane-Ends. on the Heatherbell Road, some fifteen miles from Pangburn Park, where, in addition to his regular or irregular calling, he generally kept a racing-like runaway, that whisked a light spring-cart through the country by night, freighted with pigeons, poultry, game, dripping—which latter item our readers doubtless know includes every article of culinary or domestic use. He was also a purveyor of lead, lead-stealing being now one of the liberal professions.

Geordey had had a fine time of it, for the Hit-im and Hold-im shire constables were stupid and lazy, and when the short-lived Superintendent ones were appointed, it was only a trifle in his way to suborn them. So he made hay while the sun shone, and presently set up a basket-buttoned green cutaway for Sundays, in lieu of the baggy pocketed, velveteen shooting-jacket of week-days, and replaced the fox-skin cap with a bare shallow drab, with a broad brim, and a black band, encasing his substantial in cords and mahogany tops, instead of the navvie boot that laced his great bulging calves into globes. He then called himself a sporting man.

Not a fair, not a fight, not a fray of any sort, but Geordey's great square bull-headed carcase was there, and he was always ready to run his nag, or trot his nag, or match his nag in any shape or way—Mr. George Gallon's Blue Ruin, Mr. George Gallon's Flower of the West, Mr. George Gallon's Honor Bright, will be names familiar to most lovers of leather-plating. * Besides this, he did business in a smaller way. Being a pure patriot, he was a great promoter of the sports and pastimes of the people, and always travelled with a prospectus in his pocket of some raffle for a watch, some shoot-ing-match for a fat hog, some dog or some horse to be disposed of in a surreptitious way, one of the conditions always being, that a certain sum was to be spent by the winner at Mr. Gallon's, of the Hose and Crown, at the Four Lane-ends on the Heatherbell Road.

Such was the worthy selected by Monsieur Rougier to guard his interests in the matter. But how the communication was made, or what were the instructions given, those who are acquainted with the wheels within wheels, and the glorious mystification that prevails in all matters relating to racing or robbing, will know the impossibility of narrating Even Sir Moses was infected with the prevailing epidemic, and returned from hunting greatly subdued in loquacity. He wanted to be on for a £5 or two, but couldn't for the life of him make out which was to be the right side. So he was very chary of his wine after dinner, and wouldn't let Cuddy have any brandy at bed-time—"Dom'd if he would."

CHAPTER XLIII. SIR MOSES PERPLEXED—THE RENDEZVOUS FOR THE RACE.

THE great event was ushered in by one of those fine bright autumnal days that shame many summer ones, and seem inclined to carry the winter months fairly over into the coming year. The sun rose with effulgent radiance, gilding the lingering brown and yellow tints, and lighting up the landscape with searching, inquisitorial scrutiny. Not a nook, not a dell, not a cot, not a curl of smoke but was visible, and the whole scene shone with the vigour of a newly burnished, newly varnished picture. The cattle stood in bold relief against the perennially green fields, and the newly dipped lambs dotted the hill-sides like white marbles. A clear bright light gleamed through the stems of the Scotch fir belt, encircling the brow of High Rays Hill, giving goodly promise of continued fineness.

* We append one of Mr. Gallon's advertisements for a horse, which is very characteristic of the man:— "A Flash high-stepping SCREW WANTED. Must be very fast, steady in single harness, and the price moderate. Blemishes no object. Apply, by letter, real name and address, with full description, to Mr. George Gallon, Rose and Crown, Four-Lane-ends. Hit-im and Hold-im shire."

Sir Moses, seeing this harbinger of fair from his window as he dressed, arrayed himself in his best attire, securing his new blue and white satin cravat with a couple of massive blood-stone pins, and lacing his broad-striped vest with a multiplicity of chains and appendant gew-gaws. He further dared the elements with an extensive turning up of velvet. Altogether he was a great swell, and extremely well pleased with his appearance.

The inmates of the Park were all at sixes and sevens that morning, Monsieur having left Billy to be valeted by the footman, whose services were entirely monopolised by Cuddy Flintoff and Sir Moses. When he did at length come, he replied to Billy's enquiry "how his horse was," that he was "quite well," which was satisfactory to our friend, and confirmed him in his opinion of the superiority of his judgment over that of Wetun and the rest. Sir Moses, however, who had made the tour of the stables, thought otherwise, and telling the Tiger to put the footboard to the back of the dog-cart, reserved the other place in front for his guest. A tremendous hurry Sir Moses was in to be off, rushing in every two or three minutes to see if Billy wasn't done his breakfast, and at last ordering round the vehicle to expedite his movements. Then he went to the door and gave the bell such a furious ring as sounded through the house and seemed well calculated to last for ever.

Billy then came, hustled along by the ticket-of-leave butler and the excitable footman, who kept dressing him as he went; and putting his mits, his gloves, this shawl, cravat, and his taper umbrella into his hands, they helped him up to the seat by Sir Moses, who forthwith soused him down, by touching the mare with the whip, and starting off at a pace that looked like trying to catch an express train. Round flew the wheels, up shot the yellow mud, open went the lodge gates, bark went the curs, and they were presently among the darker mud of the Marshfield and Greyridge Hill Road.

On, on, Sir Moses pushed, as if in extremis.

"Well now, how is it to be?" at length asked he, getting his mare more by the head, after grinding through a long strip of newly-laid whinstone: "How is it to be? Can this beggar of yours ride, or can he not?" Sir Moses looking with a scrutinising eye at Billy as he spoke.

"Yarse, he can ride," replied Billy, feeling his collar; "rode the other day, you know."

Sir Moses. "Ah, but that's not the sort of riding I mean. Can he ride across country? Can he ride a steeple-chase, in fact?"

Mr. Pringle. "Yarse, I should say he could," hesitated our friend.

Sir Moses. "Well, but it won't do to back a man to do a thing one isn't certain he can do, you know. Now, between ourselves," continued he, lowering his voice so as not to let the Tiger hear—"Cuddy Flintoff is no great performer—more of a mahogany sportsman than any thing else, and it wouldn't take any great hand to beat him."

Billy couldn't say whether Monsieur was equal to the undertaking or not, and therefore made no reply. This perplexed Sir Moses, who wished that Billy's downy face mightn't contain more mischief than it ought. It would be a devil of a bore, he thought, to be done by such a boy. So he again took the mare short by the head, and gave expression to his thoughts by the whip along her sides. Thus he shot down Walkup Hill at a pace that carried him half way up the opposing one. Still he couldn't see his way—dom'd if he could—and he felt half inclined not to risk his "fi-pun" note.

In this hesitating mood he came within sight of the now crowd-studded rendezvous.

Timberlake toll bar, the rendezvous for the race, stands on the summit of the hog-backed Wooley Hill, famous for its frequent sheep-fairs, and commands a fine view over the cream of the west side of Featherbedfordshire, and by no means the worst part of the land of Jewdea, as the wags of the former country call Hit-im and Hold-im shire.

Sir Moses had wisely chosen this rendezvous, in order that he might give Lord Ladythorne the benefit of the unwelcome intrusion without exciting the suspicion of the farmers, who would naturally suppose that the match would take place over some part of Sir Moses's own country. In that, however, they had reckoned without their host. Sir Moses wasn't the man to throw a chance away—dom'd if he was.

The road, after crossing the bridge over Bendibus Burn, being all against collar, Sir Moses dropped his reins, and sitting back in his seat, proceeded to contemplate the crowd. A great gathering there was, horsemen, footmen, gigmen, assmen, with here and there a tinkling-belled liquor-vending female, a tossing pie-man, or a nut-merchant. As yet the spirit of speculation was not aroused, and the people gathered in groups, looking as moudy as men generally do who want to get the better of each other. The only cheerful faces on the scene were those of Toney Loftus, the pike-man, and his wife, whose neat white-washed, stone-roofed cottage was not much accustomed to company, save on the occasion of the fairs. They were now gathering their pence and having a let-off for their long pent-up gossip.

Sir Moses's approach put a little liveliness into the scene, and satisfied the grumbling or sceptical ones that they had not come to the wrong place. There was then a general move towards the great white gate, and as he paid his fourpence the nods of recognition and How are ye's? commenced amid a vigorous salute of the muffin bells. *Tinkle tinkle tinkle, buy buy buy*, toss and try! toss and try! *tinkle tinkle tinkle*. Barcelona nuts, crack 'em and try 'em, crack 'em and try 'em; the invitation being accompanied with the rattle of a few in the little tin can.

"Now, where are the jockeys?" asked Sir Moses, straining his eye-balls over the open downs.

"They're coomin. Sir Moses, they're coomin," replied several voices; and as they spoke, a gaily-dressed man, on a milk-white horse, emerged from the little fold-yard of Butterby farm, about half a mile to the west, followed by two distinct groups of mounted and dismounted companions, who clustered round either champion like electors round a candidate going to the hustings.

133

"There's Geordey Gallon!" was now the cry, as the hero of the white horse shot away from the foremost group, and came best pace across the rush-grown sward of the sheep-walk towards the toll-bar. "There's Geordey Gallon! and now we shall hear summut about it;" whereupon the scattered groups began to mingle and turn in the direction of the coming man.

It was Mr. Gallon,—Gallon on his famous trotting hack Tippy Tom,—a vicious runaway brute, that required constant work to keep it under, a want that Mr. Gallon liberally supplied it with. It now came yawning and boring on the bit, one ear lying one way, the other another, shaking its head like a terrier with a rat in its mouth, with a sort of air that as good as said. "Let me go, or I'll either knock your teeth down your throat with my head, or come back over upon you." So Mr. Gallon let him go, and came careering along at a leg-stuck-out sort of butcher's shuffle, one hand grasping the weather-bleached reins, the other a cutting-whip, his green coat-laps and red kerchief ends flying out, his baggy white cords and purple plush waistcoat strings all in a flutter, looking as if he was going to bear away the gate and house, Toney Loftus and wife, all before him. Fortunately for the byestanders there was plenty of space, which, coupled with the deep holding ground and Mr. Gallon's ample weight—good sixteen stone—enabled him to bring the white nag to its bearings; and after charging a flock of geese, and nearly knocking down a Barcelona-nut merchant, he got him manoeuvred in a semicircular sort of way up to the gate, just as if it was all right and plain sailing. He then steadied him with a severe double-handed jerk of the bit, coupled with one of those deep ominous *wh-o-o ah's* that always preceded a hiding. Tippy Tom dropped his head as if he understood him.

All eyes were now anxiously scrutinising Gallon's great rubicund double-chinned visage, for, in addition to his general sporting knowledge and acquirements, he was just fresh from the scene of action where he had doubtless been able to form an opinion. Even Sir Moses, who hated the sight of him, and always declared he "ought to be hung," vouchsafed him a "good morning, Gallon," which the latter returned with a familiar nod.

He then composed himself in his capacious old saddle, and taking off his white shallow began mopping his great bald head, hoping that some one would sound the key-note of speculation ere the advancing parties arrived at the gate. They all, however, seemed to wish to defer to Mr. Gallon—Gallon was the man for their money, Gallon knew a thing or two, Gallon was up to snuff,—go it, Gallon!

****

"What does anybody say 'boot it Frenchman?" at length asked he in his elliptical Yorkshire dialect, looking round on the company.

"What do you say 'boot it Frenchman, Sir Moses?" asked he, not getting an answer from any one.

"Faith, I know nothing," replied the Baronet, with a slight curl of the lip.

"Nay, yeer tied to know summut, hooever," replied Gallon, rubbing his nose across the back of his hand; "yeer tied to know summut, hooever. Why, he's a stoppin' at yeer house, isn't he?"

"That may all be," rejoined Sir Moses, "without my knowing anything of his riding. What do you say yourself? you've seen him."

"Seen him!" retorted Gallon, "why he's a queer lookin' chap, ony hoo—that's all ar can say: haw, haw, haw."

"You won't back him, then?" said Sir Moses, inquiringly.

"Hardly that," replied Gallon, shaking his head and laughing heartily, "hardly that, Sir Moses. Ar'll tell you whatar'll do, though," said he, "just to mak sport luike, ar'll tak yeer two to one—two croons to one," producing a greasy-looking metallic-pencilled betting-book as he spoke.

Just then a move outside the ring announced an arrival, and presently Mr. Heslop came steering Cuddy Flintoff along in his wife's Croydon basket-carriage, Cuddy's head docked in an orange-coloured silk cap, and his whole person enveloped in a blue pilot coat with large mother-of-pearl buttons. The ominous green-pointed jockey whip was held between his knees, as with folded arms he lolled carelessly in the carriage, trying to look comfortable and unconcerned.

"Mornin', Flintoff, how are ye?" cried Sir Moses, waving hie hand from his loftier vehicle, as they drew up.

"Mornin', Heslop, how goes it? Has anybody seen anything of Monsieur?" asked he, without waiting for an answer to either of these important inquiries.

"He's coming, Sir Moses," cried several voices, and presently the Marseillaise hymn of liberty was borne along on the southerly breeze, and Jack's faded black hunting-cap was seen bobbing up and down in the crowd that encircled him, as he rode along on Paul Straddler's shooting pony.

Jack had been at the brandy bottle, and had imbibed just enough to make him excessively noisy.

"Three cheers for Monsieur Jean Rougier, de next Emperor of de French!" cried he, rising in his stirrups, as he approached the crowd, taking off his old brown hunting-cap, and waving it triumphantly, "Three cheers for de best foxer, de best fencer, de best fighter in all Europe!" and at a second flourish of the cap the crowd came into the humour of the thing, and cheered him lustily. And then of course it was one cheer more for Monsieur; and one cheer more he got.

"Three cheers for ould England!" then demanded Mr. Gallon on behalf of Mr. Flintoff, which being duly responded to, he again asked "What onybody would do 'boot it Frenchman?"

"Now, gentlemen," cried Sir Moses, standing erect in his dogcart, and waving his hand for silence: "Now, gentlemen, listen to me!" Instead of which somebody roared out, "Three cheers for Sir Moses!" and at it they went again, *Hooray, hooray, hooray*, for when an English mob once begins cheering, it never knows when to stop. "Now, gentlemen, listen to me," again cried he, as soon as the noise had subsided. "It's one o'clock, and it's time to proceed to business. I called you here that there might be no unnecessary trespass or tampering with the ground, and I think I've chosen a line that will enable you all to see without risk to yourselves or injury to anyone" (applause, mingled with a tinkling of the little bells). "Well now," added he, "follow me, and I'll show you the way;" so saying, he resumed his seat, and passing through the gate turned short to the right, taking the diagonal road leading down the hill, in the direction of Featherbedfordshire.

"Where can it be?" was then the cry.

"I know," replied one of the know-everything ones.

"Rainford, for a guinea!" exclaimed Mr. Gallon, fighting with Tippy Tom. who wanted to be back.

"I say Rushworth!" rejoined Mr. Heslop, cutting in before him.

"Nothin' o' the sort!" asserted Mr. Buckwheat; "he's for Harlingson green to a certainty."

The heterogeneous cavalcade then fell into line, the vehicles and pedestrians keeping the road, while the horsemen spread out on either side of the open common, with the spirit of speculation divided between where the race was to be and who was to win.

Thus they descended the hill and joined the broad, once well-kept turnpike, whose neglected milestones still denoted the distance between London and Hinton—London so many miles on one side, Hinton so many miles on the other—things fast passing into the regions of antiquity. Sir Moses now put on a little quicker, and passing through the village of Nettleton and clearing the plantation beyond, a long strip of country lay open to the eye, hemmed in between the parallel lines of the old road and the new Crumpletin Railway.

He then pulled up on the rising ground, and placing his whip in the socket, stood up to wait the coming of the combatants, to point them out the line he had fixed for the race. The spring tide of population flowed in apace, and he was presently surrounded with horsemen, gigmen, footmen, and bellmen as before.

"Now, gentlemen!" cried Sir Moses, addressing Mr. Flintoff and Monsieur, who were again ranged on either side of his dogcart: "Now, gentlemen, you see the line before you. The stacks, on the right here," pointing to a row of wheat stacks in the adjoining field, "are the starting post, and you have to make your ways as straight as ever you can to Lawristone Clump yonder," pointing to a clump of dark Scotch firs standing against the clear blue sky, on a little round hill, about the middle of a rich old pasture on Thrivewell Farm, the clump being now rendered more conspicuous by sundry vehicles clustered about its base, the fair inmates of which had received a private hint from Sir Moses where to go to. The Baronet always played up to the fair, with whom he flattered himself he was a great favourite.

"Now then, you see," continued he, "you can't get wrong, for you've nothing to do but to keep between the lines of the rail and the road, on to neither of which must you come: and now you gentlemen," continued he. addressing the spectators generally, "there's not the slightest occasion for any of you to go off the road, for you'll see a great deal better on it, and save both your own necks and the farmers' crops; so just let me advise you to keep where you are, and follow the jockeys field by field as they go. And now, gentlemen," continued he, again addressing the competitors, "'having said all I have to say on the subject, I advise you to get your horses and make a start of it, for though the day is fine its still winter, you'll remember, and there are several ladies waiting for your coming." So saying, Sir Moses soused down in his seat, and prepared to watch the proceedings.

Mr. Flintoff was the first to peel; and his rich orange and white silk jacket, natty doeskins, and paper-like boots, showed that he had got himself up as well with a due regard to elegance as to lightness. He even emptied some halfpence out of his pockets, in order that he might not carry extra weight. He would, however, have been a great deal happier at home. There was no "yoicks, wind him," or "yoicks, push 'im up," in him now.

Monsieur did not show to so much advantage as Cuddy; but still he was a good deal better attired than he was out hunting on the Crooked-Billet day. He still retained the old brown cap, but in lieu of the shabby scarlet, pegtop trousers and opera-boots, he sported a red silk jacket, a pair of old-fashioned broad-seamed leathers, and mahogany boots—the cap being the property of Sir Moses's huntsman, Tom Findlater, the other articles belonging to Mr. George Gallon of the Rose and Crown. And the sight of them, as Monsieur stripped, seemed to inspirit the lender, for he immediately broke out with the old inquiry, "What does onybody say 'boot it Frenchman?"

"What do *you* say 'boot it Frenchman, Sir Moses?" asked he.

Sir Moses was silent, for he couldn't see his way to a satisfactory investment; so, rising in his seat, he holloaed out to the grooms, who were waiting their orders outside the crowd, to "bring in the horses."

"Make way, there! make way, there!" cried he, as the hooded and sheeted animals approached and made up to their respective riders.

"Takeoff his nightcap! take off his nightcap!" cried Jack, pulling pettedly at the strings of the hood; "take off his nightcap!" repeated he, stamping furiously, amid the laughter of the bystanders, many of whom had never seen a Frenchman, let alone a mounted one, before.

The obnoxious nightcap being removed, and the striped sheet swept over his tail, Mr. Rowley Abingdon's grey horse Mayfly Blood showing himself as if he was in a dealer's yard, for as yet he had not ascertained what he was out for. A horse knows when he is going to hunt, or going to exercise, or going to be shod, or going to the public house, but these unaccustomed jaunts puzzle him. Monsieur now proceeded to inform him by clutching at the reins, as he stood preparing for a leg-up on the wrong side.

"The other side, mun, the other side," whispered Paul Straddler in his ear; whereupon Monsieur passed under the horse's head, and appeared as he ought. The movement, however, was not lost on Sir Moses, who forthwith determined to back Cuddy. Cuddy might be bad, but Monsieur must be worse, he thought.

"I'll lay an even five on Mr. Flintoff!" cried he in a loud and audible voice. "I'll lay an even five on Mr. Flintoff," repeated he, looking boldly round. "Gallon, what say you?" asked he, appealing to the hero of the white horse.

"Can't be done, Sir Moses, can't be done," replied Gallon, grinning from ear to ear, with a shake of his great bull head. "Tak yeer three to two if you loike," added he, anxious to be on.

Sir Moses now shook his head in return.

"Back myself, two pound ten—forty shillin', to beat dis serene and elegant Englishman!" exclaimed Jack, now bumping up and down in his saddle as if to establish a seat.

"Do you owe him any wages?" asked Sir Moses of Billy in an under-tone, wishing to ascertain what chance there was of being paid if he won.

"Yarse, I owe him some," replied Billy; but how much he couldn't say, not having had Jack's book lately.

Sir Moses caught at the answer, and the next time Jack offered to back himself, he was down upon him with a "Done!" adding, "I'll lay you an even pund if you like."

"With all my heart, Sare Moses Baronet," replied Jack gaily; adding, "you are de most engagin', agreeable mans I knows; a perfect beauty vidout de paint."

Gallon now saw his time was come, and he went at Sir Moses with a "Weell, coom, ar'le lay ye an even foive."

"Done!" cried the Baronet.

"A tenner, if you loike!" continued Gallon, waxing valiant.

Sir Moses shook his head.

"Get me von vet sponge, get me von vet sponge," now exclaimed Jack, looking about for the groom.

"Wet sponge! What the deuce do you want with a wet sponge?" demanded Sir Moses with surprise.

"Yet sponge, just damp my knees leetle—make me stick on better," replied Jack, turning first one knee and then the other out of the saddle to get sponged.

"O dom it, if it's come to that, I may as well have the ten," muttered Sir Moses to himself. So, nodding to Gallon, he said "I'll make it ten."

"Done!" said Gallon, with a nod, and the bet was made—Done, and Done, being enough between gentlemen.

"Now, then," cried Sir Moses, stepping down from his dogcart, "come into the field, and I'll start you."

Away then the combatants went, and the betting became brisk in the ring. Mr. Flintoff the favourite at evens.

CHAPTER XLIV. THE RACE ITSELF.

FROM the Nettleton cornstacks to Lawristone Clump was under two miles, and, barring Bendibus Brook, there was nothing formidable in the line—nothing at least to a peaceably disposed man pursuing the even tenor of his way, either on horseback or in his carriage along the deserted London road.

Very different, however, did the landscape now appear to our friend Cuddy Flintoff as he saw it stretching away in diminishing perspective, presenting an alternating course of husbandry stubble after grass, wheat after stubble, seeds after wheat, with perhaps pasture again after fallow. Bendibus, too, as its name indicates, seemed to be here, there, and everywhere; here, as shown by the stone bridge on the road,—there, as marked by the pollard willows lower down—and generally wherever there was an inconvenient breadth and irregularity of fence. The more Mr. Flintoff looked at the landscape, the less he liked it. Still he had a noble horse under him in General Havelock—a horse that could go through deep as fast as he could over grass, and that only required holding together and sitting on to carry him safe over his fences. It was just that, however, that Cuddy couldn't master. He couldn't help fancying that the horse would let him down, and he didn't like the idea.

Mayfly, on the other hand, was rather skittish, and began prancing and capering as soon as he got off the road into the field.

"Get 'im by de nob! get 'im by de nob!" cried Jack, setting up his shoulders. "Swing 'im round by de tail! swing 'im round by de tail!" continued he, as the horse still turned away from his work.

"Ord dom it, that's that nasty crazy brute of old Rowley Abingdon's, I do declare!" exclaimed Sir Moses, getting out of the now plunging horse's way. "Didn't know the beggar since he was clipped. That's the brute that killed poor Cherisher,—best hound in my pack. Take care, Monsieur! that horse will eat you if he gets you off."

"Eat me!" cried Jack, pretending alarm; "dat vod be vare unkind."

Sir Moses. "Unkind or not, he'll do it, I assure you."

"Oh, dear! oh! dear!" cried Jack, as the horse laid back his ears, and gave a sort of wincing kick.

"I'll tell you what," cried Sir Moses, emboldened by Jack's fear, "I'll lay you a crown you don't get over the brook."

"Crown, sare! I have no crowns," replied Jack, pulling the horse round. "I'll lay ve sovereign—von pon ten, if vou like."

"Come, I'll make it ten shillings. I'll make it ten shillings," replied Sir Moses: adding, "Mr. Flintoff is my witness."

"Done!" cried Monsieur. "Done! I takes the vager. Von pon I beats old Cuddy to de clomp, ten shillin' I gets over de brook."

"All right!" rejoined Sir Moses, "all right! Now," continued he, clapping his hands, "get your horses together—one, two, three, and *away!*"

Up bounced Mayfly in the air; away went Cuddy amidst the cheers and shouts of the roadsters—"*Flintoff! Flintoff! Flinfoff!! The yaller! the yaller! the yaller!*" followed by a general rush along the grass-grown Macadamised road, between London and Hinton.

"Oh, dat is your game, is it?" asked Jack as Mayfly, after a series of minor evolutions, subsided on all fours in a sort of attitude of attention. "Dat is your game, is it!" saying which he just took him short by the head, and, pressing his knees closely into the saddle, gave him such a couple of persuasive digs with his spurs as sent him bounding away after the General. "*Go it, Frenchman!*" was now the cry.

"Go it! aye he *can* go it," muttered Jack, as the horse now dropped on the bit, and laid himself out for work. He was soon in the wake of his opponent.

The first field was a well-drained wheat stubble, with a newly plashed fence on the ground between it and the adjoining pasture; which, presenting no obstacle, they both went at it as if bent on contending for the lead, Monsieur *sacré*ing, grinning, and grimacing, after the manner of his adopted country; while Mr. Flintoff sailed away in the true jockey style, thinking he was doing the thing uncommonly well.

Small as the fence was, however, it afforded Jack an opportunity of shooting into his horse's shoulders, which Cuddy perceiving, he gave a piercing view holloa, and spurred away as if bent on bidding him goodbye. This set Jack on his mettle; and getting back into his seat he gathered his horse together and set too, elbows and legs, elbows and legs, in a way that looked very like frenzy.

The *feint* of a fall, however, was a five-pound note in Mr. Gallon's way, for Jack did it so naturally that there was an immediate backing of Cuddy. "*Flintoff! Flintoff! Flintoff! The yaller! the yaller! the yaller!*" was again the cry.

The pasture was sound, and they sped up it best pace, Mr. Flintoff well in advance.

137

The fence out was nothing either—a young quick fence set on the ground, which Cuddy flew in Leicestershire style, throwing up his right arm as he went. Monsieur was soon after him with a high bucking jump.

They were now upon plough,—undrained plough, too, which the recent rains bad rendered sticky and holding. General Havelock could have crossed it at score, but the ragged boundary fence of Thrivewell farm now appearing in view, Mr. Flintoff held him well together, while he scanned its rugged irregularities for a place.

"These are the nastiest fences in the world," muttered Cuddy to himself, "and I'll be bound to say there's a great yawning ditch either on this side or that. Dash it! I wish I was over," continued he, looking up and down for an exit. There was very little choice. Where there weren't great mountain ash or alder growers laid into the fence, there were bristling hazel uprights, which presented little more attraction. Altogether it was not a desirable obstacle. Even from the road it looked like something. "*Go it, Cuddy! Go it!*" cried Sir Moses, now again in his dogcart, from the midst of the crowd, adding, "It's nothing of a place!"

"Isn't it," muttered Cuddy, still looking up and down, adding, "I wish you had it instead of me."

"Ord dom it, go at it like a man!" now roared the Baronet, fearing for his investments. "Go at it for the honour of the hunt! for the honour of Hit-im and Hold-im shire!" continued he, nearly stamping the bottom of his dog-cart out. The mare started forward at the sound, and catching Tippy Tom with the shafts in the side, nearly upset Geordey Gallon, who, like Sir Moses, was holloaing on the Frenchman. There was then a mutual interchange of compliments. Meanwhile Cuddy, having espied a weak bush-stopped gap in a bend of the hedge, now walks his horse quietly up to it, who takes it in a matter-of-course sort of way that as good as says, "What *have* you been making such a bother about." He then gathers himself together, and shoots easily over the wide ditch on the far side, Cuddy hugging himself at its depth as he lands. Monsieur then exclaiming, "Dem it, I vill not make two bites of von cherry," goes at the same place at the rate of twenty miles an hour, and beat beside Cuddy ere the latter had well recovered from his surprise at the feat. "Ord rot it!" exclaimed he, starting round, "what d'ye mean by following a man that way? If I'd fallen, you'd ha' been a-top of me to a certainty."

"Oh, never fear," replied Monsieur, grinning and flourishing his whip. "Oh, never fear, I vod have 'elped you to pick up de pieces."

"Pick up the pieces, sir!" retorted Cuddy angrily. "I don't want to pick up the pieces. I want to ride the race as it should be."

"Come then, old cock," cried Monsieur, spurring past, "you shall jomp 'pon me if you can." So saying, Jack hustled away over a somewhat swampy enclosure, and popping through an open bridle-gate, led the way into a large rich alluvial pasture beyond.

Jack's feat at the boundary fence, coupled with the manner in which he now sat and handled his horse, caused a revulsion of feeling on the road, and Gallon's stentorian roar of "The *Frenchman! the Frenchman!*" now drowned the vociferations on behalf of Mr. Flintoff and the "yaller." Sir Moses bit his lips and ground his teeth with undisguised dismay. If Flintoff let the beggar beat him, he—-he didn't know what he would do. "*Flintoff! Flintoff!*" shrieked he as Cuddy again took the lead.

And now dread Rendibus appears in view! There was no mistaking its tortuous sinuosities, even if the crowd on the bridge had not kept vociferating, "The bruk! the bruk!"

"The bruk be hanged!" growled Cuddy, hardening his heart for the conflict. "The bruk be hanged!" repeated he, eyeing its varying curvature, adding, "if ever I joke with any man under the rank of a duke again, may I be capitally D'd. Ass that I was," continued he, "to take a liberty with this confounded Frenchman, who cares no more for his neck than a frog. Dashed, if ever I joke with any man under the rank of a prince of the blood royal," added he, weaving his eyes up and down the brook for a place.

"*Go at it full tilt!*" now roars Sir Moses from the bridge; "go at it full tilt for the honour of Hit-im and Hold-im shire!"

"Honour of Hit-im and Hold-im shire be hanged!" growled Cuddy; "who'll pay for my neck if I break it, I wonder!"

"Cut along, old cock of vax!" now cries Monsieur, grinning up on the grey. "Cut along, old cock of vax, or I'll be into your pocket."

"*Shove him along!*" roars stentorian-lunged Gallon, standing erect in his stirrups, and waving Monsieur on with his hat. "*Shove him along!*" repeats he, adding, "he'll take it in his stride."

Mayfly defers to the now-checked General, who, accustomed to be ridden freely, lays back his vexed ears for a kick, as Monsieur hurries up. Cuddy still contemplates the scene, anxious to be over, but dreading to go. "Nothing so nasty as a brook," says he; "never gets less, but may get larger." He then scans it attentively. There is a choice of ground, but it is choice of evils, of which it is difficult to choose the least when in a hurry.

About the centre are sedgy rushes, indicative of a bad taking off, while the weak place next the ash involves the chance of a crack of the crown against the hanging branch, and the cattle gap higher up may be mended with wire rope, or stopped with some awkward invisible stuff. Altogether it is a trying position, especially with the eyes of England upon him from the bridge and road.

"Oh, go at it, mun!" roars Sir Moses, agonised at his hesitation; "Oh, go at it, mun! It's *nothin'* of a place!"

"Isn't it," muttered Cuddy; "wish you were at it instead of me." So saying, he gathers his horse together in an undecided sort of way, and Monsieur charging at the moment, lands Cuddie on his back in the field and himself in the brook.

Then a mutual roar arose, as either party saw its champion in distress.

"*Stick to him, Cuddy! stick to him!*" roars Sir Moses.

"*Stick to him, Mouncheer! stick to him!*" vociferates Mr. Gallon on the other side.

They do as they are bid; Mr. Flintoff remounting just as Monsieur scrambles out of the brook, aud Cuddy's blood now being roused, he runs the General gallantly at it, and lands, hind legs and all, on the opposite bank. Loud cheers followed the feat.

It is now anybody's race, and the vehemence of speculation is intense.

"The red!"—"The yaller! the yaller!"—"The red!" Mr. Gallon is frantic, and Tippy Tom leads the way along the turnpike as if he, too, was in the race. Sir Moses's mare breaks into a canter, and makes the action of the gig resemble that of a boat going to sea. The crowd rush pell-mell without looking where they are going; it is a wonder that nobody is killed.

Lawristone Clump is now close at hand, enlivened with the gay parasols and colours of the ladies.

There are but three more fences between the competitors and it, and seeing what he thinks a weak place in the next, Mr. Flintoff races for it over the sound furrows of the deeply-drained pasture. As he gets near it begins to look larger, and Cuddy's irresolute handling makes the horse swerve.

"Now, then, old stoopid!" cries Jack, in a good London cabman's accent; "Now, then, old stoopid! vot are ye stargazing that way for? Vy don't ye go over or get out o' de vay?"

"*Go yourself,*'" growled Cuddy, pulling his horse round.

"Go myself!" repeated Jack; "'ow the doose can I go vid your great carcase stuck i' the vay!"

"My great carcase stuck i' the way!" retorted Cuddy, spurring and hauling at his horse. "My great carcase stuck in the way! Look at your own, and be hanged to ye!"

"Yell, look at it!" replied Jack, backing his horse for a run, and measuring his distance, he dapped spurs freely in his sides, and going at it full tilt, flew over the fence, exclaiming as he lit, "Dere, it is for you to 'zarnine."

"That feller can ride a deuced deal better than he pretends," muttered Cuddy, wishing his tailorism mightn't be all a trick; saying which he followed Jack's example, and taking a run he presently landed in the next field, amidst the cheers of the roadsters. This was a fallow, deep, wet, and undrained, and his well ribbed-lip horse was more than a match for Jack's across it. Feeling he could go. Cuddy set himself home in his saddle, and flourishing his whip, cantered past, exclaiming, "Come along old stick in the mud!"

"I'll stick i' the mod ye!" replied Jack, hugging and holding his sobbing horse. "I'll stick i' the mod ye! Stop till I gets off dis birdliming field, and I'll give you de go-bye, Cuddy, old cock."

Jack was as good as his word, for the ground getting sounder on the slope, he spurted up a wet furrow, racing with Cuddy for the now obvious gap, that afforded some wretched half-starved calves a choice between the rushes of one field and the whicken grass of the other. Pop, Jack went over it, looking back and exclaiming to Cuddy, "Bon jour! top of de mornin' to you, sare!" as he hugged his horse and scuttled up a high-backed ridge of the sour blue and yellow-looking pasture.

The money was now in great jeopardy, and the people on the road shouted and gesticulated the names of their respective favourites with redoubled energy, as if their eagerness could add impetus to the animals. "*Flintoff! Flintoff! Flintoff!*" "*The Frenchman! the Frenchman!*" as Monsieur at length dropped his hands and settled into something like a seat. On, on, they went, Monsieur every now and then looking back to see that he had a proper space between himself and his pursuer, and, giving his horse a good dig with his spurs, he lifted him over a stiff stake-and-rice fence that separated him from the field with the Clump.

"Here they come!" is now the cry on the hill, and fair faces at length turn to contemplate the galloppers, who come sprawling np the valley in the unsightly way fore-shortened horses appear to do. The road gate on the right flies suddenly open, and Tippy Tom is seen running away with

Geordey Gallon, who just manages to manouvre him round the Clump to the front as Monsieur comes swinging in an easy winner.

Glorious victory for Geordey! Glorious victory for Monsieur! They can't have won less than thirty pounds between them, supposing they get paid, and that Geordey gives Jack his "reglars." Well may Geordey throw up his shallow hat and hug the winner. But who shall depict the agony of Sir Moses at this dreadful blow to his finances? The way he dom'd Cuddy, the way he dom'd Jack, the way he swung frantically about Lawristone Clump, declaring he was ruined for ever and ever! After thinking of everybody at all equal to the task, we are obliged to get, our old friend Echo to answer "Who!"

CHAPTER XLV. HENEREY BROWN & CO. AGAIN.

THE first paroxysm of rage being over, Sir Moses remounted his dog-cart, and drove rapidly off, seeming to take pleasure in making his boy-groom (who was at the mare's head) run after it as long as he could.

"What's it Baronet off?" exclaimed Mr. Gallon, staring with astonishment at the fast-receding vehicle; "what's it, Baronet off?" repeated he, thinking he would have to go to Pangburn Park for his money.

"O dear Thom Mothes is gone!" lisped pretty Miss Mechlinton, who wanted to have a look at our hero, Mr. Pringle, who she heard was frightfully handsome, and alarmingly rich. And the ladies, who had been too much occupied with the sudden rush of excited people to notice Sir Moses's movements, wondered what had happened that he didn't come to give his tongue an airing among them as usual. One said he had got the tooth-ache; another, the ear-ache; a third, that he had got something in his eye; while a satirical gentleman said it looked mure like a B. in his bonnet.

"Ony hoo," however, as Mr. Gallon would say, Sir Moses was presently out of the field and on to the hard turnpike again.

We need scarcely say that Mr. Pringle's ride home with him was not of a very agreeable character: indeed, the Baronet had seldom been seen to be so put out of his way, and the mare came in for frequent salutations with the whip—latitudinally, longitudinally, and horizontally, over the head and ears, accompanied by cutting commentaries on Flintoff's utter uselessness and inability to do anything but drink.

He "never saw such a man—domd if ever he did," and he whipped the mare again in confirmation of the opinion.

Nor did matters mend on arriving at home; for here Mr. Mordecai Nathan met him in the entrance hall, with a very doleful face, to announce that Henerey Brown & Co., who had long been coddling up their horses, had that morning succeeded in sloping with them and their stock to Halterley Fair, and selling them in open market, leaving a note hanging to the key in the house-door, saying that they had gone to Horseterhaylia where Sir Moses needn't trouble to follow them.

"Ond dom it!" shrieked the Baronet, jumping up in the air like a stricken deer; "ond dom it! I'm robbed! I'm robbed! I'm ruined! I'm ruined!" and tottering to an arm-chair, he sank, overpowered with the blow. Henerey Brown & Co. had indeed been too many for him. After a long course of retrograding husbandry, they seemed all at once to have turned over a new leaf, if not in the tillage way, at all events in that still better way for the land, the cattle line,—store stock, with some symptoms of beef on their bones, and sheep with whole fleeces, going on all-fours depastured the fields, making Mordecai Nathan think it was all the fruits of his superior management. Alack a-day! They belonged to a friend of Lawyer Hindmarch's, who thought Henerey Brown & Co. might as well eat all off the land ere they left. And so they ate it as bare as a board.

"Ond dom it, how came you to let them escape?" now demanded the Baronet, wringing his hands in despair; "ond dom it, how came you to let them escape?" continued he, throwing himself back in the chair.

"Why really, Sir Moses, I was perfectly deceived; I thought they were beginning to do better, for though they were back with their ploughing, they seemed to be turning their attention to stock, and I was in hopes that in time they would pull round."

"Pull round!" ejaculated the Baronet; "pull round! They'll flatten me I know with their pulling;" and thereupon he kicked out both legs before him as if he was done with them altogether.

140

His seat being in the line of the door, a rude draught now caught his shoulder, which making him think it was no use sitting there to take cold and the rheumatism, he suddenly bounced up, and telling Nathan to stay where he was, he ran up stairs, and quickly changed his fine satiney, velvetey, holiday garments, for a suit of dingy old tweeds, that looked desperately in want of the washing-tub. Then surmounting the whole with a drab wide-awake, he clutched a knotty dog-whip, and set off on foot with his agent to the scene of disaster, rehearsing the licking he would give Henerey with the whip if he caught him, as he went.

Away he strode, as if he was walking a match, down Dolly's Close, over the stile, into Farmer Hayford's fields, and away by the back of the lodges, through Orwell Plantation and Lowestoff End, into the Rushworth and Mayland Road.

Doblington farm-house then stood on the rising ground before him. It was indeed a wretched, dilapidated, woe-begone-looking place; bad enough when enlivened with the presence of cattle and the other concomitants of a farm; but now, with only a poor white pigeon, that Henerey Brown & Co., as if in bitter irony, had left behind them, it looked the very picture of misery and poverty-stricken desolation.

It was red-tiled and had been rough-cast, but the casting was fast coming off, leaving fine map-like tracings of green damp on the walls,—a sort of map of Italy on one side of the door, a map of Africa on the other, one of Horseterhaylia about the centre, with a perfect battery of old hats bristling in the broken panes of the windows. Nor was this all; for, by way of saving coals, Henerey & Humphrey had consumed all the available wood about the place—stable-fittings, cow-house-fittings, pig-sty-fittings, even part of the staircase—and acting under the able advice of Lawyer Hindmarch, had carried away the pot and oven from the kitchen, and all the grates from the fire-places, under pretence of having bought them of the outgoing tenant when they entered,—a fact that the lawyer said "would be difficult to disprove." If it had not been that Henerey Brown & Co. had been sitting rent-free, and that the dilapidated state of the premises formed an excellent subject of attack for parrying payment when rent came to be demanded, it would be difficult to imagine people living in a house where they had to wheel their beds about to get to the least drop-exposed quarter, and where the ceilings bagged down from the rafters like old-fashioned window-hangings. People, however, can put up with a great deal when it saves their own pockets. Master and man having surveyed the exterior then entered.

"Well," said Sir Moses, looking round on the scene of desolation, "they've made a clean sweep at all events."

"They have that," assented Mr. Mordecai Nathan.

"I wonder it didn't strike you, when you caught them selling their straw off at night, that they would be doing something of this sort," observed Sir Moses.

"Why, I thought it rather strange," replied Mr. Nathan; "only they assured me that for every load of straw they sold, they brought back double the value in guano, or I certainly should have been more on the alert."

"Guano be hanged!" rejoined the Baronet, trying to open the kitchen window, to let some fresh air into the foul apartment; "guano be hanged! one ton of guano makes itself into twenty ton with the aid of Kentish gravel. No better trade than spurious manure-manufacturing; almost as good as cabbage-cigar making. Besides," continued he, "the straw goes off to a certainty, whereas there's no certainty about the guano coming back instead of it. Oh, dom it, man," continued he, knocking some of the old hats out of the broken panes, after a fruitless effort to open the window, "I'd have walked the bailiffs into the beggars if I could have foreseen this."

"So would I, Sir Moses," replied Mr. Nathan; "only who could we get to come in their place?"

That observation of Mr. Mordecai Nathan comprises a great deal, and accounts for much apparent good landlordism, which lets a bad tenant go on from year to year with the occasional payment of a driblet of rent, instead of ejecting him; the real fact being that the landlord knows there is no one to get to come in his place—no better one at least—and that fact constitutes one of the principal difficulties of land-owning. If a landlord is not prepared to take an out-of-order farm into his own hands, he must either put up with an incompetent non-paying tenant, or run the risk of getting a worse one from the general body of outlying incompetence. A farm will always let for something.

There is a regular rolling stock of bad farmers in every country, who pass from district to district, exercising their ingenuity in extracting whatever little good their predecessors have left in the land. These men are the steady, determined enemies to grass. Their great delight is to get leave to plough out an old pasture-held under pretence of laying it down better. There won't be a grass field on a farm but what they will take some exception to, and ask leave to have "out" as they call it. Then if they get leave, they take care never to have a good take of seeds, and so plough on and plough on, promising to lay it down better after each fresh attempt, just as a thimble-rigger urges his dupe to go on and go on, and try his luck once more, until land and dupe are both fairly exhausted. The tenant then marches, and the thimble-rigger decamps, each in search of fresh fields and flats new.

Considering that all writers on agriculture agree that grass land pays double, if not treble, what arable land does, and that one is so much more beautiful to the eye than the other, to say nothing of pleasanter to ride over, we often wonder that landlords have not turned their attention more to the increase and encouragement of grass land on their estates than they have done.

To be sure they have always had the difficulty to contend with we have named, viz., a constant hankering on the part of even some good tenants to plough it out. A poor grass-field, like Gay's hare, seems to have no friends. Each man proposes to improve it by ploughing it out, forgetful of the fact, that it may also be improved by manuring the surface. The quantity of arable land on a farm is what puts landlords so much in the power of bad farmers. If farms consisted of three parts grass and one part plough, instead of three parts plough and one part grass, no landlord need ever put up with an indifferent, incompetent tenant; for the grass would carry him through, and he could either let the farm off, field by field, to butchers and graziers, or pasture it himself, or hay it if he liked. Nothing pays better than hay. A very small capital would then suffice for the arable land; and there being, as we said before, a rolling stock of scratching land-starvers always on the look-out for out-of-order farms, so every landowner should have a rolling stock of horses and farm-implements ready to turn upon any one that is not getting justice done it. There is no fear of gentlemen being overloaded with land; for the old saying, "It's a good thing to follow the laird," will always insure plenty of applicants for any farm a landlord is leaving— supposing, of course, that he has been doing it justice himself, which we must say landlords always do; the first result we see of a gentleman farming being the increase of the size of his stock-yard, and this oftentimes in the face of a diminished acreage under the plough.

Then see what a saving there is in grass-farming compared to tillage husbandry: no ploughs, no harrows, no horses, no lazy leg-dragging clowns, who require constant watching; the cattle will feed whether master is at home or polishing St. James's Street in paper boots and a tight bearing-rein.

Again, the independence of the grass-farmer is so great. When the wind howls and the rain beats, and the torrents roar, and John Flail lies quaking in bed, fearing for his corn, then old Tom Nebuchadnezzar turns quietly over on his side like the Irish jontleman who, when told the house was on fire, replied, "Arrah, by Jasus, I'm only a lodger!" and says, "Ord rot it, let it rain; it'll do me no harm! I'm only a grass-grower!"

But we are leaving Sir Moses in the midst of his desolation, with nothing but the chilly fog of a winter's evening and his own bright thoughts to console him.

"And dom it, I'm off," exclaimed he, fairly overcome with the impurity of the place; and hurrying out, he ran away towards home, leaving Mr. Mordecai Nathan to lock the empty house up, or not, just as he liked.

And to Pangburn Park let us now follow the Baronet, and see what our friend Billy is about.

CHAPTER XLVI. THE PRINGLE CORRESPONDENCE.

MR. Pringle's return was greeted with an immense shoal of letters, one from Mamma, one with "Yammerton Grange" on the seal, two from his tailors—one with the following simple heading, "To bill delivered," so much; the other containing a vast catalogue of what a jury of tailors would consider youthful "necessaries," amounting in the whole to a pretty round sum, accompanied by an intimation, that in consequence of the tightness of the money-market, an early settlement would be agreeable—and a very important-looking package, that had required a couple of heads to convey, and which, being the most mysterious of the whole, after a due feeling and inspection, he at length opened. It was from his obsequious friend Mr. Smoothley, and contained a printed copy of the rules of the Hit-im and Hold-im shire Hunt, done up in a little red-backed yellow-lined book, with a note from the sender, drawing Mr. Pringle's attention to the tenth rule, which stipulated that the annual club subscription of fifteen guineas was to be paid into Greedy and Griper's bank, in Hinton, by Christmas-day in each year at latest, or ten per cent. interest would be charged on the amount after that.

"Fi-fi-fifteen guineas! te-te-ten per cent.!" ejaculated Billy, gasping for breath; "who'd ever have thought of such a thing!" and it was some seconds before he sufficiently recovered his composure to resume his reading. The rent of the cover he had taken, Mr. Smoothley proceeded to say, was eight guineas a-year. "Eight guineas a-year!" again ejaculated Billy; "eight guineas a-year! why I thought it was a mere matter of form. Oh dear, I can't stand this!" continued he, looking vacantly about him. "Surely, risking one's neck is quite bad enough, without paying for doing so. Lord Ladythorne never asked me for any money, why should Sir Moses? Oh dear, oh dear! I wish i'd never embarked in such a speculation. Nothing to be made by it, but a great deal to be lost. Bother the thing, I wish I was out of it," with which declaration he again ventured to look at Mr. Smoothley's letter. It went on to say, that the rent would not become payable until the next season, Mr. Treadcroft being liable for that year's rent. "Ah well, come, that's some consolation, at all events," observed our friend, looking up again; "that's some consolation, at all events," adding, "I'll take deuced good care to give it up before another year comes round."

Smoothley then touched upon the more genial subject of the hunt-buttons. he had desired Garnet, the silversmith, to send a couple of sets off the last die, one for Billy's hunting, the other for his dress coat; and he concluded by wishing our friend a long life of health and happiness to wear them with the renowned Hit-im and Hold-im shire hunt; and assuring him that he was always his, with great sincerity, John Smoothley. "Indeed," said Billy, throwing the letter down; "more happiness if I don't wear them," continued he, conning over his many misfortunes, and the great difficulty he had in sitting at the jumps. "However," thought he, "the dress ones will do for the balls," with which not uncommon consolation he broke the red seal of the Yammerton Grange letter.

This was from our friend the Major, all about a wonderful hunt his "haryers" had had, which he couldn't resist the temptation of writing to tell Billy of. The description then sprawled over four sides of letter paper, going an arrant burst from end to end, there not being a single stop in the whole, whatever there might have been in the hunt; and the Major concluded by saying, that it was by far the finest run he had ever seen during his long mastership, extending over a period of five-and-thirty years.

Glancing his eye over its contents, how they found at Conksbury Corner, and ran at a racing pace without a check to Foremark Hill, and down over the water-meadows at Dove-dale Green to Marbury Hall, turning short at Fullbrook Folly, and over the race-course at Ancaster Lawn, doubling at Dinton Dean, and back over the hill past Oakhanger Gorse to Tufton Holt, where they killed, the account being interwoven, parenthesis within parenthesis, with the brilliant hits and performances of Lovely, and Lilter, and Dainty, and Bustler, and others, with the names of the distinguished party who were out, our old friend Wotherspoon among the number, Billy came at last to a sly postscript, saying that "his bed and stall were quite ready for him whenever he liked to return, and they would all be delighted to see him." The wording of the Postscript had taken a good deal of consideration, and had undergone two or three revisions at the hands of the ladies before they gave it to the Major to add—one wanting to make it rather stronger, another rather milder, the Major thinking they had better have a little notice before Mr. Pringle returned, while Mamma (who had now got all the linen up again) inclined, though she did not say so before the girls, to treat Billy as one of the family. Upon a division whether the word "quite" should stand part of the Postscript or not, the Major was left in a minority, and the pressing word passed. His bed and stall were "quite ready," instead of only "ready" to receive him. Miss Yammerton observing, that "quite" looked as if they really wished to have him, while "ready" looked as if they did not care whether he came or not. And Billy, having pondered awhile on the Postscript, which he thought came very opportunely, proceeded to open his last letter, a man always taking those he doesn't know first.

This letter was Mamma's—poor Mamma's—written in the usual strain of anxious earnestness, hoping her beloved was enjoying himself, but hinting that she would like to have him back. Butterfingers was gone, she had got her a place in Somersetshire, so anxiety on that score was over. Mrs. Pringle's peculiar means of information, however, informed her that the Misses Yammerton were dangerous, and she had already expressed her opinion pretty freely with regard to Sir Moses. Indeed, she didn't know which house she would soonest hear of her son being at—Sir Moses's with his plausible pocket-guarding plundering, or Major Yammerton's, with the three pair of enterprising eyes, and Mamma's mature judgment directing the siege operations. Mrs. Pringle wished he was either back at Tantivy Castle, or in Curtain Crescent again.

Still she did not like to be too pressing, but observed, as Christmas was coming, when hunting would most likely be stopped by the weather, she hoped he would run up to town, where many of his friends, Jack Sheppard, Tom Brown, Harry Bean, and others, were asking for him, thinking he was lost. She also said, it would be a good time to go to Uncle Jerry's, and try to get a settlement with him, for though she had often called, sometimes by appointment, she had never been able to meet with him, as he was always away, either seeing after some chapel he was building, or attending a meeting for the conversion of the Sepoys, or some other fanatics.

The letter concluded by saying, that she had looked about in vain for a groom likely to suit him; for, although plenty had presented themselves from gentlemen wishing for high wages with nothing to do, down to those who would garden and groom and look after cows, she had not seen anything at all to her mind. Mr. Luke Grueler, however, she added, who had called that morning, had told her of one that he could recommend, who was just leaving the Honourable Captain Swellington; and being on his way to town from Doubleimupshire, where the Captain had got to the end of his tether, he would very possibly call; and, if so, Billy would know him by his having Mr. Grueler's card to present. And with renewed expressions of affection, and urging him to take care of himself, as well among the leaps as the ladies, she signed herself his most doting and loving "Mamma."

"Groom!" (humph) "Swellington!" (humph) muttered Billy, folding up the letter, and returning it to its highly-musked envelope.

"Wonder what sort of a beggar he'll be?" continued he, twirling his mustachios; "Wonder how he'll get on with Rougier?" and a thought struck him, that he had about as much as he could manage with Monsieur. However, many people have to keep what they don't want, and there is no reason why such an aspiring youth as our friend should be exempt from the penance of his station. Talking of grooms, we are not surprised at "Mamma's" difficulty in choosing one, for we know of few more difficult selections to make; and, considering the innumerable books we have on the choice and management of horses, we wonder no one has written on the choice and management of grooms. The truth is, they are as various as the horse-tribe itself; and, considering that the best horse may soon be made a second-rate one by bad grooming, when a second-rate one may be elevated to the first class by good management, and that a man's neck may be broken by riding a horse not fit to go, it is a matter of no small importance. Some men can dress themselves, some can dress their horses; but very few can dress both themselves and their horses. Some are only fit to strip a horse and starve him. It is not every baggy-corded fellow that rolls slangily along in top-boots, and hisses at everything he touches, that is a groom. In truth, there are very few grooms, very few men who really enter into the feelings and constitutions of horses, or look at them otherwise than as they would at chairs or mahogany tables. A horse that will be perfectly furious under the dressing of one man, will be as quiet as possible in the hands of another——a rough subject thinking the more a horse prances and winces, the greater the reason to lay on. Some fellows have neither hands, nor eyes, nor sense, nor feeling, nor anything. We have seen one ride a horse to cover without ever feeling that he was lame, while a master's eye detected it the moment he came in sight. Indeed, if horses could express their opinions, we fear many of them would have very indifferent ones of their attendants. The greater the reason, therefore, for masters giving honest characters of their servants.

Our friend Mr. Pringle, having read his letters, was swinging up and down the little library, digesting them, when the great Mr. Bankhead bowed in with a card on a silver salver, and announced, in his usual bland way, that the bearer wished to speak to him.

"Me!" exclaimed Billy, wondering who it could be; "Me!" repeated he, taking the highly-glazed thin pasteboard missive off the tray, and reading, "Mr. Luke Grueler, Half-Moon Street, Piccadilly."

"Grueler, Grueler!" repeated Billy, frowning and biting his pretty lips; "Grueler—I've surely heard that name before."

"The bearer, sir, comes *from* Mr. Grueler, sir," observed Mr. Bankhead, in explanation: "the party's own name, sir, is Gaiters; but he said by bringing in this card, you would probably know who he is."

"Ah! to be sure, so I do," replied Billy, thus suddenly enlightened, "I've just been reading about him. Send him in, will you?"

"If you please, sir," whispered the bowing Bankhead as he withdrew.

Billy then braced himself up for the coming interview.

A true groom's knock, a loud and a little one, presently sounded on the white-over-black painted door-panel, and at our friend's "Come in," the door opened, when in sidled a sleek-headed well put on groomish-looking man, of apparently forty or five-and-forty years of age. The man bowed respectfully, which Billy returned, glancing at his legs to see whether they were knock-kneed or bowed, his Mamma having cautioned him against the former. They were neither; on the contrary, straight good legs, well set off with tightish, drab-coloured kerseymere shorts, and continuations to match. His coat was an olive-coloured cutaway, his vest a canary-coloured striped toilanette, with a slightly turned-down collar, showing the whiteness of his well-tied cravat, secured with a gold flying-fox pin. Altogether he was a most respectable looking man, and did credit to the recommendation of Mr. Grueler.

Still he was a groom of pretension—that is to say, a groom who wanted to be master. He was hardly, indeed, satisfied with that, and would turn a gentleman off who ventured to have an opinion of his own on any matter connected with his department. Mr. Gaiters considered that his character was the first consideration, his master's wishes and inclinations the second; so if master wanted to ride, say, Rob Roy, and Gaiters meant him to ride Moonshine, there would be a trial of skill which it should be.

Mr. Gaiters always considered himself corporally in the field, and speculated on what people would be saying of "his horses."

Some men like to be bullied, some don't, but Gaiters had dropped on a good many who did. Still these are not the lasting order of men, and Gaiters had at tended the dispersion of a good many studs at the Corner. Again, some masters had turned him off, while he had turned others off; and the reason of his now being disengaged was that the Sheriff of Doubleimupshire had saved him the trouble of taking Captain Swellington's horses to Tattersall's, by selling them off on the spot. Under these circumstances, Gaiters had written to his once former master—or rather employer—Mr. Grueler, to announce his retirement, which had led to the present introduction. Many people will recommend servants who they wouldn't take themselves. Few newly married couples but what have found themselves saddled with invaluable servants that others wanted to get rid of.

Mutual salutations over, Gaiters now stood in the first position, hat in front, like a heavy father on the stage.

Our friend not seeming inclined to lead the gallop, Mr. Gaiters, after a prefatory hem, thus commenced: "Mr. Grueler, sir, I presume, would tell you, sir, that I would call upon you, sir?"

Billy nodded assent.

"I'm just leaving the Honourable Captain Swellington, of the Royal Hyacinth Hussars, sir, whose regiment is ordered out to India; and fearing the climate might not agree with my constitution, I have been obliged to give him up."

"Ah!" ejaculated Billy.

"I have his testimonials," continued Gaiters, putting his hat between his legs, and diving into the inside pocket of his cutaway as he spoke. "I have his testimonials," repeated he, producing a black, steel-clasped banker or bill-broker's looking pocket-book, and tedding up a lot of characters, bills, recipes, and other documents in the pocket. He then selected Captain Swellington's character from the medley, written on the best double-thick, cream-laid note-paper, sealed with the Captain's crest—a goose—saying that the bearer John Gaiters was an excellent groom, and might safely be trusted with the management of hunters. "You'll probably know who the Captain is, sir," continued Mr. Gaiters, eyeing Billy as he read it, "He's a son of the Right Honourable Lord Viscount Flareup's, of Flareup Castle, one of the oldest and best families in the kingdom—few better families anywhere," just as if the Peer's pedigree had anything to do with Gaiters's grooming. "I have plenty more similar to it," continued Mr. Gaiters, who had now selected a few out of the number which he held before him, like a hand at cards. "Plenty more similar to it," repeated he, looking them over. "Here is Sir Rufus Rasper's, Sir Peter Puller's, Lord Thruster's, Mr. Cropper's, and others. Few men have horsed more sportsmen than I have done; and if my principals do not go in the first flight, it is not for want of condition in my horses. Mr. Grueler was the only one I ever had to give up for overmarking my horses; and he was so hard upon them I couldn't stand it; still he speaks of me, as you see, in the handsomest manner," handing our friend Mr. Grueler's certificate, couched in much the same terms as Captain Swellington's.

"Yarse," replied Billy, glancing over and then returning it, thinking, as he again eyed Mr. Gaiters, that a smart lad like Lord Ladythorne's Cupid without wings would be more in his way than such a full-sized magnificent man. Still his Mamma and Mr. Grueler had sent Gaiters, and he supposed they knew what was right. In truth, Gaiters was one of those overpowering people that make a master feel as if he was getting hired, instead of suiting himself with a servant.

This preliminary investigation over, Gaiters returned the characters to his ample book, and clasping it together, dropped it into his capacious pocket, observing, as it fell, that he should be glad to endeavour to arrange matters with Mr. Pringle, if he was so inclined.

Our friend nodded, wishing he was well rid of him.

"It's not every place I would accept," continued Mr. Gaiters, growing grand; "for the fact is, as Mr. Grueler will tell you, my character is as good as a Bank of England note; and unless I was sure I could do myself justice, I should not like to venture on an experiment, for it's no use a man undertaking anything that he's not allowed to carry out his own way; and nothing would be so painful to my feelings as to see a gentleman not turned out as he should be."

Mr. Pringle drawled a "yarse," for he wanted to be turned out properly.

"Well, then," continued Mr. Gaiters, changing his hat from his right hand to his left, subsiding into the second position, and speaking slowly and deliberately, "I suppose you want a groom to take the entire charge and management of your stable—a stud groom, in short?"

"Yarse, I s'pose so," replied Billy, not knowing exactly what he wanted, and wishing his Mamma hadn't sent him such a swell.

"Well, then, sir," continued Mr. Gaiters, casting his eyes up to the dirty ceiling, and giving his chin a dry shave with his disengaged hand; "Well, then, sir, I flatter myself I can fulfil that office with credit to myself and satisfaction to my employer."

"Yarse," assented Billy, thinking there would be very little satisfaction in the matter.

"Buy the forage, hire the helpers, do everything appertaining to the department,—in fact, just as I did with the Honourable Captain Swellington."

"Humph," said Billy, recollecting that his Mamma always told him never to let servants buy anything for him that he could help.

"Might I ask if you buy your own horses?" inquired Mr. Gaiters, after a pause.

"Why, yarse, I do," replied Billy; "at least I have so far."

"Hum! That would be a consideration," muttered Gaiters, compressing his mouth, as if he had now come to an obstacle; "that would be a consideration. Not that there's any benefit or advantage to be derived from buying horses," continued he, resuming his former tone; "but when a man's character's at stake, it's agreeable, desirable, in fact, that he should be intrusted with the means of supporting it. I should like to buy the horses," continued he, looking earnestly at Billy, as if to ascertain the amount of his gullibility.

"Well," drawled Billy, "I don't care if you do," thinking there wouldn't be many to buy.

"Oh!" gasped Gaiters, relieved by the announcement; he always thought he had lost young Mr. Easyman's place by a similar demand, but still he couldn't help making it. It wouldn't have been doing justice to the Bank of England note character, indeed, if he hadn't.

"Oh!" repeated he, emboldened by success, and thinking he had met with the right sort of man. He then proceeded to sum up his case in his mind,—forage, helpers, horses,·horses, helpers, forage;—he thought that was all he required; yes, he thought it was all he required, and the Bank of England note character would be properly supported. He then came to the culminating point of the cash. Just as he was clearing his throat with a prefatory "Hre" for this grand consideration, a sudden rush and banging of doors foreboding mischief resounded through the house, and something occurred——that we will tell in another chapter.

CHAPTER XLVII. A CATASTROPHE.—A TÊTE-À-TÊTE DINNER

"ON, Sir, Sir, please step this way! please step this way!" exclaimed the *delirium tremens* footman, rushing coatless into the room where our hero and Mr. Gaiters were,—his shirt-sleeves tucked up, and a knife in hand, as if he had been killing a pig, though in reality he was fresh from the knife-board.

"Oh, Sir, Sir, please step this way!" repeated he, at once demolishing the delicate discussion at which our friend and Mr. Gaiters had arrived.

"What's ha-ha-happened?" demanded Billy, turning deadly pale; for his cares were so few, that he couldn't direct his fears to any one point in particular.

"Please, sir, your 'oss has dropped down in a f-f-fit!" replied the man, all in a tremble.

"Fit!" ejaculated Billy, brushing past Gaiters, and hurrying out of the room.

"Fit!" repeated Gaiters, turning round with comfortable composure, looking at the man as much as to say, what do you know about it?

"Yes, f-f-fit!" repeated the footman, brandishing his knife, and running after Billy as though he were going to slay him.

Dashing along the dark passages, breaking his shins over one of those unlucky coal-scuttles that are always in the way, Billy fell into an outward-bound stream of humanity,—Mrs. Margerum, Barbara the housemaid, Mary the Lanndrymaid, Jones the gardener's boy, and others, all hurrying to the scene of action.

Already there was a ring formed round the door, of bare-armed helpers, and miscellaneous hangers-on, looking over each other's shoulders, who opened a way for Billy as he advanced.

The horse was indeed down, but not in a fit; for he was dying, and expired just as Billy entered. There lay the glazy-eyed hundred-guinea Napoleon the Great, showing his teeth, reduced to the mere value of his skin; so great is the difference between a dead horse and a live one.

"Bad job!" said Wetun, who was on his knees at its head, looking up; "bad job!" repeated he, trying to look dismal.

"What! is he dead?" demanded Billy, who could hardly realise the fact.

"Dead, ay—he'll never move more," replied Wetun, showing his fast-stiffening neck.

"By Jove! why didn't you send for the doctor?" demanded Billy.

"Doctor! we had the doctor," replied Wetun, "but he could do nothin' for him."

"Nothin' for him!" retorted Billy; "why not?"

"Because he's rotten," replied Wetun.

"Rotten! how can that be?" asked our friend, adding, "I only bought him the other day!"

"If you open 'im you'll find he's as black as ink in his inside, rejoined the groom, now getting np in the stall and rubbing his knees.

"Well, but what's that with?" demanded Hilly. "It surely must be owing to something. Horses don't die that way for nothing."

"Owing to a bad constitution—harn't got no stamina," replied Wetun, looking down upon the dead animal.

Billy was posed with the answer, and stood mute for a while.

"That 'oss 'as never been rightly well sin he com'd," now observed Joe Bates, the helper who looked after him, over the heads of the door-circle.

"I didn't like his looks when he com'd in from 'unting that day," continued Tom Wisp, another helper.

"No, nor the day arter nonther," assented Jack Strong, who was a capital hand at finding fault, and could slur over his work with anybody.

Just then Mr. Gaiters arrived; and a deferential entrance was opened for his broadcloth by the group before the door.

The great Mr. Gaiters entered.

Treating the dirty blear-eyed Wetun more as a helper than an equal, he advanced deliberately up the stall and proceeded to examine the dead horse.

He looked first np his nostrils, next at his eye, then at his neck to see if he had been bled.

"I could have cured that horse if I'd had him in time," observed he to Billy with a shake of the head.

"Neither you nor no man under the sun could ha' done it," asserted Mr. Wetun, indignant at the imputation.

"I could though—at least he never should have been in that state," replied Gaiters coolly.

"I say you couldn't!" retorted Wetun, putting his arms a-kimbo, and sideling up to the daring intruder, a man who hadn't even asked leave to come into his stable.

A storm being imminent, our friend slipped off, and Sir Moses arrived from Henerey Brown &, Co.'s just at the nick of time to prevent a fight.

So much for a single night in a bad stable, a result that our readers will do well to remember when they ask their friends to visit them—"Love me, love my horse," being an adage more attended to in former times than it is now.

"Ah, my dear Pringle! I'm so sorry to hear about your horse! go sorry to hear about your horse!" exclaimed Sir Moses, rushing forward to greet our friend with a consolatory shake of the hand, as he came sauntering into the library, flat candlestick in hand, before dinner. "It's just the most unfortunate thing I ever knew in my life; and I wouldn't have had it happen at my house for all the money in the world—dom'd if I would," added he, with a downward blow of his fist.

Billy could only reply with one of his usual monotonous "y-a-r-ses."

"However," said the Baronet, "it shall not prevent your hunting to-morrow, for I'll mount you with all the pleasure in the world—all the pleasure in the world," repeated he, with a flourish of his hand.

"Thank ye," replied Billy, alarmed at the prospect; "but the fact is, the Major expects me back at Yammerton Grange, and——"

"That's nothin!" interrupted Sir Moses; "that's nothin; hunt, and go there after—all in the day's work. Meet at the kennel, find a fox in five minutes, have your spin, and go to the Grange afterwards."

"O, indeed, yes, you shall," continued he, settling it so, "shall have the best horse in my stable—Pegasus, or Atalanta, or Old Jack, or any of them—dom'd if you shalln't—so that matter's settled."

"But, but, but," hesitated our alarmed friend, "I—I—I shall have no way of getting there after hunting."

"O, I'll manage that too," replied Sir Moses, now in the generous mood. "I'll manage that too—shall have the dog-cart—the thing we were in to-day; my lad shall go with you and bring it back, and that'll convey you and your traps 'and all altogether. Only sorry I can't ask you to stay another week, but the fact is I've got to go to my friend Lord Lundyfoote's for Monday's hunting at Harker Crag,"—the fact being that Sir Moses had had enough of Billy's company and had invited himself there to get rid of him.

The noiseless Mr. Bankhead then opened the door with a bow, and they proceeded to a tête-à-tête dinner, Cuddy Flintoff having wisely sent for his things from Heslop's house, and taken his departure to town under pretence, as he told Sir Moses in a note, of seeing Tommy White's horses sold.

Cuddy was one of that numerous breed of whom every sportsman knows at least one—namely, a man who is always wanting a horse, a "do you know of a horse that will suit me?" sort of a man. Charley Flight, who always walks the streets like a lamplighter and doesn't like to be cheeked in his stride, whenever he sees Cuddy crawling along Piccadilly towards the Corner, puts on extra steam, exclaiming as he nears him, "How are you, Cuddy, how are you? I *don't* know of a horse that will suit you!" So he gets past without a pull-up.

But we are keeping the soup waiting—also the fish—cod sounds rather—for Mrs. Margerum not calculating on more than the usual three days of country hospitality,—the rest day, the drest day, and the pressed day,—had run out of fresh fish. Indeed the whole repast bespoke the exhausted larder peculiar to the end of the week, and an adept in dishes might have detected some old friends with new faces. Some *rechauffers* however are quite as good if not better than the original dishes—hashed venison for instance—though in this case, when Sir Moses inquired for the remains of the Sunday's haunch, he was told that Monsieur had had it for his lunch—Jack being a safe bird to lay it upon, seeing that he had not returned from the race. If Jack had been in the way then, the cat would most likely have been the culprit, or old Libertine, who had the run of the house.

Neither the Baronet nor Billy however was in any great humour for eating, each having cares of magnitude to oppress his thoughts, and it was not until Sir Moses had imbibed the best part of a pint of champagne besides sherry at intervals, that he seemed at all like himself. So he picked and nibbled and dom'd and dirted as many plates as he could. Dinner being at length over, he ordered a bottle of the green-sealed claret (his best), and drawing his chair to the fire proceeded to crack walnuts and pelt the shells at particular coals in the fire with a vehemence that showed the occupation of his mind. An observing eye could almost tell which were levelled at Henerey Brown, which at Cuddy Flintoff, and which again at the impudent owner of Tippy Tom.

At length, having exhausted his spleen, he made a desperate dash at the claret-jug, and pouring himself out a bumper, pushed it across to our friend, with a "help yourself," as he sent it. The ticket-of-leave butler, who understood wine, had not lost his skill during his long residence at Portsmouth, and brought this in with the bouquet in great perfection. The wine was just as it should be, neither too warm nor too cold; and as Sir Moses quailed a second glass, his equanimity began to revive.

When not thinking about money, his thoughts generally took a sporting turn,

Horses and hounds, and the system of kennel, Leicestershire saga, and the hounds of old Moynell,

as the song says; and the loss of Billy's horse now obtruded on his mind.

"How the deuce it had happened he couldn't imagine; his man, Wetun,—and there was no better judge—said he seemed perfectly well, and a better stable couldn't be than the one he was in; indeed he was standing alongside of his own favourite mare, Whimpering Kate,—'faith, he wished he had told them to take her out, in case it was anything infectious,—only it looked more like internal disease than anything else.—Wished he mightn't be rotten. The Major was an excellent man,—cute,——" and here he checked himself, recollecting that Billy was going back there on the morrow. "A young man," continued he, "should be careful who he dealt with, for many what were called highly honourable men were very unscrupulous about horses;" and a sudden thought struck Sir Moses, which, with the aid of another bottle, he thought he might try to carry out. So apportioning the remains of the jug equitably between Billy and himself, he drew the bell, and desired the ticket-of-leave butler to bring in another bottle and a devilled biscuit.

"That wine won't hurt you," continued he, addressing our friend, "that wine won't hurt you, it's not the nasty loaded stuff they manufacture for the English market, but pure, unadulterated juice of the grape, without a headache in a gallon of it so saying, Sir Moses quaffed off his glass and set it down with evident satisfaction, feeling almost a match for the owner of Tippy Tom. He then moved his chair a little on one side, and resumed his contemplation of the fire,—the blue lights rising among the red,—the gas escaping from the coal,—the clear flame flickering with the draught. He thought he saw his way,—yes, he thought he saw his way, and forthwith prevented any one pirating his ideas, by stirring the fire. Mr. Bankhead then entered with the bottle and the biscuit, and, placing them on the table, withdrew.

"Come, Pringle!" cried Sir Moses cheerfully, seizing the massive cut-glass decanter, "let's drink the healths of the young ladies at——, you know where," looking knowingly at our friend, who blushed. "We'll have a bumper to that," continued he, pouring himself out one, and passing the bottle to Billy.

"The young ladies at Yammerton Grange!" continued Sir Moses, holding the glass to the now sparkling fire before he transferred its bright ruby-coloured contents to his thick lips. He then quailed it off with a smack.

"The young ladies at Yammerton Grange!" faltered Billy, after filling himself a bumper.

"Nice girls those, dom'd if they're not," observed the Baronet, now breaking the devilled biscuit. "You must take care what you're about there, though, for the old lady doesn't stand any nonsense; the Major neither."

Billy said he wasn't going to try any on———.

"No—but they'll try it on with you," retorted Sir Moses; "mark my words if they don't."

"O, but I'm only there for hunting," observed Billy, timidly.

"I dare say," replied Sir Moses, with a jerk of his head, "I dare say,—but it's very agreeable to talk to a pretty girl when you come in, and those *are* devilish pretty girls, let me tell you,—dom'd if they're not,—only one talk leads to another talk, and ultimately Mamma talks about a small gold ring."

Billy was frightened, for he felt the truth of what Sir Moses said. They then sat for some minutes in silence, ruminating on their own affairs,—Billy thinking he would be careful of the girls, and wondering how he could escape Sir Moses's offer of a bump on the morrow,—Sir Moses thinking he would advance that performance a step. He now led the way.

"You'll be wanting a horse to go with the Major's harriers," observed he; "and I've got the very animal for that sort of work; that grey horse of mine, the Lord Mayor, in the five-stalled stable on the right; the safest, steadiest animal ever man got on to; and I'll make you a present of him, dom'd if I won't; for I'm more hurt at the loss of yours than words can express; wouldn't have had such a thing happen at my house on any account; so that's a bargain, and will make all square; for the grey's an undeniable good 'un—worth half-a-dozen of the Major's—and will do you some credit, for a young man on his preferment should always study appearances, and ride handsome horses; and the grey is one of the handsomest I ever saw. Lord Tootle-ton, up in Neck-and-crop-shire, who I got him of, gave three 'under'd for him at the hammer, solely, I believe, on account of his looks, for he had never seen him out except in the ring, which is all my eye, for telling you whether a horse is a hunter or not; but, however, he *is* a hunter, and no mistake, and you are most, heartily welcome to him, dom'd if you're not; and I'm deuced glad that it occurred to me to give him you, for I shall now sleep quite comfortable; so help yourself, and we'll drink Foxhunting," saying which, Sir Moses, who had had about enough wine, filled on a liberal heel-tap, and again passed the bottle to his guest.

Now Billy, who had conned over the matter in his bedroom before dinner, had come to the conclusion that he had had about hunting enough, and that the loss of Napoleon the Great afforded a favourable opportunity for retiring from the chase; indeed, he had got rid of the overpowering Mr. Gaiters on that plan, and he was not disposed to be cajoled into a continuance of the penance by the gift of a horse; so as soon as he could get a word in sideways, he began hammering away at an excuse, thanking Sir Moses most energetically for his liberality, but expressing his inability to accept such a magnificent offer.

Sir Moses, however, who did not believe in any one refusing a gift, adhered pertinaciously to his promise,—"Oh, indeed, he should have him, he wouldn't be easy if he didn't take him," and ringing the bell he desired the footman to tell Wetun to see if Mr. Pringle's saddle would fit the Lord Mayor, and if it didn't, to let our friend have one of his in the morning, and "here!" added he, as the man was retiring, "bring in tea."—And Sir Moses being peremptory in his presents, Billy was compelled to remain under pressure of the horse.—So after a copious libation of tea the couple hugged and separated for the night, Sir Moses exclaiming "Breakfast at nine, mind!" as Billy sauntered up stairs, while the Baronet ran off to his study to calculate what Henerey Brown & Co. had done him out of.

CHAPTER XLVIII. ROUGIER'S MYSTERIOUS LODGINGS—THE GIFT HORSE.

MR. Gallon's liberality after the race with Mr. Flintoff was so great that Monsieur Rougier was quite overcome with his kindness and had to be put to bed at the last public-house they stopped at, viz.—the sign of the Nightingale on the Ashworth road. Independently of the brandy not being particularly good, Jack took so much of it that he slept the clock round, and it was past nine the next morning ere he awoke. It then took him good twenty minutes to make out where he was; he first of all thought he was at Boulogne, then in Paris, next at the Lord Warden Hotel at Dover, and lastly at the Coal-hole in the Strand.

Presently the recollection of the race began to dawn upon him—the red jacket—the grey horse, Cuddy in distress, and gradually he recalled the general outline of the performance, but he could not fill it up so as to make a connected whole, or to say where he was.

He then looked at his watch, and finding it was half-past four, he concluded it had stopped,—an opinion that was confirmed on holding it to his ear; so without more ado, he bounded out of bed in a way that nearly sent him through the gaping boards of the dry-rotting floor of the little attic in which they had laid him. He then made his way to the roof-raised window to see what was outside. A fine wet muddy road shone below him, along which a straw-cart was rolling; beyond the road was a pasture, then a turnip field; after which came a succession of green, brown, and drab fields, alternating and undulating away to the horizon, varied with here and there a belt or tuft of wood. Jack was no wiser than he was, but hearing sounds below, he made for the door, and opening the little flimsy barrier stood listening like a terrier with its ear at a rat-hole. These were female voices, and he thus addressed them—"I say, who's there? Theodosia, my dear," continued he, speaking down stairs, "vot's de time o' day, my sweet?"

The lady thus addressed as Theodosia was Mrs. Windybank, a very forbidding tiger-faced looking woman, desperately pitted with the small-pox, who was not in the best of humours in consequence of the cat having got to the cream-bowl; so all the answer she made to Jack's polite enquiry was, "Most ten."

"Most ten!" repeated Jack, "most ten! how the doose can that be?"

"It is hooiver," replied she, adding, "you may look if you, like."

"No, my dear, I'll take your word for it," replied Jack; "but tell me, Susannah," continued he, "whose house is this I'm at?"

"Whose house is't?" replied the voice; "whose house is't? why, Jonathan Windybank's—you knar that as well as I do."

"De lady's not pleasant," muttered Jack to himself; so returning into the room, he began to array himself in his yesterday's garments, Mr. Gallon's boots and leathers, his own coat with Finlater's cap, in which he presently came creaking down stairs and confronted the beauty with whom he had had the flying colloquy. The interview not being at all to her advantage, and as she totally denied all knowledge of Pangburn Park, and "de great Baronet vot kept the spotted dogs," Monsieur set off on foot to seek it; and after divers askings, mistakings, and deviations, he at length arrived on Rossington hill just as the servants' hall dinner-bell was ringing, the walk being much to the detriment of Mr. Gallon's boots.

In consequence of Monsieur's *laches*, as the lawyers would say, Mr. Pringle was thrown on the resources of the house the next morning; but Sir Moses being determined to carry out his intention with regard to the horse, sent the footman to remind Billy that he was going to hunt, and to get him his things if required. So our friend was obliged to adorn for the chase instead of retiring from further exertion in that line as he intended; and with the aid of the footman he made a very satisfactory toilette,—his smart scarlet, a buff vest, a green cravat, correct shirt-collar, with unimpeachable leathers and boots.

Though this was the make-believe day of the week, Sir Moses was all hurry and bustle as usual, and greeted our hero as he came down stairs with the greatest enthusiasm, promising, of all things in the world! to show him a run.

"Now bring breakfast! bring breakfast!" continued he, as if they had got twenty miles to go to cover; and in came urn and eggs, and ham, and cakes, and tongue, and toast, and buns, all the concomitants of the meal.—At it Sir Moses went as if he had only ten minutes to eat it in, inviting his guest to fall-to also.

Just as they were in the midst of the meal a horse was heard to snort outside, and on looking up the great Lord Mayor was seen passing up the Park.

"Ah, there's your horse!" exclaimed Sir Moses, "there's your horse! been down to the shop to get his shoes looked to," though in reality Sir Moses had told the groom to do just what he was doing, viz.—to pass him before the house at breakfast-time without his clothing.

The Lord Mayor was indeed a sort of horse that a youngster might well be taken in with, grey, with a beautiful head and neck, and an elegantly set-on tail. He stepped out freely and gaily, and looked as lively as a lark.

He was, however, as great an impostor as Napoleon the Great; for, independently of being troubled with the Megrims, he was a shocking bad hack, and a very few fields shut him up as a hunter.

"Well now," said Sir Moses, pausing in his meal, with the uplifted knife and fork of admiration, "that, to my mind, is the handsomest horse in the country,—I don't care where the next handsomest is.—Just look at his figure, just look at his action.—Did you ever see anything so elegant? To my mind he's as near perfection as possible, and what's more, he's as good as he looks, and all I've got to say is, that you are most heartily welcome to him."

"O, thank'e," replied Billy, "thank'e, but I couldn't think of accepting him,—I couldn't think of accepting him indeed."

"O, but you shall," said Sir Moses, resuming his eating, "O but you shall, so there's an end of the matter.—And now have some more tea," whereupon he proceeded to charge Billy's cup in the awkward sort of way men generally do when they meddle with the tea-pot.

Sir Moses, having now devoured his own meal, ran off to his study, telling Billy he would call him when it was time to go, and our friend proceeded to dandle and saunter, and think what he would do with his gift horse. He was certainly a handsome one—handsomer than Napoleon, and grey was a smarter colour than bay—might not be quite so convenient for riding across country on, seeing the color was conspicuous, but for a hot day in the Park nothing could be more cool or delightful. And he thought it was extremely handsome of Sir Moses giving it to him, more, he felt, than nine-tenths of the people in the world would have done.

Our friend's reverie was presently interrupted by Sir Moses darting back, pen and paper in hand, exclaiming, "I'll tell ye what, my dear Pringle! I'll tell ye what! there shall be no obligation, and you shall give me fifty puns for the grey and pay for him when you please. But *mark* me!" added he, holding up his forefinger and looking most scrutinisingly at our friend, "*Only on one condition, mind! only on one condition, mind!* that you give me the refusal of him if ever you want to part with him;" and without waiting for an answer, he placed the paper before our friend, and handing him the pen, said, "There, then, sign that I. O. U." And Billy having signed it, Sir Moses snatched it up and disappeared, leaving our friend to a renewal of his cogitations.

Sir Moses having accomplished the grand "do," next thought he would back out of the loan of the dog-cart. For this purpose he again came hurrying back, pen in hand, exclaiming, "Oh dear, he was so sorry, but it had just occurred to him that he wanted the mare to go to Lord Lundyfoote's; however, I'll make it all square, I'll make it all square," continued he; "I'll tell Jenkins, the postman, to send a fly as soon as he gets to Hinton, which, I make no doubt, will be here by the time we come in from hunting, and it will take you and your traps all snug and comfortable; for a dog-cart, after all, is but a chilly concern at this time of year, and I shouldn't like you to catch cold going from my house;" and without waiting for an answer, he pulled-to the door and hurried back to his den. Billy shook his head, for he didn't like being put off that way, and muttered to himself, "I wonder who'll pay for it though." However, on reflection, he thought perhaps he would be as comfortable in a fly as finding his way across country on horseback; and as he had now ascertained that Monsieur could ride, whether or not he could drive, he settled that he might just as well take the grey to Yammerton Grange as not. This then threw him back on his position with regard to the horse, which was not so favourable as it at first appeared; indeed, he questioned whether he had done wisely in signing the paper, his Mamma having always cautioned him to be careful how he put his name to anything. Still, he felt he couldn't have got off without offending Sir Moses; and after all, it was more like a loan than a sale, seeing that he had not paid for him, and Sir Moses would take him back if he liked. Altogether he thought he might be worse off, and, considering that Lord Tootleton had given three hundred for the horse, he certainly must be worth fifty. There is nothing so deceiving as price. Only tell a youngster that a horse has cost a large sum, and he immediately looks at him, while he would pass him by if he stood at a low figure. Having belonged to a lord, too, made him so much more acceptable to Billy.

A loud crack of a whip, accompanied by a "Now, Pringle!" presently resounded through the house, and our friend again found himself called upon to engage in an act of horsemanship.

"Coming!" cried he, starting from the little mirror above the scanty grey marble mantel-piece, in which he was contemplating his moustachios; "Coming!" and away he strode, with the desperate energy of a man bent on braving the worst. His cap, whip, gloves, and mits, were all laid ready for him on the entrance hall-table; and seizing them in a cluster, he proceeded to decorate himself as he followed Sir Moses along the intricate passages leading to the stable-yard.

CHAPTER XLIX. THE SHAM DAY.

SATURDAY is a very different day in the country to what it is in London. In London it is the lazy day of the week, whereas it is the busy one in the country. It is marked in London by the coming of the clean-linen carts, and the hurrying about of Hansoms with gentlemen with umbrellas and small carpet-bags, going to the steamers and stations for pleasure; whereas in the country everybody is off to the parliament of his local capital on business. All the markets in Hit-im and Hold-im shire were held on a Saturday, and several in Featherbedfordshire; and as everybody who has nothing to do is always extremely busy, great gatherings were the result. This circumstance made Sir Moses hit upon Saturday for his fourth, or make-believe day with the hounds, inasmuch as few people would be likely to come, and if they did, he knew how to get rid of them. The consequence was, that the court-yard at Pangburn Park exhibited a very different appearance, on this occasion, to what it would have done had the hounds met there on any other day of the week. Two red coats only, and those very shabby ones, with very shady horses under them—viz., young Mr. Billikins of Red Hill Lodge, and his cousin Captain Luff of the navy (the latter out for the first time in his life), were all that greeted our sportsmen; the rest of the field being attired in shooting-jackets, tweeds, antigropolos and other anti-fox-hunting looking things.

"Good morning, gentlemen! good morning!" cried Sir Moses, waving his hand from the steps at the promiscuous throng; and without condescending to particularise any one, he hurried across for his horse, followed by our friend. Sir Moses was going to ride Old Jack, one of the horses he had spoken of for Billy, a venerable brown, of whose age no one's memory about the place supplied any information—though when he first came all the then wiseacres prophesied a speedy decline. Still Old Jack had gone on from season to season, never apparently getting older, and now looking as likely to go on as ever. The old fellow having come pottering out of the stable and couched to his load, the great Lord Mayor came darting forward as if anxious for the fray. "It's *your* saddle, sir," said Wetun, touching his forehead with his finger, as he held on by the stirrup for Billy to mount. Up then went our friend into the old seat of suffering. "There!" exclaimed Sir Moses, as he got his feet settled in the stirrups; "there, you do look well! If Miss 'um' sees you," continued he, with a knowing wink, "it'll be all over with you;" so saying, Sir Moses touched Old Jack gently with the spur, and proceeded to the slope of the park, where Findlater and the whips now had the hounds.

Tom Findlater, as we said before, was an excellent huntsman, but he had his peculiarities, and in addition to that of getting drunk, he sometimes required to be managed by the rule of contrary, and made to believe that Sir Moses wanted him to do the very reverse of what he really did. Having been refused leave to go to Cleaver the butcher's christening-supper at the sign of the Shoulder of Mutton, at Kimberley, Sir Moses anticipated that this would be one of his perverse days, and so he began taking measures accordingly.

"Good morning, Tom," said he, as huntsman and whips now sky-scraped to his advance—"morning all of you," added he, waving a general salute to the hound-encircling group.

"Now, Tom," said he, pulling up and fumbling at his horn, "I've been telling Mr. Pringle that we'll get him a gallop so as to enable him to arrive at Yammerton Grange before dark."

"Yes, Sir Moses," replied Tom, with a rap of his cap-peak, thinking he would take very good care that he didn't.

"Now whether will Briarey Banks or the Reddish Warren be the likeliest place for a find?"

"Neither, Sir Moses, neither," replied Tom confidently, "Tip-thorne's the place for us."

This was just what Sir Moses wanted.

"Tipthorne, you think, do you?" replied he, musingly. "Tipthorne, you think—well, and where next?"

"Shillington, Sir Moses, and Halstead Hill, and so on to Hatchington Wood."

"Good!" replied the Baronet, "Good!" adding, "then let's be going."

At a whistle and a waive of his hand the watchful hounds darted up, and Tom taking the lead, the mixed cavalcade swept after them over the now yellow-grassed park in a north-easterly direction, Captain Luff working his screw as if he were bent on treading on the hounds' stems.

There being no one out to whom Sir Moses felt there would be any profitable investment of attention, he devoted himself to our hero, complimenting him on his appearance, and on the gallant bearing of his steed, declaring that of all the neat horses he had ever set eyes on the Lord Mayor was out-and-out the neatest. So with compliments to Billy, and muttered "cusses" at Luff, they trotted down Oxclose Lane, through the little village of Homerton, past Dewfield Lawn, over Waybridge Common, shirking Upwood toll-bar, and down Cornforth Bank to Burford, when Tipthorne stood before them. It was a round Billesdon Coplow-like hill, covered with stunted oaks, and a nice warm lying gorse sloping away to the south; but Mr. Tadpole's keeper having the rabbits, he was seldom out of it, and it was of little use looking there for a fox.

That being the case, of course it was more necessary to make a great pretension, so halting noiselessly behind the high red-berried hedge, dividing the pasture from the gorse, Tom despatched his whips to their points, and then touching his cap to Sir Moses, said, "P'raps Mr. Pringle would like to ride in and see him find."

"Ah, to be sure," replied Sir Moses, "let's both go in," whereupon Tom opened the bridle-gate, and away went the hounds with a dash that as good as said if we don't get a fox we'll get a rabbit at all events.

"A fox for a guinea!" cried Findlater, cheering them, and looking at his watch as if he had him up already. "A fox for a guinea!" repeated he, thinking how nicely he was selling his master.

"Keep your eye on this side," cried Sir Moses to Billy. "he'll cross directly!" Terrible announcement. How our friend did quake.

"*Yap, yap, yap*," now went the shrill note of Tartar, the tarrier, "*Yough, yough, yough*" followed the deep tone of young Venturesome, close in pursuit of a bunny.

"*Crack!*" went a heavy whip, echoing through the air and resounding at the back of the hill.

All again was still, and Tom advanced up the cover, standing erect in his stirrups, looking as if half-inclined to believe it was a fox after all.

"*Eloo in! Eloo in!*" cried he, capping Talisman and Wonderful across. "Yoicks wind 'im! yoicks push him up!" continued he, thinking what a wonderful performance it would be if they did find.

"Squeak, yap, yell, squeak," now went the well-known sound of a hound in a trap. It is Labourer, and a whip goes diving into the sea of gorse to the rescue.

"Oh, dom those traps," cries Sir Moses, as the clamour ceases, adding, "no fox here, I told you so," adding, "should have gone to the Warren."

He then took out his box-wood horn and stopped the performance by a most discordant blast. The hounds came slinking out to the summons, some of them licking their lips as if they had not been there altogether for nothing.

"Where to, now, please Sir Moses?" asked Tom, with a touch of his cap, as soon as he had got them all out.

"*Tally-ho!*" cries Captain Luff, in a most stentorian strain—adding immediately, "Oh no! I'm mistaken, *It's a hare!*" as half the hounds break away to his cry.

"Oh, dom you and your noise," cries Sir Moses, in well-feigned disgust, adding—"Why don't you put your spectacles on?"

Luff looks foolish, for he doesn't know what to say, and the excitement dies out in a laugh at the Captain's expense.

"Where to, now, please, Sir Moses?" again asks Tom, chuckling at his master's displeasure, and thinking how much better it would have been if he had let him go to the supper.

"Where you please," growled the Baronet, scowling at Luff's nasty rusty Napoleons—"where you please, you said Shillington, didn't you—anywhere, only let us find a fox," added he, as if he really wanted one.

Tom then got his horse short by the head, and shouldering his whip, trotted off briskly, as if bent on retrieving the day. So he went through the little hamlet of Hawkesworth over Dippingham water meadows, bringing Blobbington mill-race into the line, much to Billy's discomfiture, and then along the Hinton and London turnpike to the sign of the Plough at the blacksmith's shop at Shillington.

The gorse was within a stone's throw of the "Public," so Luff and some of the thirsty ones pulled up to wet their whistles and light the clay pipes of gentility.

The gorse was very open, and the hounds ran through it almost before the sots had settled what they would have, and there being a bye-road at the far end, leading by a slight*détour* to Halstead Hill, Sir Moses hurried them out, thinking to shake off some of them by a trot. They therefore slipped away with scarcely a crack of the whip, let alone the twang of a horn.

"Bad work this," said Sir Moses, spurring and reining up alongside of Billy, "bad work this; that huntsman of mine," added he, in an under tone, "is the most obstinate fool under the sun, and let me give you a bit of advice," continued he, laying hold of our friend's arm, as if to enforce it. "If ever you keep hounds, always give orders and never ask opinions. Now, Mister Findlater!" hallooed he, to the bobbing cap in advance, "Now, Mister Findlater! you're well called Findlater, by Jove, for I think you'll never find at all. Halstead Hill, I suppose, next?"

"Yes, Sir Moses," replied Tom, with a half-touch of his cap, putting on a little faster, to get away, as he thought, from the spray of his master's wrath. And so with this comfortable game at cross purposes, master and servant passed over what is still called Lingfield common (though it now grows turnips instead of gorse), and leaving Cherry-trees Windmill to the left, sunk the hill at Drovers' Heath, and crossing the bridge at the Wellingburn, the undulating form of Halstead Hill stood full before them. Tom then pulled up into a walk, and contemplated the rugged intricacies of its craggy bush-dotted face.

"If there's a fox in the country one would think he'd be here," observed he, in a general sort of way, well knowing that Mr. Testyfield's keeper took better care of them than that. "Gently hurrying!" hallooed he, now cracking his whip as the hounds pricked their ears, and seemed inclined to break away to an outburst of children from the village school below.

Tom then took the hounds to the east end of the hill, where the lying began, and drew them along the face of it with the usual result, "*Nil.*" Not even a rabbit.

"Well, that's queer," said he, with well feigned chagrin, as Pillager, Petulant, and Ravager appeared on the bare ground to the west, leading out the rest of the pack on their lines. They were all presently clustering in view again. A slight twang of the horn brought them pouring down to the hill to our obstinate huntsman just as Captain Luff and Co. hove in sight on the Wellingburn Bridge, riding as boldly as refreshed gentlemen generally do.

There was nothing for it then but Hatchington Wood, with its deep holding rides and interminable extent.

There is a Hatchington Wood in every hunt, wild inhospitable looking thickets, that seem as if they never knew an owner's care, where men light their cigars and gather in groups, well knowing that whatever sport the hounds may have, theirs is over for the day. Places in which a man may gallop his horse's tail off, and not hear or see half as much as those do who sit still.

Into it Tom now cheered his hounds, again thinking how much better it would have been if Sir Moses had let him go to the supper. "*Cover hoick! Cover hoick!*" cheered he to his hounds, as they came to the rickety old gate. "I wouldn't ha' got drunk," added he to himself. "*Yoi, wind him! Yoi, rouse him, my boys!* what 'arm could it do him, my going, I wonders?" continued he to himself. "Yoi, try for him, Desp'rate, good lass! Desp'rate bad job my not gettin', I know," added he, rubbing his nose on the back of his hand; and so with cheers to his hounds and commentaries on Sir Moses's mean conduct, the huntsman proceeded from ride to road and from road to ride, varied with occasional dives into the fern and the rough, to exhort and encourage his hounds to rout out a fox; not that he cared much now whether he found one or not, for the cover had long existed on the reputation of a run that took place twelve years before, and it was not likely that a place so circumstanced would depart from its usual course on that day.

There is nothing certain, however, about a fox-hunt, but uncertainty; the worst-favoured days sometimes proving the best, and the best-favoured ones sometimes proving the worst. We dare say, if our sporting readers would ransack their memories, they will find that most of their best days have been on unpromising ones. So it was on the present occasion, only no one saw the run but Tom and the first whip. Coming suddenly upon a fine travelling fox, at the far corner of the cover, they slipped away with him down wind, and had a bona fide five and thirty minutes, with a kill, in Lord Ladythorne's country, within two fields of his famous gorse cover, at Cockmere.

"Ord! rot ye, but ye should ha' seen that, if you'd let me go to the supper," cried Tom, as he threw himself off his lathered tail-quivering horse to pick up his fox, adding, "I knows when to blow the horn and when not."

Meanwhile Sir Moses, having got into a wrangle with Jacky Phillips about the price of a pig, sate on his accustomed place on the rising ground by the old tumble-down farm-buildings, wrangling, and haggling, and declaring it was a "do." In the midst of his vehemence, Robin Snowball's camp of roystering, tinkering besom-makers came hattering past; and Robin, having a contract with Sir Moses for dog horses, gave his ass a forwarding bang, and ran up to inform his patron that "the hunds had gone away through Piercefield plantins iver see lang since:"—a fact that Robin was well aware of, having been stealing besom-shanks in them at the time.

"Oh, the devil!" shrieked Sir Moses, as if he was shot. "Oh, the devil!" continued he, wringing his hands, thinking how Tom would be bucketing Crusader now that he was out of sight; and catching up his horse, he stuck spurs in his sides, and went clattering up the stony cross-road to the west, as hard as ever the old Jack could lay legs to the ground, thinking what a wigging he would give Tom if he caught him.

"Hark!" continued he, pulling short up across the road, and nearly shooting Billy into his pocket with the jerk of his suddenly stopped horse, "Hark!" repeated he, holding up his hand, "Isn't that the horn?"

"Oh, dom it! it's Parker, the postman," added he,—"what business has the beggar to make such a row!" for, like all noisy people, Sir Moses had no idea of anybody making a noise but himself. He then set his horse agoing again, and was presently standing in his stirrups, tearing up the wretched, starvation, weed-grown ground outside the cover.

Having gained a sufficient elevation, he again pulled up, and turning short round, began surveying the country. All was quiet and tranquil. The cattle had their heads to the ground, the sheep were scattered freely over the fields, and the teams were going lazily over the clover-lays, leaving shiny furrows behind them.

"Well, that's a sell, at all events!" said he, dropping his reins. "Be b'und to say they are right into the heart of Featherbedfordshire by this time,—most likely at Upton Moss in Woodberry Vale,—as fine a country as ever man crossed,—and to think that that wretched deluded man has it all to himself!—I'd draw and quarter him if I had him, dom'd if I wouldn't," added Sir Moses, cutting frantically at the air with his thong-gathered whip.

Our friend Billy, on the other hand, was all ease and composure. He had escaped the greatest punishment that could befall him, and was so clean and comfortable, that he resolved to surprise his fair friends at Yammerton Grange in his pink, instead of changing as he intended.

Sir Moses, having strained his eye-balls about the country in vain, at length dropped down in his saddle, and addressing the few darkly-clad horsemen around him with, "Well, gentlemen, I'm afraid it's all over for the day," adding, "Come, Pringle, let us be going," he poked his way past them, and was presently retracing his steps through the wood, picking up a lost hound or two as he went. And still he was so loth to give it up, that he took Forester Hill in his way, to try if he could see anything of them; but it was all calm and blank as before; and at length he reached Pangburn Park in a very discontented mood.

In the court-yard stood the green fly that had to convey our friend back to fairy-land, away from the red coats, silk jackets and other the persecutions of pleasure, to the peaceful repose of the Major and his "haryers." Sir Moses looked at it with satisfaction, for he had had as much of our friend's society as he required, and did not know that he could "do" him much more if he had him a month; so if he could now only get clear of Monsieur without paying him, that was all he required.

Jack, however, was on the alert, and appeared on the back-steps as Sir Moses dismounted; nor did his rapid dive into the stable avail him, for Jack headed him as he emerged at the other end, with a hoist of his hat, and a "Bon jour, Sare Moses, Baronet!"

"Ah, Monsieur, comment vous portez-vous?" replied the Baronet, shying off, with a keep-your-distance sort of waive of the hand.

Jack, however, was not to be put off that way, and following briskly up, he refreshed Sir Moses's memory with, "Pund, I beat Cuddy, old cock, to de clomp; ten franc—ten shillin'—I get over de brook; thirty shillin' in all, Sare Moses, Baronet," holding out his hand for the money.

"Oh, ah, true," replied Sir Moses, pretending to recollect the bets, adding, "If you can give me change of a fifty-pun note, I can pay ye," producing a nice clean one from his pocket-book that he always kept ready for cases of emergency like the present.

"Fifty-pun note, Sare Moses!" replied Jack, eyeing it. "Fifty-pun note! I 'ave not got such an astonishin' som about me at present," feeling his pockets as he spoke; "bot I vill seek change, if you please."

"Why, no," replied Sir Moses, thinking he had better not part with the decoy-duck. "I'll tell you what I'll do, though," continued he, restoring it to its case; "I'll send you a post-office order for the amount, or pay it to your friend, Mr. Gallon, whichever you prefer."

"Veil, Sir Moses, Baronet," replied Jack, considering, "I think de leetle post-office order vill be de most digestible vay of squarin' matters."

"Va-a-ry good," cried Sir Moses, "Va-a-ry good. I'll send you one, then," and darting at a door in the wall, he slipped through it, and shot the bolt between Jack and himself.

And our hero, having recruited nature with lunch, and arranged with Jack for riding his horse, presently took leave of his most hospitable host, and entered the fly that was to convey him back to Yammerton Grange. And having cast himself into its ill-stuffed hold he rumbled and jolted across country in the careless, independent sort of way that a man does who has only a temporary interest in the vehicle, easy whether he was upset or not. Let us now anticipate his arrival by transferring our imaginations to Yammerton Grange.

CHAPTER L. THE SURPRISE.

IT is all very well for people to affect the magnificent, to give general invitations, and say "Come whenever it suits you; we shall always be happy to see you," and so on; but somehow it is seldom safe to take them at their word. How many houses has the reader to which he can ride or drive up with the certainty of not putting people "out," as the saying is. If there is a running account of company going on, it is all very well; another man more or less is neither here nor there; but if it should happen to be one of those solemn lulls that intervene between one set of guests going and another coming, denoted by the wide-apart napkins seen by a side glance as he passes the dining-room window, then it is not a safe speculation. At all events, a little notice is better, save, perhaps, among fox-hunters, who care less for appearances than other people.

It was Saturday, as we said before, and our friend the Major had finished his week's work:— paid his labourers, handled the heifers that had left him so in the lurch, counted the sheep, given out the corn, ordered the carriage for church in case it kept dry, and as day closed had come into the house, and exchanged his thick shoes for old worsted worked slippers, and cast himself into a semicircular chair in the druggeted drawing-room to wile away one of those long winter evenings that seem so impossible in the enduring length of a summer day, with that best of all papers, the "Hit-im and Hold-im shire Herald." The local paper is the paper for the country gentleman, just as the "Times" is the paper for the Londoner. The "Times" may span the globe, tell what is doing at Delhi and New York, France, Utah, Prussia, Spain, Ireland, and the Mauritius; but the paper that tells the squire of the flocks and herds, the hills and dales, the births and disasters of his native district, is the paper for his money. So it was with our friend the Major. He enjoyed tearing the half-printed halfwritten envelope off his "Herald," and holding its damp sides to the cheerful fire until he got it as crisp as a Bank of England note, and then, sousing down in his easy chair to enjoy its contents, conscious that no one had anticipated them. How he revelled in the advertisements, and accompanied each announcement with a mental commentary of his own.

We like to see country gentlemen enjoying their local papers.

Ashover farm to let, conjured up recollections of young Mr.

Gosling spurting past in white cords, and his own confident prediction that the thing wouldn't last.

Burlinson the auctioneer's assignment for the benefit of his creditors, reminded him of his dogs, and his gun, and his manor, and his airified looks, and drew forth anathemas on Burlinson in particular, and on pretenders in general.

Then Mr. Napier's announcement that Mr. Draggleton of Rushworth had applied for a loan of four thousand pounds from the Lands Improvement Company for draining, sounded almost like a triumph of the Major's own principles, Draggleton having long derided the idea of water getting into a two-inch pipe at a depth of four feet, or of draining doing any good.

And the Major chuckled with delight at the thought of seeing the long pent-up water flow in pure continuous streams off the saturated soil, and of the clear, wholesome complexion the land would presently assume. Then the editorial leader on the state of the declining corn markets, and of field operations (cribbed of course from the London papers) drew forth an inward opinion that the best thing for the land-owners would be for corn to keep low and cattle to keep high for the next dozen years or more, and so get the farmers' minds turned from the precarious culture of corn to the land-improving practice of grazing and cattle-feeding.

And thus the Major sat, deeply immersed in the contents of each page; but as he gradually mastered the cream of their contents, he began to turn to and fro more rapidly; and as the rustling increased, Mrs. Yammerton, who was dying for a sight of the paper, at length ventured to ask if there was anything about the Hunt ball in it.

"Hunt ball!" growled the Major, who was then in the hay and straw market, wondering whether, out of the twenty-seven carts of hay reported to have been at Hinton Market on the previous Saturday, there were any of his tenants there on the sly; "Hunt ball!" repeated he, running the candle up and down the page; "No, there's nothin' about it here," replied he, resuming his reading.

"It'll be on the front page, my dear," observed Mrs. Yammerton, "if there is anything."

"Well, I'll give it you presently," replied the Major, resuming his reading; and so he wens on into the wool markets, thence to the potato and hide departments, until at length he found himself floundering among the Holloway Pills, Revalenta Food, and "Sincere act of gratitude," &c., advertisements; when, turning the paper over with a wisk, and an inward "What do they put such stuff as that in for?" he handed it to his wife: while, John Bull like, he now stood up, airing himself comfortably before the fire.

No sooner was the paper fairly in Mamma's hands, than there was a general rush of the young ladies to the spot, and four pairs of eyes were eagerly glancing up and down the columns of the front page, all in search of the magical letter "B" for Ball. Education—Fall in Night Lights—Increased Bate of Interest—Money without Sureties—Iron and Brass Bedsteads—Glenfield Starch—Deafness Cured—German Yeast—Insolvent Debtor—Elkington's Spoons—Boots and Shoes,—but, alas! no Ball.

"Yes, there it is! No it isn't," now cried Miss Laura, as her blue eye caught at the heading of Mrs. Bobbinette the milliner's advertisement, in the low corner of the page, Mrs. Bobbinette, like some of her customers, perhaps, not being a capital payer, and so getting a bad place. Thus it ran—

HIT-IM AND HOLD-IM SHIRE HUNT BALL.

—Mrs. Bobbinette begs to announce to the ladies her return from Paris, with every novelty in millinery, mantles, embroideries, wreaths, fans, gloves, &c.

"Mrs. Bobbinette be banged," growled the Major, who winced under the very name of milliner; "just as much goes to Paris as I do. Last time she was there I know she was never out of Hinton, for Paul Straddler watched her."

"Well, but she gets very pretty things at all events," replied Mrs. Yammerton, thinking she would pay her a visit.

"Aye, and a pretty bill she'll send in for them," replied the Major.

"Well, my dear, but you must pay for fashion, you know," rejoined Mamma.

"Pay for fashion! pay for haystacks!" growled the Major; "never saw such balloons as the women make of themselves. S'pose we shall have them as flat as doors next. One extreme always leads to another."

This discussion was here suddenly interrupted by a hurried "hush!" from Miss Clara, followed by a "hish!" from Miss Flora; and silence being immediately accorded, all ears recognised a rumbling sound outside the house that might have been mistaken for wind, had it not suddenly ceased before the door.

The whole party was paralysed: each drawing breath, reflecting on his or her peculiar position:—Mamma thinking of her drawingroom—Miss, of her hair—Flora, of her sleeves—Harriet, of her shabby shoes—the Major, of his dinner.

The agony of suspense was speedily relieved by the grating of an iron step and a violent pull at the door-bell, producing ejaculations of, "It *is*, however!"

"Him, to a certainty!" with, "I told you so,—nothing but liver and bacon for dinner," from the Major; while Mrs. Yammerton, more composed, swept three pair of his grey worsted stockings into the well of the ottoman, and covered the old hearth-rug with a fine new one from the corner, with a noble antlered stag in the centre. The young ladies hurried out of the room, each to make a quick revise of her costume.

The shock to the nervous sensibilities of the household was scarcely less severe than that experienced by the inmates of the parlour; and the driver of the fly was just going to give the bell a second pull, when our friend of the brown coat came, settling himself into his garment, wondering who could be coming at that most extraordinary hour.

"Major at home?" asked our hero, swinging himself out of the vehicle into the passage, and without waiting for an answer, he began divesting himself of his muffin-cap, cashmere shawl, and other wraps.

He was then ready for presentation. Open went the door. "Mr. Pringle!" announced the still-astonished footman, and host and hostess advanced in the friendly emulation of cordiality. They were overjoyed to see him,—as pleased as if they had received a consignment of turtle and there was a haunch of venison roasting before the fire. The young ladies presently came dropping in one by one, each "*so* astonished to find Mr. Pringle there!" Clara thinking the ring was from Mr..Jinglington, the pianoforte-tuner; Flora, that it was Mr. Tightlace's curate; while Harriet did not venture upon a white lie at all.

Salutations and expressions of surprise being at length over, the ladies presently turned the weather-conversation upon Pangburn Park, and inquired after the sport with Sir Moses, Billy being in the full glory of his pink and slightly soiled leathers and boots, from which they soon diverged to the Hunt ball, about which they could not have applied to any better authority than our friend. He knew all about it, and poured forth the volume of his information most freely.

Though the Major talked about there being nothing but liver and bacon for dinner, he knew very well that the very fact of there being liver and bacon bespoke that there was plenty of something else in the larder. In fact he had killed a south-down,—not one of your modern muttony-lambs, but an honest, home-fed, four-year-old, with its fine dark meat and rich gravy; in addition to which, there had been some minor murders of ugly Cochin-China fowls,—to say nothing of a hunted hare, hanging by the heels, and several snipes and partridges, suspended by the neck.

It is true, there was no fish, for, despite the railroad, Hit-im and Hold-im shire generally was still badly supplied with fish, but there was the useful substitute of cod-sounds, and some excellent mutton-broth; which latter is often better than half the soups one gets. Altogether there was no cause for despondency; but the Major, having been outvoted on the question of requiring notice of our friend's return, of course now felt bound to make the worst of the case—especially as the necessary arrangements would considerably retard his dinner, for which he was quite ready. He had, therefore, to smile at his guest, and snarl at his family, at one and the same time.—Delighted to see Mr. Pringle back.—Disgusted at his coming on a Saturday.—Hoped our hero was hungry.—Could answer for it, he was himself,—with a look at Madam, as much as to say, "Come, you go and see about things and don't stand simpering there."

But Billy, who had eaten a pretty hearty lunch at Pangburn Park, had not got jolted back into an appetite by his transit through the country, and did not enter into the feelings of his half-famished host. A man who has had half his dinner in the shape of a lunch, is far more than a match for one who has fasted since breakfast, and our friend chatted first with one young lady, and then with another, with an occasional word at Mamma, delighted to get vent for his long pent-up flummery. He was indeed most agreeable.

Meanwhile the Major was in and out of the room, growling and getting into everybody's way, retarding progress by his anxiety to hurry things on.

At length it was announced that Mr. Pringle's room was ready; and forthwith the Major lit him a candle, and hurried him upstairs, where his uncorded boxes stood ready for the opening keys of ownership.

"Ah, there you are!" cried the Major, flourishing the composite candle about them; "there you are! needn't mind much dressing—only ourselves—only ourselves. There's the boot-jack,—here's some hot water,—and we'll have dinner as soon as ever you are ready." So saying, he placed the candle on the much be-muslined toilette-table, and, diving into his pocket for the key of the cellar, hurried off to make the final arrangement of a feast.

Our friend, however, who was always a dawdling leisurely gentleman, took very little heed of his host's injunctions, and proceeded to unlock and open his boxes as if he was going to dress for a ball instead of a dinner; and the whole party being reassembled, many were the Major's speculations and enquiries "what could he be about?" "must have gone to bed," "would go up and see," ere the glad sound of his opening door announced that he might be expected. And before he descended a single step of the staircase the Major gave the bell such a pull as proclaimed most volubly the intensity of his feelings. The ladies of course were shocked, but a hungry man is bad to hold, and there is no saying but the long-pealing tongue of the bell saved an explosion of the Major's. At all events when our friend came sauntering into the now illuminated drawing-room, the Major greeted him with, "Heard you coming, rang the bell, knew you'd be hungry, long drive from Sir Moses's here;" to which Billy drawled a characteristic "Yarse," as he extinguished his candle and proceeded to ingratiate himself with the now elegantly attired ladies, looking more lovely from his recent restriction to the male sex.

The furious peal of the bell had answered its purpose, for he had scarcely got the beauties looked over, and settled in his own mind that it was difficult to say which was the prettiest, ere the door opened, the long-postponed dinner was announced to be on the table, and the Major, having blown out the composites, gladly followed the ladies to the scene of action.

And his host being too hungry to waste his time in apologies for the absence of this and that, and the footboy having plenty to do without giving the dishes superfluous airings, and the gooseberry champagne being both lively and cool, the dinner passed off as pleasantly as a luncheon, which is generally allowed to be the most agreeable sociable meal of the day, simply because of the absence of all fuss and pretension. And by the time the Major had got to the cheese, he found his temper considerably improved. Indeed, so rapidly did his spirits rise, that before the cloth was withdrawn he had well-nigh silenced all the ladies, with his marvellous haryers,—five and thirty years master of haryers without a subscription,—and as soon as he got the room cleared, he inflicted the whole hunt upon Billy that he had written to him about, an account of which he had in vain tried to get inserted in the Featherbedfordshire Gazette, through the medium of old 'Wotherspoon, who had copied it out and signed himself "A Delighted Stranger." Dorsay Davis, however, knew his cramped handwriting, and put his manuscript into the fire, observing in his notice to correspondents that "A Delighted Stranger" had better send his currant jelly contributions to grandmamma, meaning the Hit-im and Hold-im shire Herald. So our friend was victimised into a *viva voce* account of this marvellous chase, beginning at Conksbury corner and the flight up to Foremark Hill and down over the water meadows to Dove-dale Green, &c., interspersed with digressions and explanations of the wonderful performance of the particular members of the pack, until he scarcely knew whether a real run or the recital of one was the most formidable. At length the Major, having talked himself into a state of excitement, without making any apparent impression on his guest's obdurate understanding, proposed as a toast "The Merry Haryers," and intimated that tea was ready in the drawing room, thinking he never had so phlegmatic an auditor before. Very different, however, was his conduct amid the general conversation of the ladies, who thought him just as agreeable as the Major thought him the contrary. And they were all quite surprised when the clock struck eleven, and declared they thought it could only be ten, except the Major, who knew the odd hour had been lost in preparing the dinner. So he moved an adjournment, and proclaimed that they would breakfast at nine, which would enable them to get to church in good time. Whereupon mutual good-nights were exchanged, our friend was furnished with a flat candlestick, and the elder sisters retired to talk him over in their own room; for however long ladies may be together during the day, there is always a great balance of conversation to dispose of at last, and so the two chatted and talked until midnight.

Next morning they all appeared in looped-up dresses, showing the party-coloured petticoats of the prevailing fashion, which looked extremely pretty, and were all very well—a great improvement on the draggletails—until they came to get into the coach, when it was found, that large as the vehicle was, it was utterly inadequate for their accommodation. Indeed the door seemed ludicrously insufficient for the ingress, and Miss Clara turned round and round like a peacock contending with the wind, undecided which way to make the attempt. At last she chose a bold sideways dash, and entered with a squeeze of the petticoat, which suddenly expanded into its original size, but when the sisters had followed her example there was no room for the Major, nor would there have been any for our hero had not Mamma been satisfied with her own natural size, and so left space to squeeze him in between herself and the fair Clara. The Major then had to mount the coach box beside old Solomon, and went growling and grumbling along at the extravagances of fashion, and wondering what the deuce those petticoats would cost, he was presently comforted by seeing two similar ones circling over the road in advance, which on overtaking proved to contain the elegant Miss Bushels, daughters of his hind at Bonnyrigs farm, whereupon he made a mental resolution to reduce Bushel's wages a shilling a week at least.

This speedy influx of fashion and abundance of cheap tawdry finery has well nigh destroyed the primitive simplicity of country churches. The housemaid now dresses better—finer at all events—than her mistress did twenty years ago, and it is almost impossible to recognise working people when in their Sunday dresses. Gauze bonnets, Marabout feathers, lace scarfs, and silk gowns usurp the place of straw and cotton print, while lace-fringed kerchiefs are flourished by those whose parents scarcely knew what a pocket-handkerchief was. There is a medium in all things, but this mania for dress has got far beyond the bounds of either prudence or propriety; and we think the Major's recipe for reducing it is by no means a bad one.

We need scarcely say, that our hero's appearance at church caused no small sensation in a neighbourhood where the demand for gossip was far in excess of the supply. Indeed, we fear many fair ladies' eyes were oftener directed to Major Yammerton's pew than to the Reverend Mr. Tightlace in the pulpit. Wonderful were the stories and exaggerations that ensued, people always being on the running-up tack until a match is settled, after which, of course, they assume the running-down one, pitying one or other victim extremely—wouldn't be him or her for anything—Mr. Tightlace thought any of the young ladies might do better than marry a mere fox-hunter, though we are sorry to add that the fox-hunter was far more talked of than the sermon. The general opinion seemed to be that our hero had been away preparing that dread document, the proposals for a settlement; and there seemed to be very little doubt that there would be an announcement of some sort in a day or two—especially when our friend was seen to get into the carriage after the gay petticoats, and the little Major to remount the box seat.

And when at the accustomed stable stroll our master of harryers found the gallant grey standing in the place of the bay, he was much astonished, and not a little shocked to learn the sad catastrophe that had befallen the bay.

"Well, he never heard anything like that!—*dead*! What, do you mean to say he absolutely died on your hands without any apparent cause?" demanded the Major; "must have been poisoned surely;" and he ran about telling everybody, and making as much to do as if the horse had still been his own. He then applied himself to finding out how Billy came by the grey, and was greatly surprised to learn that Sir Moses had given it him. "Well, that was queer," thought he, "wouldn't have accused him of that." And he thought of the gift of Little Bo-peep, and wondered whether this gift was of the same order.

CHAPTER LI. MONEY AND MATRIMONY.

MONEY and matrimony! what a fine taking title! If that does not attract readers, we don't know what will. Money and matrimony! how different, yet how essentially combined, how intimately blended! "No money, no matrimony," might almost be written above some doors. Certainly money is an essential, but not so absorbing an essential as some people make it. Beyond the expenditure necessary for a certain establishment, a woman is seldom much the better for her husband's inordinate wealth. We have seen the wife of a reputed millionaire no better done by than that of a country squire.

Mr. Prospero Plutus may gild his coach and his harness, and his horses too, if he likes, but all the lacker in the world will not advance him a step in society; therefore, what can he do with his surplus cash but carry it to the "reserve fund," as some Joint-Stock Bankers pretend to do. Still there is a money-worship among us, that is not even confined to the opposite sex, but breaks out in veneration among men, just as if one man having half a million or a million pieces of gold could be of any advantage to another man, who only knows the rich man to say "How d'ye do?" to. A clever foreigner, who came to this country some years ago for the honestly avowed purpose of marrying an heiress, used to exclaim, when any one told him that another man had so many thousands a year, "Vell, my good friend, vot for that to me? I cannot go for be marry to him!" and we never hear a man recommended to another man for his wealth alone, without thinking of our foreign friend. What earthly good can Plutus's money do us? We can safely say, we never knew a rich man who was not uncommonly well able to take care of his cash. It is your poor men who are easy about money. To tell a young lady that a young gentleman has so many thousands a year is very different; and this observation leads us to say, that people who think they do a young man a kindness by exaggerating his means or expectations, are greatly mistaken. On the contrary, they do him an injury; for, sooner or later, the lawyers know everything, and disappointment and vexation is the result.

Since our friend Warren wrote his admirable novel, "Ten Thousand a Year," that sum has become the fashionable income for exaggerators. Nobody that has anything a year has less, though we all know how difficult a sum it is to realise, and how impossible it is to extract a five-pound note, or even a sovereign, from the pockets of people who talk of it as a mere bagatelle. This money mania has increased amazingly within the last few years, aided, no doubt, by the gigantic sums the Joint-Stock Banks have enabled penniless people to "go" for.

When Wainwright, the first of the assurance office defrauders by poison, was in prison, he said to a person who called upon him, "You see with what respect they treat me. They don't set me to make my bed, or sweep the yard, like those fellows," pointing to his brother prisoners; "no, they treat me like a gentleman. They think I'm in for ten thousand pounds." Ten thousand pounds! What would ten thousand pounds be nowadays, when men speculate to the extent of a quarter or may be half a million of money? Why Wainwright would have had to clean out the whole prison on the present scale of money delinquency. A hundred thousand pounder is quite a common fellow, hardly worth speaking of. There was a time when the greediest man was contented with his plum. Now the cry is "More! more!" until some fine morning the crier is "no more" himself.

This money-craving and boasting is all bad. It deceives young men, and drives those of moderate income into the London clubs, instead of their marrying and settling quietly as their fathers did before them. They hear of nothing but thousands and tens of thousands until they almost believe in the reality, and are ashamed to encounter the confessional stool of the lawyers, albeit they may have as much as with prudence and management would make married life comfortable. Boasting and exaggeration also greatly misleads and disappoints anxious "Mammas," all ready to believe whatever they like, causing very likely promising speculations to be abandoned in favour of what turn out great deal worse ventures. Only let a young man be disengaged, professionally and bodily, and some one or other will be sure to invest him with a fortune, or with surprising expectations from an uncle, an aunt, or other near relation. It is surprising how fond people are of fanning the flame of a match, and how they will talk about what they really know nothing, until an unfortunate youth almost appears to participate in their exaggerations. Could some of these Leviathans of fortune know the fabulous £ s. d. colours under which they have sailed, they would be wonderfully astonished at the extent of their innocent imposture. Yet they were not to blame because people said they had ten thousand a year, were richest commoners in fact. Many would then understand much unexplained politeness, and appreciate its disinterestedness at its true value. Captain Quaver would see why Mrs. Sunnybrow was so anxious that he should hear Matilda sing; Mr. Grist why Mrs. Snubwell manoeuvred to get him next Bridget at dinner; and perhaps our "Richest Commoner" why Mrs. Yammerton was so glad to see him back at the Grange.

CHAPTER LII. A NIGHT DRIVE.

PEOPLE who travel in the winter should remember it isn't summer, and time themselves accordingly. Sir Moses was so anxious to see Monsieur Rougier off the premises, in order to stop any extra hospitality, that he delayed starting for Lundyfoote Castle until he saw him fairly mounted on the gift grey and out of the stable-yard; he then had the mare put to the dog-cart, and tried to make up for lost time by extra speed upon the road. But winter is an unfavourable season for expedition; if highways are improving, turnpikes are getting neglected, save in the matter of drawing the officers' sinecure salaries, and, generally speaking, the nearer a turnpike is to a railway, the worse the turnpike is, as if to show the wonderful advantage of the former. So Sir Moses went flipping and flopping, and jipping and jerking, through Bedland and Hawksworth and Washingley-field, but scarcely reached the confines of his country when he ought to have been nearing the Castle. It was nearly four o'clock by the great gilt-lettered clock on the diminutive church in the pretty village of Tidswell, situated on the banks of the sparkling Lune, when he pulled up at the sign of the Hold-away Harriers to get his mare watered and fed. It is at these sort of places that the traveller gets the full benefit of country slowness and stupidity. Instead of the quick ostler, stepping smartly up to his horse's head as he reins up, there is generally a hunt through the village for old Tom, or young Joe, or some worthy who is either too old or too idle to work. In this case it was old bow-legged, wiry Tom Brown, whose long experience of the road did not enable him to anticipate a person's wants; so after a good stare at the driver, whom at first he thought was Mr. Meggison, the exciseman; then Mr. Puncheon, the brewer; and lastly, Mr. Mossman, Lord Polkaton's ruler; he asked, with a bewildered scratch of his head, "What, de ye want her put oop?"

"Oop, yes," replied Sir Moses; "what d'ye think I'm stopping for? Look alive; that's a good fellow," added he, throwing him the reins, as he prepared to descend from the vehicle.

"Oh, it's you, Sir Moses, is it," rejoined the now enlightened patriarch, "I didn't know you without your red coat and cap;" so saying, he began to fumble at the harness, and, with the aid of the Baronet, presently had the mare out of the shafts. It then occurred to the old gentleman that he had forgotten the key of the stable. "A sink," said he, with a dash of his disengaged hand, "I've left the key i' the pocket o' mar coat, down i' Willy Wood's shop, when ar was helpin' to kill a pig—run, lad, doon to Willy Wood," said he to a staring by-standing boy, "and get me mar coat," adding to Sir Moses, as the lad slunk unwillingly away, "he'll be back directly wi' it." So saying, he proceeded to lead the mare round to the stable at the back of the house.

When the coat came, then there was no pail; and when they got a pail, then the pump had gone dry; and when they got some water from the well, then the corn had to be brought from the top of the house; so, what with one delay and another, day was about done before Sir Moses got the mare out of the stable again. Night comes rapidly on in the short winter months, and as Sir Moses looked at the old-fashioned road leading over the steepest part of the opposite hill, he wished he was well on the far side of it. He then examined his lamps, and found there were no candles in them, just as he remembered that he had never been to Lundy-foote Castle on wheels, the few expeditions he had made there having been performed on horseback, by those nicks and cuts that fox-hunters are so famous at making and finding. "Ord dom it," said he to himself, "I shall be getting benighted. Tell me," continued he, addressing the old ostler, "do I go by Marshfield and Hengrove, or——"

"No, no, you've no business at noughter Marshfield nor Hengrove," interrupted the sage; "veer way is straight oop to Crowfield-hall and Roundhill-green, then to Brackley Moor and Belton, and so on into the Sandywell-road at Langley. But if ar were you," continued he, beginning to make confusion worse confounded, "ar would just gan through Squire Patterson's Park here," jerking his thumb to the left to indicate the direction in which it lay.

"Is it shorter?" demanded Sir Moses, re-ascending the vehicle.

"W-h-o-y no, it's not shorter," replied the man, "but it's a better road rayther—less agin collar-like. When ye get to the new lodge ye mun mind turn to the right, and keep Whitecliffe Law to the left, and Lidney Mill to the right, you then pass Shimlow tilery, and make straight for Roundhill Green, and Brackley Moor, and then on to Belton, as ar toll'd ye afoor—ye can't miss yeer way," added he, thinking he could go it in the dark himself.

"Can't I?" replied Sir Moses, drawing the reins. He then chucked the man a shilling, and touching the mare with the point of the whip, trotted across the bridge over the Lane, and was speedily brought up at a toll-bar on the far side.

It seems to be one of the ordinances of country life, that the more toll a man pays the worse road he gets, and Sir Moses had scarcely parted with his sixpence ere the sound running turnpike which tempted him past Squire Patterson's lodge, ran out into a loose, river-stoned track, that grew worse and worse the higher he ascended the hill. In vain he hissed, and jerked, and jagged at the mare. The wheels revolved as if they were going through sea-sand. She couldn't go any faster.

It is labour and sorrow travelling on wheels, with a light horse and a heavy load, on woolly winter roads, especially under the depressing influence of declining day—when a gorgeous sunset has no charms. It is then that the value of the hissing, hill-rounding, plain-scudding railway is appreciated. The worst line that ever was constructed, even one with goods, passengers, and minerals all mixed in one train, is fifty times better than one of these ploughing, sobbing, heart-breaking drives. So thought Sir Moses, as, whip in hand, he alighted from the vehicle to ease the mare up the steep hill, which now ran parallel with Mr. Patterson's rather indifferent park wall.

What a commentary on consequence a drive across country affords, One sees life in all its phases—Cottage, House, Grange, "Imperial John" Hall, Park, Tower, Castle, &c. The wall, however, is the true index of the whole. Show me your wall and I'll tell you what you have. There is the five hundred—by courtesy, thousand—a year wall, built of common stone, well embedded in mortar, extending only a few yards on either side of the lodgeless green gate. The thousand—by courtesy, fifteen hundred—a year wall, made of the same material, only the mortar ceases at the first convenient bend of the road, and the mortared round coping of the top is afterwards all that holds it together. Then there is the aspiring block and course wall, leading away with a sweep from either side of a handsome gateway, but suddenly terminating in hedges. The still further continued wall, with an abrupt juncture in split oak paling, that looks as if it had been suddenly nipped by a want-of-cash frost. We then get to the more successful all-round-the-park alike efforts of four or five thousand a-year—the still more solid masonry and ornamental work of "Ten Thousand a Year," a Warren wall in fact, until at length we come to one so strong and so high, that none but a man on a laden wain can see over it, which of course denotes a Ducal residence, with fifty or a hundred thousand a year. In like manner, a drive across country enables a man to pick up information without the trouble of asking for it.

The board against the tree at the corner of the larch plantation, stating that "Any one trespassing on these grounds, the property of A. B. C. Sowerby, Esq., will, &c., with the utmost, &c.," enables one to jump to the conclusion that the Westmoreland-slated roof we see peering among the eagle-winged cedars and luxuriant Scotch firs on the green slope to the left, is the residence of said Sowerby, who doesn't like to be trespassed upon. A quick-eyed land-agent would then trace the boundaries of the Sowerby estate from the rising ground, either by the size of its trees, its natural sterility, or by the rough, gateless fences, where it adjoins the neighbouring proprietors.

Again, the sign of the Smith Arms at a wayside public-house, denotes that some member of that illustrious family either lives or has property in that immediate neighbourhood, and as everybody has a friend Smith, we naturally set about thinking whether it is our friend Smith or not. So a nobleman's coronet surmounting his many-quartered coat-of-arms, suggests that the traveller is in the neighbourhood of magnificence; and if his appearance is at all in his favour, he will, perhaps, come in for a touch, or a demi-touch, of the hat from the passers-by, the process being almost mechanical in aristocratic parts. A board at a branch road with the words "To Lavender Lodge only," saves one the trouble of asking the name of the place towards which we see the road bending, while a great deal of curious nomenclature may be gleaned from shop-fronts, inn-signs, and cart-shafts.

But we are leaving Sir Moses toiling up the hill alongside of his dog-cart, looking now at his watch, now at his jaded mare, now at Mr. Patterson's fragile park wall, thinking how he would send it over with his shoulder if he came to it out hunting. The wall was at length abruptly terminated by a cross-road intersecting the hill along a favourable fall of the ground, about the middle of it, and the mare and Sir Moses mutually stopped, the former to ease herself on the piece of level ground at the junction, the latter to consider whether his course was up the hill or along the more inviting line to the left.

"Marshfield," muttered he to himself, "is surely that way, but then that old buffer said I had no business at Marshfield. Dom the old man," continued he, "I wish I'd never asked him anything about it, for he has completely bewildered me, and I believe I could have found my way better without."

So saying, Sir Moses reconnoitered the scene; the balance of the fat hill in front, with the drab-coloured road going straight up the steepest part of it, the diverging lines either way; above all, the fast closing canopy around. Across the road, to the right, was a paintless, weather-beaten finger-post, and though our friend saw it had lost two of its arms, he yet thought the remaining ones might give him some information. Accordingly, he went over to consult it. Not a word, no, not a letter was legible. There were some upright marks, but what they had stood for it was impossible to decipher. Sir Moses was nonplussed. Just at this critical moment, a rumbling sound proceeded from below, and looking down the hill, a grey speck loomed in the distance, followed by a darker one a little behind. This was consoling; for those who know how soon an agricultural country becomes quiet after once the labourers go to their homes can appreciate the boon of any stirrers.

Still the carts came very slowly, and the quick falling shades of night travelled faster than they. Sir Moses stood listening anxiously to their jolting noises, thinking they would never come up. At the same time, he kept a sharp eye on the cross-road, to intercept any one passing that way. A tinker, a poacher, a mugger, the veriest scamp, would have been welcome, so long as he knew the country. No one, however, came along. It was an unfrequented line; and old Gilbert Price, who worked by the day. always retired from raking in the mud ruts on the approach of evening. So Sir Moses stood staring and listening, tapping his boot with his whip, as he watched the zig-zag course of the grey up the hill. He seemed a good puller, and to understand his work, for as yet no guiding voice had been heard. Perhaps the man was behind. As there is always a stout pull just before a resting-place, the grey now came to a pause, to collect his energies for the effort.

Sir Moses looked at his mare, and then at the carts halting below, wondering whether if he left her she would take off. Just as he determined to risk it, the grey applied himself vigorously to the collar, and with a grinding, ploughing rush, came up to where Sir Moses stood.

The cart was empty, but there was a sack-like thing, with a wide-awake hat on the top, rolling in the one behind.

"Holloo, my man!" shouted Sir Moses, with the voice of a Stentor.

The wide-awake merely nodded to the motion of the cart.

"*Holloo, I say!*" roared he, still louder.

An extended arm was thrown over the side of the cart, and the wide-awake again nodded as before.

"The beggar's asleep!" muttered Sir Moses, taking the butt-end of his whip, and poking the somnambulist severely in the stomach.

A loud grunt, and with a strong smell of gin, as the monster changed his position, was all that answered the appeal.

"The brute's drunk," gasped Sir Moses, indignant at having wasted so much time in waiting for him.

The sober grey then made a well-rounded turn to the right, followed by the one in the rear, leaving our friend enveloped in many more shades of darkness than he was when he first designed him coming. Night had indeed about closed in, and lights began to appear in cottages and farm-houses that sparsedly dotted the hill side.

"Well, here's a pretty go," said Sir Moses, remounting the dogcart, and gathering up the reins; "I'll just give the mare her choice," continued he, touching her with the whip, and letting her go. The sensible animal took the level road to the left, and Sir Moses's liberality was at first rewarded by an attempted trot along it, which, however, soon relaxed into a walk. The creaking, labouring vehicle shook and rolled with the concussion of the ruts.

He had got upon a piece of township road, where each surveyor shuffled through his year of office as best he could, filling up the dangerous holes in summer with great boulder stones that turned up like flitches of bacon in winter. So Sir Moses rolled and rocked in imminent danger of an upset. To add to his misfortunes, he was by no means sure but that he might have to retrace his steps: it was all chance.

There are but two ways of circumventing a hill, either by going round it or over it; and the road, after evading it for some time, at length took a sudden turn to the right, and grappled fairly with its severity. The mare applied herself sedulously to her task, apparently cheered by the increasing lights on the hill. At length she neared them, and the radiant glow of a blacksmith's shop cheered the drooping spirit of the traveller.

"Holloo, my man!" cried Sir Moses, at length, pulling up before it.

"Holloo!" responded the spark-showering Vulcan from within.

"Is this the way to Lord Lundyfoote's?" demanded Sir Moses, knowing the weight a nobleman's name carries in the country.

"Lord Lundyfoote's!" exclaimed Osmand Hall, pausing in his work; "Lord Lundyfoote's!" repeated he; "why, where ha' you come from?"

"Tidswell," replied Sir Moses, catting off the former part of the journey.

"Why, what set ye this way?" demanded the dark man, coming to the door with a red-hot horse-shoe on a spike, which was nearly all that distinguished him from the gloom of night; "ye should never ha' coom'd this way; ye should ha' gone by Marshfield and Hengrove."

"Dom it, I said so!" ejaculated the Baronet, nearly stamping the bottom of his gig out with vexation. "However, never mind," continued he, recollecting himself, "I'm here now, so tell me the best way to proceed."

This information being at length accorded, Sir Moses proceeded; and the rest of the hill being duly surmounted, the dancing and stationary lights spreading o'er the far-stretching vale now appeared before him, with a clustering constellation, amid many minor stars scattered around, denoting the whereabouts of the castle.

It is always cheering to see the far end of a journey, distant though the haven be, and Sir Moses put on as fast as his lampless condition would allow him, trusting to his eyes and his ears for keeping on the road. Very much surprised would he have been had he retraced his steps the next morning, and seen the steep banks and yawning ditches he had suddenly saved himself from going over or into by catching at the reins or feeling either wheel running in the soft.

At length he reached the lodges of the massive variously-windowed castle, and passing gladly through them, found, on alighting at the door, that, instead of being late for dinner as he anticipated, his Lordship, who always ate a hearty lunch, was generally very easy about the matter, sometimes dining at seven, sometimes at eight, sometimes in summer even at nine o'clock. The footman, in reply to Sir Moses inquiring what time his Lordship dined, said he believed it was ordered at seven, but he didn't know when it would be on the table.

Being an ardent politician, Lord Lundyfoote received Sir Moses with the fellow-feeling that makes us wondrous kind cordiality, and dived so energetically into his subject, as soon as he got the weather disposed of, as never to wait for an answer to his question, whether his guest would like to take anything before dinner, the consequence of which was, that our poor friend was nearly famished with waiting. In vain the library time-piece ticked, and chimed, and struck; jabber, jabber, jabber, went his voluble Lordship; in vain the deep-toned castle-clock reverberated through the walls—on, on he went, without noticing it. until the butler, in apparent despair, took the gong, and gave it such a beating just outside the door, that he could scarcely hear himself speak. Sir Moses then adroitly slipped in the question if that was the signal for dressing; to which his Lordship having yielded a reluctant "Yes," he took a candle from the entering footman, and pioneered the Baronet up to his bedroom, amid a running commentary on the state of the country and the stability of the ministry. And when he returned he found his Lordship distributing his opinions amoung an obsequious circle of neighbours, who received all he said with the deference due to a liberal dispenser of venison; so that Sir Moses not only got his dinner in comparative peace, but warded his Lordship off the greater part of the evening.

CHAPTER LIII. MASTER ANTHONY THOM.

THE two-penny post used to be thought a great luxury in London, though somehow great people were often shy of availing themselves of its advantages, indeed of taking their two-penny-posters in. "Two-penny-posters," circulars, and ticketed shops, used to be held in about equal repugnance by some. The Dons, never thought of sending their notes or cards of invitation by the two-penny post. John Thomas used always to be trotted out for the purpose of delivery. Pre-paying a letter either by the two-penny post or the general used to be thought little short of an insult. Public opinion has undergone a great change in these matters. Not paying them is now the offence. We need scarcely expatiate on the boon of the penny post, nor on the advantage of the general diffusion of post-offices throughout the country, though we may observe, that the penny post was one of the few things that came without being long called for: indeed, so soon as it was practicable to have it, for without the almost simultaneous establishment of railways it would have been almost impossible to have introduced the system. The mail could not have carried the newspaper traffic and correspondence of the present day. The folded tablecloths of *Times*, the voluminous *Illustrated News*, the *Punch's*, the huge avalanches of papers that have broken upon the country within the last twenty years. Sir Moses Mainchance, unlike many country gentlemen, always had his letters forwarded to him where-ever he went. He knew it was only the trouble of writing a line to the Post-office, saying re-direct my letters to so-and-so, to have what he wanted, and thus to keep pace with his correspondence. He was never overpowered with letters when he came home from a visit or tour, as some of our acquaintance are, thus making writing doubly repugnant to them.

The morning after his arrival at Lundyfoote Castle brought him a great influx of re-directed letters and papers. One from Mr. Heslop, asking him to meet at his house on the Friday week following, as he was going to have a party, one from Signior Quaverini, the eminent musician, offering his services for the Hunt ball: one from Mr. Isinglass, the confectioner, hoping to be allowed to supply the ices and refreshment as usual; another (the fifth), from Mr. Mossman, about the damage to Mr. Anthill's sown grass; an envelope, enclosing the card and terms of Signior Dulcetto, an opposition musician, offering lower terras than Quaverini; a note from Mr. Paul Straddler, telling him about a horse to be bought dog cheap; and a "dead letter office" envelope, enclosing a blue ink written letter, directed to Master Anthony Thom, at the Inn-in-the-Sands Inn, Beechwood Green, stating that the party was not known at the address, reintroduces Mr. Geordey Gallon, a gentleman already known to the reader.

How this letter came to be sent to Sir Moses was as follows:—

When Mr. Geordey Gallon went upon the "Torf," as he calls it, becoming, as he considered, the associate of Princes, Prime Ministers, and so on, he bethought him of turning respectable, and giving up the stolen-goods-carrying-trade,—a resolution that he was further confirmed in by the establishment of that troublesome obnoxious corps the Hit-im-and-Hold-im-shire Rural Police.

To this end, therefore, he gradually reduced the number of his Tippy-Tom-jaunts through the country by night, intimating to his numerous patrons that they had better suit themselves elsewhere ere he ceased travelling altogether.

Among the inconvenienced, was our old friend Mrs. Margerum, long one of his most regular customers; for it was a very rare thing for Mr. Gallon not to find a carefully stitched-up bundle in the corner of Lawyer Hindmarch's cattle-shed, abutting on the Shillburn road as he passed in his spring cart.

To remedy this serious inconvenience, Mrs. Margerum had determined upon inducting her adopted son, Master Anthony Thom, into the about-to-be-relinquished business; and Mr. Gallon having made his last journey, the accumulation of dripping caused by our hero's visit to Pangburn Park made it desirable to have a clearing-out as soon as possible.

To this end, therefore, she had written the letter now sent to Sir Moses; but, being a very prudent woman, with a slight smattering of law, she thought so long as she did not sign her surname at the end she was safe, and that no one could prove that it was from her. The consequence was, that Anthony Thom not having shifted his quarters as soon as intended, the letter was refused at the sign of the Sun-in-the-Sands, and by dint of postmark and contents, with perhaps a little *malice prepense* on the part of the Post-master, who had suffered from a dishonest housekeeper himself, it came into the hands of Sir Moses. At first our master of the hounds thought it was a begging-letter, and threw it aside accordingly; but in course of casting about for a fresh idea wherewith to propitiate Mr. Mossman about the sown grass, his eye rested upon the writing, which he glanced at, and glanced at, until somehow he thought he had seen it before. At length he took the letter up, and read what made him stare very much as he proceeded. Thus it run:—

"PANGBURN PARK, Thursday Night.

"My own ever dear Anthony Thom,

"*I write to you, trusting you will receive this safe, to say that as Mr. George Gallon has discontinued travelling altogether, I must trust to you entirely to do what is necessary in futur, but you must be most careful and watchful, for these nasty Pollis fellers are about every where, and seem to think they have a right to look into every bodies basket and bundle. We live in terrible times, I'm sure, my own beloved Anthony Thom, and if it wasn't for the hope that I may see you become a great gentleman, like Mr. George Gallon, I really think I would forswear place altogether, for no one knows the anxiety and misery of living with such a nasty, mean, covetous body as Old Nosey.*"

"Old Nosey!" ejaculated Sir Moses, stopping short in his reading, and feeling his proboscis; "Old Nosey! dom it, can that mean me? Do believe it does—and it's mother Margerum's handwriting—dom'd if it isn't," continued he, holding the letter a little way off to examine and catch the character of the writing; "What does she mean by calling me a nasty, covetous body? I that hunt the country, subscribe to the Infirmary, Agricultural Society, and do everything that's liberal and handsome. I'll Old Nosey her!" continued he, grinding his teeth, and giving a vigorous flourish of his right fist; "I'll Old Nosey her! I'll turn her out of the house as soon as ever I get home, dom'd if I won't," said Sir Moses quivering with rage as he spoke. At length he became sufficiently composed to resume his reading—

"*-No one knows the anxiety and misery of living with such a nasty, mean, covetous body as Old Nosey, who is always on the fret about expense, and thinks everybody is robbing him.*"

"Oh, dom it, that means me sure enough!" exclaimed Sir Moses; "that's on account of the row I was kicking up t'other day about the tea—declared I drank a pound a week myself. I'll tea her!" continued he, again turning to the letter and reading,—

"*-I declare I'd almost as soon live under a mistress as under such a shocking mean, covetous man.*"

"Would you?" muttered Sir Moses; adding, "you shall very soon have a chance then." The letter thus continued,—

"*-The old feller will be away on Saturday and Sunday, so come afore lightning on Monday morning, say about four o'clock, and I'll have everything ready to lower from my window.*"

"Oh the deuce!" exclaimed Sir Moses, slapping his leg; "Oh the deuce! going to rob the house, I declare!"

"*-To lower from my window*" read he again, "*for it's not safe trusting things by the door as we used to do, now that these nasty knavish Pollis fellers are about; so now my own beloved Anthony Thom, if you will give a gentle whistle, or throw a little bit of soft dirt up at the window, where you will see a light burning, I'll be ready for you, and you'll be clear of the place long afore any of the lazy fellers here are up,—for a set of nastier, dirtier drunkards never were gathered together.*"

"Humph!" grunted Sir Moses, "that's a cut at Mr. Findlater." The writer then proceeded to say,—

"*—But mind my own beloved Anthony Thom, if any body questions you., say it's a parcel of dripping, and tell them they are welcome to look in if they like, which is the readiest way of stopping them from doing so. We have had a large party here, including a young gent from that fine old Lord Ladythorne, who I would dearly like to live with, and also that nasty, jealous, covetous body Cuddy Flintoff, peeping and prying about everywhere as usual. He deserves to have a dish-clout pinned to his tail.*"

"*He, he, he!*" chuckled Sir Moses, as he read it

"-I shall direct this letter by post to you at the sign of the Sun in the Sands, unless I can get it conveyed by a private hand. I am half in hopes Mr. Gallon may call, as there is going to be a great steeple match for an immense sum of money, £200 they say, and they will want his fine judgment to direct matters. Mr. Gallon is indeed a man of a thousand."

"Humph!" grunted Sir Moses, adding, "we are getting behind the curtain now." He then went on reading,—

"—Oh my own dear darling Anthony Thom! what would I give to see you a fine gentleman like Mr. George Gallon. I do hope and trust, dearest, that it may yet come to pass; but we must make money, and take care of our money when made, for a man is nothing without money. What a noble example you have before you in Mr. George Gallon! He was once no better nor you, and now he has everything like a gentleman,—a hunting horse to ride on, gold studs in his shirt, and goose for his dinner. O my own beloved Anthony Thom, if I could but see you on a white horse, with a flowered silk tie, and a cut velvet vest with bright steel buttons, flourishing a silver-mounted whip, how glad, how rejoiced it would make me. Then I shouldn't care for the pryings and grumblings of Old Nosey, or the jealous watchings of the nasty, waspish set with which one is surrounded, for I should say my Anthony Thom will revenge and protect me, and make me comfortable at last. So now my own dearest Anthony Thom, be careful and guarded in coming about here, for I dread those nasty lurkin Pollis men more nor can I say, for I never knew suspicious people what were good for any thing themselves; and how they ever come to interduce such nasty town pests into the quiet peaceful country, I can't for the life of me imagine; but Mr. George Gallon, who is a man of great intellect, says they are dangerous, and that is partly why he has given up travelling; so therefore my own dearest Anthony Thom be guarded, and mind put on your pee jacket and red worsted comforter, for I dread these hoar frosts, and I'll have everything ready for my darling pet, so that you won't be kept waiting a moment; but mind if there's snow on the ground you don't come for fear of the tracks. I think I have littel more to say this time, my own darling Anthony Thom, except that I am, my own dear, dear son,

"Your ever loving mother,
"Sarah."

"B-o-o-y Jove!" exclaimed Sir Moses, sousing himself down in an easy chair beside the table at which he had been writing "b-o-y Jove, what a production! Regular robber, dom'd if she's not. Would give something to catch Master Anthony Thom, in his red worsted comforter, with his parcel of dripping. Would see whether I'd look into it or not. And Mr. Geordey Gallon, too! The impudent fellow who pretended not to know the Frenchman. Regular plant as ever was made. Will see whether he gets his money from me. Ten punds the wretch tried to do me ont of by the basest deceit that ever was heard of. Con-found them, but I'll see if I can't be upsides with them all though," continued he, writhing for vengeance. And the whole of that day, and most of that night, and the whole of the following day when hunting at Harker Crag, he was thinking how he could manage it. At length, as he was going quietly home with the hounds, after only an indifferent day's sport, a thought struck him which he proceeded to put in execution as soon as he got into the house. He wrote a note to dear Lord Repartee, saying, if it would be quite convenient to Lady Repartee and his Lordship, he would be glad to stay all night with them before hunting Filberton forest; and leaving the unfolded note on the library table to operate during the night, he wrote a second one in the morning, inquiring the character of a servant; and putting the first note into the fire, he sealed the second one, and laid it ostentatiously on the hall table for the post.

We take it we all have some ambitious feeling to gratify—all have some one whom we either wish to visit, or who we desire should visit us. We will candidly state that our ambition is to dine with the Lord Mayor. If we could but achieve that great triumph, we really think we should rest satisfied the rest of our life. We know how it would elevate us in the eyes of such men as Cuddy Flintoff and Paul Straddler, and what an advantage it would be to us in society being able to talk in a familiar way of his Lordship (Lordship with a capital L., if you please, Mr. Printer).

Thus the world proceeds on the aspiring scale, each man looking to the class a little in advance of his own.

"O knew they but their happiness, of men the happiest" are the sporting country gentlemen who live at home at ease—unvexed alike with the torments of the money-maker and the anxieties of the great, and yet sufficiently informed and refined to be the companions of either—men who see and enjoy nature in all her moods and varieties, and live unfettered with the pomp and vexation of keeping up appearances, envying no one, whoever may envy them. If once a man quits this happy rank to breast the contending billows of party in hopes of rising to the one above it, what a harvest of discord he sows for his own reaping. If a man wants to be thoroughly disgusted with human nature, let him ally himself unreservedly to a political party. He will find cozening and sneaking and selfishness in all their varieties, and patriotic false pretences in their most luxuriant growth. But we are getting in advance of our subject, our thesis being Mr. and Mrs. Wotherspoon.

Our snuffy friend Spoon was not exempt from the ambitious failings of lesser men. His great object of ambition was to get Major Yammerton to visit him—or perhaps to put it more correctly, his great object of ambition was to visit Major Yammerton. But then, unfortunately, it requires two parties to these bargains; and Mrs. Yammerton wouldn't agree to it, not so much because old Spoon had been a butler, but because his wife (our pen splutters as it writes the objection) his wife had been a—a—housekeeper. A handsome housekeeper she was, too, when she first came into the country; so handsome, indeed, that Dicky Boggledike had made two excursions over to their neighbour, Farmer Flamstead, to see her, and had reported upon her very favourably to the noble Earl his august master.

Still Mrs. Yammerton wouldn't visit her. In vain Mrs. Wotherspoon sent her bantams' eggs, and guinea fowls' eggs, and cuttings from their famous yellow rose-tree; in vain old Spoon got a worn-out horse, and invested his nether man in white cords and top boots to turn out after the harriers; in vain he walked a hound in summer, and pulled down gaps, and lifted gates off their hinges in winter—it all only produced thanks and politeness. The Yammertons and they were very good How-do-you-do? neighbours, but the true beef-and-mutton test of British friendship was wanting. The dinner is the thing that signs and seals the acquaintance.

Thus they had gone on from summer to summer, and from season to season, until hope deferred had not only made old Spoon's heart sick, but had also seen the white cords go at the knees, causing him to retire his legs into the military-striped cinnamon-coloured tweeds in which he appears in:

n addition to muffling his legs, he had begun to mutter and talk about giving up hunting,—getting old,—last season—and so on, which made the Major think he would be losing one of the most personable of his field. This made him pause and consider how to avert the misfortune. Hunted hares he had sent him in more than regular rotation: he had liquored him repeatedly at the door; the ladies had reciprocated the eggs and the cuttings, with dahlias, and Sir Harry strawberry runners; and there really seemed very little left about the place wherewith to propitiate a refractory sportsman. At this critical juncture, a too confiding hare was reported by Cicely Bennett, farmer Merry field's dairymaid, to have taken up her quarters among some tussuckey brambles at the north-east corner of Mr. Wotherspoon's cow pasture—a most unusual, indeed almost unprecedented circumstance, which was communicated by Wotherspoon in person to the Major at the next meet of the hounds at Girdle Stone Green, and received with unfeigned delight by the latter.

"You don't say so!" exclaimed he, wringing the old dandy's hand; "you don't say so!" repented he, with enthusiasm, for hares were scarce, and the country good; in addition to which the Major knew all the gaps.

"*I do*," replied Spoon, with a confident air, that as good as said, you may take my word for anything connected with hunting.

"Well, then, I'll tell you what we'll do," rejoined the Major, poking him familiarly in the ribs with his whip, "I'll tell you what we'll do; we'll have a turn at her on Tuesday—meet at your house, eh? what say you to that?"

"With all my heart," responded the delighted Wotherspoon, adding, in the excitement of the moment, "S'pose you come to breakfast?"

"Breakfast," gasped the Major, feeling he was caught. "Dash it, what would Mrs. Yammerton say? Breakfast!" repeated he, running the matter through his mind, the wigging of his wife, the walk of his hound, the chance of keeping the old boy to the fore if he went—go he would. "With all my heart," replied he, dashing boldly at the oiler; for it's of no use a man saying he's engaged to breakfast, and the Major felt that if the worst came to the worst, it would only be to eat two, one at home, the other with Spoon.

So it was settled, much to Mr. and Mrs. Wotherspoon's satisfaction, who were afterwards further delighted to hear that our friend Billy had returned, and would most likely be of the party. And most assiduously they applied themselves to provide for this, the great event of their lives.

CHAPTER LIV. MR. WITHERSPOON'S DEJEUNER À LA FOURCHETTE.

IVY BANK 'Power (formerly caled Cow gate Hill), the seat of Jeames Wotherspoon Esquire, stands on a gentle eminence about a stone's throw from the Horseheath and Hinton turnpike road, and looks from the luxuriance of its ivy, like a great Jack-in-the-green. Ivy is a troublesome thing, for it will either not grow at all or it grows far too fast, and Wotherspoon's had rairly overrun the little angular red brick, red tiled mansion, and helped it to its new name of Ivy Bank Tower. If the ivy flourished, however, it was the only thing about the place that did; for Wotherspoon was no farmer, and the 75a,:5r. 18p, of which the estate consisted, was a very uninviting looking property. Indeed Wotherspoon was an illustration of the truth of Sydney Smith's observation that there are three things which every man thinks he can do, namely, drive a gig, edit a newspaper, and farm a small property, and Spoon bought Cowgate Hill thinking it would "go of itself." as they say of a horse, and that in addition to the rent he would get the farmer's profit as well, which he was told ought to be equal to the rent. Though he had the Farmers' Almanack, he did not attend much to its instructions, for if Mrs. Wotherspoon wanted the Fe-a-ton, as she called it, to gad about the country in, John Strong, the plough-boy footman "loused" his team, and arraying himself in a chocolate-coloured coat, with a red striped vest and black velveteens, left the other horse standing idle for the day. So Spoon sometimes caught the season and sometimes he lost it; and the neighbours used to hope that he hadn't to live by his land. If he caught the season he called it good management; if he didn't he laid the blame upon the weather, just as a gardener takes the credit for all the good crops of fruit, and attributes the failures to the seasons. Still Spoon was not at all sensible of his deficiencies, and subscribed a couple of guineas a year to the *Harrowford Agricultural Society*, in return for which he always had the toast of the healths of the tenant farmers assigned to him, which he handled in a very magnificent and condescending way, acknowledging the obligations the landowners were under to them, and hoping the happy union would long subsist to their mutual advantage; indeed, if he could only have got the words out of his mouth as fast as he got the drink into it, there is no saying but he might some day have filled the presidential chair. Now, however, a greater honour even than that awaited him, namely, the honour of entertaining the great Major Yammerton to breakfast. To this end John Strong was first set to clean the very dirty windows, then to trim the ivy and polish the brass knocker at the door, next to dig the border, in which grew the famous yellow rose, and finally to hoe and rake the carriage-drive up to the house; while Mrs. Wotherspoon, aided by Sally Brown, her maid-of-all-work, looked out the best blue and gold china, examined the linen, selected a tongue, guillotined the poultry, bespoke the eggs, and arranged the general programme of the entertainment.

The Major thought himself very sly, and that he was doing the thing very cleverly by nibbling and playing with his breakfast on the appointed morning, instead of eating voraciously as usual; but ladies often know a good deal more than they pretend to do, and Mrs. Yammerton had seen a card from Mrs. Wotherspoon to their neighbour, Mrs. Broadfurrow, of Blossomfield Farm, inviting Broadfurrow and her to a "*déjeuner à la fourchette*" to meet Major Yammerton and see the hounds. However, Mrs. Yammerton kept the fact to herself, thinking she would see how her Major would manoeuvre the matter, and avoid a general acquaintance with the Wotherspoons. So she merely kept putting his usual viands before him, to try to tempt him into indulgence; but the Major, knowing the arduous part he would have to perform at the Tower, kept rejecting all her insidious overtures for eating, pretending he was not altogether right. "Almond pudding hadn't agreed with him," he thought. "Never did—should have known better than take it," and so on.

Our dawdling hero rather discontented his host, for instead of applying himself sedulously to his breakfast, he did nothing but chatter and talk to the young ladies, as if there was no such important performance before them as a hare to pursue, or the unrivalled harriers to display. he took cup after cup, as though he had lost his reckoning, and also the little word "no" from his vocabulary. At length the Major got him raised from the table, by telling him they had two miles farther to go than they really had, and making for the stable, they found Solomon and the footman whipper-in ready to turn out with the hounds. Up went our sportsmen on to their horses, and forth came the hounds wriggling and frolicking with joy. The cavalcade being thus formed, they proceeded across the fields, at the back of the house, and were presently passing up the Hollington Lane. The gift grey was the first object of interest as soon as they got well under way, and the Major examined him attentively, with every desire to find fault.

"Neatish horse," at length observed he, half to himself, half to our friend; "neatish horse—lightish of bone below the knee, p'raps, but still by no means a bad shaped 'un."

Still though the Major could'nt hit off the fault, he was pretty sure there was a screw loose somewhere, to discover which he now got Billy to trot the horse, aud cauter him, and gallop him, successively.

"Humph!" grunted he, as he returned after a brush over the rough ground of Farthingfield Moor; "he has the use of his legs—gets well away; easy horse under you, I dessay?" asked he.

Billy said he was, for he could pull him about anywhere; saying which he put him boldly at a water furrow, and lauded handsomely on the far side.

"Humph!" grunted the Major again, muttering to himself, "May be all right—but if he is, it's devilish unlike the Baronet, giving him. Wish he would take that confounded moon-eyed brute of mine and give me my forty puns back."

"And he gave him ye, did he?" asked the Major, with a scrutinising stare at our friend.

"Why—yarse—no—yarse—not exactly," replied Billy, hesitating. "The fact is, he offered to give me him. and I didn't like taking him, and so, after a good deal to do, he said I might give him fifty pounds for him, and pay him when it suited me."

"I twig," replied the Major, adding, "then you have to pay fifty pounds for him, eh?"

"Or return him," replied Billy, "or return him. He made me promise if ever I wanted to part with him, I would give him the refusal of him again."

"Humph!" grunted the Major, looking the horse over attentively. "Fifty puns," muttered he to himself,—"must be worth that if he's sound, and only eight off. Wouldn't mind giving fifty for him myself," thought he; "must be something wrong about him—certain of that—or Sir Moses wouldn't have parted with him;" with which firm conviction, and the full determination to find out the horse's weak point, the Major trotted along the Bodenham Road, through the little hamlet of Maywood, thence across Faulder the cattle jobber's farm, into the Heath-field Road at Gilden Bridge. A quarter of a mile further, and Mr. Wotherspoon's residence was full in sight.

The "Tower" never, perhaps, showed to greater advantage than it did on this morning, for a bright winter's sun lit up the luxuriant ivy on its angular, gable-ended walls, nestling myriads of sparrows that flew out in flocks at the approach of each visitor.

"What place is this?" asked our hero, as, at a jerk of the Major's head, Solomon turned off the road through the now propped-open gate of the approach to the mansion.

"Oh, this is where we meet," replied the Major; "this is Mr. Wotherspoon's, the gentleman you remember out with us the day we had the famous run when we lost the hare at Mossheugh Law—the farm by the moor, you know, where the pretty woman was churning—you remember, eh?"

"O, ah!" repeated Billy: "but I thought they called his place a Tower,—Ivy something Tower," thinking this was more like two great sentry boxes placed at right angles, and covered with ivy than anything else.

"Well, yes; he calls this a Tower," replied the Major, seeing by Billy's face that his friend had not risen in his estimation by the view of his mansion. "Capital feller Spoon, though," continued he, "must go in and pay our respects to him and his lady." So saying, he turned off the road upon the closely eaten sward, and, calling to Solomon to stop and let the hounds have a roll on the grass, he dismounted, and gave his horse in charge of a fustian-clad countryman, telling him to walk him about till he returned, and he would remember him for his trouble. Our friend Billy did the same, and knocking the mud sparks off his boots against the well pipe-clayed door-steps, prepared to enter the Tower. Before inducting them, however, let us prepare the inmates for their reception.

Both Mr. and Mrs. Wotherspoon had risen sufficiently early to enable them to put the finishing stroke to their respective arrangements, and then to apparel themselves for the occasion. They were gorgeously attired, vieing with the rainbow in the colour of their clothes. Old Spoon, indeed, seemed as if he had put all the finery on he could raise, and his best brown cauliflower wig shone resplendent with Macassar oil. He had on a light brown coat with a rolling velvet collar, velvet facings and cuffs, with a magnificent green, blue, and yellow striped tartan velvet vest, enriched with red cornelian buttons, and crossed diagonally with a massive Brazilian gold chain, and the broad ribbon of his gold double-eye-glasses. He sported a light blue satin cravat, an elaborately worked ruby-studded shirt front, over a pink flannel vest, with stiff wrist-bands well turned up, showing the magnificence of his imitation India garnet buttons. On his clumsy fingers he wore a profusion of rings—a brilliant cluster, a gold and opal, a brilliant and sapphire, an emerald half-hoop ring, a massive mourning, and a signet ring,—six in all,—genuine or glass as the case might be, equally distributed between the dirty-nailed fingers of each hand. His legs were again encased in the treacherous white cords and woe-begone top-boots that were best under the breakfast table. He had drawn the thin cords on very carefully, hoping they would have the goodness to hang together for the rest of the day.

Mrs. Wotherspoon was bedizened with jewellery and machinery lace. She wore a rich violet-coloured velvet dress, with a beautiful machinery lace chemisette, fastened down the front with large Cairngorum buttons, the whole connected with a diminutive Venetian chain, which contrasted with the massive mosaic one that rolled and rattled upon her plump shoulders. A splendid imitation emerald and brilliant brooch adorned her bust, while her well-rounded arms were encircled with a mosaic gold, garnet and turquoise bracelet, an imitation rose diamond one, intermixed with pearl, a serpent armlet with blood-stone eyes, a heavy jet one, and an equally massive mosaic gold one with a heart's ease padlock. Though in the full development of womanhood, she yet distended her figure with crinoline, to the great contraction of her room.

The two had scarcely entered the little parlour, some twelve feet square, and Spoon got out his beloved Morning Post, ere Mr. and Mrs. Broadfurrow were seen wending their way up the road, at the plodding diligent sort of pace an agricultural horse goes when put into harness; and forthwith the Wotherspoons dismissed the last anxieties of preparation, and lapsed into the easy, unconcerned host and hostess. When John Strong threw open the door, and announced Mr. and Mrs. Broadfurrow, they were discovered standing over the fire, as if d'ejeuner à la fourchette giving was a matter of every day's occurrence with them. Then, at the summons, they turned and came forward in the full glow of cordiality, and welcomed their guests with all the fervour of sincerity; and when Mrs. Wotherspoon mounted the weather for a trot with Mrs. Broadfurrow, old Spoon out with his engine-turned gold snuff-box, and offered Broadfurrow a pinch ere he threw his conversation into the columns of his paper. The offer being accepted, Wotherspoon replenished his own nose, and then felt ready for anything. He was in high feather. He sunk his favourite topic, the doings of the House of Lords, and expatiated upon the Princess Royal's then approaching marriage. Oh, dear, he was so glad. He was so glad of it—glad of it on every account—glad of it on the Princess's account—glad of it on her most gracious Majesty's account. Bless her noble heart! it almost made him feel like an old man when he remembered the Prince Consort leading her to the hymeneal altar herself. Well, well, life was life, and he had seen as much of it as most men; and just as he was going to indulge in some of his high-flown reminiscences, the crack of a hunting whip sounded through the house, and farmer Nettlefold's fat figure, attired in the orthodox green coat and white cords of the Major Yammerton's hunt was seen piled on a substantial brown cob, making his way to the stables at the back of the Tower. Mr. Nettlefold, who profanely entered by the back door, was then presently announced, and the same greetings having been enacted towards him, Wotherspoon made a bold effort to get back to the marriage, beginning with "As I was observing," when farmer Rintoul came trotting up on his white horse, and holloaed out to know if he could get him put up.

"Oh, certainly," replied Wotherspoon, throwing up the window, when a sudden gust of wind nearly blew off his wig, and sadly disconcerted the ladies by making the chimney smoke.

Just at this moment our friend appeared in sight, and all eyes were then directed to the now gamboling tongue-throwing hounds, as they spread frisking over the green.

"What beauties!" exclaimed Mrs. Wotherspoon, pretending to admire them, though in reality she was examining the Point de Paris lace on Mrs. Broadfurrow's mantle—wondering what it would be a yard, thinking it was very extravagant for a person like her to have it so broad. Old Spoon, meanwhile, bustled away to the door, to be ready to greet the great men as they entered.

"Major Yammerton and Mr. Jingle!" announced John Strong, throwing it open, and the old dandy bent nearly double with his bow.

"How are ye, Wotherspoon?" demanded our affable master, shaking him heartily by the hand, with a hail-fellow-well-met air of cordiality. "Mr. Pringle you know," continued he, drawing our friend forward with his left hand, while he advanced with his right to greet the radiant Mrs. Wotherspoon.

The Major then went the round of the party, whole handing Mrs. Broadfurrow, three fingering her husband, presenting two to old Rintonl, and nodding to Nettlefold.

"Well, here's a beautiful morning," observed he, now Colossus-of-Rhodesing with his clumsily built legs—"most remarkable season this I ever remember during the five-and-thirty years that I have kept haryers—more like summer than winter, only the trees are as bare of leaves as boot-trees, *haw, haw, haw.*"

"*He, he, he,*" chuckled old Wotherspoon, "v-a-a-ry good, Major, v-a-a-ry good," drawled he, taking a plentiful replenishment of snuff as he spoke.

Breakfast was then announced, and the Major making up to the inflated Mrs. Wotherspoon tendered his arm, and with much difficulty piloted her past the table into the little duplicate parlour across the passage, followed by Wotherspoon with Mrs. Broadfurrow and the rest of the party.

And now the fruits of combined science appeared in the elegant arrangement of the breakfast-table, the highly polished plate vieing with the snowy whiteness of the cloth, and the pyramidical napkins encircling around. Then there was the show pattern tea and coffee services, chased in wreaths and scrolls, presented to Mr. Wotherspoon by the Duke of Thunderdownshire on his marriage; the Louis Quatorze kettle presented to Mrs. Wotherspoon by the Duchess, with the vine-leaf-patterned cake-basket, the Sutherland-patterned toast-rack, and the tulip-patterned egg-stand, the gifts and testimonials of other parties.

Nor was the entertainment devoted to mere show, for piles of cakes and bread of every shape and make were scattered profusely about, while a couple of covered dishes on the well polished little sideboard denoted that the fourchette of the card was not a mere matter of form. Best of all, a group of flat vine-leaf encircling Champagne glasses denoted that the repast was to be enlivened with the exhilarating beverage.

The party having at length settled into seats, Major Yammerton on Mrs. Wotherspoon's right, Mr. Pringle on her left, Mrs. Broadfurrow on Spoon's right, her husband on his left, with Rintoul and Nettlefold filling in the interstices, breakfast began in right earnest, and Mrs. Wotherspoon having declined the Major's offer of assisting with the coffee, now had her hands so full distributing the beverages as to allow him to apply himself sedulously to his food. This he did most determinedly, visiting first one detachment of cakes, then another, and helping himself liberally to both hashed woodcocks and kidneys from under the covers. His quick eye having detected the Champagne glasses, and knowing Wotherspoon's reputed connoisseurship in wines, he declined Mrs. Wotherspoon's tea, reserving himself for what was to follow. In truth, Spoon was a good judge of wine, so much so that he acted as a sort of decoy duck to a London house, who sent him very different samples to the wine they supplied to the customers with whom he picked up. He had had a great deal of experience in wines, never, in the course of a longish life having missed the chance of a glass, good, bad, or indifferent. We have seen many men set up for judges without a tithe of Wotherspoon's experience. Look at a Club for instance. We see the footman of yesterday transformed into the butler of to-day, giving his opinion to some newly joined member on the next, with all the authority of a professor—talking of vintages, and flavours, and roughs and smooths, and sweets, and drys, as if he had been drinking wine all his life. Wotherspoon's prices were rather beyond the Major's mark, but still he had no objection to try his wine, and talk as if he would like to have some of the same sort. So having done ample justice to the eatables he turned himself back in his chair and proceeded to criticise Mrs. Wotherspoon's now slightly flushed face, and wonder how such a pretty woman could marry such a snuffy old cock. While this deliberate scrutiny was going on, the last of the tea-drinkers died out, and at a pull of the bell, John Strong came in, and after removing as many cups and saucers as he could clutch, he next proceeded to decorate the table with Champagne glasses amid the stares and breath-drawings of the company.

While this interesting operation was proceeding, the old dandy host produced his snuff-box, and replenishing his nose passed it on to Broadfurrow to send up the table, while he threw himself back in his chair and made a mental wager that Strong would make a mistake between the Champagne and the Sillery. The glasses being duly distributed, and the Major's eye at length caught, our host after a prefatory throat-clearing hem thus proceeded to address him, individually, for the good of the company generally.

"Major Yammerton," said he, "I will take the liberty of recommending a glass of Sillery to you.—The sparkling, I believe, is very good, but the still is what I particularly pride myself upon and recommend to my friends."

"Strong!" continued he, addressing the clown, "the Sillery to Major Yammerton," looking at Strong as much as to say, "you know it's the bottle with the red cord round the neck."

The Major, however, like many of us, was not sufficiently versed in the delicacies of Champagne drinking to prefer the Sillery, and to his host's dismay called for the sparkling-stuff that Wotherspoon considered was only fit for girls at a boarding school. The rest of the party, however, were of the Major's opinion, and all glasses were eagerly held for the sparkling fluid, while the Sillery remained untouched to the master.

It is but justice to Wotherspoon to add, that he showed himself deserving of the opportunity, for he immediately commenced taking two glasses to his guest's one.

That one having been duly sipped and quaffed and applauded, and a becoming interval having elapsed between, Mr. Wotherspoon next rose from his chair, and looking especially wise, observed, up the table "that there was a toast he wished—he had—he had—he wished to propose, which he felt certain under any—any (panse) circumstances, would be (pause again) accepted—he meant received with approbation (applause), not only with approbation, but enthusiasm," continued he, hitting off the word he at first intended to use, amid renewed applause, causing a slight "this is my health," droop of the head from the Major—"But when," continued the speaker, drawing largely on his snuff-box for inspiration, "But when in addition to the natural and intrinsic (pause) merit of the (hem) illustrious individual" ("Coming it strong," thought the Major, who had never been called illustrious before,) "there is another and a stronger reason," continued Wotherspoon, looking as if he wished he was in his seat again—"a reason that comes 'ome to the 'earts and symphonies of us all (applause). ("Ah, that's the hounds," thought the Major, "only I 'spose he means sympathies.") "I feel (pause) assured," continued Mr. Wotherspoon, "that the toast will be received with the enthusiasm and popularity that ever attends the (pause) mention of intrinsic merit, however (pause) 'umbly and inadequately the (pause) toast may be (pause) proposed," (great applause, with cries of no, no,) during which the orator again appealed to his snuff-box. He knew he had a good deal more to say, but he felt he couldn't get it out. If he had only kept his seat he thought he might have managed it. "I therefore," said he, helping Mrs. Broadfurrow to the sparkling, and passing the bottle to her husband while he again appealed to the Sillery, "beg to propose, with great sincerity, the 'ealth of Her most gracious Majesty The Queen! The Queen! God bless her!" exclaimed Wotherspoon, holding up a brimming bumper ere he sunk in his chair to enjoy it.

"With all my heart!" gasped the disgusted Major, writhing with vexation—observing to Mrs. Wotherspoon as he helped her, and then took severe toll of the passing bottle himself, "by Jove, your husband ought to be in Parliament—never heard a man acquit himself better"—the Major following the now receding bottle with his eye, whose fast diminishing contents left little hopes of a compliment for himself out of its contents. He therefore felt his chance was out, and that he had been unduly sacrificed to Royalty. Not so, however, for Mr. Wotherspoon, after again charging his nose with snuff, and passing his box round the table while he collected his scattered faculties for the charge, now drew the bell-cord again, and tapping with his knife against the empty bottle as "Strong" entered, exclaimed, "Champagne!" with the air of a man accustomed to have all the wants of life supplied by anticipation. There's nobody gets half so well waited upon as an old servant.

This order being complied with, and having again got up the steam of his eloquence, Mr. Wotherspoon arose, and, looking as wise as before, observed, "That there was another toast he had to propose, which he felt (pause) sure would (pause) would be most agreeable and acceptable to the meeting,—he meant to say the party, the present party (applause)—under any circumstances (sniff, snuff, sneeze); he was sure it would be most (snuff) acceptable, for the great and distinguished (pause), he had almost said illustrious (sniff), gentleman (pause), was—was estimable"—"—was estimable (pause) and glorious in every relation of life.

"This is me, at all events," thought the Major, again slightly drooping his too bashful head, as though the shower-bath of compliment was likely to be too heavy for him. (applause), and keeps a pack of hounds second to none in the kingdom (great applause, during which the drooping head descended an inch or two lower). I need not after that (snuff) expression of your (sniff) feelings (pause), undulate on the advantage such a character is of to the country, or in promoting (pause) cheerful hospitality in all its (pause) branches, and drawing society into sociable communications; therefore I think I shall (pause) offer a toast most, most heartily acceptable (sniff) to all your (snuff) feelings, when I propose, in a bumper toast, the health of our most— most distinguished and—and hospitable host—guest, I mean—Major Yammerton, and his harriers!" saying which, the old orator filled himself a bumper of Sillery, and sent the sparkling beverage foaming and creaming on its tour. He then presently led the charge with a loud, "Major! your very good health!"

"Major, your very good health!"

"Your very good health, Major!"

"Major, your very good health!" then followed up as quickly as the glasses could be replenished, and the last explosion having taken place, the little Major arose, and looked around him like a Bantam cock going to crow. He was a man who could make what he would call an off-hand speech, provided he was allowed to begin with a particular word, and that word was "for." Accordingly, he now began with,—

"Ladies and gentlemen, For the very distinguished honour you have thus most unexpectedly done me, I beg to return you my most grateful and cordial thanks. (Applause.) I beg to assure you, that the 'steem and approbation of my perhaps too partial friends, is to me the most gratifying of compliments; and if during the five-and-thirty years I have kept haryers, I have contributed in any way to the 'armony and good fellowship of this neighbourhood, it is indeed to me a source of unfeigned pleasure. (Applause.) I 'ope I may long be spared to continue to do so. (Renewed applause.) Being upon my legs, ladies and gentlemen," continued he, "and as I see there is still some of this most excellent and exhilarating beverage in the bottle (the Major holding up a halfemptied one as he spoke), permit me to conclude by proposing as a toast the 'ealth of our inestimable 'ost and 'ostess—a truly exemplary couple, who only require to be known to be respected and esteemed as they ought to be. (Applause.) I have great pleasure in proposing the 'ealth of Mr. and Mrs. Wotherspoon! (Applause.) Mrs. Wotherspoon," continued he, bowing very low to his fair hostess, and looking, as he thought, most insinuating, "your *very* good 'ealth! Wotherspoon!" continued he, standing erect, and elevating his voice, "Your very good 'ealth!" saying which he quaffed off his wine, and resumed his seat as the drinking of the toast became general.

Meanwhile old Wotherspoon had taken a back hand at the Sillery, and again arose, glass in hand, to dribble out his thanks for the honour the Major and company had done Mrs. Wother-spoon and himself, which being the shortest speech he had made, was received with the greatest applause.

All parties had now about arrived at that comfortable state when the inward monitor indicates enough, and the active-minded man turns to the consideration of the "next article, mem,"—as the teasing shop-keepers say, The Major's "next article," we need hardly say, was his haryers, which were still promenading in front of the ivy-mantled tower, before an admiring group of pedestrians and a few sorrily mounted horsemen,—old Duffield, Dick Trail, and one or two others,—who would seem rather to have come to offer up their cattle for the boiler, than in expectation of their being able to carry them across country with the hounds. These are the sort of people who stamp the farmers' hedges down, and make hare hunting unpopular.

172

"Well, sir, what say you to turning out?" now asked our Master, as Wotherspoon still kept working away at the Sillery, and maundering on to Mr. Broadfurrow about the Morning Post and high life.

"Well, sir, what you think proper," replied Spoon, taking a heavy pinch of snuff, and looking at the empty bottles on the table.

"The hare, you say, is close at hand," observed our master of hounds.

"Close at hand, close at hand—at the corner of my field, in fact," assented Wotherspoon, as if there was no occasion to be in a hurry.

"Then let's be at her!" exclaimed the Major rising with wine-inspired confidence, and feeling that it would require a very big fence to stop him with the hounds in full cry.

"Well, but we are going to see you, ain't we?" asked Mrs. Wotherspoon.

"By all means," replied our Master; adding, "but hadn't you better get your bonnet on?"

"Certainly," rejoined Mrs. Wotherspoon, looking significantly at Mrs. Broadfurrow; whereupon the latter rose, and with much squeezing, and pardoning, and thank-you-ing, the two succeeded in effecting a retreat. The gentlemen then began kicking their legs about, feeling as though they would not want any dinner that day.

CHAPTER LV. THE COUNCIL OF WAR.—POOR PUSS AGAIN!

WHILE the ladies were absent adorning themselves, the gentlemen held a council of war as to the most advisable mode of dealing with the hare, and the best way of making her face a good country. The Major thought if they could set her a-going with her head towards Martinfield-heath, they would stand a good chance of a run; while Broadfurrow feared Borrowdale brook would be in the way.

"Why not Linacres?" asked Mr. Rintoul, who preferred having the hounds over any one's farm but his own.

"Linacres is not a bad line," assented the Major thoughtfully; "Linacres is not a bad line, 'specially if she keeps clear of Minsterfield-wood and Dowland preserve; but if once she gets to the preserve it's all U. P., for we should have as many hares as hounds in five minutes, to say nothing of Mr. Grumbleton reading the riot act among us to boot."

"I'll tell ye how to do, then," interposed fat Mr. Nettlefold, holding his coat laps behind him as he protruded his great canary-coloured stomach into the ring; "I'll tell you how to do, then. Just crack her away back over this way, and see if you can't get her for Witherton and Longworth. Don't you mind," continued he, button-holeing the Major, "what a hunt we had aboot eighteen years since with a har we put off old Tommy Carman's stubble, that took us reet away over Marbury Plot, the Oakley hill, and then reet down into Woodbury Yale, where we killed?"

"To be sure I do!" exclaimed the delighted Major, his keen eyes glistening with pleasure at the recollection. "The day Sam Snowball rode into Gallowfield bog and came out as black as a sweep—I remember it well. Don't think I ever saw a better thing. If it had been a—a—certain somebody's hounds (*he, he, he!*), whose name I won't mention (*haw, haw, haw!*), we should never have heard the last of it (*he, he, he!*)."

While this interesting discussion was going on, old Wotherspoon who had been fumbling at the lock of the cellaret, at length got it open, and producing therefrom one of those little square fibre-protected bottles, with mysterious seals and hieroglyphical labels, the particoloured letters leaning different ways, now advanced, gold-dotted liquor-glass in hand, towards the group, muttering as he came, "Major Yammerton, will you 'blege me with your 'pinion of this Maraschino di Zara, which my wine merchants recommend to me as something very 'tickler," pouring out a glass as he spoke, and presenting it to his distinguished guest.

"With all my heart," replied the Major, who rather liked a glass of liquor; adding, "we'll all give our opinion, won't we, Pringle?" appealing to our hero.

"Much pleasure," replied Billy, who didn't exactly know what it was, but still was willing to take it on trust.

"That's right," rejoined old Spoon; "that's right; then 'blege me," continued he, "by helping yourselves to glasses from the sideboard," nodding towards a golden dotted brood clustering about a similarly adorned glass jug like chickens around a speckled hen.

At this intimation a move was made to the point; and all being duly provided with glasses, the luscious beverage flowed into each in succession, producing hearty smacks of the lips, and "very goods" from all.

"Well, I think so," replied the self-satisfied old dandy; "I think so," repeated he, replenishing his nose with a good pinch of snuff; "Comes from Steinberger and Leoville, of King Street, Saint Jeames's—very old 'quaintance of mine—great house in the days of George the Fourth of festive memory. And, by the way, that reminds me," continued he, after a long-drawn respiration, "that I have forgotten a toast that I feel (pause) we ought to have drunk, and—"

"Let's have it now then," interrupted the Major, presenting his glass for a second helping.

"If you please," replied "Wotherspoon, thus cut short in his oration, proceeding to replenish the glasses, but with more moderate quantities than before.

"Well, now what's your toast?" demanded the Major, anxious to be off.

"The toast I was about to propose—or rather, the toast I forgot to propose," proceeded the old twaddler, slowly and deliberately, with divers intermediate sniffs and snuffs, "was a toast that I feel 'sured will come 'ome to the 'arts and symphonies of us all, being no less a—a—(pause) toast than the toast of the illustrious (pause), exalted—I may say, independent—I mean Prince— Royal Highness in fact—who (wheeze) is about to enter into the holy state of matrimony with our own beloved and exalted Princess (Hear, hear, hear). I therefore beg to (pause) propose that we drink the 'ealth of His Royal (pause) 'Ighness Prince (pause) Frederick (snuff) William (wheeze) Nicholas (sniff) Charles!" with which correct enunciation the old boy brightened up and drank off his glass with the air of a man who has made a clean breast of it.

"Drink both their 'ealths!" exclaimed the Major, holding up his glass, and condensing the toast into "The 'ealths of their Royal Highnesses!" it was accepted by the company with great applause.

Just as the last of the glasses was drained, and the lip-smacking guests were preparing to restore them to the sideboard, a slight rustle was heard at the door, which opening gently, a smart black velvet bonnet trimmed with cerise-coloured velvet and leaves, and broad cerise-coloured ribbons, piloted Mrs. Wotherspoon's pretty face past the post, who announced that Mrs. Broadfurrow and she were ready to go whenever they were.

"Let's be going, then," exclaimed Major Yammerton, hurrying to the sideboard and setting down his glass. "How shall it be, then? How shall it be?" appealing to the company. "Give them a view or put her away quietly?—give them a view or put her away quietly?"

"Oh, put her away quietly," responded Mr. Broadfurrow, who had seen many hares lost by noise and hurry at starting.

"With her 'ead towards Martinfield?" asked the Major.

"If you can manage it," replied Broadfurrow, well knowing that these sort of feats are much easier planned than performed.

"'Spose we let Mrs. Wotherspoon put her away for us," now suggested Mr. Rintonl.

"By all means!" rejoined the delighted Major; "by all means! She knows the spot, and will conduct us to it. Mrs. Wotherspoon," continued he, stumping up to her as she now stood waiting in the little passage, "allow me to have the honour of offering you my arm;" so saying, the Major presented it to her, observing confidentially as they passed on to the now open front door, "I feel as if we were going to have a clipper!" lowering the ominous hat-string as he spoke.

"Solomon! Solomon!" cried he, to the patient huntsman, who had been waiting all this lime with the hounds. "We are going! we are going!"

"Yes, Major," replied Solomon, with a respectful touch of his cap.

"Now for it!" cried the Major, wheeling sharp round with his fair charge, and treading on old Wotherspoon's gouty foot, who was following too closely behind with Mrs. Broadfurrow on his arm, causing the old cock to catch up his leg and spin round on the other, thus splitting the treacherous cords across the knee.

"*Oh-o-o-o!*" shrieked he, wrinkling his face up like a Norfolk biffin, and hopping about as if he was dancing a hornpipe.

"*Oh-o-o-o!*" went he again, on setting it down to try if he could stand.

"I really beg you ten thousand pardons!" now exclaimed the disconcerted Major, endeavouring to pacify him. "1 really beg you ten thousand pardons; but I thought you were ever so far behind."

"So did I, I'm sure," assented Mrs. Wotherspoon.

"You're such a gay young chap, and step so smartly, you'd tread on any body's heels," observed the Major jocularly.

"Well, but it was a pincher, I assure you," observed Wotherspoon, still screwing up his mouth.

At length he got his foot down again, and the assault party was reformed, the Major and Mrs. Wotherspoon again leading, old Spoon limping along at a more respectful distance with Mrs. Broadfurrow, while the gentlemen brought up the rear with the general body of pedestrians, who now deserted Solomon and the hounds in order to see poor puss started from her form. Solomon was to keep out of sight until she was put away.

Passing through the little American blighted orchard, and what Spoon magnificently called his kitchen garden, consisting of a dozen grass-grown gooseberry bushes, and about as many winter cabbages, they came upon a partially-ploughed fallow, with a most promising crop of conch grass upon the unturned part, the hungry soil looking as if it would hardly return the seed.

"Fine country! fine country!" muttered the Major, looking around on the sun-bright landscape, and thinking he could master it whichever way the hare went. Up Sandywell Lane for Martinfield Moor, past Woodrow Grange for Linacres, and through Farmer Fulton's fold-yard for Witherton. .

Oh, yes, he could do it; and make a very good show out of sight of the ladies.

"Now, where have you her? where have you her?" whispered he, squeezing Mrs. Wotherspoon's plump arm to attract her attention, at the same time not to startle the hare.

"O, in the next field," whispered she, "in the next field," nodding towards a drab-coloured pasture in which a couple of lean and dirty cows were travelling about in search of a bite. They then proceeded towards it.

The gallant Major having opened the rickety gate that intervened between the fallow and it, again adopted his fair charge, and proceeded stealthily along the high ground by the ragged hedge on the right, looking back and holding up his hand for silence among the followers.

At length Mrs. Wotherspoon stopped. "There, you see," said she, nodding towards a piece of rough, briary ground, on a sunny slope, in the far corner of the field.

"I see!" gasped the delighted Major; "I see!" repeated he, "just the very place for a hare to be in—wonder there's not one there always. Now," continued he, drawing his fair charge a little back, "we'll see if we can't circumvent her, and get her to go to the west. Rintoul!" continued he, putting his hand before his mouth to prevent the sound of what he said being wafted to the hare. "Rintoul! you've got a whip—you go below and crack her away over the hill, that's a good feller, and we'll see if we can't have something worthy of com-mem-mo-ration"—the Major thinking how he would stretch out the run for the newspapers—eight miles in forty minutes, an hour and twenty with only one check—or something of that sort.

The pause thrilled through the field, and caused our friend Billy to feel rather uncomfortable, he didn't appreciate the beauties of the thing.

Rintoul having now got to his point, and prepared his heavy whip-thong, the gallant band advanced, in semicircular order, until they came within a few paces of where the briars began. At a signal from the Major they all hailed. The excitement was then intense.

"I see her!" now whispered the Major into Mrs. Wotherspoon's ear. "I see her!" repeated he, squeezing her arm, and pointing inwardly with his thong-gathered whip.

Mrs. Wotherspoon's wandering eyes showed that she did not participate in the view.

"Don't you see the tuft of fern just below the thick red-berried rose bush a little to the left here?" asked the Major; "where the rushes die out?"

Mrs. Wotherspoon nodded assent.

"Well, then, she's just under the broken piece of fern that lies bending this way. You can see her ears moving at this moment."

Mrs. Wotherspoon's eyes brightened as she saw a twinkling something.

"*Now then, put her away!*" said the Major gaily.

"She won't bite, will she?" whispered Mrs. Wotherspoon, pretending alarm.

"Oh, bite, no!" laughed the Major; "hares don't bite—not pretty women at least," whispered he. "Here take my whip and give her a touch behind," handing it to her as he spoke.

Mrs. Wotherspoon having then gathered up her violet-coloured velvet dress a little, in order as well to escape the frays of the sharp-toothed brambles as to show her gay red and black striped petticoat below, now advanced cautiously into the rough sea, stepping carefully over this tussuck and t'other, avoiding this briar and that, until she came within whip reach of the fern. She then paused, and looked back with the eyes of England upon her.

"*Up with her!*" cried the excited Major, as anxious for a view as if he had never seen a hare in his life.

Mrs. Wotherspoon then advanced half a step farther, and protruding the Major's whip among the rustling fern, out sprang—what does the reader think?—A GREAT TOM CAT!

"*Tallyho!*" cried Billy Pringle, deceived by the colour.

"*Hoop, hoop, hoop!*" went old Spoon, taking for granted it was a hare.

Crack! resounded Rintoul's whip from afar.

"*Haw, haw, haw!* never saw anything like that!" roared the Major, holding his sides.

"Why, it's a cat!" exclaimed the now enlightened Mrs. Wotherspoon, opening wide her pretty eyes as she retraced her steps towards where he stood.

"Cat, ay, to be sure, my dear! why, it's your own, isn't it?" demanded our gallant Master.

"No; ours is a grey—that's a tabby," replied she, returning him his whip.

"Grey or tab, it's a cat," replied the Major, eyeing puss climbing up a much-lopped ash-tree in the next hedge.

"Why, Spoon, old boy, don't you know a cat when you see her?" demanded he, as his chagrined host now came pottering towards them.

"I thought it was a hare, 'pon honour, as we say in the Lords," replied the old buck, bowing and consoling himself with a copious pinch of snuff.

"Well, it's a sell," said the Major, thinking what a day he had lost.

"D-a-a-vilish likely place for a hare," continued old Wotherspoon, reconnoitring it through his double eye-glasses; "D-a-a-vilish likely place, indeed."

"Oh, likely enough," muttered the Major, with a chuck of his chin, "likely enough,—only it isn't one, *that's all!*"

"Well, I wish it had been," replied the old boy.

"So do I," simpered his handsome wife, drawing her fine lace-fringed kerchief across her lips.

The expectations of the day being thus disappointed, another council of war was now held, as to the best way of retrieving the misfortune. Wotherspoon, who was another instance of the truth of the observation, that a man who is never exactly sober is never quite drunk, was inclined to get back to the bottle. "Better get back to the house," said he, "and talk matters quietly over before the fire;" adding, with a full replenishment of snuff up his nose, "I've got a batch of uncommonly fine Geisenheimer that I would like your 'pinion of, Major," but the Major, who had had wine enough, and wanted to work it off with a run, refused to listen to the tempter, intimating, in a whisper to Mrs. Spoon, who again hung on his arm, that her husband would be much better of a gallop.

And Mrs. Wotherspoon, thinking from the haziness of the old gentleman's voice, and the sapient twinkling of his gooseberry eyes, that he had had quite enough wine, seconded this view of the matter; whereupon, after much backing and bowing, and shaking of hands, and showing of teeth, the ladies and gentlemen parted, the former to the fire, the latter to the field, where the performance of the pack must stand adjourned for another chapter.

CHAPTER LVI. A FINE RUN!—THE MAINCHANCE CORRESPONDENCE.

HE worst of these *dejeuners à la fourchette*, and also of luncheons, is, that they waste the day, and then send men out half-wild to ride over the hounds or whatever else comes in their way. The greatest funkers, too, are oftentimes the boldest under the influence of false courage; so that the chances of mischief are considerably increased. The mounted Champagne bottle smoking a cigar, at page 71, is a good illustration of what we mean. We doubt not Mr. Longneck was very forward in that run.

All our Ivy Tower party were more or less primed, and even old Wotherspoon felt as if he could ride. Billy, too, mounted the gallant grey without his usual nervous misgivings, and trotted along between the Major and Rintoul with an easy Hyde Park-ish sort of air. Rintonl had intimated that he thought they would find a hare on Mr. Merryweather's farm at Swayland, and now led them there by the fields, involving two or three little obstacles—a wattled hurdle among the rest—which they all charged like men of resolution. The hurdle wasn't knocked over till the dogs'-meatmen came to it.

Arrived at Swayland, the field quickly dispersed, each on his own separate hare-seeking speculation, one man fancying a fallow, another a pasture: Rintonl reserving the high hedge near the Mill bridle-road, out of which he had seen more than one whipped in his time. So they scattered themselves over the country, flipping and flopping all the tufts ard likely places, aided by the foot-people with their sticks, and their pitchings and tossings of stones into bushes and hollows, and other tempting-looking retreats.

The hounds, too, ranged far and wide, examining critically each likely haunt, pondering on spots where they thought she had been, but which would not exactly justify a challenge.

While they were all thus busily employed, Rintoul's shallow hat in the air intimated that the longed-for object was discerned, causing each man to get his horse by the head, and the foot-people to scramble towards him, looking anxiously forward and hurriedly back, lest any of the riders should be over them. Rintoul had put her away, and she was now travelling and stopping, and travelling and stopping, listening and wondering what was the matter. She had been coursed before but never hunted, and this seemed a different sort of proceeding.

The terror-striking notes of the hounds, as they pounced upon her empty form, with the twang of the horn and the cheers of the sportsmen urging them on, now caused her to start; and, laying back her long ears, she scuttled away over Bradfield Green and up Ridge Hill as hard as ever she could lay legs to the ground.

"Come along, Mr. Pringle! come along, Mr. Pringle!" cried the excited Major, spurring up, adjusting his whip as if he was going to charge into a solid square of infantry. He then popped through an open gate on the left.

The bustling beauties of hounds had now fallen into their established order of precedence, Lovely and Lilter contending for the lead, with Bustler and Bracelet, and Ruffler and Chaunter, and Ruin and Restless, and Dauntless and Driver, and Dancer and Flaunter and others striving after, some giving tongue because they felt the scent, others, because the foremost gave it.—So they went truthfully up the green and over the hill, a gap, a gate, and a lane serving the bustling horsemen.

The vale below was not quite so inviting to our "green linnets" as the country they had come from, the fields being small, with the fences as irregular as the counties appear on a map of England. There was none of that orderly squaring up and uniformity of size, that enables a roadster to trace the line of communication by gates through the country.—All was zigzag and rough, indicating plenty of blackthorns and briers to tear out their eyes. However, the Champagne was sufficiently alive in our sportsmen to prevent any unbecoming expression of fear, though there was a general looking about to see who was best acquainted with the country. Rintoul was now out of his district, and it required a man well up in the lin to work them satisfactorily, that is to say, to keep them in their saddles, neither shooting them over their horses' heads nor swishing them over their tails. Our friend Billy worked away on the grey, thinking, if anything, he liked him better than the bay He even ventured to spur him.

The merry pack now swing musically down the steep hill, the chorus increasing as they reach the greener regions below. The fatties, and funkers, and ticklish forelegged ones, begin who-a-ing and g-e-e-ntly-ing to their screws, holding on by the pommels and cantrells, and keeping their nags' heads as straight as they can. Old Wotherspoon alone gets off and leads down. He's afraid of his horse slipping upon its haunches. The sight of him doing so emboldens our Billy, who goes resolutely on, and incautiously dropping his hand too soon, the grey shot away with an impetus that caused him to cannon off Broadfurrow and the Major and pocket himself in the ditch at the bottom of the hill. Great was the uproar! The Richest Commoner in England was in danger! Ten thousand a-year in jeopardy! "Throw yourself off!"

"Get clear of him!"

"Keep hold of him!"

"Mind he doesn't strike ye!" resounded from all parts, as first the horse's head went up, and then his tail, and then his head again, in his efforts to extricate himself.

At length Billy, seizing a favourable opportunity, threw himself off on the green sward, and, ere he could rise, the horse, making a desperate plunge, got out, and went staling away with his head in the air, looking first to the right and then to the left, as the dangling reins kept checking and catching him.

"Look sharp or you'll loss him!" now cried old Duffield, as after an ineffectual snatch of the reins by a passing countryman, the horse ducked his head and went kicking and wriggling and frolicking away to the left, regardless of the tempting cry of the hounds.

The pace, of course, was too good for assistance—and our friend and the field were presently far asunder.

Whatever sport the hounds had—and of course they would have a clipper—we can answer for it Mr. Pringle had a capital run; for his horse led him a pretty Will-o'-the-wisp sort of dance, tempting him on and on by stopping to eat whenever his rider—or late rider, rather—seemed inclined to give up the chase, thus deluding him from field to lane and from lane to field until our hero was fairly exhausted.—Many were the rushes and dashes and ventures made at him by hedgers and ditchers and drainers, but he evaded them all by laying back his ears and turning the battery of his heels for the contemplation, as if to give them the choice of a bite or a kick.

At length he turned up the depths of the well-known Love Lane, with its paved *trottoir*, for the damsels of the adjoining hamlets of East and West Woodhay to come dry-shod to the gossip-shop of the well; and here, dressed in the almost-forgotten blue boddice and red petticoat of former days, stood pretty Nancy Bell, talking matrimonially to Giles Bacon, who had brought his team to a stand-still on the higher ground of the adjoining hedge, on the field above.

Hearing the clatter of hoofs, as the grey tried first the hard and then the soft of the lane, Bacon looked that way; and seeing a loose horse he jumped bodily into the lane, extending his arms and his legs and his eyes and his mouth in a way that was very well calculated to stop even a bolder animal than a horse. He became a perfect barrier. The grey drew up with an indignant snort and a stamp of his foot, and turning short round he trotted back, encountering in due time his agitated and indignant master, who had long been vowing what a trimming he would give him when he caught him. Seeing Billy in a hurry,—for animals are very good judges of mischief, as witness an old cock how he ducks when one picks up a stone,—seeing Billy in a hurry we say, the horse again wheeled about, and returned with more leisurely steps towards his first opponent. Bacon and Nancy were now standing together in the lane; and being more pleasantly occupied than thinking about loose horses, they just stood quietly and let him come towards them, when Giles's soothing w-ho-o-ays and matter-of-course style beguiled the horse into being caught.

Billy presently came shuffling up, perspiring profusely, with his feet encumbered with mud, and stamping the thick of it off while he answered Bacon's question as to "hoo it happened," and so on, in the grumpy sort of way a man does who has lost his horse, he presented him with a shilling, and remounting, rode off, after a very fine run of at least twenty minutes.

The first thing our friend did when he got out of sight of Giles Bacon and Nancy, was to give his horse a good rap over the head with his whip for its impudent stupidity in running away, causing him to duck his head and shake it, as if he had got a pea or a flea in hiss ear.—He then began wheeling round and round, like a dog wanting to lie down, much to Billy's alarm, for he didn't wish for any more nonsense. That performance over, he again began ducking and shaking his head, and then went moodily on, as if indifferent to consequences. Billy wished he mightn't have hit him so hard.

When he got home, he mentioned the horse's extraordinary proceedings to the Major, who, being a bit, of a vet. and a strong suspector of Sir Moses' generosity to boot, immediately set it down to the right cause—megrims—and advised Billy to return him forthwith, intimating that Sir Moses was not altogether the thing in the matter of horses; but our friend, who kept the blow with the whip to himself, thought he had better wait a day or two and see if the attack would go off.—In this view he was upheld by Jack Rogers, who thought his old recipe, "leetle drop gin," would set him all right, and proceeded to administer it to himself accordingly. And the horse improved so much that he soon seemed himself again, whereupon Billy, recollecting Sir Moses's strenuous injunctions to give him the refusal of him if ever he wanted to part with him, now addressed him the following letter:—

"Yammerton Grange.

"Dear Sir Moses,

"*As I find I must return to town immediately after the hunt ball, to which you were so good as invite me, and as the horse you were so good as give me would be of no use to me there, I write, in compliance with my promise to offer him back to you if ever I wanted to part with him, to say that he will be quite at your service after our next day's hunting, or before if you like, as I dare say the Major will mount me if I require it. He is a very nice horse, and I feel extremely obliged for your very handsome intentions with regard to him, which, under other circumstances, I should have been glad to accept. Circumstanced as I am, however, he would be wasted upon me, and will be much better back in your stud.*

"I will, therefore, send him over on hearing from you; and you can either put my I.O.U. in the fire, or enclose it to me by the Post.

"Again thanking you for your very generous offer, and hoping you are having good sport, I beg to subscribe myself,

"Dear Sir Moses,

"Yours very truly,

"Wm. PRINGLE

"To Sir Moses Mainchance, Bart.,

"Pangburn Park."

And having sealed it with the great seal of state, he handed it to Rougier to give to the postman, without telling his host what he had done.

The next post brought the following answer:—

"*Many, very many thanks to you, my dear Pringle, for your kind recollection of me with regard to the grey, which I assure you stamps you in my opinion as a most accurate and excellent young man.—You are quite right in your estimate of my opinion of the horse; indeed, if I had not considered him something very far out of the common way, I should not have put him into your hands; but knowing him to be as good as he's handsome, I had very great satisfaction in placing him with you, as well on your own account as from your being the nephew of my old and excellent friend and brother baronet, Sir Jonathan Pringle—to whom I beg you to make my best regards when you write.*

"Even were it not so, however, I should be precluded from accepting your kind and considerate offer for only yesterday I sent Wetun into Doubleimupshire, to bring home a horse I've bought of Tom Toweler, on Paul Straddler's recommendation, being, as I tell Paul, the last

178

I'll ever buy on his judgment, unless he turns out a trump, as he has let me in for some very bad ones.

"But, my dear Pringle, ain't you doing yourself a positive injustice in saying that you would have no use for the grey in town? Town, my dear fellow, is the very place for a horse of that colour, figure, and pretension; and a very few turns in the Park, with you on his back, before that best of all pennyworths, the chair-sitting swells, might land you in the highest ranks of the aristocracy—unless, indeed, you are booked elsewhere, of which, perhaps, I have no business to inquire.

"I may, however, as a general hint, observe to the nephew of my old friend, that the Hit-im and Hold-imshire Mammas don't stand any nonsense, so you will do well to be on your guard. No; take my advice, my dear fellow, and ride that horse in town.—It will only be sending him to Tat.'s if you tire of him there, and if it will in any way conduce to your peace of mind, and get rid of any high-minded feeling of obligation, you can hand me over whatever you get for him beyond the 50 L.—And that reminds me, as life is uncertain, and it is well to do everything regularly, I'll send my agent, Mr. Mordecai Nathan, over with your I.O.U., and you can give me a bill at your own date—say two or three months—instead, and that will make vs all right and square, and, I hope, help to maintain the truth of the old adage, that short reckonings make long friends,—which I assure you is a very excellent one.

"And now, having exhausted both my paper and subject, I shall conclude with repeating my due appreciation of your kind recollection of my wishes; and with best remembrances to your host and hostess, not forgetting their beautiful daughters, whom I hope to see in full feather at the ball, I remain,

"My dear Pringle.

"Very truly and sincerely, yours,

"Moses Mainchance.

"To Wm. Pringle"

We need scarcely add that Mr. Mordecai Nathan followed quickly on the heels of the letter, and that the I. O. U. became a short-winded bill of exchange, thus saddling our friend permanently with the gallant grey. And when Major Yammerton heard the result, all the consolation Billy got from him was, "*I told you so*," meaning that he ought to have taken his advice, and returned the horse as unsound.

With this episode about the horse, let us return to Pangburn Park.

CHAPTER LVII. THE ANTHONY THOM TRAP.

SIR Moses was so fussy about his clothes, sending to the laundry for this shirt and that, censuring the fold of this cravat and that, inquiring after his new hunting ties and best boots, that Mrs. Margerum began to fear the buxom widow, Mrs. Vivian, was going to be at Lord Repartee's, and that she might be saddled with that direst of all dread inflictions to an honest conscientious housekeeper, a teasing, worreting, meddling mistress. That is a calamity which will be best appreciated by the sisterhood, and those who watch how anxiously "widowers and single gentlemen" places are advertised for in the newspapers, by parties who frequently, not perhaps unaptly, describe themselves as "thoroughly understanding their business."

Sir Moses, indeed, carried out the deception well; for not only in the matter of linen, but in that of clothes also, was he equally particular, insisting upon having all his first-class daylight things brought out from their winter quarters, and reviewing them himself as they lay on the sofa, ere he suffered Mr. Bankhead to pack them.

At length they were sorted and passed into the capacious depths of an ample brown leather portmanteau, and the key being duly turned and transferred to the Baronet, the package itself was chucked into the dog-cart in the unceremonious sort of way luggage is always chucked about. The vehicle itself then came to the door, and Sir Moses having delivered his last injunctions about the hounds and the horses, and the line of coming to cover so as to avoid public-houses, he ascended and touching the mare gently with the whip, trotted away amid the hearty—"well shut of yous" of the household. Each then retired to his or her private pursuits; some to drink, some to gamble, some to write letters, Mrs. Margerum, of course, to pick up the perquisites. Sir Moses, meanwhile, bowled away ostentatiously through the lodges, stopping to talk to everybody he met, and saying he was going away for the night.

Bonmot Park, the seat of Lord Repartee, stands about the junction of Hit-im and Hold-imshire, with Featherbedfordshire. Indeed, his great cover of Tewington Wood is neutral between the hunts, and the best way to the park on wheels, especially in winter time, is through Hinton and Westleak, which was the cause of Sir Moses hitting upon it for his deception, inasmuch as he could drive into the Fox and Hounds Hotel; and at Hinton, under pretence of baiting his mare without exciting suspicion, and there make his arrangements for the night. Accordingly, he took it very quietly after he got clear of his own premises, coveting rather the shades of evening that he had suffered so much from before, and as luck would have it by driving up Skinner Lane, instead of through Nelson Street, he caught a back view of Paul Straddler, as for the twenty-third time that worthy peeped through the panes of Mrs. Winship, the straw-bonnet maker's window in the market-place, at a pretty young girl she had just got from Stownewton. Seeing his dread acquaintance under such favourable circumstances, Sir Moses whipped Whimpering Kate on, and nearly upset himself against the kerb-stone as he hurried up the archway of the huge deserted house,—the mare's ringing hoofs alone, announcing his coming.

Ostler! Ostler! Ostler! cried he in every variety of tone, and at length the crooked-legged individual filling that and other offices, came hobbling and scratching his head to the summons. Sir Moses alighting then, gave him the reins and whip; and wrapper in hand, proceeded to the partially gas-lit door in the archway, to provide for himself while the ostler looked after the mare.

Now, it so happened, that what with bottle ends and whole bottles, and the occasional contributions of the generous, our friend Peter the waiter was even more inebriated than he appears at page 263; and the rumbling of gig-wheels up the yard only made him waddle into the travellers' room, to stir the fire and twist up a bit of paper to light the gas, in case it was any of the despised brotherhood of the road.—He thought very little of bagmen—Mr. Customer was the man for his money. Now, he rather expected Mr. Silesia, Messrs. Buckram the clothiers' representative, if not Mr. Jaconette, the draper's also, about this time; and meeting Sir Moses hurrying in top-coated and cravated with the usual accompaniments of the road, he concluded it was one of them; so capped him on to the commercial room with his dirty duster-holding hand.

"Get me a private room, Peter; get me a private room," demanded the Baronet, making for the bottom of the staircase away from the indicated line of scent.

"Private room," muttered Peter.

"Why, who is it?"

"Me! me!" exclaimed Sir Moses, thinking Peter would recognise him.

"Well, but whether are ye a tailor or a draper?" demanded Peter, not feeling inclined to give way to the exclusiveness of either.

"Tailor or draper! you stupid old sinner—don't you see it's me—me Sir Moses Mainchance?"

"Oh, Sir Moses, Sir, I beg your pardon, Sir," stammered the now apologising Peter, hurrying back towards the staircase. "I really begs your pardon, Sir; but my eyes are beginning to fail me, Sir—not so good as they were when Mr. Customer hunted the country.—Well Sir Moses, Sir, I hope you're well, Sir; and whether will you be in the Sun or the Moon? You can have a fire lighted in either in a minute, only you see we don't keep fires constant no ways now, 'cept in the commercial room.—Great change, Sir Moses, Sir, since Mr. Customer hunted the country; yes, Sir, great change—used to have fires in every room, Sir, and brandy and—"

"Well, but," interrupted Sir Moses, "I can't sit freezing up stairs till the fire's burnt up.—You go and get it lighted, and come to me in the commercial-room and tell me when it's ready; and here!" continued he, "I want some dinner in an hour's time, or so."

"By all means, Sir Moses. What would you like to take, Sir Moses?" as if there was everything at command.

Sir Moses—"Have you any soup?"

Peter—"Soup, Sir Moses. No, I don't think there is any soup."

Sir Moses—"Fish; have you any fish?"

Peter—"Why, no; I don't think there'll be any fish to-day, Sir Moses."

Sir Moses—"What have you, then?"

Peter—(Twisting the dirty duster), "Mutton chops—beef steak—beef steak—mutton chops—boiled fowl, p'raps you'd like to take?"

Sir Moses—"No. I shouldn't (*muttering*, most likely got to be caught and killed yet.) Tell the cook," continued he, speaking up, "to make on a wood and coal fire, and to do me a nice dish of mutton chops on the gridiron; not in the frying-pan mind, all swimming in grease; and to boil some mealy potatoes."

Peter—"Yes, Sir Moses; and what would you like to have to follow?"

"*Cheese!*" said Sir Moses, thinking to cut short the inquiry.

"And hark'e." continued Sir Moses: Don't make a great man of me by bringing out your old battered copper showing-dishes; but tell the cook to send the chops up hot and hot, between good warm crockery-ware plates, with ketchup or Harvey sauce for me to use as I like."

"Yes, Sir Moses," replied Peter, toddling off to deliver as much of the order as he could remember.

And Sir Moses having thawed himself at the commercial-room fire, next visited the stable to see that his mare had been made comfortable, and told the ostler post-boy boots to be in the way, as he should most likely want him to take him out in the fly towards night. As he returned, he met Bessey Bannister, the pretty chambermaid, now in the full glow of glossy hair and crinoline, whom he enlisted as purveyor of the mutton into the Moon, in lieu of the antiquated Peter, whose services he was too glad to dispense with.—It certainly is a considerable aggravation of the miseries of a country inn to have to undergo the familiarities of a dirty privileged old waiter.

So thought Sir Moses, as he enjoyed each succeeding chop, and complimented the fair maiden so on her agility and general appearance, that she actually dreamt she was about to become Lady Mainchance.

CHAPTER LVIII. THE ANTHONY THOM TAKE.

SIR Moses Mainchance, having fortified himself against the night air with a pint of club port, and a glass of pale brandy after his tea, at length ordered out the inn fly, without naming its destination to his fair messenger. These vehicles, now so generally scattered throughout the country, are a great improvement on the old yellow post-chaise, that made such a hole in a sovereign, and such a fuss in getting ready, holloaing, "Fust pair out!" and so on, to give notice to a smock-frocked old man to transform himself into a scarlet or blue jacketed post-boy by pulling off his blouse, and who, after getting a leg-up and a ticket for the first turnpike-gate, came jingling, and clattering, and cracking his dog-whip round to the inn door, attracting all the idlers and children to the spot, to see who was going to get into the "chay." The fly rumbles quietly round without noise or pretension, exciting no curiosity in any one's mind; for it is as often out as in, and may only be going to the next street, or to Woodbine Lodge, or Balsam Bower, on the outskirts of the town, or for an hour's airing along the Featherbedfordshire or the old London road. It does not even admit of a pull of the hair as a hint to remember the ostler as he stands staring in at the window, the consequence of which is, that the driver is generally left to open the door for his passenger himself. Confound those old iniquities of travelling!—a man used never to have his hand out of his pocket. Let not the rising generation resuscitate the evil, by contravening the salutary regulation of not paying people on railways.

Sir Moses hearing the sound of wheels, put on his wraps; and, rug in hand, proceeded quietly down stairs, accompanied only by the fair Bessey Bannister, instead of a flight of dirty waiters, holloaing "Coming down! coming down! now then! look sharp!" and so on.

The night was dark, but the ample cab-lamps threw a gleam over the drab and red lined door that George Beer the driver held back in his hand to let his customer in.

"Good night, my dear," said Sir Moses, now slyly squeezing Miss Bannister's hand, wondering why people hadn't nice clean quiet-stepping women to wait upon them, instead of stuck-up men, who thought to teach their masters what was right, who wouldn't let them have their plate-warmers in the room, or arrange their tables according to their own desires.—With these and similar reflections he then dived head-foremost into the yawning abyss of a vehicle. "Bang" went the door, and Beer then touched the side of his hat for instructions where to go to.

"Let me see," said Sir Moses, adjusting his rug, as if he hadn't quite made up his mind. "Let me see—oh, ah! drive me northwards, and I'll tell you further when we stop at the Slopewell turnpike-gate:" so saying Sir Moses drew up the gingling window, Beer mounted the box, and away the old perpetual-motion horse went nodding and knuckling over the uneven cobble-stone pavement, varying the motion with an occasional bump and jump at the open channels of the streets. Presently a smooth glide announced the commencement of Macadam, and shortly after the last gas-lamp left the road to darkness and to them. All was starlight and serene, save where a strip of newly laid gravel grated against the wheels, or the driver objurgated a refractory carter for not getting out of his way. Thus they proceeded at a good, steady, plodding sort of pace, never relaxing into a walk, but never making any very vehement trot.

At the Slopewell gate Sir Moses told Beer to take a ticket for the Winterton Burn one; arrived at which, he said, "Now go on and stop at the stile leading into the plantation, about half a mile on this side of my lodges," adding, "I'll walk across the park from there;" in obedience to which the driver again plied his whip along the old horse's ribs, and in due time the vehicle drew up at the footpath along-side the plantation.—The door then opened, Sir Moses alighted and stood waiting while the man turned his fly round and drove off, in order to establish his night eyes ere he attempted the somewhat intricate passage through the plantation to his house.

The night, though dark, was a good deal lighter than it appeared among the gloom of the houses and the glare of the gaslights at Hinton; and if he was only well through the plantation, Sir Moses thought he should not have much difficulty with the rest of the way. So conning the matter over in his mind, thinking whereabouts the boards over the ditch were, where the big oak stood near which the path led to the left, he got over the stile, and dived boldly into the wood.

The Baronet made a successful progress, and emerged upon the open space of Coldnose, just as the night breeze spread the twelve o'clock notes of his stable clock through the frosty air, upon the quiet country.

"All right," said he to himself, sounding his repeater to ascertain the hour, as he followed the tortuous track of the footpath, through cowslip pasture, over the fallow and along the side of the turnip field; he then came to the turn from whence in daylight the first view of the house is obtained.

A faint light glimmered in the distance, about where he thought the house would be situate.

"Do believe that's her room," said Sir Moses, stopping and looking at the light. "Do believe that's her signal for beloved Anthony Thom. If I catch the young scoundrel," continued he, hurrying on, "I'll—I'll—I'll break every bone in his skin." With this determination, Sir Moses put on as fast as the now darker lower ground would allow, due regard being had to not missing his way.

At length he came to the cattle hurdles that separated the east side of the park from the house, climbing over which he was presently among the dark yews and hollies, and box-bushes of the shrubbery. He then paused to reconnoitre.—The light was still there.—If it wasn't Mrs. Margerum's room, it was very near it; but he thought it was hers by the angle of the building and the chimneys at the end. What should he do?—Throw a pebble at the window and try to get her to lower what she had, or wait and see if he could take Anthony Thom, cargo and all? The night was cold, but not sufficiently so, he thought, to stop the young gentleman from coming, especially if he had his red worsted comforter on; and as Sir Moses threw his rug over his own shoulders, he thought he would go for the great haul, at all events; especially as he felt he could not converse with Mrs. Margerum à la Anthony Thom, should she desire to have a little interchange of sentiment. With this determination he gathered his rug around him, and proceeded to pace a piece of open ground among the evergreens, like the Captain of a ship walking the quarter-deck, thinking now of his money, now of his horses, now of Miss Bannister, and now of the next week's meets of his hounds.—He had not got half through his current of ideas when a footstep sounded upon the gravel-walk; and, pausing in his career, Sir Moses distinctly recognised the light patter of some one coming towards him. He down to charge like a pointer to his game, and as the sound ceased before the light-showing window, Sir Moses crept stealthily round among the bushes, and hid behind a thick ground-sweeping yew, just as a rattle of peas broke upon the panes.

The sash then rose gently, and Sir Moses participated in the following conversation:—

Mrs. Margerum (from above)—"O, my own dearly beloved Anthony Thom, is that you, darling! But don't, dear, throw such big 'andfulls, or you'll be bricking the winder."

Master Anthony Thom (from below)—"No, mother; only I thought you might be asleep."

Mrs. Margerum—"Sleep, darling, and you coming! I never sleep when my own dear Anthony Thom is coming! Bless your noble heart! I've been watching for you this—I don't know how long."

Master Anthony Thom—"Couldn't get Peter Bateman's cuddy to come on."

Mrs. Margerum—"And has my Anthony Thom walked all the way?"

Master Anthony Thom—"No; I got a cast in Jackey Lishman the chimbley-sweep's car as far as Burnfoot Bridge. I've walked from there."

Mrs. Margerum—"Bless his sweet heart! And had he his worsted comforter on?"

Master Anthony Thom—"Yes; goloshes and all."

Mrs. Margerum—"Ah, goloshes are capital things. They keep the feet, warm, and prevent your footsteps from being heard. And has my Anthony Thom got the letter I wrote to him at the Sun in the Sands?"

Master Anthony Thom—"No, never heard nothin' of it."

Mrs. Margerum—"No! Why what can ha' got it?"

Master Anthony Thom—"Don't know.—Makes no odds.—I got the things all the same."

Mrs. Margerum—"O, but my own dear Anthony Thom, but it does. Mr. Gerge Gallon says it's very foolish for people to write anything if they can 'elp it—they should always send messages by word of mouth. Mr. Gallon is a man of great intellect, and I'm sure what he says is right, and I wish I had it back."

Master Anthony Thom—"O, it'll cast up some day, I'll be bound.—It's of no use to nobody else."

Mrs. Margerum—"I hope so, my dear. But it is not pleasant to think other folks may read what was only meant for my own Anthony Thom. However, it's no use crying over spilt milk, and we must manish better another time. So now look out, my beloved, and I'll lower what I have."

So saying, a grating of cord against the window-sill announced a descent, and Master Anthony Thom, grasping the load, presently cried, "All right!"

Mrs. Margerum,—"It's not too heavy for you, is it, dear?" *Master Anthony Thom* (hugging the package)—"O, no; I can manish it. When shall I come again, then, mother?" asked he, preparing to be off.

Mrs. Margerum—"Oh, bless your sweet voice, my beloved. When shall you come again, indeed? I wish I could say very soon; but, dearest, it's hardly safe, these nasty pollis fellers are always about, besides which, I question if old Nosey may be away again before the ball; and as he'll be all on the screw for a while, to make up for past expense, I question it will be worth coming before then. So, my own dear Anthony Thom, s'pose we say the ball night, dear, about this time o' night, and get a donkey to come on as far as the gates, if you can, for I dread the fatigue; and if you could get a pair of panniers, so much the better, you'd ride easier, and carry your things better, and might have a few fire-bricks or hearth-stones to put at the top, to pretend you were selling them, in case you were stopped—which, however, I hope won't be the case, my own dear; but you can't be too careful, for it's a sad, sinful world, and people don't care what they say of their neighbours. So now, my own dearest Anthony Thom, good night, and draw your worsted comforter close round your throat, for colds are the cause of half our complaints, and the night air is always to be dreaded; and take care that you don't overheat yourself, but get a lift as soon as you can, only mind who it is with, and don't say you've been here, and be back on the ball night. So good night, my own dearest Anthony Thom, and take care of yourself whatever you do, for——"

"Good night, mother," now interrupted Anthony Thom, adjusting the bundle under his arm, and with repeated "Good night, my own dearest," from her, he gave it a finishing jerk, and turning round, set off on his way rejoicing.

Sir Moses was too good a sportsman to holloa before his game was clear of the cover; and he not only let Anthony Thom's footsteps die out on the gravel-walk, but the sash of Mrs. Margerum's window descend ere he withdrew from his hiding-place and set off in pursuit. He then went tip-toeing along after him, and was soon within hearing of the heavily laden lad.

"Anthony Thom, my dear! Anthony Thom," whispered he, coming hastily upon him as he now turned the corner of the house.

Anthony Thom stopped, and trembling violently exclaimed, "O Mr. Callon. is it you?"

"Yes, my dear, it's me," replied Sir Moses, adding, "you've *got* a great parcel, my dear; let me carry it for you," taking it from him as he spoke.

"*Shriek! shriek! scream!*" now went the terrified Thom, seeing into whose hands he had fallen. "O you dom'd young rascal," exclaimed Sir Moses, muffling him with his wrapper,—"I'll draw and quarter you if you make any noise. Come this way, you young miscreant!" added he, seizing him by the worsted comforter and dragging him along past the front of the house to the private door in the wall, through which Sir Moses disappeared when he wanted to evade Mon s. Rougier's requirements for his steeple-chase money.

That passed, they were in the stable-yard, now silent save the occasional stamp of the foot or roll of the halter of some horse that had not yet lain down. Sir Moses dragged his victim to the door in the corner leading to the whipper-in's bedroom, which, being open, he proceeded to grope his way up stairs. "Harry! Joe! Joe! Harry!" holloaed he, kicking at the door.

Now, Harry was away, but Joe was in bed; indeed he was having a hunt in his sleep, and exclaimed as the door at length yielded to the pressure of Sir Moses' foot. "'Od rot it! Don't ride so near the hounds, man!"

"Joe!" repeated Sir Moses, making up to the corner from whence the sound proceeded. "Joe! Joe!" roared he still louder.

"O, I beg your pardon! I'll open the gate!" exclaimed Joe, now throwing off the bed-clothes and bounding vigorously on to the floor.

"Holloa!" exclaimed he, awaking and rubbing his eyes. "Holloa! who's there?"

"Me," said Sir Moses, "me,"—adding: "Don't make a row, but strike a light as quick as you can; I've got a bag fox I want to show you."

"Bag fox, have you?" replied Joe, now recognising his master's voice, making for the mantel-piece and feeling for the box. "Bag fox, have you? Dreamt we were in the middle of a run from Ripley Coppice, and that I couldn't get old Crusader over the brook at no price." He then hit upon the box, and with a scrape of a lucifer the room was illuminated.

Having lit a mould candle that stood stuck in the usual pint-bottle neck, Joe came with it in his hand to receive the instructions of his master.

"Here's a dom'd young scoundrel I've caught lurking about the house," said Sir Moses, pushing Anthony Thom towards him "and I want you to give him a good hiding."

"Certainly, Sir Moses; certainly," replied Joe, taking Anthony Thom by the ear as he would a hound, and looking him over amid the whining and whimpering and beggings for mercy of the boy.

"Why this is the young rascal that stole my Sunday shirt off Mrs. Saunders's hedge!" exclaimed Joe, getting a glimpse of Anthony Thom's clayey complexioned face.

"No, it's not," whined the boy. "No, it's not. I never did nothin' o' the sort."

"Nothin' o' the sort!" retorted Joe, "why there ain't two hugly boys with hare lips a runnin' about the country," pulling down the red-worsted comforter, and exposing the deformity as he spoke.

"It's you all over," continued he, seizing a spare stirrup leather, and proceeding to administer the buckle-end most lustily. Anthony Thom shrieked and screamed, and yelled and kicked, and tried to bite; but Joe was an able practitioner, and Thom could never get a turn at him.

Having finished one side, Joe then turned him over, and gave him a duplicate beating on the other side.

"There! that'll do: kick him down stairs!" at length cried Sir Moses, thinking Joe had given him enough; and as the boy went bounding head foremost down, he dropped into his mother's arms, who, hearing his screams, had come to the rescue.

Joe and his master then opened the budget and found the following goods:—

2 lb. of tea, 1 bar of brown soap in a dirty cotton night-cap, marked C. F.; doubtless, as Sir Moses said, one of Cuddy Flintoff's.

"Dom all such dripping," said Sir Moses, as he desired Joe to carry the things to the house. "No wonder that I drank a great deal of tea," added he, as Joe gathered them together.

"Who the deuce would keep house that could help it?" muttered Sir Moses, proceeding on his way to the mansion, thinking what a trouncing he would give Mrs. Margerum ere he turned her out of doors.

1 lb. of coffee
3 lb. of brown sugar
3 lb. of starch
1 lb. of currants
1 lb. of rushlights
1 roll of cocoa
2 oz. of nutmegs
1 lb. of mustard
1 bar of pale soap
1 lb. of orange peel
1 bottle of capers
1 quail of split pras

CHAPTER LIX. ANOTHER COUNCIL OF WAR.—MR. GALLON AT HOME.

MRS. Margerum having soothed and pressed her beautiful boy to her bosom, ran into the house, and hurrying on the everlasting pheasant-feather bonnet in which she was first introduced to the reader, and a faded red and green tartan cloak hanging under it, emerged at the front door just as Sir Moses and Joe entered at the back one, vowing that she would have redress if it cost her a fi' pun note. Clutching dear Anthony Thom by the waist, she made the best of her way down the evergreen walk, and skirting the gardens, got upon the road near the keeper's lodge. "Come along, my own dear Anthony Thom," cried she, helping him along, "let us leave this horrid wicked hole.—Oh, dear! I wish I'd never set foot in it; but I'll not have my Anthony Thom chastised by any nasty old clothesman—no, that I won't, if it cost me a fifty pun note"—continued she, burning for vengeance. But Anthony Thom had been chastised notwithstanding, so well, indeed, that he could hardly hobble—seeing which, Mrs. Margerum halted, and again pressing him to her bosom, exclaimed, "Oh, my beloved Anthony Thom can't travel; I'll take him and leave him at Mr. Hindmarch's, while I go and consult Mr. Gallon."—So saying, she suddenly changed her course, and crossing Rye-hill green, and the ten-acre field adjoining, was presently undergoing the *wow-wow wow-wow* of the farmer lawyer'o dog, Towler. The lawyer, ever anxious for his poultry, was roused by the noise; and after a rattle of bolts, and sliding of a sash, presented his cotton night-capped head at an upper window, demanding in a stentorian voice "who was there?"

"Me! Mr. Hindmarch, me! Mrs. Margerum; for pity's sake take us in, for my poor dear boy's been most shemfully beat."

"Beat, has he!" exclaimed the lawyer, recognising the voice, his ready wit jumping to an immediate conclusion; "beat, has he!" repeated he, withdrawing from the window to fulfil her behest, adding to himself as he struck a light and descended the staircase, "that'll ha' summut to do with the dripping, I guess—always thought it would come to mischief at last." The rickety door being unbolted and opened, Mrs. Margerum and her boy entered, and Mrs. Hindmarch having also risen and descended, the embers of the kitchen fire were resuscitated, and Anthony Thom was examined by the united aid of a tallow candle and it. "Oh, see! see!" cried Mrs. Margerum, pointing out the wales on his back,—"was there ever a boy so shemfully beat? But I'll have revenge on that villainous man,—that I will, if it cost me a hundred pun note."—The marks seen, soothed, and deplored, Mr. Hindmarch began inquiring who had done it. "Done it! that nasty old Nosey," replied Mrs. Margerum, her eyes flashing with fire; "but I'll make the mean feller pay for it," added she,—"that I will."

"No, it wasn't old No-No-Nosey, mo-mo-mother," now sobbed Anthony Thom, "it was that nasty Joe Ski-Ski-Skinner."

"Skinner, was it, my priceless jewel," replied Mrs. Margerum, kissing him, "I'll skin him; but Nosey was there, wasn't he, my pet?"

"O, yes, Nosey was there," replied Anthony Thom, "it was him that took me to Ski-Ski-Skinner"—the boy bursting out into a fresh blubber, and rubbing his dirty knuckles into his streaming eyes as he spoke.

"O that Skinner's a bad un," gasped Mrs. Margerum, "always said he was a mischievous, dangerous man; but I'll have satisfaction of both him and old Nosey," continued she, "or I'll know the reason why."

The particulars of the catastrophe being at length related (at least as far as it suited Mrs. Margerum to tell it), the kettle was presently put on the renewed fire, a round table produced, and the usual consolation of the black bottle resorted to. Then as the party sat sipping their grog, a council of war was held as to the best course of proceeding. Lawyer Hindmarch was better versed in the law of landlord and tenant—the best way of a tenant doing his landlord,—than in the more recondite doctrine of master and servant, particularly the delicate part relating to perquisites; and though he thought Sir Moses had done wrong in beating the boy, he was not quite sure but there might be something in the boy being found about the house at an unseasonable hour of the night. Moreover, as farming times were getting dull, and the lawyer was meditating a slope *à la* Henerey Brown & Co.? he did not wish to get mixed up in a case that might bring him in collision with Sir Moses or his agent, so he readily adopted Mrs. Margerum's suggestion of going to consult Mr. George Gallon. He really thought Mr. Gallon would be the very man for her to see. Geordey was up to everything, and knew nicely what people could stand by, and what they could not; and lawyer Hindmarch was only sorry his old grey gig-mare was lame, or he would have driven her up to George's at once. However, there was plenty of time to get there on foot before morning, and they would take care of Anthony Thom till she came back, only she must be good enough not to return till nightfall; for that nasty suspicious Nathan was always prowling about, and would like nothing better than to get him into mischief with Sir Moses.—And that point being settled, they replenished their glasses, and drank success to the mission; and having seen the belaboured Anthony Thom safe in a shakedown, Mrs. Margerum borrowed Mrs. Hindmarch's second best bonnet, a frilled and beaded black velvet one with an ostrich feather, and her polka jacket, and set off on foot for the Rose and Crown beer-shop, being escorted to their door by her host and hostess, who assured her it wouldn't be so dark when she got away from the house a bit.

And that point being accomplished, lawyer and Mrs. Hindmarch retired to rest, wishing they were as well rid of Anthony Thom, whom they made no doubt had got into a sad scrape, in which they wished they mightn't be involved.

A sluggish winter's day was just dragging its lazy self into existence as Mrs. Margerum came within sight of Mr. Gallon's red-topped roof at the four lane ends, from whose dumpy chimney the circling curl of a wood fire was just emerging upon the pure air. As she got nearer, the early-stirring Mr. Gallon himself crossed the road to the stable, attired in the baggy velveteen shooting-jacket of low with the white cords and shining pork-butcher's top-boots of high life. Mr. Gallon was going to feed Tippy Tom before setting off for the great open champion coursing meeting to be held on Spankerley Downs, "by the kind permission of Sir Harry Fuzball, Baronet," it being one of the peculiar features of the day that gentlemen who object to having their game killed in detail, will submit to its going wholesale, provided it is done with a suitable panegyrick. "By the kind permission of Sir Harry Fuzball, Baronet," or "by leave of the lord of the manor of Flatshire," and so on; and thus every idler who can't keep himself is encouraged to keep a greyhound, to the detriment of a nice lady-like amusement, and the encouragement of gambling and poaching.

Mr. Gallon was to be field steward of this great open champion meeting, and had been up betimes, polishing off Tippy Tom; which having done, he next paid a similar compliment to his own person; and now again was going to feed the flash high-stepping screw, ere he commenced with his breakfast.

Mrs. Margerum's "*hie Mr. Gallon, hie!*" and up-raised hand, as she hurried down the hill towards his house, arrested his progress as he passed to the stable with the sieve, and he now stood biting the oats, and eyeing her approach with the foreboding of mischief that so seldom deceives one.

"O Mr. Gallon! O Mr. Gallon!" cried Mrs. Margerum, tottering up, and dropping her feathered head on his brawny shoulder.

"*What's oop? What's oop?*" eagerly demanded our sportsman, fearing for his fair character.

"O Mr. Gallon! *such* mischief! *such* mischief!"

"Speak, woman! speak!" demanded our publican; "say, *has he cotched ye?*"

"Yes, Gerge, yes," sobbed Mrs. Margerum, bursting into tears. "To devil he has!" exclaimed Mr. Gallon, stamping furiously with his right foot, "Coom into it hoose, woman; coom into it boose, and tell us'arl aboot it." So saying, forgetting Tippy Toni's wants, he retraced his steps with the corn, and flung frantically into the kitchen of his little two-roomed cottage.

"Here, lassie!" cried he, to a little girl, who was frying a dish of bubble-and-squeak at the fire. "Here, lassie, set doon it pan loike, aud tak this corn to it huss, and stand by while it eats it so saying he handed her the sieve, and following her to the door, closed it upon her.

"Noo," said he to Mrs. Margerum, "sit doon and tell us arl aboot it. Who cotched ye? Nosey, or who?"

"0 it wasn't me! It was Anthony Thom they caught, and they used him most shemful; but I'll have him tried for his life ofore my Lord Size, and transported, if it costs me all I'm worth in the world."

"Anthony Thom was it?" rejoined Mr. Gallon, raising his great eye-brows, and staring wide his saucer eyes, "Anthony Thom was it? but he'd ha' nothin' upon oi 'ope?"

"Nothin', Gerge," replied Mrs. Margerum, "nothin'—less now it might just appen to be an old rag of a night-eap of that nasty, covetous body Cuddy Flintoff; but whether it had a mark upon it or not I really can't say."

"O dear, but that's a bad job," rejoined Mr. Gallon, biting his lips and shaking his great bull-head; "O dear, but that's a bad job. you know I always chairged ye to be careful 'boot unlawful goods."

"You did, Gerge! you did!" sighed Mrs. Margerum; "and if this old rag had a mark, it was a clear oversight. But, O dear!" continued she, bursting into tears, "how they did *beat* my Anthony Thom!" With this relief she became more composed, and proceeded to disclose all the particulars.

"Ah, this 'ill be a trick of those nasty pollis fellers," observed Mr. Gallon thoughtfully, "oi know'd they'd be the ruin o' trade as soon as ever they came into it country loike—nasty pokin', pryin', mischievous fellers. Hoosomiver it mun be seen to, aud that quickly," continued he. "for it would damage me desp'rate on the Torf to have ony disturbance o' this sorrt, and we mun stop it if we can.

"Here, lassie!" cried he to the little girl who had now returned from the stable, "lay cloth i' next room foike, and then finish the fryin'; and oi'll tell ye what," continued he, laying his huge hand on Mrs. Margerum's shoulder, "oi've got to go to it champion coorsin' meetin', so I'll just put it hus into harness and droive ye round by it Bird-i'-the-Bush, where we'll find Carroty Kebbel, who'll tell us what te do, for oi don't like the noight-cap business some hoo," so saying Mr. Gallon took his silver plated harness down from its peg in the kitchen, and proceeded to caparison Tippy Tom, while the little girl, now assisted by Mrs. Margerum, prepared the breakfast, and set it on the table. Rather a sumptuous repast they had, considering it was only a way-side beer-shop; bubble-and-squeak, reindeer-tongue, potted game, potted shrimps, and tea strikingly like some of Sir Moses's. The whole being surmounted with a glass a-piece of pure British gin, Mr. Gallon finished his toilette, and then left to put the high-stepping screw into the light spring-cart, while Mrs. Margerum reviewed her visage in the glass, and as the openworks clock in the kitchen struck nine, they were dashing down the Heatherbell-road at the rate of twelve miles an hour.

CHAPTER LX. MR. CARROTY KEBBEL.

MR. Carroty Kebbel was a huge red-haired, Crimean-bearded, peripatetic attorney, who travelled from petty sessions to petty sessions, spending his intermediate time at the public houses, ferreting out and getting up cases. He was a roistering ruffian, who contradicted everybody, denied everything, and tried to get rid of what he couldn't answer with a horse-laugh. He was in good practice, for he allowed the police a liberal per-centage for bringing him prosecutions, while his bellowing bullying insured him plenty of defences on his own account. He was retained by half the ragamuffins in the country. He had long been what Mr. Gallon not inaptly called his "liar," and had done him such good service as to earn free quarters at the Rose and Crown whenever he liked to call. He had been there only the day before, in the matter of an *alibi* he was getting up for our old hare-finding friend Springer, who was most unhandsomely accused of night-poaching in Lord Oilcake's preserves, and that was how Mr. Gallon knew where to find him. The Crumpletin railway had opened out a fine consecutive line of petty sessions, out of which Carrots had carved a "home circuit" of his own. He was then on his return tour.

With the sprightly exertions of Tippy Tom, Gallon and Mrs. Margerum were soon within sight of the Bird-in-the-Bush Inn, at which Gallon drew up with a dash. Carrots, however, had left some half-hour before, taking the road for Farningford, where the petty sessions were about to be held; and though this was somewhat out of Gallon's way to Spankerley Downs, yet the urgency of the case determined him to press on in pursuit, and try to see Carrots. Tippy Tom, still full of running, went away again like a shot, and bowling through Kimberley toll-bar with the air of a man who was free, Gallon struck down the Roughfield road to the left, availing himself of the slight fall of the ground to make the cart run away with the horse, as it were, and so help him up the opposing hill. That risen, they then got upon level ground; and, after bowling along for about a mile or so, were presently cheered with the sight of the black wide-awake crowned lawyer striding away in the distance.

Carrots was a disciple of the great Sir Charles Napier, who said that a change of linen, a bit of soap, and a comb were kit enough for any one; and being only a two-shirts-a-week man, he generally left his "other" one at such locality as he was likely to reach about the middle of it, so as to apportion the work equally between them. This was clean-shirt day with him, and he was displaying his linen in the ostentatious way of a man little accustomed to the luxury. With the exception of a lavender-and-white coloured watch-ribbon tie, he was dressed in a complete suit of black-grounded tweed, with the purple dots of an incipient rash, the coat having capacious outside pockets, and the trousers being now turned np at the bottoms to avoid the mud; "showing" rhinoceros hide-like shoes covering most formidable-looking feet. Such was the monster who was now swinging along the highway at the rate of five miles an hour, in the full vigour of manhood, and the pride of the morning. At the sight of him in advance, Mr. Gallon just touched Tippy Tom with the point of the whip, which the animal resented with a dash at the collar and a shake of the head, that as good as said, "You'd better not do that again, master, unless you wish to take your vehicle home in a sack." Mr. Gallon therefore refrained, enlisting the aid of his voice instead, and after a series of those slangey-whiney *yaah-hoo! yaah-hoo's!* that the swell-stage-coachmen, as they called the Snobs, used to indulge in to clear the road or attract attention, Mr. Gallon broke out into a good downright "Holloa, Mr. Kebbel! Holloa!"

At the sound of his name, Carrots, who was spouting his usual exculpatory speech, vowing he felt certain no bench of Justices would convict on such evidence, and so on, pulled up; and Mr. Gallon, waving his whip over his head, he faced about, and sat down on a milestone to wait his coming. The vehicle was presently alongside of him.

"Holloa, George!" exclaimed Carrots, rising and shaking hands with his client. "Holloa! What's up? Who's this you've got?" looking intently at Mrs. Margerum.

"I'll tell you," said George, easing the now quivering-tailed Tippy Tom's head; "this is Mrs. Margerum you've heard me speak 'boot; and she's loike to get into a little trooble loike; and I tell'd her she'd best see a 'liar' as soon as she could."

"Just so," nodded Kebbel, anticipating what had happened. "You see," continued Mr. Gallon, winding his whip thong round the stick as he spoke "in packing up some little bit things in a hurry loike, she put up a noight cap, and she's not quoite sure whether she can stand by it or not, ye know."

"I see," assented Carrots; "and they've got it, I 'spose?"

"I don't know that they got it," now interposed Mrs. Margerum; "but they got my Anthony Thom, and beat him most shameful. Can't I have redress for my Anthony Thom?"

187

"We'll see," said Carrots, resuming his seat on the milestone, and proceeding to elicit all particulars, beginning with the usual important inquiry, whether Anthony Thom had said anything or not. Finding he had not, Carrots took courage, and seemed inclined to make light of the matter. "The groceries you bought, of course," said he, "of Roger Rounding the basket-man—Roger will swear anything for me; and as for the night-cap, why say it was your aunt's, or your niece's, or your sister's—Caroline Somebody's—Caroline Frazer's, Charlotte Friar's, anybody's whose initials are C. F."

"O! but it wasn't a woman's night-cap, sir, it was a man's; the sort of cap they hang folks in; and I should like to hang Old Mosey for beating my Anthony Thom," rejoined Mrs. Margerum.

"I'm afraid we can't hang him for that," replied Mr. Kebbel, laughing. "Might have him up for the assault, perhaps."

"Well, have him up for the assault," rejoined Mrs. Margerum; "have him up for the assault. What business had he to beat my Anthony Thom?"

"Get him fined a shilling, and have to pay your own costs, perhaps," observed Mr. Kebbel; "better leave that alone, and stick to the parcel business—better stick to the parcel business. There are salient points in the case. The hour of the night is an awkward part," continued he, biting his nails; "not but that the thing is perfectly capable of explanation, only the Beaks don't like that sort of work, it won't do for us to provoke an inquiry into the matter."

"Just so," assented Mr. Gallon, who thought Mrs. Margerum had better be quiet.

"Well, but it's hard that my Anthony Thom's to be beat, and get no redress!" exclaimed Mrs. Margerum, bursting into tears.

"Hush, woman! hush!" muttered Mr. Gallon, giving her a dig in the ribs with his elbow; adding, "ye mun de what it liar tells ye."

"I'll tell you what I can do," continued Mr. Kebbel, after a pause. "They've got my old friend Mark Bull, the ex-Double-im-up-shire Super, into this force, and think him a great card. I'll get him to go to Sir Moses about the matter; and if Mark finds we are all right about the cap, he's the very man to put Mosey up to a prosecution, and then we shall make a rare harvest out of him," Carrots rubbing his hands with glee at the idea of an action for a malicious prosecution.

"Ay, that'll be the gam," said Mr. Gallon, chuckling,—"that'll be the gam; far better nor havin' of him oop for the 'sult."

"I think so," said Mr. Kebbel, "I think so; at all events I'll consider the matter; and if I send Mark to Sir Moses, I'll tell him to come round by your place and let you know what he does; but, in the meantime," continued Kebbel, rising and addressing Mrs. Margerum earnestly, "*don't you answer any questions* to anybody, and tell Anthony Thom to hold his tongue too, and I've no doubt Mr. Gallon and I'll make it all right;" so saying, Mr. Kebbel shook hands with them both, and stalked on to his petty-sessional practice.

Gallon then coaxed Tippy Turn round, and, retracing his steps as far as Kimberley gate, paid the toll, and shot Mrs. Margerum out, telling her to make the best of her way back to the Rose and Crown, and stay there till he returned. Gallon then took the road to the right, leading on to the wide-extending Spankerley Downs; where, unharnessing Tippy Tom under lea of a secluded plantation, he produced a saddle and bridle from the back of the cart, which, putting on, he mounted the high-stepping white, and was presently among the coursers, the greatest man at the meeting, some of the yokels, indeed, taking him for Sir Harry Fuzball himself.

But when Mr. Mark Bull arrived at Sir Moses's, things had taken another turn, for the Baronet, in breaking open what he thought was one of Mrs. Margerum's boxes, had in reality got into Mr. Bankhead's, where, finding his ticket of leave, he was availing himself of that worthy's absence to look over the plate prior to dismissing him, and Sir Moses made so light of Anthony Thom's adventure that the Super had his trouble for nothing. Thus the heads of the house—*the* Mr. and Mrs. in fact, were cleared out in one and the same day, by no means an unusual occurrence in an establishment, after which of course Sir Moses was so inundated with stories against them, that he almost resolved to imitate his great predecessor's example and live at the Fox and Hounds Hotel at Hinton in future. To this place his mind was now more than ordinarily directed in consequence of the arrangements that were then making for the approaching Hunt Ball, to which long looked-for festival we will now request the company of the reader.

CHAPTER LXI. THE HUNT BALL.—MISS DE GLANCEY'S REFLECTIONS.

THE Hit-im and Hold-im shire hunt balls had long been celebrated for their matrimonial properties, as well for settling ripe flirtations, as for bringing to a close the billing and cooing of un-productive love, and opening fresh accounts with the popular firm of "Cupid and Co." They were the greenest spot on the memory's waste of many, on the minds of some whose recollections carried them back to the romping, vigorous Sir Roger de Coverley dances of Mr. Customer's time,—of many who remembered the more stately glide of the elegant quadrille of Lord Martingal's reign, down to the introduction of the once scandalising waltz and polka of our own. Many "Ask Mamma's" had been elicited by these balls, and good luck was said to attend all their unions.

Great had been the changes in the manners and customs of the country, but the one dominant plain gold ring idea remained fixed and immutable. The Hit-im and Hold-im shire hunt ball was expected to furnish a great demand for these, and Garnet the silversmith always exhibited an elegant white satin-lined morocco case full in his window, in juxtaposition with rows of the bright dress-buttons of the hunt, glittering on beds of delicate rose-tinted tissue paper.

All the milliners far and wide used to advertise their London and Parisian finery for the occasion, like our friend Mrs. Bobbinette,—for the railway had broken through the once comfortable monopoly that Mrs. Russelton and the Hinton ones formerly enjoyed, and had thrown crinoline providing upon the country at large. Indeed, the railway had deranged the old order of things; for whereas in former times a Doubleimnpshire or a Neck-and-Crop shire sportsman was rarely to be seen at the balls, aud those most likely under pressure of most urgent "Ask Mamma" circumstances, now they came swarming down like swallows, consuming a most unreasonable quantity of Champagne—always, of course, returning and declaring it was all "gusberry." Formerly the ball was given out of the Hit-im and Hold-im shire hunt funds; but this unwonted accession so increased the expense, that Sir Moses couldn't stand it, dom'd of he could; and he caused a rule to be passed, declaring that after a certain sum allowed by the club, the rest should be paid by a tax on the tickets, so that the guest-inviting members might pay for their friends. In addition to this, a sliding-seale of Champagne was adopted, beginning with good, and gradually relaxing in quality, until there is no saying but that some of the late sitters might get a little gooseberry. Being, however, only a guest, we ought not perhaps to be too critical in the matter, so we will pass on to the more general features of the entertainment.

We take it a woman's feelings and a man's feelings with regard to a ball are totally different and distinct.

Men—unmarried men, at least—know nothing of the intrinsic value of a dress, they look at the general effect on the figure. Piquant simplicity, something that the mind grasps at a glance and retains—such as Miss Yammerton's dress in the glove scene—is what they like. Many ladies indeed seem to get costly dresses in order to cover them over with something else, just as gentlemen build handsome lodges to their gates, and then block them out of sight by walls.

But even if ball-dresses were as attractive to the gentlemen as the ladies seem to think them, they must remember the competition they have to undergo in a ball-room, where great home beauties may be suddenly eclipsed by unexpected rivals, and young gentlemen see that there are other angels in the world besides their own adored ones. Still balls are balls, and fashion is fashion, and ladies must conform to it, or what could induce them to introduce the bits of black of the present day into their coloured dresses, as if they were just emerging from mourning. Even our fair friends at Yammerton Grange conformed to the fashion, and edged the many pink satin-ribboned flounces of their white tulle dresses with narrow black lace—though they would have looked much prettier without.

Of all the balls given by the members of the Hit-im and Hold-im shire hunt, none had perhaps excited greater interest than the one about to take place, not only on account of its own intrinsic merits as a ball, but because of the many tender emotions waiting for solutions on that eventful evening. Among others it may be mentioned that our fat friend the Woolpack, whose portrait adorns page 241, had confided to Mrs. Rocket Larkspur, who kept a sort of register-office for sighers, his admiration of the fair auburn-haired Flora Yammerton; and Mrs. Rocket having duly communicated the interesting fact to the young lady, intimating, of course, that he would have the usual "ten thousand a year," Flora had taken counsel with herself whether she had not better secure him, than contend with her elder sister either for Sir Moses or Mr. Pringle, especially as she did not much fancy Sir Moses, and Billy was very wavering in his attentions, sometimes looking extremely sweet at her, sometimes equally so at Clara, and at other times even smiling on that little childish minx Harriet. Indeed Mrs. Rocket Larkspur, in the multiplicity of her meddling, had got a sort of half-admission from that young owl, Rowley Abingdon, that he thought Harriet very pretty, and she felt inclined to fan the flame of that speculation too.

Then Miss Fairey, of Yarrow Court, was coming, and it was reported that Miss de Glancey had applied for a ticket, in order to try and cut her out with the elegant Captain Languisher, of the Royal Hollyhock Hussars. Altogether it was expected to be a capital ball, both for dancers and lookers-on.

People whose being's end and aim is gaiety, as they call converting night into day, in rolling from party to party, with all the means and appliances of London, can have little idea of the up-hill work it is in the country, getting together the ingredients of a great ball. The writing for rooms, the fighting for rooms—the bespeaking of horses, the not getting horses—the catching the train, the losing the train—above all, the choosing and ordering those tremendous dresses, with the dread of not getting those tremendous dresses, of their being carried by in the train, or not fitting when they come. Nothing but the indomitable love of a ball, as deeply implanted in a woman's heart as the love of a hunt is in that of a man, can account for the trouble and vexation they undergo.

But if 'tis a toil to the guests, what must it be to the givers, with no friendly Grange or Gunter at hand to supply everything, guests included, if required, at so much per head! Youth, glorious youth, comes to the aid, aud enters upon the labour with all the alacrity that perhaps distinguished their fathers.

Let us now suppose the absorbing evening come; and that all-important element in country festivities, the moon shining with silvery dearness as well on the railway gliders as on the more patient plodders by the road. What a converging there was upon the generally quiet town of Hinton; reminding the older inhabitants of the best days of Lord Martingal and Mr. Customer's reigns. What a gathering up there was of shining satins and rustling silks and moire antiques, white, pink, blue, yellow, green, to say nothing of clouds of tulle; what a compression of swelling eider-down and watch-spring petticoats; and what a bolt-upright sitting of that happy pride which knows no pain, as party after party took up and proceeded to the scene of hopes and fears at the Fox and Hounds Hotel and Posting House.

The ball-room was formed of the entire suite of first-floor front apartments, which, on ordinary occasions, did duty as private rooms—private, at least, as far as thin deal partitions could make them so—and the supper was laid out in our old acquaintance the club-room, connected by a sort of Isthmus of Suez, with a couple of diminutive steps towards the end to shoot the incautious becomingly, headforemost, into the room.

Carriages set down under the arched doorway, and a little along the passage the Blenheim was converted into a cloak-room for the ladies, where the voluminous dresses were shook out, and the last hurried glances snatched amid anxious groups of jostling arrivals. Gentlemen then emerging from the commercial room rejoined their fair friends in the passage, and were entrusted with fans and flowers while, with both hands, they steered their balloon-like dresses up the red druggetted staircase.

Gentlemen's balls have the advantage over those given by ladies, inasmuch as the gentlemen must be there early to receive their fair guests; and as a ball can always begin as soon as there are plenty of gentlemen, there are not those tedious delays and gatherings of nothing but crinoline that would only please Mr. Spurgeon.

The large highly-glazed, gilt-lettered, yellow card of invitation, intimated nine o'clock as the hour; by which time most of the Hinton people were ready, and all the outlying ones were fast drawing towards the town. Indeed, there was nothing to interfere with the dancing festivities, for dinner giving on a ball night is not popular with the ladies—enough for the evening being the dance thereof. Country ladies are not like London ones, who can take a dinner, an opera, two balls, and an at-home in one and the same night. As to the Hinton gentlemen, they were very hospitable so long as nobody wanted anything from them; if they did, they might whistle a long time before they got it. If, for instance, that keeper of a house of call for Bores, Paul Straddler, saw a mud-sparked man with a riding-whip in his hand, hurrying about the town, he would after him, and press him to dine off, perhaps, "crimped cod and oyster sauce, and a leg of four year old mutton, with a dish of mince pies or woodcocks, whichever he preferred;" but on a ball night, when it would be a real convenience to a man to have a billet, Paul never thought of asking any one, though when he met his friends in the ball, and heard they had been uncomfortable at the Sun or the Fleece, he would exclaim, with well-feigned reproach, "Oh dash it, man, why didn't you come to me?"

But let us away to the Fox and Hounds, and see what is going on.

To see the repugnance people have to being early at a ball, one would wonder how dancing ever gets begun. Yet somebody must be there first, though we question whether any of our fair readers ever performed the feat; at all events, if ever they did, we will undertake to say they have taken very good care not to repeat the performance.

The Blurkinses were the first to arrive on this occasion, having only themselves to think about, and being anxious, as they said, to see as much as they could for their money. Then having been duly received by Sir Moses and the gallant circle of fox-hunters, and passed inwardly, they took up a position so as to be able to waylay those who came after with their coarse compliments, beginning with Mrs. Dotherington, who, Blurkins declared, had worn the grey silk dress she then had on, ever since he knew her.

Jimmy Jarperson, the Laughing Hyæna, next came under his notice, Blurkins telling him that his voice grated on his ear like a file; asking if any body else had ever told him so.

Mrs. Rocket Larkspur, who was duly distended in flaming red satin, was told she was like a full-blown peony; and young Treadcroft was asked if he knew that people called him the Woolpack.

Meanwhile Mrs. Blurkins kept pinching and feeling the ladies' dresses as they passed, making a mental estimate of their cost. She told Miss Yammerton she had spoilt her dress by the black lace.

A continuously ascending stream of crinoline at length so inundated the room, that by ten o'clock Sir Moses thought it was time to open the ball; so deputing Tommy Heslop to do the further honours at the door, he sought Lady Fuzball, and claimed the favour of her hand for the first quadrille.

This was a signal for the unmated ones to pair; and forthwith there was such a drawing on of gloves, such a feeling of ties, such a rising on tiptoes, and straining of eyes, and running about, asking for Miss This, and Miss That, and if anybody had seen anything of Mrs. So-and-so.

At length the sought ones were found, anxiety abated, and the glad couples having secured suitable *vis-à-vis*, proceeded to take up positions.

At a flourish of the leader's baton, the enlivening "La Traviata" struck up, and away the red coats and black coats went sailing and sinking, and rising and jumping, and twirling with the lightly-floating dresses of the ladies.

The "Pelissier Galop" quickly followed, then the "Ask Mamma Polka," and just as the music ceased, and the now slightly-flushed couples were preparing for a small-talk promenade, a movement took place near the door, and the elegant swan-like de Glancey was seen sailing into the room with her scarlet-geranium-festooned dress set off with eight hundred yards of tulle! Taking her chaperone Mrs. Roseworth's arm, she came sailing majestically along, the men all alive for a smile, the ladies laughing at what they called her preposterous dimensions.

But de Glancey was not going to defeat her object by any premature condescension; so she just met the men's raptures with the slightest recognition of her downcast eyes, until she encountered the gallant Captain Languisher with lovely Miss Fairey on his arm, when she gave him one of her most captivating smiles, thinking to have him away from Miss Fairey in no time.

But Miss de Glancey was too late! The Captain had just "popped the question," and was then actually on his way to "Ask Mamma," and so returned her greeting with an air of cordial indifference, that as good as said, "Ah, my dear, you'll not do for me."

Miss de Glancey was shocked. It was the first time in her life that she had ever missed her aim. Nor was her mortification diminished by the cool way our hero, Mr. Pringle, next met her advances. She had been so accustomed to admiration, that she could ill brook the want of it, and the double blow was too much for her delicate sensibilities. She felt faint, and as soon as she could get a fly large enough to hold herself and her chaperone, she withdrew, the mortification of this evening far more than counterbalancing all the previous triumphs of her life.

One person more or less at a ball, however, is neither here nor there, and the music presently struck np again, and the whirling was resumed, just as if there was no such person as Miss de Glancey in existence. And thus waltz succeeded polka, and polka succeeded quadrille, with lively rapidity—every one declaring it was a most delightful ball, and wondering when supper would be.

At length there was a lull, and certain unmistakeable symptoms announced that the hour for that superfluous but much talked of meal had arrived, whereupon there was the usual sorting of consequence to draw to the cross table at the top of the room, with the pairing off of eligible couples who could be trusted alone, and the shirking of Mammas by those who were not equally fortunate. Presently a movement was made towards the Isthmus of Suez, on reaching which the rotund ladies had to abandon their escorts to pilot their petticoats through the straits amid the cries of "take care of the steps!" "mind the steps at the end!" from those who knew the dangers of the passage. And thus the crinoline came circling into the supper room—each lady again expanding with the increased space, and reclaiming her beau. Supper being as we said before a superfluous meal, it should be light and airy, something to please the eye and tempt the appetite; not composed of great solid joints that look like a farmer's ordinary, or a rent-day dinner with "night mare" depicted on every dish. The Hit-im and Hold-im shire hunt balls had always been famous for the elegance of their supper, Lord Ladythorne kindly allowing his Italian confectioner, Signor Massaniello, to superintend the elegancies, that excited such admiration from the ladies as they worked their ways or wedged themselves in at the tables, but whose beauty did not save them from destruction as the evening advanced. At first of course the solids were untouched, the tongues, the hams, the chickens, the turkeys, the lobster salads, the nests of plover eggs, the clatter patter being relieved by a heavy salvo of Champagne artillery. Brisk was the demand for it at starting, for the economical arrangement was as well known as if it had been placarded about the room. When the storm of corks had subsided and clean plates been supplied, the sweets, the jellies, the confectionery were attacked, and occasional sly sorties were made against the flower sugar vases and ornaments of the table. Then perspiring waiters came panting in with more Champagne fresh out of the ice, and again arm-extended the glasses hailed its coming, though some of the Neck-and-Crop-shire gentlemen smacked their lips after drinking it, and pronounced it to be No. 2. Nevertheless they took some more when it came round again. At length the most voracious cormorant was appeased, and all eyes gradually turned towards the sporting president in the centre of the cross table.

We have heard it said that the House of Commons is the most appalling and critical assembly in the world to address, but we confess we think a mixed party of ladies and gentlemen at a sit-down supper a more formidable audience.

We don't know anything more painful than to hear a tongue-tied country gentleman floundering for words and scrambling after an idea that the quick-witted ladies have caught long before he comes within sight of his subject. Theirs is like the sudden dart of the elastic greyhound compared to the solemn towl of the old slow-moving "southern" hound after its game.

Sir Moses, however, as our readers know, was not one of the tongue-tied sort—on the contrary, he had a great flow of words and could palaver the ladies as well as the gentlemen. Indeed he was quite at home in that room where he had coaxed and wheedled subscriptions, promised wonders, and given away horses without the donees incurring any "obligation." Accordingly at the fitting time he rose from his throne, and with one stroke of his hammer quelled the remaining conversation which had been gradually dying out in anticipation of what was coming. He then called for a bumper toast, and after alluding in felicitous terms to the happy event that so aroused the "symphonies" of old Wotherspoon, he concluded by proposing the health of her Majesty the Queen, which of course was drunk with three times three and one cheer more. The next toast, of course, was the ladies who had honoured the Ball with their presence, and certainly if ever ladies ought to be satisfied with the compliments paid them, it was on the present occasion, for Sir Moses vowed and protested that of all beauties the Hit-im and Hold-im shire beauties were the fairest, the brightest, and the best; and he said it would be a downright reflection upon the rising generation if they did not follow the Crown Prince of Prussia's excellent example, and make that ball to be the most blissful and joyous of their recollections. This toast being heartily responded to, Sir Moses leading the cheers, Sir Harry Fuzball rose to return thanks on behalf of the ladies, any one of whom could have done it a great deal better; after which old Sir George Persiflage, having arranged his lace-tipped tie, proposed the health of Sir Moses, and spoke of him in very different terms to what Sir Moses did of Sir George at the hunt dinner, and this, answer affording Sir Moses another opportunity—the good Champagne being exhausted—he renewed his former advice, and concluded by moving an adjournment to the ball-room. Then the weight of oratory being off, the school broke loose as it were, and all parties paired off as they liked. Many were the trips at the steps as they returned by the narrow passage to the ball-room. The "Ask Mamma" Polka then appropriately struck up, but polking being rather beyond our Baronet's powers he stood outside the ring rubbing his nose and eyeing the gay twirlers, taking counsel within himself what he should do. The state of his household had sorely perplexed him, and he had about come to the resolution that he must either marry again or give up housekeeping and live at Hinton. Then came the question whom he should take? Now Mrs. Yammerton was a noted good manager, and in the inferential sort of way that we all sometimes deceive ourselves, he came to the conclusion that her daughters would be the same. Clara was very pretty—dom'd if she wasn't—She would look very well at the head of his table, and just at the moment she came twirling past with Billy Pringle, the pearl loops of her pretty pink wreath dancing on her fair forehead. The Baronet was booked; "he would have her, dom'd if he wouldn't," and taking courage within himself as the music ceased, he claimed her hand for the next quadrille, and leading her to the top of the dance, commenced joking her about Billy, who he said would make a very pretty girl, and then commenced praising herself. He admired her and everything she had on, from the wreath to her ribbon, and was so affectionate that she felt if he wasn't a little elevated she would very soon have an offer. Then Mammas, and Mrs. Rocket Larkspurs, and Mrs. Dotherington, and Mrs. Impelow, and many other quick-eyed ladies followed their movements, each thinking that they saw by the sparkle of Clara's eyes, and the slight flush of her pretty face, what was going on. But they were prématuré. Sir Moses did not offer until he had mopped his brow in the promenade, when, on making the second slow round of the room, a significant glance with a slight inclination of her handsome head as she passed her Mamma announced that she was going to be Lady Mainchance!

Hoo-ray for the Hunt Ball!

Sold again and the money paid! as the trinket-sellers say at a fair.

Another offer and accepted say we. Captain and Mrs. Languisher, Sir Moses and Lady Mainchance. Who wouldn't go to a Hit-im-and-Hold-im-shire hunt ball?

Then when the music struck up again, instead of fulfilling her engagements with her next partner. Clara begged to be excused—had got a little headache, and went and sat down between her Mamma and her admiring intended; upon which the smouldering fire of surmise broke out into downright assertion, and it ran through the room that Sir Moses had offered to Miss Yammerton. Then the indignant Mammas rose hastily from their seats and paraded slowly past, to see how the couple looked, pitying the poor creature, and young gentlemen joked with each other, saying—"Go thou and do likewise." and paired off to the supper room to acquire courage from the well iced but inferior Champagne.

And so the ardent ball progressed, some laying the foundations for future offers, some advancing their suits a step, others bringing them to we hope, a happy termination. Never was a more productive hunt ball known, and it was calculated that the little gentleman who rides so complacently on our first page exhausted all his arrows o the occasion.

When the mortified Miss de Glancey returned to her lodgings at Mrs. Sarsnet the milliner's, in Verbena Crescent, she bid Mrs. Roseworth good-night, and dismissing her little French maid to bed, proceeded to her own apartment, where, with the united aid of a chamber and two toilette-table candles, she instituted a most rigid examination, as well of her features as her figure, in her own hand-mirror and the various glasses of the room, and satisfied herself that neither her looks nor her dress were any way in fault for the indifference with which she had been received. Indeed, though she might perhaps be a little partial, she thought she never saw herself looking better, and certainly her dress was as stylish and looming as any in the ball-room.

Those points being satisfactorily settled, she next unclasped the single row of large pearls that fastened the bunch of scarlet geraniums into her silken brown hair; and taking them off her exquisitely modelled head, laid them beside her massive scarlet geranium bouquet and delicate kid gloves upon the toilette-table. She then stirred the fire; and wheeling the easy-chair round to the front of it, took the eight hundred yards of tulle deliberately in either hand and sunk despondingly into the depths of the chair, with its ample folds before her. Drawing her dress up a little in front, she placed her taper white-satined feet on the low green fender, and burying her beautiful face in her lace-fringed kerchief, proceeded to take an undisturbed examination of what had occurred. How was it that she, in the full bloom of her beauty and the zenith of her experience, had failed in accomplishing what she used so easily to perform? How was it that Captain Langnisher seemed so cool, and that supercilious Miss eyed her with a side-long stare, that left its troubled mark behind, like the ripple of the water after a boat. And that boy Pringle, too, who ought to have been proud and flattered by her notice, instead of grinning about with those common country Misses?

All this hurt and distressed our accomplished coquette, who was unused to indifference and mortification. Then from the present her mind reverted to the past; aud stirring the fire, she recalled the glorious recollections of her many triumphs, beginning with her school-girl days, when the yeomanry officers used to smile at her as they met the girls out walking, until Miss Whippey restricted them to the garden during the eight days that the dangerous danglers were on duty. Next, how the triumph of her first offer was enhanced by the fact that she got her old opponent Sarah Snowball's lover from her—who, however, she quickly discarded for Captain Capers—who in turn yielded to Major Spankley.

Dicer, and the grave Mr. Woodhouse all in tow together, each thinking himself the happy man and the others the cat's-paw, until the rash Hotspur Smith exploded amongst them, and then suddenly dwindled from a millionaire into a mouse. Other names quickly followed, recalling the recollections of a successful career. At last she came to that dread, that fatal day, when, having exterminated Imperial John, and with the Peer well in hand, she was induced, much against her better judgment, to continue the chase, and lose all chance of becoming a Countess. Oh, what a day was that! She had long watched the noble Earl's increasing fervour, and marked his admiring eye, as she sat in the glow of beauty and the pride of equestrianism; and she felt quite sure, if the chase had ended at the check caused by the cattle-drover's dog, he would have married her. Oh, that the run should ever have continued! Oh, that she should ever have been lured on to her certain destruction! Why didn't she leave well alone? And at the recollection of that sad, that watery day, she burst into tears and sobbed convulsively. Her feelings being thus relieved, and the fire about exhausted, she then got out of her crinoline and under the counterpane.

CHAPTER LXII. LOVE AT SECOND SIGHT.—CUPID'S SETTLING DAY.

A sudden change now came over the country.—The weather, which had been mild and summer-like throughout, changed to frost, binding all nature up in a few hours. The holes in the streets which were shining with water in the gas-lights when Miss de Glancey retired to bed, had a dull black-leaded sort of look in the morning, while the windows of her room glistened with the silvery spray of ferns and heaths and fancy flowers.—The air was sharp and bright, with a clear blue sky overhead, all symptomatic of frost, with every appearance of continuing.—That, however, is more a gentleman's question than a lady's, so we will return within doors.

Flys being scarce at Hinton, and Miss de Glancey wishing to avoid the gape and stare of the country town, determined to return by the 11.30 train; so arose after a restless night, and taking a hurried breakfast, proceeded, with the aid of her maid, to make one of those exquisite toilettes for which she had so long been justly famous. Her sylph-like figure was set off in a bright-green terry-velvet dress, with a green-feathered bonnet of the same colour and material, trimmed with bright scarlet ribbons, and a wreath of scarlet flowers inside.—A snow-white ermine tippet, with ermine cuffs and muff, completed her costume. Having surveyed herself in every mirror, she felt extremely satisfied, and only wished Captain Languisher could see her. With that exact punctuality which constant practice engenders, but which sometimes keeps strangers sadly on the fret, the useful fly was at length at the door, and the huge box containing the eight hundred yards of tulle being hoisted on to the iron-railed roof, the other articles were huddled away, and Miss de Glancey ascending the steps, usurped the seat of honour, leaving Mrs. Roseworth and her maid to sit opposite to her. A smile with a half-bow to Mrs. Sarsnet, as she now stood at the door, with a cut of the whip from the coachman, sent our party lilting and tilting over the hard surface of the road to the rail.

The line ran true and smooth this day, and the snorting train stopped at the pretty Swiss cottage station at Fairfield just as Mrs. Roseworth saw the last of the parcels out of the fly, while Miss de Glancey took a furtive peek at the passengers from an angle of the bay window, at which she thought she herself could not be seen.

Now, it so happened that the train was in charge of the well-known Billy Bates, a smart young fellow, whose good looks had sadly stood in the way of his preferment, for he never could settle to anything; and after having been a footman, a whipper-in, a watcher, a groom, and a grocer, he had now taken up with the rail, where he was a great favourite with the fair, whom he rather prided himself upon pairing with what he considered appropriate partners. Seeing our lovely coquette peeping out, it immediately occurred to him, that he had a suitable *vis-à-vis* for her—a dashing looking gent., in a red flannel Emperor shirt, a blue satin cravat, a buff vest, aud a new bright-green cut-away with fancy buttons; altogether a sort of swell that isn't to be seen every day.

"This way, ladies!" now cried Billy, hurrying into the first-class waiting-room, adjusting the patent leather pouch-belt of his smart green-and-red uniform as he spoke. "This way, ladies, please!" waving them on with his clean white doeskin-gloved hand towards the door; whereupon Miss de Glancey, drawing herself up, and primming her features, advanced on to the platform, like the star of the evening coming on to the stage of a theatre.

Billy then opened the frosty-windowed door of a carriage a few paces up the line; whereupon a red railway wrapper-rug with brown foxes' heads being withdrawn, a pair of Bedford-corded legs dropped from the opposite seat, and a dogskin gloved hand was protruded to assist the ascent of the enterer. A pretty taper-fingered primrose-kidded one was presently inside it; but ere the second step was accomplished, a convulsive thrill was felt, and, looking up, Miss de Glancey found herself in the grasp of her old friend Imperial John!

"O Mr. Hybrid!" exclaimed she, shaking his still retained hand with the greatest cordiality; "O Mr. Hybrid! I'm so *glad* to see you! I'm so *glad* to meet somebody I know!" and gathering herself together, she entered the carriage, and sat down opposite to him.

Mrs. Roseworth then following, afforded astonished John a moment to collect his scattered faculties, yet not sufficient time to compare the dread. "*Si-r-r-r!* do you *mean to insult me!*" of their former meeting, with the cordial greeting of this. Indeed, our fair friend felt that she had a great arrear of politeness to make up, and as railway time is short, she immediately began to ply her arts by inquiring most kindly after His Highness's sister Mrs. Poppeyfield and her baby, who she heard was *such* a sweet boy; and went on so affably, that before Billy Bates arrived with the tickets, which Mrs. Roseworth had forgotten to take, Imperial John began to think that there must have been some mistake before, and Miss de Glancey couldn't have understood him. Then, when the train was again in motion, she applied the artillery of her eyes so well—for she was as great an adept in her art as the Northumberland horse-tamer is in his—that ere they stopped at the Lanecroft station, she had again subjugated Imperial John;—taken his Imperial reason prisoner! Nay more, though he was going to Bowerbank to look at a bull, she actually persuaded him to alight and accompany her to Mrs. Roseworth's where we need scarcely say he was presently secured, and in less than a week she had him so tame that she could lead him about, anywhere.

The day after the ball was always a busy one in Hit-im-and-Hold-em-shire. It was a sort of settling day, only the parties scattered about the country instead of congregating at the "corner." Those who had made up their minds overnight, came to "Ask Mamma" in the morning, and those who had not mustered sufficient courage, tried what a visit to inquire how the young lady was after the fatigue of the ball would do to assist them. Those who had got so far on the road as to have asked both the young lady and "Mamma," then got handed over to the more business-like inquiries of Papa—when Cupid oft "spreads his light wings and in a moment flies." Then it is that the tenable money exaggerations come out—the great expectations dwindling away, and the thousands a-year becoming hundreds. We never knew a reputed Richest Commoner's fortune that didn't collapse most grievously under the "what have you got, and what will you do?" operation. But if it passes Papa, the still more dread ordeal of the lawyer has to be encountered when one being summoned on either side, a hard money-driving bargain ensues, one trying how much he can get, the other how little he can give—until the whole nature and character of the thing is changed. Money! money! money! is the cry, as if there was nothing in the world worth living for but those eternal bits of yellow coin. But we are getting in advance of our subject, our suitor not having passed the lower, or "Ask-Mamma" house.

Among the many visited on this auspicious day were our fair friends at Yammaerton Grange, our Richest Commoner having infused a considerable degree of activity into the matrimonial market. There is nothing like a little competition for putting young gentlemen on the alert. First to arrive was our friend Sir Moses Mainchance, who dashed up to the door in his gig with the air of a man on safe ground, saluting Mamma whom he found alone in the drawing-room, and then the young ladies as they severally entered in succession. Having thus sealed and delivered himself into the family, as it were, he enlarged on the delights of the ball—the charming scene, the delightful music, the excellent dancing, the sudden disappearance of de Glancey and other the incidents of the evening. These topics being duly discussed, and cake and wine produced, "Mamma" presently withdrew, her example being followed at intervals by Flora and Harriet.

Scarcely had she got clear of the door ere the vehement bark of the terrier called her attention to the front of the house, where she saw our fat friend the Woolpack tit-tup-ing up on the identical horse Jack Rogers so unceremoniously appropriated on the Crooked Billet day. There was young Treadcroft with his green-liveried cockaded groom behind him, trying to look as unconcerned as possible, though in reality he was in as great a fright as it was well possible for a boy to be. Having dismounted and nearly pulled the bell out of its socket with nervousness, he gave his horse to the groom, with orders to wait, and then followed the footman into the dining-room, whither Mrs. Yammerton had desired him to be shown.

Now, the Woolpack and the young Owl (Rowley Abingdon), had been very attentive both to Flora and Harriet at the ball, the Woolpack having twice had an offer on the tip of his tongue for Flora, without being able to get it off.

Somehow his tongue clave to his lips—he felt as if his mouth was full of claggum. He now came to see if he could have any better luck at the Grange.

Mrs. Yammerton had read his feelings at the ball, and not receiving the expected announcement from Flora, saw that he wanted a little of her assistance, so now proceeded to give it. After a most cordial greeting and interchanges of the usual nothings of society, she took a glance at the ball, and then claimed his congratulations on Clara's engagement, which of course led up to the subject, opening the locked jaw at once; and Mamma having assured the fat youth of her perfect approval and high opinion of his character, very soon arranged matters between them, and produced Flora to confirm her. So she gained two sons-in-law in one night. Miss Harriet thus left alone, took her situation rather to heart, and fine Billy, forgetful of his Mamma's repeated injunctions and urgent entreaties to him to return now that the ball was over, and the hunting was stopped by the frost, telling him she wanted him on most urgent and particular business, was tender-hearted enough on finding Harriet in tears the next day to offer to console her with his hand, which we need not say she joyfully accepted, no lady liking to emulate "the last rose of summer and be left blooming alone." So all the pretty sisters were suited, Harriet perhaps the best off, as far as looks at least went.

But, when in due course the old "what have you got and what will you do?" inquiries came to be instituted, we are sorry to say our fine friend could not answer them nearly so satisfactorily as the Woolpack, who had his balance-sheets nearly off by heart. Billy replying in the vacant *negligé* sort of way young gentlemen do, that he supposed he would have four or five thousand a-year, though when asked why he thought he'd have four or five thousand a-year, he really could not tell the reason why. Then when further probed by our persevering Major, he admitted that it was all at the mercy of uncle Jerry, and that his Mamma had said their lawyer had told her he did not think pious Jerry would account except under pressure of the Court of Chancery, whereupon the Major's chin dropped, as many a man's chin has dropped, at the dread announcement. It sounds like an antidote to matrimony. Even Mrs. Yammerton thought under the circumstances that the young Owl might be a safer speculation than fine Billy, though she rather leant, to fine Billy, as people do lean to strangers in preference to those they knew all about. Still Chancery was a choker. Equity is to the legal world what Newmarket is to the racing world, the unadulterated essence of the thing. As at Newmarket there is none of the fun and gaiety of the great race-meetings, so in Chancery there is none of the pomp and glitter and varied incident that rivets so many audiences to the law courts.

All is dull, solemn, and dry—paper, paper, paper—a redundancy of paper, as if it were possible to transfer the blush of perjury to paper. Fifty people will make affidavits for one that will go into a witness-box and have the truth twisted out of them by cross-examination. The few strangers who pop into court pop out again as quickly as they can, a striking contrast to those who go in in search of their rights—though wrestling for one's rights under a pressure of paper, is very like swimming for one's life enveloped in a salmon-net. It is juries that give vitality to the administration of justice. A drowsy hum pervades the bar, well calculated for setting restless children to sleep, save when some such brawling buffoon as the Indian juggler gets up to pervert facts, and address arguments to an educated judge that would be an insult to the mind of a petty juryman. One wonders at men calling themselves gentlemen demeaning themselves by such practices. Well did the noble-hearted Sir William Erie declare that the licence of the bar was such that he often wished the offenders could be prosecuted for a misdemeanour. We know an author who made an affidavit in a chancery suit equal in length to a three-volume novel, and what with weighing every word in expectation of undergoing some of the polished razors keen of that drowsy bar, he could not write fiction again for a twelvemonth. As it was, he underwent that elegant extract Mr. Verde, whose sponsors have done him such justice in the vulgar tongue, and because he made an immaterial mistake he was held up to the Court as utterly unworthy of belief! We wonder whether Mr. Verde's character or the deponent's suffered most by the performance. But enough of such worthies. Let all the bullies of the bar bear in mind if they have tongues other people have pens, and that consideration for the feelings of others is one of the distinguishing characteristics of gentlemen.

CHAPTER LXIII. A STARTLING ANNOUNCEMENT.

HE proverbial serenity of Poodles was disturbed one dull winter afternoon by our old friend General Binks banging down the newly-arrived evening paper with a vehemence rarely witnessed in that quiet quarter. Mr. Dorfold, who was dosing as usual with outstretched leg's before the fire, started up, thinking the General was dying. Major Mustard's hat dropped off, Mr. Pioser let fall the "Times Supplement," Mr. Crowsfoot ceased conning the "Post" Alemomh, the footman, stood aghast, and altogether there was a general cessation of every thing—Beedles was paralyzed.

The General quickly followed up the blow with a tremendous oath, and seizing Colonel Callender's old beaver hat instead of his own new silk one, flung frantically out of the room, through the passage and into St. James's Street, as if bent on immediate destruction.

All was amazement! What's happened the General Something must have gone wrong with the General! The General—the calmest, the quietest, the most, placid man in the world—suddenly convulsed with such a violent paroxysm. He who had neither chick nor child, nor anything to care about, with the certainty of an Earldom, what *could* have come over him?

"I'll tell you," exclaimed Mr. Bullion who had just dropped in on his way from the City: "I'll tell you," repeated he. taking up the paper which the General had thrown down. "*His bank's failed!* Heard some qweerish hints as I came down Cornhill:" and forthwith! Bullion turned to the City article, and ran his accustomed eye down its contents.

"Funds opened heavily. Foreign stocks quiet. About £20,000 in bar gold. The John Brown arrived from China. Departure of the Peninsular Mail postponed," and so on; but neither failures, nor rumours of failures, either of bankers or others, were there.

Very odd—what could it be, then? must be something in the paper. And again the members resolved themselves into a committee of the whole house to ascertain what it was.

The first place that a lady would look to for the solution of a mystery of this sort, is, we believe, about the last place that a man would look to, namely, the births, deaths, and marriages;

and it was not until the sensation had somewhat subsided, and Tommy White was talking of beating up the General's quarter in Bury Street, to hear what it was, that his inseparable—that "nasty covetous body Cuddy Flintoff," who had been plodding very perseveringly on the line, at length hit off what astonished him as much as we have no doubt it will the reader, being neither more nor less than the following very quiet announcement at the end of the list of marriages:—

"This morning, at St. Barnabas, by the Rev. Dr. Duff, the Right Hon. The Earl of Ladythorne, to Emma, widow of the late Wm, Pringle, Esq."

The Earl of Ladythorne married to Mrs. Pringle! Well done our fair friend of the frontispiece! The pure white camellias are succeeded by a coronet! The borrowed velvet dress replaced by anything she likes to own. Who would have thought it!

But wonders will never cease; for on this eventful day Mr. George Gallon was seen driving the Countess's old coach companion, Mrs. Margerum, from Cockthorpe Church, with long white rosettes flying at Tippy Tom's head, and installing her mistress of the Rose and Crown, at the cross roads; thus showing that truth is stranger than fiction. "George," we may add, has now taken the Flying Childers Inn at Eversley Green, where he purposes extending his "Torf" operations, and we make no doubt will be heard of hereafter.

Of our other fair friends we must say a few parting words on taking a reluctant farewell.

Though Miss Clara, now Lady Mainchance, is not quite so good a housekeeper as Sir Moses could have wished, she is nevertheless extremely ornamental at the head of his table; and though she has perhaps rather exceeded with Gillow, the Major promises to make it all right by his superior management of the property. Mr. Mordecai Nathan has been supplanted by our master of "haryers," who has taken a drainage loan, and promises to set the water-works playing at Pangburn Park, just as he did at Yammerton Grange. He means to have a day a week there with his "haryers," which, he says, is the best way of seeing a country.

Miss de Glancey has revised Barley Hill Hall, for which place his Highness now appears in Burke's "Landed Gentry," very considerably; and though she has not been to Gillow, she has got the plate out of the drawing-room, and made things very smart. She keeps John in excellent order, and rides his grey horse admirably. Blurkins says "the grey mare is the better horse," but that is no business of ours.

Of all the brides, perhaps, Miss Flora got the best set down; for the Woolpack's house was capitally furnished, and he is far happier driving his pretty wife about the country with a pair of pyebald ponies, making calls, than in risking his neck across country with hounds—or rather after them.

Of all our beauties, and thanks to Leech we have dealt in nothing else, Miss Harriet alone remains unsettled with her two strings to her bow—fine Billy and Rowley Abingdon; though which is to be the happy man remains to be seen.

We confess we incline to think that the Countess will be too many for the Yammertons; but if she is, there is no great harm done; for Harriet is very young, and the Owl is a safe card in the country where men are more faithful than they are in the towns. Indeed, fine Billy is almost too young to know his own mind, and marrying now would only perhaps involve the old difficulty hereafter of father and son wanting top boots at the same time, supposing our friend to accomplish the difficult art of sitting at the Jumps.

So let us leave our hero open. And as we have only aimed at nothing but the natural throughout, we will finish by proposing a toast that will include as well the mated and the single of our story, as the mated and the single all the world over, namely, the old and popular one of "The single married, and the married happy!" drunk with three times three and one cheer more! HOO-RAY!

197

Printed in Great Britain
by Amazon

72260719R00119